The World's Finest Mystery and Crime Stories

■ ■ ■

Fifth Annual Collection

Forge Books Edited by Ed Gorman and Martin H. Greenberg

The World's Finest Mystery and Crime Stories
First Annual Collection

The World's Finest Mystery and Crime Stories
Second Annual Collection

The World's Finest Mystery and Crime Stories
Third Annual Collection

The World's Finest Mystery and Crime Stories
Fourth Annual Collection

The World's Finest Mystery and Crime Stories
Fifth Annual Collection

The World's Finest Mystery and Crime Stories

■ ■ ■

FIFTH ANNUAL COLLECTION

Edited by
ED GORMAN
and
MARTIN H. GREENBERG

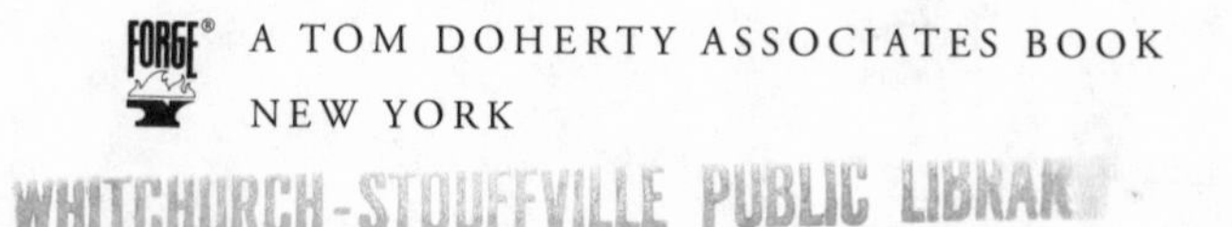

A TOM DOHERTY ASSOCIATES BOOK
NEW YORK

This is a work of fiction and nonfiction. All the characters and events portrayed in the stories in this collection are either fictitious or are used fictitiously.

THE WORLD'S FINEST MYSTERY AND CRIME STORIES: FIFTH ANNUAL COLLECTION

This book is printed on acid-free paper.

Edited by James Frenkel

A Forge Book
Published by Tom Doherty Associates, LLC
175 Fifth Avenue
New York, NY 10010

www.tor.com

Forge® is a registered trademark of Tom Doherty Associates, LLC.

ISBN 0-765-31146-1 (hc)
EAN 978-0765-31146-7 (hc)
ISBN 0-765-31147-X (pbk)
EAN 978-0765-31147-4 (pbk)

First Edition: October 2004

Printed in the United States of America

0 9 8 7 6 5 4 3 2 1

Copyright Acknowledgments

■ ■ ■

"The Year in Mystery and Crime Fiction: 2003," by Jon L. Breen. Copyright © 2004 by Jon L. Breen.

"A 2003 Yearbook of Crime and Mystery," by Edward D. Hoch. Copyright © 2004 by Edward D. Hoch.

"World Mystery Report: Great Britain," by Maxim Jakubowski. Copyright © 2004 by Maxim Jakubowski.

"World Mystery Report: Canada," by Edo van Belkom. Copyright © 2004 by Edo van Belkom.

"World Mystery Report: Germany," by Thomas Wörtche. Copyright © 2004 by Thomas Wörtche.

"The Year 2003 in Mystery Fandom," by George A. Easter. Copyright © 2004 by George A. Easter.

"Cowboy Grace," by Kristine Kathryn Rusch. Copyright © 2003 by Kristine Kathryn Rusch. First published in *The Silver Gryphon*, edited by Gary Turner and Marty Halpern, Golden Gryphon Press. Reprinted by permission of the author.

"Palace in the Pines," by Doug Allyn. Copyright © 2003 by Doug Allyn. First published in *Ellery Queen's Mystery Magazine*, July 2003. Reprinted by permission of the author.

"Offenders," by Mat Coward. Copyright © 2003 by Mat Coward. First published in *The Mammoth Book of Future Cops*, edited by Maxim Jakubowski and M. Christian, Robinson Publishing. Reprinted by permission of the author.

"Bet on Red," by Jeff Abbott. Copyright © 2003 by Jeff Abbott. First published in *High Stakes*, edited by Robert J. Randisi, Signet. Reprinted by permission of the author.

"Doctor's Orders," by Judith Cutler. Copyright © 2003 by Judith Cutler. First published in *Birmingham Noir*, edited by Joel Lane and Steve Bishop, Tindal Street Press. Reprinted by permission of the author and her agents, the Stuart Krichevsky Literary Agency.

"Esther Gordon Framlingham," by Antony Mann. Copyright © 2003 by Antony Mann. First published in *Crimewave 7: The Last Sunset*, TTA Press (www.tta.com). Reprinted by permission of the author.

"Nighthawks," by John Lutz. Copyright © 2003 by John Lutz. First published in *Flesh & Blood: Guilty as Sin*, edited by Max Allan Collins and Jeff Gelb, Mysterious Press. Reprinted by permission of the author.

"Low Tide," by Dick Lochte. Copyright © 2003 by Dick Lochte. First published in *Flesh & Blood: Guilty as Sin*, edited by Max Allan Collins and Jeff Gelb, Mysterious Press. Reprinted by permission of the author.

"Starting Over," by Carol Anne Davis. Copyright © 2003 by Carol Anne Davis. First published in *Green for Danger*, edited by Martin Edwards, Do-Not Press. Reprinted by permission of the author.

"Dreams of Jeannie," by Catherine Dain. Copyright © 2003 by Catherine Dain. First published in *Dreams of Jeannie and Other Stories*, Five Star Publishing. Reprinted by permission of the author.

"The Face of Ali Baba," by Edward D. Hoch. Copyright © 2003 by Edward D. Hoch. First published in *Ellery Queen's Mystery Magazine*, December 2003. Reprinted by permission of the author.

"Take My Word for It and You Don't Have to Answer," by Robert S. Levinson. Copyright © 2003 by Robert S. Levinson. First published in *Ellery Queen's Mystery Magazine*, December 2003. Reprinted by permission of the author.

"The Maids," by G. Miki Hayden. Copyright © 2003 by G. Miki Hayden. First published in *Blood on Their Hands*, edited by Lawrence Block, Berkley Prime Crime. Reprinted by permission of the author.

"Black Heart and Cabin Girl," by Shelley Costa. Copyright © 2003 by Shelley Costa. First published in *Blood on Their Hands*, edited by Lawrence Block, Berkley Prime Crime. Reprinted by permission of the author.

■ ■ ■

We'd like to dedicate this book to
the librarians who fight the good fight every day.

—Ed Gorman and Martin H. Greenberg

Contents

The Year in Mystery and Crime Fiction: 2003

Jon L. Breen

■ ■ ■

The crime fiction community, which has always been good at respecting and preserving its history, did an especially good job in 2003. Call it the Year of the Scholarly Edition, not only from the speciality imprints but from university presses and mainstream series devoted to reprinting the classics.

It was an especially big year for recognition of nineteenth-century female pioneers of the genre. Duke University Press offered paired novels by Metta Fuller Victor (1831–85), *The Dead Letter & The Figure Eight*, and the better-known Anna Katharine Green (1846–1935), *That Affair Next Door & Lost Man's Lane*, both omnibus volumes with introductions by Catherine Ross Nickerson. Modern Library brought out a new edition, including over sixty pages of notes and other editorial paraphernalia, of *The Trail of the Serpent* (1860) by Mary Elizabeth Braddon (1837–1914), best remembered as the author of *Lady Audley's Secret*. This earlier book is claimed by editor Chris Willis to be "probably the first British detective novel."

Moving on to twentieth-century writers, Everyman's Library added James M. Cain to their catalog with an omnibus comprising *The Postman Always Rings Twice, Double Indemnity, Mildred Pierce*, and *Selected Stories*, including a meaty introduction by Robert Polito and a chronology of Cain's life and times. The Feminist Press at the City University of New York included Dorothy B. Hughes's *In a Lonely Place* (1947) in its Femmes Fatales: Women Write Pulp series, with an afterword by Lisa Maria Hogeland and a publisher's foreword that assumes a broad and somewhat fuzzy definition of pulp. Volume 280 of *The Dictionary of Literary Biography* was comprised of everything relevant to a single novel apart from the text itself: *Dashiell Hammett's The Maltese Falcon: A Documentary Volume*, edited by Richard Layman with the assistance of George Parker Anderson.

The most ambitious project of The Battered Silicon Dispatch Box, that prolific Canadian publisher of Sherlockiana and vintage detective fiction, was *The Complete Annotated Father Brown*, presenting in two large format volumes all fifty-three stories about G.K. Chesterton's detecting priest, chronologically arranged, with new and original illustrations, critical commentaries by Pasquale Accardo, and notes by John Peterson. For copyright reasons, the set is available for sale only in Canada, but publisher George Vanderburgh advises he can fill individual orders received from outside Canada at Box 204, Shelburne, Ontario LON 1SO. From that same battered box came *The Thinking Machine Omnibus*, a complete edition of Jacques Futrelle's early twentieth-century stories of an irascible scientist sleuth, and *The Max Carrados Portfolio*, gathering all the stories about Ernest Braman's blind detective.

Some quick snapshots of other noteworthy events of 2003: Bob Napier's long-running fanzine *Mystery and Detective Monthly* came to a planned but still regretted end with issue #200, while another venerable outlet for fannish reviews and opinion, Steve Lewis's *Mystery*File*, launched a comeback. . . . The annual Bouchercon was held in that most hard-boiled and noirish of American cities, Las Vegas. . . . In honor of the centenary of the great suspense master Cornell Woolrich (1903–68), biographer Francis M. Nevins held a December celebration at Manhattan's Mercantile Library in the midst of a blizzard and edited a new collection of Woolrich stories, *Night and Fear* (Carroll & Graf/Penzler), not actually published until early 2004. . . . When the Fox Movie Channel announced a series of Charlie Chan films, the objections of Asian-American pressure groups to that benign and admirable character flared anew, causing Fox first to cancel the series, then to bookend showings with sensitivity training sessions.

Among the prominent mystery voices stilled were a challenging and original novelist whose artistic impulses were better than his commercial instincts, Nicolas Freeling, creator of the prematurely buried Van der Valk; and one of the most influential and well-loved editors of mystery fiction, first at Walker and later at Mysterious Press, Sara Ann Freed. For a full account of the year's necrology, see Edward D. Hoch's yearbook.

Best Novels of the Year 2003

The following fifteen were the most impressive crime novels I read and reviewed in 2003. As usual, they cover a range of styles and approaches, with a stronger representation of humor and satire than usual (see Anderson, Elton, Hall, McBain, Mcdonald, and Simon). I'll repeat my standard disclaimer: I don't pretend to cover the whole field—with today's volume of new books, no single reviewer does. But try to find fifteen better.

Keith Ablow, *Psychopath* (St. Martin's Minotaur). The latest case for forensic psychiatrist Frank Clevenger is an extraordinary variation on the Jekyll-and-Hyde theme.

James Anderson, *The Affair of the 39 Cufflinks* (Poisoned Pen). Return to Alderley, that murder-prone British stately home of the 1930s, in a superb tongue-in-cheek novel of detection.

Ken Bruen, *The Guards* (St. Martin's Minotaur). In his first major assault on the American market, the immensely gifted and original Irish writer introduces Galway cop-turned-private-eye Jack Taylor.

Ben Elton, *Dead Famous* (Black Swan/Trafalgar). First published in Britain in 2001 but not distributed in the U.S. until 2003, this satirical but classically plotted account of a murder-plagued reality TV show was my book of the year. (Also highly recommended is Elton's 2002 novel *High Society* [Bantam U.K. Trafalgar].)

DeLoris Stanton Forbes: *The Perils of Marie Louise* (Five Star). An unconventional family saga from one of crime fiction's most restlessly inventive writers.

Parnell Hall, *Manslaughter* (Carroll & Graf/Penzler). New York private eye Stanley Hastings is consistently one of the most entertaining characters in contemporary mystery fiction.

Carolyn Hart, *Letter from Home* (Berkley). A mystery set on the World War II home front in small-town Oklahoma may be the best novel ever from the multi-award-winning author.

P.D. James, *The Murder Room* (Knopf). A museum of Britain in the 1930s is the scene for the latest typically complex, enthralling, and (yes) a little too long case for Scotland Yard's poetic policeman Adam Dalgliesh.

Stuart M. Kaminsky, *Not Quite Kosher* (Forge). Chicago cop Abe Lieberman, one of the great characters in contemporary crime fiction, may outlive the author's Toby Peters and Pofirio Rostnikov.

Dean Koontz, *Odd Thomas* (Bantam). A psychic detective story of great ingenuity from one of the bestseller list's most prolific and versatile permanent residents. *The Face* (Bantam), another supernatural mystery, is nearly as good.

Ed McBain, *Fat Ollie's Book* (Simon and Schuster). The latest in the 87th Precinct series is most notable for its pointed satire of the cop/author phenomenon.

Gregory Mcdonald, *Flynn's World* (Pantheon). In this academic comedy, Boston cop Francis Xavier Flynn makes a welcome return after a nineteen-year hiatus.

James Sallis, *Cypress Grove* (Walker). A small-town mystery for movie buffs, noir devotees, and admirers of lyrical prose.

Roger L. Simon, *Director's Cut* (Atria). Has counterculture private eye Moses Wine, here handling security for an independent film shoot in Prague, changed his politics shockingly rightward? If you share Simon's abrasive sense of humor, you may not care.

Jill Paton Walsh and Dorothy L. Sayers, *A Presumption of Death* (St. Martin's Minotaur). The second of these posthumous collaborations continuing the Lord Peter Wimsey/Harriett Vane saga is more Walsh and less Sayers but another admirable job.

Subgenres

Private eyes. Ed Gorman's Iowan Sam McCain was in good form in *Everybody's Somebody's Fool* (Carroll & Graf), and Michael Connelly's Harry Bosch segued from L.A. cop to sleuth-for-hire in *Lost Light* (Little, Brown). While I've been slow to appreciate Janet Evanovich's New Jersey bounty hunter Stephanie Plum, *To the Nines* (St. Martin's) gave me a lot of laughs. The most unconventional private eye on the current scene is Alexander McCall Smith's Botswana sleuth Precious Ramotswe, who makes her fourth appearance in *The Kalahari Typing School for Men* (Pantheon), utterly charming but not really a crime or mystery novel.

Classical puzzles. They're thin on the ground these days, but along with the Anderson, Elton, Hall, and Walsh/Sayers titles on my top fifteen, try Jane Haddam's *Conspiracy Theory* (St. Martin's Minotaur), featuring one of the last surviving great detectives, Gregor Demarkian.

Amateur sleuths. Joyce Krieg's *Murder Off Mike* (St. Martin's Minotaur) introduced a promising new sleuth in talk-radio host Shauna J. Bogart. Another first novel, Meredith Blevins's semi-supernatural *The Hummingbird Wizard* (Forge), brought us Annie Szabo and her colorful family-by-marriage of Gypsies. Ray Bradbury's *Let's All Kill Constance* (Morrow) marked the return of his unnamed writer/sleuth in mid-century Hollywood. Also in strong form were Donna Andrews's Meg Langslow in *Crouching Buzzard, Leaping Loon* (St. Martin's Minotaur/Dunne); Dean James's Simon Kirby-Jones in *Faked to Death* (Kensington); Lyn Hamilton's Lara McClintoch in *The Thai Amulet* (Berkley); and Ralph McInerny's Father Dowling in *Last Things* (St. Martin's Minotaur).

Police. Among the series cops stylishly walking their beats were Ken Bruen's Brant and Roberts in the London-based *Blitz* (Do-Not/Dufour); Tony Hillerman's Navajo Tribal Police Joe Leaphorn and Jim Chee in *The Sinister Pig* (HarperCollins); and Paula L. Woods's L.A. detective Charlotte Justice in *Dirty Laundry* (Ballantine). J. D. Robb, writing in ostensible collaboration with alter ego Nora Roberts, brought science fictional Eve Dallas into the second half of *Remember When* (Putnam). Two small-town lawmen made notable debuts: Henry Kisor's Deputy Sheriff Steve Martinez of Michigan's Upper Peninsula in *Season's Revenge* (Forge), and Alice Blanchard's Oklahoma police chief Charlie Grover in *The Breathtaker* (Warner).

Lawyers. Series advocates in reliable form included Lisa Scottoline's Rosato and Associates in *Dead Ringer* (HarperCollins); William Bernhardt's Ben Kincaid in *Death Row* (Ballantine); and Perri O'Shaughnessy's Nina Reilly in *Presumption of Death* (Delacorte).

Crooks. Andrew Vachss's *The Getaway Man* (Vintage/Random) approximates the tough crime novels of the Gold Medal days. Larry King and Thomas H. Cook's *Moon Over Manhattan* (New Millennium) is a criminous farce and much better than the celebrity byline would lead you to expect. Julius Fast's *A Trunkfull of Trouble* (Gryphon), the first mystery in forty-five years by the very first Edgar winner, features a slightly dim mob gopher who misunderstands his instructions on where to put a not-quite-dead body.

Historicals. The western-mystery hybrid (less rare than you might think) was well represented by Ed Gorman's *Relentless* (Berkley) and Suzann Ledbetter's *A Lady Never Trifles with Thieves* (Pocket Books). London and Egypt of the 1890s figure in Anne Perry's *Seven Dials* (Ballantine), from her Charlotte and Thomas Pitt series. Also in strong new cases were Peter Tremayne's eighth-century Irish advocate Sister Fidelma in *Smoke in the Wind* (St. Martin's Minotaur); Michael Jecks's fourteenth-century duo of Baldwin Furnshill and Simon Puttock in *The Templar's Penance* (Headline/Trafalgar Square); and none other than Queen Elizabeth I in Karen Harper's *The Queene's Christmas* (St. Martin's Minotaur/Dunne). Two novels, each distinguished in its own way, cast Dr. Joseph Bell (Sherlock Holmes's model) as detective and Arthur Conan Doyle as Watson: Howard Engel's *Mr. Doyle and Dr. Bell* (Overlook) and David Pirie's *The Night Calls* (St. Martin's Minotaur).

Thrillers. The series character is not a person but a place, California's Soledad County, in Marcia Muller's *Cyanide Wells* (Mysterious). Donald E. Westlake's *Money for Nothing* (Mysterious) masterfully mixes comedy and intrigue; while Gayle Lynds proves in *Robert Ludlum's The Altman Code* (St. Martin's) that in the right hands, even the "franchise" novel can be worth the discriminating reader's attention. Adam Hall's *Quiller Balalaika* (Carroll & Graf/Penzler) is the first U.S. publication of the final novel in one of the most distinguished of the Cold War spy series, first published in Britain in 1996. I called cartoonist Peter Steiner's *A French Country Murder* (St. Martin's Minotaur/ Dunne) a sort of espionage cozy, combining a quiet, leisurely style with a wild thriller plot.

Short Stories

It was another banner year for single-author collections. Two of the finest contemporary masters of the shorter form were collected for the first time. Both Crippen & Landru and Five Star offered volumes by Brendan DuBois, *The Dark Snow and Other Mysteries*

A 2003 Yearbook of Crime and Mystery

Edward D. Hoch

■ ■ ■

Collections and Single Stories

Aird, Catherine. *Chapter and Hearse, and Other Mysteries*. London: Macmillan. Seventeen stories featuring Inspector Sloane and other characters. (U.S. edition: St. Martin's, 2004)

Albert, Susan Wittig. *An Unthymely Death and Other Garden Mysteries*. New York: Berkley. Ten stories, four new, featuring China Bayles, herb-shop owner, with sidebar gardening tips. The new stories are mainly noncriminous.

Asimov, Isaac. *The Return of the Black Widowers*. New York: Carroll & Graf. Seventeen stories from the popular series, six previously uncollected, plus two pastiches by William Brittain and editor Charles Ardai. Introduction by Harlan Ellison.

Bellem, Robert Leslie. *Corpse on Ice, From the Case Files of Dan Turner, P.I., Volume II*. Bloomington, IL: Black Dog Books. Four stories from *Spicy Detective* and *Hollywood Detective* 1935–43.

———. *Roscoes in the Night*. Silver Spring, MD: Adventure House. Thirteen newly collected pulp stories about Dan Turner, Hollywood detective. Edited by John Wooley.

Bourdain, Anthony. *The Bobby Gold Stories*. London & New York: Bloomsbury. Twelve connected short stories about a security man for a Manhattan nightclub.

Bradbury, Ray. *Bradbury Stories*. New York: Morrow. One hundred stories, 1947–96, mainly fantasy but including crime stories from *Ellery Queen's Mystery Magazine, Manhunt, Playboy*, and elsewhere. (Contents different from *The Stories of Ray Bradbury*, 1980.)

Breen, Jon L. *J. B. Must Die: An Ed Gorgon Story*. Norfolk, VA: Crippen & Landru. A new story in a separate pamphlet accompanying the limited edition of *Kill the Umpire*.

———. *Kill the Umpire: The Calls of Ed Gorgon*. Norfolk, VA: Crippen & Landru. Sixteen stories, one new, 1971–2003, mainly from *EQMM*. Includes a checklist of Breen's novels and short stories.

Cain, James M. *The Postman Always Rings Twice, Double Indemnity, Mildred Pierce, and Selected Stories*. New York: Knopf/Everyman's Library. A Cain omnibus containing three novels and five previously collected short stories, 1928–39. Introduction by Robert Polito.

Cameron, Vicki. *Clue Mysteries*. Philadelphia: Running Press. Fifteen brief whodunits using the characters from the "Clue" board game.

Carraher, Philip J. *Alias Simon Hawkes: Further Adventures of Sherlock Holmes in New*

York. Bloomington, IN: 1stbooks Library. A novelette and three short stories, two of them locked-room mysteries.

Cave, Hugh B. *Come into My Parlor: Tales from Detective Fiction Weekly*. Norfolk, VA: Crippen & Landru. Eleven stories and novelettes from a popular pulp magazine, 1936–40.

———. *Desperate Character*. Norfolk, VA: Crippen & Landru. A single story from *Detective Fiction Weekly*, 7/9/38, in a pamphlet accompanying the limited edition of *Come Into My Parlor*.

———. *The Stinging 'Nting and Other Stories*. Bloomington, IN: Black Dog Books. Four stories from *Far East Adventure Stories* and *Man Stories*, 1931, including one detective story.

Chandler, Raymond. *Raymond Chandler's Marlowe: The Authorized Philip Marlowe Graphic Novel*. New York: iBooks. Graphic adaptations of three Chandler short stories by Jerome Charyn, David Lloyd, and Ryan Hughes.

Chesterton, G. K. *The Complete Annotated Father Brown*. Shelburne, Ont., Canada: The Battered Silicon Dispatch Box. All fifty-three stories, with footnotes by John Peterson, critical commentary by Pasquale Accardo, and original magazine illustrations.

Cody, Liza. *Lucky Dip and Other Stories*. Norfolk, VA: Crippen & Landru. Seventeen stories, two new, 1988–2003. Includes a Liza Cody checklist. (See also under *Nonfiction.)*

Coel, Margaret. *My Last Goodbye*. Mission Viejo, CA: A.S.A.P. Publishing. A single new short story in the author's Arapaho Ten Commandments series. Introduction by Nancy Pickard.

Collins, Max Allan. *Quarry's Greatest Hits*. Waterville, Maine: Five Star. A 1987 novel, *Primary Target*, and three short stories about hit man Quarry. Introduction by Ed Gorman.

Cook, Thomas H. *The Lesson of the Season*. New York: The Mysterious Bookshop. A single new story in a pamphlet published for customers of a Manhattan bookstore.

Coward, Mat. *Do the World a Favour and Other Stories*. Waterville, Maine: Five Star. Fourteen stories, two new, 1993–2003.

Dain, Catherine. *Dreams of Jeannie and Other Stories*. Waterville, Maine: Five Star. Eleven stories, one new, and an article, 1990–2003.

DeAndrea, William L. *Murder—All Kinds*. Norfolk, VA: Crippen & Landru. All eleven of the late author's short mystery stories, one previously unpublished, including four about Matt Cobb and two Sherlockian adventures. Introduction by Jane Haddam.

Deaver, Jeffery. *Twisted: The Collected Stories of Jeffery Deaver*. New York: Simon & Schuster. Sixteen stories, including a new Lincoln Rhyme Christmas story.

De Bra. Lemuel. *Slaves of the Silver Serpent*. Fitzroy Vic, Australia: Black Dog Books. Crime stories and one detective story. (2002)

Eccles, Marjorie. *Account Rendered and Other Stories*. London: Robert Hale. Twelve suspense stories.

Ellroy, James. *Destination: Morgue*. London: Century. The title novella and fifteen nonfiction pieces.

Estleman, Loren D. *Silent Thunder*. New York: ibooks. Reprint of a 1989 novel, together with one uncollected short story.

Fearn, John Russell. *Liquid Death and Other Stories*. Holicong, PA: Wildside Press. The title novella and nine stories of mystery and weird menace, three previously unpublished, mainly from *Thrilling Mystery Stories*. Edited by Philip Harbottle. (2002)

Fortune, Mary. *The Detectives' Album, Stories of Crime and Mystery from Colonial Australia*. Shelburne, Ont., Canada: The Battered Silicon Dispatch Box. Thirteen stories, 1867–1913, from the *Australian Journal*, narrated by young police officer Mark Sinclair. Edited by Lucy Sussex.

Frazee, Steve. *Nights of Terror*. Waterville, Maine: Five Star. Eight western stories, some criminous. Edited by Eric Frazee.

Futrelle, Jacques. *Jacques Futrelle's "The Thinking Machine."* New York: Modern Library. Twenty-one stories, plus two introductory vignettes. Edited by Harlan Ellison.

———. *The Thinking Machine Omnibus*. Shelburne, Ont., Canada: The Battered Silicon Dispatch Box. All the Thinking Machine stories, including thirteen previously uncollected, as well as three pastiches by Carolyn Wells and a Sherlockian pastiche by Futrelle. Edited by Stan Smith.

Garfield, Brian. *The Hit and The Marksman*. Waterville, Maine: Five Star. A 1970 novel and a new novelette.

Gault, William Campbell. *Marksman and Other Stories*. Norfolk, VA: Crippen & Landru. Twelve stories, 1940–57, half about private eye Joe Puma. Edited by Bill Pronzini, afterword by Gault's daughter Shelley.

Healy, Jeremiah. *Cuddy—Plus One*. Norfolk, VA: Crippen & Landru. Thirteen uncollected stories about private eye Cuddy, plus one about a woman attorney first published as by "Terry Devane."

———. *Off-Season and Other Stories*. Waterville, Maine: Five Star. Eleven nonseries stories, two new, including the new title novella.

———. *The Safest Little Town in Texas*. Norfolk, VA: Crippen & Landru. A single story in a pamphlet accompanying the limited edition of *Cuddy—Plus One*.

Henderson, C. J. *The Occult Detectives of C. J. Henderson*. Marietta, GA: Marietta Publishing. Thirteen fantasies. (2002)

Hess, Joan. *Big Foot Stole My Wife! and Other Stories*. Waterford, Maine: Five Star. Eleven stories, 1990–99, two from the author's Maggody series.

———. *The Deadly Ackee and Other Stories*. Waterville, Maine: Five Star. A 1988 novel, originally published as by "Joan Hadley," and four short stories, one about Sheriff Arly Hanks.

Hoch, Edward D. *The Iron Angel and Other Tales of the Gypsy Detective*. Norfolk, VA: Crippen & Landru. Fifteen stories about Romanian sleuth Michael Vlado, mainly from *EQMM*, 1985–2000.

———. *The Wolfram Hunters*. Norfolk, VA: Crippen & Landru. A single story from *The Saint Magazine*, 3/64, in a pamphlet accompanying the limited edition of *The Iron Angel*.

Jaynes, Roger. *Sherlock Holmes: A Duel with the Devil*. London: Breese Books. Two new novelettes and a story about Holmes's continuing battle with Professor Moriarty.

Keating, H.R.F. *Majumdar Uncle: An Inspector Ghote Story*. Norfolk, VA: Crippen & Landru. A single new story in a Christmas pamphlet for the publisher's friends and customers.

Kersh, Gerald. *Karmesin: The World's Greatest Criminal—or Most Outrageous Liar*. Norfolk, VA: Crippen & Landru. Seventeen stories from various sources, 1936–62, all but one reprinted in *EQMM*. Edited by Paul Duncan.

King, C. Daly. *The Complete Curious Mr. Tarrant*. Norfolk, VA: Crippen & Landru.

Twelve stories, eight from a previous collection plus four newly collected, three from *EQMM*. Two fantasies. Introduction by Edward D. Hoch.

Kurland, Michael. *Images, Lollygags & Conceits*. Brooklyn: Gryphon Books. A mixed collection of crime, mystery, SF, and fantasy. Introduction by Richard A. Lupoff.

Lawrence, Margery. *The Casebook of Miles Pennoyer, Volume One*. Ashcroft, B.C., Canada: Ash-Tree Press. The first six of twelve adventures of a psychic sleuth, two previously unpublished in North America. Volume Two will follow early in 2004.

Lawson, James A. *Hard Guy, The Collected Adventures of "Hard Guy" Dallas Duane*. Bloomington, IL: Black Dog Books. Four stories about a private eye in the oil fields, from *Spicy Western, Spicy Adventure*, and *Fighting Western*, 1937–45.

Lumley, Brian. *Harry Keogh: The Necroscope & Other Heroes*. New York: Tor. Eight stories, three new, about psychic detectives and vampire hunters.

Lupoff, Richard A. *Claremont Tales II*. Urbana, IL: Golden Gryphon Press. Thirteen fantasy and mystery stories, one new. (2002)

Lutz, John. *Endless Road and Other Stories*. Waterville, Maine: Five Star. A 1971 novel, *The Truth of the Matter*, and four stories, 1996–99.

Marlowe, Stephen. *Drum Beat: The Chester Drum Casebook*. Waterville, Maine: Five Star. Five stories, 1960–73, plus a 1965 novel, *Drum Beat—Dominique*. Introduction by Bill Pronzini.

McCloy, Helen. *The Pleasant Assassin and Other Cases of Dr. Basil Willing*. Norfolk, VA: Crippen & Landru. All ten stories about Willing from *EQMM*, 1948–79, in the publisher's ninth volume of Lost Classics. Introduction by B. A. Pike.

Mitchell, Basil, & Frederic Arnold Kummer. *The Adventures of Shirley Holmes*. Shelburne, Ont., Canada: The Battered Silicon Dispatch Box. A 1933 play, a novelization of the play, and a single short story, these last two from *Mystery* magazine, 1933.

Mortimer, John. *Rumpole and the Primrose Path*. New York: Viking. Six new stories about the British barrister.

Muller, Marcia. *Time of the Wolves*. Waterville, Maine: Five Star Western. Ten stories, one new, one co-authored with Bill Pronzini, with historical or modern western settings, including two about Sharon McCone and one about Elena Oliverez.

Nevins, Francis M. *Leap Day and Other Stories*. Waterville, Maine: Five Star. Fourteen stories, 1973–2002, including one each about Loren Mensing, Milo Turner, and Gene Holt. Introduction by Jon L. Breen.

Oates, Joyce Carol. *Small Avalanches and Other Stories*. New York: HarperCollins. A mixed collection of twelve stories involving teenagers, about half criminous, two from *EQMM*.

Peters, Elizabeth. *Liz Peters, PI*. Norfolk, VA: Crippen & Landru. A single short story from a 1991 anthology in a pamphlet issued for the Malice Domestic convention.

Porges, Arthur. *The Mirror and Other Strange Reflections*. Ashcroft, B.C., Canada: Ash-Tree Press. Twenty-eight stories, one new, 1950–2002, mainly fantasy, six from *Alfred Hitchcock's Mystery Magazine*. Edited by Mike Ashley. (2002)

———. *Stately Homes and the Blunt Instrument*. Pebble Beach, CA: The Pondicherry Press. A single new Sherlockian pastiche. (2002)

Prichard, Kate & Hesketh. *The Experiences of Flaxman Low*. Ashcroft, B.C. Canada: Ash-Tree Press. Twelve stories from *Pearson's Magazine*, 1898–99, in the latest volume of the Occult Detectives Library. Edited by Jack Adrian.

Pronzini, Bill. *Burgade's Crossing.* Waterville, Maine: Five Star Western. Ten stories about western detectives Carpenter and Quincannon, one new, the others previously collected.

———. *Scenarios: A "Nameless Detective" Casebook.* Waterville, Maine: Five Star. Fourteen stories, 1968–2002, five previously uncollected, one a collaboration with Marcia Muller.

Pronzini, Bill, & Barry N. Malzberg. *"Do I Dare to Eat a Peach?"* Norfolk, VA: Crippen & Landru. A single story from a 1982 anthology reprinted in a pamphlet accompanying the limited edition of *Problems Solved.*

———. *Problems Solved.* Norfolk, VA: Crippen & Landru. Twenty-two stories, two new, 1972–2003. Preface by Pronzini, afterword by Malzberg.

Rhea, Nicholas. *Constable in the Wilderness.* London: Robert Hale. New untitled short stories.

Riccardi, Ted. *The Oriental Casebook of Sherlock Holmes.* New York: Random House. Nine new stories about Holmes's three years in the Orient.

Rusch, Kristine Katherine. *The Retrieval Artist and Other Stories.* Waterville, Maine: Five Star. Contains one futuristic private-eye story.

Sheffield, Charles. *The Amazing Dr. Darwin.* Riverdale, NY: Baen Books. Six novelettes featuring Charles Darwin's grandfather. An expanded version of a 1982 collection. (2002)

Shiel, M. P. *Prince Zaleski.* Carlton, North Yorkshire, U.K.: Tartarus Press. The four published Zaleski stories, plus an unpublished story and a fragment, both collaborations with John Gawsworth. (2002)

Sladek, John. *Maps: The Uncollected John Sladek.* Holicong, PA: Wildside Press. Mystery and fantasy stories.

Spillane, Mickey. *Primal Spillane: Early Stories 1941–1942.* Brooklyn: Gryphon Books. Uncollected early stories. Introduction by Max Allan Collins.

Willeford, Charles. *The Second Half of the Double Feature.* New Albany, IN: Wit's End. Twenty-five stories, vignettes, and sketches, many previously unpublished, two from *AHMM.*

White, Fred M. *The Romance of the Secret Service Fund.* Shelburne, Ont., Canada: The Battered Silicon Dispatch Box. Six Newton Moore secret service stories from *Pearson's Magazine,* 1900. Edited by Douglas G. Greene.

Woolrich, Cornell. *Night and Fear: A Centenary Collection of Stories by Cornell Woolrich.* New York: Carroll & Graf. Fourteen uncollected stories, mainly from 1936–43. Edited by Francis M. Nevins.

Wright, Eric. *A Killing Climate: The Collected Mystery Stories.* Norfolk, VA: Crippen & Landru. Fifteen stories including two Canadian Arthur Ellis Award winners, plus a new Charlie Salter novella and an Eric Wright checklist.

———. *Lodgings for the Night.* Norfolk, VA: Crippen & Landru. A new story in a pamphlet accompanying the limited edition of *A Killing Climate.*

Anthologies

Ashley, Mike, ed. *The Mammoth Book of Roman Whodunnits.* London: Robinson. Twenty stories, all but three new. Introduction by Steven Saylor.

Block, Lawrence, ed. *Blood on Their Hands.* New York: Berkley. Nineteen new stories in an anthology from Mystery Writers of America.

Bracken, Michael, ed. *Fedora II: More Private Eyes and Tough Guys.* Doylestown, PA: Betancourt. Fourteen new stories in the second anthology of a series.

———, ed. *Hardboiled.* Doylestown, PA: Betancourt. Fourteen new private-eye stories and one poem.

Breen, Jon L., ed. *Mystery: The Best of 2002.* New York: ibooks. Fourteen stories from various sources.

Burton, Peter, ed. *Death Comes Easy: The Gay Times Book of Murder Stories.* London: Millivres Books. Stories by gay writers.

Chabon, Michael, ed. *McSweeney's Mammoth Treasury of Thrilling Tales.* New York: Vintage. A mixed collection of twenty new stories, many criminous, some fantasy.

Collins, Max Allan, & Jeff Gelb, eds. *Flesh & Blood: Guilty as Sin: Erotic Tales of Crime and Passion.* New York: Mysterious Press. Twenty-three new stories.

Connelly, Michael, ed. *The Best American Mystery Stories 2003.* Boston: Houghton Mifflin. Twenty stories from various sources. Series editor: Otto Penzler.

Daheim, Mary; Carolyn Hart, Jane Isenberg, Shirley Rousseau Murphy. *Motherhood Is Murder.* New York: Avon. Four new novelettes about mothers.

Deaver, Jeffery, ed. *A Hot and Sultry Night for Crime.* New York: Berkley. Twenty new stories in an anthology from Mystery Writers of America.

Edwards, Martin, ed. *Green for Danger.* London: The Do-Not Press. Twenty stories, all but two new, in an anthology from Britain's Crime Writers Association. Foreword by Hilary Bonner.

———, ed. *Mysterious Pleasures.* London: Little Brown. A fiftieth anniversary anthology from CWA with twenty-three stories, eight new. Foreword by Hilary Bonner.

Frazier, Sunny; JoAnne Lucas, & Cora Ramos. *Valley Fever: Where Murder Is Contagious.* McKinleyville, CA: Fithian Press. Twenty-eight new suspense stories set in the San Joaquin Valley.

Freedman, Cheryl, & Caro Soles, eds. *Bloody Words: The Anthology.* Toronto: Baskerville Books. Twelve prize winners in a contest conducted over the past five years in conjunction with the Canadian mystery conference Bloody Words, plus a thirteenth new story.

Furst, Alan, ed. *The Book of Spies: An Anthology of Literary Espionage.* New York: Modern Library. Excerpts from fourteen novels by twentieth-century writers.

Gorman, Ed, ed. *Kittens, Cats and Crime.* Waterville, Maine: Five Star. Eleven stories, eight new. Introduction by John Helfers.

Harvey, John. ed. *Men from Boys.* London: Heinemann. Sixteen stories and a novella, all but three new, from male crime writers.

Iakovou, Takis & Judy; Steven F. Havill, Jane Rubino, Peter Abresch. *Deadly Morsels.* Toronto: Worldwide. Four new short novels about food.

Jakubowski, Maxim, ed. *The Best British Mysteries.* London: Allison & Busby. First in a planned annual series, with twenty-five stories published during 2002.

Jakubowski, Maxim, & M. Christian, eds. *The Mammoth Book of Future Cops.* London: Robinson. Thirty-three stories, thirteen new.

Kurland, Michael, ed. *My Sherlock Holmes: Untold Stories of the Great Detective.* New York: St. Martin's. Thirteen new stories narrated by characters other than Dr. Watson.

Lovisi, Gary, ed. *Pulp Crime Classics*. Brooklyn, NY: Gryphon. Thirteen stories from *Manhunt* and other digest-size magazines of the 1950s.

Price, Robert, ed. *Lin Carter's Anton Zarnak, Supernatural Sleuth*. Marietta, GA: Marietta Publishing. All of Carter's Zarnak fantasies, plus thirteen tales about the character by other writers. (2002)

Randisi, Robert J., ed. *High Stakes: 8 Sure-Bet Stories of Gambling and Crime*. New York: Signet. Eight stories, six new.

Reaves, Michael, & John Pelan, eds. *Shadows over Baker Street: New Tales of Terror*. New York: Del Rey/Ballantine. Eighteen new Sherlockian tales of detection and fantasy.

Schooley, Kerry J., & Peter Sellers, eds. *Hard Boiled Love: An Anthology of Noir Love*. Toronto: Insomniac Press. Twelve stories, five new.

Slater, Susan; Ed Gorman, Irene Marcuse, & Michael Jahn. *Crooks, Crimes and Christmas*. Toronto: Worldwide. Four new novelettes.

Nonfiction

Barnett, Colleen. *Mystery Women: An Encyclopedia of Leading Women Characters in Mystery Fiction, Vol. III (1990–1999)*. Scottsdale, AZ: Poisoned Pen Press. More than five hundred entries on female sleuths.

Campbell, Andrea. *Making Crime Pay*. New York: Allworth Press. A writer's guide to criminal law, evidence, and procedure.

Carter, David. *Georges Simenon*. U.K.: Pocket Essentials. A ninety-six-page paperback containing a brief biography of Simenon, checklists of his novels and short stories in English translation, film and TV adaptations, and reference material.

Chesterton, G. K. *G. K. Chesterton's Sherlock Holmes*. Ashcroft, B.C., Canada: Calabash Press/Baker Street Irregulars. Chesterton's twenty-one illustrations for an unpublished edition of the complete Sherlock Holmes. Includes six brief essays, four by Chesterton. Introduction and appreciation of Chesterton by editor Steven Doyle.

Christopher, Joe R. *Anthony Boucher's Celebrated Detectives*. Stephenville, TX: Chorazin Press. A fourteen-page pamphlet of limericks and comments about Boucher's various sleuths.

Clarke, Stephen P. *The Lord Peter Wimsey Companion (Revised and Expanded Edition)*. West Sussex, UK: Dorothy L. Sayers Society. Expanded to 773 pages from the original 563-page 1985 edition published by The Mysterious Press.

Cody, Liza. *White Knights & Giggling Bimbos*. Norfolk, VA: Crippen & Landru. A pamphlet containing a new essay on Chandler and private eyes, included with the limited edition of *Lucky Dip*.

Day, Barry, ed. *Sherlock Holmes: In His Own Words and in the Words of Those Who Knew Him*. Cutten, CA: Taylor Publishing. Quotations from the original stories.

Deeck, William F. *The Complete Deeck on Corbett*. Lincoln, NE: iUniverse, Inc. A booklet collecting articles and reviews on the less-than-classic novels of mystery writer James Corbett (1887–1958).

Derie, Kate. *The Deadly Directory 2003*. Tucson, AZ: Deadly Serious Press. An annual guide to the mystery world, listing booksellers, publishers, magazines, fan groups, conferences, awards, etc.

Herbert, Rosemary. *Whodunit? A Who's Who in Crime & Mystery Writing*. Oxford &

New York: Oxford University Press. Hundreds of entries from *The Oxford Companion to Crime & Mystery Writing* (1999), augmented by 101 new entries. Preface by Dennis Lehane.

Hubin, Allan J. *Crime Fiction IV: A Comprehensive Bibliography 1749–2000*. Shelburne, Ont., Canada: The Battered Silicon Dispatch Box. The final edition of the most complete and authoritative guide to mysteries, in five volumes listing more than 109,000 novels and 7,000 short-story collections, or in a CD-ROM edition from Locus Press, Oakland, CA.

Jacobson, Jeanne M., & Jennie G. Jacobson. *Detecta-Crostics: Puzzles of Mystery*. Carmel, IN: The Crum Creek Press. Mystery puzzles made up of anagrams and acrostics, dealing with well-known books, authors, and characters.

Layman, Richard. *Dashiell Hammett's The Maltese Falcon: A Documentary Volume*. Detroit: Gale. A scholarly companion to the classic novel.

Locke, John, ed. *Pulp Fictioneers*. Silver Spring, MD: Adventure House. A collection of essays on the pulps from writing journals of the era.

Lovisi, Gary. *Souvenirs of Sherlock Holmes*. Brooklyn, NY: Gryphon. Articles on collectible Sherlockiana.

Lyle, Doug. *Murder and Mayhem: A Doctor Answers Medical and Forensic Questions for Mystery Writers*. New York: St. Martin's. A collection of previously published columns.

Marks, Jeffrey. *Atomic Renaissance: Women Mystery Writers of the 1940s and 1950s*. Lee's Summit, MO: Delphi Books. Studies of seven popular writers of the period.

McGilligan, Patrick. *Alfred Hitchcock: A Life in Darkness and Light*. New York: ReganBooks/HarperCollins. An 850-page biography of the famed director.

Meaker, Marijane. *Highsmith: A Romance of the 1950s*. San Francisco: Cleis Press. A memoir by Patricia Highsmith's former lover, author of a number of suspense novels as "Vin Packer."

Moss, Robert F., ed. *Raymond Chandler: A Literary Reference*. Detroit: Gale. Documents and illustrations on Chandler's life and work. (2002; trade paperback: Carroll & Graf, New York, 2003)

Niebuhr, Gary Warren. *Make Mine a Murder: A Reader's Guide to Mystery and Detective Fiction*. Westport, CT: Libraries Unlimited. A guide for librarians.

Peters, Elizabeth, & Kristen Whitbread, eds. *Amelia Peabody's Egypt: A Compendium*. New York: Morrow. An illustrated guide to the Egypt of Peters's long-running mystery series.

Polt, Richard, & Fender Tucker, eds. *Wild About Harry*. Shreveport, LA: Ramble House. Reviews of Harry Stephen Keeler's mysteries from the Keeler News fanzine.

Rennison, Nick, ed. *Bloomsbury Good Reading Guide to Crime Fiction*. London: Bloomsbury. Expanded and updated edition of a guide first published in 1990 by Kenneth & Valerie McLeish, with more than 110 new authors added.

Roth, Martin. *The Crime Writer's Reference Guide: 1001 Tips for Writing the Perfect Murder*. Studio City, CA: Michael Wiese Productions. Revised edition of a detailed guide for novelists and screenwriters. Foreword and updated information by Rey Verdugo.

Swanson, Jean, & Dean James. *The Dick Francis Companion: The Complete Guide to the Beloved Mysteries of Dick Francis—from Plot Summaries to Character Profiles and More*. New York: Berkley. An A–Z resource for Dick Francis fans, covering novels, short stories, characters, and settings. Includes a new interview with Francis.

Tucker, Fender, & Richard Polt, eds. *Wild About Harry: 22 Reviews of Harry Stephen Keeler Novels*. Shreveport, LA: Ramble House. Reviews by members of the Keeler Society.

Watt, Peter Ridgeway, & Joseph Green. *The Alternative Sherlock Holmes: Pastiches, Parodies and Copies*. London: Ashgate Press. A discussion, with bibliographic data, of virtually all non-Doylean Holmes fiction.

Wheat, Carolyn. *How to Write Killer Fiction: The Funhouse of Mystery and the Roller Coaster of Suspense*. Santa Barbara, CA: John Daniel/Perseverance Press. Tips for aspiring mystery authors.

Wilson, Andrew. *Beautiful Shadow: A Life of Patricia Highsmith*. London & New York: Bloomsbury. A biography of the author of *Strangers on a Train* and the Ripley novels.

Zeman, Barry T. *The Gleam in Bugsy Siegal's Eye: A Bibliography of Mystery Fiction About Las Vegas and Gambling*. Las Vegas: Bouchercon 34. A twenty-six-page bibliography distributed at the Bouchercon mystery convention.

Obituaries

William C. Anderson (1920–2003). Author of two crime novels, *Penelope, the Damp Detective* (1974) and *Lady Bluebeard* (1994).

Michael David Anthony (1942–2003). British author of three novels about Colonel Richard Harrison, Anglican church official, starting with *The Becket Factor* (1990).

George Axelrod (1922–2003). Well-known playwright and screenwriter who published a single crime novel, *Blackmailer* (1952).

George Baxt (1923–2003). Well-known screenwriter and author of over two dozen mystery novels starting with *A Queer Kind of Death* (1966), five of them featuring gay black detective Pharoah Love. He also created a second series about Sylvia Plotkin and Max Van Larsen beginning with the Edgar-nominated *A Parade of Cockeyed Creatures* (1967), and a celebrity mystery series starting with *The Dorothy Parker Murder Case* (1984).

Fenton Bresler (1929–2003). British journalist and author who published an Edgar-nominated biography, *The Mystery of Georges Simenon* (1983).

Sylvia K. Burack (c. 1916–2003). Retired editor and publisher of *The Writer*, which often used articles by mystery writers. Many were collected in *The Writers' Handbook* (1975) and *Writing Suspense and Mystery Fiction* (1977), both edited by Burack and her late husband A. S. Burack. She was the 1998 recipient of MWA's Raven Award.

Larry Burkett (1939–2003). Author of a single futuristic suspense novel, *The Thor Conspiracy* (1995).

W(illiam) J(ohn) Burley (1914–2002). British author of some twenty-five mystery novels, twenty of them featuring Superintendent Charles Wycliffe introduced in *Three Toed Pussy* (1968).

Keith Campbell (1914–2003). Pseudonym of Keith Campbell West-Watson, author of eight mystery novels, 1941–54, unpublished in America.

Charles Baxter Clement (1940–2002). Author of a single suspense novel, *Limit Bid! Limit Bid!* (1984).

Hal Clement (1922–2003). Pseudonym of Harry Clement Stubbs, well-known science fiction writer and author of three SF mystery novels, notably *Needle* (1950). His 1942 short story "Proof" is considered the first successful melding of SF with the mystery genre.

Bruce Cook (1932–2003). Author of the Chico Cervantes private eye novels, starting with *Mexican Standoff* (1988) and, under the pseudonym of "Bruce Alexander," ten Sir John Fielding mysteries starting with *Blind Justice* (1994).

William Copeland (1911–2003). Film and television writer who authored a single intrigue novel, *Five Hours from Isfahan* (1975).

Lucy Cores (1914–2003). Author of four mystery novels, 1943–64, notably *Let's Kill George* (1946).

Ann Cornelisen (1926–2003). Author of a single suspense novel, *Any Four Women Could Rob the Bank of Italy* (1985).

Maurice Croll (1907–2002). Author of a single suspense novel, *Little Miss David—and Goliath* (1980).

Hume Cronyn (1911–2003). Famed actor who wrote adaptations for two Hitchcock films, *Rope* (1948) and *Under Capricorn* (1949).

Amanda Cross (1926–2003). Pseudonym of well-known feminist scholar Carolyn Heilbrun, creator of Professor Kate Fansler who appeared in some fourteen novels beginning with *In the Last Analysis* (1964) and a collection *The Collected Stories* (1997).

Dola de Jong (1911–2003). Author of a single adult mystery, *The Whirligig of Time* (1964), and an Edgar nominee for a juvenile mystery in 1963.

John De St. Jeor (1936–2003). Co-author, with Brian Shakespeare, of a single suspense novel, *The Patriot Game* (1973).

Carolyn House Doty (1941–2003). Author of a single suspense novel *Whisper* (1992).

John Gregory Dunne (1932–2003). Well-known novelist and screenwriter who authored three suspense novels, notably *True Confessions* (1977).

Leslie Edgley (1912–2002). Author of eight mystery novels, 1946–71, plus six more as "Robert Bloomfield," notably *From This Death Forward* and *Vengeance Street* (both 1952), and single novels as "Michael Gillian" and "Brook Hastings," the latter in collaboration with his wife Mary.

Lloyd Arthur Eshbach (1910–2003). SF writer and publisher, founder of Fantasy Press, who also published short mysteries in *Scientific Detective Monthly, The Saint,* and *Double-Action Detective.*

Howard Fast (1914–2003). Best-selling author of historical fiction who published two suspense novels under his own name, one as "Walter Ericson," and twenty as "E. V. Cunningham," notably *Sylvia* (1960) and *Sally* (1967), some reissued as by Fast.

John R. Feegel (1932–2003). Former chief medical examiner of Tampa, Florida, and author of five thrillers starting with the MWA Edgar winner for best paperback, *Autopsy* (1975).

Lewis Feuer (1912–2003). Author of a single Sherlockian novel, *The Case of the Revolutionist's Daughter* (1983).

Elizabeth Foote-Smith (1913–2003). Author of two novels about Will Woodfield, beginning with *A Gentle Albatross* (1976).

Sara Ann Freed (c. 1945–2003). Editor-in-chief of Mysterious Press and senior editor for Warner Books, co-editor of *The Mysterious Press Anniversary Anthology* (2001). Winner of the 1999 Ellery Queen Award from MWA.

Nicholas Freeling (1927–2003). British author of some forty detective novels, including eleven about Amsterdam's Inspector Van der Valk, notably *Because of the Cats, Gun*

Before Butter (both 1963), *Double-Barrel* (1964), and *The King of the Rainy Country* (1966, MWA Edgar winner).

Giles (Alexander Esme) Gordon (1940–2003). British SF writer and literary agent who authored a single suspense novel, *Girl with Red Hair* (1974), unpublished in America.

Gary Gottesfeld (c. 1942–2003). Former president of the Southern California chapter of MWA and author of five paperback thrillers starting with *The Violet Closet* (1989).

Mab Graff (1918–2003). Author of a single mystery novel, *Clangor in the Bell Tower* (1978).

Winston Graham (1910–2003). British historical novelist and mystery writer, author of twenty-five crime novels notably *The Little Walls* (1955, CWA Gold Dagger winner), *Marnie* (1961, filmed by Hitchcock), and *The Walking Stick* (1967).

Oriel Gray (1920–2003). Australian author of a single suspense novel and a Sherlockian play, 1987–90.

A(lvin) C(arl) Greene (1923–2002). Author of a single crime novel, *The Santa Claus Bank Robbery* (1972).

Ken Grimwood (1944–2003). Winner of the 1987 World Fantasy Award who also wrote a single crime novel, *The Voice Outside* (1982).

Marjory Hall (1908–2003). Author of two romantic suspense novels, 1974–77.

Richard (Victor) Hall (1937–2003). Author of two Patrick Costello novels with Australian settings, unpublished in America.

David K. Harford (1947–2003). Short-story writer, frequent contributor to *AHMM* from 1991 on, notably with "A Death of the Ho Chi Minh Trail," one of a series based on his experences as a military police officer in Vietnam.

Gladys M. Heldman (1922–2003). Author of tennis books and founder of *World Tennis* magazine, who published a single suspense novel, *The Harmonetics Investigation* (1979).

Richard Himmel (1920–2000). Author of fourteen novels, 1950–82, some about private eye Johnny Maguire.

Stanley Hopkins, Jr. (1923–2002). Pseudonym of Blythe Morley, who published two novels about sleuth Peter Marrell in 1943–44.

Donald (Lamont) Jack (1924–2003). Canadian author of five novels in the Bandy Papers series, some criminous.

Sebastien Japrisot (1931–2003). Pseudonym of Jean Baptiste Rossi, well-known French author of at least eight mystery novels, several of which were filmed, notably *The 10:30 from Marseilles* (1963), also published as *The Sleeping Car Murders*.

Audrey Jessup (c. 1928–2003). English/Canadian short-story writer who co-edited *The Ladies' Killing Circle* (1995) and other mystery anthologies.

Robert F. Jones (1934–2003). Author of a single suspense novel, *Blood Tide* (1990).

Elia Kazan (1909–2003). Renowned stage and film director who wrote a single suspense novel, *The Assassins* (1972).

Edward Keyes (1927–2002). Author of a single suspense novel, *Double Dare* (1981).

William Krasner (1917–2003). Author of six suspense novels, 1949–85, beginning with *Walk the Dark Streets*, and a short story in *EQMM*, 11/53.

Virginia Lanier (1930–2003). Author of six novels about bloodhound trainer Jo Beth Sidden starting with Anthony Award-winner *Death in Bloodhound Red* (1995).

Jacqueline La Tourrette (1926–2002). Author of nine novels of romantic suspense, starting with *The Joseph Stone* (1971).

Emma McCloy Layman (1910–2002). Author of a single suspense novel *Airesboro Castle* (1974), unpublished in America.

Michael Leahey (1956–2003). Author of two mystery novels, *Broken Machines* (2000) and *The Pale Green Horse* (2002).

Norman Lewis (1908–2003). British travel and suspense writer, author of some fifteen novels, 1949–87, notably *Cuban Passage* (1982).

Helen Lillie (1915–2003). Journalist and author of two gothic suspense novels, 1970–73.

Eddie Little (c. 1955–2003). Author of *Another Day in Paradise* (1998), a fictionalized account of his criminal life.

Caroline Llewellyn (1948–2000). Pen name of Carolyn Llewellyn Champlin, Canadian-American author of four suspense novels, 1988–96.

Gavin Lyall (1932–2003). Popular British author of at least thirteen thrillers and spy novels, beginning with *The Wrong Side of the Sky* (1961) and followed by CWA Silver Dagger winners *The Most Dangerous Game* (1963) and *Midnight Plus One* (1965).

Dorothea Malm (1915–2003). Author of six romantic suspense novels starting with *Claire: Memoirs of a Governess* (1957).

Leon N. Mandel (1928–2002). Co-author, with Philip Finch, of a single suspense novel, *Murder So Real* (1978), under the pseudonym of Al Bird.

Elizabeth Mansfield (1925–2003). Pseudonym of Paula Schwartz, author of two paperbound historical mysteries, 1978–79.

Anthony Masters (1940–2003). British author of three novelizations of the *Minder* TV series, each containing four untitled stories. Also published four mysteries as by "Richard Tate," another under his own name, and one in collaboration with Nicholas Barker.

John McAleer (1923–2003). Author of a single mystery novel, *Coign of Vantage; or The Boston Athenaeum Murders* (1988), and a 1978 Edgar winner for his biography of Rex Stout.

Manuel Vasquez Montalban (c. 1939–2003). Spanish poet and mystery writer, creator of Barcelona private eye Pepe Carvalho, featured in twenty novels.

Douglas Anne Munson (c. 1949–2003). Woman author of a single suspense novel, *El Nino* (1990), who followed it with two others under the pseudonym of "Mercedes Lambert," with a fourth to be published posthumously.

Joan Lowery Nixon (1927–2003). Author of over 140 books and a record four-time MWA Edgar winner for her young adult novels *The Kidnapping of Christina Lattimore* (1979), *The Séance* (1980), *The Other Side of Dark* (1986), and *The Name of the Game Was Murder* (1993).

Saliee O'Brien (1908–2002). Pseudonym of Frances Leroy Janas, author of five romantic thrillers in paperback, 1972–76.

Marc Olden (c. 1934–2003). Author of twenty-six action and suspense novels, and an additional nine under the pseudonym of "Robert Hawkes." One paperback Olden novel, *They've Killed Anna* (1977), was an Edgar nominee.

Wendy Owen (c. 1930–2002). Author of two suspense novels, 1966–68, unpublished in America.

Martin Page (1938–2003). Author of two suspense novels, notably *The Man Who Stole the Mona Lisa* (1984).

Jane Rice (1913–2003). Horror and fantasy writer who published four gothic suspense tales in *AHMM* during the 1980s. "The Crossroads" was reprinted in *The Year's Best Mystery and Suspense Stories 1986*.

Richard D. Ridyard (c. 1914–2003). Author of three suspense novels, 1980–92, unpublished in America.

Margaret Ritter (1922–2003). Author of three suspense novels, 1972–79.

Peter Rondinone (1954–2002). Author of a mixed collection of short stories, *The Digital Hood* (1998), some criminous.

Robert Ross (c. 1918–2003). Retired advertising executive who collaborated with Martin Woodhouse on two historical thrillers unpublished in the U.S., and then won the MWA Edgar for first mystery with *A French Finish* (1977).

Steven D. Ryan (1948–2002). Author of a single suspense novel, *O'Leary's Law* (2000).

Antonis Samarkis (1919–2003). Author of a single suspense novel, *The Flaw* (1969).

John B. Sanford (1904–2003). Author of a single suspense novel, *Seventy Times Seven* (1939).

Thomas Savage (1915–2003). Mainstream author who published a single suspense novel, *Midnight Line* (1976).

Harold C. Schonberg (1915–2003). Pulitzer Prize–winning music critic for the *New York Times* who reviewed mysteries for the *Times* from 1972 to 1995 under the pseudonym of "Newgate Callendar."

Carol Shields (1935–2003). Pulitzer Prize–winning Canadian author who published a single suspense novel, *Swann* (1989).

Bill Shoemaker (1931–2003). Famed former jockey who turned to mystery writing with *Stalking Horse* (1994) and two later novels, said to have been ghostwritten by Dick Lochte.

Jan Smid (?–2002). Czech author of a number of mysteries with New York settings, unpublished in America.

Derek Smith (1926–2003). British author whose work included a locked-room novel, *Whistle Up the Devil* (1953), unpublished in America, and a second novel published only in Japan.

Dan Sontup (1922–2003). Contributor to *EQMM* and many other mystery magazines who published two novels in 1962 under the pseudonyms of "John Clarke" and "David Saunders." Former New York chapter president of MWA.

Gretchen (Burnham) Sprague (1926–2003). Author of an Edgar-winning juvenile mystery, *Signpost to Terror* (1967), and three adult mysteries featuring sleuth Martha Patterson.

Peter Stone (1930–2003). Well-known screenwriter and dramatist who published a novelization of his film *Charade* in 1964.

Bill Strutton (1923–2003). British television and screenwriter who authored two suspense novels, 1957–73.

Karen Duke Sturges (c. 1932–2002). Author of two novels about sleuth Phoebe Mullins, beginning with *Death of a Baritone* (1999).

Peter Tinniswood (1936–2003). British scriptwriter and novelist who authored a single suspense novel, *Shemerelda* (1981), unpublished in America.

Neal Travis (1940–2002). Author of two marginal crime novels, 1979–86.

John Trench (1920–2003). British author of four mystery and suspense novels, 1953–63, three about archaeologist Martin Cotterell.

Michio Tsuzuki (c. 1929–2003). Japanese mystery writer and translator, first editor of the Japanese edition of *EQMM.*

Leon Uris (1924–2003). Best-selling author of *Exodus* whose work included two suspense novels, *The Angry Hills* (1955) and *Topaz* (1967), the latter filmed by Hitchcock.

Doug Warren (1925–2002). Author of three paperback novels, 1959–75.

Victor Wartofsky (1931–2003). Author of a single suspense novel, *Prescription for Justice* (1987).

John Weatherhead (c. 1924–2003). British author of three suspense novels, notably *Transplant* (1968), unpublished in America.

James Welch (1940–2003). Author of a single suspense novel, *The Death of Jim Loney* (1979).

Vicki Mason White (?–2002). Author of two paperback mysteries, *Deadly Paradise* (1996) and *Deadly Demise* (1997).

David Williams (1926–2003). British author of some two dozen novels, mainly about merchant banker Mark Treasure, notably *Unholy Writ* (1976), *Treasure up in Smoke* (1978), and *Murder for Treasure* (1980). Fifteen of his short stories, from *EQMM* and other sources, are collected in *Criminal Intentions* (2001).

Sloan Wilson (1920–2003). Well-known author of *The Man in the Gray Flannel Suit* who published a single suspense novel, *The Greatest Crime*, in 1980.

Robin W. Winks (1930–2003). Yale history professor who wrote extensively about the mystery in *Modus Operandi* (1982) and in several books he edited, *Detective Fiction* (1980), *Colloquium on Crime* (1986), and the two-volume *Mystery and Suspense Writers: The Literature of Crime, Detection & Espionage* (1998), which earned him an Edgar Award.

William Woolfolk (1917–2003). Novelist and comic-book writer who published nine suspense novels, 1954–89, as well as three others as by "Winston Lyon."

Edward Young (1913–2003). Author of a single spy novel, *The Fifth Passenger* (1963).

Paul Zindel (1936–2003). Pulitzer Prize–winning playwright who published two suspense novels, 1979–84.

World Mystery Report: Great Britain

Maxim Jakubowski

■ ■ ■

After two years in which the Crime Writers Association Gold Dagger for best crime and mystery novel of the year went to a book in translation (respectively to Henning Mankell and Jose Carlos Somoza), some were betting against the odds for the unthinkable possibility of a hat trick when the short list was announced. It featured Italian writer Carlos Lucarelli's *Almost Blue* and Russian Boris Akunin's *The Winter Queen*. Could the parochial shores of Anglo-Saxon crime writing be breached again? Had the judges been enjoying their European holidays too much?

It was not to be, however, and the Gold Dagger was unsurprisingly awarded to a stalwart favorite: Minette Walters, for *Fox Evil*, while the Silver Dagger runner-up award was given to Morag Joss for *Half Broken Things*. In addition to the aforementioned foreign guests left on the starting line, the other books shortlisted were Robert Littell's *The Company* and Robert Wilson's *The Blind Man of Seville*. The list for best first novel for the John Creasey Memorial Dagger included C. J. Sansom's *Dissolution*, Rod Duncan's *Backlash*, and the winner was U.S. author William Landay for the impressive *Mission Flats*. An abbreviated shortlist that was compensated by the splendid comic presence of Peter Lovesey at the awards ceremony disguised as John Creasey and actually fooling many present with a witty cabaret act full of wonderful and wicked private jokes.

Robert Littell's massive CIA saga was also on the shortlist for the Ian Fleming Steel Dagger for thrillers (which goes to show that one judge's thriller is another man's crime and mystery story, so blurred are the genre demarcations these days . . .), together with Lee Child's *Persuader*, Roger Jon Ellory's *Candlemoth*, Lucretia Grindle's *The Nightspinners*, Gerald Seymour's *Traitor's Kiss*, Henry Porter's *Empire State*, and the eventual winner, Dan Fesperman's *The Small Boat of Great Sorrows*.

Historical mystery still thrives in the British marketplace with no period left untouched and the Ellis Peters Historical Dagger went to Andrew Taylor's *The American Boy*, with Tom Bradby's *The White Russian*, C. J. Samson's above debut, Olen Steinhauer's *The Bridge of Sighs*, Gillian Linscott's *Blood on the Wood*, Lee Jackson's *London Dust*, and Italian writer Marcello Fois's *The Advocate* making up the list of worthy nominations.

On the short-story front, Jerry Sykes, for "Closer to the Flame," won the prize for the second time, a splendid achievement by a young author who has yet to publish his first novel.

On a less celebratory note, 2003 also saw the passing of some major names in the British crime-writing firmament including Nicolas Freeling, creator of Van der Valk, Castang, and many thrillers set in Europe where he lived his last few decades; W. J. Burley who will be best remembered for his Wycliffe mysteries; the much-loved David Williams; Michael David Anthony; and Winston Graham, whose *Marnie* was adapted by Hitchcock for the movies but who later mostly worked in the field of historical sagas.

London's Crime Scene Festival entered its fourth year at the National Film Theatre on the South Bank and again proved popular, with U.S. Guests of Honor Janet Evanovich and Walter Mosley a main attraction, alongside the crème de la crème of the British scene, including Lindsey Davis, John Connolly, Martina Cole, Marian Babson, Mark Billingham, Martyn Waites, Michael Marshall, Peter Robinson, Russell James, Lauren Henderson, Edward Marston, Anne Perry, Stella Duffy, and thirty others all participating. The focus was this year on Georges Simenon with a varied program of films, TV adaptations, and panels, which included the presence of his son John Simenon, his biographer Patrick Marnham, actor Herbert Lom, who was featured in a notorious Simenon film adaptation, and Eurocrime experts like Cara Black and David Hewson. The festival, which combines literary and film events, opened with the world premiere of Joel Schumacher's *Veronica Guerin*, followed by an onstage interview with the director and the main star, the actress Cate Blanchett. The 2004 festival is already set for July 8 to 11, with the focus being on both Graham Greene and Margery Allingham, on the occasion of their centenary.

The demise of the Dead on Deansgate Festival was confirmed this year after a year when the Waterstone's book chain held it without the assistance of the CWA, but the gap was soon filled by a new event in Harrogate in Yorkshire in July, one week after Crime Scene, with the established literary festival there setting up a Crime and Mystery stream, organized by a committee of authors, agents, and publishers. Their first line-up was impressive, with many of the organizers pulling in many personal favors, and in addition to many of the Crime Scene participants, also featured Colin Dexter and Jeffery Deaver.

On the retail front, this was yet another year in which the bookselling trade traveled farther down the dangerous path of chain and supermarket domination, and a landscape of endangered independents. London's Crime In Store that had been limping on for years finally went under with debts of over a quarter million pounds in the late spring, before an investor bought the assets from the receivers and reopened it again in the summer as Crime On Store, which soon closed again within months after failing to pay its rent and with publishing houses unwilling to provide credit to the reconstructed company. Murder One, on the other hand, will be celebrating its fifteenth successful year this summer and soldiers on, making crime pay.

There were no new players on the publishing front. Most major publishers enjoyed a good year, and all the existing independents survived with equal poise, often catching in their nets authors that the big houses are disposing of and making them work due to smaller overheads.

The success story of the year was undoubtedly the emergence of Alexander McCall Smith's Botswana Mama Ramotswe mysteries. Published for several years by a small Scottish publisher, Polygon, they had been bubbling under outside of the chains' radars. These amiable mysteries, featuring Botswana's cozy answer to Miss Marple, were, following their success in the U.K., picked up by Time Warner and given considerable clout, which catapulted them onto the bestseller lists, although the fifth volume, *The Full Cupboard of Life*, appeared first from Polygon. Arguably crime too was Mark Haddon's remarkable *The Curious Case of the Dog in the Night-Time*. Published in two versions, one for children and one for adults, it scooped literary awards, what with a strong Sherlockian connection.

Major titles of 2003 included new books by Jake Arnott (*Truecrime*), Robert Barnard (*A Cry from the Dark*), Mark Billingham (*Lazybones*), Simon Brett (*Murder in the Museum*), Martina Cole (*The Know*), John Connolly (*Bad Men*), Lindsey Davis's annual Falco caper (*The Accusers*), Michael Dibdin's Zen case (*Medusa*), Christopher Fowler—a major horror writer turning to crime (*Full Dark House*), Nicci French (*The Land of the Living*), Frances Fyfield (*Seeking Sanctuary*), Jonathan Gash's latest Lovejoy caper (*The Ten Word Game*), Robert Goddard (*Days Without Number*), P. D. James's new Dalgliesh conundrum (*The Murder Room*), Peter Lovesey (*The House Sitter*), Val McDermid (*A Distant Echo*) and a paperback original Lindsay Gordon mystery as V. L. McDermid (*Hostage for Murder*), David Peace's final volume in his harrowing Ridings Quartet (*1983*), Anne Perry (*Seven Dials* and *No Graves As Yet*), Ian Rankin (*A Question of Blood*), Ruth Rendell's new Wexford case (*Babes in the Wood*) and a stand-alone (*The Rottweiler*), Peter Robinson's next Inspector Banks installment (*The Summer that Never Was*), and Minette Walters (*Disordered Minds*).

Other notable crime and mystery books, many by writers still criminally overlooked in the U.S.A, worth mentioning would include (and this is just skimming the year's publications and bears witness to the diversity of the current publishing scene) *Touching the Dark* by Jane Adams; *No Birds Singing* by Vivien Armstrong; *Fair Exchange Is Robbery* by Jeffrey Ashford; *Private View* by Meg Atkins; *Not Quite a Geisha* by Marian Babson; *Reflection* by Jo Bannister; *Chapter and Verse* by Colin Bateman; *Bishop's Brood* by Simon Beaufort; *Caught Out in Cornwall*, a final, posthumous book by Janie Bolitho; *Monsieur Pamplemousse Hits the Headlines* by Michael Bond; *When the Dead Cry Out* by Hilary Bonner, this year's Chair of the Crime Writers' Association; *Blind to the Bone* by Stephen Booth, this year's recipient of the Crime in the Library Dagger; *Vixen* by Ken Bruen; *Dead Heat* by Caroline Carver; *A Dark Night Hidden* by Alys Clare; *Burial of Ghosts* by Anne Cleeves; *The Damascened Blade* by Barbara Cleverly; *Angel and the Deadly Secret* by Anthea Cohen; *Dead Ringer* by Judith Cook; *Place of Safety* by Natasha Cooper; *Holloway Falls* by Neil Cross; *More Sinned Against* by Charles Cumming; *Meeting of Minds* by Clare Curzon; *Dying to Deceive* and *Power Shift* by Judith Cutler; *Kiss It Away* by Carol Anne Davis; *Remember Me* by Sarah Diamond; *Death and the Jubilee* by David Dickinson; Roman mystery *Murder Imperial*, Eastern whodunit *The Plague Lord*, Egyptian mystery *An Evil Spirit Out of the West*, Brother Athelstan case *House of Shadows*, and Alexander whodunit *The Gates of Hell* by the ever prolific Paul Doherty, uncrowned king of the historical mystery; *Weathercock* by Glen Duncan; *Cradle Song* by Robert Edric; *Skeleton Room* and *The Plague Maiden* by Kate Ellis; *Murder on the Internet* by Ron Ellis; *Waking Raphael* by Leslie Forbes; *Mission Canyon* by Meg Gardiner, a U.S. author living in the U.K.; *The Serpent in the Garden* by Janet Gleeson; *Alms for Oblivion* by Philip Gooden; *Watching Out* by Anne Granger; *Killer in Winter* by Susanna Gregory; *Mortal Taste* by J. M. Gregson; *Better than Death* by Georgie Hale; *Dead Reckoning* by Patricia Hall; *Snatch* and *Down the Garden Path* by Gerald Hammond; *Murder of Innocence* by Veronica Heley; *Forget Me Not* by Manda Sue Heller, the first in an Italian-set series; *Season of the Dead* by David Hewson; *Hot Potato* by Joyce Holms; *On Dangerous Ground* by Lesley Horton; *Blood Ties* by C. C. Humphreys; *Dead Light* by Graham Hurley; *Light Fantastic* by Graham Ison; *Death at Versailles* by Jane Jakeman; *The Girl with the Long Back* by Bill James; *Walking the Shadows* by Donald

James; *No One Gets Hurt* by Russell James; *Fallen Gods*, a Skinner case, and *Unnatural Justice*, an Oz Blackstone thriller, by Quintin Jardine; *The Outlaws of Ennor* and *The Templar's Penance* by Michael Jecks; *The Last Red Death* by Paul Johnston; *Water Lily* by Susanna Jones; *Half Broken Things* by Morag Joss; *The Dreaming Detective* by H.R.F. Keating; *Cold Blood* by Susan Kelly; *The Murder Exchange* by Simon Kernick; *An Orkney Murder* and *The Gowrie Conspiracy* by Alanna Knight; *Fear in the Forest* by Bernard Knight; *Death in the Valley of Shadows* by Deryn Lake; *Nothing like the Night* by David Lawrence; *Blood on the Wood* by Gillian Linscott; *Dead Letters* by Joan Lock; *Circles and Squares* and *Mortal Instruments* by John Malcolm; *The Frost Fair* by Edward Marston; *Endangering Innocents* by Priscilla Masters; *The Shadow Chaser* by John Matthews; *Perfectly Dead* by Iain McDowall; *Sanctum* by Denise Mina; *The Ambitious Stepmother* by Fidelis Morgan; *Weaving Shadows* by Margaret Murphy; *Some Bitter Taste* by Magdalen Nabb; *Harem* by Barbara Nadel; *Somebody Else* by Reggie Nadelson; *No Escape* by Hilary Norman; *Acid Lullaby* by Ed O'Connor; *A Guilty Heart* by Julie Parsons; *Limestone Cowboy* by Stuart Pawson; *Last Tango in Aberystwyth* by Malcolm Pryce; *As Bad as It Gets* by Julian Rathbone; *Apple of My Eye* by Patrick Redmond; *Summertime* by Liz Rigbey; *Angel on the Inside* by Mike Ripley; *Dangerous Sea* by David Roberts; *The Legatus Mystery* by Rosemary Rowe; *No Laughing Matter* and *Dirty Work* by Betty Rowlands; *Backlash* by Denise Ryan; *Blue Noon* by Robert Ryan; *The Eagle and the Wolves* by Simon Scarrow; *Nine Men Dancing* by Kate Sedley; *First Drop* by Zoe Sharp; *Selling Grace* by Simon Shaw; *Home From Home* by Carol Smith; John B. Spencer's posthumous *Grief*; *Death Left Hungry* and *The Enemy Within* by Sally Spencer; *Blindfold* by Lyndon Stacey; *Bitter Blue* by Cath Staincliffe; *Tell Me Lies* by Tony Strong; *The American Boy* by Andrew Taylor; *Second Act* by Marilyn Todd; *Market for Murder* by Rebecca Tope; *Badger's Moon* by Peter Tremayne; *Maxwell's Inspection* by M. J. Trow; *All Roads Leadeth* by Peter Turnbull; *Born Under Punches* by Martyn Waites; *Copy Cat* by Gillian White; *The Prince of Wales* by John Williams; *Hello Bunny Alice* by Laura Wilson; *Tripletree* by Derek Wilson; and *Vote For Murder* by David Wishart.

Debut novels that could well hold much promise for future criminal careers kept on pouring down the grapevine. Worth noting are: *Nirvana Bites* by Debi Alper; *The Dead* by Ingrid Black; *Making Love* by Marius Brill; *The Sixth Lamentation* by William Brodrick; *Savage Tide* by Glen Chandler; *Candlemoth* by Roger Jon Ellory; *The Fiend in Human* by John MacLachlan Gray; *The Nightspinners* by Lucretia Grindle; *Mister Candid* by Jules Hardy; *Down Cemetery Road by* Mick Herron; *The Crime Tsar* by Nichola McAuliffe; *The End of the Line* by K. T. MacCaffrey, *Feast of Carrion* by Keith MacCarthy; *Dragon's Eye* by Andy Oakes; *The Lamplighter* by Anthony O'Neill; *Box* by Mark Powell; *Looking for Mt Nobody* by Sue Rann; *Tower of Silence* by Sarah Rayne; *Winter's End* by John Rickards; *Dissolution* by C. J. Sansom; *Outside the White Lines* by Chris Simms; *The Cardamom Club* by Jon Stock; *The Stepmother* by Simon Tolkien (grandson of *Lord of the Rings* creator); *Nowhere's Child* by Francesca Weisman; *Practice to Deceive* by David Williams; and *Dr. Mortimer and the Carved Head Mystery* by Gerard Williams. Which of these writers will we hear from again?

On the thrillers front lines we also had much to read, including novels by Paul Adam (*Flash Point*), Ted Allbeury (*Due Process*), Campbell Armstrong (*White Rage*), Michael Asher (*Sandstorm*), Tom Bradby (*The White Russian*), Lee Child (*Persuader*), John Creed (*The Day of the Dead*), Murray Davies (*Collaborator*), Michael Dobbs (*Never Surrender*), Clive Egleton (*Assassination Day* and *Spy's Ransom*), Frederick Forsyth (*Avenger*), Brian

Freemantle (*Two Women*), John Fullerton (*Hostile Place*), Reg Gadney (*The Scholar of Extortion*), Jack Higgins (*Bad Company*), Bill James (*Man's Enemies*), Gordon Kent (*Hostile Contact*), Paul Kilduff (*The Headhunter*), Stephen Leather (*The Eye Witness*), Peter May (*The Runner*), Hector Macdonald (*The Hummingbird Saint*), Andy MacNab (*Dark Winter*), Henry Porter (*Empire State*), Michael Ridpath (*Fatal Error*), Chris Ryan (*Greed*), Gerald Seymour (*Traitor's Kiss*), Terence Strong (*Cold Monday*), and Guy Walters (*The Leader*).

As usual there was a relative paucity of short-story collections and anthologies, but some made their way to the light nonetheless: Catherine Aird's collection *Chapter and Hearse*; Martin Edwards's CWA anniversary anthology, *Mysterious Pleasures*, and the annual CWA collection, *Green for Danger*; John Harvey's rite of passage anthology *Men from Boys*; and my own inaugural annual *Best British Mysteries*, which the W. H. Smith chain even TV-advertised.

All in all, something for everyone. As can be demonstrably seen, British crime and mystery in 2003 aimed to please, if not to murder.

So get reading. Or else . . .

WORLD MYSTERY REPORT: CANADA

Edo van Belkom

■ ■ ■

In 2003 the Crime Writers of Canada reached a significant milestone with its 200th member, the highest the association's membership has ever been. Also in 2003, Maureen Jennings (*Let Loose the Dogs*, *Poor Tom Is Cold*) became president of the CWC, replacing Mary Jane Maffini (*Little Boy Blues*), who held the position for two years. Barbara Fradkin took on the position of national vice president.

In 2003, one of the last few print versions of the CWC Newsletter *Fingerprints* (Cheryl Freedman, editor; cheryl@worldhouse.com) did a feature on three Canadian mystery bookstores: Prime Crime Books (Ottawa), Sleuth of Baker Street (Toronto), and Whodunit Mystery Bookstore (Winnipeg). Included with the article was a list of the top five sellers from each store for the previous year and shows some definite nationalist tendencies in terms of the origins of the top books on the lists.

Prime Crime Books (www.members.rogers.com/prime.crime): 1.*Little Boy Blues* by Mary Jane Maffini, Rendezvous Press (Mary Jane Maffini was a former co-owner of the store) 2.*Once Upon a Time* by Barbara Fradkin, Rendezvous Press 3.*Undertow* by Thomas Rendell Curran, Breakwater Books 4.*Death in Holy Orders* by P. D. James, Ballantine 5.*Aftermath* by Peter Robinson, McClelland & Stewart.

Sleuth of Baker Street (www.sleuthofbakerstreet.com): 1.*Black Dog* by Stephen Booth, Scribner 2.*Dancing with the Virgins* by Stephen Booth, Scribner 3.*Blood on the Tongue* by Stephen Booth, Scribner 4.*The Eyre Affair* by Jasper F. Forde, Viking 5.*Place of Execution* by Val McDermid, St. Martin's Minotaur. Whodunit?

Mystery Bookstore (www.whodunitcanada.com): 1.*Macaws of Death* by Karen Dudley, Turnstone Press 2.*Bolshevik's Revenge* by Allan Levine, Great Plains Public 3.*Traitor to Memory* by Elizabeth George, Bantam 4.*Death in Holy Orders*, by P. D. James, Ballantine 5.*P Is for Peril* by Sue Grafton, Putnam.

The Arthur Ellis Awards celebrated their twentieth anniversary in 2003 with a gala banquet, June 4 at the Ontario Club in downtown Toronto. The AE Awards were first presented in 1984, with just three nominees for best novel and just a single award going to Eric Wright's *The Night the Gods Smiled.* That year Derrick Murdoch was presented with the Chairman's Award for Lifetime Achievement, which was subsequently renamed as the Derrick Murdoch Award. Twenty years later, AE Awards are handed out in six categories, including one for writing in French. In the past, other categories have included a category for Best Genre Criticism/Reference (1991 & 1992) and Best Play (1994).

Master of ceremonies for this year's event was Margaret Cannon, longtime mystery reviewer for the national newspaper the *Globe and Mail.* Cannon also received the Derrick Murdoch Award, which is presented by the CWC president to a person who has contributed a great deal either to the CWC or to Canadian crime writing as a whole. Other AE winners were: Best First Novel, *Midnight Cab* by James W. Nichol, Knopf Canada; Best Novel, *Blood of Others* by Rick Mofina, Kensington; Best Short Story, "Bottom Walker" by James Powell, *Ellery Queen's* May 2002; Best Nonfiction, *Covert Entry* by Andrew Mitrovica, Random House Canada; Best Juvenile, *Break and Enter* by Norah McClintock, Scholastic Canada; Best Crime Writing in French, *Le rouge ideal* by Jacques Coté, Alire. To contact the Crime Writers of Canada: 3007 Kingston Rd. Box 113, Toronto, ON, M1M 1P1.

In related award news, Robert J. Sawyer's mystery/science fiction crossover novel *Illegal Alien* won Japan's top science fiction award, the Seiun, for best foreign novel of the year. An Aurora Award went to editor Edo van Belkom for his young adult horror anthology *Be Very Afraid!* which features a mix of horror and mystery stories for young readers.

In book news, Rick Mofina's Arthur Ellis Award–nominated Rocky Mountain thriller *Cold Fear* was translated into Norwegian and published in June 2003 by Bladkompaniet of Oslo. *Cold Fear* was also optioned by national broadcaster CTV for a possible made-for-TV movie. Richard King's first novel, *That Sleep of Death*, was translated into French as *Le Libraire a du Flair* and published by Libre Expression. J. Robert Janes's Kohler/St. Cyr novel, *Flykiller*, published by Orion/McArthur, was the only Canadian nominee for the Hammett Award given by the International Association of Crime Writers for a work of literary excellence in the field of crime writing by a U.S. or Canadian author. And Canadian crime-writing veteran Eric Wright had a collection published by Crippen & Landru entitled *A Killing Climate*. The book features a brand-new Charlie Salter written specifically for the collection after Wright realized he didn't have enough stories to fill the book.

Mystery Readers Journal, a thematic quarterly mystery review, ended the year with an issue (Vol. 19, No. 3) focusing on "Cool Canadian Crime." The issue features essays by Lou Allin, Giles Blunt, James Coggins, Shelly Costa, Thomas Rendell Curran, Vicki Delany, William Deverell, Barbara Fradkin, Laurence Gough, Lyn Hamilton, Kenneth J. Mackay, Timothy Heald, Mary Jane Maffini, H. Mel Malton, Art Montague, James Powell, Peter Sellers, Caro Soles, and Eric Wright.

The Many Trials of One Jane Doe was a made-for-TV movie that aired on CBC in September. The film told the story of Jane Doe, a Toronto woman who was raped and who eventually sued the Toronto Police, and won, for failing to warn the people in her neighborhood that a serial rapist was on the loose.

Finally, Bloody Words V was held in June at the Lord Elgin Hotel in downtown Ottawa for the first time (after four years in Toronto). International guest of honor was Val McDermid, while Canadian guests were Howard Engel and Eric Wright. Mary Jane Maffini served as toastmaster. Visit www.bloodywords.com for more details. Coming to Toronto in 2004, Bouchercon 35.

World Mystery Report: Germany

Thomas Wörtche

■ ■ ■

Is there really a frail revival of a specific German culture of crime fiction? This was the thesis of some critics about the year 2003. Indeed, after years of stagnation, the market has begun to move again—but in which direction?

The tsunami of simply made, so-called *Regionalkrimis* (mysteries set in certain small German provinces, to be sold and read only in those very places) has lost its power—maybe they are still being produced and even read, but nobody seems to care about them anymore. The chief proponents of this trend, like Jacques Berndorff (Grafit), are shifting the settings of their novels into big cities like Berlin. But this doesn't help, because urban crime requires different ways of narration—a task probably too big for local heroes. *Regionalkrimi*, this aberration of a form, will soon be forgotten or remain as a mere footnote to the literary history of the genre.

The decline of these cute little booklets came parallel to the decline of the various Internet chat rooms concerning mysteries. During previous years we saw eager debating, tempests in a teapot about any topic you may imagine; nowadays chatting fans and self-declared experts seem to have lost any impact and drive they once possessed. Only those few professionally made Web sites seem to survive, like the internationally praised and appreciated www.kaliber38.de or the daily media-service www.alligatorpapiere.de.

Syndikat, the organization of many but by no means all German crime writers, meanwhile desperately tries to get some glitz to camouflage its tristesse—by featuring prominent amateur crime writers like porn star Dolly Buster or TV-news anchorman Ulrich Wickert. Also, the eventization of book launchings and readings at locations like coffin storehouses or aquariums seems to be over the top. The sales of German replica novels (woven by no-name-authors and copying international success formulas) can have decent sales only because some publishers (like the imprints of Random House or the Holtzbrinck group) cooperate with supermarket chains like Aldi. Offers like three novels in one volume for five euros also are the usual marketing strategy for mainstream mystery authors like Elizabeth George. This trend continues to have consequences for hard-core crime writers and the engaged publishers that are too small to compete: Distel Verlag, the specialist for the French *néo-polar*, has to make a break (or even give up), with authors like William Marshall, Jerome Charyn, James Crumley, Lawrence Block, James Sallis et al. Many established authors have problems finding new publishers, and interesting newcomers like Jonathan Lethem or David Grand (both with Tropen Verlag) are by definition a minority program for their respective publishers—the novels of such authors are under suspicion of being "too complicated."

On the other hand, the concept of global crime works so well that it seems to be something copied by major houses. When Unionsverlag *metro* started with this concept in 2000, the majors seemed to smile indulgently at the effort. But 2003 again was a successful year for *metro* with two best-selling authors: Leonardo Padura of Cuba and Nury Vittachi of Hong Kong—and a new big name, Liza Cody, on the list and with international awards (the Premio Camões and the Juan-Rulfo-Award) for *metro*-author Rubem Fonseca from Brazil. Logically the majors hurried to follow, coming up with Tibet novels by Eliot Pattison (Ruetten & Loening), Botswana novels by Alexander McCall Smith (Nymphenburger), or Turkey novels by Barbara Nadel (Ullstein). There was even one novel, *Hotel Bosporus* by Turkish female author Esmahan Aytol (Diogenes), specifically designed for the German market, where *metro*-author Celil Oker had opened up the doors for Turkish crime novels.

The trend toward reviving crime fiction also gave good support for at least three German authors who keep writing not out of sheer calculation and where luckily pushed by the trend: First, D. B. Blettenberg won the National branch of the German Critics Award for Crime Fiction (the Deutscher Krimi Preis, DKP) for his novel *Berlin Fidschitown* (Pendragon Verlag), set in Berlin and Bangkok, dealing with the Vietnam war, which is—in a way—still going on in the underground, in the catacombs, underground tubes, and Nazi bunkers of Berlin today, where Vietnamese gangs meet for shootouts and struggles about their shares of the drug and porn market. *Fidschi*, by the way, is a pejorative word for Asians in German.

Second, Manuela Martini was able to establish herself among serious authors with her second novel, *Barrier Reef* (Bastei), set in Australia, and Marcus Starck delivered another novel from down under: *Sex Dot Com* (with Pulp Master). The time seems to be over when German writers, on the seventh line of the book, send their German cops to exotic places to help the dull local police solve cases.

But all in all it is my impression that the big hype of the recent years is petering out: Crime fiction as the big, taken-for-granted cash cow is out. It loses ground to fantasy, romance, maritime stuff, or mainstream novels.

The flirtation with mainstream that some crime novels entertain may impress the highbrow literary pages, but not the readers. The worst hype last year was a novel called *Eismond* by Jan Costin Wagner (Eichborn)—an unintentionally funny novel about an inept Finnish policeman who is so sympathetic with a serial killer that he can't catch the villain and has to wait until the killer freezes to death on the cop's doorstep. The novel is narrated in lyrical prose, enough to push the lyrical quality button (according to Mr. Pavlov), but not enough to give this fairy tale any plausibility, let alone any logic or suspense.

The winners of 2003's Deutscher Krimi Preis illustrate the quirky situation quite well. D. B. Blettenberg, as mentioned above, won the national contest; second was Anne Chaplet with her novel *Schneesterben* (Verlag Antje Kunstmann)—Anne Chaplet is the well-known pseudonym of a well-known essayist and her mysteries are solid *whodunits* in the British tradition, combined with the optimistic ideology of the Agatha Christie approach to crime and murder. Anne Chaplet novels supply the needs of the educated middle-class readers, who know for sure what a mystery is and do not accept new experiences. Third in the national section was Heinrich Steinfest's novel *Ein sturer Hund* (with Piper)—an absolutely outstanding novel by the shy Austrian-Australian author who lives in Germany and writes the German language of a Robert Musil on drugs. The story about a British secret-service bounty killer who is hunted down by a Chinese-

Austrian private eye is a wonderfully absurd and grotesque piece of prose out of the spirits of irony and parody. Steinfest stands very alone, the quality of and the idea behind his books are inimitable. He is as untypical of any trend, wave, or market calculation as possible.

The international section was won by French female writer Fred Vargas, *Fliehe weit und schnell* (with Aufbau Verlag), another author who is unique. The novel starts with the suggestion that the Black Death is back in modern-day Paris and presents bizarre and witty characters and situations galore just to tell, in the end, a sad family story. Second international rank is for George Pelecanos's two novels (*The Sweet Flower* and *Right as Rain*), a very astonishing choice, since Pelecanos is not very present on the German market and published by at least two publishers (DuMont and Rotbuch). But it shows that hard-boiled American crime fiction still has true friends and fans over here. Another hard-boiled hit, rank 3, Bangkok-based Canadian author Christopher G. Moore with *Cut Out* (Unionsverlag-*metro*), a very personal story about private eye Vincent Calvino going to genocide-shaken Cambodia during the times of U.N. administration.

The results of the DKP show clearly: The trend is no-trend. All interesting books of 2003 are not to be pigeonholed; they follow only their author's individual style or taste (if there is one at all), but no other formula. Friedrich Ani sends his cop Tabor Süden from Munich to northeast Germany in *Gottes Tochter* (Droemer-Knaur), a novel that rewrites Shakespeare's *Romeo and Juliet* under East-West circumstances. Monika Geier uses her setting, the Palatium, a region near the Rhine River and France, intentionally not for folkoric purposes, but for a grown-up police procedural, *Stein sei ewig* (with Ariadne), about what the job does to a female cop. And Nobert Horst, a writing real-life cop, puts together a grim, realistic mosaic of narrative bits and bites to his first novel *Leichensache* (Goldmann).

Politics, this is also remarkable, was no topic of German crime fiction last year. No post 9/11 novel, no conspiracy novel of importance. The economic crisis in Germany is still of no issue. And the return of international political thrillers didn't happen here. That Alan Furst is back or also Robert Littell or that there is a new Ross Thomas edition in the States—no item here. Patricia Highsmith is honored with a complete works edition (Diogenes), celebrated by the literary pages but not by readers; the first and only Eric Ambler biography (by Stefan Howald, also at Diogenes) went by nearly unnoticed; the same is true for a new Charles Willeford edition (Alexander Verlag).

Of course, the rock-solid international sellers—Val McDermid (Droemer-Knaur), Peter Robinson (Ullstein), Reginald Hill (Europa Verlag), Stephen Booth and Ian Rankin (both Random House) find their true audience. But they all needed several books to be established, and it seems big publishing houses are less and less patient. At the moment Jillian Hoffman's *Cupido* (Wunderlich) is being bombed into the market with such an amount of PR money that you can bet, if this launch fails, the author will vanish forever.

So, 2003 was a year of nervousness, of curiosity for things to come, and of faint hope that somewhere, somebody is working out a new road map for the genre.

The Year 2003 in Mystery Fandom

George A. Easter

■ ■ ■

Mystery Conventions

The granddaddy of all mystery conventions is Bouchercon and in 2003 it was held in Sin City—Las Vegas, Nevada. Somehow it just seemed fitting. Fans were treated to many special events, including a grand opening ceremony hosted by Lee Child. The Barry Awards were presented in front of a crowd of over a thousand fans and guests. Two icons of mystery fiction, James Lee Burke and Ruth Rendell, were guests of honor. Convention members attended panels on a wide variety of mystery subjects, giving fans a chance to see their favorite authors up close and personal. As each set of panels ended, there was always a rush to the book dealers' room to buy books written by authors they had just listened to for the previous hour. And that brings us to the subject of the booksellers' room.

At each convention there is always a large dealers room filled with books for sale from many dealers who come from all over the country and even Canada and the U.K. When a Bouchercon convenes, the dealers room becomes the largest mystery bookstore in the world, offering a wide variety of books, from vintage collectibles to the newest hardcover or paperback on the market. It also becomes a focal point for meeting friends, authors, and fellow fans.

Bouchercons are always bustling events. Authors come to meet the fans, but also to do business with their editors, publishers, and agents. Writers generally aren't as accessible at Bouchercon as they are when they attend the smaller regional mystery conventions such as Left Coast Crime, and Malice Domestic, which attract 150+ writers and several hundreds of fans.

This year's Bouchercon culminated with an awards luncheon at which the Anthony Awards were presented.

Bouchercon 2004 will be held in Toronto, Canada (www.bouchercon2004.com). The guests of honor will be Peter Robinson, Jeremiah Healy, and Lindsey Davis. For more information on the conventions, go to www.deadlypleasures.com or enter the name of the convention in an Internet search engine.

Mystery Fan Awards 2003

The major fan awards in mystery fiction are the Anthony Awards, the Agatha Awards, the Macavity Awards, and the Barry Awards. Following are the 2003 winners, for works published in 2002.

Anthony Awards 2003

Voted on by attendees of Bouchercon 2003
Best Novel: Michael Connelly, *City of Bones*
Best First Novel: Julia Spencer-Fleming, *In the Bleak Midwinter*
Best Paperback Original: Robin Burcell, *Fatal Truth*
Best Short Story: Marcia Talley, "Too Many Cooks" in *Much Ado About Murder*
Best Nonfiction/Critical Work: Jim Huang, ed., *They Died in Vain: Overlooked, Underappreciated, and Forgotten Mystery Novels*

Agatha Awards 2003

Voted on by attendees of the Malice Domestic XV Convention
Best Novel: Donna Andrews, *You've Got Murder*
Best First Novel: Julia Spencer-Fleming, *In the Bleak Midwinter*
Best Nonfiction: Jim Huang, ed. *They Died in Vain: Overlooked, Underappreciated, and Forgotten Mystery Novels*
Best Short Story: "The Dog that Didn't Bark" by Margaret Maron, *Ellery Queen's Mystery Magazine* (December 2002)

Macavity Awards 2003

Voted on by subscribers to *Mystery Readers International Journal*
Best Novel: S. J. Rozan, *Winter and Night*
Best First Novel: Julia Spencer-Fleming, *In the Bleak Midwinter*
Best Biographical/Critical: Jim Huang, ed., *They Died in Vain: Overlooked, Underappreciated, and Forgotten Mystery Novels*
Best Short Story: "Voice Mail" by Janet Dawson (*Scam and Eggs*, Five Star)

Barry Awards 2003

Voted on by subscribers of *Deadly Pleasures Mystery* magazine
Best Novel: Michael Connelly, *City of Bones*
Best First Novel: Julia Spencer-Fleming, *In the Bleak Midwinter*
Best British Crime Novel: John Connolly, *The White Road*
Best Paperback Original: Danielle Girard, *Cold Silence*

Mystery Magazines 2003

One of the most popular ways that mystery fans keep up with what is going on in the world of mystery fiction is by subscribing to one or more mystery magazines. The most popular of the current fan magazines continue to prosper:

Mystery Scene, published five times a year, available at a cost of $32.00 per year (two years for $60.00; three years for $90.00). Eighty-eight pages of articles and reviews. Heavy emphasis on author contributions. at www.mysteryscenemag.com.

Mystery News, published bimonthly for a cost of $25.00 per year. Newspaper format includes cover interview, columns, articles, many reviews, and listing of current and upcoming books. Black Raven Press, PMB 152, 105 E. Townline Rd, Vernon Hills, IL 60061 or order at www.blackravenpress.com.

Mystery Readers International Journal, published quarterly at an annual cost of $28.00. Each issue treats a mystery theme. Calendar year 2003 featured Mysteries South of the Mason-Dixon Line; Music and Mysteries: Overtures; Music and Mysteries: Part II; and Cool Canadian Crime. P.O. Box 8116, Berkeley, CA 94707 or order at www.mysteryreaders.org.

Drood Review, published bimonthly at an annual cost of $20.00. Articles and reviews in a newsletter format. Also extensive previews of upcoming books. 484 E. Carmel Dr., #378, Carmel, IN 46032 or order at www.droodreview.com.

Deadly Pleasures, published quarterly at an annual cost of $18.00. Eighty-four pages of articles, reviews, news, and regular columns, including the popular Reviewed to Death column. P.O. Box 969, Bountiful, UT 84011 or order at www.deadlypleasures.com.

The year 2003 saw the demise of one long-standing mystery fanzine, *Mystery & Detective Monthly*, which ceased publication with its two hundredth issue. Its editor, Bob Napier, is to be congratulated on its long and successful run.

THE MYSTERY INTERNET IN 2003

The Internet is changing the way fans interact, find information, and buy books. With the proliferation of author Web sites, it also has given fans a means to communicate directly with authors whose works they read. I finished an enjoyable mystery thriller yesterday and went to the author's site where I found her e-mail address. I wanted to thank her for the pleasurable experience I had in reading her book and to tell her that there would be a very favorable review appearing in the next issue of *Deadly Pleasures*. In the old days—before e-mail—that would have been impossible to do. There would have been no way I could find out the author's address and even if I did, I probably wouldn't have gone to the trouble of typing a letter, addressing it, putting on a stamp, and taking it to the post office. Today I got a gracious reply from her.

Author Web sites are very helpful in keeping the fan informed of upcoming books, of author appearances, and of personal information about the writer. Access to the Internet is like having a gigantic and mostly current encyclopedia of mystery fiction writers at one's fingertips.

Internet bulletin boards are another interesting way for fans to interact. Join in—you might enjoy it.

CHANGING OF THE MYSTERY GUARD 2003

Each year the mystery fiction genre experiences a changing of the guard. Longtime mystery fans mourn the deaths of some of the old guard and celebrate the arrival of some very talented newcomers. The year 2003 saw the passing of Janie Bolitho, Howard Fast (who wrote mysteries as E. V. Cunningham), Sebastien Japrisot, Gavin Lyall, John Sherwood, Bruce Cook (who also wrote as Bruce Alexander), Amanda Cross, Virginia Lanier, Manuel Vazquez Montalban, and David Williams. And it saw first novels published by future stars such as William Landay, Roger Jon Ellory, Mark Haddon, Erin Hart, Robert Heilbrun, Babs Horton, Jim Kelly, Simon Kernick, Joyce Krieg, Jay MacLarty, Chris Simms, Olin Steinhauer, Wallace Stroby, Sarah Stewart Taylor, P. J. Tracy, Lono Waiwaiole, Jacqueline Winspear, and Edward Wright.

Kristine Kathryn Rusch

Cowboy Grace

■ ■ ■

Kristine Kathryn Rusch is an award-winning mystery, romance, science fiction, and fantasy writer. She has written many novels under various names, including Kristine Grayson for romance and Kris Nelscott for mystery. Her novels have made the bestseller lists—even in London—and have been published in fourteen countries and thirteen different languages. Her awards range from the Ellery Queen Readers Choice Award to the John W. Campbell Award. She is the only person in the history of the science fiction field to have won a Hugo Award for editing and a Hugo Award for fiction. Her short work has been reprinted in six Year's Best collections. Currently, she is writing a series in all four of her genres: the Retrieval Artist series in science fiction; the Smokey Dalton series in mystery (written as Kris Nelscott); the Fates series in romance (written as Kristine Grayson); and the upcoming Fantasy Life series in fantasy. We are very pleased to lead off this year's collection with "Cowboy Grace," her novella from the Silver Gryphon *anthology published by Golden Gryphon Press, and which was nominated for the Mystery Writers of America's Edgar Award for best short fiction. How many of us have just wanted to take off, to leave our own lives behind and head out for the horizon? Grace, the quiet, understated woman in this story, does just that, with results she couldn't possibly have expected.*

Every woman tolerates misogyny," Alex said. She slid her empty beer glass across the bar, and tucked a strand of her auburn hair behind her ear. "How much depends on how old she is. The older she is the less she notices it. The more she expects it."

"Bullshit." Carole took a drag on her Virginia Slim, crossed her legs, and adjusted her skirt. "I don't tolerate misogyny."

"Maybe we should define the word," Grace said, moving to the other side of Carole. She wished her friend would realize how much the smoking irritated her. In fact, the entire night was beginning to irritate her. They were all avoiding the topic du jour: the tiny wound on Grace's left breast, stitches gone now, but the skin still raw and sore.

"Mis-ah-jenny," Carole said, as if Grace were stupid. "Hatred of women."

"From the Greek," Alex said. "*Misos* or hatred and *gyne* or women."

"Not," Carole said, waving her cigarette as if it were a baton, "misogamy, which is also from the Greek. Hatred of marriage. Hmm. Two male *misos* wrapped in one."

The bartender, a diminutive woman wearing a red-and-white cowgirl outfit, complete with fringe and gold buttons, snickered. She set down a napkin in front of Alex and gave her another beer.

"Compliments," she said, "of the men at the booth near the phone."

Alex looked. She always looked. She was tall, busty, and leggy, with a crooked nose thanks to an errant pitch Grace had thrown in the ninth grade, a long chin, and eyes the color of wine. Men couldn't get enough of her. When Alex rebuffed them, they slept with Carole and then talked to Grace.

The men in the booth near the phone looked like corporate types on a junket. Matching gray suits, different ties—all in a complementary shade of pink, red, or cranberry—matching haircuts (long on top, styled on the sides), and differing goofy grins.

"This is a girl bar," Alex said, shoving the glass back at the bartender. "We come here to diss men, not to meet them."

"Good call," Carole said, exhaling smoke into Grace's face. Grace agreed, not with the smoke or the rejection, but because she wanted time with her friends. Without male intervention of any kind.

"Maybe we should take a table," Grace said.

"Maybe." Carole crossed her legs again. Her mini was leather, which meant that night she felt like being on display. "Or maybe we should send drinks to the cutest men we see."

They scanned the bar. Happy Hour at the Oh Kaye Corral didn't change much from Friday to Friday. A jukebox in the corner, playing Patty Loveless. Cocktail waitresses in short skirts and ankle boots with big heels. Tin stars and Wild West art on the walls, unstained wood and checkered tablecloths adding to the effect. One day, when Grace had Alex's courage and Carole's gravelly voice, she wanted to walk in, belly up to the bar, slap her hand on its polished surface, and order whiskey straight up. She wanted someone to challenge her. She wanted to pull her six-gun and have a stare-down, then and there. Cowboy Grace, fastest gun in the West. Or at least in Racine on a rainy Friday night.

"I don't see cute," Alex said. "I see married, married, divorced, desperate, single, single, never-been-laid, and married."

Grace watched her make her assessment. Alex's expression never changed. Carole was looking at the men, apparently seeing whether or not she agreed.

Typically, she didn't.

"I dunno," she said, pulling on her cigarette. "Never-Been-Laid's kinda cute."

"So try him," Alex said. "But you'll have your own faithful puppy dog by this time next week, and a proposal of marriage within the month."

Carole grinned and slid off the stool. "Proposal of marriage in two weeks," she said. "I'm that good."

She stubbed out her cigarette, grabbed the tiny leather purse that matched the skirt, adjusted her silk blouse, and sashayed her way toward a table in the middle.

Grace finally saw Never-Been-Laid. He had soft brown eyes, and hair that needed trimming. He wore a shirt that accented his narrow shoulders, and he had a laptop open on the round table. He was alone. He had his feet tucked under the chair, crossed at the ankles. He wore dirty tennis shoes with his Gap khakis.

"Cute?" Grace said.

"Shhh," Alex said. "It's a door into the mind of Carole."

"One that should remain closed." Grace moved to Carole's stool. It was still warm.

Grace shoved Carole's drink out of her way, grabbed her glass of wine, and coughed. The air still smelled of cigarette smoke.

Carole was leaning over the extra chair, giving Never-Been-Laid a view of her cleavage, and the guys at the booth by the phone a nice look at her ass, which they seemed to appreciate.

"Where the hell did that misogyny comment come from?" Grace asked.

Alex looked at her. "You want to get a booth?"

"Sure. Think Carole can find us?"

"I think Carole's going to be deflowering a computer geek and not caring what we're doing." Alex grabbed her drink, stood, and walked to a booth on the other side of the Corral. Dirty glasses from the last occupants were piled in the center, and the red-and-white checkered vinyl tablecloth was sticky.

They moved the glasses on the edge of the table and didn't touch the dollar tip, which had been pressed into a puddle of beer.

Grace set her wine down and slid onto her side. Alex did the same on the other side. Somehow they managed not to touch the tabletop at all.

"You remember my boss?" Alex asked as she adjusted the tiny fake gas lamp that hung on the wall beside the booth.

"Beanie Boy?"

She grinned. "Yeah."

"Never met him."

"Aren't you lucky."

Grace already knew that. She'd heard stories about Beanie Boy for the last year. They had started shortly after he was hired. Alex went to the company Halloween party and was startled to find her boss dressed as one of the Lollipop Kids from the Wizard of Oz, complete with striped shirt, oversized lollipop, and propeller beanie.

"Now what did he do?" Grace asked.

"Called me honey."

"Yeah?" Grace asked.

"And sweetie, and dollface, and sugar."

"Hasn't he been doing that for the last year?"

Alex glared at Grace. "It's getting worse."

"What's he doing, patting you on the butt?"

"If he did, I'd get him for harassment, and he knows it."

She had lowered her voice. Grace could barely hear her over Shania Twain.

"This morning one of our clients came in praising the last report. I wrote it."

"Didn't Beanie Boy give you credit?"

"Of course he did. He said, 'Our little Miss Rogers wrote it. Isn't she a doll?"

Grace clutched her drink tighter. This didn't matter to her. Her biopsy was benign. She had called Alex and Carole and told them. They'd suggested coming here. So why weren't they offering a toast to her life? Why weren't they celebrating, really celebrating, instead of rerunning the same old conversation in the same old bar in the same old way. "What did the client do?"

"He agreed, of course."

"And?"

"And what?"

"Is that it? Didn't you speak up?"

"How could I? He was praising me, for God's sake."

Grace sighed and sipped her beer. Shania Twain's comment was that didn't impress her much. It didn't impress Grace much either, but she knew better than to say anything to Alex.

Grace looked toward the middle of the restaurant. Carole was standing behind Never-Been-Laid, her breasts pressed against his back, her ass on view to the world, her head over his shoulder peering at his computer screen.

Alex didn't follow her gaze like Grace had hoped. "If I were ten years younger, I'd tell Beanie Boy to shove it."

"If you were ten years younger, you wouldn't have a mortgage and a Mazda."

"Dignity shouldn't be cheaper than a paycheck," she said.

"So confront him."

"He doesn't think he's doing anything wrong. He treats all the women like that."

Grace sighed. They'd walked this road before. Job after job, boyfriend after boyfriend. Alex, for all her looks, was like Joe McCarthy protecting the world from the Red Menace: she saw antifemale everywhere, and most of it, she was convinced, was directed at her.

"You don't seem very sympathetic," Alex said.

She wasn't. She never had been. And with all she had been through in the last month, *alone* because her two best friends couldn't bear to talk about the Big C, the lock that was usually on Grace's mouth wasn't working.

"I'm not sympathetic," Grace said "I'm beginning to think you're a victim in search of a victimizer."

"That's not fair, Grace," Alex said. "We tolerate this stuff because we were raised in an antiwoman society. It's gotten better, but it's not perfect. You tell those Xers stuff like this and they shake their heads. Or the new ones. What're they calling themselves now? Generation Y? They were raised on Title IX. Hell, they pull off their shirts after winning soccer games. Imagine us doing that."

"My cousin got arrested in 1977 in Milwaukee on the day Elvis Presley died for playing volleyball," Grace said. Carole was actually rubbing herself on Never-Been-Laid. His face was the color of the red checks in the tablecloth.

"What?"

Grace turned to Alex. "My cousin. You know, Barbie? She got arrested playing volleyball."

"They didn't let girls play volleyball in Milwaukee?"

"It was ninety degrees, and she was playing with a group of guys. They pulled off their shirts because they were hot and sweating, so she did the same. She got arrested for indecent exposure."

"God," Alex said. "Did she go to jail?"

"Didn't even get her day in court."

"Everyone gets a day in court."

Grace shook her head. "The judge took one look at Barbie, who was really butch in those days, and said, 'I'm sick of you girls coming in here and arguing that you should have equal treatment for things that are clearly unequal. I do not establish Public Decency laws. You may show a bit of breast if you're feeding a child, otherwise you are in violation of—some damn code. Barbie used to quote the thing chapter and verse."

"Then what?" Alex asked.

"Then she got married, had a kid, and started wearing nail polish. She said it wasn't as much fun to show her breasts legally."

"See?" Alex said. "Misogyny."

Grace shrugged. "Society, Alex. Get used to it."

"That's the point of your story? We've been oppressed for a thousand years and you say, 'Get used to it'?"

"I say Brandi Chastain pulls off her shirt in front of millions—"

"Showing a sports bra."

"—and she doesn't get arrested. I say women head companies all the time. I say things are better now than they were when I was growing up, and I say the only ones who oppress us are ourselves."

"I say you're drunk."

Grace pointed at Carole, who was wet-kissing Never-Been-Laid, her arms wrapped around his neck and her legs wrapped around his waist. "She's drunk. I'm just speaking out."

"You never speak out."

Grace sighed. No one had picked up the glasses and she was tired of looking at that poor drowning dollar bill. There wasn't going to be any celebration. Everything was the same as it always was—at least to Alex and Carole. But Grace wanted something different.

She got up, threw a five next to the dollar, and picked up her purse.

"Tell me if Carole gets laid," Grace said, and left.

Outside, Grace stopped and took a deep breath of the humid, exhaust-filled air. She could hear the clang of glasses even in the parking lot and the rhythm of Mary Chapin Carpenter praising passionate kisses. Grace had had only one glass of wine and a lousy time, and she wondered why people said old friends were the best friends. They were supposed to raise toasts to her future, now restored. She'd even said the "b" word and Alex hadn't noticed. It was as if the cancer scare had happened to someone they didn't even know.

Grace was going to be forty years old in three weeks. Her two best friends were probably planning a version of the same party they had held for her when she turned thirty. A male stripper whose sweaty body repulsed her more than aroused her, too many black balloons, and aging jokes that hadn't been original the first time around.

Forty years old, an accountant with her own firm, no close family, no boyfriend, and a resident of the same town her whole life. The only time she left was to visit cousins out east, and for what? Obligation?

There was no joy left, if there'd ever been any joy at all.

She got into her sensible Ford Taurus, bought at a used-car lot for well under Blue Book, and drove west.

It wasn't until she reached Janesville that she started to call herself crazy, and it wasn't until she drove into Dubuque that she realized how little tied her to her hometown.

An apartment without even a cat to cozy up to, a business no more successful than a dozen others, and people who still saw her as a teenager wearing granny glasses, braces, and hair too long for her face. Grace, who was always there. Grace the steady, Grace the smart. Grace, who helped her friends out of their financial binds, who gave them a shoulder to cry on, and a degree of comfort because their lives weren't as empty as her own.

When she had told Alex and Carole that her mammogram had come back suspicious, they had looked away. When she told them that she had found a lump, they had looked frightened.

I can't imagine life without you, Gracie, Carole had whispered.

Imagine it now, Grace thought.

The dawn was breaking when she reached Cedar Rapids, and she wasn't really tired. But she was practical, had always been practical, and habits of a lifetime didn't change just because she had run away from home at the age of thirty-nine.

She got a hotel room and slept for eight hours, got up, had dinner in a nice steak place, went back to the room, and slept some more. When she woke up Sunday morning to bells from the Presbyterian Church across the street, she lay on her back and listened for a good minute before she realized they were playing "What a Friend We Have in Jesus." And she smiled then, because Jesus had been a better friend to her in recent years than Alex and Carole ever had.

At least Jesus didn't tell her his problems when she was praying about hers. If Jesus was self-absorbed he wasn't obvious about it. And he didn't seem to care that she hadn't been inside a church since August of 1978.

The room was chintz, the wallpaper and the bedspread matched, and the painting on the wall was chosen for its color not for its technique. Grace sat up and wondered what she was doing here, and thought about going home.

To nothing.

So she got in her car and followed the Interstate, through Des Moines, and Lincoln and Cheyenne, places she had only read about, places she had never seen. How could a woman live for forty years and not see the country of her birth? How could a woman do nothing except what she was supposed to from the day she was born until the day she died?

In Salt Lake City, she stared at the Mormon Tabernacle, all white against an azure sky. She sat in her car and watched a groundskeeper maintain the flowers, and remembered how it felt to take her doctor's call.

A lot of women have irregular mammograms, particularly at your age. The breast tissue is thicker, and often we get clouds.

Clouds.

There were fluffy clouds in the dry desert sky, but they were white and benign. Just like her lump had turned out to be. But for a hellish month, she had thought about that lump, feeling it when she woke out of a sound sleep, wondering if it presaged the beginning of the end. She had never felt her mortality like this before, not even when her mother, the only parent she had known, had died. Not even when she realized there was no one remaining of the generation that had once stood between her and death.

No one talked about these things. No one let her talk about them either. Not just Alex and Carole, but Michael, her second in command at work, or even her doctor, who kept assuring her that she was young and the odds were in her favor.

Young didn't matter if the cancer had spread through the lymph nodes. When she went in for the lumpectomy almost two weeks ago now, she had felt a curious kind of relief, as if the doctor had removed a tick that had burrowed under her skin. When he had called with the news that the lump was benign, she had thanked him calmly and continued with her day, filing corporate tax returns for a consulting firm.

No one had known the way she felt. Not relieved. No. It was more like she had received a reprieve.

The clouds above the Tabernacle helped calm her. She plugged in her cell phone for the first time in days and listened to the voice-mail messages, most of them from Michael, growing increasingly worried about where she was.

Have you forgotten the meeting with Boyd's? he'd asked on Monday.

Do you want me to file Charlie's extension? he'd demanded on Tuesday.

Where the hell are you? he cried on Wednesday and she knew, then, that it was okay to call him, that not even the business could bring her home.

Amazing how her training had prepared her for moments like these and she hadn't even known it. She had savings, lots of them, because she hadn't bought a house even though it had been prudent to do so. She had been waiting, apparently, for Mr. Right, or the family her mother had always wanted for her, the family that would never come. Her money was invested properly, and she could live off the interest if she so chose. She had just never chosen to before.

And if she didn't want to be found, she didn't have to be. She knew how to have the interest paid through offshore accounts so that no one could track it. She even knew a quick and almost legal way to change her name. Traceable, but she hadn't committed a crime. She didn't need to hide well, just well enough that a casual search wouldn't produce her.

Not that anyone would start a casual search. Once she sold the business, Michael would forget her, and Alex and Carole, even though they would gossip about her at Oh Kaye's every Friday night for the rest of their lives, wouldn't summon the energy to search.

She could almost hear them now: *She met some guy*, Carole would say. *And he killed her*, Alex would add, and then they would argue until last call, unless Carole found some man to entertain her, and Alex someone else to complain to. They would miss Grace only when they screwed up, when they needed a shoulder, when they couldn't stand being on their own. And even then, they probably wouldn't realize what it was they had lost.

Because it amused her, she had driven north to Boise, land of the white collar, to make her cell call to Michael. Her offer to him was simple: cash her out of the business and call it his own. She named a price, he dickered halfheartedly, she refused to negotiate. Within two days, he had wired the money to a blind money market account that she had often stored cash in for the firm.

She let the money sit there while she decided what to do with it. Then she went to Reno to change her name.

Reno had been a surprise. A beautiful city set between mountains like none she had ever seen. The air was dry, the downtown tacky, the people friendly. There were bookstores and slot machines and good restaurants. There were cheap houses and all-night casinos and lots of strange places. There was even history, of the Wild West kind.

For the first time in her life, Grace fell in love.

And to celebrate the occasion, she snuck into a quickie wedding chapel, found the marriage licenses, took one, copied down the name of the chapel, its permit number, and all the other pertinent information, and then returned to her car. There she checked the boxes, saying she had seen the driver's licenses and birth certificates of the people involved, including a fictitious man named Nathan Reinhart, and *violà!* she was married. She had a new name, a document the credit card companies would accept, and a new beginning all at the same time.

Using some of her personal savings, she bought a house with lots of windows and a view of the Sierras. In the mornings, light bathed her kitchen, and in the evenings, it caressed her living room. She had never seen light like this—clean and pure and crisp. She was beginning to understand why artists moved west to paint, why people used to exclaim about the way light changed everything.

The lack of humidity, of dense air pollution, made the air clearer. The elevation brought her closer to the sun.

She felt as if she were seeing everything for the very first time.

And hearing it, too. The house was silent, much more silent than an apartment, and the silence soothed her. She could listen to her television without worrying about the people in the apartment below, or play her stereo full blast without concern about a visit from the super.

There was a freedom to having her own space that she hadn't realized before, a freedom to living the way she wanted to live, without the rules of the past or the expectations she had grown up with.

And among those expectations was the idea that she had to be the strong one, the good one, the one on whose shoulder everyone else cried. She had no friends here, no one who needed her shoulder, and she had no one who expected her to be good.

Only herself.

Of course, in some things she was good. Habits of a lifetime died hard. She began researching the best way to invest Michael's lump-sum payment—and while she researched, she left the money alone. She kept her house clean and her lawn, such as it was in this high desert, immaculate. She got a new car and made sure it was spotless.

No one would find fault with her appearances, inside or out.

Not that she had anyone who was looking. She didn't have a boyfriend or a job or a hobby. She didn't have anything except herself.

She found herself drawn to the casinos, with their clinking slot machines, musical come-ons, and bright lights. No matter how high tech the places had become, no matter how clean, how "family-oriented," they still had a shady feel.

Or perhaps that was her upbringing, in a state where gambling had been illegal until she was twenty-five, a state where her father used to play a friendly game of poker—even with his friends—with the curtains drawn.

Sin—no matter how sanitized—still had appeal in the brand-new century.

Of course, she was too sensible to gamble away her savings. The slots lost their appeal quickly, and when she sat down at the blackjack tables, she couldn't get past the feeling that she was frittering her money away for nothing.

But she liked the way the cards fell and how people concentrated—as if their very lives depended on this place—and she was good with numbers. One of the pit bosses mentioned that they were always short of poker dealers, so she took a class offered by one of the casinos. Within two months, she was snapping cards, raking pots, and wearing a uniform that made her feel like Carole on a bad night.

It only took a few weeks for her bosses to realize that Grace was a natural poker dealer. They gave her the busy shifts—Thursday through Sunday nights—and she spent her evenings playing the game of cowboys, fancy men, and whores. Finally, there was a bit of an Old West feel to her life, a bit of excitement, a sense of purpose.

When she got off at midnight, she would be too keyed-up to go home. She started bringing a change of clothes to work, and after her shift, she would go to the casino next door. It had a great bar upstairs—filled with brass, Victorian furnishings, and a real hardwood floor. She could get a sandwich and a beer. Finally, she felt like she was becoming the woman she wanted to be.

One night, a year after she had run away from home, a man sidled up next to her. He had long blond hair that curled against his shoulders. His face was tanned and lined, a bit too thin. He looked road-hardened—like a man who'd been outside too much, seen too much, worked in the sun too much. His hands were long, slender, and callused. He wore no rings, and his shirt cuffs were frayed at the edges.

He sat beside her in companionable silence for nearly an hour, while they both stared at CNN on the big screen over the bar, and then he said, "Just once I'd like to go someplace authentic."

His voice was cigarette growly, even though he didn't smoke, and he had a Southern accent that was soft as butter. She guessed Louisiana, but it might have been Tennessee or even northern Florida. She wasn't good at distinguishing Southern accents yet. She figured she would after another year or so of dealing cards.

"You should go up to Virginia City. There's a bar or two that looks real enough."

He snorted through his nose. "Tourist trap."

She shrugged. She'd thought it interesting—an entire historic city, preserved just like it had been when Mark Twain lived there. "Seems to me if you weren't a tourist there wouldn't be any other reason to go."

He shrugged and picked up a toothpick, rolling it in his fingers. She smiled to herself. A former smoker then, and a fidgeter.

"Reno's better than Vegas, at least," he said. "Casinos aren't family friendly yet."

"Except Circus Circus."

"Always been that way. But the rest. You get a sense that maybe it ain't all legal here."

She looked at him sideways. He was at least her age, his blue eyes sharp in his leathery face. "You like things that aren't legal?"

"Gambling's not something that should be made pretty, you know? It's about money, and money can either make you or destroy you."

She felt herself smile, remember what it was like to paw through receipts and tax returns, to make neat rows of figures about other people's money. "What's the saying?" she asked. "Money is like sex—"

"It doesn't matter unless you don't have any." To her surprise, he laughed. The sound was rich and warm, not at all like she had expected. The smile transformed his face into something almost handsome.

He tapped the toothpick on the polished bar, and asked, "You think that's true?"

She shrugged. "I suppose. Everyone's idea of what's enough differs, though."

"What's yours?" He turned toward her, smile gone now, eyes even sharper than they had been a moment ago. She suddenly felt as if she were on trial.

"My idea of what's enough?" she asked.

He nodded.

"I suppose enough is that I can live off the interest in the manner in which I've become accustomed. What's yours?"

A shadow crossed his eyes and he looked away from her. "Long as I've got a roof over my head, clothes on my back, and food in my mouth, I figure I'm rich enough."

"Sounds distinctly unAmerican to me," she said.

He looked at her sideways again. "I guess it does, don't it? Women figure a man should have some sort of ambition."

"Do you?"

"Have ambition?" He bent the toothpick between his fore and middle fingers. "Of course I do. It just ain't tied in with money, is all."

"I thought money and ambition went together."

"In most men's minds."

"But not yours?"

The toothpick broke. "Not anymore," he said.

Three nights later, he sat down at her table. He was wearing a denim shirt with silver snaps and jeans so faded that they looked as if they might shred around him. That, his hair, and his lean look reminded Grace of a movie gunslinger, the kind that cleaned a town up because it had to be done.

"Guess you don't make enough to live off the interest," he said to her as he sat down.

She raised her eyebrows. "Maybe I like people."

"Maybe you like games."

She smiled and dealt the cards. The table was full. She was dealing 3-6 Texas Hold 'Em and most of the players were locals. It was Monday night and they all looked pleased to have an unfamiliar face at the table.

If she had known him better she might have tipped him off. Instead she wanted to see how long his money would last.

He bought in for one hundred dollars, although she had seen at least five hundred in his wallet. He took the chips, and studied them for a moment.

He had three tells. He fidgeted with his chips when his cards were mediocre and he was thinking of bluffing. He bit his lower lip when he had nothing, and his eyes went dead flat when he had a winning hand.

He lost the first hundred in forty-five minutes, bought back in for another hundred, and managed to hold on to it until her shift ended shortly after midnight. He sat through dealer changes and the floating fortunes of his cards. When she returned from her last break, she found herself wondering if his tells were subconscious after all. They seemed deliberately calculated to let the professional poker players around him think that he was a rookie.

She said nothing. She couldn't, really—at least not overtly. The casino got a rake and they didn't allow her to do anything except deal the game. She had no stake in it anyway. She hadn't lied to him that first night. She loved watching people, the way they played their hands, the way the money flowed.

It was like being an accountant, only in real time. She got to see the furrowed brows as the decisions were made, hear the curses as someone pushed back a chair and tossed in that last hand of cards, watch the desperation that often led to the exact wrong play. Only as a poker dealer, she wasn't required to clean up the mess. She didn't have to offer advice or refuse it; she didn't have to worry about tax consequences, about sitting across from someone else's auditor, justifying choices she had no part in making.

When she got off, she changed into her tightest jeans and a summer sweater and went to her favorite bar.

Casino bars were always busy after midnight, even on a Monday. The crowd wasn't there to have a good time but to wind down from one—or to prepare itself for another. She sat at the bar, as she had since she started this routine, and she'd been about to leave when he sat next to her.

"Lose your stake?" she asked.

"I'm up four hundred dollars."

She looked at him sideways. He didn't seem pleased with the way the night had gone—not the way a casual player would have been. Her gut instinct was right. He was someone who was used to gambling—and winning.

"Buy you another?" he asked.

She shook her head. "One's enough."

He smiled. It made him look less fierce and gave him a rugged sort of appeal. "Everything in moderation?"

"Not always," she said. "At least, not anymore."

Somehow they ended up in bed—her bed—and he was better than she imagined his kind of man could be. He had knowledgeable fingers and endless patience. He didn't seem to mind the scar on her breast. Instead he lingered over it, focusing on it as if it were an erogenous zone. His pleasure at the result enhanced hers and when she finally fell asleep, somewhere around dawn, she was more sated than she had ever been.

She awoke to the smell of frying bacon and fresh coffee. Her eyes were filled with sand, but her body had a healthy lethargy.

At least, she thought, he hadn't left before she awoke.

At least he hadn't stolen everything in sight.

She still didn't know his name, and wasn't sure she cared. She slipped on a robe and combed her hair with her fingers and walked into her kitchen—the kitchen no one had cooked in but her.

He had on his denims and his hair was tied back with a leather thong. He had found not only her cast-iron skillet but the grease cover that she always used when making bacon. A bowl of scrambled eggs steamed on the counter, and a plate of heavily buttered toast sat beside it.

"Sit down, darlin'," he said. "Let me bring it all to you."

She flushed. That was what it felt like he had done the night before, but she said nothing. Her juice glasses were out, and so was her everyday ware, and yet somehow the table looked like it had been set for a *Gourmet* photo spread.

"I certainly didn't expect this," she said.

"It's the least I can do." He put the eggs and toast on the table, then poured her a cup of coffee. Cream and sugar were already out, and in their special containers.

She was slightly uncomfortable that he had figured out her kitchen that quickly and well.

He put the bacon on a paper-towel-covered plate, then set that on the table. She hadn't moved, so he beckoned with his hand.

"Go ahead," he said. "It's getting cold."

He sat across from her and helped himself to bacon while she served herself eggs. They were fluffy and light, just like they would have been in a restaurant. She had no idea how he got that consistency. Her home-scrambled eggs were always runny and undercooked.

The morning light bathed the table, giving everything a bright glow. His hair seemed even blonder in the sunlight and his skin darker. He had laugh lines around his mouth, and a bit of blond stubble on his chin.

She watched him eat, those nimble fingers scooping up the remaining egg with a slice of toast, and found herself remembering how those fingers had felt on her skin.

Then she felt his gaze on her, and looked up. His eyes were dead flat for just an instant, and she felt herself grow cold.

"Awful nice house," he said slowly, "for a woman who makes a living dealing cards."

Her first reaction was defense—she wanted to tell him she had other income, and what did he care about a woman who dealt cards, anyway?—but instead, she smiled. "Thank you."

He measured her, as if he expected a different response, then he said, "You're awfully calm considering that you don't even know my name. You don't strike me as the kind of woman who does this often."

His words startled her, but she made sure that the surprise didn't show. She had learned a lot about her own tells while dealing poker, and the experience was coming in handy now.

"You flatter yourself," she said softly.

"Well," he said, reaching into his back pocket, "if there's one thing my job's taught me, it's that people hide information they don't want anyone else to know."

He pulled out his wallet, opened it, and with two fingers removed a business card. He dropped it on the table.

She didn't want to pick the card up. She knew things had already changed between them in a way she didn't entirely understand, but she had a sense from the fleeting expression she had seen on his face that once she picked up the card she could never go back.

She set down her coffee cup and used two fingers to slide the card toward her. It identified him as Travis Delamore, a skip tracer and bail bondsman. Below his name was a phone number with a 414 exchange.

Milwaukee, Wisconsin, and the surrounding areas. Precisely the place someone from Racine might call if they wanted to hire a professional.

She slipped the card into the pocket of her robe. "Is sleeping around part of your job?"

"Is embezzling part of yours?" All the warmth had left his face. His expression was unreadable except for the flatness in his eyes. What did he think he knew?

She made herself smile. "Mr. Delamore, if I stole a dime from the casino, I'd be instantly fired. There are cameras everywhere."

"I mean your former job, Ms. Mackie. A lot of money is missing from your office."

"I don't have an office." His use of her former name made her hands clammy. What had Michael done?

"Do you deny that you're Grace Mackie?"

"I don't acknowledge or deny anything. When did this become an inquisition, Mr. Delamore? I thought men liked their sex uncomplicated. You seem to be a unique member of your species."

This time he smiled. "Of course we like our sex uncomplicated. That's why we're having this discussion this morning."

"If we'd had it last night, there wouldn't be a this morning."

"That's my point." He downed the last of his orange juice. "And thank you for the acknowledgment, Ms. Mackie."

"It wasn't an acknowledgment," she said. "I don't like to sleep with men who think me guilty of something."

"Embezzlement," he said gently, using the same tone he had used in bed. This time, it made her bristle.

"I haven't stolen anything."

"New house, new name, new town, mysterious disappearance."

The chill she had felt earlier grew. She stood and wrapped her robe tightly around her waist. "I don't know what you think you know, Mr. Delamore, but I believe it's time for you to leave."

He didn't move. "We're not done."

"Oh, yes, we are."

"It would be a lot easier if you told me where the money was, Grace."

"Do you always get paid for sex, Mr. Delamore?" she asked.

He studied her for a moment. "Don't play games with me, honey."

"Why not?" she asked. "You seem to enjoy them."

He shoved his plate away as if it had offended him. Apparently this morning wasn't going the way he wanted it to either. "I'm just telling you what I know."

"And I'm just asking you to leave. It was fun, Travis. But it certainly wasn't worth this."

He stood and slipped his wallet back into his pocket. "You'll hear from me again."

"This isn't high school," she said, following him to the door. "I won't be offended if you fail to call."

"No," he said as he stepped into the dry desert air. "You probably won't be offended. But you will be curious. This is just the beginning, Grace."

"One person's beginning is another person's ending," she said as she closed and locked the door behind him.

The worst thing she could do, she knew, was panic. So she made herself clean up the kitchen as if she didn't have a care in the world, and she left the curtains open so that he could see if he wanted to. Then she went to the shower, making it long and hot. She tried to scrub all the traces of him off of her.

For the first time in her life, she felt cheap.

Embezzlement. Something had happened, something Michael was blaming on her. It would be easy enough, she supposed. She had disappeared. That looked suspicious enough. The new name, the new car, the new town, all of that added to the suspicion.

What had Michael done? And why?

She got out of the shower and toweled herself off. She was tempted to call Michael, but she certainly couldn't do it from the house. If she used her cell, the call would be traceable too. And if she went to a pay phone, she would attract even more suspicion. She had to consider that Travis Delamore was following her, spying on her.

In fact, she had to consider that he had been doing that for some time.

She went over all of their conversation, looking for clues, mistakes she might have made. She had told him very little, but he had asked a lot. Strangely—or perhaps not so strangely anymore—all of their conversations had been about money.

Carole would have been proud of her. Grace had finally let her libido get the better of her. Alex would have been disgusted, reminding her that men couldn't be trusted.

What could he do to her besides cast suspicion? He was right. Without the money, he had nothing. And she had a job, no criminal record, and no suspicious investments.

But if he continued to follow her, she could go after him. The bartender had seen them leave her favorite bar together. She had an innocent face, she'd been living here for a year, got promoted, was well liked by her employer. Delamore had obviously flirted with her while he played poker the night before, and the casino had cameras.

They probably had records of all the times he had watched her before she noticed him.

It wouldn't take much to make a stalking charge. That would get her an injunction in the least, and it might scare him off.

Then she could find out why he was so sure he had something on her. Then she could find out what it was Michael had done.

The newly remodeled ladies' room on the third floor of the casino had twenty stalls and a lounge complete with smoking room. It had once been a small rest room, but the reconstruction had taken out the nearby men's room and replaced it with more stalls. The row of pay phones in the middle stayed, as a convenience to the customers.

Delamore wouldn't know that she called from those pay phones. No one would know.

She started using the third-floor ladies' room on her break and more than once had picked up the receiver on the third phone and dialed most of her old office number. She'd always stop before she hit the last digit, though. Her intuition told her that calling Michael would be wrong.

What if Delamore had a trace on Michael's line? What if the police did?

A week after her encounter with Delamore, a week in which she used the third-floor ladies' room more times than she could count, she suddenly realized what was wrong. Delamore didn't have anything on her except suspicion. He had clearly found her—that hadn't been hard, since she really hadn't been hiding from anyone—and he had probably checked her bank records for the money he assumed she had embezzled from her former clients. But the money she had gotten from the sale of the business was still in that hidden numbered account—and would stay there.

Her native caution had served her well once again.

She had nothing to hide. It didn't matter what some good-looking skip trace thought. Her life in Racine was in the past. A part of her past that she couldn't avoid, any more than she could avoid the scar on her breast—the scar that Delamore had clearly used to identify her, the bastard. But past was past, and until it hurt her present, she wasn't going to worry about it.

So she stopped making pilgrimages to the third-floor women's room, and gradually, her worries over Delamore faded. She didn't see him for a week, and she assumed—wrongly—that it was all over.

He sat next to her at the bar as if he had been doing it every day for years. He ordered a whiskey neat, and another "for the lady," just like men in her fantasies used to do. When he looked at her and smiled, she realized that the look didn't reach his eyes.

Maybe it never had.

"Miss me, darlin'?" he asked.

She picked up her purse, took out a five to cover her drink, and started to leave. He grabbed her wrist. His fingers were warm and dry, their touch no longer gentle. A shiver started in her back, but she willed the feeling away.

"Let go of me," she said.

"Now, Gracie, I think you should listen to what I have to say."

"Let go of me," she said in that same measured tone, "or I will scream so loud that everyone in the place will hear."

"Screams don't frighten me, doll."

"Maybe the police do. Believe me, *hon,* I will press charges."

His smile was slow and wide, but that flat look was in his eyes again, the one that told her he had all the cards. "I'm sure they'll be impressed," he said, reaching into his breast pocket with his free hand. "But I do believe a warrant trumps a tight grip on the arm."

He set a piece of paper down on the bar itself. The bartender, wiping away the remains of another customer's mess, glanced her way as if he were keeping an eye on her.

She didn't touch the paper, but she didn't shake Delamore's hand off her arm, either. She wasn't quite sure what to do.

He picked up the paper, shook it open, and she saw the strange bold-faced print of a legal document, her former name in the middle. "Tell you what, Gracie. How about we finish the talk we started the other morning in one of those dark, quiet booths over there?"

She was still staring at the paper, trying to comprehend it. It looked official enough. But then, she'd never seen a warrant for anyone's arrest before. She had only heard of them.

She had never imagined she'd see her own name on one.

She let Delamore lead her to a booth at the far end of the bar. He slid across the plastic, trying to pull her in beside him, but this time, she shook him off. She sat across from him, perched on the seat with her feet in the aisle, purse clutched on her lap. Flee position, Alex used to call it. You Might Be a Loser and I Reserve the Right to Find Someone Else, was Carole's name for it.

"If I bring you back to Wisconsin," he said, "I get a few thousand bucks. What it don't say on my card is that I'm a bounty hunter."

"What an exciting life you must lead," Grace said dryly.

He smiled. The look chilled her. She was beginning to wonder how she had ever found him attractive. "It's got its perks."

It was at that moment she decided she hated him. He would forever refer to her as a perk of the job, not as someone who had given herself to him freely, someone who had enjoyed the moment as much as he had.

All that gentleness in his fingers, all those murmured endearments. Lies.

She hated lies.

"But," he was saying, "I see a way to make a little more money here. I don't think you're a real threat to society. And you're a lot of fun, more fun than I would've expected, given how you lived before you moved here."

The bartender came over, his bar towel over his arm. "Want anything?"

He was speaking to her. He hadn't even looked at Delamore. The bartender was making sure she was all right.

"I don't know yet," she said. "Can you check back in five minutes?"

"Sure thing." This time he did look at Delamore, who grinned at him. The bartender shot him a warning glare.

"Wow," Delamore said as the bartender moved out of earshot. "You have a defender."

"You keep getting off track," Grace said.

Delamore shrugged. "I like talking to you."

"Well, I find talking with you rather dull."

He raised his eyebrows. "You didn't think so a few days ago."

"As I recall," she said, "we didn't do a lot talking."

His smile softened. "That's my memory too."

She clutched her purse tighter. It always looked so glamorous in the movies, finding the right person, having a night of great sex. And even if he rode off into the sunset never to be seen again, everything still had a glow of perfection to it.

Not the bits of sleaze, the hardness in his expression, the sense that what he wanted from her was something she couldn't give.

"You know, the papers said that Michael Holden went into your old office, and put a gun in his mouth and pulled the trigger. Then the police, after finding the body, discovered that most of the money your clients had entrusted to your firm had disappeared."

She couldn't suppress the small whimper of shock that rose in her throat.

Delamore noted it and his eyes brightened. "Now, you tell me what happened."

She had no idea. She had none at all. But she couldn't tell Delamore that. She didn't even know if the story was true.

It sounded true. But Delamore had lied before. For all she knew he was some kind of con man, out to get her because he smelled money.

He was watching her, his eyes glittering. She could barely control her expression. She needed to get away.

She stood, still clutching her purse like a schoolgirl.

"Planning to leave? I wouldn't do that if I were you." His voice had turned cold. A shiver ran down her spine, but she didn't move, just stared down at him unable to turn away.

"One call," he said softly, "and you'll get picked up by the Nevada police. You should sit down and hear what I have to say."

Her hands were shaking. She sat, feeling trapped. He had finally hooked her, even though she hadn't said a word.

He leaned forward. "Now listen to me, darling. I know you got the money. I been working this one a long time, and I dug up the records. Michael closed all those accounts right after you disappeared. That's not a coincidence."

Her mouth was dry. She wanted to swallow, but couldn't.

" 'Member our talk about money? One of those first nights, here in this bar?"

She was staring at him, her eyes wide and dry as if she'd been driving and staring at the road for hours. It felt like she had forgotten to blink.

"I told you I don't need much, and that's true. But I'm getting tired of dragging people back to their parole officers or for their court date, or finding husbands who'd skipped out on their families and then getting paid five grand or two grand. Then people question your expenses, like you don't got a right to spend a night in a motel or eat three squares. Or they demand to know why you took so danged long to find someone who'd been hiding so good no cop could find them."

His voice was so soft she had to strain to hear it. In spite of herself, she leaned forward.

"I'm forty-five years old, doll," he said. "And I'm getting tired. You got one pretty little scar. Did you notice all the ones I got? On the job. Yours is the first case in a while where I didn't get a beating." Then he grinned. "At least, not a painful one."

She flushed, and her fingers tightened on the purse. Her hands were beginning to hurt. Part of her, a part she'd never heard from before, wanted to take that purse and club him in the face. But she didn't move. If she moved, she would lose any control she had.

"So," he said, "here's the deal. I like you. I didn't expect to, but I do. You're a pretty little thing, and smart as a whip, and this is probably going to be the only crime you'll ever commit, because you're one of those girls who just knows better, aren't you?"

She held her head rigidly, careful so that he wouldn't take the most subtle movement for a nod.

"And I think you got a damn fine deal here. The house is nice—lots of light—and the town obviously suits you. I met those friends of yours, the ballbuster and the one who thinks she's God's Gift to Men, and I gotta say it's clear why you left."

Her nails dug into the leather. Pain shot through the tender skin at the top of her fingers.

"I really don't wanna ruin your life. It's time I make a change in mine. You give me fifty grand, and I'll bury everything I found about you."

"Fifty thousand dollars?" Her voice was raspy with tension. "For the first payment?"

His eyes sparkled. "Onetime deal."

She snorted. She knew better. Blackmailers never worked like that.

"And maybe I'll stick around. Get to know you a little better. I could fall in love with that house myself."

"Could you?" she asked, amazed at the dry tone she'd managed to maintain.

"Sure." He grinned. That had been the look that had made her go weak less than a week ago. Now it sent a chill through her. "You and me, we had something."

"Yeah," she said. "A one-night stand."

He laughed. "It could be more than that, darlin'. It took you long enough, but you might've just found Mr. Right."

"Seems to me you were the one who was searching." She stood. He didn't protest, and she was glad. She had to leave. If she stayed any longer, she'd say something she would regret.

She tucked her purse under her arm. "I assume the drink's on you," she said, and then she walked away.

He didn't follow her—at least not right away. And she drove in circles before going home, watching for his car behind hers, thinking about everything he had said. Thinking about her break, her freedom, the things she had done to create a new life.

The things that now made her look guilty of a crime she hadn't committed.

She didn't sleep, of course. She couldn't. Her mind was too full—and her bed was no longer a private place. He'd been there, and some of him remained, a shadow, a laugh. After an hour of tossing and turning, she moved to the guest room and sat on the edge of the brand new unused mattress, clutching a blanket and thinking.

It was time to find out what had happened. Delamore knew who she was. She couldn't pretend anymore. But he wasn't ready to turn her in. That gave her a little time.

She took a shower, made herself a pot of coffee, and a sandwich that she ate slowly. Then she went to her office, sat down in front of her computer, and hesitated. The moment she logged on was the moment that all her movements could be traced. The moment she couldn't turn back from.

But she could testify to the conversation she'd had with Delamore, and the bartender would back her up. She wouldn't be able to hide her own identity should the police come for her, and so there was no reason to lie. She would simply say that she was concerned about her former business partner. She wanted to know if any of what Delamore told her was true.

It wouldn't seem like a confession to anyone but him.

She logged on, and used a search engine to find the news.

It didn't take her long. Amazing how many newspapers were online. Michael's death created quite a scandal in Racine, and the pictures of her office—the bloody mess still visible inside—were enough to make the ham on rye that she'd had a few moments ago turn in her stomach.

Michael. He'd been a good accountant. Thorough, exacting. Nervous. Always so nervous, afraid of making any kind of mistake.

Embezzlement? Why would he do that?

But that was what the papers had said. She dug farther, found the follow-up pieces. He'd raised cash, using clients' accounts, to bilk the company of a small fortune.

And Delamore was right. The dates matched up. Michael had stolen from her own clients to pay her for her own business. He had bought the business with stolen money.

She bowed her head, listening to the computer hum, counting her own breaths. She had never once questioned where he had gotten the money. She had figured he'd gotten a loan, had thought that maybe he'd finally learned the value of savings.

Michael. The man who took an advance on his paycheck once every six months. Michael, who had once told her he was too scared to invest on his own.

I wouldn't trust my own judgment, he had said.

Oh, the poor man. He had been right.

The trail did lead to her. The only reason Delamore couldn't point at her exactly was because she had stashed the cash in a blind account. And she hadn't touched it.

Not yet.

She'd been living entirely off her own savings, letting the money from the sale of her business draw interest. The nest egg for the future she hadn't planned yet.

Delamore wanted fifty thousand dollars from her. To give that to him, she'd have to tap the nest egg.

How many times would he make her tap it again? And again? Until it was gone of course. Into his pocket. And then he'd turn her in.

She wiped her hand on her jeans. It was a nervous movement, meant to calm herself down. She had to think.

If the cops could trace her, they would have. They either didn't have enough on her or hadn't made the leap that Delamore had. And then she had confirmed his leap with the conversation tonight.

She got up and walked away from the computer. She wouldn't let him intrude. He had already taken over her bedroom. She needed to have a space here, in her office, without him.

There was no mention of her in the papers, nothing that suggested she was involved. The police would have contacted the Reno police if they had known where she was. Even if they had hired Delamore to track her, they might still not have been informed about her whereabouts. Delamore wanted money more than he wanted to inform the authorities about where she was.

Grace sat down in the chair near the window. The shade was drawn, but the spot was soothing nonetheless.

The police weren't her problem. Delamore was.

She already knew that he wouldn't be satisfied with one payment. She had to find a way to get rid of him.

She bowed her head. Even though she had done nothing criminal she was thinking like one. How did a woman get rid of a man she didn't want? She could get a court order, she supposed, forcing him to stay away from her. She could refuse to pay him and let the cards fall where they might. Years of legal hassle, maybe even an arrest. She would certainly lose her job. No casino would hire her, and she couldn't fall back on her CPA skills, not after being arrested for embezzlement.

Ignoring him wasn't an option either.

Then, there was the act of desperation. She could kill him. Somehow. She had always thought that murderers weren't methodical enough. Take an intelligent person, have her kill someone in a thoughtful way, and she would be able to get away with the crime.

Everywhere but in her own mind. No matter how hard she tried, no matter how much he threatened her, she couldn't kill Delamore.

There had to be another option. She had to do something. She just wasn't sure what it was.

She went back to the computer and looked at the last article she had downloaded. Michael had stolen from people she had known for years. People who had trusted her, believed in her and her word. People who had thought she had integrity.

She frowned. What must they think of her now? That she was an embezzler too? After all those years of work, did she want that behind her name?

Then again, why should she care about people she would never see again?

But she would see them every time she closed her eyes. Elderly Mrs. Vezzetti and her poodle, trusting Grace to handle her account because her husband, God rest his soul, had convinced her that numbers were too much for her pretty little head. Mr. Heitzkey, who couldn't balance a checkbook if his life depended on it. Ms. Andersen, who had taken Grace's advice on ways to legally hide money from the IRS—and who had seemed so excited when it worked.

Grace sighed.

There was only one way to make this right. Only one way to clear her conscience and to clear Delamore out of her life.

She had to turn herself in.

She did some more surfing as she ate breakfast and found discount tickets to Chicago. She had to buy them from round-trip Chicago to Reno (God bless the casinos for their cheap airfare deals) and fly only the Reno to Chicago leg. Later she would buy another set, and not use part of it. Both of those tickets were cheaper than buying a single round-trip ticket out of Reno to Racine.

Grace made the reservation, hoping that Delamore wasn't tracking round-trips that started somewhere else, and then she went to work. She claimed a family emergency, got a leave of absence, and hoped it would be enough.

She liked the world she had built here. She didn't want to lose it because she hadn't been watching her back.

Twenty-four hours later, she and the car she rented in O'Hare were in Racine. The town hadn't changed. More churches than she saw out west, a few timid billboards for Native American Casinos, a factory outlet mall, and bars everywhere. The streets were grimy with the last of the sand laid down during the winter snow and ice. The trees were just beginning to bud, and the flowers were poking through the rich black dirt.

It felt as if she had gone back in time.

She wondered if she should call Alex and Carole, and then decided against it. What would she say to them, anyway? Instead, she checked into a hotel, unpacked, ate a mediocre room-service meal, and slept as if she were dead.

Maybe in this city, she was.

The district attorney's office was smaller than Grace's bathroom. There were four chairs, not enough for her, her lawyer, the three assistant district attorneys, and the DA himself. She and her lawyer were allowed to sit, but the assistant DAs hovered around the bookshelves and desk like children who were waiting for their father to finish business. The DA himself sat behind a massive oak desk that dwarfed the tiny room.

Grace's lawyer, Maxine Jones, was from Milwaukee. Grace had done her research before she arrived and found the best defense attorney in Wisconsin. Grace knew that Maxine's services would cost her a lot—but Grace was gambling that she wouldn't need Maxine for more than a few days.

Maxine was a tall, robust woman who favored bright colors. In contrast she wore debutante jewelry—a simple gold chain, tiny diamond earrings—that accented her toffee-colored skin. The entire look made her seem both flamboyant and powerful, combinations that Grace was certain helped Maxine in court.

"My client," Maxine was saying, "came here on her own. You'll have to remember that, Mr. Lindstrom."

Harold Lindstrom, the district attorney, was in his fifties, with thinning gray hair and a runner's thinness. His gaze held no compassion as it fell on Grace.

"Only because a bounty hunter hired by the police department found her," Lindstrom said.

"Yes," Maxine said. "We'll concede that the bounty hunter was the one who informed her of the charges. But that's all. This man hounded her, harassed her, and tried to extort money out of her, money she did not have."

"Then she should have gone to the Reno police," Lindstrom said.

An assistant DA crossed her arms as if this discussion was making her uncomfortable. It was making Grace uncomfortable. Never before had she been discussed as if she weren't there.

"It was easier to come here," Maxine said. "My client has a hunch, which if it's true, will negate the charges you have against her and against Michael Holden."

"Mr. Holden embezzled from his clients with the assistance of Ms. Reinhart."

"No. Mr. Holden followed standard procedure for the accounting firm."

"Embezzlement is standard procedure?" Lindstrom was looking directly at Grace.

Maxine put her manicured hand on Grace's knee, a reminder to remain quiet.

"No. But Mr. Holden, for reasons we don't know, decided to end his life, and since he now worked alone, no one knew where he was keeping the clients' funds. My client," Maxine added, as if she expected Grace to speak, "would like you to drop all charges against her and to charge Mr. Delamore with extortion. In exchange, she will testify against him, and she will also show you where the money is."

"Where she hid it, huh?" Lindstrom said. "No deal."

Maxine leaned forward. "You don't have a crime here. If you don't bargain with us, I'll go straight to the press, and you'll look like a fool. It seems to me that there's an election coming up."

Lindstrom's eyes narrowed. Grace held her breath. Maxine stared at him as if they were all playing a game of chicken. Maybe they were.

"Here's the deal," he said, "if her information checks out, then we'll drop the charges. We can't file against Delamore because the alleged crimes were committed in Nevada."

Maxine's hand left Grace's knee. Maxine templed her fingers and rested their painted tips against her chin. "Then, Harold, we'll simply have to file a suit against the city and the county for siccing him on my client. A multimillion-dollar suit. We'll win, too. Because she came forward the moment she learned of a problem. She hasn't been in touch with anyone from here. Her family is dead, and her friends were never close. She had no way of knowing what was happening a thousand miles away until a man you people sent started harassing her."

"You said he's been harassing you for a month," Lindstrom said to Grace. "Why didn't you come forward before now?"

Grace looked at Maxine who nodded.

"Because," Grace said, "he didn't show me any proof of his claims until the night before I flew out. You can ask the bartender at the Silver Dollar. He saw the entire thing."

Lindstrom frowned at Maxine. "We want names and dates."

"You'll get them," Maxine said.

Lindstrom sighed. "All right. Let's hear it."

Grace's heart was pounding. Here was her moment. She suddenly found herself hoping they would all believe her. She had never lied with so much at stake before.

"Go ahead, Grace," Maxine said softly.

Grace nodded. "We had run into some trouble with our escrow service. Minor stuff, mostly rudeness on the part of the company. It was all irritating Michael. Many things were irritating him at that time, but we weren't close, so I didn't attribute it to anything except work."

The entire room had become quiet. She felt slightly light-headed. She was forgetting to breathe. She forced herself to take a deep breath before continuing.

"In the week that I was leaving, Michael asked me how he could go about transferring everything from one escrow company to another. It required a lot of paperwork, and he didn't trust the company we were with. I thought he should have let them and the new company handle it, but he didn't want to."

She squeezed her hands together, reminded herself not to embellish too much. A simple lie was always best.

"We had accounts we had initially set up for clients in discreet banks. I told Michael to go to one of those banks, place the money in accounts there, and then when the new escrow accounts were established, to transfer the money to them. I warned him not to take longer than a day in the intermediate account."

"We have no record of such an account," the third district attorney said.

Grace nodded. "That's what I figured when I heard that he was being charged with embezzlement. I can give you the names of all the banks and the numbers of the accounts we were assigned. If the money's in one of them, then my name is clear."

"Depending on when the deposit was made," Lindstrom said. "And if the money's all there."

Grace's light-headedness was growing. She hadn't realized how much effort bluffing took. But she did know she was covered on those details at least.

"You may go through my client's financial records," Maxine said. "All of her money is accounted for."

"Why wouldn't he have transferred the money to the new escrow accounts quickly, like you told him to?" Lindstrom asked.

"I don't know," Grace said.

"Depression is a confusing thing, Harold," Maxine said. "If he's like other people who've gotten very depressed, I'm sure things slipped. I'm sure this wasn't the only thing he failed to do. And you can bet I'd argue that in court."

"Why did you leave Racine so suddenly?" Lindstrom asked. "Your friends say you just vanished one night."

Grace let out a small breath. On this one she could be completely honest. "I had a scare. I thought I had breast cancer. The lumpectomy results came in the day I left. You can check with my doctor. I was planning to go after that—maybe a month or more—but I felt so free, that I just couldn't go back to my work. Something like that changes you, Mr. Lindstrom."

He grunted as if he didn't believe her. For the first time in the entire discussion, she felt herself get angry. She clenched her fingers so hard that her nails dug into her palms. She wouldn't say any more, just like Maxine had told her to.

"The banks?" Lindstrom asked.

Grace slipped a small leather-bound ledger toward him. She had spent a lot of time drawing that up by hand in different pens. She hoped it would be enough.

"The accounts are identified by numbers only. That's one of the reasons we liked the banks. If he started a new account, I won't know its number."

"If they're in the U.S., then we can get a court order to open them," Lindstrom said.

"Check these numbers first. Most of the accounts were inactive." She had to clutch her fingers together to keep them from trembling.

"All right," Lindstrom said and stood. Maxine and Grace stood as well. "If we discover that you're wrong—about anything—we'll arrest you, Ms. Reinhart. Do you understand?"

Grace nodded.

Maxine smiled. "We're sure you'll see it our way, Harold. But remember your promise. Get that creep away from Grace."

"Right now, your client's the one we're concerned with, Maxine." Lindstrom's cold gaze met Grace's. "I'm sure we'll be in touch."

Grace thought the eight o'clock knock on her hotel-room door was room service. She'd ordered another meal from them, unable to face old haunts and old friends. Until she had come back, she had never even been in a hotel in Racine, so she felt as if she weren't anywhere near her old home. Now if she could only get different local channels on the television set, her own delusion would be complete.

She undid the locks, opened the door, and stepped away so that the waiter could bring his cart/table inside.

Instead, Delamore pulled the door back. She was so surprised to see him that she didn't try to close him out. She scuttled away from him toward the nightstand, and fumbled behind her back for the phone.

His cheeks were red, and his eyes sparkling with fury. His anger was so palpable, she could feel it across the room.

"What kind of game are you playing?" he snapped, slamming the door closed.

She got the phone off the hook without turning around. "No game."

"It is a game. You got away from me, and then you come here, telling them that I've been threatening you."

"You have been threatening me." Her fingers found the bottom button on the phone—which she hoped was "O." If the hotel operator heard this, she'd have to call security.

"Of course I'd been threatening you! It's my job. You didn't want to come back here and I needed to drag you back. Any criminal would see that as a threat."

"Here's what you don't understand," Grace said as calmly as she could. "I'm not a criminal."

"Bullshit." Delamore took a step toward her. She backed up farther and the end table hit her thighs. Behind her she thought she heard a tinny voice ask a muted question. The operator, she hoped.

Grace held up a hand. "Come any closer and I'll scream."

"I haven't done anything to you. I've been trying to catch you."

She frowned. What was he talking about? And then she knew. The police had put a wire on him. The conversation was being taped. And they—he—was hoping that she'd incriminate herself.

"You're threatening me now," she said. "I haven't done anything. I talked to the DA today. I explained my situation and what I think Michael did. He's checking my story now."

"Your lies."

"No," Grace said. "You're the one who's lying, and I have no idea why."

"You bitch." He lowered his voice the angrier he got. Somehow she found that even more threatening.

"Stay away from me."

"Stop the act, Grace," he said. "It's just you and me. And we both know you're not afraid of anything."

Then the door burst open and two hotel security guards came in. Delamore turned and as he did, Grace said, "Oh, thank God. This man came into my room and he's threatening me."

The guards grabbed him. Delamore struggled, but the guards held him tightly. He glared at her. "You're lying again, Grace."

"No," she said and stepped away from the phone. He glanced down at the receiver, on its side on the table, and cursed. Even if he hadn't been wired, she had a witness.

The guards dragged him away and Grace sank onto the bed, placing her head in her hands. She waited until the shaking stopped before she called Maxine.

Grace had been right. Delamore had been wearing a wire, and her ability to stay cool while he attacked had preserved her story. That incident, plus the fact that the DA's office had found the money exactly where she had said it would be, in the exact amount that they had been looking for, went a long way toward preserving her credibility. When detectives interviewed Michael's friends one final time, they all agreed he was agitated and depressed, but he would tell no one why. Without the embezzlement explanation, it simply sounded as if he were a miserable man driven to the brink by personal problems.

She had won, at least on that score. Her old clients would get their money back, and they would be off her conscience. And nothing, not even Delamore, would take their place.

Delamore was under arrest, charged with extortion, harassment, and attempting to tamper with a witness. Apparently, he'd faced similar complaints before, but they had never stuck. This time, it looked as if they would.

Grace would have to return to Racine to testify against him. But not for several months. And maybe, Maxine said, not even then. The hope was that Delamore would plead and save everyone the expense of a trial.

So, on her last night in Racine, perhaps forever, Grace got enough courage to call Alex and Carole. She didn't reach either of them; instead she had to leave a message on their voice mail, asking them to meet her at Oh Kaye's one final time.

Grace got there first. The place hadn't changed at all. There was still a jukebox in the corner and cocktail waitresses in short skirts and ankle boots with big heels. Tin stars and Wild West art on the walls, unstained wood and checkered tablecloths adding to the effect. High bar stools and a lot of lonely people.

Grace ignored them. She sashayed to the bar, slapped her hand on it, and ordered whiskey neat. A group of suits at a nearby table ogled her and she turned away.

She was there to diss men not to meet them.

Carole arrived first, black miniskirt, tight crop top, and cigarette in hand. She looked no different. She hugged Grace so hard that Grace thought her ribs would crack.

"Alex had me convinced you were dead."

Grace shook her head. "I was just sleeping around."

Carole grinned. "Fun, huh?"

Grace thought. The night had been fun. The aftermath hadn't been. But her life was certainly more exciting. She didn't know if the trade-off was worth it.

Alex arrived a moment later. Her auburn hair had grown, and she was wearing boots beneath a long dress. The boots made her look even taller.

She didn't hug Grace.

"What the hell's the idea?" Alex snapped. "You vanished—kapoof! What kind of friend does that?"

In the past, Grace would have stammered something, then told Alex she was exactly right and Grace was wrong. This time, Grace set her whiskey down.

"I told you about my lumpectomy," Grace said. "You didn't care. I was scared. I told you that, and you didn't care. When I found out I didn't have cancer, I called you to celebrate, and you didn't care. Seems to me you vanished first."

Alex's cheeks were red. Carole stubbed her cigarette in an ashtray on the bar's wooden rail.

"Not fair," Alex said.

"That's what I thought," Grace said.

Carole looked from one to the other. Finally, she said, very softly, "I really missed you, Gracie."

"I thought some misogynistic asshole picked you up and killed you," Alex said.

"Could have happened," Grace said. "Maybe it nearly did."

"Here?" Carole asked. "At Oh Kaye's?"

Grace shook her head. "It's a long story. Are you both finally ready to listen to me?"

Carole tugged her miniskirt as if she could make it longer. "I want to hear it."

Alex picked up Grace's whiskey and tossed it back. Then she wiped off her mouth. "What did I tell you, Grace? Women always tolerate misogyny. You should have fought him off."

"I did," Grace said.

Alex's eyes widened. Carole laughed. "Our Gracie has grown up."

"No," Grace said. "I've always been grown-up. You're just noticing now."

"There's a story here," Alex said, slipping her arm through Grace's, "and I think I need to hear it."

"Me, too." Carole put her arm around Grace's shoulder. "Tell us about your adventures. I promise we'll listen."

Grace sighed. She'd love to tell them everything, but if she did, she'd screw up the case against Delamore. "Naw," Grace said. "Let's just have some drinks and talk about girl things."

"You gotta promise to tell us," Alex said.

"Okay," Grace said. "I promise. Now how about some whiskey?"

"Beer," Alex said.

"You see that cute guy over there?" Carole asked, pointing at the suits.

Grace grinned. Already, her adventure was forgotten. Nothing changed here at Oh Kaye's. Nothing except Cowboy Grace, who'd finally bellied up to the bar.

Doug Allyn

PALACE IN THE PINES

■ ■ ■

Author of seven novels and more than eighty short stories, Doug Allyn's background includes Chinese language studies at Indiana University and extended duty in Southeast Asia during the Vietnam war. Later, he studied creative writing and criminal psychology at the University of Michigan while moonlighting as a songwriter/guitarist in the rock band Devil's Triangle. He currently reviews books for the Flint Journal *while maintaining a full-time writing schedule. His short stories have garnered both critical and commercial acclaim and have been awarded numerous prizes, including the Robert L. Fish for best first story, the Edgar Allan Poe Award, the American Mystery Award, the Derringer Award twice, and the Ellery Queen Readers Award six times. Doug counts among his career highlights drinking champagne with Mickey Spillane and waltzing with Mary Higgins Clark. "Palace in the Pines," our selection for this year, was the Ellery Queen Readers Award–winning story for 2003, and it's a masterpiece, a tale of love and murder set in the idyllic forests of Michigan.*

I was hoping he'd be magical. If I meet a car salesman I expect a spiel. A politician? A handshake and a pitch for my vote. So I thought Geno LaRosa might show me a trick or two. Find a quarter in my ear. Or make my troubles disappear.

TV Guide called Geno LaRosa the hippest magician in America. A new-wave Houdini—pop magic for the new millennium. He was a regular guest on the *Tonight Show* and *Letterman*, with his own specials on HBO and Showtime, where he made elephants and city buses vanish. I don't have cable, so I've never seen his shows. But I knew who he was.

I just couldn't figure out what he wanted. LaRosa is a big star. I run a low-rent construction company in Valhalla, northern Michigan. Upstate. Waaay upstate. Big lake country. The boondocks. Sometimes cell phones work up here, sometimes not. Relay towers are too few and far apart. We have plenty of trees, though. Pine forests, cedar swamps, rolling hills teeming with white birch, poplar, and balsam. Trees and more trees. A few small towns are linked by narrow ribbons of two-lane blacktop. But we have a lot more trees than people.

When my dad said Geno LaRosa called and asked me to meet him in the middle of noplace along the Lake Huron shore, I figured it was one of my buddies goofing. Or maybe Dad got the name wrong. Some days he can't remember mine.

But it was no joke. A limo was idling on the shoulder of the road, a uniformed driver leaning against the door. I wheeled my pickup truck in behind it.

A man and woman were in front of the limo, arguing about something. She was a stunner, tall and dark, her face framed by a perfect bouffant, every hair precisely in place. A New York supermodel. Or could have been.

Her buddy was square as a barrel with a salt-and-pepper beard. Looked like a bear in a business suit.

Geno LaRosa was sitting alone, halfway up the hillside. He waved, so I made my way up to him.

He looked more like a grad student than a TV star. A good-looking guy. Photogenic. Intelligent eyes, lean jaw, shaggy mop dyed blond, fashionable two-day stubble. Dressed casually, blue jeans, Yale sweater, white tennies.

Not magical, though. All business. I introduced myself. Geno nodded politely, but didn't offer to shake hands. "I'll be frank, Mr. Shea, you aren't my first choice for this project. Not even my third." He handed me a folio. I recognized the architects, Cohen and Harding, a big firm, out of Detroit. And out of my league.

Flipping past the survey and title I found the master blueprints, scanned them. Blinked. Then examined them more closely, trying to quiet my heartbeat. This was big. A private home, log construction. Bigger than anything I'd ever done. Bigger than I'd ever seen. And I really needed the work. A job like this could . . .

And then it hit me. Damn, I'd never get this job. The more I looked at the plans, the further my heart sank. My company was just too small. He'd probably called me out here to satisfy some bank requirement for multiple bids. Damn, damn, damn.

"Looks like an interesting project," I said, rolling up the drawings. "Tell me about it."

"It's all there in the plans—"

"It'll take me an hour to scan these properly, Mr. LaRosa. I'm sure you're a busy man. So am I. And since we're both standing here, why don't you just tell me what you want? Exactly. Unless you'd rather call the next builder on your list."

He glanced at me sharply, looking me over for the first time. I'm no fashion plate. Sandy hair cropped short for quick showers. Jeans and a T-shirt, faded but not fashionable. The tattoo on my arm covers a nasty burn scar from a welding torch. A poster boy for the working class. I expected to be blown off. Instead, he nodded. And actually smiled.

"Fair enough, Mr. . . . ? I'm sorry, I've forgotten your name."

"Shea. Dan Shea."

"Of course. Here's what I want, Mr. Shea. A house. Right here, on this hillside. Three stories, twenty-seven rooms, nine thousand square feet. Full-width balconies on all floors, facing Lake Huron. Five-car attached garage over there, ten-car garage with living quarters for staff on the far side of the hill. You with me so far?"

"Sure. A monster house with staff quarters close by but out of sight. I noticed you specified log construction. Are you a big Abe Lincoln fan or do you just like to make things tough for contractors?"

"It's a bit more complicated than that. Are you familiar with the Chinese principles of feng shui?"

"I've read about them, sure. The basic idea is that an ideal house should contain all the natural elements—wood, fire, and water—and face in the proper direction."

"Which in this case will be northeast, toward the lake and the rising sun. I had a Tibetan shaman flown here to bless the site. He said it was a magical spot."

"It's a great-looking hill, all right," I acknowledged. "How much land do you have here?"

"Twenty-five hundred acres. Completely undeveloped woods and swampland. I also bought the airfield outside Valhalla. I'm a licensed pilot and I have my own Lear jet. Weather permitting, Detroit's only forty minutes away."

"This far north, the weather doesn't always cooperate, Mr. LaRosa. And your site's pretty isolated."

"So it is. Do you know what I do for a living, Mr. Shea?"

"Sort of. You're a magician. On TV."

"It's a great life, but I spend a lot of time traveling. Sometimes it all starts to feel . . . ephemeral. I tell jokes, do some illusions, and it's on to the next theater, the next town, the next country. Hotels, motels, airports. Places and faces start to blur. Sometimes I really need to get away from all that."

"You've picked the right spot, then. You're fifteen miles from Valhalla, which pretty much qualifies this place as the middle of nowhere."

"That's precisely why I chose it. I want my home to be a haven, Mr. Shea. A log fortress away from the world. I want it to have roots, to belong here, on this spot. As though someone built it centuries ago and it will stand a thousand years after we're gone. I want timbers that grew in this ground and stones from these hills. Whenever possible, I'd prefer to use local craftsmen, men who care about their work. Still with me?"

I chewed my lip, thoughtfully looking over the site. Rough country. Only one road, but there was a county power line a mile or so to the south. . . . Doable. I felt the conviction growing in my gut. I could make something wonderful happen here. The hillside sloped gently down to the lapping waters of Lake Huron, roses growing wild along the shore, towering pines, white and red, the breeze whispering through their boughs. And for a moment, only a moment, I caught a glimpse of what the house would look like.

Magnificent. A palace. In the pines.

"You're smiling," LaRosa said. "Is something funny?"

"If it is, the joke's probably on me. Straight up, Mr. LaRosa, the architectural firm that did your plans recommended a half-dozen builders. I don't see my name on their list. So why am I here?"

"The realtor who sold us the property recommended you. Said you had grit and ambition, a young man on the move. Not unlike myself."

"I've got a great crew and we do first-class work, but we've never built anything this size. All the contractors on your architect's list are reputable. So why didn't you . . . ?" And suddenly I knew. "Hell, you did call them, didn't you? And they all tried to talk you out of it, right?"

He nodded. "Something like that. One problem with being an entertainer, nobody takes a clown seriously. Three different contractors pooh-poohed the idea of building with local materials. Impractical. They said a house this size has to be fabricated offsite, everything precut to size at a factory, then freighted in and assembled. Like a Tinkertoy. Better quality, less expensive, and a lot simpler to build. What do you think of that, Mr. Shea? Are they right?"

"Definitely simpler to build," I admitted, scanning the plans again. "Not necessarily cheaper. Freighting in the logs and using two or three factory work crews at once would speed up construction, but they'd be in a hurry to finish up and get out. Local crews, custom fitting timbers at the site, would definitely take more time, but the craftsmanship would be superior. And they're used to working with local materials."

"How much time difference are we talking about?"

"Precut at the factory, the project could be done in . . . twenty-four to twenty-eight weeks. With local materials, add another month, minimum."

"Two contractors claimed it couldn't be done at all. Something about logs from this part of the country being too short?"

I digested that one, flipping through to the specifications page. "Logs in precut structures of this size are usually ponderosa pine from big timber farms out West. They grow 'em in fields like wheat, straight as telephone poles. Michigan pines live through more weather. Wind, snow. The wood's denser and . . . ah. Here's the problem. Seventy-foot rafters and purlins. Wow. They were right. Local timbers don't grow nearly this long."

"So it can't be done?"

"I didn't say that. My daddy says there are at least three ways to do anything, you just have to find 'em. Here are your options. One, use local timbers for the walls, floors, and ceilings and import longer logs for the rafters and main beams. The problem is, the grain will be visibly different. Western pine is cleaner, fewer gnarls, less character. Twenty feet overhead, it'll look phony. Option two, use structural steel instead of log rafters, box it in with local pine. If it's done right, the seams won't show, and you can dispense with some of these support corbels, here and here, in the great room and the dining room. Open them up to the sun a little more."

"You said three ways. What's the third option?"

"You've already heard it. Precut the logs at a factory, truck them in. If you wanted to do that, I wouldn't be here."

"What I want is in those plans. I love to travel but I need a place of my own, too. Something real. Something . . . substantial."

"This'll be substantial, all right. It'll be a palace, in the pines."

"A palace in the pines." He nodded, smiling. "I like the sound of that. So, what do you think? Can you build me a palace, Mr. Shea?"

"As I said, a bigger company could—"

"All I've gotten from bigger companies is a lot of guff about why it's impossible. I do the impossible for a living. Straight up, Shea, can you make this happen or not?"

"Yes, sir. I can build your palace, Mr. LaRosa. Exactly the way you want it, rocks, trees, feng shui, the works. I can get it done."

"Fair enough. Leo! Clarissa! Come up here! Conference!" Leo and the lady started climbing up, but the going was rough. High heels and tight skirts aren't designed for north-country hillsides. "How long will construction take, Mr. Shea?"

"I'll have to check the plans—"

"Ballpark," he interrupted impatiently. "If I want to spend Christmas here, will I be able to?"

I thought a moment. "Sure. I can't promise the outbuildings, but barring a disaster we can have the main house livable by December."

"Terrific," he said as the other two came stumbling up. "Leo, Mr. Shea's going to handle this project for me. Haggle enough to earn your ten percent, but make it happen, clear?"

Leo looked me over, taking my measure in a millisecond. He wasn't impressed. "Whatever you say, Geno. We'll get it done."

"Clarissa, Shea here promises the house will be livable by Christmas. We could get married over the holidays, invite some people up, work in the wedding and a house-warming between Vegas and the Japanese tour. Does that work for you?"

She frowned, then nodded. "Sure. We can do that."

"Great. I don't want anything heavy, now. No press, no fans, just the usual suspects and—"

"It's covered," Clarissa said with a flash of irritation. "Don't worry, I'll take care of it."

"That's my girl. Now, about the house. Mr. Shea here says he's up for the job but he's never built a palace before. I need someone here to coordinate this, deal with problems and make decisions on the spot. I can't be worrying about wallpaper patterns while I'm onstage in Berlin. I want you to stay and oversee the project."

"Me?" Clarissa echoed. "But—"

"It has to be you, Clare. I'll be on tour in Europe for May and June, Brazil after that. A million things are going to come up here and you know what I like. I want this place perfect for us. You're the only one I trust to make it that way."

She started to argue, then opted not to. "Okay," she said, eyeing me doubtfully. "I'll handle it."

"Great. Done deal. I have to be in Iowa by seven so I gotta go. Mr. Shea can find you a place to stay somewhere nearby. I'll call you from Des Moines, love. Come on, Leo."

And that was it. Most of my clients spend more time choosing bathroom rugs than LaRosa took for a mansion. Geno and his manager hurried down the hillside to the limo and roared off down the dirt road.

Leaving me with his fiancée. Eyeing each other like stray dogs.

"Clarissa Landis," she said, offering her hand, breaking the ice. "And you are . . . ?"

"Dan Shea," I said, still shaken by the suddenness of it all. An hour ago I was scrounging for a job to cover my mortgage payment. Now I had the biggest project I'd ever seen dumped in my lap. And I had to finish it by Christmas. I opened the plans to the site layout, trying to orient myself.

"So," Clarissa said. "How do we make this work?"

Lost in the plans, I scarcely heard her.

"Wrong," she said, gently folding the plans closed, facing me. "That's not how it's going to work, Mr. Shea. Let's get things straight from the git-go. Geno hired you because he thinks you can do the job. But he didn't get where he is by ducking tough decisions. When it comes to business, he's a hard-nose. The moment he thinks you can't hack it, you'll be gone. And I'll be the one grading your report card. Do we understand each other?"

"I'm not sure. How much do you know about construction, Miss Landis?"

"Call me Clare. Not much, but I can learn. I'm no bimbo, Mr. Shea. I'm a CPA with a master's degree in contract law. I've negotiated every project and contract Geno's been involved with for the past five years."

"I thought Leo was the business manager."

"Leo's a haggler. He lines up deals, I close them and follow through afterward to make sure everything works. But I'm not your enemy, Mr. Shea. I'm on your side. I want this to go well. And finish on time. By Christmas."

"I expect so. Have you two been engaged long?"

She glanced at her watch. "About four and a half minutes, give or take."

I blinked. "You mean . . . ?"

"Right, that was it. Geno's proposal, wedding plans, housewarming, the whole bit. Happily ever after in a heartbeat. And it's okay. A moonlight proposal on bended knee would have been cute but it's not Geno. And I'd marry him at the bottom of a well if he asked me to. He's a marvelous man."

"He must be. And I see what you mean about making tough decisions in a hurry."

"Really? You think proposing to me was a tough decision?"

It was the first time I'd seen her smile. An impish smile, a little crooked in one corner. Supermodel beauty, intelligence, plus a sense of humor? I felt a pang of envy. Geno was a lucky guy. And so was I, if I could make this work.

"There's a joke in the construction business, Miss—sorry—Clare. A guy's haggling with a builder. I'm pretty handy, he says. Suppose I help you? Will that change the price?

"Sure, the builder says. With your help, I'll do the job for a thousand bucks. If you don't help, it'll be five hundred."

Her smile faded. "That's a joke?"

"An old one. The point is—"

"I get the point, Mr. Shea. I'm not sure you got mine. I won't tell you how to build Geno's palace, but I'm going to make damned sure it's finished exactly as planned and on schedule. If you have questions, I'll get answers; if you have problems, I'll help solve them. But if I think you're the problem, I'll solve that, too. Clear?"

"Clear."

"Good. When do we start?"

"It's not that simple. I'll need a written contract and a deposit before—"

"No problem," she interrupted. "I'll have Leo fax a working agreement to us at your offices. Geno told him to make this happen, so the terms will be more than fair and I have power of attorney to sign for Geno. How big a deposit will you need?"

I flipped through the plans to the architects' construction cost estimates. And swallowed. It was nearly seven million. My end would be fourteen percent of that. More money than I'd ever seen in my life. Clare glanced over my shoulder.

"The standard deposit is half down, correct?"

"That's normal, but—"

"Tell you what, I'll have a hundred thousand deposited in your personal account this afternoon as a binder. We'll keep a working balance, say, three million, in a joint corporate account. I'll be your financial officer for this project. I may not know construction, but I can crunch numbers faster than IBM. Tell me what you need, I'll make it happen. I'll need a place to stay. What's available?"

"There's a Holiday Inn outside the village, plus a couple of nice bed-and-breakfasts—"

"The Holiday Inn will do. I'm used to motels. Shall we go?" But as she turned to leave, she hesitated, looking around as though seeing it, really taking it all in, for the first time. The swaying pines, the hillside rolling down to the lake, waves nuzzling the shore. "My God," she said softly, "what an incredibly lovely spot this is."

She was right. It was. And I wondered if anything I could build here, even a mansion, would be worthy of this magical ground. But I had to admit that Geno's fiancée, sun-dappled, with the spring breeze tousling her perfect hair, belonged in a palace.

We met that evening in the Holiday Inn's private dining room. A business dinner to discuss the nuts and bolts of getting the project under way. But it was personal, too. We traded histories and ideas, fumbling our way toward the working relationship we'd need to get this thing done.

Clare was strictly New York City. Grew up broke but artsy. Her father was a struggling stage director, her mom a part-time actress. Clare worked her way through CCNY, hired on with the William Morris talent agency after graduation.

Geno LaRosa was one of their biggest clients. After she got him out of a Jersey casino contract, he hired her for his personal staff. No hanky-panky, strictly business.

She'd been with him five years, the last two as his girlfriend. And now his fiancée. She was so happy she practically bubbled. And I couldn't help wondering if any woman's eyes would ever shine like that for me. I grew up hardscrabble poor in the north country. Quit school to support my family. Clawed my way up from timberjack to carpenter to crew boss of my own company. Put two sisters and my little brother through college. My dad lives with me now, takes care of the house, cooks a little.

"He doesn't work with you?" Clare asked.

"He's busted up. Logging accident took one leg twenty years back. He's drifty when he drinks. Worse when he doesn't. He takes some looking after."

"You're not married?"

"No time. You don't meet many women at north-woods construction sites. Unless you count she-bears."

"I think you could do better than a bear, Mr. Shea. Do you have anything against working with women?"

"Not really. My bookkeeper's a nice lady, seventy-two. But construction's a different deal. Working in rough country isn't like building in the city. Big trees falling, heavy machinery plowing unstable ground. Screw up in the city, you get sued. Make a mistake out here, you wind up minus a leg, like my dad. Or maybe dead. It's hard, dirty work. And risky. It's no place for a woman."

"No?" she smiled, leaning back. "We'll see about that."

She showed up at the hillside the next day, wearing shiny new hobnailed boots, a flannel work shirt, and pristine jeans. Even had her hair tied back in a ponytail. Like she'd stepped out of a fashion layout in a Marshall Field's catalog. In that getup, anyone else would have looked ridiculous. Clare just looked like her own younger sister. Not as sophisticated, but even prettier. To me, anyway.

The site was already a madhouse. Puck Paquette, my big, slow Canuck foreman, was marking off the foundation for the concrete contractor while the rest of my crew cleared the site, cutting brush and dropping trees, prepping the hilltop for major surgery.

I kept an eye on things, but mostly I worked the phone, lining up the list of subcontractors we'd need for this job, everything from electricians to iron workers.

Fortunately it was early in the season, and the sheer size of the project made it easy to collect crews. In a part of the country where an early snow can steal two months' wages, everyone was happy to sign on. It had been a long winter. We were all hungry as bears.

But not greedy. Not yet. That would come later, when they realized how big the job was and how much money was involved. I had a backup list for every contractor I hired.

The first one who tried to jack up his price would be fired on the spot. No discussion, no appeal. Gone. A lesson to the others.

I've always been an easy boss. Too easy, maybe. LaRosa's palace was my big chance, and I was already picking up attitude from the owner. Geno wasn't the only one who could make hard decisions in a hurry.

After a few hours of hovering around the site, Clare asked me to put her to work. I'd half expected the request after her remarks the night before, considered trying to talk her out of it. Decided to teach her a lesson instead.

So I loaned her my smallest chain saw, a Stihl sixteen-incher, and took twenty minutes to teach her the basics: how to hold it, where to notch a trunk, to crank the saw wide open before starting a cut. Woodcraft 101. Then I turned her loose on a copse of seedling jack pines, none taller than five feet, the easiest, safest job on the site.

Clare waded in with a will. I went back to work with the layout crew, marking boundaries, driving stakes. But keeping an eye on Clare as well. I figured she'd fade in the first twenty minutes.

She didn't. She kept at it nonstop for nearly two hours before I noticed the telltale signs of fatigue. I approached cautiously. More Woodcraft 101. Never startle somebody who's swinging a chain saw. Unless you want your body parts scattered over a wide area.

"Yo," I called, stepping into her line of vision. "Take five."

"I'm okay," she said, straightening, licking sweat off her upper lip. "Really."

"Actually, you're doing great for a rookie," I admitted, "but you're tiring now. Some people slow down, some speed up. You're speeding up. Tired people make little mistakes, only there aren't any minor mistakes with chain saws. Take a break."

"You're the boss," she said, easing down the saw, looking around. "Wow, the hill's half bald already. Your men work fast."

"Knocking trees down is easy. Putting something half as pretty in their place is the hard part." She leaned against a big pine, catching her breath as I pointed out the various crews, explained what each group was doing, then outlined the order of battle for the next few weeks.

Grading would begin as soon as we finished clearing, then we'd run in a temporary power line for electric lights and pour the foundation and footings. Then the real work would start.

She took it all in and asked a few pointed questions. A very bright woman. Then she picked up her chain saw.

"You really don't have to do this, you know," I said.

"I know. And any minimum-wage high-school kid could probably do a better job than I will. But I want to do it. When we're finished, this will be my house, too. I'll be married here, raise my children here if we're lucky. So I don't want to be a spectator, Mr. Shea. I want to have a hand in building some small part of it, every step of the way. Will you help me do that?"

"It'll be my pleasure, Miss Landis. Every step of the way."

"And if I get underfoot, you'll tell me, right?"

"You'll be the first to know. Promise."

"Thanks," she said, giving me a quick peck on the cheek. "It means a lot to me. Now, out of my way, bozo, I've got trees to drop." Setting her hard hat at a jaunty angle, she did a perfect lumberjack swagger back to her little copse. Leaving me smiling in spite of myself.

I went back to work, too, but I found it hard to concentrate. At odd moments Clare's elfin smile kept flickering across the video screen of my memory. And I could still feel the warmth of her lips against my cheek.

By midsummer, the house was already taking shape. The foundations were down and dry, power and sewer lines were laid, and the walls were rising. Building with logs is vastly different from standard construction. In a stick-built house, you raise the framework first, roof it over, then side it. With the interior protected from the elements, several crews can work at once, electricians and plumbers, for example. The whole process speeds up.

With logs, everything waits for the walls, and they're raised exactly as they were back in Abe Lincoln's day, stacked up one stick at a time, each one matched and hand-fitted to the one below. LaRosa's palace was far too large for single logs to span any part of it, so we had to butt them end to end, which meant more matching and hand-fitting. It's like assembling a 3-D jigsaw puzzle with slippery pieces that weigh three hundred pounds each. Tricky, dangerous work.

Ordinarily, the first five tiers are stacked by hand, but since we were going up three stories, I set cranes up at opposite ends of the building and ran two stacking crews simultaneously, dawn to dark, then continued working another four hours by artificial light.

Clare came out to the site almost every day, helping in small ways, gofering, carrying planks. Something. But she spent most of her days on the phone, arranging deliveries, badgering or sweet-talking suppliers, making sure the materials were delivered to the site on time and in the proper order.

She was really good at it. Without her help, the sheer size of the project and the thousand petty problems that cropped up every damned day would have snowed me under. But they didn't. Because Clare coped with them, carrying the load for me.

Puck Paquette, my grizzly-sized foreman, adopted Clare like a stray pup. Taught her the lore of lumberjacking and woodcraft, and to curse like a logger. Clare soaked it up, loving every minute.

She also had a sharp eye for problems. Too sharp, sometimes. She cornered me during a lunch break at the site, pulling me aside.

"One of your crew is drunk."

"Which one?"

"A welder. The dark one, with the ponytail. Looks like an Indian."

"He is an Indian. Ojibwa, full blood. His name's Mafe Rochon. But he's not just a welder. He's a freakin' genius with a torch."

"He's also loaded."

"Nah, he drinks but he's not wrecked. See this tattoo on my arm? It covers a scar I got with a cutting torch. I was lucky. At three thousand degrees, flesh doesn't burn, it vaporizes. With a torch, your margin for error is exactly zero, especially when you're working high steel. If Mafe was loaded, he'd be dead already."

"I can't believe you're defending him."

"Hey, I'm defending us. If we want to finish by Christmas, I need the best men I can get. I don't like Mafe, he's a troublemaker and a mean drunk. But there aren't five guys on the planet as good as he is with a torch. I need him."

"Then talk to him about his drinking before he kills himself or somebody else."

"Yes, ma'am. I'll definitely talk to him."

And I did. And Mafe told me to screw off, which I expected. But he did cut back on the wine for a while. I settled for that. So did Clare. She knew he was still drinking, but let it pass. A very quick study.

Most days flew by in a blur. Clare would track me down at the site, rattle off a list of problems that needed my attention. I'd make a decision or she would, and on to the next. We had working dinners twice a week but I was too exhausted to be of much use. Once I fell asleep at the table in mid sentence. Clare booked a room for me at the inn to save me the drive home.

After ordering the desk not to wake me before ten, she hit the site the next morning to get things under way. I woke late, charged out to the job in a rage. Which Clare promptly jollied away. If I was too beat to eat, I wasn't sharp enough to boss work crews through a fourteen-hour day.

She was right. But more important, she made her point without pulling rank or busting my chops. A remarkable woman. Smart, lovely, likable. And despite the pressures and problems, we were becoming friends. Good friends. The kind who talk about real things. Life, love, and What It's All About. Buds.

And maybe slightly more than that. On my part, anyway. But I wouldn't admit it, even to myself. Kept pushing it to the back of my mind. I was working like a madman on the biggest job I'd ever seen, let alone bossed. Building a goddamn magnificent mansion. A palace in the pines.

This job could change my life, set me up financially, open doors to deals I could scarcely imagine. I wasn't about to blow it all over a dumb-ass schoolboy crush on the owner's fiancée. And that's all it was. A crush. Puppy love. On a one-way street.

Geno LaRosa only showed up at the site twice. The first time was during the final fury of topping off the walls. Men screaming at each other, cranes roaring, timbers soaring skyward.

He didn't stay long. Clare showed him around for half an hour, then they left in his limo. Geno seemed a bit awed by it all. Intimidated by the chaos he'd created. The dirt, the noise. Or maybe he only wanted to be alone with Clare. At the Holiday Inn. I was glad he didn't hang around the site. A star underfoot was a distraction for the crews. As to where he and Clare went and what they did? I tried not to think about that. Hated the scenes flitting through my imagination. I handled it. But I wasn't much fun to be around for a few days.

Geno's second visit changed everything.

By late July we had the walls up, floors down, and a roof overhead. After the colossal battle of wrestling timbers into place atop a sixty-foot wall, installing wiring, plumbing, paneling was almost a pleasure. There were still a million problems to solve, and a mountain of work to be done, but the scale was smaller.

Logistics were crucial now, making sure each crew had what they needed in the right order. Plumbing and wiring before paneling and fixtures. Windows and doors installed with slip joints to allow for settling, with every step of the work okayed by the county building and electrical inspectors.

We were still under tremendous pressure, but it wasn't the craziness of rough construction. I was more of a field general than a combat commander now. It felt good.

I'd gotten into the habit of coming out to the site at sunrise, strolling through the mansion with a cup of coffee, checking everyone's handiwork, plotting out my day.

I knew Geno LaRosa was planning to visit sometime during the week, so I wasn't surprised to find a Lincoln limo parked beside a bulldozer. There were no lights showing, no one around. LaRosa probably left the car and rode into town with Clare. To the Holiday Inn. Damn.

I couldn't keep the pictures out of my mind. Geno and Clare together, in her room. They haunted me as I stalked the halls of his half-built palace. Trying to concentrate on my work. And failing.

I almost fell over them. In the master bedroom, third floor, with a balcony and a magnificent view of the lake.

It had no doors yet, and I wasn't expecting anyone. I wanted to check the windows for plumb, but I didn't get that far. Two steps into the room I froze. Something was out of place.

A sleeping bag. Sprawled in the center of the floor. Geno LaRosa was wrapped up in it, snoring softly, his forearm across his eyes, dead to the world.

As I started to tiptoe back out, I realized Clare was in the shadows at the balcony window, watching the dawn break on the horizon, tinting Lake Huron a burnished bronze.

She was barefoot, wearing nothing but Geno's shirt, her dark hair loose about her shoulders. Framed in the morning glow, she was so achingly lovely that for a moment I couldn't move. Couldn't even breathe. Felt a pain in my chest so deep I thought I might break in half.

Maybe I groaned. Or perhaps Clare sensed my presence. She turned. And our eyes met and held. And I couldn't help myself. Everything I felt for her, all the words, the emotions, were in that look. But there was no reply for me. Only sympathy. And kindness. The wordless compassion of one friend for another.

And then she looked away. Tugged Geno's shirt closed and turned back to the dawn. As though I wasn't there at all.

And perhaps for her, I wasn't.

I backed out quietly, made my way down to my truck, and sat behind the wheel. Shaking. When the work crews arrived, I helped the electricians wire up the basement, staying as far from that third-floor master bedroom as I could.

Geno and Clare found me later in the morning. LaRosa congratulated me on how quickly the home was taking shape and we discussed trouble spots in the construction. He made a few suggestions and his ideas were sound. Clare was right, he was a bright guy. Quick as a Pentium chip.

But at one point, when Clare was explaining the technique we used to set the rafters in place, I noticed Geno eyeing her in an odd way. Frowning.

And it dawned on me how different she was from the fashion plate who'd stumbled up the hillside in high heels that first day. Her hair was tied back now, the sun and wind had reddened her cheeks, highlighting a few freckles.

I thought she was far more beautiful now. But Geno had proposed to Clarissa Landis, the impeccable New York mannequin. And I wondered what he thought of this brash country girl in the flannel shirt and boots who could laugh it up with lumberjacks.

Geno flew out the next day, headed for Spain on the final leg of his European tour. Clare and I got back to work. But not back to normal. That sunrise moment in the master bedroom was there between us.

I'm not a subtle man. I don't lie worth a damn and I'm not good at concealing my emotions. She knew exactly how I felt now. She read it in my eyes that morning. But we never spoke of it. We continued working together, meeting for dinner once or twice a week as though nothing had happened.

But it had. I'd changed. Everything I'd ever wanted, everything I considered important had turned upside down. I've always put my work first. Had to. To support my family and make my way in this world. Never doubted it was the right thing to do.

Until now. When I realized I was working like a dog to build a magnificent mansion so the woman I loved could live happily ever after in it. With another man.

A cosmic joke. On me. But I wasn't sophisticated enough to laugh it off. It hurt too much. I felt as if my heart had been seared with Mafe Rochon's acetylene torch. All I know is work, so I poured my pain into building the palace. And took my rage out on the men.

The construction continued at a furious pace, but the pressure was building. Tempers were fraying. I was pushing too hard and I knew it. But I was too angry to back off. Something had to break. And it did.

A cup.

We were in the private dining room at the Holiday Inn going over invoices. Clare was sipping coffee when the cup slipped out of her hand, slopping cappuccino all over the paperwork.

Grumbling, I was mopping up the mess when she bounced a soggy napkin wad off my forehead. I nearly blew my stack. Dammit, this was serious! The plans could have been ruined—

She whizzed another paper wad past my ear and I just couldn't resist the mischief in her eyes. Ducking below the table, I threw a french fry back at her. She countered with half a sandwich and our business dinner erupted into a food fight free-for-all, dodging around the room pelting each other with napkin bombs and potato wads, laughing so hard the manager stuck her nose in to check on the noise. And got splattered for her trouble.

Afterward, as we were picking up the papers, sorting them out, Clare touched my arm. "Danny, I know you have feelings for me, and I care for you, too, but . . ."

"But not enough."

"Not the same way. You have to let this go. It'll wreck everything if you don't."

"I don't know if I can, Clare. I've tried, but . . ."

"You have to. This is the happiest time of my life, and helping you build this house has been a wonderful part of it. Don't ruin it for me, Danny. Please."

"Okay. If that's what you want, enough said. Forget about it. I've been handling trouble all my life. I'll handle this, too. I promise."

"I'll drink to that," she said, pouring us both a fresh mug of coffee. But as we raised them in a toast to seal the bargain, Clare's cup slipped from her fingers. Again.

I thought she was still kidding around. But she wasn't.

The next day, Mafe Rochon came in wrecked. He was working on the second-floor balcony, tack-welding curlicues onto the cast-iron railing, sparks flying, singing to himself in French. Happy as a clam, drunk as a lord. I could smell it on him five feet away.

I tapped him on the shoulder. He glanced up, gave me a bleary grin, and went back to his work. I was about to yank him to his feet when Puck Paquette grabbed my arm, hauled me off.

"What the hell you doing, Danny?"

"Firing Rochon's ass! He's drunk. I warned him."

"Warnin's don't mean nothin' to Mafe. He's a stone wino, you know that. Knew it when you hired him. He stayed sober a week after that last time you talked to him. Mean as a grizzly with the crabs. He ain't too drunk to work. I been keepin' an eye on him."

"Then you'd better watch him a damn sight closer, Puck! If I catch him drinking on the job again it'll be your ass, too—"

"Mr. Shea! Puck! You'd better get down here!" one of the carpenters yelled from the kitchen.

We were both sprinting downstairs before he finished. The panic in his voice cut through the noise like a hacksaw.

"It's Miss Landis," he explained as I bulled past him into the kitchen. Clare was sitting on the floor, her back against a cabinet.

"Sorry," she said sheepishly. "I fell."

"What happened?" I asked, kneeling beside her.

"I don't know. My knees just wobbled and, um . . . I can't seem to make my legs work, Danny. I'm not hurt or anything. If I can just rest here a minute—"

"Not a chance," I said, scooping her up in my arms. "Hold the fort, Puck, I'm taking Clare into town."

Valhalla is too small for a hospital. All we have is a doc-in-the-box clinic run by a Mormon couple from Utah. They did some quick tests, didn't like the results, and promptly sent Clare off in an ambulance down to University Hospital in Ann Arbor. I followed in my pickup. Pedal to the metal all the way.

At the U they ran more tests. Nobody said much, but they frowned a lot. I wanted to call Geno and notify Clare's parents but she forbade it. No point in worrying anybody. Not until we knew something.

I tried to stay in touch with the project, talked to Puck every day, worked out the construction snags as best I could over the phone.

Puck never said it, but I knew what he was thinking. This was my project, a monster of a job. It needed me. What the hell was I doing babysitting the boss's girlfriend in Ann Arbor?

He was dead-ass right and I knew it. But I didn't care.

It took ten days of tests and retests, EMGs, CAT scans, MRIs before they finally told us what it all meant.

By then Clare had been assigned to a specialist, a neurologist, Dr. Khalid. Tall, bald, and beige. And gentle. Eyes sad as a spaniel. We were in his office at U hospital. Clare was in a wheelchair, hospital policy. And necessary. Despite the small army of doctors she'd seen, her sense of balance remained undependable. Sometimes she could walk normally. Sometimes she fell.

"I wish I knew an easy way to tell you this, Clare," Khalid said quietly. "The tests aren't totally conclusive, but our preliminary diagnosis is amyotrophic lateral sclerosis."

"Lou Gehrig's disease," Clare said flatly. It wasn't a question.

"I'm afraid so."

"Afraid of what?" I put in. "What's this Gehrig's disease?"

"A motor disturbance of the nervous system," Khalid explained. "The initial symptoms are weakness in the hands, spasticity or weakness in the legs—"

"—followed by difficulty swallowing and speaking," Clare finished for him. "I've been reading up on my symptoms."

"Okay, fine," I said. "That's what it is. What do we do about it?"

"Very little, I'm afraid," Khalid said. "There are palliative drugs that can make you more comfortable, Miss Landis, but at present there's no cure. Nor any effective treatment. I'm very sorry."

There was a long silence.

"This is crap," I said, flushing, feeling my rage roiling up. I was one second away from punching out Dr. Khalid or the wall. I needed to hit something.

"Danny—"

"No! It really is! This giant frickin' hospital, all these doctors, all this high-tech equipment, and you can't fix somebody who's having a little trouble with her legs?"

"The diagnosis is only preliminary," Dr. Khalid reminded me. "It'll be several months before we can be absolutely certain."

"Why? How will you know?"

"Her symptoms will exacerbate. ALS sometimes progresses very rapidly and I've seen Clare's condition deteriorate in the short time she's been here. The prognosis in such cases is grave."

"No pun intended, I hope," Clare said briskly. "How much time are we talking about here?"

"That's impossible to say with certainty."

"Then give me a ballpark figure, Doctor. I need a number I can understand. Are we talking months? Years?"

"Not years. The normal progression of ALS is from nine to eighteen months," Khalid said. "Your case seems particularly aggressive. You're already having difficulty walking. If the disorder continues at its present rate, your other motor functions may be impaired in a matter of months. You're going to need full-time care, Miss Landis. And soon."

"For how long?"

"Six months, perhaps a year. I'm very—"

"Sorry," Clare finished. "You said that already. So am I."

I drove her back to Valhalla myself. No need for an ambulance now. There was no rush. I headed north on I-75 with the woman I loved, a five-hour drive through some of the loveliest scenery on the planet on a sunny August afternoon. The darkest day of my life.

"There are other hospitals," I said.

"University Hospital's one of the best in the country. I checked. And I saw at least a dozen specialists there. They can't all be wrong."

"I want them to be."

"So do I. But I don't have time to waste on wishful thinking. I'm still trying to get my head around all this, Danny. Dammit! I was so close to having it all. Geno, the palace, maybe even a family. It's not fair."

"No, it's not. What are you going to do?"

"I don't know. Count my blessings, I guess."

"What blessings?"

"Hey, I don't have to worry about getting fat or going gray or having my husband dump me for a waitress."

"How can you joke about this?"

"Because I can't stand whiners and feeling sorry for myself won't help. Okay, it's a lousy break, and some of my dreams won't come true. Reality check. Most people slave away their whole lives and never even catch a glimpse of a dream. At least I came close. Almost close enough to touch it."

"It's still not fair."

"Nope, but there's nothing we can do about that. Solving problems is what we do best. So let's deal with this one. For openers, I don't want anyone else to know about this. It stays between us, Danny. Tell them I'm having back trouble. The wheelchair is only a precaution. Okay?"

"But what about your folks? And Mr. LaRosa?"

"They're my problem, I'll tell them . . . when I'm ready. I need to get everything back on track first. I know that staying at the hospital with me had to cost you. How far behind schedule are we?"

"Forget the damned schedule, Clare. It doesn't matter."

"Wrong, it matters to me. We've worked too long and too hard on this to quit now. I want to see it finished."

"For Geno?" I asked bitterly.

"Of course. But mostly for me. I hate hospitals. I've never had any fun in one. I want to live in my own house, that I helped to build. Even if it's only for a little while. I don't want to die in a hospital, Danny."

"You won't," I said. "I promise."

Architects hate redrawing their plans in the middle of a project, so I didn't bother consulting Detroit. Especially since the changes were serious.

The outside stairways were thirty feet across with a shallow, twelve-to-one rise. Ripping out the railings to add a wheelchair ramp trashed the aesthetics of the entry but at least the job wasn't complicated. Carpentry 101.

The interior was tougher. The great hall had broad, curving staircases at either end that rose three stories, lined with handcrafted wrought-iron bannisters. Installing Stair-Glide chair lifts would have destroyed all of Mafe Rochon's intricate ironwork without really solving the problem.

Clare wouldn't be able to negotiate any kind of ramp for long. She was going to need an elevator.

A small dumbwaiter ran from the kitchen to the upper floors, so we already had an elevator shaft, of sorts. But adapting it to accept a full-size elevator cab meant doubling the interior dimensions. We'd have to completely gut a section of the house we'd just finished. On all three floors. With every foot of it checked and approved by state inspectors.

I never hesitated. Puck was ripping out woodwork to build the new shaft even before I'd finished altering the plans.

None of this came cheap. The elevator, a top-of-the-line Access system, ran nearly thirty thousand. The ramps, remodeling, and installation would easily triple that figure.

The modifications were going to bump the bottom line by almost a hundred grand, and my agreement required that I inform Mr. LaRosa of any overrun above ten thousand. Clare asked me to hold off, so I did. I was breaking my contract, my word, and the law. And I didn't give a damn.

All I cared about was finishing the palace as soon as humanly possible. Not for LaRosa or the money. For Clare.

I ripped into the work like a madman, surly as a gut-shot grizzly. Driven by desperation and anguish. And pain. And rage.

Bullying and begging by turns, I drove the crews even harder. Fourteen-hour shifts became normal. Then sixteen. We started having minor accidents, the mistakes men make when they're tired. There was some grumbling. Talk of a walkout or a slow-down.

I quashed it by firing the first man I heard mouthing off. The others got the message. Like it or not, the palace was still the biggest job any of us had ever seen. Nobody quit. But we were all running on fumes, strung out, taut as guy wires. Only a word away from a major blowup.

Ten days after we returned from University Hospital, Clare finally got up the nerve to tell Geno what had happened. I don't know what was said or how he took it. She only told me that Geno and his manager would be flying in on Sunday. She wanted to meet them at the house, privately. I could give the crews the day off.

And she asked one other favor. She wanted to talk with Geno alone in their third-floor bedroom. Could I arrange that?

The elevator had arrived on site but wasn't installed yet. So on that Sunday, I carried Clare up the three flights to her room in my arms.

I was surprised at how little she weighed. And how haggard and drawn she'd become in only two weeks. She looked exhausted.

Dr. Khalid was right; the disease was moving aggressively, wasting her muscles, killing her by inches. And yet to me, at that moment, she'd never been so beautiful. And carrying her up to that bedroom to wait for the man she loved was the hardest goddamn thing I've ever done.

Two limousines arrived an hour later, one with Geno and his manager, Leo Holtzer, the second with one of Leo's assistants, Teddy something, and a woman, slim, blond, and very New York.

LaRosa asked me to show the group around, and went trotting briskly up the stairs, two at a time. I watched him part of the way, envying his effortless grace. Looks, brains, talent, and big bucks to boot. No wonder Clare was in love with him.

I tried to play tour guide for Leo and company but they clearly weren't interested. So I parked them on the back deck in the sunshine with a decent bottle of wine, and left them to chat.

I passed the time strolling the grounds, checking our progress. Staying as far from the master bedroom as I could. I was on the back deck, admiring Rochon's railing welds, when Geno came down. He looked awful—ashen, eyes red. Shaken. He'd obviously been crying. He huddled with Leo a moment, then the two of them waved me over, away from the others.

LaRosa's eyes lanced through me like lasers. "You should have told me!" he hissed.

"Clare asked me not to."

"You work for me, Shea, not for Clare. And you'd better remember that from here on. Clear?"

"Yes, sir."

"Good. Sorry. I know this isn't your fault. But it's such a god-awful thing. To see her like that . . ." His voice trailed away. Then he gathered himself, took a deep breath. "The wedding's off, of course, but I want the house finished anyway—"

"What do you mean, it's off?"

"We agreed it would be pointless now, to say nothing of the legal complications. Besides, marry an invalid? With my lifestyle? How long before I'd resent her? Or she'd resent me?"

"She doesn't have very long."

"Neither do I. I'm only a step or two below the top of the entertainment world, a notch away from being a household name. I can't afford to slow down now, not for anything. Not for anyone. Clare understands that."

"But she loves you."

"And I'll do what I can for her. But derailing my life, wrecking my career, won't help either of us. Or pay the bills. Including yours. You're out of line, Shea. You're my contractor, not my conscience. I didn't authorize those ramps or the elevator. They're coming out of your end. And I want them gone. They're an eyesore."

"But Clare—"

"Won't be living here. Nor will I. Don't you get it? This dream is over. Clare will need full-time care. I'll arrange for that, of course, but it can't be here. I simply can't afford a ten-million-dollar rest home. Finish the house, Shea, make it presentable. But no more changes, no more overruns. I'm putting it on the market and if it sells I can't guarantee the new owners will keep you on. If you have any questions, work them out with Leo. I'm going into town for dinner. Tell Clare I'll see her before I go. But after today, I want her off the property. Permanently. We're done. Clear?"

I was too stunned to answer. LaRosa took that as a reply and strode off. His two assistants trotted after him like lap dogs. Halfway to the limo, the girl took his arm. And it wasn't for balance. Clare was right. When it came to business, Geno was a hardnose. He was cutting his losses and moving on.

Leo noticed my stare.

"Don't worry about him, bucko, you've got grief of your own. You've violated a half-dozen clauses of your contract. I could fire you right now."

"Go ahead."

"Bringing in a new contractor is too much hassle. But you'd better get back on the winning side, and quick."

"Winning side?"

"In the end it'll come down to money. It always does. Clare and Geno have been together five years. She'll probably hire a lawyer, sue for palimony. Maybe she'll ask you to testify about what a cold-hearted bastard Geno is. Don't even think about it. We know all about you two."

"About what?"

"The quiet little dinners, the nights you spent at the Holiday Inn together. The way you dumped your responsibilities to hold her hand down in Ann Arbor. If there's a lawsuit—"

"How much do you weigh?" I interrupted.

"Weigh? What the hell does that—"

"Just wondering. I've worked construction all my life, so I do a lot of heavy lifting. You look pretty chunky to me, Leo, but I figure I can throw you all the way to that limo down there. Give or take a bounce. And if you're not gone in the next three seconds, we're gonna find out."

"Are you out of your tree? You can't threaten me—"

"One," I counted. "Two—"

He didn't wait for three. And for a fat city boy, he could move pretty fast.

Clare was exactly where I'd left her, in her wheelchair in the third-floor master bedroom, staring out over the lake.

"Is he gone?"

"They've all gone," I said. "Geno said he'd be back later. To, um . . ." I coughed. "Clare, he's coming to say good-bye."

"He wants to move me to a rest home in New York. Better medical care, not so isolated. Away from all the construction dirt and noise. Leo's already made the arrangements. Funny, making arrangements used to be my job."

"Maybe it's the right thing to do."

"No, not for me. I feel alive here. I love the chaos and the cursing and the sawdust in the air. It smells like the future. Like hope. And Geno still needs this palace, this . . . sanctuary, whether he knows it or not. I can tell he's been worrying himself sick over me. He looks peaked. Probably hasn't been eating right. Don't you think he looked thin?"

"Clare, don't ask what I think of Geno LaRosa. You don't want to know."

"Poor Danny," she said with a wan smile. "Don't worry, Geno's much too decent to throw me out of here. In the end he'll do the right thing for me and this house. He just needs a little time to think. He'll change his mind. You'll see."

"Maybe you're right. Shall I take you downstairs?"

"No, I'd rather wait for Geno here."

"It'll be dark soon, Clare. There's no electricity on this floor."

"Then leave me some candles. These days I look better by candlelight anyway. But I'd like to wait alone, if you don't mind, Danny. I've got some thinking to do."

"Whatever you say. I'll find some candles, then I'll leave you two alone to talk. I'll stop by later in case you need a ride to town."

"Thanks. Just don't come blundering into our bedroom again, okay?"

"Not a chance. I'm still blushing from the last time."

"Yeah, right. Pervert." She laughed, and so did I. Couldn't help it. Clare's laugh is as contagious as the flu. I'd almost forgotten how fine it was. Hadn't heard it lately.

I went home, fed my dogs, and sat with my dad awhile. Avoiding the palace. Partly out of jealousy. If Geno and Clare were making up or making out, I didn't want to know about it.

But it was partly out of fear as well. I really couldn't afford to lose this job. I desperately needed the work and the money. So I didn't want to see Geno LaRosa again. I might be tempted to try a little magic on him. Like rearranging his face.

Dusk was settling over the hills when I drove back to the site. It was after seven, but Geno's limo was still there. No driver in sight, he must have come alone. I could see candlelight flickering in the master bedroom. So they were still up there. Together. Damn.

I switched on my truck radio and settled in to wait. A month's worth of exhaustion rolled over me like a dark wave, carrying me down and down . . .

When I woke it was full dark. After ten. No light was showing in the house now. But Geno's limo hadn't moved.

I wasn't sure what to make of that.

The limo was long gone the next morning when the crews clocked in. At eleven, I called an early lunch-break meeting in the great room. Standing a few steps up the staircase, I explained the change in our situation to the men. Told them the house was up for sale and we could be replaced without notice.

"If anyone wants to bail out, all I ask is a couple of days to find a replacement. You can draw your wages at the end of the week, no hard feelings. Any takers?"

No one raised a hand.

"Hell," Puck said, "we've already spent more time in this place than Mr. New York Big Shot. Screw 'im if he wants to sell. I've never worked on a frickin' mansion before, probably never will again. I want to see this one finished, slicked up and shinin' in the sun."

Nods and murmurs ran through the group. They'd stick. And I had to swallow a lump in my throat. These were good men, skilled craftsmen, hard workers, every one. I'd pushed them to the max and beyond but they still wouldn't quit. They deserved better luck. "Yo, Danny," Mafe Rochon called. "This sudden change of heart Mr. LaRosa had—you don't suppose he's mad 'cause he found out you been bangin' his girlfriend, do ya?"

I turned away, shrugging off the jibe. Letting it pass. Clamping the lid on my anger. Mafe was half buzzed, as usual, just running his mouth. It didn't mean anything and I couldn't afford any trouble now.

Let it go.

Let it go, let it go. And I did! Whirling, I vaulted the railing, tackling Mafe Rochon from the stairway, hitting him chest high, pulling him down. Cursing, we wrestled around on the floor until Mafe got a boot in my chest and kicked me off halfway across the room.

Scrambling to our feet, we lit into each other. No science, no skill, hammering away like hockey players, trying to land one monster punch!

Puck tried to pull us apart, caught a wild backhand that bloodied his nose and sat him down hard, gagging. No one else stepped in. They formed a rough ring around us instead and let us go at it. This had been coming on for a while. Get the hell out of the way, boys! Let 'er rip!

I'd jumped Mafe in a red-eyed fury. It passed the first time he grazed me with a right cross. Drunk or sober, Rochon had an iron-worker's power in his fists. If I couldn't finish him fast, he'd pound me down and stomp me into dog meat.

Ducking under his guard, I drove a hard left hook into his beer belly, following with an overhand right that opened a gash under his eye. He didn't even blink. Countered with an elbow to the throat that nearly broke my jaw!

We'd both drawn blood now. And tasted our own. Panting, sparring cautiously, we circled each other, glaring like pit bulls, looking for an opening.

"All right, that's enough!" somebody yelled. "Break it up, you two."

If Mafe heard, he gave no sign. Instead he lowered his head and rushed me. Bulling into my chest, he smashed me into the wall of fight fans like a pile driver, sending a half-dozen men sprawling in a wild tangle. Bystanders scrambled to get out of the way as Mafe and I grappled again.

Somebody grabbed my arm from behind. Twisting free, I whirled, fist cocked—and found myself facing a cop. A big cop. In uniform. With his riot baton raised, ready to open my skull.

Another officer prodded Mafe back with his night stick as a half-dozen policemen surrounded the crowd. Carrying shotguns.

"Whoa up," I said, opening my hands, backing away. "I'm cool. What's all this?"

"I could ask you the same thing, sport. What the hell is this supposed to be? A fight club?"

"No. It's . . . just a little lunch-hour boxing match that got out of hand."

"Didn't look much like boxing to me."

"So maybe we're not very good." I lowered my hands. "What are you guys doing here? I know the neighbors didn't complain. We don't have any."

"I'm Sergeant Macafee, Michigan State Police. I'm looking for the owner, a Mr. Geno LaRosa. Who's in charge here?"

"That would be me. I'm the contractor, Dan Shea. Mr. LaRosa isn't here."

"I told you he'd say that," Leo Holtzer said, pushing through the crowd.

"Cool off, Mr. Holtzer," Macafee said, "I'll handle this. When did you see LaRosa last, Mr. Shea?"

"He was here last night. Had a long talk with his fiancée, Clare Landis."

"What time did he leave?"

"I . . . can't say for sure. I didn't actually see him. His car was here when I came by to give Miss Landis a ride back to town. That would have been seven, seven-thirty. I didn't want to interrupt them, so I waited. Must have nodded off. When I woke up, the limo was gone. I drove Clare into town, went home. That's all I can tell you."

"He's lying!"

"Put a cork in it, Holtzer! I won't tell you again. Can anybody vouch for your story, Mr. Shea?"

"I don't know. Clare, I guess."

"Damned right she will," Leo spat. "They're in it together!"

"In what together? What the hell's going on?"

"Mr. LaRosa is missing," Macafee said, reading my face. "He was supposed to be in Las Vegas last night. Didn't show. We found his car at the county airport. His private plane is still parked on the apron. He obviously never left, but nobody seems to know where he is."

"I don't know anything about that, but I can tell you he's not here."

"Maybe not, but we can't just take your word for it. You men! I want you all to stay right where you are, in the middle of this room. Don't talk to each other and don't move around. Anyone who does is a collar. Understood?"

"Twenty-five grand!" Leo shouted. "Twenty-five thousand dollars to any man who can help us locate Geno LaRosa! I know he's here! I know Shea did him harm. What do you say?"

"Dammit, Holtzer—" Macafee began.

"Wait a minute," Mafe Rochon said. "There's a fresh patch of cement in the basement. It wasn't there Saturday when we quit."

"What about that, Shea?" Macafee asked.

"Sure there's fresh cement down there." I shrugged. "This is a construction site, Sarge. I realigned a drain Sunday. So what?"

"So we'll search the building first," Macafee said. "Then you can show me that new drain."

A half-dozen cops and two police dogs went through the house, top to bottom. It was a thorough search but it didn't take long. With so many walls unfinished you could see through most of the building end to end. Couldn't hide a cat in it.

One dog freaked at some blood spots near the staircase but it was fresh, from Puck's broken nose. They didn't find anything else. Leaving four men to watch my crew, Macafee had Rochon lead us down to the basement. It was a shambles. We'd been storing our scrap lumber down here and the cops had ripped the stacks apart. They'd even torn open the crates containing the bathtubs and appliances, the elevator cab and its motor.

"Jeez, Macafee, you clowns have cost me a month's work down here," I griped. "Who's gonna pay for this mess?"

"That's not your problem," Leo snapped. "You're fired, Shea. And you're going to jail!"

"The new concrete's over here," Mafe said, pointing to a patch about six feet by four. Grave size.

"The drains come down the north wall and run through there," I pointed out. "They were misaligned. I straightened them up."

"Maybe." Macafee nodded. "I want to see what's under there anyway. Bust it up."

"You bust it up, pal. Fatso here just fired me."

"I'll break it up," Rochon said, grabbing a sledgehammer. "Hell, for twenty-five thou I'd bust up my daddy in the town square."

"You'd have to ask your mama first. To find out who he was."

"Damn you, Danny!" Mafe lunged at me with the hammer.

Macafee blocked his path, pointing toward the fresh cement. "Back off, Rochon. Take it out on the cement."

Mafe set to work with a will. Glowering at me between blows, he pulverized the concrete, raising a cloud of acrid dust, pelting us all with stone chips. At the bottom he found an eight-inch drainpipe. Neatly aligned. Nothing else. They even brought the dogs down for a sniff. The German shepherds wrinkled their noses at the bitter stench of quick-dry cement and turned away, tails drooping. They looked almost as disappointed as Mafe.

"If you're done screwing around down here, Sergeant, I need to get my men back to work," I said. "It's a big property, though. Twenty-five hundred acres of piney woods, swamps, and sinkholes. If you boys plan on searching it, you'd best get started. Might take awhile."

Macafee scanned my face.

"You seem awfully certain we won't find him, Mr. Shea. Why is that? Because you know where he is?"

"Nope."

"But you're not surprised he's missing?"

"The guy came to his dream house yesterday and found out his fiancée is dying. Maybe he went off by himself to think things through. Wouldn't you?"

"I might," Macafee admitted. "But I wouldn't disappear without a trace."

"That's because you're a cop. I put up buildings, you chase crooks. Geno LaRosa makes elephants and skyscrapers disappear. Making himself disappear would be kid stuff. I expect he'll turn up again when he wants to."

"You're saying this is a publicity stunt?" Macafee asked.

"I sure hope so. The man pays my wages."

"He's lying!" Leo ranted, red-faced with fury. "I want him arrested."

"For what?" Macafee asked. "He's right. We aren't certain there's actually been a crime. And it's at least possible this is some kind of stunt."

"A stunt? In this two-bit backwater? Are you out of your mind? I want this property searched! Every inch of it!"

"That's not possible," Macafee said. "Not today, anyway. It'd take an army to search two thousand acres. I don't have the authority to order it just because your boss missed a nightclub date. We're done here. For now."

"Then I order you to escort Shea and his men off this property! They're fired! All of them."

"You can't fire us, Leo. My contract is with Geno LaRosa, not you. He told me to finish this house by Christmas and you've already cost us half a day. If I were you, I'd leave with these officers. Construction sites are dangerous places. Especially for civilians."

Leo glanced around at the hard-eyed crew surrounding him and swallowed. "All right. I'll go. But you won't get away with this, Shea. Geno's not just a performer, he's an industry, a multinational corporation. Television, DVDs, computer games. I'll have the studio put up a million-dollar reward. Geno's fans will rip this dump apart looking for him. I'll have studio attorneys bury you in lawsuits. You'll never finish this job or any other. Before I'm through, you'll be building outhouses in prison. You're finished!" He turned and stalked out. Macafee and his men went with him.

"Another satisfied customer," Puck said. "Now what?"

"Back to work, that's why we're here. We've got a contract, remember?"

"What about Holtzer? If he was serious about that reward, he could cause real problems. We can't work and guard this place at the same time."

"I know. The plans called for a security fence after the house is finished. We'll just have to build it now, that's all. Just in case."

"Okay." Puck nodded. "I'll see to it."

"What about me?" Mafe Rochon asked sourly. "Have I got a job or not?"

"That depends. I don't have time to fight you, Mafe. Besides, you hit too damn hard. You gonna give me any more problems?"

"Nah." He grinned, massaging the mouse under his eye. "I figure with the cops and that Holtzer fella you got trouble enough, Danny. I'd kinda like to stick around. See how it all turns out."

"All right, then. We're burnin' daylight, guys. Let's roll."

Puck's fence wasn't pretty. Chain-link, ten feet high, topped with razor wire. The original plans called for fieldstone pillars and wrought-iron spikes. We could install them after we finished the main house. Assuming we got the chance.

Reporters and curiosity seekers started coming by in a steady stream, blowing their horns outside the gate, gawking, taking pictures.

The fence kept them at bay, but it wouldn't for long. The tabloids were already printing rumors—SUPERSTAR MAGICIAN MURDERED?; MAGIC MAN GENO'S MYSTERIOUS DISAPPEARANCE!—and I knew that five minutes after Leo posted his big-buck reward, the stampede would be on. Fence or no fence, they would bury us.

But I couldn't let myself worry about it. No time. I added a third shift, working around the clock now, twenty-four/seven. I was on the job for almost every minute of it, storming around like a demon, catching catnaps when I could. But in my heart I knew I was only killing time. Trying not to think. Waiting for the ax to fall.

A few days later, it finally came down. Clare called me at the site. We hadn't talked since the Sunday Geno vanished. She'd been ill, holed up in the Holiday Inn, avoiding reporters. She said Leo Holtzer and the studio lawyers were flying in that night for a meeting. I had to be there or they could fire me without a hearing.

Hell, who were we kidding? They were going to fire me anyway. Holtzer would see to that. I thought about ducking it, just to spite him. This would be his big moment. Payback time. Nothing I could say would change anything.

I went anyway. No choice. I couldn't leave Clare to face the wolves alone.

But as I drove out of the gate that night, I stopped a moment for one final look.

Even unfinished, with half the windows installed, the mansion was magnificent. My palace in the pines. We were so close. Two more months and . . . But I wasn't going to get those months. Geno was right. This dream was over.

Two security goons posted at the Holiday Inn conference-room door frisked me and checked my identification before letting me pass.

Inside, Leo was sitting at the conference table flanked by a half-dozen guys in suits. I scarcely noticed them. All I could see was Clare.

She was in her wheelchair, alone, near the head of the table. She looked terrible. Gaunt, hopeless. She didn't even look up when I walked in.

"Mr. Shea?" The suit beside Leo rose. "I'm Abel Reisch, senior corporate counsel for OmniTel Studios. Take a seat, please." He didn't offer to shake hands. Neither did I. Reisch was tall, hawkfaced, graying at the temples. He introduced the other guys at the table, all corporate officers with OmniTel. I didn't catch their names. Leo was gloating like a schoolyard bully. I let it pass. Mafe Rochon was right. I had troubles enough.

"This isn't a formal hearing, Mr. Shea," Reisch said. "It's strictly a private, corporate inquiry. But it will be recorded, and considering the gravity of the situation, perhaps you'd prefer to have an attorney present?"

"No."

"As you wish." One of the suits placed a laptop on the table and set it to Record. Reisch stated his name, the date, identified the rest of us, and noted that I'd declined a lawyer.

"The tabloids are full of innuendos that imply you were involved in the death or disappearance of Geno LaRosa, Mr. Shea. Leo here believes it, too. For the record, Mr. Shea, did you kill Geno LaRosa?"

I blinked. "Wow, you don't kid around, do you? No, I didn't kill Geno and I have no idea where he is."

"What did you expect him to say?" Leo snapped.

"You told the police his disappearance might be deliberate?" Reisch continued, ignoring the interruption.

"I only said it was possible. He got some very bad news that day about Miss Landis. Maybe he wanted to drop out, think things over."

"And how do you think he might have accomplished this?"

"No idea. I'm a contractor. Turning lumber into houses is as magical as I get. You people know more about this sort of thing than I do."

"Unfortunately, we don't. Which is the purpose of this meeting. When did you see Mr. LaRosa last?"

"That Sunday. The day he disappeared."

"And did he give you any indication of his intentions?"

"We only talked about the house. He said he wanted it finished. Asked me to speed things up, in fact."

"Because he intended to sell it and fire you!" Leo spat.

"Is that true?" Reisch asked.

"Mr. LaRosa didn't say anything like that to me. Leo brought it up after the police tore the place apart looking for Geno."

"The state police have assured me it was a thorough search. Would you agree?"

"They had search dogs and went through the house top to bottom. Even smashed up some of the concrete in the basement. Looked pretty darn thorough to me."

"But they didn't search the entire property, did they?" Reisch pressed. "Twenty-five hundred acres of wilderness. Do you think the police should search the property, Mr. Shea?"

"Where they search is their business."

"So you'd have no objection?" His eyes were locked on mine, probing my thoughts like radar.

"No, why should I?"

"Miss Landis? Would you have any objections to the police searching the grounds?"

"No." Clare's voice was barely a whisper.

"Very well, we're agreed. I'll ask the state police to do a complete search of the grounds, the airfield, and anywhere else they think appropriate. OmniTel will cover any and all expenses. Personally, I doubt that they'll find anything. Geno was far too good an illusionist to leave any traces."

"What?" Leo asked, dumbfounded. "What are you saying?"

"That OmniTel's public position will essentially be a question mark. We don't know where Geno LaRosa is, or what happened to him. But privately, off the record, we'll admit that after a thorough investigation, we tend to agree with Mr. Shea. That Geno vanished deliberately, as the ultimate expression of his art. And that in time he will return. When he chooses to."

"Have you lost your mind, Abel?" Leo blurted. "You can't be serious!"

"Leo, I've tolerated your outbursts to this point because of your long association with Geno. But it's time for a reality check. Mr. LaRosa has been a valued employee of OmniTel for years—"

"You're damned right! He earned millions for you!"

"And he will continue to do so," Reisch went on. "We're getting offers for movies about his life, the networks want to rerun his cable TV specials. With DVDs, action toys, video games, advertising tie-ins, the profit potential is enormous."

"And you're willing to let Shea get away with murder? Just to make a few bucks?"

"Turn that off!" Reisch snapped at the exec with the laptop. "You don't get it, Leo. Dead, Geno is just another victim. A few minutes of airtime on the six o'clock news, then oblivion. But missing? Vanished? Geno becomes immortal, a legend greater than Houdini. Or Jimmy Hoffa."

"But he's dead! They killed him, I'm sure of it!"

"I'd be careful about making unfounded allegations, Leo. Clare is in delicate health and the corporation will react aggressively to any threats. Especially since you have no legal standing in the matter."

"No standing? I'm Geno's agent, for God's sake!"

"If he's dead, you no longer have a client, Leo. And if you go to the press, we'll sue you for defamation and cut off your royalties. Be reasonable. As long as Geno remains . . . missing, you'll continue to receive your full percentage of his earnings. But you really can't afford a war with OmniTel. Take a walk, cool off. I'll meet you in the bar later. We'll work something out."

Holtzer glanced down the table looking for allies. Found only cold stares. He started to argue, then shook his head. And stalked out.

One of the execs glanced a question at Reisch.

"Don't worry, Leo's a bright fella," Reisch said. "He'll come around. And you, Mr. Shea? Do you have any . . . questions?"

"Mr. Reisch, all I want is to finish Mr. LaRosa's house as planned. Will I be able to do that?"

"Of course. We can make it a centerpiece. The magician's mysterious mansion, brooding by the lakeshore, waiting for his return. I do have a small favor to ask, though."

"What favor?"

"As she's in failing health, Clare would like to move into the house as soon as possible. A room or two will suffice. Can you arrange that, Mr. Shea?"

"Of course. No problem."

"Good." Reisch smiled. "I like your attitude, Mr. Shea. We're going to get along famously. From now on, you just concentrate on your work. If anyone bothers you—police, reporters, anyone at all—just refer them to me. And I'll make them . . . disappear."

"Like magic?" I asked.

"Exactly."

And that was it. Almost.

As the meeting broke up, Reisch took me aside, away from the others. "One other small matter, Mr. Shea. If by chance you happen to . . . stumble across any remains? Bury them. Deep. You wouldn't want to ruin Geno's chance for immortality. Would you?"

And he smiled. And shook my hand.

Mr. Reisch proved as good as his word. Reporters had been stopping by my house, bugging my father. I called Abel Reisch's office. End of story. They never came back.

We finished the main house ahead of schedule in early December. And earned a whopping bonus from OmniTel. A very merry Christmas present for the crews. And for me.

Clare lives there now, in the third-story bedroom. But it's not the dream home she envisioned. It's a prison. From her window she can see the fence, and the barbed wire. And even armed guards.

They're necessary. Ever since Geno vanished, wackos from all over the planet have been finding their way to the mansion.

They linger outside the gates like zombies. Some burn candles. Some sing. Some just stare.

Waiting.

As Clare does. She's wheelchair-bound now. Speaks with difficulty. Needs help to eat. When death finally comes, it will be a blessing for her. A release.

There are worse things than death.

Watching the woman I love dying by inches every day. Knowing she loved another man so much she'd rather see him dead than let him go.

I found Geno at the bottom of the elevator shaft that night. I don't know how she did it. Perhaps she pushed him. Or just led him to the elevator door, and in the candlelight, he assumed . . .

I don't want to know. I don't care.

I only knew that I couldn't let her die in a hospital. Or in a cell. But even on two thousand acres, you can't hide a body anymore. With all the high-tech gear police have nowadays, I knew they'd find it.

If there was a body to find.

I have a burn scar on my arm. From a torch. And I was lucky. Because at three thousand degrees, flesh doesn't burn. It vaporizes.

But not right away. Even with Rochon's torch set at the maximum, it took hours. Hours. And the sizzling and the ghastly stench . . .

In the end, only a fine gray ash remained. Like cement dust.

The police actually found Geno when they broke up that floor. They just didn't recognize him.

But I didn't get away with anything. Not really. The horror of that night haunts me. It stains my soul. I can't sleep. Can't eat.

I think Clare knows. When they searched the basement and found nothing, she must have guessed. We've never spoken of it.

But in a way, I suppose we each got what we wanted. Or a part of it.

I'm financially set, and the publicity about the palace has attracted more clients than I can handle.

Clare won't die in a hospital. She'll live out her days in that house. With the man she loved. And as her days grow short, she spends them in the past. Dreaming of happier times. With him. But in the end, only Geno got it all. He wanted fame and he's a legend now. Immortal. Greater than Houdini.

And his magnificent house turned out exactly as he planned. A massive log castle that truly belongs where it is.

Built of native trees and stones from the fields around it, the mansion looks as if it's been there for centuries and will stand a thousand years after we're gone.

I built it. But it was Geno's dream. His palace in the pines.

He'll always be a part of it now.

And so will Clare.

And so will I.

Mat Coward

OFFENDERS

■ ■ ■

Mat Coward is a British writer in many genres. His short stories have been nominated for the Edgar and the Dagger, broadcast on BBC Radio, and published in numerous anthologies, magazines, and e-zines in the U.K., U.S., Japan, and Europe. His first collection, Do the World a Favour and Other Stories, *was published by Five Star in 2003. His most recent novel is* Over and Under, *published by Five Star, the third in his mystery series featuring Detective Inspector Don Packham and Detective Constable Frank Mitchell. Among his recent books in the U.K. is a short history of British radio comedy, in the "Pocket Essentials" series. The story picked for this collection is a rare foray into science fiction, as he tackles the all-too-precarious right to free speech in a future locked-down England in "Offenders."*

At the Joke Squad, we'd never been busier. It was midwinter, and in my experience the cold weather makes people say things out loud that they'd normally keep to themselves.

DS Geraint Brook didn't seem the kind who bothered much about censoring his speech, though that was probably nothing to do with the weather. He'd been posted to us temporarily, from his usual perch at Robbery/Organized Crime, and he wasn't happy about it.

"No offense, Barney," he said as we wandered around the New Scotland Yard parking lot, trying to find the car we'd been assigned, "but the stuff the Joke Squad deals with is trivial crap. I spend my days bagging proper villains, and that's where I should be now."

"First of all, we don't call it the Joke Squad," I lied, slinging my overnight bag into the trunk. "It's the Offense-Related Offenses Section."

"Even the name's stupid."

"We police inappropriateness-related offenses. We do not arrest people for telling jokes." That's not strictly true. We do arrest people for telling jokes—but because they contravene the law, not because they're jokes. "Under human rights legislation, people have the right not to be offended."

Geraint got into the passenger seat, and I started the engine. "Human rights is just a beard," he said. "The world's falling apart, so the powers clamp down on dissent. It's their automatic instinct."

"You're not in favor of religious tolerance, for instance?"

"Oh, bollocks! Listen, you can't give a right to one man, without taking it away from another. Freedom is like matter—it can be neither created nor destroyed. Yeah? You give a guy the basic human right of freedom of speech, you're denying his neighbor the basic human right not to be insulted. Or vice versa."

I concentrated on my driving for a while.

Geraint looked out of his window at the London traffic. At the fourth set of lights, he said, "Sorry, mate, I don't mean to have a go at you. Truth is, we've got a big one on at Robbery—a gene piracy job—which I've spent almost a *year* working on. And I'm going to miss the denouement so we can go and pick up some daft Yank student for . . . whatever it was you said we were picking her up for."

"Possession and Dissemination of Material Contrary to the Unity of the Homeland."

"Which means what, exactly?"

"She's been reported for having a poster on her bedroom wall ridiculing the U.S. president."

"A poster!" Geraint grunted. "Not an offense under British or European law, is it?"

I was trying to be patient. I'd met Geraint before, at Met sports-and-socials, and I liked him. But he was being deliberately thick this morning. "No, it's not, but it is an offense under U.S. law."

"And the U.S.A. does not recognize any boundaries to its writ. So this poor tart gets fast-track extradited." He shook his head, either in disgust or for show. "Why should we collect their garbage? What are they going to do, bomb us?"

I pulled over. Geraint looked surprised and a little worried. Which was what I wanted. I switched off the engine, and turned to face him. "Listen, mate, there's something you should know about me, just in case it's a bit of gossip you've missed. It's a private matter and I only mention it now to avoid future embarrassment. OK?"

"Barney, I'm sorry if I've—"

"Don't worry, it's only this: my father was collateralized during the bombing of Edinburgh." Dad worked in a factory ten miles from the Scottish Parliament—the presumed target, after it had repeatedly refused to privatize its social services to an American multinational. Technically, of course, the U.S.A. didn't do the bombing; the multinational did, and five years later was fined almost a million dollars for doing so.

"Oh, shit. Mate, I'm really—"

"So, if you have any opinions about Britain's diplomatic relations with America . . ."

He held out his hands in front of him, either side of his face. "I'll keep them to myself. Apologies."

"Good man."

We drove on quietly. Geraint fidgeted. Eventually, he said what I'd known he'd have to say. Everyone always does. "Barney, I've got to ask. Tell me to sod off, but don't you hate them? The Yanks?"

"I don't hate Americans. They're just people same as us."

"Oh, yeah, sure. But—"

"Look, Geraint, one thing my father's death taught me—be realistic. Either we cooperate with the Americans in arresting their citizens over here, or they'll do it themselves without us. You want the policing of this country handed over to the Americans direct?"

"Hell, no! Hasn't worked very well in Spain, has it?"

"And it is sort of reciprocal, to be fair. I've just finished the paperwork on an Irish guy they nicked for us at an airport in Connecticut."

"Nicked for what?"

"Telling Irish jokes." I let him start to splutter, then I said, "No, he made a joke to a friend about hijacking, at Heathrow. It was caught on tape." I didn't add that the man wasn't arrested at the time of the offense because, until the tape had been enhanced by Customs officers investigating an entirely separate case, the joke was inaudible at a distance of more than thirty centimeters.

As we pulled into the U.S. embassy's parking lot, Geraint said, "We've actually got to have one of the bastards in the car with us, have we?"

"Don't worry. In my squad we know how to deal with Feds. They're just a bunch of square-headed, slow-witted, single-brain-cell organisms in ill-fitting suits."

The Fed assigned to us knocked on the window. She was tall, slim, and rather lovely.

"Blimey!" said Geraint.

She shook hands. "Agent Hilda Westlake, Office for the Defense of the Homeland. Hi."

"You're black," I said. I hadn't intended to say it aloud.

"Yep," she said. "It's not against the law, not yet."

I couldn't get over that. As I pulled into the traffic, I just couldn't stop thinking about it. It was incredible. I'd never encountered anything like this before. A Yank official had made a *joke.*

Two hours later we arrived at the West University campus, and fifteen minutes after that we were knocking on the door of Elaine Cassidy's room. Geraint had been silent for most of the journey. I could see his point, though I didn't say as much: our job was to collect Cassidy, and drive her to Heathrow. It wasn't exactly brain work.

"No reply," I said, and knocked again.

Hilda Westlake moved me gently to one side. And turned the door handle.

There was a fair amount of blood, all of it dry. A young woman—Elaine Cassidy, presumably—lay on the floor, her nose smashed beyond recognition. Next to her was a very large book.

"Oh, shit," said Hilda.

"We can still take her to the airport," said Geraint. "With any luck the plane will crash and no one will ever be the wiser."

"We'd better call the local cops," said Hilda. "We don't do murders."

A look passed between me and Geraint. I suppose I felt sorry for him, missing his big case and all. "Don't worry," I said. "My pal Geraint here, he's done more murders than you've had commendations."

"Won't they make trouble if we steal their case?"

Geraint laughed. "They're privatized down here, they don't want murders. Murder eats up resources, and all you get at the end—if you're lucky—is one conviction."

"And no revenue," I added.

"I don't know . . ."

"Listen, Agent Westlake," said Geraint. "In the privatized areas, if you want a cop in a hurry you call in a burglary in progress, say you've got the robbers locked in your vault with your jewel collection. You call in a murder, they'll tell you to phone back during office hours."

"Well, I don't know . . ."

"We'll have to liaise eventually, yeah, but believe me the locals aren't going to fight us for possession of a manpower-gobbling case involving the daughter of rich foreigners."

She looked at me. "How do you know she's rich?"

I shrugged. "Who else goes to university?" I thought it would be easier for Hilda to agree if she didn't actually have to say it, so I changed the subject. "What was she studying?"

"Law. What else does anyone study these days?"

Geraint joined in. "And what was the nature of the complaint against her— a poster, was it?"

Hilda checked her notes. "A poster of the president as a pig."

"Right," I said. "Subversive *and* subtle. So, where is the poster? Shouldn't it be on the wall somewhere?"

It was a three-meter-square room. Bed, books, stereo, lots of shoes. Small statuette of Jesus. Small bathroom, en suite. No posters on the walls at all.

"Maybe she got to hear about the complaint, destroyed the evidence."

"Or maybe," said Geraint, "there never was a poster—malicious complaint?"

Hilda screwed up her face. It was a surprisingly attractive gesture. "We get very few maliciouses. The penalties are . . . significant."

"You must get malicious *anonymous* complaints."

She looked uncomfortable. "Anonymous is kind of a gray area."

"You know who made the complaint in this instance?"

She checked her notes again. "Another law student. Name of Kelly Norton." She frowned. "Actually, that's unusual—the complainant isn't American. She's native. I mean, British."

"*Native?*" Even the good-looking ones have all the social graces of a thunderstorm. "Well, let's see if she's in her mud hut, shall we?"

She wasn't in her mud hut. She was in the student bar, drinking white wine and lemonade with six or seven tall, handsome friends. We detached her from them by means of our charming manner and our ID cards, and she led us to a quiet seating area overlooking lawns, an ornamental fountain, a razor-wire fence, and one of the biggest slum towns in Western Europe. It was a kilometer away, in a shallow valley, but on a bright day you could hear it as clearly as you could see it.

"Kelly, my name is Detective Sergeant Barney Garner, and this is Agent Hilda Westlake." We'd left Geraint at the crime scene to do some preliminaries, him having the relevant know-how.

Kelly Norton chewed her lip and nodded. "You're here about Elaine?"

"Tell us why you complained about her to the embassy," said Hilda.

"Well, she had this poster on her wall—it was, like, really rude. It was a photo of your president, but they'd jiggered it so he looked like a pig."

"Right. And you took offense at this?"

"Wouldn't you? It was disgusting."

I thought her expression of moral outrage a little overdone. But then, as Hilda had said, a complaint from a "native" was unusual. So presumably she was an unusual native.

"So you rang the embassy hotline?"

"Sure. Will she be deported?"

Hilda wrote on her pad, and didn't reply. "Now, when did you see this poster?"

"The evening before last. I rang straightaway."

"Was that the only time you saw it?"

The complainant swallowed heavily, "Um . . . I don't remember." For the first time, she switched her attention from Agent Westlake to me. She gave me a half smile, and twisted a length of her brown hair around her fingers.

"Where did you see it?" I asked.

"In her room—I said. It was on her wall."

"And what were you doing in her room?"

Kelly switched back to Hilda. She seemed to have regained her confidence. "Oh, right. I went there to borrow her hair dryer. Mine had blown."

"So Elaine's a friend, then?"

"Not really. I hardly know her at all. We're in a few of the same classes, we live on the same corridor, but we don't mix in the same crowds. You know, the Americans pretty much keep to themselves . . ." She trailed off. "Um—no offense."

Hilda nodded. "So why go to her for a hair dryer?"

"I did knock on a few doors along the corridor before I got to hers. A lot of people had already gone out for the night. She was the first one who answered."

"Whereabouts was the poster?" I asked. "Where on the wall?"

"Well . . . like, just above her desk."

Hilda said, "Did you get the hair dryer?"

"Ah, no, She, like, didn't have one." She gave the sentence a questioning inflection. I took that to mean that this bit, at least, was the truth.

"A fight over a boy?" We were walking back to the dead girl's room, trying to figure out a believable reason for Kelly to have informed on Elaine. And while we were at it, a motive for murder by persons unknown.

"Boyfriend trouble doesn't usually end in murder."

"These days?" she said. "Everything ends in murder. These *varsity* types, they're desperate to get married as young as possible—means they don't have to endure too much sex."

I smiled, and looked at her sideways. "You're an unusual American, you know. It's hard to tell when you're being serious."

"Always," said Hilda. "I work for the federal government, Sergeant. I never joke."

"Right. More than your job's worth."

"More than my life's worth."

Geraint looked a lot happier now that he was doing some proper, morbid work. "No prints on the big law book. Blood, but no prints. As for Elaine, she's been dead since last night. No sign of recent sexual activity, forced or unforced. She *has* been in a fight, though."

I looked around the room. A place for everything, and everything in its place. "Doesn't look like robbery."

"Only thing obviously missing," he agreed, "is the Material Contrary to the Unity of the Homeland."

"The poster," said Hilda. "Right. Well, I guess things are pretty grim outside the campus walls, but I can't think an anti-American poster is worth much."

"It's not anti-American," I said. "Anti-president, not the same thing."

They both ignored me. "Her virtue's intact," said Geraint, "and so is her sound system. Seems reasonable to guess that the killer had a personal motive."

"This poster," I asked. "Is it one you've seen before?"

Hilda shrugged. "Not offhand. But she could have made it herself. There must be a hundred new posters every day."

"Your department isn't having much effect then, is it?" said Geraint.

"Sergeant, we're not the gestapo, whatever you may have heard."

"What I'd heard," he replied, "was that you *are* the gestapo."

She snorted. "Yeah? Well, what does that make you guys? Vichy enforcers?"

I interrupted. She was pretty when she was angry, but he wasn't. "I notice there's no CCTV in the corridor here."

"You're kidding!" Hilda slapped her head, probably in despair at the backwardness of the natives. "A building full of rich people's kids and there's no cameras?"

"Privacy," said Geraint. "The rich are very big on that—especially the rich young. They're in and out of each other's rooms, smoking, drinking, flirting, doing drugs . . . they think they're too rich to die."

"This one wasn't," I said, taking out my phone. "I suppose we'd better get her moved."

A search of the residence block's rubbish area failed to produce the President Pig poster.

"I don't believe there ever was a poster," said Geraint. "You don't have any record of this girl? I mean, as far as you know, she stands up for the national anthem, follows American football, always votes for the government?"

"She's too young to vote."

"Whatever. She's not known to your lot—or her family, or her associates?"

"No, but when someone's away from home for the first time, mixing with—well, mixing with . . ."

"Natives," I said. "Sure. Untrustworthy lot, the hairy natives."

"My point being, Sergeant, people change."

"If Elaine Cassidy changed," said Geraint, "the campus security office is going to know."

"If you can trust native security," I added.

The head of campus security was a large woman in a small office. Her badge read "Bone." I assumed it was her name. She claimed to have no special knowledge of Elaine Cassidy.

"Obviously, we keep a special eye on our American students."

"Why?" Geraint asked. "Are they the most troublesome?"

She didn't answer that. She didn't need to. She kept a special eye on the Americans because balkanized Britain is balkanized not so much regionally, as along responsibility lines. Bonn rules the economy—but anything to do with security, you jump when D.C. says jump.

"And you kept a special eye on Elaine?"

"Of course. But as I said, there was never any hint of anything worrying."

Hilda said, "Did you know a complaint had been made about her to my office?"

Bone bristled. "In *theory*, campus security is given a courtesy call before you lot turn up. Evidently, your phones weren't working today."

"We don't really bother with theory, ma'am," said Geraint. "We're public servants."

Not private crap like you, he meant—and Bone knew it. "No doubt you'll keep me informed of your progress," she said, by way of dismissal.

"Looks like you've had a wasted journey, Agent Westlake," I said as we watched Elaine Cassidy's body being removed, packed in what appeared to be a giant speaker for a rock gig. That's the nice thing about the private sector: discretion guaranteed.

"You might be right, but the death of a U.S. citizen is still an embassy matter. I'm on the spot, I might as well hang around."

"Overseeing the natives."

She put a hand on my arm until I met her eyes. "You know something, Barney, you're not a bad-looking guy. You're good at your job. You have your own hair. So tell me—why does this *native* shit upset you so much? You suffering from empire envy, like every other little Englishman I've met since I came here?"

"All right," I said. "Since you ask. What bothers me is the way America still gives itself imperial airs, when the truth is your empire's as dead as ours is. Your country's in as big a mess as we are—worse in some ways. For instance, how many universities have you got in the U.S.?"

She looked genuinely amused. "This isn't a *university*. Come on! This is a finishing school for rich kids! Most of them foreign."

"If you girls have finished," said Geraint, "I suggest we go and get a drink."

"How about lunch?" said Hilda.

He grinned. "That's what I said."

Geraint drove. As we left the campus, Hilda said, "We're not going to the student bar? We could talk to a few of Elaine's pals."

"That wouldn't be a drink. That'd be work."

It took a few minutes for me and Hilda to realize where he was taking us. She wasn't thrilled. "Jesus, you have to be joking!"

I was pretty shocked myself, but I wasn't going to show it. "This'll be a new experience for you, Agent Westlake. Back home, you wouldn't go onto an estate like this except in a convoy of tanks, am I right?"

She wobbled her head at me. It's something only American women can do, and only black American women can do convincingly. "Sure. Except maybe to visit with my folks."

From a distance it looked like something a nuke had left behind. From close up, it wasn't so bad—from close up it looked like something that had been rebuilt from salvage, ten years *after* a nuke. There were shops, houses, pubs. Human beings. Parked cars and burger bars. The poverty was obvious, but it wasn't what I'd imagined; it looked like somewhere people lived.

At first I thought all the shops were closed. Then, as we drove slowly on, I saw people coming and going from them and realized that they were kept boarded up all the time, except for a small space for the door. Extreme fear of crime—presumably based, unlike in the nicer areas, on actual experience—is a classic sign of chronic poverty. On the other hand, it must also be a sign that you've still got something worth stealing. Steel shutters as a sign of hope? Well, there weren't many other candidates for the job.

"What are we looking for, Geraint?"

"A student bar."

Hilda gave him the look she'd have given a penniless drunk who asked her for a kiss. She must have done a course in incredulity. "What—*here*?"

"It'll be on the outskirts, but far enough in to make it count."

"You seriously think kids from that college come slumming it down here?"

He shook his head. "*Slumming it* is an overly pejorative term. They're young and alive, Hilda. The day they leave college they become middle-aged. Their lives are over, and their careers begin. Some of them—not a majority, maybe not very many, but some—will want to breathe some unfiltered air once or twice. They know it's the only chance they'll ever get."

"Unless they're very unlucky," I said.

"There's a student bar in every major slum city. In Robbery we find them . . . you know. Useful."

It was Hilda, in fact, who spotted the student bar, on our second drive-round. She saw a group of students—they couldn't have been anything else, their clothes so well made and ill-treated—emerging from a dark doorway onto a bright pavement. A bit drunk, but mostly stoned on their own daring and independence.

We curbed up next to them, and I got out. "Ladies, gentlemen. Would you like a lift back to college?"

A tall boy with floppy blond hair and big shoulders looked me up and down. Mostly down. "There's seven of us. What are we going to do—sit on your laps?" Their laughter was slightly nervous, which I took to mean that they knew who we were.

"OK," said Geraint, from his side of the hood. "We'll just have a quick chat. Are any of you lot American?"

This round of laughter was scornful. "Hardly," said the blond boy. "The Yanks don't come down here."

"Why not?"

"They stick to their own." He watched Hilda stretch herself out of the backseat, legs first. "Can't say I blame them."

She gave him a smile. Lent it to him, anyway. "You ever ask them to come with you?"

"Ah . . . nope."

"They wouldn't be welcome?"

"No offense, love, but—we don't want anything to do with them, they don't want anything to do with us."

"What about a girl called Elaine Cassidy," I said. "Any of you know her?"

"*Knew* her, you mean. I heard she was dead."

"Where did you hear that?"

"Everyone's talking about it."

"So," said Geraint. "You've been raising a few glasses to her memory, right?"

The blond boy just shut his eyes, very slowly, then turned his back on us and led his posse homeward. I suppose he opened his eyes before he got there.

Back at the college parking lot, I said, "We never did get that drink."

"Nah," said Geraint. "Students can drink in those places. Cops can't. Students have got money."

"If the Yanks don't mix with the natives, it's hard to see how Elaine could've got into a situation with one that would've got her killed." Geraint finished his beer and his sandwich with a single swallow. "Horrible stuff they serve in these college bars. It is cheap, mind."

"So you're saying it must've been an American who killed her?"

"Only," said Hilda, "if what we've been told is true, and the two tribes don't mix at all. I'd like to hear that from an American student."

Taking her at her word, Geraint went and fetched her one. A thin boy, already balding, who'd been sitting at a corner table, on his own, staring miserably at a cup of coffee. From the body language, I gathered he came reluctantly.

"From the look on your face," I said, "I gather you've heard about Elaine Cassidy."

"What do *you* care? Native cops aren't going to bother about a dead Yank."

It must have been the mood I was in, or perhaps the horrible beer, but his comment made me both sad and angry. More angry than sad, I decided after a moment's contemplation. "That's crap, you silly little boy. How can you think that? A young girl's killed and you think we're—"

"Barney," said Hilda, leaning across my space. "The guy's just repeating what he's heard. Isn't that right, young man?"

He'd barely glanced at her until then. I'd noticed that with a lot of well-off Americans; black people were invisible to them. "You're a Yank?"

She widened her eyes and crossed her hands over her breasts. "With an accent like mine? How dare you!"

He smiled. "Sorry—I meant, you're an American."

"North Carolina. Say, did you know Elaine well?"

"I don't know. All the American students know each other. We've got no choice."

"What can you tell us about her?"

"You mean why was she killed? No idea. I don't think she had any enemies. She was a quiet girl, just worked at her studies."

"Not a party girl?"

"*Hardly.*"

"Not much of a mixer? She didn't have a boyfriend?"

"Look, she used to eat with the rest of us. Came to the Thanksgiving Ball. But mostly, she was kind of . . ."

Hilda spoke quietly, as if it were just the two of them there. The young master and his favorite maid. "Kind of standoffish?"

"I wouldn't want to say that. That sounds like a criticism. But, you know, she came from a very important family."

"Old money?"

"Old money, old power. Sure. It's sort of like, if we hadn't been a minority here—well, you know, back home she wouldn't have had much to do with us."

After lunch, Geraint and I had another look around Elaine's room. We still couldn't see anything there that suggested much of a life beyond her law studies. Even her CD collection was clean. Mostly Christian rock, and Britney retrospectives; nothing that was on the U.S. Surgeon General's Index.

"She didn't have any friends," said Geraint. "I'd bet on it."

"And therefore no enemies?"

"Ah, now. I wouldn't bet on that." He was examining the walls with an illuminated glass.

Agent Westlake finished her phone call, and joined us. "Well, our local office knows nothing about the poster. It's not one that's doing the rounds, anyway. Which doesn't mean it doesn't exist."

"But it is suggestive," said Geraint.

"Well, yes."

"Tell you something else—there's been no poster on any of the walls of this room since it was last painted. You get a forensic team in here, they'll tell you the same."

"So," I said, "if Kelly Norton *didn't* see a subversive poster, why did she say she did?"

"We could ask her," Hilda suggested.

"No." Geraint was tapping a pen against his teeth. "First, let's talk to the security hag."

"We already did."

"Yeah, but last time we were polite."

Ms. Bone started off on the attack. "You didn't tell me I had a dead student in the place! Thanks very much, that came as a nice surprise."

"Oh," said Geraint, "so that was one aspect of the business you didn't already know about?"

"So much for interagency cooperation!" She stopped seething at Hilda, and looked at Geraint. "What do you mean?"

"I mean, when did you first know about the complaint against Elaine Cassidy?"

She looked at each of us in turn, then at nothing.

"At the moment," Geraint went on, "this is a fairly small matter concerning the withholding of evidence pertaining to a criminal investigation, but—"

"Actually, Geraint," I interrupted, "that *isn't* a small matter."

He cupped his chin in his hand. "Oh, yeah—you're right, Barney. It isn't, is it?"

Bone wasn't as rattled by this superb performance as I'd hoped she might be. "Believe me, gentlemen, I know the law. I've been in private security all my life. I have a primary duty of care to my employers—you don't believe me, check the case law."

A lot of lawyers earn a lot of money arguing over that very point—which has precedence, contract or law? So far the consensus seems to be that if you break the law you're in big trouble . . . whereas if you break your contract you're in big trouble. It's an answer the lawyers are happy with.

"Listen," said Hilda, "I understand. But your duty here is surely clear: to minimize—since you're too late to prevent—damage to this institution's reputation. Now if you fail to do that, and the university loses money as a result, I guess they could sue you. Is that right? That's how it works back home, anyhow."

The security woman wedged her buttocks into a swivel chair and gave Hilda a look as if it was all her fault. The murder, and her buttocks. "Elaine Cassidy came to me yesterday morning, to say that a malicious complaint had been made against her. She berated me for allowing such a thing to happen. I don't know how she thought I was supposed to stop it, but there you are."

"How did she know?"

With evident pleasure, Bone directed her reply at Hilda. "One of her daddy's pals works at the embassy."

I asked, "Did she know who'd made the complaint?"

"Oh, yes," said Bone. "Daddy's mole was fully informative."

"That might sound a bit weird, Kelly, but believe me that's how it works—and if you see a lawyer, he'll tell you the same thing."

A frightened girl, being questioned in a car. Me in the driving seat, Geraint Brook next to Kelly Norton on the backseat, Agent Westlake outside, leaning against the car talking on her phone. Geraint's last remark was intended to pass as an offer of legal representation, should anyone ever ask.

"We have proof that you made a malicious complaint to the U.S. embassy against Elaine." That wasn't quite a lie; we had a reasonably strong case, at any rate. Certainly more than enough to get a magistrate to sign an indefinite detention order. "Now obviously that's a lesser crime than murder—"

She started crying.

"—but like I say, my advice to you is to tell us about the murder, straight out. You understand all that?"

Kelly nodded. We waited. We weren't waiting for her to decide, just to stop crying. She'd already decided.

"Start with why you made the complaint, Kelly."

"Just to teach the Yanks a lesson. I hate them. We all do."

"Elaine especially?"

"I don't know. She was so stuck-up."

"So there never was a poster of the president as a pig?"

She shook her head, and tear debris spattered the upholstery. "No. When the investigators got here I was just going to say, *Oh, she must've got rid of it, it was there yesterday.*"

"What did you think would happen to her?"

"I don't know. When they couldn't find the poster I suppose I just thought it would fizzle out." She looked up at Geraint, as if expecting to find an ally. "But it'd leave a nice big stain on her precious family name, wouldn't it?"

"Things didn't work out that way."

"Elaine found out what I'd done. I don't know how. She went whining to that fat bitch in security, Ms. Bone. So Bone called me in. Told me that unless I could persuade Elaine not to complain about *me*, I'd be in big trouble. The Yanks would believe Elaine, not me."

"That hadn't occurred to you?"

"I don't know. I didn't think it was all going to be such a big thing."

"How did Ms. Bone know the poster didn't exist?"

"You kidding? They check our rooms at least once a week. They think we don't know. She said my only hope was to see Elaine, just say it was all a joke, and beg her to use her contacts to—you know—get the whole thing dropped."

"Doesn't sound like an idea Elaine Cassidy would have gone for."

"Crazy idea. She was *really* enjoying herself. First time I've seen her smile since she arrived at this place. She was getting haughtier and snottier and then she started *slapping* me, and . . ."

"And that big textbook was the nearest thing to hand?"

"Really," said Kelly, "if you think about it, it was self-defense."

"I wouldn't bother with that in court," said Geraint. "It never worked for the French Resistance."

I was surprised by Hilda Westlake's tact in waiting outside, not insisting on being part of the interrogation. I chose to think it was tact, rather than a desire not to be involved more than necessary in a matter so rich in potential fallout for all concerned.

"Kelly's admitted the killing, and we've charged her with murder," I told her. "We'll drive her over to the local police-u-like franchise and process her."

Hilda glanced over to the car. "How did you get her to confess? You had basically nothing."

"Well," I said, "Geraint convinced her that it was in her best interests."

Geraint joined us, and gave Hilda a big smile. Not a friendly one, but a big one.

"What," said Hilda, "she's going for manslaughter? After stopping to wipe her prints off the weapon?"

"Nope. I explained to her that murder takes precedence over false allegations regarding the Possession or Dissemination of President Pig."

Then Hilda got it. She looked half impressed, half annoyed, which was about what I'd expected. "Right. So if she's serving time for murder, we won't be able to extradite her for the other thing. Nice work, Sergeants. Not sure if I've ever had my time so comprehensively wasted."

"Thank you," said Geraint.

Hilda looked at me, with what could almost have been a slight question in her eyes. "Your friend took that as a compliment, Barney."

"You all right to make your own way back to London, Agent Westlake?" said Geraint. "We need to deliver our passenger."

She carried on looking at me for a while, then she shrugged and turned away. As we drove off, I watched her in the mirror. She had her back to me and was on the phone and she didn't turn around.

Jeff Abbott

BET ON RED

■ ■ ■

Jeff Abbott is the nationally bestselling, award-winning author of seven novels of mystery and suspense, including the Anthony Award nominee A Kiss Gone Bad; *the Agatha and Macavity Award winner* Do Unto Others; The Only Good Yankee; Promises of Home; *and* Distant Blood. *The second Whit Mosley novel,* Black Jack Point, *was nominated for an Edgar Allan Poe Award, an Anthony Award, and a Barry Award. His latest novel,* Cut and Run, *was released in 2003 and was an Edgar Allan Poe Award nominee for Best Paperback Original. His short story "Bet on Red," first published in the anthology* High Stakes, *was an Edgar nominee for Best Short Story. The story evokes the dreamlike nature of Las Vegas, where anybody's luck can turn on a dime, allegiances are as solid as desert mirages, and a hit man out to remove a thorn in his boss's side may just end up working in a much more profitable partnership, if he can stay one step ahead of everyone else.*

I'll make a bet with you," Bobby said. He was bourbon-drunk and he leaned close to Sean's ear to talk over the arpeggios of the piano music, the never-ending chimes of the slot machines, the high roar of gamblers who, just for a moment, were beating the odds.

"I'm listening." Sean thought it was about time to head up to his room, tired of talking to Bobby, just tired period. Bobby was scaring off all the women with his overeager laughing, raising his glass to passing beauties like an idiot dink. It was a shame, really; this was Bobby's last night to be with a woman and the odds weren't pretty. Sean was supposed to get rid of Bobby tomorrow, take him out into the desert outside of Vegas, shoot him, bury him deep in the dry earth, and then fly back to Houston with Vic's hundred grand and pretend he hadn't set foot on the Strip recently.

"I bet"—Bobby gestured with his near-empty glass—"I can nail that pretty little redhead at the end of the bar."

Sean looked. Pretty was an understatement. She was gorgeous, hair that soft color of auburn that made Sean's throat catch, skin flawless as a statue's, dressed tastefully in a little black number that suggested a firm, ripe figure but didn't give away too much of the show. She was sitting alone, not looking at anyone, not trying to make eye contact. Maybe a high-class hooker, maybe not. Maybe just waiting on her boyfriend to finish at the craps table. She was drinking white wine and she cradled the stem of the glass between her palms, like she was keeping a delicate bird from taking wing.

"You aim high," Sean said.

"I got the gun for it," Bobby said.

"And you could impress her with all the cash you got," Sean said. At least temporarily. Sean thought about Vic's money, neat bricks of green he would have to hide in his checked bag tomorrow morning, wishing now he was driving from Vegas to Houston, but what a dreary endless drive it would have been. He didn't dislike Bobby, didn't like the idea of killing him, but orders were orders and when Vic gave them, you listened.

"Listen, man, that's Vegas for you. The air is thick with constant possibility, you never know which way the ball's gon' drop and then you're broke or rich, all in an instant," Bobby said. "I'm feeling like the ball's dropping my way. She's been looking at me."

"Looking ain't buying," Sean said. "And the keno screen's above your head, buddy."

"But see, that's all Vegas is about. The potential of every single moment." Bobby pulled a wad from his pants pockets, twenties rolled into a thick burrito, and Sean thought, *This is why Vic wants you dead, you dummy.*

"A thousand bucks says I get her," Bobby said.

Sean said nothing. A thousand bucks. Money in his pocket he could take and not feel guilty for taking and keeping after Bobby was dead. If he shot Bobby and then pocketed the money, that would be stealing from Vic, his boss—an unwise move. But if he won the cash from Bobby, then that was fair. Fair as could be. Plus it would be funny to watch Bobby try with the perfect redhead, and hell, if Bobby won, he'd die happier. Harmless. Sean felt an odd tug of friendship for Bobby, soon to die, with his heavy earnest face flush with life.

"And if you do bed her, what do I have to pay?" Sean said.

"Man," Bobby said, "that happens, I'll have already won."

"That's not a fair bet," Sean said.

"Tell you what, I win," Bobby said, "and you help me straighten out this misunderstanding with Vic. You tell him I've got the deals working just the way he wants."

Vic had sent Bobby to Vegas to shut down his drug operation, sell out the remaining supplies, clean the last hundred grand through the Caymans, pull up stakes, and kiss Vegas good-bye. The Feds and the locals were cracking down hard and Vic didn't have enough friends in town to make dealing worthwhile. Bobby didn't want to give up Vegas. And instead of taking three days to wrap up the project Bobby had taken a week, living off Vic's account at the King Midas, apparently doing nothing but drinking and betting and generally not closing shop in any great hurry, keeping the money tied up. And Vic was killing mad.

"That's really between you and Vic," Sean said. "It's your business, Bobby."

"Yeah, but you got his ear more than I do. You could help me a lot. I got the feeling he was a little irritated with me the last time we talked. He doesn't get that it took me longer than I thought it would to collect all the money."

Bobby was fun but dumber than a stump. It didn't matter how long it truly took to gather funds and close shop, it mattered how long Vic gave you to get the work done. Sean finished his beer. Bobby didn't have a chance in hell with the redhead. This was betting with a dead man, and Sean was the house. "Okay," he said. "You're on."

Bobby finished his drink, motioned to the bartender for another. "Observe, grasshopper," he said, moving down toward the redhead.

"Good luck," Sean said, meaning it, being nice, ordering himself another beer for the floor show.

It took about twenty minutes. Sean watched, trying not to watch, Bobby easing onto the stool next to the woman. Sean kept waiting for her to tell Bobby to get lost, to name her price, to ask the bartender to tell Bobby to leave her alone. But instead she gave Bobby a soft, kind smile, talked with him, a little shyly at first, then laughed, let him order her another glass of wine. Once she looked toward Sean, seeing him watching them, maybe having noticed him sitting with Bobby before, knowing he was the friend watching his friend make a move. But she didn't smile at Sean and she looked right back at Bobby, who was now playing it cool, not overeager like he had been in the hour before.

They finally got up when she finished her second glass of wine and headed into the acre of casino proper, Bobby giving Sean a knowing wiggle of eyebrow and a subtle thumbs-up with his hand at his side, Sean raising his beer in toast, surprised, the redhead never glancing Sean's way.

See you in the morning, Bobby mouthed.

Sean watched them head out into the hubbub of the slot machines and gaming tables, smiling for a minute. Well, it was one sweet way to spend your last night on earth. The angels were on Bobby's side. Sean downed his beer, went out to the roulette table, bet twice on black, watched the ball fall wrong both times, his chips vanish. He didn't really like betting. He remembered that a little too late.

Sean tried Bobby's hotel room early the next morning, about seven, figuring the guy would be sacked out, sleeping late on the last day of his life.

"Yeah?" A woman's voice, sleepy. But polite. Smoke and purr in her voice. Bobby must have done right by her.

"Is Bobby there?"

"He's in the shower. May I have him call you?" May, not can. The redhead was a nice lady.

"No, thanks, I'll just call him later." Not wanting to leave his name.

"May I tell him who's calling—" she started but Sean hung up. Got himself showered and dressed, fast, now wanting to get the job done, collect Bobby and the money, kill the poor guy, go home.

Sean called Bobby's room again. No answer, fifteen minutes after he first called. He didn't leave a message on the voice-mail system, decided he didn't want to stop by Bobby's room, risk the redhead seeing his face again. Bobby was a breakfast eater, loving the cheap but lavish Vegas buffets, and so Sean headed down to the restaurant. It was crowded with tourist gamblers in vacation clothing, a few bored teenagers, some conventioneering high-tech geeks wearing golf shirts with corporate logos on the pockets.

No Bobby working through a fat omelette, alone or with the redhead. Sean got coffee and a plate of eggs and bacon and sat down in a corner booth, wearing his sunglasses. If Bobby came in, he could excuse himself quickly, tell Bobby to come to his room in an hour, let him enjoy his last meal.

They didn't show. Maybe Bobby'd taken the redhead out for a nicer breakfast than one might find here at the King Midas. Maybe down to Bellagio or Mandalay Bay.

Sean finished his breakfast, checked his cell phone. One message. From Vic.

"Hey, bud," Vic said. "Just calling to see if you're knocking 'em dead in Vegas." That Vic. His little code was a scream. "Hope you're winning big. Call me when you're back."

A niggle of panic started in his stomach. Sean ignored it, finished his coffee, kept scanning the crowd for Bobby's blond hair, for the boom of his voice. Nothing. Tried Bobby's cell phone. No answer.

Sean waited another thirty minutes, tried Bobby's room again, got nothing. He went up to the room, used the extra key Bobby had given him when he got to Vegas yesterday. Nothing. Bed a mess, Bobby's clothes still in the closet. The slightest scent of perfume was in the air, the redhead smelled like rose petals and spice. But the bathroom was clean, the shower dry, the towels hanging in maid-hung precision.

He's in the shower. But no one had showered in this room.

"No, no, no," Sean said to himself. "Not after I was a nice guy." He ran from the room, his heart thick in his chest, and headed straight down to the lobby.

Sean drove his rental car down the Strip, then to Sahara Avenue, to the leased office Vic had rented when he and Bobby set up the Vegas operation two months ago, before Vic started feeling pressure from the Feds and decided Vegas made him overextended. The sign on the door read PRIORI CONSULTING, which Vic and Bobby had thought clever, because a consultant could mean it was any kind of business, and the legal term sounded respectable and fancy.

Sean had a key and he tried the lock.

The door opened. The office was simple, just a desk and a chair and a laptop computer. A motivational poster on the wall said ACHIEVE, with some dink standing atop a mountain summit at dawn, arms raised in triumph. Like that was supposed to impress Sean or Vic, hard evidence of Bobby's absent work ethic. No Bobby. Sean locked the door behind him, set the dead bolt.

He went straight to the vault in the back room of the office. Opened it with the combination Vic had given him, not wanting Bobby to know he knew the combo, not wanting to make a big deal about the money.

It was gone. Every last sweet brick of green was gone.

Sean sat in the King Midas bar, peeling the label off his beer in long strips, thinking, *This is my skin when Vic gets hold of me.*

Bobby was gone.

Sean felt like control over his own fate had danced right out of his arms, like he was one of those losers who surrendered all to the spinning roulette ball, waiting for it to drop into red or black or a sacred number, every hope in the world wrapped up on how that damned ball fell. Now his generous act was going to screw over his life big time. Maybe the redhead would show back up here, if she were a working girl or a guest. He thought she might be a working girl; not many women came to Vegas alone. Maybe she knew where Bobby had run to. But she had lied about the shower, he believed, Bobby maybe paid her to lie. Give him a head start on his run.

Sean didn't know a soul in Vegas who could help him find Bobby, didn't know any of the street-level dealers Bobby recruited, and he had not known what else to do other than go back to the bar, cancel his flight to Houston, and pray he got a lead on Bobby.

He had started to call Vic twice, hung up before finishing the number. Not knowing what he could say, almost laughing because he was afraid, scared in a way he didn't want to admit, trying to imagine the words coming from his mouth: *Bobby wanted to get laid, and it just didn't seem likely, so I let him out of my sight. We had a bet. Sorry.*

He switched to vodka martinis and was deep into his second when she came in and sat at the bar.

At first he blinked, not sure it was the same redhead. But it was, this time in leather pants and a white ruffled blouse, simple but stylish. She looked relaxed and she didn't look over at him. She ordered a glass of pinot grigio.

Sean counted to one hundred, waiting to see if Bobby trailed in behind her. Please, Jesus. But no Bobby. Sean got up from the bar stool, took his martini glass with him, eased next to her. She glanced at him.

"I'm Bobby's friend," he said in a low voice.

"I know. And you're probably a little more shaken," she said, glancing a his martini, "than stirred." Her smile was cool, not shy, not surprised. Expecting to see him, maybe even happy about it.

"Where is he?" Sean asked.

She took a dainty sip of wine. "He's resting. Comfortably."

"Where?" Trying to keep his voice calm.

"Someplace you won't find him."

"I can look pretty freaking hard, honey. Tell me where he is. Right now."

She ran a fingernail along the stem of her glass and let a few heavy seconds pass before she answered. "You're not really in a position to make demands."

"Not in a crowded bar."

"Not anywhere," she said. "You need to remember that. I'm not working alone. You're being watched wherever you go."

He was silent for several seconds, thinking, *What the hell is this?* "I'll remember," he said. There was nothing to be gained by threatening her. Play it cool, he decided, play along, and get her alone and then she'd talk. She was enjoying the driver's seat, relishing it a bit too much, and that was a mistake.

"So this is the deal," the redhead said. "Bobby had a hundred grand in cash on him. You get ten grand, just to tell one white lie. Tell Vic you took care of Bobby but that he had already blown the hundred grand gambling."

"And Vic just believes me?" Sean said.

"We both know," she said, "that yes, Vic will believe you. If you want, we'll get a statement from a couple of blackjack and baccarat dealers that a guy matching Bobby's description blew through a hundred grand in the past week."

"What about the rest of the money?"

"Not your concern. But Bobby walks and gets a new life somewhere else."

"And still has every reason to tell the cops about Vic. And me. No way."

"Sean," she said. "Do you think Bobby would do jail well?"

He surprised them both by laughing. She gave him back a smile, and the intelligence was sharp in her face, she was clearly no dumb bunny-Vegas-lay. "Actually, no, Bobby wouldn't do jail well at all. Be dead or someone's punk in five minutes."

"So you and I both know he's not going to run to the police or the FBI and talk about Vic."

"But he might go into WitSec, cut a deal that keeps him out of jail," Sean said.

Her smile faded. "That's a risk you take. You're not getting close to him," she said. "I've offered you the deal."

"Usually with Vic," he said, "I bring back a finger as proof." This was a lie but he wanted to see her reaction. Vic would think he was a freak if he hauled back a bloodied finger.

"In your carry-on or in your checked luggage?" Not blinking, not afraid at his announcement.

"In a Baggie, actually."

"Messy at security, and I don't believe you."

"Who are you?" he asked.

"You can call me Red."

"I'm impressed with the setup. You in with Bobby from the beginning?"

"I never met him until last night," she said.

"I think that's the first lie you've told me," he said.

"Think what you like," Red said. Her smile went crooked and she took a sip of her white wine. "Tell me. How were you going to spend the bet? The thousand bucks?"

"He told you, huh?"

"Yes." She watched the bartender approach them and she shook her head. The barkeep went back to the other end of the bar.

"Fishing gear, I guess."

"Fishing gear." She said it like how she might say *urine sample*. "I am so flattered that it was my maidenly virtue versus accessorizing your bass boat."

Despite himself, he felt a blush creep up his collar.

Now Red gave him a sly sideways glance. "You want to make a bet with me, Sean?"

"No. I want to conclude our business and never see you again."

"Now you've hurt my feelings," she said with a coy pout.

"I'll bet you heal fast," Sean said.

"Bobby said you were ex-military."

"Yeah, I was a grunt once."

"I've always thought military men had a sense of honor."

"I do," Sean said.

"I have a sense of honor, too. I won't screw you over, you won't screw me and Bobby over. We're all happier. Do we have a deal?"

"Don't kid yourself that I want to cut a deal with you, honey. What if I say no?"

"Then you'll be killed," Red said. "How does that sound?"

He watched her face, chewed the last olive in his martini, swallowed the small puddle of vodka at the glass's bottom. Watched her face for a hint of bluff and didn't see any. "Bobby sure got smart since he got to town."

"This town forces you to be smarter, Sean," she said and now she smiled at him and it seemed genuine, like they hadn't discussed big money and death.

"It hasn't worked on me yet," Sean said.

"You're plenty smart, hon," Red said. "So agree to this. Come to the Misty Moor Bar—off the Strip, near the Convention Center—in two hours. Alone and unarmed. Break either rule and you're dead. You'll get your money then. You will then be expected to leave Vegas immediately; we'll even escort you to the airport."

She swung her legs off the bar stool, pulled a ten from her purse.

"I'll buy your wine," Sean said. "You can buy my drink at the other bar."

She tucked the bill back inside. "Thanks. I'll see you then," she said. "And Sean?"

"What?"

"It's nothing personal. Bobby likes you. So do I."

Red turned and walked out, and he debated as to whether he should follow her. He counted to twenty, left money on the counter by the bill, got up from the bar stool, headed out, and hung back in the casino's crowd.

She never looked back to see if he trailed her. But if she wasn't working alone, as she said, then her partners might be watching him this very moment. He stayed back as far as he dared, weaving through the slot-machiners hooting at their triple cherries, past a rail-thin lady carrying a bucket of coins with all the care she would give the Holy Grail, past honeymooners nuzzling in the lobby. She headed past the bell attendants dressed like ancient Greeks. There was no taxi line at the moment and she quickly ducked into a cab with a promo for a wireless phone service mounted on the trunk, a monkey wearing eyeglasses talking on a cellular.

As soon as her cab pulled out of the circular driveway he grabbed a taxi, told the Nigerian driver to head down the Strip, and said, "See that cab up ahead? With the monkey talking on the phone? Follow it, please."

"Excuse?"

"The ad on the back. See?" She was five cars ahead of them, her driver changing lanes, and Sean could taste his own panic in his mouth, sour and coppery. "Jesus, keep up, don't lose them, but don't get too close."

"Ah," the driver said. "No trouble is wanted."

"That's my girlfriend," he said, "and I think she's dumping me to go back to her husband. I don't want trouble, I just want to know, 'cause if she's leaving me, I'm just gonna go back to my wife."

The Nigerian made a low noise in his throat that sounded like *Americans* but said nothing more.

Screw this meeting on her turf. He wasn't about to risk Vic's rage for a measly ten grand. Let her take him straight to Bobby. He would end their little game tonight, and then get the hell out of town.

The cab took her to a small house, in an older, quiet residential area distant from all the neon and glam. Not a well-to-do neighborhood but not too scruffy. He told the driver to let him off at the corner from where her cab had turned, and shoved fifty at the Nigerian, who babbled thanks and revved off. Sean sprinted away from the corner, out of her line of sight. He couldn't see Red but her cab was pulling away from a house nine homes down from where he was, marked with a decorative covered-wagon mailbox.

This was, he decided, a good hideout for Bobby. Quiet neighborhood, probably not a lot of crime, older folks who kept an eye on each other. Maybe it was the woman's house, although she looked like she came from money. Or had money. The easy, unafraid confidence she had with him, the nice clothes she'd worn both nights.

He felt a lava-heat anger with Bobby; oddly, he didn't wish Red ill at the moment and his reaction surprised himself. He liked her; Vic would have liked her too, but she had chosen the wrong side. She was the kind of girl he'd like to have taken back to Houston, taken out to dinner with Vic, she would have made Sean look good, would have had fun with him. Stupid Bobby, getting himself and this cool girl killed.

Sean headed for the next street, which ran parallel to the street she'd stopped on. In case she'd seen the cab, gotten suspicious. If she'd seen him, she and Bobby would run and that might be the end of the money and of Sean.

He walked down a street called Pelican Way—where the hell were there pelicans in Nevada? he wondered—counting houses, just giving her and Bobby time to relax, letting them start to get ready for meeting him at the bar. He counted nine houses, stopped in front of one. Brick, a one-car carport, wind chimes hanging by the front door, the trim and shutters needing a fresh coat of paint.

This ranch-style should be directly behind Red's house. He changed his plan. The house was dark, entirely so, no cars in the small driveway, old oil leaks marring the carport's concrete. The house next door was dark, too, although the house on the other side had a single light gleaming on its porch. He turned like he belonged here, and walked, casually, straight up the driveway. He went through the carport, paused at the fence, listened for the rasp of dog breath, and then opened the gate and went inside.

The backyard was empty except for a swing set, an old barbecue, dusty patio furniture in need of a wash. Sean went to the fence and tiptoed onto the rail, peering into Red's backyard. Three lights on in the house. A kitchen with an old-style bay window. Then he saw Red talking on the phone, moving from the kitchen table to the counter, sipping from a water bottle, moving back again. He ducked back down under the fence. Waited a minute. Looked again.

Now the kitchen was empty. He watched, counted to two hundred. Didn't see movement in the house. Counted to two hundred again, looked. All appeared quiet.

No guards, no dogs. The thought that Red must be part of a rival drug ring in town, convinced Bobby to switch sides, occurred to him but then he thought not. She didn't seem the gang type. Maybe she really was just working with him, no one else, a heist by just her and her Bobby. He hoped. It would make his work easier.

Sean went over the fence, dropped down, sprinted for the patio. He had a Glock under his jacket and as he ran he pulled it free. He got to the patio, waited against the door. Listened. The soft buzz of the TV sounded, a videotape playing in it. Sounded like an old John Wayne movie, the distinctive rise and fall of the Duke saying, "Hell, yes, I'm back in town."

Then he heard Red's voice, soft, gentle: "I'll be back in a little while, all right? Enjoy the movie." No answer from whoever she was talking to.

Sean moved away from the door. He heard a door open to his right, into the one-car garage. Light footsteps, just one person, heels, a woman's step. Red, alone. Then a car starting, pulling out of the driveway, headlights flickering on at the last moment. She had a car but had taken a taxi to King Midas so he couldn't follow her to a parked car in the lot. Smart girl. Sean stayed still, counted to one hundred. He went around to the carport, tried the door to the house. Locked.

He popped the glass pane in the door, and it tinkled, sure loud enough for Bobby to hear inside the house. So he worked quick, reaching inside, fingers fumbling to unlock the door.

There was no dead bolt. Instead, there was another key lock. Bobby was locked in from both sides. Weird. He leveled his pistol into the broken glass, waiting for Bobby to barrel out at the sound of the break-in, but there was no sound in the darkened house except the melodramatic score of the Western, faint as a whisper.

Sean waited ten seconds, felt a tremble of panic thumping his guts, and decided standing there waiting for Bobby to charge the door wasn't going to work. He went back to the patio and kicked in the glass door. Loud shattering noise. Two houses down a dog barked, sharp and hard, twice; then quiet. Sean counted to twenty. Nothing. No concerned neighbors popping a head over the fence.

Sean flicked open the door handle, slid the door open.

The room was a sunken den and the kitchen was to his right, and a hallway went off at a left angle. He waited, his gun leveled at the opening and waited some more. He could hear the sound of horses riding hard and stopping, of John Wayne mouthing a good-natured threat, of a polite man answering with an oozy official tone.

Sean inched down the hallway, the gun out like he'd learned in his days in the army. A feeble spill of light—from a television—came from a room at the end of the hall. He moved toward it, calming his breathing, listening for the sound of Bobby moving, and finally Sean charged fast into the room, going through the door, covering the room with his gun.

Bobby was there. Both hands cuffed to a bed, gagged with a cloth jammed in his mouth and duct tape masking his mouth, ribboning into his hair. One of his eyes was bruised. He was shirtless, dressed only in the khakis from last night with a wet circle of stain on the front, and he smelled like he needed a shower. A pile of pillows kept his head propped up. A little television with a VCR player stood on a scruffy bureau, the John Wayne movie playing.

Sean stared for a moment, then shook his head.

Bobby groaned, made pleading noises behind the gag. Sean muted the TV, left the tape running, John Wayne swaggering across a saloon. He sat on the edge of the bed.

"Are you going to scream if I take this off?" Sean asked. "I mean, Vegas is just full of possibilities, isn't it, Bobby? So you said."

Bobby shook his head.

Sean pulled the tape and gag from Bobby's head, not worrying about the threads of hair that ripped free with the industrial tape, and Bobby said, "Oh, thank God, man, thank God, Sean. I knew you'd find me. Get me the hell out of here."

Sean sat down on the edge of the bed. "Tell me what's happened." Calm. Curious to hear what the story was, because this tied-up-and-bound-gig was not what he expected.

"That bitch, man, she's crazy. Drugged me and tied my ass up. Christ, she's *nuts*. Untie me, man."

"Just a minute," Sean said. "You're not in with her?"

"In with her?" Bobby stared. He jerked at the handcuffs. "Do I look it?"

"I went to your office looking for your sorry ass," Sean said. "And all of Vic's money is missing. The whole hundred grand."

Bobby's lips—chapped and blistered from the tape—turned into a frown. "Holy shit. She must've taken it."

"She was in your hotel room when I called this morning."

"Shit, man, she slipped something into my drink and knocked my ass out. I woke up here, she must've snuck me out of the hotel somehow, she's got inside help. She probably took all my keys, took the money. Unhook me, Sean, Jesus, let's get the hell out of here." An edge in his voice; Sean thought he was about to cry.

"God, you're dumb. You are so unrelentingly dumb. Did she bring the money here?"

"I don't know, I don't know, just untie me, please, before she gets back here!"

"No hurry." Sean checked his watch. "Because she's heading off to meet me at a bar. She's negotiating on your behalf, buddy, for me to tell Vic that you're dead and for you to keep all his money."

Bobby struggled against the shackles, pulling his head up from the pillows. "That's a goddamned lie, I'm not trying to steal Vic's money! She's set you up. Listen, untie me, we'll wait for her to come back and then we'll make her tell us who she's working for."

"You never saw her before?"

"No, man, I swear it. *Swear it!*"

"But she knows your business. She knows about you working for Vic. She knows my name. She knows there was a safe in the office and she got the combo. You must've seen her before."

"No, I swear."

"Then you must've blabbed to somebody, and that's who she's working with."

"No, never, never," Bobby said but his voice dropped a notch, spurred by a jiggle of memory, a thought of a mistake made and now wished away.

"Right, Bobby. Never would you make a mistake. You wear my ass out just listening to you."

"Listen, Sean, she's the bad guy, not me. We can get the money back. Together."

Sean said nothing for a moment, thinking it out, feeling very tired and then wired, all at once. He stood up. Went and searched the house carefully and efficiently. There was scant furniture in the house, he decided it was a rental.

"Sean?" Bobby called quietly. "Sean?"

"Just a minute. Hush," Sean said. No sign of the money anywhere. It wasn't here. He went back to the bedroom, Bobby watching him with eyes glassy with sick fear.

"Sean, you're my friend, Vic's my friend, you know I had nothing to do with this girl's scheme."

"You know, I believe you, Bobby," Sean said. "Had to chase the wrong girl, didn't you?" He nearly laughed. He had made his decision.

"Yeah, I guess," Bobby said.

"Did you get her?" Sean asked, wondering what he'd say.

"No," Bobby said after a moment.

"Then I guess I win the bet," Sean said.

"Well, that was a bad bet to make," Bobby said.

"That's real true." Sean stood up, turned up John Wayne. Real loud.

Sean had thought the "Misty Moore" was maybe a bar named after the owner, some chick named Misty, but instead it was Moor without the *e* on the end, and when he went inside he noticed a silver thistle above the bar and the waitresses wore tams on their heads and snug miniskirt kilts across their asses and the wallpaper was plaid. He spotted Red sitting in a very private back corner booth, drinking her white wine. The bar was not terribly crowded, a dozen conventioneers watching a basketball game on the big screen, a few locals. He slid into the booth, sitting next to her, not across from her.

"You take the low road," he said, "and I'll take the high road."

"Cute. Scotland was one of the few cultures not raided by Vegas," Red said. She was very calm. "Then *Braveheart* came out and they opened up this place. If you get drunk, they'll paint your face blue."

A waitress approached them and asked Sean what he would drink. "Scotch," he said. "Obviously."

"You're a few minutes late," Red said when the waitress walked off. "Fortunately I'm patient and forgiving."

"More reason to admire you," he said. "Let's get to it."

"I've got your ten thousand," she said. "You still agreeing to lie to Vic, let Bobby walk?"

"Actually, the deal has changed, Red." He kept his voice low and the waitress returned with his Scotch, set it down in front of him, walked off back to the bar.

Red was very still. "Changed?"

"You have the hundred grand. You also have a dead man in your house. You know, your house at 118 Falcon Street. Where you had the John Wayne movie marathon playing." He saw the shift in her face, saw she believed him now. "So, baby, I can call the police, from that phone right over there in the corner, and I figure they can be at your house faster than you or anybody else can be dragging Bobby's body out to your car. You'll have a lot of questions to answer."

"So will you," she said, staying calm.

"No, I won't. Because I sure don't know you, and you can't prove that I know you. Or that I knew Bobby."

"You would have been seen with him at the hotel."

"Maybe. Maybe those folks don't talk after Vic calls his friends at the casino. But Bobby boy's dead in your house."

"I haven't shot a gun anytime recently. They have chemical tests . . ."

"I wouldn't waste a good bullet on Bobby. Smothered with a pillow, sweetheart," Sean said. "How hard they got to look for a new suspect?"

Red took a microscopic sip of her wine. She set the glass down carefully. "So. What now?"

"Who else here's with you?" he asked.

"No one."

"You had help in getting Bobby out of the King Midas. So don't lie to me. It makes me want to call 911." He smiled at her, touched her hand gently. "You're no longer running the show, sweetness."

She let two beats pass. "The guy in the windbreaker at the bar. He's my partner." Sean allowed himself a very quick glance. The guy was watching them, not threatening, not worried, and he glanced into his beer right when Sean looked at him. The guy was big but had a softness to his hands and his mouth, had a nervousness to him that made Sean feel confident.

"How'd you find out about Bobby and the money?" Sean asked.

She gestured to the waitress for another glass of wine, and he knew then she would tell him, that he had her. "My partner works for an office equipment leasing company. He delivered Bobby's office equipment for him when he got started. Late in the day, he and Bobby got to talking. Ended up going out for a beer. Bobby doesn't like to be alone, ever, and here he was new in a big town where he didn't know nobody. They got to be drinking buddies and Bobby'd give my partner a little coke now and then, when he came to town. One night Bobby drank too much, talked plenty. The safe combo, Jesus, Bobby stuck the numbers on a sticky note in his desk drawer. Not the brightest star in the sky."

"And you were the handy redhead."

"It's not natural," Red said. "I spent $250 on this hair color at a really uppity salon on the Strip after Bobby told my friend he dug redheads."

"Looks good," Sean said.

"Thank you," she said.

Sean looked back at the bar and now her partner kept his stare back on Sean. "Your friend appears to be a little nervous," he said. "Are we going to have a problem?"

"No."

"He more than a friend?"

"My brother."

"Oh, please."

"No, really, he is. No joke."

"I love a family that works together," Sean said. "Okay, wave Bubba over here."

She did and at first the brother, uncool, acted like he didn't see her. But then she stood up and said, "Garry, come here, please," clear as a bell and Garry got up and came and sat across from Sean and Red. His mouth was thin. Scared, in over his head.

Sean didn't smile, didn't say hello or offer his hand. "So, the two of you thought you could screw me over."

"Not you," Red said, "Bobby and Vic. Jesus, you act like it was personal." Her smile warmed a degree. "I told you it wasn't."

"Doesn't matter," Sean said. "You got a dead guy in your house. What I don't have is what I came here for, Vic's money. Now. I give you guys credit, the scheme was clever. You get rid of Bobby, get the money, and make Vic think that Bobby's on the run so he never, ever comes hunting for you."

"Thank you," Red said.

"You're welcome," Sean said. "I want that money here on this table in ten minutes or I'm calling the police and telling them that there's a funny smell coming from y'all's guest bedroom."

Garry went white as salt. Red took a calm sip of her wine.

"And if we don't cooperate, you get nothing," she said. "You get screwed over just as bad as us, because Vic'll kill you, won't he?"

"Of course not," Sean said.

"Really? You'll have failed in your errand and he's not gonna take it lightly," Red said. "Bobby told me all about him, and we did some checking on him. People piss themselves when Vic comes into a room."

"Maybe Bobby did. He's easily impressed," Sean said and for the first time Red laughed.

"He was impressed with you, Sean. He liked you. Truly."

Sean felt a pang of regret, wanted to close his eyes, but instead put a hard stare on his face. "Don't tell me that, you'll make me feel bad."

"I'll make you feel worse," Red said. "If you send us to jail, you go home empty-handed. You'll never get your money because we'll give it to the cops, cut a deal to tell all we know about you and Vic and Bobby, and you're just as dead as we are. So call 911, Sean. We'll sit here and wait."

"For God's sakes . . ." Garry said.

"Hush now," Red said. "Sean's thinking. He needs his quiet time."

They had him by the throat just as surely as he had them. Standoff.

"So there's no way out for any of us," Red said, "unless we work together. And unless you're willing to get out from under Vic's thumb."

"I'm not under his thumb," Sean said.

"There's two types of people in this world," Red said. "Bosses and errand boys. Bobby, at least during his time in Vegas, he got to be a boss. But you're always gonna be

Vic's errand boy, aren't you? He could've kept his business running in Vegas, given it to you, let you take the risk. And the reward." She leaned forward and he could smell the rose perfume he'd smelled in Bobby's hotel room with its lie-dry shower, the soft scent of wine on her breath. "Are you always going to be an errand boy, Sean?"

He said nothing, watching her.

"I mean, say Vic was out of the picture, you could take over in Vegas. There's a whole infrastructure of dealers and customers in place, ready for someone smarter than Bobby to step in. Make more money than an errand boy ever would. I could help you, Sean. We could get rid of Vic. Together. It beats sending each other to prison." And she gave him a wry grin.

"I can't just kill Vic. The rest of his organization would come after me like an army." That was all of ten guys, but it was enough.

"Not if something happened to him here. Away from them, where they couldn't know exactly what had happened. Maybe the same trouble that happened to Bobby. A rival gang. Vic dies, you take over the operation before the other gang can, you're a hero. End of story."

"What," Sean said, "are you suggesting?" Feeling another rush of decision, of possibility, imagining a roulette ball spinning in her smile.

"Tell me," Red said, "does Vic like redheads?"

The King Midas bar, two nights later, was quieter than the first time Sean had been in here with Bobby, a different bartender, tonight a black woman with a soft Jamaican accent. Vic watched her walk to the other side of the bar. They were at a back table, but with a good view of the curved teak of the bar.

"These Caribes," Vic said. "They're everywhere. If you grew up on an island, why would you want to move to a goddamned desert?" He coughed once, sipped hard at his vodka and tonic. "It's pissing me off."

"Change of pace." Sean cleared his throat. "I'm sorry this has turned into a hassle, but I'm confident we can catch the bastards that kidnapped Bobby."

"You got a lead on these assholes?" Vic said. He took another tense swallow of vodka.

"Asians from Los Angeles, moving east," Sean said. "That's the word on the street." The lie was easy now, practiced in his mind, and it made sense.

Vic frowned. "Let 'em kill Bobby for all I care. Why should I meet with them?"

"Listen, he talks before he dies, and they've got the information to bring you down," Sean said. "They can feed it to informants, cut a deal to trade you to the cops on a platter if any of their chiefs get caught. You need Bobby back in one piece. Plus, they're being too clever, wanting to meet, wanting more money. Greed is stupid in this case. We'll kill them."

"Christ," Vic said. "You're sure this ain't a trap they're setting?"

"I'm sure," Sean said and he saw Red walk in. Same little black dress as before but now her hair was rich coffee brown, bobbed short, like Sean knew Vic liked. "They're not that smart."

"Christ," Vic said. "I want them dead when we're done, you hear me?"

"I hear you," Sean said. "Listen, try to relax. This is Vegas. Have some fun. We can't do anything until the meeting tomorrow, man. Chill out. You want to go see a show?"

Vic said, "Jesus, no, sitting in a chair for two hours would drive me nuts." He finished his vodka, ordered another. Sean waited, giving him time, not wanting to force it. Finally Vic saw her.

"Check out the sweet treat at the bar," Vic said.

"Which?"

"Five stools from the right. The tasty brunette."

"She's out of your league, Vic, too pretty." Pushing Vic's button.

Vic raised an eyebrow but wasn't mad. Smiling at the challenge. "This from the little league."

"I'm just saying, she looks like she's happy alone," Sean said. "She wouldn't want to talk to some guy who's all stressed about his business. Not thinking about having a good time."

"Hey, I want her, I can get her," Vic said.

Sean smiled. "You think so, Vic? How about a little bet?"

Judith Cutler

Doctor's Orders

■ ■ ■

Prize-winning short-story writer Judith Cutler is the author of two acclaimed series of crime novels set in Birmingham. The Dying series features amateur sleuth Sophie Rivers (Dying to Deceive), *while in a police procedural series Inspector Kate Power* (Power Shift) *lives up to her name. They will shortly be joined in their fight against injustice by painter and decorator Caffy Tyler, who made her first appearance in* Scar Tissue. *A former secretary of the Crime Writers' Association, Judith has taught creative writing at Birmingham University, and has run occasional writing courses elsewhere (including a maximum security prison and an idyllic Greek island). "Doctor's Orders" first appeared in the British anthology* Birmingham Noir, *and takes a look at what might go on behind closed doors in any shop in England (or America, for that matter), and how a young wife with nowhere to turn may take matters into her own hands.*

Meena Sangra twisted and tugged at the bright new gold ring. It was too tight to let her scratch the rash developing underneath. But there wasn't time to worry about that. She stooped for another attack on the piles of newspapers. The binder tape cut into yesterday's blisters.

There. The last pile in place, ready for the paperboy. Poor little thing: he didn't look strong enough to carry such a load. And he was so well spoken: she could understand his accent, at least, and he always made sure his nouns agreed with his verbs. She could trust his personal pronouns, too. So many of the people here in Smethwick seemed to find them difficult. "Us are off down the market," for instance: what did they mean by that? Her father would never have permitted such sloppiness. He had learned English from a teacher straight from England: he had the purest vowels, the most clipped enunciation, of all their acquaintances. He regretted deeply that even the good girls' school his daughter had attended had English teachers who were not native born—time and again he would mock her accent when she drove with him on his rounds in the old Morris. Meena swallowed hard. Part of her was glad that he wasn't alive to see to what depths she had been brought; half resented his early death, which had reduced her to this.

Putting her hand to the small of her back she straightened. Five past six. Vinod would be expecting his tea by now. And her mother-in-law must be bathed and dressed. Although the routine was less than a week old, it irked already.

Oh, my daughter, that you should have come to this, she heard her father lamenting.

She looked down at the ring. In England, Father had told her, the Christians used to marry "for better, for worse, for richer, for poorer." Neither her Hindu nor her civil marriage ceremony had used those precise words, but she understood them very clearly on this cold wet morning. The words "worse" and "poorer" had the heaviest weight.

The marriage broker had given her mother to understand that Vinod was a rich businessman. He had shown her photographs of the home she was to expect, a spacious five-bedroomed house in the Birmingham suburb of Harborne: "Very, very fine," he'd insisted. "A big wide road, lined with trees. The houses have such big gardens, front and back, that you cannot hear the big cars as they rush back and forth. And Mr. Sangra has a fine car: look, there it is, in front of the garage. Neighbors? Oh, millionaires to a man. You have to be to live on Lordswood Road."

Her dying mother was happy to take the broker at his word. And however independent Meena had wanted to be, life in India as a woman not quite young anymore, with no family to support her, seemed less attractive than a traditional marriage. In her rush to escape the empty family home, Meena had even agreed to get together a dowry. The broker insisted that it was still the norm for decent Hindu women in England, whatever the law in India might be. What were a few hundred pounds, anyway? Even as she started to realize her capital, she heard her father say, as clearly as if he'd been at her shoulder, *Keep something in reserve, my child.* So she would not sell, but insisted on renting out the old family house. And before she handed the keys over, she took a spade and dug as deep as she could, so deep that no monsoon flood would wash away the earth, and no drought make cracks deep enough to show what she had buried. One day her new husband might be grateful for her forethought.

"Meena! Where are you? Come here at once!"

"Coming, Mother-in-law!" She ran upstairs to the best bedroom, recoiling at the smell of old woman and old woman's urine. Perhaps she would get used to it. Her father had got used to unpleasant smells. He'd conducted postmortems on the long dead, so that one day he could become not just a family doctor but a famous pathologist. He'd come home stinking of the morgue: Meena could almost smell him now. But instead she gagged at the old woman and her chamber pot, and had to dress the former and empty the latter. *There, Father, you'd be pleased I got those right.*

The old woman was fat and arthritic. It didn't take her father to diagnose that. But he had made himself unpopular among fat, arthritic old ladies by telling them that the best way to deal with their aches and pains was to get up and walk to market, as fast as they could. Lying in bed made them worse, he'd insisted. Mother-in-law had sniffed when Meena had relayed the advice, clear as if her father had spoken it from beyond the grave.

"Walk to market?" she'd repeated in disbelief. "That's what *you're* here for: to run to the market."

Or at least to the shops. Smethwick was well provided with shops selling familiar food: vegetables and spices lit up the eyes and nose with their freshness. She loved shopping. Even when the cold rain drenched down, she could bury her nose in a box full of methi and imagine herself at home. And there were shops selling cosmetics and saris to dazzle the eye and empty the purse. Not that her purse had much in it. It seemed it was the custom in Smethwick for men to dole out housekeeping money a coin or two at a time. She'd have to ask Vinod when she wanted more clothes. It seemed she even had to ask him when she wanted a simple walk along the High Street to Smethwick library. For they were not living in a house on Lordswood Road, Harborne. Not yet. They were living at the back of their shop. And when she asked him when they were moving to the house in the glossy color photographs, he had hit her. Not very hard. There was no bruise to show on her cheek, but she needed mouthwash for the ulcers that came up. Ask Vinod for extra money? Thank goodness for her father's voice, telling her that ordinary salt dissolved in hot water was as good as anything she could buy from a pharmacist.

When she got used to English money, Vinod told her to make herself useful in the shop. She obeyed. Despite her efforts, it was clear he preferred to keep an eye on her. But one day Mother-in-law had an appointment with the doctor and needed Vinod to drive her. No, the car wasn't the gleaming Jaguar in the photo. To be fair, it wasn't an old Morris, either, but something in between. An Orion, that was it. Blue, with a scrape along one side.

"The girl comes with me!" Mother-in-law had insisted. "Someone has to help me undress."

Visibly Vinod agonized: Mother or making money? The latter won. *See, Father—I haven't forgotten.*

She still had difficulty distinguishing what the locals said. Everyone had the same whining gabble, whether it was the old white men coming in, whippets at heels, for a couple of ounces of rough tobacco, or the proud Sikh women with more bright Indian gold than she'd seen outside a jeweler's shop. It was one of the old men who asked her, "Wor'appened to the other one, me love?"

"Other one?" she repeated.

"Ah. The other wench. Not so old as you, but not so pretty, neither. Worked here nigh on a year, dae her, Tom?" He addressed another old man, his upper lip stained by the snuff she now sold him.

"Ah. Then her went away."

Meena smiled politely, but for the first time wished her husband were here beside her, if only to translate. "Wench?" she ventured.

The first man slapped his thigh. "Yow doe half talk funny. Like them folk at the BBC."

"Wench," his friend put in with a helpful smile. "Someone like yourself as might be. And her was here for a bit, and then her went away. Go back to Pakistan, did she?"

Pakistan? What were they talking about? If only they would speak English! It was best to smile as she took their money and carefully counted the right change and say, "I'm afraid I've no idea. You would have to ask my husband about this wench."

The old men exchanged a glance. She'd no idea why, no idea what it meant. But the incident made her uneasy.

Mother-in-law was in a terrible mood when she came home. As Meena bent to ease off her sandals, a huge clout knocked her off balance. "You and your exercise! So much for you and your exercise!"

Meena had no idea what she meant. But she knew her ear was ringing, and that the wrist that she'd landed on was already swelling. *A cold cloth, wrapped tight. That's best for a sprain*, her father told her. So she gathered herself up and headed for the sink.

"Where do you think you're going? You pauper: a slut with a dowry your size, and you think you can go where you want? Come back here!" Mother-in-law's voice thundered around the small room.

"I've hurt my wrist, Mother-in-law."

"Poor girl. Come here: let me see!" The old woman sounded contrite.

Meena approached, squatting, as before, at her feet. As she laid the damaged hand in the old woman's there was another thunderous blow, this time to the other ear.

By now Meena was crying—shock, pain, anger. Vinod must hear of this. She stumbled into the shop. Vinod was stacking shelves. There was no one else to be seen. By now the pain in her wrist was so bad she knew she had broken a bone. She ought to find a doctor. She blurted it all out to Vinod, who carried on methodically placing one tin of cat food on another, just as if she didn't exist.

When the shelf was complete, he turned to her, and boxed both ears. "You think my customers want to hear my wife sniveling and wailing like a mad woman? You think that's the way to make my customers happy so that they buy and we can have that house on Lordswood Road, Harborne? You think that? Let me tell you, wife, a woman who wants medical treatment will have to come up with more dowry. Let me assure you of that."

"But there's the Health Service. It's all free!"

"Not dentists!" And he slapped her so hard across the mouth that she could swear that her teeth moved in their sockets.

In their bedroom, she rocked herself backward and forward like a sick child. She didn't know which part of her body hurt the most. Sick, dizzy, and bleeding where he had taken her by force, she wept for her father, and the books he had read aloud to her when she had a fever he couldn't cure or a sorrow he couldn't soothe away. Cinderella, that was who she felt like. With her family already calling for their supper.

Grabbing a tea towel, she bound the throbbing, swollen wrist as tightly as she dared. Keeping it tucked as far from their eyes as she could, she picked over dhal and peeled garlic with as little movement as she could manage. She managed to press the chapatis into a semblance of a decent size and thickness. But when she came to lift the big heavy frying pan, she had to admit defeat. Tonight she would have to use one of the lightweight saucepans her mother-in-law despised. Once they had been nonstick, but Mother-in-law insisted on the vigorous use of scouring pads.

As she fried onions and added pinches of *dhania* and *jeera*, she tried to blot out what was happening. But it was all too clear. She'd read of countless women who had disappeared after marriages. Sometimes the pitiful remains of their poor charred bodies were found. Sometimes they were not. And it was clear that the police turned the blindest of eyes. Who'd ever heard of the husband or mother-in-law being brought to justice? Not in the whole of India, so far as she knew. Some women did contrive a risky escape: they told of beatings and cruelty like her own. Worse. It was the dowry their husbands wanted, the dowry and a domestic slave. And the police shook their heads in disbelief that their families should have so blatantly broken the law by handing over a dowry in the first place. If the Indian police were so unsympathetic, what could she hope for from these strange English people whose accents she could not penetrate and who didn't even know their personal pronouns?

No, it was to herself that she must look for salvation. Back home she had a house, after all, and the cache buried deep in the herb garden. But that was thousands of miles and an expensive air ticket away. Somehow, somehow, she must save odd pennies of change from her shopping, and hide them until she had enough. Months? Years? Who knew how long it would take.

Keep a low profile, daughter, her father said over her shoulder.

After three weeks, she had saved two pound coins and seventy-three pence. And gained a fresh black eye. The blue and purple marks on her wrist had subsided to grayish yellow smears. She was learning how to deal with the nightly rapes, using the breathing system her father had recommended for women in labor too poor for the painkillers they needed. She would smile and scrape before her mother-in-law, and flatter her husband. But she knew that she might as well have been nice to tigers. All the good meals and subservience in the world wouldn't stop them turning on her when the mood took them.

One Tuesday it did.

She was in the shop, stacking packets of cigarettes behind the counter. Vinod was dealing with Lottery tickets. Not daring to turn around, she recognized the voice of the man with the whippet. Quickly, silently, she passed Vinod the tobacco he'd want.

Vinod might not have registered her efficiency; the old man did.

"Ah, you'm got a good wench there, mate. I was asking her the other day, what happened to the other one? Where's she gone? Back to Pakistan?"

Vinod said dismissively, "Oh, that young cousin of mine. She's gone back to India. To get married. Very hardworking girl."

He was talking too fast. Meena knew there was something wrong.

"No better than this wench here. You know how to pick them, all right, Mr. Patel. I'll say that for you."

Vinod barely waited till the door had pinged shut before he gabbled, "Ah! These stupid old men. Calling us all Pakistanis, and all Mr. Patel."

Appease, appease!

Meena clicked her tongue in disapproval, as was expected, and continued with the cigarettes. She did not want to talk, after all. She wanted to think. So "wench" meant "woman." And as far as she could recall, there'd been no mention in the broker's report about any dependent cousins working in the Sangra business empire. No respectable bachelor would have an unmarried female in his household, not without a wife to chaperone her. Even his mother would not do. Almost absentmindedly she scratched the rash on her ring finger.

She wasn't surprised when Vinod made a swift excuse and left the shop. He was going to speak to his mother. He was going to make sure they told the same story.

Meena took especial trouble with the meals that day: they could have no complaints there. She tried to ask Vinod sensible questions—even suggested, very tentatively, that they might free up floor space in the shop by storing stuff in the cellar.

"Damp," he said, as swiftly as he'd dismissed the old man.

Soon the tigers decided to strike. At least the old one did.

Meena was kneeling at her feet, cutting her toenails. The nails were thick, twisted into strange shapes. The scissors were clearly inadequate: they needed the sort of strong clippers her father had used on his mother's feet, so long ago she'd almost forgotten. Perhaps the momentary lapse in concentration was to blame. She had pulled on a nail and hurt the old woman. The yells brought Vinod dashing up. Before she knew it, she was on her knees, and Vinod was unbuckling his belt.

When she recovered consciousness she was in pitch-darkness. For a moment she thought she'd died. For another, longer moment, she wished she had.

Use your wits, my child, her father told her. *Come on: think! Where are you?*

Rolling onto her knees, she made her fingers explore. Small square tiles—the sort they had in the kitchen. If she crawled slowly forward, she might find—yes, a wall. Systematically working around, she found steps, and the rough wood of a door. No, not dead. Just locked in the cellar. She hauled herself up so that she could sit on the bottom step. Quickly she lay down again. It wasn't just the pain, though she was afraid of fainting again. It was the fear of Vinod finding her somewhere he hadn't thrown her.

Deep breaths. That was it. The sort she used at night when Vinod took her. But something else penetrated the fog of her mind. A smell.

Of course there was a smell. Vinod had explained only a few hours ago that it was damp.

Her father might have been holding her hand: *My child, this is why we have to work quickly. That smell means someone is dead under there.*

There had been an earthquake—just a small one, not terrible enough to bring the world's press in—and she and her father had been among those struggling to claw out the living before they too started to give of that strange sweet smell. The same sweet smell she was breathing in now. That first time, with her father, she'd managed not to vomit. Now, holding her nose, breathing through her mouth, she might manage again. She knew it was vital—yes, Father, literally a matter of life and death—that she betray no hint to Vinod or his mother that she suspected something—some*one*—might be buried in the cellar.

Next time Vinod took Mother-in-law to the doctor, Meena bribed the paperboy to watch the shop and dashed down to the cellar, taking a flashlight out of stock. Yes! The red quarry tiles were very slightly disarranged, over in the far corner. Half of her wanted to lift one to see if what she feared was correct. The other half feared dirt under the fingernails. She fled back upstairs.

As soon as the shop was empty, she prised some money from the Air Ambulance collecting box and replenished the till.

When a florid card invited them to a family wedding in Leicester, Meena wondered briefly if they would want her presentable enough to take with them, and that for a week she might be spared any beatings. For a day or so it seemed she might be right. But the old woman's arthritis flared up: she would have to stay behind. And it didn't take Father's whisper in her ear to tell Meena that she would have to stay behind to look after her. Well, a night without Vinod's attentions must be a bonus, even if the old woman would be sulky and vicious-tempered at missing the celebrations.

Once the old woman was snoring, Meena crept down to the cellar. No, she was crazy. She couldn't believe it. Of course she could smell damp.

Damp, yes—and something else. You know what that something else is! Courage, my daughter: evidence—that's what the English police will want.

Meena nodded. Even the Indian police wouldn't argue with a body in a cellar.

Yes, there was a scrap of cotton: her predecessor had been reduced to the cheapest of saris. And a skein of long black hair. Poor woman. Meena didn't want to see any more.

Oh, you coward! You think the police will take the word of an Indian woman without a bone or two to show them?

The thought made her gag. She was concentrating so hard on not vomiting, she didn't hear the door creak open.

"You bitch! You interfering bitch! Well, there's no help for it now! You'll have to stay down here till Vinod comes back. He'll know what do!"

No. Meena wasn't going to stay down here with only a half-exposed skull for company. She hurtled toward the old woman, who stepped back so quickly she lost her footing. There was a dreadful thud as her head hit the step. She slithered down, little by little. Meena was paralyzed. She could hear the breath rattling in Mother-in-law's throat: she knew she was dying.

She ought to call an ambulance. The police. She knew she ought. And show them the hair and the sari. But what if they thought she'd killed the old woman? Vinod would certainly swear she had. Blindly, desperately, she pulled up more tiles, dashing into the kitchen for a knife to slice aside the damp earth. Scrabbling, dragging, at long last she got the old woman into the grave only just deep enough for her bulk. The earth she'd displaced? Thank God it was still night, and she could sprinkle it over the backyard, under the old TV and carpet Vinod had dumped there. All the time she worked, she tried to work out what to do next.

If she robbed the till and fled, Vinod would set the police on her. There was no doubt about that. And she knew they'd soon find an errant woman. Interpol. The Indian police. She'd be hounded down and imprisoned for life.

Well, was that any worse than what she'd suffered recently?

Meena washed and dressed very carefully. There was no telltale earth under her fingernails. If she looked tired and pale when she opened the shop for the paperboy on Sunday morning, no one would be surprised. The customers were used to averting eyes from her bruised arms and swollen face. In fact, the shop did its usual brisk business, the whippet man buying extra tobacco to celebrate his birthday. To his amazement, she pressed an extra packet on him.

When Vinod returned, still bleary though it was after midday, she was ready for him. Bringing tea as he took his place—still in his best clothes—at the till, she asked polite questions about the wedding, and replied indifferently to his questions about his mother. It was after three when he decided he ought to see her.

Meena locked the shop and flicked over the CLOSED sign. The people of Smethwick would just have to wonder why they'd packed up so early.

Vinod was calling and calling, both for his mother and—now—for Meena. She went to the cellar head to wait for him. She had both the flashlight and the heavy frying pan in her hands.

Keep your voice steady, daughter. Remember, you have to win this argument. Put down that pan. Right out of sight. Your only weapon must be your brain.

She returned the pan to the kitchen.

"So where the hell is she?" Vinod shook her.

"If you calm down I'll show you." She stood back deferentially to let him go first: he'd see nothing sinister in that.

He stood on the step below her. Yes, with that pan she could have smashed his skull quite easily—are you sure you're right, Father? "Your mother's down there." She pointed with the beam of light from the flashlight. But she pointed to the corner where the young woman was buried. "Oh, no. I've got it wrong. That's where the other body is, isn't it? No, I wouldn't advise touching me. Or you might well join them." She pressed a finger into his back. Just as they did on the films. Just as they did on the films, he believed it was a knife. He raised his hands. "Be quiet and listen. I have enough evidence to have you taken to prison."

"But Mother—you've killed her!"

"In fact, she had a heart attack or something. But it might take time for the pathologist to find that out. Stand still, I tell you." She drove in her fingernail more firmly. "I shall be leaving England as soon as I can get a flight. To pay for the flight I need money from you."

He was ready to turn and bluster. She pressed harder.

"You don't deserve it, but I'm offering you a chance. What is a thousand pounds, five thousand pounds, to spare yourself prison? You'll buy two tickets, in fact, one for me, one for your mother. Different flights, I think. That should buy you a little time. The only time you'll ever hear from me is if I learn you've remarried. Yes, Vinod, you've got to stay here in Smethwick for the rest of your life. No more wives, no more dowries, no more dreams about Lordswood Road, Harborne."

"But—"

"Is it a deal, Vinod? Because frankly, if it isn't, I don't reckon much for your chances. Not if the police find you locked in here with the bodies of two dead women." Another fingernail stab. "Down the steps."

It didn't take long for him to agree. While he whimpered and snuffled in darkness, she used his credit card to book tickets. She raided the till for cash and slipped out to buy a new sari and travel bag.

She toyed with leaving him in darkness forever, but it would look better if the street saw him waving her off in an A1 taxi. The club class flight was comfortable. The pounds sterling she flourished were quite enough to compensate the people who'd been renting her house. She dug at her leisure. In time, she acquired a new passport under a new name, and then a visa for the States.

She was waiting for the taxi to take her to the airport when she heard her father's voice again. *My child, this is your last chance. Write that letter to the English police now.*

"But what about our bargain? I promised I wouldn't split."

And after all he did to you, my daughter, you think you're bound by a promise?

Obedient as always, she reached for pen and paper.

Antony Mann

ESTHER GORDON FRAMLINGHAM

■ ■ ■

Antony Mann is an Australian writer currently living in Oxford, U.K., with his wife, Judy, and young son, Zachary. His short fiction has appeared in many magazines and journals, including The Third Alternative, Crimewave, London Magazine, *and* Ellery Queen's Mystery Magazine. *He was the 1999 winner of the U.K. Crime Writers' Association Short Story Dagger for "Taking Care of Frank." His fiction has twice received Honorable Mentions in Ellen Datlow and Terri Windling's* The Year's Best Fantasy & Horror *series, and in 2000 his story "Gunned Down" was broadcast on BBC Radio 4 as one of only five stories selected nationwide for their New Writers' Week. "Esther Gordon Framlingham," originally published in* Crimewave, *and from his short-story collection* Milo & I, *has been shortlisted for the 2003 CWA Short Fiction Dagger. A good writer can find criminous elements practically anywhere, and Antony Mann is no exception. In this short story, he gets to the heart of a problem plaguing more than one mystery writer today—the problem of originality.*

How about a late seventeenth-century Russian peasant?" I asked. Across the room, my agent Myra raised an eyebrow.

"North or south?"

"South."

"Been done."

"Ah, I meant north," I said quickly. Myra shook her head.

"Sorry, been done," she said. "Sheila Trescothick's Ivan the Irascible series. Ivan's an irascible Russian peasant, disliked by all and sundry in his small northern Russian village, tolerated only because of his extraordinary ability to solve the most perplexing of crimes."

"Yeah yeah, I get the idea. Okay. Try this on for size." I read from the bottom of my list. "A nineteenth-century Peruvian goatherd, male, between thirteen and sixteen years old, an amateur sleuth who solves crimes across the local mountain community?"

"Nu-uh. Stan Archer. The Miguel Goatchild books."

I didn't think it was necessary that Myra smile so hugely, but you can't say she didn't have a sense of humor. She all but clapped her hands in merriment. A slim and businesslike thirty-five with wavy auburn hair and sharp, intelligent eyes, she'd been taking fifteen percent of my very little for three years now.

"Oh, yeah." I nodded. "I've heard of them. Vaguely."

"They've won awards," said Myra.

"Of course they have. Works of genius."

The room was as light as the small windows and the overtaxed bulb in the frilly shade would allow. The main office was out the door left. Out there, clacking and ringing noises sank meekly into the thick carpet. This was reception, where Myra sat her writers down for chats. It smelled of my grandfather's aftershave. He was dead. One wall—floor to ceiling—was devoted entirely to books on shelves, both fiction and nonfiction, hardback and soft. These were the books that over the years Myra had sold on behalf of her clients. It was impressive. It said, *I'm a successful agent, I place lots of manuscripts*, and as always, I was impressed. But not one of them was mine.

I sighed and turned my attention back to my list. I'd started with thirty-six brilliant ideas for crime-fiction sleuths that didn't yet exist. Or so I'd thought. Now, there remained only one not crossed off. "Myra, don't piss me around now, because this is my last shot. Are you sitting comfortably? A dominant Neanderthal male at the time of the Cro-Magnon . . ."

Myra was already shaking her head.

"No?" I whispered.

"Merlene Trent's Ug Oglog novels. You mean to say you don't know them?"

"They've won awards?"

"They're big in New Zealand."

"Lucky New Zealand. May it sink without a ripple, both islands. Well, that's that. By my reckoning, there's now a fictional detective for every profession across every social class from each and every region in the entire history of mankind, including the future, parallel universes, and q-space."

"What can I say? Crime fiction's going through a purple patch."

I took my cup from the glass table between us and poured the dark tepid coffee down my throat. Like it was going to quench my thirst.

"So unless a writer dies—or gets murdered—there isn't a single opening left for a series gumshoe. And I'm stuck trying to write one-offs."

"No, no, that's no good," said Myra.

"I've got a great idea for one. There's this zeppelin pilot, see, and he gets drunk one night and accidentally kills the son of a wealthy local politician in a bar fight. He panics and runs off, but then this other guy who was at the bar finds him and blackmails him into flying the zeppelin into the Arctic Circle where the rich politician is secretly mining . . ."

"Nobody reads one-offs," said Myra firmly, stopping me in mid-plot. "If there isn't a recurring central character from book to book, readers simply get muddled and don't know what's happening. Sure, a resilient few can cope, but others tend to lose all sense of direction, even when they're sitting down. They get confused and worried. Some throw up. Do you really want to be responsible for making people ill?"

"Yes."

"I'm sorry, Paul," said Myra, as though she'd just told me no, she didn't want to change her gas supplier, not today, not any day. "Maybe if you'd been lead singer of a trendy Brit pop band, if you were a stand-up comic or celebrity gardener, you could get away with it."

"So what are you saying? That I'm all washed up before I get started? That it doesn't matter what I write, it won't find a publisher? This sucks. I'm going back to law school."

"I like your writing, Paul. I think you've got potential. That's why I'm going to tell you this. Esther Gordon Framlingham is dead."

"Who?"

"Esther Gordon Framlingham. She wrote the Father Rufus mysteries."

"Really? The little old lady with curly white hair and spectacles? I thought that was Mary Margaret Whitmore."

"It was Esther Gordon Framlingham too. They both have white hair."

"Oh. Dead, huh? That's a shame. Father Rufus, you say?" Now that I thought about it, I knew those books! Between Father Quentin and Father Septus in the alphabet, sixteenth-century abbot, sixteenth-century Exeter. "Yeah, yeah, I read some when I was growing up. They're kind of fruity, aren't they?"

"Fruity? No. Maybe you're thinking of Father Rastus. This is Father Rufus. There's no fruit. Anyhow, if you'll just let me finish my fucking thought for a change, what I was going to say was, Cantor isn't certain anymore that they want Esther Gordon Framlingham dead."

"Publishers can do that now, bring people back to life?"

"No no, well not the midsize ones like Cantor anyway. She's dead, but they haven't released the news yet."

"Crikey, does her family know?"

"Not yet. She's been a recluse for decades anyway."

"How did she die?"

"Boredom. Shut up and let me finish. Cantor would ideally like to keep the Father Rufus series going indefinitely, maybe even until the world is destroyed by a giant asteroid or consumed in the final implosion of the universe. Rufus is a brand name, and of course there's the TV series."

I filled Myra's pause, because she just left it out there for me.

"And they want someone to step into Esther Gordon Framlingham's shoes, ghostwrite the Rufus books?"

I filled another.

"And you want me to do it? Wouldn't that mean writing under her name?"

"To begin with. Esther Gordon Framlingham was frankly churning out shite toward the end there, and sales were drooping like my husband's dick. Cantor wants a team player, someone energetic and enthusiastic to become part of the brand."

"Someone who'll write for peanuts and do what they're told."

"You got it."

"I always thought you were a lesbian."

"Married twelve years this March. And so what if I'm gay? You threatened by that? But enough about me. The point is, Cantor might eventually be willing to let a new writer come up with their own books. If said writer can demonstrate increased sales with the ghostwritten stuff. And, of course, when society moves on and new gumshoe professions develop."

"How about lifestyle coach?" I said. "I've always wanted to write about a mystery-solving lifestyle coach, at any rate for the last four seconds. You can't say it's not contemporary, and no one else has . . ."

"Anne Portman. The Ralph de Silvian mysteries. De Silvian is a lifestyle coach who solves murders while coaching . . ."

"Yeah yeah, put a sock in it yourself for a change. I get the picture."

"Good. If you've got it, then don't go losing it. Anyhow, there is just the one other catch that I've omitted as yet to tell you about. Cantor has asked me to audition *two* writers for the Esther Gordon Framlingham job. You and one other."

And, she could do basic arithmetic.

"Who's the other lucky fool?"

"Jack Pantango."

"Doesn't ring a bell."

"That's the idea. The one who comes up with the best synopsis and three chapters in the next fortnight gets the nod."

"Didn't Esther Gordon Framlingham leave any story lines behind?"

"At least four hundred, but you don't get to see them unless you win."

"What if I don't like the idea of writing Father Rufus books?"

"Have a ball at law school."

Sleuth. Gumshoe. Detective. Private eye. They're all just another name for soft-spoken tonsured fifteenth-century cleric. I didn't do any research. I didn't need to. The more I thought about it, the more I vividly remembered the Father Rufus books from my childhood. It was my dad who bought the whole set by mail order, except for the ones that hadn't yet been written. I liked them so much I would always get to them first and devour them in a sitting. *The White Raven. Candlestyx. The False Witch. The Third Chamber.*

I recalled Dad reading them by the fire on chilly winter evenings. Whenever he finished one, he'd toss it into the flames, and reflectively watch it burn. What was he thinking about? Fire? Books? Books on fire? They were big thick volumes, but quick to read, and it wasn't exactly a huge fireplace. We were never cold, though.

It took me no more than a couple of days to thrash out the synopsis. I came up with a clever plot: this ship's captain gets drunk one night in an inn, see? And accidentally kills the son of a wealthy local nobleman during a fight. He panics and runs off, but then this other guy who was at the inn finds him and blackmails him into sailing the ship to the Arctic Circle where the rich nobleman is running a secret mining operation. Then Father Rufus is called in to solve all the assorted murders and associated mysteries that would no doubt crop up from time to time.

I was halfway through Chapter One when Jack Pantango got in touch.

He was ten years younger than me, and that was only the start of what irked me about him. For some reason he'd wanted to meet in The Juniper Tree, a crummy pub a half mile from Liverpool Street Station, which for me meant an inconvenient trek up from Tooting Broadway by tube. The Juniper Tree was undecorated in olive green wall carpet and those stupid bar mirrors covered in swirly bits that reflect life in swirls. The place was replete with fruit machines going ding, and tired-looking blue-collar types at the bar who'd never figured out how to get some expression into their faces.

Pantango himself was lean and boy-faced, good-looking, with his dark hair slicked back behind his ears.

"For some reason, I thought you'd be older," I was saying. "What are you? Twenty-two? Twenty-three?"

Across the table, Pantango was using the tips of his fingers to edge his half pint of lime-and-lemonade in a circle, watching the ice try to keep up as the glass moved around it. He was from the East End, and spoke deliberately, as though it was me who was the idiot.

"Mr. Gadd, it's like this."

"Call me Paul," I said.

"I won't, if you don't mind. It'll make it easier what I have to say, if we keep it on a business footing."

"Ha, that sounds a bit serious." My attempt at a laugh betrayed me somewhat by sticking fast to the insides of my throat. "Congratulations, by the way, on getting in on this Esther Gordon Framlingham audition. Have you been on Myra's books for long?"

"Who?"

"She's not your agent? Well, congrats anyway. It's very young to be expecting to land this sort of job, so don't be too disappointed if it's me who ends up with the banana. But don't feel you don't have a chance, because I honestly think you do."

"End up with the banana? What the fuck are you talking about?" He stopped spinning the glass and raised his voice, and the heads of blokes at the bar moved the inch required for their eyes to note what was going on. I got annoyed again as I realized I was up against an authentic cheeky chappy Cockney geezer who no doubt didn't balk at having to punch people in the face. Plus he was probably a supergifted natural writer who'd be great on TV and radio and look smooth on the back of a jacket sleeve, who'd most likely soon write the definitive London working-class novel on the proceeds of the Esther Gordon Framlingham job. Which should have been mine.

"Is that a South American name?" I said. "Pantango? You do look a bit Spanish."

Though I only meant to a little, I was making him angry a lot, and now, in my general direction, he poked at the air with his finger.

"Mr. Gadd," he said, keeping something nasty corked up that I was glad not to see. "Believe me, I want to say this twice, but if it does end up being only once, then you've saved yourself a smashed kneecap. The Esther Gordon Framlingham job is Jack Pantango's, right? It's a payday for me that I'm not going to miss, plus apparently there's other perks that go with. Like there's chicks and drugs, yeah? So get it fucking straight. There's no discussion on this that won't lead to some breakage."

The further annoyance, of this upstart punk who wanted to steal my big chance referring to himself in the third person as though he could present himself objectively to the world at large—a habit I've always despised, even in myself—was the last straw. Though by his expression he was almost begging me to, I had no choice but to protest.

"Sorry," I said, standing and draining my glass in one. "I've been working toward this Esther Gordon Framlingham thing for the last five years. Actually, I haven't been working toward it at all, but it'll have to do until something better comes along. Do what you have to, but don't forget, a writer writes with his brain, not his kneecaps. I cite as an example that French guy who was paralyzed but still wrote a book using his eyelid to press down the keys on his typewriter? Or what was it? Come to think of it, it couldn't have been that." I turned to the assembled heads at the bar, all now facing in my direction, assaulting me with their mild amusement and indifference. "Does anyone remember the name of that book, or the guy's name even? I never read it myself. Anyway, don't forget him!"

With that, I walked out, turning no more than four or five times to see if Pantango was following. But he just sat there, staring at me, a small, hard smile on his face, and I could tell, he would soon be beating my fucking head in.

As it turned out, he didn't want to beat me up. He wanted to kill me. I found out soon enough when, halfway along the darkest stretch of the lane that ran from The Juniper Tree toward Liverpool Street Station, where the only real illumination in fifty yards came from the filthed-up windows of a heat-trap chippie selling last month's grease in tonight's batter, he came at me from the shadows near a roll-up corrugated doorway with a blade that somehow found light enough to glint back into my eyes.

It turned out also that, even supposing he was a young upstart writer of some talent, he was lousy at killing people. Lunging forward to puncture my squawk of surprise, he tripped on the cobbles of the footpath and his feet skittered out from under him. In retrospect, it was comical, the way he twisted as he fell, the way the air and city smog was forced from his lungs with a grunt as he hit the ground. Even funnier, if you're amused by that kind of thing, was the way the knife in his hand went straight through his eye into his brain. Ha ha. Ha.

I would have called the police, or at least simply walked away, but I was still finding Jack Pantango pretty annoying, not least because he'd just tried to stab me. So, avoiding the spreading pool of blood, I searched his pockets for wallet and keys. I had a vague notion of finding out where he lived and breaking in. On the slim chance his Esther Gordon Framlingham idea was superior to my own, I could steal it with impunity.

It was his wallet that told me he wasn't Jack Pantango at all. According to his driver's license, Gardner Beam had been twenty-five years old, and had lived in Bow, and had looked less like a thug in real life than in passport-sized photos. I also found a sheet of ruled notebook paper, folded in four. On it someone had written, in inverted commas, "Jack Pantango," and an address in Highgate.

It was dark, but early still, so I bought an A–Z from the kiosk at Liverpool Street and caught the tube across town. Pantango lived in a modern block of flats halfway up North Hill, a corner place set back behind a laurel hedge—three stories of pocket-sized balconies painted white, faintly luminous in the moonlight amid the beige brickwork.

I got through the security entrance on the coattails of an old man in a black business suit who didn't see me. He was halfway up the first flight of stairs before the front door had gently squeezed against my foot.

It was a woman who opened the door to apartment nine. Maybe because I hadn't buzzed she was expecting to see a neighbor—she opened her mouth to speak, then shut it again, and I saw a shadow of trepidation cross her eyes.

"Yes?"

She was fiftyish, a short frump in a kitchen-curtain floral dress that was keeping her ample bosom in check. Her hair was stiff and dark and looked like a wooden salad bowl, something you'd maybe pay a tenner for at a crafts fair, inverted and plonked on her head.

"Hi," I said. "I'm looking for Jack Pantango."

That made her start, and she would have shut the door in my face if I hadn't stuck out a hand and stopped her.

"I don't mean to be rude, but it's important. Is he home?"

She didn't turn around and look back into the apartment like I thought she might have done if he'd been there. She just stared straight at me, then sighed deeply, and her shoulders sagged along with her face.

"You'd better come in."

"It's okay for *you*," she said, not bothering to hide the bitterness. "You're not all that fat and you're not that old."

"Thanks very much."

We sat in her kitchen, at the table, drinking weak tea by the light of the fluorescent tube. The wall tiles were gaudy with cutesy kitten pictures, and there was a plastic water filter near the sink. She was a Jackie, not a Jack, but she was a Pantango.

"Me?" she went on. "I'm fifty-four and plain ugly. I'm a part-time surveyor with an arthritic left knee. Do you really think I could ever make it as a writer? What publisher is going to want to promote *me*?"

"What about your writing?"

"What's it got to do with that? Sure, if I had some claim to fame. Christ, why didn't I become a politician? Or a bus driver?"

"Do something quirky, like wheel a microwave around the Outer Hebrides. Write about that," I said. "Are you a virgin? That'd help."

"Maybe, but only if I was proud of it. That's why I hired Beam, you see? He was going to be my public face, do the interviews and appearances when I got famous, and I was going to pay him a retainer from my royalties. Plus he was a cheap Cockney thug, so I thought he could scare you off into the bargain."

"You didn't tell him that being a writer meant that he'd get lots of women and drugs, did you?"

"I thought that might make the deal more attractive."

"He believed you on that?"

She refilled my cup.

"I'm sorry about the knife thing. Did he really try to kill you?"

"I think that was just for his own enjoyment." I said, "Jesus, Jackie, what was the point? The Esther Gordon Framlingham job, it's faceless anyway! It's anonymous hack work for a few bucks!"

"Oh, but it could lead to other things, don't you think?" she said, almost plaintively.

"Oh, it could do," I said. "But for me, not for you."

It was simple enough. Pantango didn't have a choice. In return for me not going to the police about Gardner Beam, she left the way clear for me to secure the Esther Gordon Framlingham gig.

I finished my Father Rufus chapters, then sent them off to Myra, and a week or so later she called me into her office.

"This is good stuff," she told me as she slapped the typescript down onto the reception-room table. "The writing is tight. The characters are real. The story is strong."

I was grinning in anticipation.

"And it's funny," said Myra, "because Jack Pantango rang me during the week and told me she was no longer interested. Wouldn't say why. But that leaves just you."

"You knew Jack Pantango was a woman?"

"Of course I knew he was a woman. He's one of my people."

"Christ, why didn't you tell me?"

"Why the fuck should I? What's it to you? Anyhow, you didn't get the job."

There was nothing I could say to that which wouldn't come out all sulky and disappointed and wrong, so I said, "Why not? You just told me yourself you liked what I wrote! What's the problem? This isn't fair!"

"What's the problem?" She slid the chapters over. "I wanted synopsis and three chapters on Father Rufus. You've given me *Brother* Rufus."

"I've . . . what?"

"I don't want sixteenth-century Exeter! I want fifteenth-century Bath! I want Esther Gordon Framlingham, not Edna Williams Dickinson!"

Bloody hell, I'd written about the wrong detective. Sure, a mistake anyone could have made, but could I really have *remembered* it all so wrong, those vivid unimpeachable memories, my father by the fire with a book, my father, the book, the fire? How clear it still seemed.

"Whoops," I said. "But no harm done. Let's just switch the dates and places, and make it a Father Rufus story anyway."

"What, and destroy the authenticity? No thanks, buster. In any case, I was going to tell you this if you *had* got the job, so I'll tell you now too. Cantor has decided to keep Esther Gordon Framlingham breathing a while longer. So there's no big break."

"What do you mean, keep her breathing and there's no big break? I thought that was the precise reason there *was* a big break!"

"There's another teensy thing I neglected to tell you. The real Esther Gordon Framlingham has actually been dead sixteen years. When I told you that Cantor was looking for someone to ghostwrite the Esther Gordon Framlinghams, maybe I should have said they were really looking for someone to replace the Esther Gordon Framlingham ghostwriter who's been churning the books out for the last decade and a half. But now they've changed their minds and kept it to the status quo. Sorry about that."

"Esther Gordon Framlingham has been dead sixteen years?"

"Her flesh has."

"Does her family know?" In a way, I was relieved. I was a big fan of Brother Rufus, but Father Rufus I could take or leave. But I had an idea. "Hey, what about this? Contemporary fifty-something virginal female part-time surveyor from Highgate with an arthritic left knee."

"*Part-time* surveyor, you say? Because of course you know the Donna Cable mysteries by Rod Binks, but I think she's full-time . . ."

"Definitely part-time," I said.

"Hmmm. Interesting. You might have hit on something. Why don't you write me synopsis and three chapters?"

John Lutz

NIGHTHAWKS

■ ■ ■

Two-time Shamus Award–winner John Lutz has produced more than thirty novels and two hundred short stories. His SWF Seeks Same *was the basis for the 1992 movie* Single White Female *starring Bridget Fonda and Jennifer Jason Leigh. Recent books include* The Night Spider *and a collection of his short fiction* Endless Road and Other Stories. *He splits his time between Webster Groves, Missouri, and sunny Florida. He is a master of the spare, lean, fast-moving short mystery story, and our selection for this year, "Nighthawks," is no exception. First published in the most recent* Flesh & Blood *erotic mystery anthology* Guilty as Sin, *it is an unflinching glimpse into the mind of a lonely woman, and the lengths to which she'll go to end her solitude.*

What was she doing here?

Amy often asked herself that, shying away from the answer every time. She looked around at the rest of the people in Nighthawks, all about her age—thirty something—and most of them smiling and having a good time. The place was large, and though the music was loud there was room for tables toward the back, where it was dim and something like quiet and people could talk and understand each other.

Well, they could talk and come to an understanding.

Amy sat at one of those tables where she had a good view of the dance floor. The band was live and in desperate good cheer, playing the hits. During the fast tunes with lots of drums and bass, most people on the crowded floor danced alone, or fast danced barely touching hands. During the slow tunes, they clung to each other as if they were drowning.

"Ready?" the barmaid whose name was Nancy asked Amy, suddenly appearing at her elbow.

Amy nodded. "You bet."

She watched Nancy glide among the tables, then along the edge of the dance floor toward the long bar. There were a lot of illuminated, brightly colored liquor advertisements behind the bar, and softly colored lights from sconces set all around the lounge, with more of the glowing advertisements mounted here and there on the walls. The total effect was a flattering, uniform light, faintly pink, that softened features, did wonders for the complexion, and temporarily deleted years and wisdom. The bar itself was always busy by this time, eight o'clock, with patrons perched on or standing alongside stools, and others massed behind them waiting for an opening so they could order drinks.

Ollie, the regular bartender and part owner of Nighthawks, was a huge man in his forties who had once been a light-heavyweight professional boxer. He'd gained weight since then, and would have to fight heavyweight now. Amy liked him. He was always friendly to everyone, and especially the women in a protective way. And his massive bulk and thickened, once-handsome features commanded respect from some of the men who couldn't hold their liquor and wanted to hold everything else.

But the biggest thing behind the bar, where you might expect to see a mirror, was the painting. A print, actually, much larger than the original. The owner of Nighthawks was a big fan of the artist Edward Hopper and his famous painting, after which the lounge was named. Amy often sat studying the painting, the stark image of a city diner late at night. Visible through the window were three lonely people at the counter, and the white-uniformed guy who waited on them. Inhabitants of a spare, cruel world. Everyone in the painting looked tired. Or bored. Definitely lonely. Difficult to know for sure what they were thinking. For some reason they were up late. For some reason they couldn't or wouldn't sleep. Not yet. Amy could understand why the owner liked the painting.

"Mind if a sexy single man sits down with you?" a voice asked behind Amy.

Amy knew that the voice, deep and throaty though it was, didn't belong to a man; it was Janice's.

Janice Walker was Amy's age and worked with her at Needlington, where they manufactured speedometers for cars. Janice came to Nighthawks for the same reason Amy did, to meet men. Not that there weren't plenty of men working at Needlington. It was just that they were either married or the kind you'd just as soon not meet. It was the first time the two women had seen each other today, though it was Friday, a workday. Amy had taken most of the day off for a doctor's appointment, and Janice had gotten off work at the plant just three hours ago.

"Sit your handsome, penile self down," Amy said, pulling out a chair for Janice. Nancy arrived with Amy's second margarita, and Janice sat down and ordered a whiskey sour. Like Amy, she was a reasonably attractive brunette, though Amy felt that her figure was certainly better than Janice's, who was a little light on top. Amy's face was heart-shaped and retained some of youth's innocence. Janice's features were leaner and harsher, with a tautness as if she'd perversely had cosmetic surgery to make herself appear older. Unlike Amy, she'd been married, and to a man who talked with his fists. Janice had told Amy that the day they'd met at Needlington two years ago. Though both women hadn't captured the knack of long-term relationships with the opposite sex, neither had given up, so they became friends and sometimes referred to themselves as sister stalkers. Neither liked to think of herself as prey.

"How long you been here?" Janice asked. She had her tight dark skirt and a blue sweater on today, maybe some kind of bra that made her boobs look larger and gave her improbable uplift.

"One drink," Amy said.

"You look morose."

"Do I? I'm just sitting here as usual, denying reality."

"You shouldn't be ironic; it's a turnoff. None of these guys has walked over here and asked if he could kiss every part of you?"

"Not yet." Amy licked salt from her glass rim and took a sip of margarita. "That one over there, sitting at the end of the bar, gives me the glance now and then." She nodded toward a slender, dark-haired man, mid-thirties, coiled on a bar stool in the way of the tall and wiry, staring into the beer mug he was holding with both hands. "He looks like he oughta be playing Hamlet, doesn't he?"

Janice turned back from staring at the man. "Yeah. He's almost too pretty to be a guy. Like he's the kind that might leave you testing HIV positive."

"You're being kinda rough on him."

"Am I? That kind of tragic figure has his appeal, but you better leave him to enjoy his suffering alone."

"You know him?"

"Of him. All I need to know. Used to work at Needlington. His name is Jerry. I don't know his last name." Janice leaned closer to Amy and lowered her voice. "Rumor is he tested positive."

"Oh? Just rumor?"

"Strong rumor, and good enough for me. They say it's the reason he had to quit rather than be fired. That way he walked away with severance pay. He's a looker, but I wouldn't get near him. Not that I don't feel sorry for him, but he's not the kind of ladykiller I dream about."

"He probably wouldn't be in here if he was gay," Amy said speculatively.

"True. But maybe he goes both ways."

"Should I care?"

Janice stared at her. "Aren't you the liberated hussy?"

Another sip of margarita. "Yeah, maybe I am." Amy didn't completely believe Janice, who had a way of stretching the truth. "If he's in here to date, like we are, you're saying he's a mass murderer."

Janice looked startled. "Well, I wouldn't say that."

"Of course," Amy said, staring into her drink the way Jerry was staring into his beer, "we're all going to die."

Janice gave her phlegmy laugh. "Sure we are. But you know what they say: timing in death is everything."

Maybe time is everything, Janice thought.

A tall man wearing a horrible green sports coat that looked as if it had been tailored from pool-table felt ambled over with intense casualness and asked Janice to dance. Amy had seen him before, even danced with him. His name was Harvey, she was pretty sure. All she really remembered about him other than that was that he had bad breath.

For several minutes Amy sat and watched Harvey and Janice slow dance. They might be a longtime married couple, she mused, with as many years behind them as ahead. Harvey leaned down and kissed Janice on the neck beneath her left ear. Janice grinned over at Amy, who felt slightly nauseated.

Jerry, she noticed, had gotten down from his stool at the bar. He was dancing with a short, Latin-looking girl Amy hadn't seen before. They were standing far apart and talking animatedly, looking into each other's eyes. Amy wondered if the woman knew she was dancing with a mass murderer. The music ended, Jerry and his partner said a few more words to each other, then they split and the woman sashayed back to her table while Jerry ignored her and walked back toward the bar. Typical male rutter, Amy thought. Probably struck out, so he no longer gave a fuck about the woman. But she liked the way Jerry walked, like a lean western gunfighter who might draw and fire any second. Something lethal in that walk.

The band had swung into another slow number before too many dancers left the floor. Janice and Harvey had hit it off and were going around again. Amy didn't know why, or at least at that point wasn't sure why, but she stood up and intercepted Jerry the mass murderer before he reached his still vacant bar stool.

He noticed her approach and stopped, staring at her like a carnivore who couldn't believe one of the wary herd was actually approaching him. The closer she got, the handsomer was Jerry. Lean but well muscled, tanned and tendoned and tight. Clean white shirt under a well-cut blue blazer, wearing Levi's and thin-soled buffed moccasins. It had probably taken him a while before the mirror to get that one thick lock of curly dark hair to dangle just so over his forehead. Johnny Ringo in town and cruising for action.

"I saw you out there dancing," Amy said, "and figured you were worse than I was. It gave me the confidence to approach you."

He smiled at her. Great teeth. "Show me what I'm doing wrong," he said, and held out his hand for her.

On the dance floor he was surprisingly smooth, and knew how to lead if you got up next to him like the Latin woman hadn't. She could feel his lean body working.

"You spend a lotta time in here?" he asked.

"It seems like a lot."

"So you live around here?"

She smiled up at him. "I live wherever I am."

He returned the smile, not yet able to believe this all the way. "I'm Jerry," he said.

"Amy Fortrell."

"Sounds like a soap-opera name."

"Jerry sounds like a first name."

"Oh. Sorry. It's Jerry Graves."

"What about you? Do you live around here?"

"Depends on the definition."

"That's vague," Amy said, tired of circling and fencing, of wasting time. "Maybe we should be more specific with each other. Maybe you should show me exactly where you live."

He was staring curiously at her, still disbelieving his good luck. "Why?"

"So I can find it next time."

As they left together, the Latin woman was staring.

He lived in a small apartment with a threadbare imitation oriental carpet and old walnut furniture so dark it was almost black. There was a coffee table, two end tables with matching blue lamps, a framed painting of a vase of flowers that wasn't very good. In a corner sat an ancient television with a coiled wire on top where a cable box or VCR might have sat. The apartment was clean, though, and a glance into the small kitchen detected no unwashed dishes.

What am I doing here? Amy asked herself, as she'd asked herself earlier that evening in Nighthawks, as if momentarily bobbing to the surface of a dream. But she knew what she was doing there.

She knew.

"Where's the bed?" she asked.

"It folds down from the wall."

"Show me," she said, thinking Jerry had the longest eyelashes she'd ever seen on a man.

What passed for the bedroom in the apartment was an area behind a large three-part folding screen with Chinese figures on it. The screen concealed a small bureau and chair, and a table with a lamp made from a big ceramic jug. Jerry moved the table and lamp a few feet to the side, then pulled a Murphy bed down from where it was folded into the wall. Amy had never seen a Murphy bed before and was surprised when it emerged from the wall already, if sloppily, made. There were even a couple of soft pillows that had been pinned between mattress and wall and were now regaining their plumpness. Under one of the pillows was yesterday's newspaper, the sports page. Jerry absently tossed it aside.

They made love fiercely on the soft and squealing old bed, holding tight to each other as if a hurricane might try to separate them. Amy knew the reason for their desperate lovemaking, but Jerry didn't know of her secret knowledge. As he rolled off her she saw a reddened scab on his back, but she didn't mention it.

She lay on her back staring at the pattern of cracks in the ceiling, feeling a bead of perspiration slowly tracking down her right breast. Her heart was pounding and her blood roared like a wild river in her ears.

"You're amazing," Jerry said, sitting up next to her on the sweat-damp mattress. He bent down and licked the bead of perspiration from her breast, then stood up and walked to a wall switch. The paddle fan above the bed began revolving slowly, casting more shadow than air.

"It's missing a few speeds," he explained, returning to the bed.

"You're not missing any speed at all," Amy said.

He laughed, grabbing her, and they wrestled. The old Murphy bed's springs were howling.

"Don't you have a neighbor we might disturb?" Amy asked.

"Maybe," Jerry said, pinning her to the mattress and nuzzling her ear. "I don't give a fuck."

"Oh, yes you do!" Amy said, laughing. She knew she sounded like a woman more interested in sex than in love, but she didn't care.

He kissed her, and her dread had to wait in the distance.

When he pulled away this time, she was smiling. Loneliness was over.

It was perfect for more than a month. She never asked him about why he'd lost his job at Needlington. He never asked her how come she hadn't heard about him and his problems. She went into work every day but saw less and less of Janice. Amy thought it best not to confide in her friend about this current hot affair. Jerry disappeared from time to time during the day, saying he was going job hunting. She didn't believe him and didn't care if he was lying. His unemployment checks came regularly in the mail, so she supposed he was at least going through the motions of looking for work so he wouldn't be dropped from the dole. But if he wasn't really looking very hard, she couldn't blame him. One thing she'd learned, there came a time in life when you had to think of yourself, even pamper yourself. Maybe that should be dismissed as the philosophy of the young. Maybe sometimes the young got it right.

But when Amy came home from work with a headache one afternoon, Jerry surprised her. He'd told her he'd be gone until evening, and as usual she hadn't asked where. When she opened the door at a few minutes past two, then walked to the kitchen sink to get a glass of water and glanced out the window, there he was sitting beneath the scraggly oak tree in the backyard. He was slumped in a webbed old aluminum lounge chair with one foot propped up on an empty cardboard box.

Amy carried her glass of water and went down the back stairs and outside.

She must have been downwind; she smelled the marijuana from twenty feet away.

He didn't notice her approach, or he might have flicked away the joint.

"Are you nuts?" she asked, glancing back at the wall of apartment windows behind her. "Anybody looking outside can see you."

He appeared surprised to find her there but didn't look particularly guilty. He was wearing a sleeveless T-shirt and his curly dark hair was mussed, the way she liked it. "They'll see me smoking a cigarette, is all."

She moved toward him, and he tossed the half-smoked joint away. It landed between some flowers bordering the walk and smoldered. He smiled sadly up at her. "Does it really make any difference?"

She swallowed. "No, I suppose not."

"Why did you come home early?"

"Headache," she said.

"Still got it?"

"No."

They went upstairs, undressed, and made love with a new seriousness and intentness. They were both perspiring furiously and his kisses smelled like grass. He stared into her eyes as he mounted her and began thrusting, and she stared back and gave him every part of herself, to the farthest corner of her soul.

When they were finished they lay side by side exhausted, the paddle fan flailing away above them. It was humming and ticking and moving only warm air. There were bite marks on Jerry's chest and shoulders. Amy knew there were similar marks on her neck, some on her breasts. She knew her fingernails had raked patterns of possession in his back.

"I don't want to live without you," she said.

"That's the idea," he told her.

They were both still breathing hard enough that the bedsprings sang beneath them. Amy was so happy she considered not keeping the doctor's appointment she had tomorrow.

But in the morning she felt differently, and she did keep it.

And that changed everything.

Amy knew Janice had been surprised when she phoned and asked if they could meet at Nighthawks the next evening. But Amy had to tell someone before she told Jerry, who had driven to the next town to look for work and wasn't due to return until late that night.

When they were settled at a table where they could talk, Janice said, "Since you weren't at work today, I figured you might be sick."

"I did go to the doctor this morning," Amy said. "I didn't come in to work this afternoon because I felt . . . I don't know, I guess like complaining to somebody."

Janice gave her an odd look. "This is about Jerry?"

"This is about a cruel trick."

"I warned you about him, Amy."

"It isn't what you think. It's been fantastic. It's worked all the way with Jerry."

Janice smiled at her as if she were hopeless. Amy knew what she must be thinking: all the way with Jerry couldn't be very much farther.

Nancy arrived with a margarita for Amy, a whiskey sour for Janice, and a bowl of pretzels and mixed nuts.

"My cancer is in remission!" Amy blurted out, as soon as Nancy was out of earshot.

Janice gave her an astounded look. "*What* cancer?"

"I'm told now it might not even *be* cancer. Six weeks ago the doctors analyzed my MRI and CAT scan tests and told me I had a spot on my brain that figured to be a tumor. It was in an inoperable place and they thought it was probably malignant. This morning I went in for the results of more tests, and the spot is half its original size. They tell me they must have misdiagnosed it the first time. They still aren't sure what it is, but now their guess is that it's a blood mass, possibly from a mild aneurysm, and it might disappear altogether. It certainly isn't cancerous."

"But you thought it was and you didn't tell me! Or anyone else, did you?"

"I couldn't. I didn't want to believe it."

"My God, Amy!"

"Crazy as it sounds, I thought if I told someone it might . . . well, make it all the way true." Amy took a sip of margarita. Janice had reached across the table and was gripping her free hand. Her eyes were moist. Amy said, "You're a good friend, Janice . . ."

Janice swallowed, then dabbed at her eyes with the white paper napkin that had come with her drink. "I guess that explains Jerry. Did you tell *him*? I mean six weeks ago, when you thought you didn't have long to live?"

"Not then or now."

Janice sat back, looking at her old friend, obviously wondering how well she really knew Amy. "I don't understand. Why don't you tell him now? You have wonderful news to share."

"I can't." Amy bowed her head and tears came. "I mean, that's the cruel trick I was talking about. The irony. At least it might be ironic, what happens to me. Maybe my good news is only temporary. Not that I don't deserve whatever happens. Jerry and I both thought we were living the last, best parts of our lives together. Running out of time on earth together. And maybe we still are, only on a different timetable. We're both caught in a trap. Christ, Janice, how can I burden a sick man with all that guilt? How can I tell him?"

Janice shook her head in disbelief. "Wait a sec, Amy. Let me catch up. *Jerry's* sick?"

Amy gazed across the table through a blur of tears, surprised. "Of course he is. You know, he's HIV positive . . ."

"Jesus! Jerry has AIDS?"

"I don't know if it's gone that far yet. I think I've seen some symptoms. We don't talk about it. We have a kind of tacit understanding."

"So you both thought you'd die together," Janice said. "And now he might have given you . . . Oh, Amy! When did you find out he was ill?"

Amy withdrew her hand that was about to lift her glass and cocked her head to the side. "Six weeks ago, when you told me."

"When *I* told you? Amy, I never said Jerry had AIDS!"

"But you did!" Amy's mind was whirling. "Right here at this table. You said that was why he lost his job at Needlington. He tested positive and somehow the company found out about it. He had to quit rather than risk his severance pay."

"Amy, he tested positive for drugs! Somebody in Personnel told me his urine sample showed he'd recently ingested narcotics!"

Amy slumped back in her chair, not noticing she'd spilled part of her drink on her jeans. Janice was right! She hadn't actually said *what* Jerry had tested positive for! Amy had filled in the blanks and filled them in wrong. Oh, *how* wrong!

Then the shock of what Janice had said began to wear off, and something light and wonderful rushed in. How happy, how joyous Amy was that she'd misunderstood Janice! Jerry was going to live! She was going to live! Their love was going to live! Nothing was forever, but right now, all the time in eternity seemed to be theirs. Amy's gaze fell on the *Nighthawks* print behind the bar. Never had she felt so far removed from the lonely souls in the sparse, desolate diner!

She stood up, rummaged in her purse, and tossed a crumpled twenty-dollar bill on the table to pay for the drinks.

Janice was staring up at her, trying to process yet another development. "Amy, where are you going?"

"I've got to get to the stores before they close. I need flowers, candles, and champagne! Two bottles! I want to be waiting for Jerry when he comes home tonight."

"Amy!" Janice's sharp tone stopped her.

"I'm so happy for you!" Janice said when Amy turned to look back.

As soon as Amy closed the apartment door behind her, she realized Jerry was already home. She knew from the faint noises, the warmth, and the scent.

She could hear the familiar singing of the old Murphy bed's springs behind the trifold screen. She could see the rhythmic interplay of shadows cast by the dim light near the bed.

Not even thinking to put down her bouquet of freshly cut flowers, or the paper sacks that held French champagne bottles and her new silk nightgown, she walked silently to look behind the screen.

Jerry was making love to another woman. On top of her, holding her legs folded back, grunting each time he powered himself into her. Amy could hear her moans. One of her hands was clinging to his bare back, the other waving wildly in the air as if trying to grasp something that wasn't there.

Amy must have made a sound. Or maybe Jerry simply somehow knew she was there.

He stopped his mad thrusting, raised himself up on his elbows, and peered back at Amy. The woman craned her neck to see where he was staring. A thin face, blond hair, startled eyes—Amy recognized her from Accounting at Needlington. Pamela, she thought her name was.

"Jesus!" the woman whose name might be Pamela said.

Jerry let out a long breath. "No," he said, gasping for air, "it's Amy." Making a joke of it. Trying to.

Amy didn't remember gripping the neck of one of the champagne bottles, didn't remember moving to the bed. Jerry said, "Ow!" Once. Said nothing the second time the heavy bottle struck his skull hard enough to crush it.

"Jesus!" Pamela screamed, trying to work herself out from beneath Jerry's inert body. They were both slick with perspiration and she couldn't get a grip on him that didn't slip off. She started kicking her long legs, the backs of her thighs still red where Jerry had held her. "Jesus!" she screamed again.

"Amy," Amy corrected her, and swung the bottle sideways across Pamela's face.

Pamela somehow flung herself out from beneath Jerry and fell to the other side of the bed. Amy walked around the foot of the bed and saw that she was frantically digging among the pile of her clothes on the floor, in her purse. Did she have a gun in there. Amy didn't care.

Pamela stood up, blood streaming down her face, one eye closed. She didn't have a gun; she had a knife. No, a long nail file.

Amy stepped toward her, the champagne bottle raised, feeling the sting of the metal file piercing her shoulder and breast. She brought the bottle down on Pamela's head again and again, this time hard enough to break the glass and send glistening shards and foam over Pamela's face there on the floor.

Absently, Amy stared down at the nail file protruding from the top of her left breast. Then she looked at Pamela's nude body, streaked with blood and champagne. Pamela was a big woman, lodged between the bed and the wall. She looked dead but she might not be. Still, it would take her a while to get unstuck, the way one of her legs was bent beneath her.

Amy's expression didn't change as she pulled the metal nail file from her breast and tossed it on the floor. Jerry looked dead, too, the way one of his eyes was open and the other closed, but he might not be. It was hard to know for sure when people were really dead.

Amy went into the kitchen and got a proper knife.

Now Amy knew for sure what the *Nighthawks* painting meant. She wished she could be part of it, safely inside the starkly illuminated diner and away from life's irony and tricks. The people in the painting weren't lonely—they were there so they *wouldn't* be lonely. Outside the diner's glass windows was the night, and inside was light and the comfort of coffee and conversation. Not that the diners and the short-order cook behind the counter weren't sad. They knew, and the painter Hopper knew, that the diner was only a temporary shelter in an inevitable journey, a stop along the way. The irony and loneliness were out there waiting. The night would always return, and one time forever.

Amy thought a lot about the famous painting, sometimes actually trying to will herself into it. The guards let her keep a torn-out color illustration of it that she'd found in a magazine and taped to her cell wall on Death Row.

The magazine was *Time*.

Dick Lochte

Low Tide

■ ■ ■

Dick Lochte is the author of the award-winning Sleeping Dog *(recently named one of the 100 Favorite Mysteries of the Century by the Independent Booksellers Association) and the short-story collection* Lucky Dog and Other Tales of Murder, *both of which feature his irascible private eye, Leo Bloodworth, and his teenage assistant, Serendipity. He is also the coauthor, with attorney Christopher Darden, of several legal thrillers, including* The Last Defense. *Short stories are a great way for authors to experiment with characters and scenarios that would fall outside a series' character's world. In "Low Tide," also published in* Flesh & Blood: Guilty as Sin, *Lochte does just that, revealing a dark underbelly to sunny California, which, by the way, is where he also makes his home.*

Shay studied the customer's driver's license. It had been issued by the State of California approximately two years before. It stated that the name of the woman standing across the counter was Noreen Waldman and that she'd been born eighteen years ago. Her photo indicated that since she'd posed for the DMV Noreen had gone through a few changes. The brunette bangs and rosy cheeks had been traded in for a platinum rooster cut and a chalk-powdered face accentuated by jet eyebrows and purple-black lipstick. Instead of a pressed schoolgirl blouse, Noreen was wearing a boutique-tattered T-shirt over latticed black spandex tights.

The bank was located on L.A.'s Sunset Strip, an area not known for its conservative style of dress, but the girl was pushing it, Shay thought. And her orchid musk was almost as toxic as sewer gas.

But she did have a body on her.

"That's a screamin' corsage," Noreen Waldman said, pointing a black fingernail at the violet flower pinned to Shay's blouse. "I'm going org just looking at it."

Shay responded with a brief, patronizing smile. She placed the ID on the marble counter and picked up the check Noreen Waldman wanted to cash. It was for the sum of fifteen hundred dollars and no cents from Aristo Escorts, Inc., made out to "Nasty Wald." Shay looked at the girl and raised a questioning eyebrow.

"*Nom de* business," the girl said.

Trying to ignore another blast of the orchid musk, Shay turned the check over. It was properly endorsed. "How would you like it?" she asked.

"In my hand."

"I mean, in what denominations, large or small?"

"Like my men, big and hard."

Shay felt the blood rising to her face. She glanced at her cash drawer and saw nothing larger than hundreds. The bank had a prescribed limit to the amount a teller was allowed to keep there. The big bills were in a drawer below, near the carpet. Shay bent down and retrieved three five hundred dollar notes.

Nasty stared at the bills on the marble counter. "Can't you find me a Grover down there?"

Trying to hide her annoyance, Shay drew back two of the bills and hunkered down again, exchanging them for a one thousand dollar note from the bottom drawer.

Nasty smiled at her, folded the crisp bills once, then twice. Watching Shay watching her, she slid them inside the front of her tights. "My bank box," she said. "Big bills keep it nice and smooth." She touched herself. "Wanna feel?"

Shay stared at her without expression or reply.

"Well, *c'est la vie*," Nasty said and blew her an orchid-scented kiss.

Shay watched the girl strut to the door.

"You okay?"

Taylor, the security guard, was standing at the counter in his gray uniform, holstered pistol on his hip. His ordinary, almost handsome face registered concern.

"I'm fine," she said.

"Problem with Morticia?"

"Nope."

"Smells like a two-bit whore," Taylor said.

"She's a little more expensive than that," Shay said.

"Strictly low tide," Taylor said. When Shay didn't respond, he added, "You know, what's left on the beach after—"

"I got it," Shay said.

He made her nervous. She hadn't seen anything about it in the rulebook, but she assumed the bitchy bank manager wouldn't be too crazy about tellers yakking it up with the bank guard during business hours.

"Flower looks better on you than it did on the vine," he said, pointing to the violet bud.

"It was sweet of you."

"It's called a Princess," he said. "You up for a taco at lunch?"

She'd been working at the Sunset Branch for only eight days. Her second day, she'd made the mistake of letting Taylor share her table at the Mucho Taco down the block. She'd thought he might be able to bring her up to speed on gossip about her coworkers and the manager, Sylvia Berg. But Taylor, a stolid man in his mid-forties whose half-day security turn was supplementing a retirement check from the army, seemed totally indifferent to office politics.

He was one of those God-and-country guys, full of talk about honor and integrity and all that happy horseshit. But he apparently had a thing for her. That morning he'd brought her the flower. A proud part-time security guard. Jesus!

"No taco today, Taylor," she said.

"Tomorrow?"

"We'll see."

She was watching him reluctantly amble back to his position near the door when a considerably more appealing figure caught her eye. Young, wearing an expensive Italian-cut cocoa-brown suit, narrow in the waist, broad in the shoulders. Deep-tanned, with blond hair that, combed straight back, was long enough to whisk against the collar of his black silk shirt. His eyes were hidden behind very dark sunglasses so thin and smoothly curved they resembled a burglar's mask.

She was amused by the overall effect. Buccaneer businessman.

He was headed toward her when, suddenly, a rumpled, bearded figure plunged in front of him clutching a deposit slip and a wad of cash. The buccaneer businessman shrugged and moved to the teller on her right. Greg something. She could remember the teller's full name if she concentrated.

But her new customer wouldn't let her. He shoved his money and deposit slip at her. "Hurry it up, honey," he said. "Got things to see, people to do."

"Yes, sir," she said.

"Shay."

The teller, Greg Whatever, was calling her. His face was pale. Silently, he showed her a slip of notepaper. His customer, the buccaneer, was smiling at her.

"What part of 'in a hurry' don't you understand?" her customer asked nastily.

"Y-yes, sir. Just a second."

The neatly typed note read: "My partner is watching with a gun. Take two stacks of five-hundred-dollar bills from bottom drawer. Place on counter. No alarm, no harm."

Greg was at his bottom drawer, complying with the request.

Shay searched the room. Business as usual. Taylor stood beside the front door, pointing a customer toward the area known as the platform, where the bank's service reps sat. Sylvia the manager was absent. Probably in the alley catching a smoke. Great timing.

Shay bent down and found two stacks of five-hundred-dollar bills. Twenty-five to a stack, tightly wrapped. Twenty-five thousand dollars.

"Hey, honey," her customer said. "What the hell are you doin'? I said I'm in a hurry. Chop, chop."

Then there was a softer voice, almost a whisper. "One more peep out of that hairy mouth and my partner will shoot you in your fucking head. Dig? Good boy. Now, I'll take that off your hands."

Shay arose. The buccaneer businessman was standing next to her customer, his back hiding his actions from Taylor. No one else in the bank seemed to notice that a robbery was taking place. The bearded customer stood wide-eyed and frozen as the blond man added his bills to Shay's packs and slipped the combination into his inside coat pocket. Then he took a sideways step and retrieved Greg's packets.

"Thanks for your cooperation," he said quietly. "Stay chilled for five minutes. My partner will leave and nobody bleeds."

He turned and calmly walked toward the door. He stumbled on the way and Taylor grabbed him and helped him regain his balance. The blond man smiled gratefully and Shay could see his lips form the words "Thanks, officer."

Then he was gone.

Shay, Greg, and the bearded customer stood like statues for about a minute, with the tension growing nearly unbearable. Then the bearded customer threw himself to the floor, shouting, "It's a robbery, goddammit!"

Faces turned their way. Taylor was the first to react, charging toward them, hand on holster. He scowled at the customer in the fetal position on the floor.

"It was the guy in the brown suit," Greg said in a rush. "With the shades."

"His partner's here with a gun," Shay said.

Taylor scanned the frightened and startled faces on the scattered customers. "Not likely. Hit the alarm."

"Done," Greg shouted at Taylor who was racing to the front door. "And he's got a dye pack."

A dye pack. Shay couldn't believe it. She'd pegged Greg as a total wuss. But he'd had balls enough to slip the buccaneer a dye pack along with a stack of real bills. Two to three minutes after exposure to the microwave signal at the bank doors, the dye pack would explode covering the buccaneer with red paint, dying that long blond hair, sending blinding tear gas past those expensive sunglasses, maybe even scorching that beautifully tailored suit.

Convinced that there was no longer any danger, the bearded customer rose to his feet just as the branch manager Sylvia Berg approached from the rear of the bank. "What's going on?" she demanded.

"We've been robbed, Sylvia," Shay said.

"Dammit." The bank manager wheeled around, looking at the startled customers. "Where's my security?"

"He ran off after the guy," Greg said.

Sylvia pursed her lips, then turned to Shay. "Your station?"

"And Greg's."

"How much?"

"Twenty-five thousand," Shay said.

"Twelve thousand five hundred," Greg said, adding smugly, "And a dye pack."

"You were carrying that much? You know the bank's policy—"

"The robber made us get it from the bottom drawer," Greg said.

"He knew about the bottom drawer? I have to call Mysner." Joseph Mysner was the bank's head of security.

The bearded customer said, "You in charge?"

"Yes, sir. I'm the branch manager, Sylvia Berg."

"Well, Sylvia, you're out another nine hundred bucks, too. That's what he took off me."

"The robber took your money, Mr. . . . ?"

"Calusia. Chick Calusia. Yeah. He took my cash. And it's this broad's fault."

Sylvia's unblinking, birdlike green eyes shifted to Shay.

"My fault?"

"If you'd got off your ass and deposited my cash, I'd of been out of here."

"Shay?" Sylvia asked.

"I'm sorry. This 'gentleman' started to hand me his deposit—which was for only six hundred dollars by the way—and that's when the robber—"

"Excuse me, sister. You move like you being paid by the hour. I was standin' here for ten fucking minutes waiting for you to get it in gear. And the amount was nine hundred fucking dollars."

"Sylvia, that's not—"

"We'll discuss this in a—"

Sylvia was interrupted by the sound of gunfire from out on Sunset. All conversation stopped in the bank. People turned toward the front door, curious, afraid.

A young man with spiked hair and tattoo-covered arms banged against the door, backed up, and tried again. This time, he got it open. "Call the cops," he shouted, ducking down, hands protecting the back of his partially shaved head. "There's a dude out in the street, wailin' with a gun. Crazy. Covered in red paint."

Shay's heart skipped a beat.

Ignoring Sylvia and the bearded man, she rushed to the teller gate, fumbled it open, and headed for the front door. She heard Sylvia calling her name. Screw her.

Shay stepped from the bank to a glare-bright, shockingly subdued Sunset Boulevard. Traffic had stopped. People were pressed against the sides of buildings. Everyone seemed to be staring at the red-dye-stained figure sitting in the middle of the street, keening in pain, hands pressed against his tearing eyes. His discarded gun was at his side.

It was the bank guard, Taylor.

His eyes stung so much his mind wasn't working. One side of his chest seemed to be aflame. His eyes felt like they'd been hit by acid. He knew he was down and in trouble. He just couldn't sort out what had happened. Had he been shot? Stabbed? Maybe he could start to figure it out if he opened his eyes. But they hurt so bad. What hurt even worse was that he'd fucked up, dishonored himself.

He was brought back to some semblance of reality by a woman calling his name. He recognized the voice. The beautiful teller. Shay.

"We've got to get you out of the street," she said.

Car horns began to blare.

He nodded.

She bent beside him, guided his arm around her shoulders. "Up we go."

Even through the pain and confusion he was vitally aware of her body rubbing against his as they struggled. Then he was up. Not quite balanced, but up. She hugged his waist, her firm breasts pressing against his arm as she walked him slowly toward the bank. His eyes were wet, still burning, but he was catching up to the situation. "My gun," he said.

"In the street. I'll get it in a second."

"Christ! Did I shoot anybody?" he asked.

"Not that I can see," she said, propping him against the front of the bank.

Blinking through the tears, he watched her blurred image run back into the street, bend down, and retrieve his gun. What a goddamned woman! And what a goddamn disgrace he was.

They fired his ass, of course.

His chest was tender from the dye pack, but the skin wasn't even broken. An optometrist from the neighboring discount glasses store checked his eyes and bathed them in some kind of fluid.

The burning had just about disappeared when the bank's security officer Joseph Mysner showed up with John Pinella, the head of American Guard Services, the guy Taylor worked for. Mysner looked like a college footballer gone to seed, big, balding, and red-faced. At about half his size, Pinella was a sleek, olive-complexioned man wearing a wrinkle-free pin-striped suit and a faintly amused smile.

Taylor sat quietly in the bank's conference room while Sylvia Berg and the two men discussed his pathetic response to the robbery. They all seemed to be on the same page: he'd fucked up royally. He couldn't disagree.

When the bank reps left to "confab" with the arriving FBI agents, Pinella sighed and shook his head. "You really fucked the duck, my boy."

Taylor looked down at the bright stains on his hands. He had them under his chin, too. "Guess that's why my face is so red, huh?"

"It's the gunplay I don't get," Pinella said. "That the way you did it in the MPs? Shoot first?"

The question shook Taylor. But there was no way Pinella could know about the way he did it in the MPs, no way anyone alive could. "I never took a dye pack to the chest and face before," he said. "I coulda sworn I'd been hit by incoming, Cap." Pinella liked his men to call him Cap.

"That's the other thing. You let the goddamned perp slip the pack into your jacket pocket."

Right. That's what really galled him. The son of a bitch had played him. Just like the towelhead had played him that night in Kuwait City. But he'd found the Arab scam artist again and regained some of his self-respect. He felt his fury rising, but this wasn't the place for it. He took some deep breaths and said, "You think I like being played for an asshole, Cap?"

Pinella's face softened a little. "Guess not," he said.

"It'd be nice to get out of here. Go to bed and nurse my wounds."

"Not gonna happen, guy. Not for a while. You got cops to talk to, and FiBIes, and paperwork like you've never seen. Lucky nobody got hurt."

"Except me," Taylor said. "Maybe I should check in with a lawyer."

Pinella frowned. "Don't piss me off, Taylor. You already put us in the soup. Be a good boy and we'll find you something to do. Night watchman. Something."

Key-ryst. Night goddamned watchman. If only he could get his hands on that fucking Mr. Slick, he'd . . . aw, what the hell!

Taylor staggered from the conference room in search of cops and/or feds. He desperately wanted to do what he had to and get the hell away from the bank, from the scene of his humiliation and failure.

He wasn't sure how he felt about seeing Shay, but he needn't have worried. She wasn't in the main room. Probably off somewhere being questioned. Debriefed. He hated jargon like that. It was one of the things he didn't miss from the MPs.

Shay had expected to stay the full day at the bank, but she was out and away by three in the afternoon. And once again at liberty.

She'd asked for it. There was about an hour in which she sat around waiting to give her deposition. And another hour, roughly, before the representatives of law and order were finished with her. At that point she and Sylvia got into a discussion about Chick Calusia and the amount of his deposit.

"Since the robber took Mr. Calusia's deposit slip with his money," Sylvia had told her, "it's your word against his."

"So?"

"So, we're depositing nine hundred dollars into Mr. Calusia's account," Sylvia said. "And to minimize the bank's exposure to possible legal action initiated by Mr. Calusia, you're going to personally apologize to him for any inconvenience or indignity he may have experienced."

"I don't think so," Shay said.

"This isn't a discussion. If you wish to continue working here at the bank—"

"Fuck the bank," Shay replied. "Fuck Mr. Calusia and, Sylvia, especially, fuck you."

Shay was feeling remarkably alive as she drove through the afternoon traffic. She was approaching the house when she recognized a woman driving past in a periwinkle-blue Miata convertible, her short platinum hair dancing in the wind.

It took a few seconds for Shay to weigh the odds of her crossing paths with Nasty Wald again that day. She didn't put much stock in coincidence.

Taylor was lying on his couch in his underwear watching TV when the door buzzer sounded. He'd been there for nearly an hour, sipping vodka from a half-gallon plastic jug and trying to get his mind off the humiliation he'd suffered. On the small screen, a woman in a dress cut down to her pierced navel appeared to be singing while a shirtless stud, standing behind her, kissed her neck and ran a hand the size of a phone book down her firm thigh. Taylor had the sound turned down as far as it would go. He hated contemporary music. But he was a big fan of videos.

He'd seen this particular one before and he knew that as a result of the stud's rubbing, or something, the singer's nipples were about to burgeon under the gauzy gown. Whoever was at his door started to knock.

Annoyed, he called out, "Go away."

"It's me. Shay."

Taylor grabbed the remote and clicked off the TV right in the middle of the nipple shot, then rolled off the couch. "Minute," he told her. He looked down and saw that he was poking out of his skivvies. He staggered to the bedroom and grabbed a ratty striped bathrobe from the floor where he'd dropped it a couple days ago. When he got to the front door, his fingers struggled with the slip lock before it came free.

Then she was standing in the doorway. Outlined by the dim lighting in the hall she reminded him of the way women looked in movies when he was in the first throws of puberty. The Angie Dickinson kind of blonde—full-bodied, golden-haired, the back light adding an irresistible air of streetlamp mystery.

She was wearing the same clothes she'd had on earlier at the bank. But her blouse had lost its press, its top buttons were undone, and her legs were bare under her skirt. "Okay if I come in?" she asked.

"Wha—oh, sure. Yeah."

He was embarrassed by the place. It was a cheap furnished apartment in a lousy section of town. But she didn't seem to care about the surroundings, one way or another, "I was worried about you," she said.

"I'm okay." He kicked sections of the morning paper out of the way, opening a path to the couch. "Sit down. Can I, uh, get you something?"

"Maybe later," she said. "Right now, you should get dressed and come with me."

"What?"

"You stoned, Taylor?" she asked, not reprimanding him, merely curious.

"I'm okay," he said, a little defensively.

Her eyes dropped to his crotch and she smiled. "I guess you are glad to see me," she said. His dick was poking through the robe.

Mortified, he tucked himself away.

She moved closer and to his surprise and pleasure placed her hand on his erection. “That’s some icebreaker,” she said. Then she rose on tiptoe to kiss him. Her lips were soft and moist and he felt them part as her tongue slid past.

His battered body shivered as her pelvis rubbed against him, her tongue exploring his mouth. Then she pulled away, breathing heavily. “That was . . . good for openers,” she said.

He reached for her, but she danced away. “Not just yet. There’s something more important for us to take care of.”

“I don’t think so,” Taylor said, reaching for her again.

“I know where he is,” she said. “Right this minute.”

Taylor’s boozy, sex-revved mind couldn’t take the shift. “He?”

“The man who robbed the bank.”

He blinked. “You found him? How?”

“The freak-show girl who came in just before him. The one you called low tide. She drove by me a while ago and it got me to thinking. She made me open my bottom drawer. Then the crook showed and he knew where we keep the big bills. Anyway, she drove past and I followed her right to the bastard.

“I was going to call the police. But I got fired today, too. So I don’t give a damn about the money or the bank. But I do give a damn about you and I hate the way you’ve been fucked over. All your talk about honor and pride, I figured you for the kind of guy who’d rather do the job himself.”

“You got that right,” he said. Goddamn, but she was one of a kind! “Where are they?”

“Get dressed and I’ll show you,” she said.

It was at that moment that Taylor discovered something new about himself. He wanted her more than he wanted revenge. “They can wait,” he said, pulling her to him.

“There’s no time—” she began. But her resistance was halfhearted. When they kissed, the fever he was feeling seemed to infect her, too. Her hand pushed his robe aside just as his went beneath her skirt.

The couch was only a few feet away, but they didn’t get that far. They made love on the hard floor, the sheets of the discarded morning paper crackling and tearing beneath them. She wasn’t wearing anything under the skirt. He slid right into her.

Taylor was nearly delirious with pleasure. When he thought about it later, he wondered if part of his euphoria wasn’t due to the prospect of getting his hands on that smug fucking bank robber.

“What do we do if they’re gone?” Shay said as Taylor’s battered, pea-green Chevy bounced along the freeway.

“Find ’em again.” He liked having her with him, liked everything about her. But, in his postcoital mood, romance was losing its battle with revenge. Even with her hand on his lap.

The hand moved and he felt himself stirring. But it was the Beretta Centurion stuck behind his belt that she touched. “This isn’t the same gun . . .”

“At the bank? Hell no. That one’s in a bag in some evidence locker. This is something I picked up overseas.”

“You ever . . . use it?”

"There was a time something happened, kinda like what went down at the bank. This Kuwaiti asshole set me up."

"What'd he do?"

"Tried to disgrace me, to make me less a man," Taylor said. He wasn't about to provide her with any of the details.

"Turn here," Shay said.

The canyon road took an abrupt upward angle. As they continued following the road, the dinner-hour traffic thinned to almost nothing. The higher they went, the fewer houses they passed. The occasional streetlights did a lousy job of chasing the night away.

Inside the car, there wasn't much conversation, until:

"There," Shay said, pointing to a shadowy two-story wooden house tucked into a notch in the canyon wall. A shiny black Porsche Boxter was parked near a wooden stairwell that led to an upper-level entrance. A light was on deep in the house.

Taylor gave the place a snapshot glance, then continued up the canyon just far enough to be out of view from the house. He hugged the canyon wall, leaving enough room for other cars to pass if the drivers were careful. "Only the Porsche," he said. "The girl's?"

"She was driving a Miata. He must be alone."

"Or they both left in her car."

"I don't think so," Shay said. "If they'd gone somewhere together, he'd have wanted to drive the Boxter, right? Mr. Macho."

"Probably," Taylor said. "I'll go see." He opened his door.

She slid over to get out too. "No. You stay," he said. He pulled the Beretta from his belt.

"What's your plan?" she asked, eyes on the gun.

"That's why I want you to stay here," he said. "So you won't know."

He eased the car door shut. Shay's face looked pale in moonlight. Pale and beautiful and troubled. He leaned through the open window and kissed her on the lips. It was a cool almost passionless kiss.

"It'll be fine," he said.

He was expecting her to say something like "Be careful." Or maybe "Don't shoot unless you have to."

She said, "Any hint of trouble, honey, shoot the son of a bitch."

She was definitely one in a million.

The left side of the house came within inches of the canyon wall. On the other side a high wooden gate guarded what appeared to be a narrow path to the rear. The gate was locked. That left the door at the top of the stairs.

Taylor climbed the heavy wooden steps quickly and soundlessly. As he approached the front door, he could hear music, Samba, maybe. The door was cracked an inch or so. He used the gun barrel to push it open farther.

Light filtered through a glass wall at the rear of the house. There was enough of it to illuminate a room with a few pieces of cheap wicker furniture. A couple of chairs, a matching table, a sofa with cushions of a dark color that might have been black or midnight-blue. The floor was unfinished; the walls bare. The only things that suggested human occupancy were the odors of the punk girl's cheap orchid perfume and something even more repellent.

Taylor moved cautiously and quietly across the concrete, stepping down into a sunken area that had no furniture at all. The glass wall looked out on a brightly lit patio with a wooden deck and a small dark pool constructed to resemble a lagoon. A stream flowed into it from a fake waterfall that seemed to extend from the canyon wall. The music was coming from a medium-sized boom box on the deck, between a couple of cheap lawn chairs. A beer bottle was on its side near the boom box.

Satisfied that the pool area was deserted, Taylor moved to the right, where a narrow hall led to a shadowy bedroom. The odors intensified. Decaying orchids and sex and, overriding them both, the nearly toxic smell of feces and urine. Holding his breath, Taylor stood at the doorway to the bedroom, getting a quick fix on it before stepping in.

It, too, drew its light from the patio, through an open sliding-glass door. It was the only room in the place that looked lived in. Clothes were thrown around, male and female. A wastebasket overflowed with cleaner's bags and wrappers. The bed looked well used, with what appeared to be black silk sheets rumpled enough for the mattress to peek through. From his position, Taylor could see nothing to account for the terrible smell.

Near the foot of the bed was a pile of loose thousand-dollar bills and a packet of money that still had the bank seal attached. If the loot was still around . . .

Taylor took a step into the bedroom and immediately regretted it. His peripheral vision picked up a naked arm pointing a gun directly at him from a corner of the room.

Taylor froze, then slowly raised his hands, slipping his finger from the trigger guard of the gun but not dropping the weapon. He didn't know what else to do. He figured the robber would tell him. Or shoot him.

There was only silence.

He turned his head in what he hoped was a nonthreatening manner.

The man with the gun was the same one who'd robbed the bank and humiliated him. He wasn't looking so good. He was naked, huddled in the corner, his skin waxy and tinged with blue. His gun arm was propped on top of a wicker table. His head rested against a wall, unblinking eyes flat and cloudy, staring at the doorway without seeing it.

Taylor was reasonably sure the man was dead, but he still took a sideways step out of the line of fire. His eyes were watering from the stench, his stomach churning, as he cautiously approached the naked body. Blood, now crusted, had flowed from three holes in the bank robber's chest and stomach. He was seated in his own excrement, not that he minded the discomfort.

Taylor reached over the table and grabbed the barrel of the naked man's gun. But he couldn't pry it loose without breaking fingers. There was no pulse in the man's neck. He was definitely an ex-human. Let him keep the fucking gun if it meant so much to him.

Taylor felt a breeze against his neck and turned quickly.

Shay stood at the bedroom door, a handkerchief pressed to her nose. In her other hand she held a gun. Everybody had one these days, it seemed.

"I . . . was worried," she said, lowering the weapon. "Is he dead?"

"None deader," Taylor said.

"I didn't hear . . . You didn't . . . ?"

"Shoot him? No. This happened a while ago. He's already starting to stiffen up," he said, walking toward her. "Let's get out of here."

"The freak must have killed him."

"That's a good bet. C'mon. Before I toss."

"Look at all the money," Shay said behind the kerchief.

"Yeah. Stomach full of bullets and he still was able to scare her off before she could grab any of it."

"You think that's what happened?"

Taylor nodded. "Let's get out of here."

"Shame to leave all that money." She moved into the room. Shoving the handkerchief into a pocket, she grabbed a handful of the loose bills.

They'd been covering something small and violet.

Taylor blinked, but the violet object didn't go away. It was the Princess flower he'd given Shay that morning.

She saw it, too. "Well, shit," she said and pointed her gun at him. It was a nice little Walther, he noticed. A good choice. "Better drop that piece of yours, huh, Taylor."

She threw the money back on the pile and picked up his Beretta. A gun in each hand, she said, "Let's take this out on the patio. It's getting a little close in here."

Shay followed Taylor out into a warm night and the sound of samba music and the gurgling of the fake waterfall. It was a relief to breathe, to clean some of the stench from her nostrils.

"Whoo-eee," she said, using her clothed elbow to slide the door shut behind them. "I always knew Del was full of shit, but c'mon now."

"What happened, Shay? You catch him with the punk bimbo?"

"You want to turn off that music?" she said. "I don't much feel like a mambo right now."

It took him a second to find the off button on the boom box.

"Now sit, Taylor," she said. "We have to talk."

"It won't do us any good if we're caught here with ol' Del," he said.

"This place is pretty isolated."

"Miss Low Tide might come back."

"I hope not," she said. "Three's a crowd. Sit."

The lawn chair scraped against the deck under his weight.

"Lie back," she said. "That way we can talk without me worrying about you making some stupid macho move." She perched on the edge of the remaining chair. "First off, I didn't kill Del. It must've been the psycho bitch. I saw her driving away."

"You Del's wife?"

"No way. We played around a little. That was about three years ago, when I was still an honest, underpaid teller at a bank in Arizona. Del picked me up in a bar. He fucked me and together we fucked the bank. Then we fucked more banks. Once I wised up a little, saw the kind of fella he was, I ended the romance. Too many deadly diseases out there. Del couldn't keep it in his pants and he didn't believe in rubbers. Since then, we've just been business partners, me getting jobs at banks and him robbing 'em."

"How does Miss Low Tide fit in?" Taylor asked.

She shrugged. "My guess is he picked her up today. It was just like him to be hustling tramps on the street in front of a bank he was about to rob."

"Why'd she shoot him? Lovers' quarrel?"

"Who the hell knows? Maybe she saw the money, tried to kill him but screwed up. He was able to get his own gun and chase her off."

He had his head cocked to one side, looking at her with an odd smile. She suspected he was wondering if she was bullshitting him, if she'd been the one who'd put the holes in Del. Was there something on her face for him to read? Maybe that she'd left the bank earlier than Del had expected and saw the crew-cut bitch driving away. That the goddamned house had been reeking of the stink of orchids and their lovemaking. That fucking Del hadn't even bothered to put his clothes back on or change the sheets.

Could he tell that Del, the insatiable bastard, had thrown her down on that still-damp bed and fucked her and then gone out to the patio for the beer that he'd been drinking? Could Taylor see it in her eyes that she'd put her clothes back on, found the money and one of Del's several guns, and called out sweetly for him to come back to the bedroom?

He'd been at the patio door, smug and with a hard-on, when she shot him twice. But the bastard didn't fall. He staggered toward her and she lost it. Dropped the money and shot him again. He fell on the bed and she thought that had to be the end of it. But as she moved toward the fallen loot, he rolled over on the bed. In his hand was his gun, the one he slept with.

She stumbled back without the cash, firing again as she ran from the room.

Breathless, she paused near the front door, considering the situation. She'd shot him what? Three, maybe four times? How long could it take for the blood to run out of him?

There was no sound from the bedroom. Just the fucking radio music out on the patio.

"Hey, Del," she called out. "How's it hanging?"

"Come on in and see, baby."

Shit. He didn't sound that weak. So what? She could outwait him. Then grab the loot and drift away. But . . . the cash was minimal, compared to the more than four hundred grand Del had stashed away in bank boxes across the state. He used to joke that he wasn't stealing the money, he was merely moving it around from one bank to another. She'd made it her business to keep track of the locations and the various fake names he'd used. And she could do a fair job of imitating his handwriting. But she couldn't stand in for him. She'd needed a man to front the deal.

That was when she'd thought of Taylor.

She was a little startled when he asked, "Why'd you come to my apartment, Shay? What am I doing here?"

"I'll level with you," she said. "At the bank, I thought you were a nice enough guy, but there wasn't anything there for me. Then Del messed you up. When I saw you like that, blind and in pain, I felt . . . I'm not sure what I felt. But it was something . . . different. Intimate." The weird thing was that she wasn't lying, exactly.

"That's good?"

"Yeah. Intimacy. Something I've been missing."

"It'd help me to believe that," Taylor said, "if you put down the guns."

She hesitated, then thought what the hell? She needed him, needed his cooperation. Considering the sort of lovesick way he was looking at her, she didn't think she needed the guns. She placed them on the deck. "Better?"

"Much." He leaned forward and picked up her Walther. Sniffed it and smiled. "Sorry, but I had to make sure."

"I know," she said. The gun she'd used, one of Del's many, was resting at the bottom of the canyon. She stood slowly. "Maybe we'd better collect my stuff, clean up a little, and get going."

"There's no hurry, like you said." He shifted his legs to make room for her.

She sat down, facing him. She felt a slight unease because she couldn't quite read his mood. But she was a firm believer in her sexual attraction. She was convinced she could seduce him into joining her in collecting Del's loot. She placed a hand on his arm. "After the . . . incident at the bank today," she said, "I wanted to stay with you while you were recovering. But Sylvia and that security guy insisted I go with them."

She tenderly touched one of the red splotches on his neck. He closed his eyes, apparently enjoying her touch. "What happened after you left the bank?" he asked.

"I drove here."

"Del was alive?"

"Yes. I told him I'd decided to end the partnership. He wasn't happy. I was packing a bag when he grabbed me and dragged me to the front of the house. He threw me out, told me never to come back. I said I wanted my things. He laughed at me. Slammed and locked the door. There wasn't much else I could do, so I drove away. When I reached the bottom of the drive, Little Miss Punk passed me driving up."

"Why didn't you tell me all this before?"

"I . . . didn't want you to know I was involved in the robbery." Was that true? Good lies always had a little truth hidden in them. She didn't want to lose him. Was it more than just the money? Maybe. "I was afraid you'd throw me out, too."

"I'd never do that," he said.

She pressed against him, resting her head on his chest. His arm went around her shoulders. "I love you, Taylor," she said. "It just might work, you and me."

His body relaxed. His hand moved a strand of her hair so that he could kiss her ear. "You and me," he whispered.

Something was definitely happening to her. She was no longer conning him. She was falling in love with him. Either that or she was conning herself.

"I don't want any secrets between us," he said.

"No secrets," she agreed, curious now as to where he was headed.

"You asked me about the Kuwaiti who screwed me over," he said. "Still want to hear the story?"

"If you want to share it," she said.

"Seven years ago in the Persian Gulf, during my last tour of duty. About eight o'clock at night. A pretty local girl waved down my jeep near this town of Kazimah. Her boyfriend had gotten pissed at her and left her out there on the road to hitch back to Kuwait City. She was a secretary for one of the oil companies, she said. The whole thing was a lie. A setup."

"A setup for what?" Shay asked.

"My partner, Jeb Cooley, and I were scheduled that night to guard an army warehouse. While the girl and I were . . . while we were at her place, her lover and some other guys bounced a lead pipe off of Jeb's skull and cleaned out the warehouse. Nothing crucial like arms or medicine. Just cases of whiskey, wine, beer, Coca-Cola, little foil pouches of macadamia nuts—crap like that—all of it about to be sent out to temporary officers' clubs throughout the area. Over a hundred grand in booze and snacks, worth three times that on the Kuwaiti black market."

"You must've got in terrible trouble."

"No. I told everybody I'd had a flat tire. They were suspicious, of course, and on my ass for a while, but since I wasn't really involved in the robbery there was no way they could find any evidence. Still, the suspicion was there. Jeb, who'd been as close to me as a brother, put in for a new partner. And that was that for my military career."

"Why didn't you try to catch the real thieves?" she asked.

He smiled ruefully. "That was the beauty of it. If I'd brought in the Kuwaiti who planned the break-in, the story about me and the girl would have come out. I would have gotten off the hook for the theft, but I'd have been found guilty of dereliction of duty. By keeping the lie I could at least get an honorable discharge and collect a pension."

"So the guy who pulled the robbery walked away free and clear."

"Not exactly," Taylor said. "I found him and I beat him with my gun butt until my arm got tired. He never recovered."

"You killed him?" She seemed shocked.

"Don't you think he deserved it? He robbed me of my good name and my self-respect and he forced me to give up the only job I ever loved."

"Oh, honey," she said, hugging him. Then a question popped into her head. Without thinking, she began, "What happened to the g . . ." She censored herself.

But not soon enough. "The girl?" he asked. "What happened to her?"

"I guess. Did you ever see her again?"

"Once more," he said. "The guy—the one I pistol-whipped to death—there'd been nothing personal in what he did. I was just somebody in the way of his plan, so he had me removed. But the girl—she made it very personal. I had no choice. I did the only thing I could."

Shay was frowning now. She didn't really want to know, but she heard herself asking, "Wha—what did you do to her?"

"What I had to," Taylor said. "I did this." He pointed her own Walther against her taut stomach.

She barely got out the word "No," before he pulled the trigger.

Taylor rested Shay's body on the chair. Her cheek was still warm when he kissed it. He dabbed at his tears. Then he wiped the Walther clean. He wiped the power button of the boom box, too. He was glad the white-haired freak hadn't participated in the robbery, in his humiliation. Taking a human life gave him no pleasure.

He paused for one final look at Shay. "You and me," he said.

He reentered the dreadful bedroom and tossed Shay's Walther onto the roiled king-size. Holding his breath, he wiped his prints from the barrel of Del's pistol.

As he made his way to the door, he was stopped by the pile of cash. Over thirty-five thousand dollars. A nice bundle of found money. But it was stolen goods. Tainted. It offered no temptation to a man who prided himself on honor and integrity.

Taylor bent down and reached past the money to pick up the wilted violet flower. He took that away with him. He thought he'd get it laminated. Carry it in his wallet. Once the red dye and the burns wore off, it would give him something to remember Shay by.

Carol Anne Davis

Starting Over

■ ■ ■

Carol Anne Davis had been writing for several years, aided by a small-business start-up program in England, before her first novel, Shrouded, *was published by Do-Not Press in 1998. It was followed by the novels* Safe as Houses *and* Noise Abatement, *and the true-crime book* Women Who Kill: Profiles of Female Serial Killers. *Her true-crime features and reviews appear in monthly magazines, and she also has been a true-crime columnist for the British mystery magazine* Shots *since 2002, writing about everything from Murderous Mothers through to Killers on the Ward. She has also appeared (shaken but not stirred) at various literary events, including Crime Scene and Dead on Deansgate. Her most recent true-crime book,* Children Who Kill, *and her new dark crime novel,* Kiss It Away, *were both published in 2003. "Starting Over," published in the anthology* Green for Danger, *finds a parole officer out in the English countryside trying to keep tabs on a group of ex-cons who just can't seem to resist falling back into their old ways.*

"You mean they've all moved here for no apparent reason?" Jennifer asked. It was her first day as a parole officer in rural Wiltshire though she had a decade's worth of experience.

Gail beamed at her. "They have indeed."

Jennifer had heard through the grapevine that the woman was called Gullible Gail. Hell, she didn't even have a lock on the reception-room drawer that contained the Hob Nobs. Now the ex-cons were relocating to the countryside to live on her patch.

"Why would London prisoners come here?" she asked with genuine curiosity. "There's only casual farmwork on offer and there are virtually no shops."

"There's the Spar," Gail said, "And the mobile library."

"Gail—most of our clients can't read."

For a second the older woman's mouth drooped, then it curved upward again. "Ah, but it rents out videos of the countryside for a pound a time."

The kind of videos her clients had been making didn't involve cute fox cubs or harvest mice—though the occasional donkey made a manually excited appearance. Hoping that the ex-cons had exited the movie business, Jennifer switched on her new computer and logged onto the Internet.

"I need to see what Wiltshire has to offer parolees," she explained to Gail who was peering benignly over her shoulder.

"Oh, can you work that Web thing? One of our clients has her own Web site," she replied.

"She has? What's her name?"

Gail mentioned a prisoner who had recently spent time in Holloway for breaking and entering. "But she's a completely reformed character. She's become a writer now."

Further alarm bells went off in Jennifer's head. "Writers don't make much money in their first few years."

"Ah, but she's offering a tutoring service. You know how there's a writers group called The Nine Novelists and another called Seven Scribes? Well, she's called herself The Voluptuous One."

A few online searches later, Jennifer found herself staring at The Voluptuous One's official site. The front page showed the former prisoner in a black blouse that she hadn't yet found time to button. The side split of her skirt was equally open to the elements. "One-to-one tuition a specialty," the wording under her nipples read.

"She must have conquered her childhood dyslexia," Gail said with genuine admiration. "She's come so far."

Unsure whether to laugh or cry, Jennifer switched off the machine. She'd never thought that prostitution should be illegal, especially the behind-closed-doors type that The Voluptuous One was clearly engaged in. So she'd turn a blind eye to the woman's new career if she continued to commit a victimless crime.

But what else had been going on in this pretty part of the country? As Gail's senior officer—albeit her junior in age by twenty years—Jennifer had the right to peruse the woman's lilac-scented reports. Taking a deep breath, she started right away.

One of the first problems seemed to be the number of men who'd served time for bestiality and were now living closer to cows than might be considered proper. Jennifer made a mental note to become a vegan rather than drink the local milk.

"These prisoners who were arrested in the fields . . ." she said to Gail.

Gail beamed. "No need to worry. I've fixed them all up with nice girlfriends."

"Your girlfriends?" Jennifer asked faintly.

"No, dear, girlfriends of The Voluptuous One."

Had the area been turned into one huge knocking shop? Should she inform the Center for Communicable Diseases?

"Let's go to the village immediately," Jennifer said.

Gail picked up a purple mobile with a cartoon coot on it. "The clients gave me this and said I could phone them whenever . . ."

Jennifer quickly took it from her. "I think it's time they had a big surprise."

"You'll be so impressed when you see what they've done with the place," Gail promised as they lurched along the country roads in her canary-yellow Lada. Several sheep backed away—and Jennifer swore one crossed its back legs—at the sight of a vehicle. "They've turned the place into an ideal village. I'll take you to the knitting group which they hold in Maggie's home."

Maggie, as far as Jennifer could remember, was the wife of an old lag who'd served twenty years for armed robbery. And Maggie herself had managed to smoke sixty a day off a social security check and still have enough cash left for an ankle-length mink coat.

At Jennifer's insistence, Gail brought the Lada to a tire-shrieking halt some distance from Maggie's villa and both parole officers entered the back door on foot. Six women were knitting busily in the plushy carpeted living room.

"It's only me," Gail called as they walked in.

Twelve knitting needles immediately stopped clickety-clacking. Jennifer stared at the six balaclavas they'd been working on.

"It's brass monkeys weather here in the winter," Maggie said defensively, returning to her plain and purl.

Gail nodded understandingly. "If you need a wolens' allowance from the social fund . . ."

"They're up to something," Jennifer said as they walked back to the car. Or rather they walked back to where the car had been: all that remained was the tire tracks.

"No, that's why they moved here," Gail assured her as they started the long walk back to the parole office. "They want to mend their ways and know that in the country there's less opportunity for crime."

Three weeks later Jennifer wondered anew about the opportunities for crime when she gave a con-artist-turned-local-handyman cash for a steering wheel security lock. He handed her a fiver in change and it didn't seem quite dry.

"Finding enough work here to keep you busy, are you, Neville?" she asked, remembering how his record had involved everything from credit card scams to money laundering.

Neville looked around the empty workshop. "Oh, aye."

Unconvinced, Jennifer drove on to the center of the village and parked behind Fred the Fence's barn. Suddenly she heard the unmistakable clatter of a printing press. Were they actually printing their own money? Jennifer dashed into the workshop just as the press began to spew out the covers of a glossy magazine.

Fred jumped when he saw her, then smiled. "Is Gail not bringing us sultana cake anymore?"

"She's gone into Salisbury to buy herself a new car—well, a reconditioned one."

"It's a sad day when a man's so broke that he has to steal a Lada," Fred said.

"You're doing alright yourself?" Jennifer asked. Judging by his glossy leather shoes and waxed jacket he was doing wonderfully. She just wasn't sure how he managed it off his social security check.

"Aye, we've been given a small European grant to set up this magazine," Fred explained. He held up one of the covers and Jennifer could see that it was called *Starting Over*. "It's a magazine run by ex-prisoners for ex-prisoners," Fred said.

"You write it all by yourself?" Jennifer queried, remembering how the man had always spelled phonetically.

"No, all the ex-cons contribute—and some are former editors," Fred said happily.

Maybe he really had hit on something. After all, as a parole officer she had very limited time with each parolee—but if they pooled their information they could help each other find affordable housing, sympathetic new employers, and even a husband or wife.

Jennifer got back to the office ten minutes before Gail arrived in an elderly four-wheeled drive.

"Gail, you may be right. They really are trying to turn over a new leaf," she said and told her all about the magazine.

The following weekend, Jennifer was at a Winning Ways in Wiltshire conference and ended up having lunch with a patisserie entrepreneur from the neighboring village. She told him how the ex-cons had impressively rewritten their own life stories by producing

Starting Over and he suggested that she submit a copy for the annual competition to find the Local Business of the Year.

"Nominees aren't told that they've been entered for the competition unless they reach the shortlist," he added, reaching for another slice of lardy cake. "So don't tell a soul. Just hand in a copy of the magazine to my bakery."

It was difficult keeping her secret from Gail but luckily the woman seemed to be preoccupied with fitting new security locks to her vehicle and to her Hob Nobs drawer. (There had been several break-ins in the area that Jennifer put down to bored local children.) She casually asked Fred the Former Fence for a copy of *Starting Over* but he explained that demand was such that they were completely sold out.

"How about saving me a copy of the next issue?" she asked, keeping her tone lighthearted.

"You can bet on it," Fred said—but when publication day arrived he claimed that every copy was earmarked for subscribers at home and abroad.

She simply couldn't get hold of a copy without arousing the parolee's suspicions, Jennifer told her new acquaintance as they sat in the ground-floor tearoom of his five-story bakery.

"Leave it to me," he said between mouthfuls of Marlborough bun, "I know someone in the post office who deals with the bulk deliveries."

Jennifer winced, hating the fact that he was going to steal a copy. But she was determined that her boys would have the chance of a sheepskin fleece from the woolen mill and a side of beef from the local abattoir that together formed the top business prize.

Shortly after The Great Magazine Robbery, the bakery entrepreneur phoned her at home.

"Jennifer, you're not going to believe this."

His voice sounded so strange that she wondered if he had choked on a fig roll.

But when she saw the copy of *Starting Over* that he'd purloined, the words stuck in her own throat. The inside front cover offered The Dummy's Guide to Safecracking while page one proudly displayed Jemmy of the Month. Page two looked at Credit Card Counterfeiting and page three featured a working girl with her price card. Jennifer noticed that lip service was particularly reasonable but that whippings didn't come cheap. Meanwhile the center spread was Houses of the Rich & Famous that included arrows showing various windows and doors.

The classifieds were also a rich source of employment with requests for everything from getaway drivers to doctors specializing in gunshot wounds. Not to be outdone, the travel section offered suitcases with false compartments and ready-in-two-hours' passports while the miscellaneous section had adverts for offshore bank accounts, thermal lance hire, and police band radios.

"My car's outside if you want a lift to the police station," the baker said weakly.

Jennifer hesitated. "If we go to the police now you'll have to admit that your friend stole the magazine. And my bosses will think I was naive not to have known about all of this so I'll probably get demoted." She looked sadly at the advert from a plastic surgeon promising that the patient's own mother wouldn't recognize him afterward. "Do you think we could wait a couple of months, then send it in anonymously?"

"That sounds like an excellent solution," the man said—and this time they both reached for a large triangle of chocolate sponge.

The next day Jennifer put in for a transfer back to the Birmingham office explaining that she'd found the Wiltshire patch hard to manage due to the distance from the office to the parolees' village. She also said that the men were running a magazine but refused to issue her with a copy and that she was slightly troubled by this.

Jennifer knew that the wheels of parole officedom grind exceedingly slow so long before anyone official looked into the magazine the police would be sent the baker's anonymous copy. She'd come out of the whole affair looking reasonable as she was the only one who had voiced her concerns.

Concern eventually spread throughout the parole system and photocopies of *Starting Over* were sent to various judicial VIPs. Several plastic surgeons and a Harley Street doctor immediately contributed to the brain drain by relocating overseas.

As for Fred the Fence and the other guys? They were forcibly relocated closer to the sea, specifically to HMP Maidstone. There they are putting their editing skills to less lucrative use by running the prison magazine. Meanwhile The Voluptuous One's tutoring is widely sought after and the suicide rate among lonely farmers has gone right down.

Catherine Dain

DREAMS OF JEANNIE

■ ■ ■

Catherine Dain was raised in Reno, Nevada, the setting for the Freddie O'Neal mystery series. The Freddie O'Neal series has received two nominations for the Shamus Award from the Private Eye Writers of America, one for Lay It on the Line *and a second for* Lament for a Dead Cowboy. *Other books in the series are* Sing a Song of Death, Walk a Crooked Mile, Bet Against the House, The Luck of the Draw, *and* Dead Man's Hand. *Her other novels include* Angel in the Dark, A New Age Mystery; Darkness at the Door, A New Age Mystery; Death of the Party, A Faith Cassidy Mystery; *and* Follow the Murder, A Faith Cassidy Mystery. *A short-story collection,* Dreams of Jeannie and Other Stories, *is available from Five Star in 2003. She lives with Angel, her calico cat, in California. Her story chosen for this year's anthology, "Dreams of Jeannie," is the title story of her single-author collection published by Five Star Publishing, and gives psychic and amateur detective Mariana Morgan the confounding case of a young woman who keeps dreaming about death and destruction—but for whom?*

I am so tired of clients insisting that their dreams of a terrorist attack are clairvoyant," Mariana snapped. "The dreams are the body's attempts to call attention to stress. Personal stress combined with the anxiety of the collective unconscious, that's all. How long is it going to take before we go on to the next fad?"

She leaned against the jewelry counter, hoping for some attention, but Deirdre was devoting herself to polishing earrings and didn't look up. Deirdre ran Enchantment, a small store and metaphysical center, with impressive attention to detail.

"Well, the sleeping-with-Bill dreams persisted a couple of years after his presidency ended," Deirdre answered calmly. "So I think we're going to be hearing about terrorists for a while. You'd better find a way to deal with your own stress so you can nod and listen when your clients express theirs. Right now, I suggest you go outside, take a psychic shower, clear your chakras, and come in again."

Mariana straightened up, uncertain whether to follow Deirdre's advice or argue with her. Clearing her chakras before the next client arrived for a psychic reading was a good idea. But she had half an hour, and arguing felt more satisfying.

"Why don't you hold a workshop on dreams?" she asked. "Teach people something instead of letting them muddle through on their own."

"Why don't you?" Deirdre responded.

"Because I don't know enough about dreams. I can give people intuitive help, but I don't know theory, so I can't teach them to help themselves. You can."

"All right." Deirdre finished polishing the silver moon-and-stars earrings she had been working on and removed the polishing glove from her left hand. She looked up at Mariana, giving her full attention. "Tell me what you've been dreaming."

"Not about terrorists." Mariana hesitated. Deirdre waited expectantly. "I dreamed about Tim dying again. And I dreamed about Marion Zimmer Bradley. And I dreamed about an earthquake."

"What did you dream about Marion Zimmer Bradley?" Deirdre was suddenly interested. Although the writer had been dead for several years, her books still sold well. Deirdre had limited shelf space for books, since she had a better mark-up on jewelry, crystals, incense, and other such items for New Age–minded shoppers, but she always had at least one copy of *Miss of Avalon* in stock.

"I dreamed I was standing in line with a group of other women, waiting to hear a great teacher speak. We were outside a temple, and the weather was warm. I could feel the perspiration on my skin. When we were allowed inside, the speaker turned out to be Marion Zimmer Bradley. But she was young, and she wasn't obese," Mariana said.

"How do you feel about Marion Zimmer Bradley?"

"I love her books."

"Okay," Deirdre said, "so either you had an out-of-body experience in which you went to hear her speak in the spirit world because the message in her books means something to you, and you wanted more, or your Higher Consciousness took her form to tell you something."

"I think I was really there. Do astral bodies sweat?"

"Why not? People cry astral tears in their dreams, why not sweat astral beads of perspiration? Do you remember what she told you?" Deirdre asked.

"No."

Deirdre shook her head with impatience.

"Ask for another dream about her, and this time remember. The message might be important—like about writing a great book. And you know why you dream about Tim dying."

"I know. Because I still miss him," Mariana said. "I know he has gone on, which is why he doesn't talk to me as often, but I still miss him. I don't know about asking for a dream about Marion Zimmer Bradley. You're better at asking for dreams than I am. My subconscious doesn't seem to pay attention. Anyway, why would Marion Zimmer Bradley give me a message about a great book?"

"Why not?" Deirdre said again. "Especially if it was just your Higher Consciousness appearing as Marion Zimmer Bradley. Your Higher Consciousness might think it's time for you to use your talent. And if you want to control your dreams, you have to practice."

This time Mariana shook her head.

"Maybe. All right. What about the earthquake?"

"This is Southern California. Wait long enough, there will be an earthquake, and then it will be a clairvoyant dream. Maybe it was nothing more than a truck going by outside, and the rumble became an earthquake in your dream consciousness. Otherwise known as random firing of synapses in your brain. Or maybe something—maybe someone—is coming to shake up your life."

"I could have come up with that myself. And I really don't want my life shaken up, thank you very much. I think I'll go clear my chakras."

Mariana pushed through the glass doors and left the shop. What she saw outside was so unattractive that she almost changed her mind. Minimall parking lots are seldom aesthetically pleasing, and the one in front of Enchantment was no exception. On this day the heavy marine layer, Southern California June gloom extending into July, had added a gray glaze to the picture. Cars, a few people, a street, and another minimall on the other side. All the colors muted, slightly drab. Maybe she could use some change in her life.

She sat down on a bench, took off her sandals so that her feet could feel the energy of the narrow strip of grass between cement and asphalt, and closed her eyes. Visualizing a waterfall of drops all the colors of the rainbow, flowing through her body, clearing her energy centers, helped more than she thought it would. When she opened her eyes, she was ready to go back to the store and see her next client.

"Mariana? I'm Jeannie Cullen, and I'm early. Can we start now?" A woman was standing between the bench and the door, barring Mariana's way. The woman's dark brown hair was wild and frizzed, and her face was flushed from crying. She was wearing a yellow tunic top that didn't go well with her blue and green floral slacks, as if she had dressed in what her hand grabbed from the closet, without paying attention. But even those colors were muted by the gray of the day.

"Of course, Jeannie," Mariana answered, allowing herself a slight twinge of annoyance that her break was over almost before it began. "Come on in the store, let me get a cup of tea, and we'll start."

Deirdre looked up and nodded as they entered.

"Okay?" she asked.

"More or less," Mariana replied.

She slipped behind the counter, dropped a bag of spicy herb tea into a cup, added hot water from the red-topped spout on the dispenser, and slipped back to the customer side.

"Follow me," she said to the distraught woman waiting for her.

Beyond the book section at the back of the store, a hallway led to a combination office and storeroom for Deirdre, two offices that she rented out, the reading room, and a larger room where evening classes were offered.

Mariana ushered Jeannie into the reading room, which wasn't much more than a large closet with a small, round table, two chairs, a framed poster of frolicking dolphins, and a potted plant that somehow managed to sustain itself in fluorescent light.

"I dreamed about a terrorist attack," Jeannie began, before Mariana could even set the timer to thirty minutes.

"Dreams are not necessarily clairvoyant," Mariana said, knowing it would be useless to tell Jeannie that she was the second person that day to come in with a dream of terrorists. Jeannie would take it for confirmation, when it was nothing of the kind. The last client's dream could be easily explained by what was going on in her life. Mariana was certain Jeannie's dream would be the same.

Jeannie glared at her. Mariana knew that she would have to be careful, or the heavy emotion that had caused the flushed face and the swollen eyes would turn to anger.

"You don't understand," Jeannie said. "And I thought you were a psychic. In the dream, my husband was the terrorist."

"I'm sorry," Mariana replied, belatedly switching her attention from herself to her client. "No wonder you're upset. You're right, I didn't take the time to tune in before I answered. What is it you want from me?"

"I want to know what's going on. I know he's involved in something, and now I get this dream that he's a terrorist, planning to blow something up. What is he doing?" Jeannie's eyes began to fill, and her voice broke.

Mariana reached down and grabbed the box of tissues from its place on the floor—there was no room on top of the table—and offered it to Jeannie. Jeannie grabbed two tissues and held them to her eyes.

"Okay," Mariana said, after she had returned the box to the floor. "Here's how we're going to handle it. I want your birthdate, then his first name and birthdate. I'm going to look at your life paths and the path of your relationship, and we'll go from there."

Jeannie glared again, distracted from her tears.

"You think it's about me," she said. "And it isn't. It's my patriotic duty to turn him in, but I need corroboration from somebody before I call the FBI."

"Birthdates," Mariana said calmly.

"I'm a Taurus and he's a Scorpio."

"I don't care about your sun signs. I'm not doing astrology. I want to know your life path cards, the archetypes of the Major Arcana that you're working through. They will help me tune in to the situation. May I have your birthdates?"

Jeannie reluctantly gave her both dates.

"His name is Eric," she added.

Mariana quickly added up the two dates.

"A nine and a one," she said. "You're a Hermit and Eric's a Magician. This has to be a difficult relationship for you under the best of circumstances. You need boundaries, you need a quiet space to get in touch with your own inner truth, and Eric has no concept of the word privacy. He also doesn't have much sense of truth."

"I know that," Jeannie said. "I know he's lying to me. And I know he's a terrorist."

"Doesn't fit the profile," Mariana said, hoping to lighten the mood a little. She didn't like the energy she was picking up from Jeannie, and she didn't like the energy path that she was tuning into as she looked at the two cards, the Hermit and the Magician.

"What kind of psychic are you? You think only Arabs are terrorists?"

"I'm sorry," Mariana said. "We haven't gotten off to a good start. Let's try again." She shuffled the cards and fanned them out on the small table. "Pick six cards, and let's look at your relationship with Eric."

"This is not about my relationship with Eric," Jeannie said, her voice rising. "This is not about me. I want to know what he's doing."

"I understand that. But if you want me to look at him, I have to start by looking at the two of you. That's the way I work," Mariana responded. "You're the one who's here, you're the one who's upset, and I need to look at the energy flow between the two of you. He may not be a terrorist. He could be lying about something else."

"He's a terrorist." Jeannie hesitated, as if she might want to argue, then quickly chose six cards and handed them to Mariana.

Mariana placed them as the base, stem, and petals of a flower, to see the direction of the energy flow. The cards confirmed her own sense that the energy between the two people wasn't good and wasn't going to get better. And there was more. She waited until the images in her head became clearer before she spoke.

"You're partly right," she said. "Eric is involved in something dangerous, and there is someone else involved. But his anger seems personal, not against the government, or anything faceless. You can't talk to him. He won't listen to you. In fact, some of his anger is toward you. The wisest course of action might be for you to move out. Would you like to see what your path looks like if you choose to do that?"

Jeannie shook her head, dismissing Mariana's question. "I know I can't talk to him. I need to talk to the FBI. How can I stop him?"

"You can't. You can't change what he does. You can only protect yourself."

"You are not helping," Jeannie said. Her hands flew around her face, disconnected, then settled back in her lap. "In the dream, he blew something up, something concrete, some kind of building. I wasn't in danger. I think you're wrong. Eric may be angry at me—he's angry at everyone right now—but he isn't going to hurt me."

"What Eric is blowing up is your marriage. Your dream was a metaphor, something that your subconscious was trying to tell you. He may not hurt you physically, but he's hurting you psychologically. You need to get out." Mariana said it flatly. She didn't like telling clients things they didn't want to hear.

"I don't need to get out. I need to get information I can take to the FBI, and you aren't giving me that," Jeannie said. She picked up her bag. "This is useless."

Mariana glanced at the timer.

"We've only used about fifteen minutes," she said. "I'll tell Deirdre to charge you for that."

"Fine."

Jeannie was out the door and halfway down the hall before Mariana caught up with her.

Deirdre barely raised an eyebrow when Mariana explained that Jeannie had called off the reading.

"I couldn't give her what she wanted," Mariana began, once Jeannie had left the store. "She decided to end the reading, and I let her."

"This is the first time a client has walked out on you, but it won't be the last," Deirdre said. "You'll have others. Some will even yell at you. And some of the ones who yell will come back for another reading, but they never apologize. It's all part of the business. Do you want to tell me about it?"

While both psychics kept their clients' secrets where outsiders were concerned, they had agreed when Mariana had first started working at the store that there would be no secrets between the two of them. Mariana thought of Deirdre as the psychic equivalent of a consulting therapist. Although Deirdre was no older than Mariana, both women in their mid-thirties, Deirdre had acknowledged her psychic talents at a younger age and had been a professional for years. For Mariana, the awakening had been later and more difficult, and it was still hard for her to discipline her talents to the constraints of the business.

When Mariana had met Deirdre, shortly after both women had lost their husbands to murder, she hadn't thought they would become friends. She still wasn't sure they were friends. So much about them was different: what they read, what they watched on television, even physical characteristics. But as she looked at Deirdre, with her short, curly blond hair and blue eyes, and thought of herself, with her long, dark hair and dark eyes, she knew that the deep similarities were more important than the surface differences.

"She dreamed her husband is a terrorist. I think it's a metaphor for what's happening in the marriage. And I hope she isn't in danger," Mariana said.

"You could always call David, see what he thinks," Deirdre said.

"Don't, Deirdre. I don't think this is a job for the police, and David would think I wanted to talk to him." Mariana had learned to deflect Deirdre's light jabs, but she wished that Deirdre hadn't mentioned the police detective. There were too many uncertainties in that relationship—if she could even call it that—and she didn't want to deal with them now. Maybe never.

"Then you need to let it go," Deirdre said. "Another psychic shower to clear your chakras, and then get ready for the next client."

"I don't have a next client."

"But you will."

Deirdre was right. Mariana had two more clients that afternoon, neither of whom had terrorist dreams. By the time she was through for the day, she was ready to leave all client concerns behind her at the store.

When she reached the small apartment above a garage a few blocks from the beach, her home in Ventura until she could figure out where to go next, Miles and Ella were waiting to be fed. And Mariana had to feed herself as well. After dinner, she settled down for an evening of watching television, curled up on the bed with the two cats.

She was laughing at an old movie on one of the cable channels when the phone rang.

"Are you watching the news?" Deirdre asked. "If not, turn it on. Your client was murdered. You may want to call David after all."

Deirdre hung up before Mariana could argue with her.

And there it was on the local news. Jean Cullen had been murdered, stabbed to death when she apparently surprised a pair of burglars. Her distraught husband, Eric Cullen, sobbed for the camera. Mariana had been wrong—it was a matter for the police.

Mariana waited until morning, after an almost sleepless night, before she picked up the phone and called David.

He returned her call just as she was getting ready to leave for the store.

"The woman who was murdered last night, Jeannie Cullen," Mariana said. "Her husband did it."

David hesitated, then said, "He couldn't have done it, Mariana. He has an alibi. Eric Cullen owns a custom auto body shop, and for the last couple of weeks he and two other men have been working into the night, restoring a classic Jaguar. They place him at the shop until after ten. Then he stopped for a late dinner, verified by a credit card slip. His wife had been dead for a couple of hours by the time he got home."

"Are you sure? Couldn't the men be covering for him?"

"Believe me, we checked. The spouse is always a suspect until proven otherwise. And burglars don't often break into a home in the middle of the evening when someone is there. Because of that, we'll look at him even harder. But the two men who swore he was working with them seem pretty reliable, and the waitress remembered him, said he didn't seem upset about anything. Why do you think he did it?"

"Because she came to see me yesterday. She said he was a terrorist, plotting something, but I told her she was the one in danger, told her to leave him. I should have called you then," Mariana said.

David laughed gently. "You can call me anytime. But I couldn't have done anything to protect Jean Cullen, you know that."

"You could have had somebody drive by her house last night," Mariana argued.

"But I wouldn't have. You know that, too. We wouldn't have done anything unless she asked for help."

Mariana did know that.

"What happens now?" she asked.

"We investigate it as a burglary that became a murder, just what it appears to be. And don't worry. We'll consider the possibility that Eric Cullen set it up himself, that he hired somebody to do it. Do you have any idea why he might have wanted to get rid of his wife?"

"No. Damn. I don't. She didn't think he was angry at her—she kept calling him a terrorist. I'll tune in later and let you know what I come up with," Mariana said.

"How about over dinner?" David asked.

This was why she hadn't wanted to call him.

"I'll think about it," she said.

"My divorce is final in November. Are you going to make me wait until then?"

"It's not that."

"Then what?"

"We live in such different worlds. I don't think it makes sense to start something that can't go anywhere."

"Would you say that to one of your clients?"

"No, I wouldn't." She would look at the energy flow between the two people, and if it was positive, as she knew it was in this case, she would tell a client not to jump ahead, not to try to guess the end of the relationship at the beginning, because too much can happen in between. People have free will. Take it a step at a time, see what it feels like. "All right. Dinner. But not tonight. I didn't sleep last night, and I'm tired. And I still have to work this afternoon."

"Okay. Tomorrow. I'll pick you up at seven."

Mariana hung up the phone, grabbed the bag that held her cards, said good-bye to the cats, and headed down the stairs to her car. She didn't like being late.

Not that it would have mattered this day. Deirdre was alone when Mariana reached the store, and the only two appointments for readings were scheduled late in the afternoon.

"So what did David say?" Deirdre asked before Mariana even had a chance to put her bag in the reading room and get a cup of tea.

"He said the husband has an alibi," Mariana replied.

"Of course," Deirdre said. "I asked for a dream of Jeannie last night. She realizes now that she was wrong, that she was in danger from her husband. It's some kind of trade, but I don't think she knows the details, even with her enhanced perspective. He's going to do something for someone else, and that's the person who murdered her."

"A dream of Jeannie," Mariana said, smiling in spite of herself.

"But she has dark brown hair," Deirdre said.

"And she spoke to you?"

"Not exactly. Her regret and her husband's anger were feelings that she transmitted. And then I saw an image of something changing hands, and a handshake, and then blood. The blood woke me up. I could be wrong on the interpretation, but I don't think so," Deirdre replied.

"How long have you been able to control your dreams—get what you ask for?" Mariana asked.

"I can't always do it. But I've been working on it for about fifteen years now, and sometimes it works." Deirdre twisted her face into mock annoyance. "It's like everything else connected with the psychic world, though. I can't always get all the information I want. Jeannie didn't tell me anything you could use to convince David that her husband is a murderer."

"Or a terrorist." Mariana lowered her voice. Two women had just entered the shop, heading for the incense display, and she didn't want to discuss the murder with them. "What could this favor be? Do you suppose he really is planning to blow something up?"

"That's as good a favor for murder as any, isn't it?" Deirdre had lowered her voice, too.

Mariana sighed. She felt like a conspirator, the way the two of them had their voices lowered and their heads together. "All right. How do we get more information? Do I read for you, or do you read for me? Or do you want to channel Baba-ji?"

"Well, it gets harder now, because we're both involved to some degree, which makes it harder to get out of the way and let the energy through, as you know." Deirdre said. "And I don't think Baba-ji would be interested in helping out on this one. He'd want to know how this project helps our spiritual growth."

"I should think bringing a murderer to justice is a good reason to go forward," Mariana said.

"I know you would, but Baba-ji would tell you that the Lords of Karma will take care of Eric Cullen, and that they don't need your help," Deirdre said calmly.

"And so . . ." Mariana prompted.

"And so I think we both ought to ask for dreams of Jeannie. She might get through to you more easily than to me, since you made a psychic connection with her shortly before she died. Let's try that first." The two women customers were standing in front of the cash register, and Deirdre moved away to ring up the purchase.

Mariana wanted something more definitive, but she knew she wasn't going to get it. She needed to prepare for her first client. Jeannie Cullen's murderer would have to wait.

The afternoon dragged for Mariana, with only two readings. Deirdre was busy, though, with a steady stream of customers, so they didn't get a chance to resume the conversation until Mariana was ready to leave.

"I'll do it," Mariana said, as Deirdre counted out her share of the money for the readings. "I'll try asking for a dream. But I want to do something else, too. I want to drive by Eric Cullen's shop and see if I can pick anything up from the energy there."

"You think you'll catch him making a bomb?" Deirdre handed Mariana the money and closed the cash register.

"No. I just want to see what the place feels like. Mind if I borrow the telephone directory? I need an address."

Mariana found the address, only because Eric Cullen had been considerate enough to list himself as owner of Top of the Line Body Shop in the Yellow Pages ad. The shop was on Thompson, in midtown Ventura, one of a number of auto repair shops in a cluster not too far from where she lived.

"Don't go in," Deirdre said.

"I'll just drive by," Mariana replied. "Although the Mustang could use a paint job."

"Call me when you get home."

Mariana shook her head, not wanting to be fussed over, and left the store.

She took the short drive to Thompson and slowed down when she reached the block, looking for a sign so that she could tell which of the small repair shops was the right one.

Top of the Line Body Shop had an address on Thompson, but was actually set back from the street, almost all the way to Front Street, the last street before the railroad tracks, the freeway, Harbor Boulevard, and the beach. Mariana decided to drive around the block to get a better look.

But there was really nothing to see. A narrow asphalt parking area with more cars than parking spaces and a garage with three racks, all of them in use. A small office. That was it.

There were five men working on the cars, all wearing dirty gray uniforms. Mariana wondered which one was Eric Cullen. She decided he had to be the big man with blond, curly hair. He seemed to be in charge.

Deirdre was right, of course. Mariana wasn't likely to catch him working on a bomb. Especially at six in the evening, with the sun still up. The thing to do was to drive by later, see if he really worked until ten.

Mariana drove home, fed the cats, fed herself, and found that she couldn't settle into her regular evening routine, tired as she was. She wanted to know what Eric Cullen was doing.

She forced herself to wait until nine o'clock before she left the house. She wrapped herself in a shawl, not because she needed protection from the elements, but because it brought her comfort.

The evening air was a comfortable sixty-five degrees, practically a year-round norm in Ventura. For about ten months of the year, the temperature rose to a high of seventy during the day and dropped to a low of fifty at night. Not much summer, but not much winter, either. Mariana couldn't complain about the cold. Still, the shawl felt good.

The short trip down Thompson didn't quite confirm Eric Cullen's alibi, but it confirmed that he might have had one. The lights were out at the four other shops that were part of the same cluster. Not at Top of the Line. Three men were still working on what appeared to be a dark blue Jaguar, and one of the men was the big blond.

Mariana couldn't think of a good reason to talk to them, so she slowly drove home again.

Deirdre was right. The only thing she could do was ask for a dream of Jeannie.

The dream came toward morning, and Mariana struggled to hold on to the images when she woke up.

She had been standing in a meadow, and Jeannie had waved to her from the other side of the stream—a transformed Jeannie, smiling, glad to see her. Then she and Jeannie were flying, hand in hand, through the night sky. The ocean was below them. Then they were over a building of some kind—Mariana couldn't quite make it out—and Jeannie wanted to take her inside, but then they were both afraid. Jeannie vanished, and Mariana woke up.

That was all.

A dream of Jeannie. *Borne like an angel on the summer air.* Except that in the song Jeannie was borne like a vapor, not an angel. Nothing was quite right.

The building. Was there a way of finding the building? Was it even in Ventura? It didn't look like a house, more like an office building, but the image had been hazy.

Mariana hurried to get ready to go to Enchantment, eager to compare dreams with Deirdre.

But Deirdre was busy with customers, and Mariana had two clients waiting, and it was the middle of the afternoon before Mariana could tell Deirdre about her trip to the body shop, and before they had a chance to compare dreams.

"Well, Jeannie certainly wants to communicate with you," Deirdre said, when Mariana had told her dream. "And your dream was more helpful than mine. All I got was the image of Jeannie lying dead on the floor while two men with gloves on messed up the living room. Neither one was a big blond."

"If you saw them, though, maybe you could pick them out of a book," Mariana said. "Mug shots."

"No. All I could tell was that they were both more brownish than blondish. They had baseball caps on, and facial hair, and jackets pulled up high. I don't think Jeannie knew them."

Mariana sighed. "David told me when we first met that psychic information was always interesting, usually right, and never helped him solve a case. I'd really like to prove him wrong."

"We have a start," Deirdre said. "We know we have to find a building near the beach."

"We?" Mariana had expected Deirdre to try to talk her out of looking for the building.

"Well, you. I have to be home to take care of the kids tonight."

"And I'm having dinner with David."

"Then after dinner you can take a nice, romantic drive along the beach and look for that building."

"I'll think about it. I'm not sure David would agree."

They were interrupted by Mariana's third client, who turned out to be her last for the afternoon. Because it was slow, Mariana checked out a little early. And because it was Saturday, she wouldn't be seeing Deirdre for the next four days.

"Call me tomorrow," Deirdre said, as Mariana prepared to leave. "Don't make me wait until Thursday to find out about your date. Or about the building, either."

"I'll call if there's anything to tell. And call me if you get another dream."

Mariana stepped out into a late afternoon that was a little sunnier than the preceding days. She still felt a chill.

By the time she had gone home, fed the cats, and put on a little fresh makeup, the chill had settled into her bones. She wished she hadn't made the date with David.

Just before seven, she heard his footsteps on the stairs.

"I'm early," he said as she opened the door.

"It's all right. I'm ready."

They walked down the stairs in silence, not speaking until they were both settled into his car.

"I thought we might go to that café on Thompson," David said, starting the engine.

"That's fine. We could drive by Eric Cullen's shop on the way, see if he's working late," Mariana replied.

David frowned. His gray moustache twitched before he answered. "If there's something you have to tell me about Jean Cullen's murder, let's get it over with before we have dinner."

"I'm not sure I have anything that will help, but Deirdre and I have both been dreaming of Jeannie."

"Okay, tell me." David turned off the engine. He leaned back in the seat and looked at her, waiting.

Mariana couldn't quite see his eyes. She wished she could see his eyes.

"Jeannie says it was two men, brownish complexion, facial hair, wearing jackets and baseball caps. She didn't know them. She thinks there was some kind of trade, that they murdered her because her husband is going to do something for someone else. There is a building involved, and I think it's near the beach. Maybe he's going to blow it up." She got it all out in one breath.

"All this from a dream," David said.

She still couldn't see his expression.

"From three dreams, actually—two of Deirdre's and one of mine."

"Anything else?"

"No." Mariana hesitated, then plunged on. "Except I was wondering if you had come up with any motives, either a motive for the burglary—something important stolen from the house—or a motive for murder."

"Nothing we could take to court. Cullen lost his wife at a convenient time. He's in debt, and the insurance money will get him out. And we heard he has a girl friend. On top of that, nothing of value was stolen from the house." David reached over and put his hand on her shoulder. "I'm telling you this because I'm treating you as part of the investigation on this case. I want to know anything either one of you picks up. Okay?"

"Does that mean we can take a drive along the beach and look for the building?"

"After dinner. But only if you promise to talk about something else from now until then."

Mariana promised. So over dinner and wine at the small café on Thompson they had one of those conversations that people have when they are avoiding talking about anything important, complete with awkward silences.

She was glad when it was over.

And he kept his promise.

"Which way?" he asked, when he had steered the car to Harbor Boulevard. He hadn't driven past Eric Cullen's shop on the way to dinner, but he did then. The lights were out, and he didn't slow down.

"I don't know. Let's try right. I think it's toward Santa Barbara, not Oxnard."

"In that case, I should have stayed on Thompson. Do you want me to pick up the freeway?"

"Yes."

It would have been a pleasant drive under other circumstances, with a full moon and a clear sky and the gentle waves breaking against the sand. But this wasn't going to work, and Mariana knew it almost at once.

"You might as well take me home," she said, even before they reached the Seacliff exit.

"Okay."

She could feel his disappointment. Until then, she hadn't realized that he wanted her to be right. There was something comforting about him wanting her to be right.

"I'm not going to ask you in," she said when he stopped the car in front of her door. Even though they weren't in the black-and-white, David accepted it as his prerogative as a police detective to park in a no-parking zone.

"I know." He leaned over and kissed her cheek. "Goodnight."

Mariana was halfway up the stairs, and David had already driven away, when it hit her. Nothing about this was quite right. They should have turned left on Harbor Boulevard.

She wasn't certain what to do, whether to go in and try to call him back, or to look for the building herself. But then a wave of urgency hit her. She had to look for the building. Now.

She walked back down to the carport, got in her car, and headed back to Harbor Boulevard, this time turning left.

When she saw the building, she recognized it at once, and wondered why she hadn't known it in the dream. It was a small, exclusive hotel, with an equally small and exclusive restaurant, a low rectangular building, dimly lit, right on the beach. And a dark blue classic Jaguar was parked in front of the restaurant.

The wave of urgency hit her again. It was quickly replaced by fear, the same fear that she had felt in the dream.

Mariana pulled over to the curb and jumped out of her car. She started running toward the restaurant, shouting as she ran.

"There's a bomb in the Jaguar! A bomb!"

She saw a door open, and a face appear.

"A bomb!" she cried again. "In the car! Run!"

People began streaming out of the restaurant, customers and staff, running away from the building.

But when the explosion came, it wasn't from the car. The entire restaurant turned into a fireball before her eyes.

Mariana stood, too stunned to say anything when a security guard appeared beside her and twisted her arm up behind her back.

"Let's sit down, right where we are, and wait for the police," he said.

Mariana nodded. That was exactly what she wanted to do.

The firefighters were the first to arrive, followed closely by three police cars. She sat locked in the back of a black-and-white until David arrived to take her home for the second time that evening.

Mariana didn't call Deirdre on Sunday. She spent much of the day recovering from the fear and the shock of the night before, a recovery made only a little easier by the sense that the spirit of Jeannie Cullen was hovering over her bed, wanting her to be all right.

Deirdre had been watching television news, though, and she left two messages that Mariana ignored. Deirdre knew she was all right. The details would have to wait until she felt like sharing them.

Only after David had called on Monday to fill in the missing pieces did Mariana pick up the phone and call Enchantment.

"The bomb target was Senator Fordham," Mariana said. "She and her husband occasionally use that particular hotel for a weekend getaway. Several people knew they would be there this weekend. And everybody knows they enjoy late dinners. Nobody raised an eyebrow when a well-dressed blond man with a briefcase parked a Jaguar out front and asked for a table. Nobody noticed when he went to the men's room and didn't come back."

"So they have Eric Cullen for the bombing, if not his wife's murder. Does David know who the co-conspirator is yet?" Deirdre asked.

"The FBI is swarming all over the case, but the rumor is that someone wanted to remove the one strong anti-war voice from the Armed Services Committee," Mariana told her. "It centers around the shop. I'm almost certain that one of Cullen's employees is the link. But I've been not-quite-right on so much, starting with my dream of an earthquake. It felt like an earthquake, but it was an explosion. I think I would have responded differently from the beginning if I had dreamed of an explosion."

"But you still succeeded in saving all those people. Is David ready to admit that he was wrong? That psychics can help solve a case?"

"He was even cheerful about it."

"So are you seeing him tonight?" Deirdre sounded like a teenager, and Mariana didn't feel like giggling with her. Not yet.

"Tonight I'm asking for a dream of Jeannie," Mariana said. "It's time to get it right, time to say thank you, and goodbye."

Edward D. Hoch

The Face of Ali Baba

■ ■ ■

Edward D. Hoch is the author of more than 850 short stories, and is believed by many to be the foremost author of short mystery fiction. Nick Velvet, a thief who—for a substantial fee—steals only items of no intrinsic value, appears in many stories. Other recurring characters are Dr. Sam Hawthorne, an elderly general practitioner, and the unusual Simon Ark, who claims to be a two-thousand-year-old Coptic priest. Hoch has also served as president of the Mystery Writers of America, and received that organization's Grand Master Award in 2001. He has not only written every type of mystery story, he's invented a few along the way as well. "The Face of Ali Baba," his contribution to this year's collection, which first appeared in EQMM, *shows him in fine form as retired secret agent Jeffery Rand tracks down a terrorist in India.*

Long ago, when he was a boy playing in the desert village of his birth, he'd had another name. But that was so far in the past he'd almost forgotten what it was. Now, to his growing band of followers and the bulk of the world's press, he was merely Ali Baba the terrorist, the man who'd planned the devastating attacks on New York and London and Paris.

The nations of the world had risen up against him, with every major intelligence service on his trail. He'd been forced to shave his beard and flee his homeland, escaping through the checkpoints in a coffin beneath the embalmed body of an old woman. Now he needed a destination, someplace where they would not think of seeking him out, yet someplace close enough so he could still contact and command his followers. His first action had been to pay a small fortune to a plastic surgeon in New Delhi to make certain changes in his appearance.

Sometime after the operation, when he was certain of its success, he ordered the surgeon and another man run down by trucks and killed. He was covering his tracks.

It was a few weeks later, in early April, when Rand's plane touched down in Pakistan. Much as he disliked the assignment that had brought him out of retirement once again, he realized that he had no one to blame but himself. The previous year he'd successfully captured a killer on Crete with links to a terrorist network, and British Intelligence had ways of remembering accomplishments like that.

This was the biggest one of all, he knew. The man known throughout the world as

Ali Baba was a terrorist and leader of terrorists. "You get this one," he'd been told, "and it could mean a knighthood from the Queen."

Rand had studied Ali Baba's photographs at length, always aware that he might look entirely different now. Some said he did not have the classic features of a true Arab, and might have a bit of Indian blood in him. It had been a year since he'd been photographed in Pakistan, and that was where the trail ended. The terrorist leader had no siblings or known relatives, nowhere he would likely go to hide. The man who would help Rand pick up the trail, in Multon, was named Hugh Draper, an Englishman who'd spent a good portion of his life in the Middle East. He had a tanned and weathered face, a product of the dry desert air in that part of Pakistan and neighboring India. A contract employee of various intelligence services, at the moment he was working for the British.

"Mr. Rand, I'm happy to give you any help I can, but you realize it must be somewhat limited. We believe Ali Baba was here and then gone, before any of us ever saw this photograph."

The picture in question appeared to show the terrorist's face, minus his familiar beard, engaged in conversation with another man. "Have you identified this man?" Rand asked.

"It is a local undertaker, Verier Rangoli. A newspaper took it months ago but didn't use it until last month when he died. Ali Baba, if that is really he, gave the photographer a fictitious name, and the few people who saw the photo didn't recognize him. It wasn't until some time after they published it that our man at the British Embassy spotted a similarity to younger pictures of Ali Baba without his beard."

"Have you questioned the photographer?"

"Of course," Draper told him. "A reporter had interviewed the undertaker for a story and then sent a photographer around for pictures. He snapped about a dozen of Rangoli talking to families and arranging funerals. He remembered this man didn't want his picture used, claimed he was arranging for the funeral of an elderly aunt. They didn't use it at first and it went into the file, but after Rangoli's death the photo editor dug it out and ran it."

"What did Rangoli die of?"

"Street accident. A truck hit him. Nothing unusual in these parts."

Rand's expertise during his years with British Intelligence had been with codes and ciphers, but he'd learned a good deal more than that. "You must have the date this photo was taken. We could check the funeral home's records for the supposed aunt."

"I've already done it. It was at the end of November. There were no burials here that week, only a body shipped back home to New Delhi in a hearse."

"What better way to slip across the border than inside a coffin?"

"These days the lids are opened at the border. We know all their tricks."

Rand thought about it. "Ali Baba is not a large man, neither in height nor weight. He might have left the country in that same coffin, concealed beneath the old woman's body."

"Who would travel hundreds of miles like that?" Draper asked.

"He only had to travel a few miles across the border. Once inside India the hearse would have stopped so he could come out of hiding."

"Would Ali Baba have chanced that?"

"No," Rand decided on further thought. "It would be safest to remain in the coffin for the entire journey. How far is it from the Indian border to New Delhi?"

"About two hundred miles. You pick up the national highway as soon as you cross and it takes you directly to the capital."

"Little more than a three-hour journey on a good highway. I think we can assume that Ali Baba escaped across the border in that coffin and then traveled all the way to the capital in it."

"If that was really him in the photo," Draper cautioned. "I have a car if you wish to make the trip."

Rand smiled. "I'm retired. I have nothing better to do than follow up on false leads."

"No wife left behind?"

"She lectures on archaeology at Reading University. I hope she's missing me about now."

New Delhi is a twentieth-century city built on a site adjoining old Delhi after India's capital was moved there from Calcutta in 1911. It took nearly twenty years to build, and with its symmetrical street layout and Western architectural style it reminded Rand of Washington, D.C. Mainly the nation's administrative center, the city also boasted a few manufacturing, printing, and textile plants. The body of the elderly woman had been consigned to the Bundi Funeral Home near the city's center, and they picked up the trail there.

Jawahar Bundi was a short swarthy man in a red turban who seemed disturbed by Rand's questions. Yes, he had received the body in question the previous November. The date of the interment was here in his records. New Delhi was not like some areas of India, where bodies were burned or left for the vultures.

"Did you open the coffin?" Rand asked.

"Of course! Three of her nephews insisted on being present when I did so, to verify that it was really their aunt."

"Did you leave them alone with the body?"

The undertaker nodded. "They wanted some private time to pray over her."

Rand nodded. "I expected as much."

He asked Bundi if he had seen a fourth person with them as they left, but the undertaker shook his head. "It was strange, though," he said, digging back in his memory. "The one nephew came out and made arrangements for the burial. He said the others had already left by the back door."

So Ali Baba, in all likelihood, had been in New Delhi four months ago. But where was he now?

Back at their hotel, Rand and Draper pondered the question. "He'd need to change his appearance," Draper decided, stating the obvious.

"Plastic surgery?"

"Probably. He shaved off his beard at once, of course, but that wouldn't be enough."

Rand considered the possibilities. "He still looked the same, minus the beard, in that Pakistan photo. He wouldn't have had time to have the surgery there before being smuggled out of the country in that coffin, but once he was here—"

"We must check the plastic surgeons," Draper agreed.

The list was not a long one even though it covered both Delhi and New Delhi. Draper's knowledge of Hindi helped immensely on the telephone, but the first two calls were not promising. "The first one refused to answer any questions on the grounds of patient confidentiality, and the second one's been dead since last month."

Rand's eyes left the front page of the English-language newspaper he'd been scanning. "Dead how?"

"Traffic accident. Hit by a truck while crossing the street."

"Wasn't that what happened to the undertaker back in Pakistan last month?"

"I believe you're right," Draper agreed. "Odd coincidence, isn't it?"

"Perhaps too odd to be a coincidence," Rand decided.

The following morning they set off on foot for the deceased surgeon's office to learn what they could about his death. It was some distance from their hotel, in old Delhi, where the streets were crowded with bicycles and cars, all openly ignoring the traffic lights. Down the block Rand could see a cow in the street, further impeding progress. The sidewalks were not much better, crowded with street musicians and, in one case, a young man carrying a cobra in an open basket as he sought a suitable place to entertain the crowds.

"That could be dangerous," Rand commented. The cobra reared its head as if preparing to strike.

"Their fangs are usually removed as a precaution," Draper assured him. "Here we are."

The building was red sandstone, like many in the city, but seemed more recent than those around it and boasted a variety of professional offices for doctors and dentists. They sought out the Chandra Clinic on the third floor. Its waiting room was crowded, but they found an Englishwoman named Susan Withers who was the office manager and willing to help.

"The clinic is continuing, though Dr. Chandra's untimely death was a blow to us all," she informed them. She appeared to be in her forties, with dark hair in a neat bun and a solemn demeanor that went well with her tweed suit.

Rand informed her they were seeking a male patient who may have had plastic surgery in late November or early December. "An Arab, perhaps."

"We make no distinction here," she told him.

"Would it be possible to check your records of Dr. Chandra's patients during that period? The surgery would probably have been on the face."

"Face work was his specialty. Many of his patients are women trying to look a bit younger. Some come here from the film studios in Bombay, or Mumbai as it's now called." She bit her lower lip, pondering their request. "Is this government business?"

"British government business," Rand made clear. "The Indian government is not involved at this point."

Susan Withers left her desk and walked to a filing cabinet. She returned with seven folders covering the period in question. "If he were still alive, Dr. Chandra would never allow this. These are all of his male patients during that period."

Rand glanced at the patient names on the file tabs. He hadn't expected to find Ali Baba's name, and the ones that were there meant nothing to him. *Guijarey, Karni, Lakshmi, Masese, Mughal, Nautch, Surai*. "Are any of these familiar?" he asked Draper.

"Can't say that they are."

Together they read over the patients' descriptions. All were in their late thirties or forties, close to Ali Baba's age, and all had addresses in India. Their heights and weights were not recorded. "Do you have any before-and-after photographs?" Rand asked.

"Dr. Chandra kept those at home. He was very proud of some of his results."

"Do you have his address? Perhaps his wife could—"

"Dr. Chandra was divorced and lived alone. I don't know what happened to his personal effects."

Rand took down the names and addresses of the seven male patients, and then asked for Dr. Chandra's address as well. Susan Withers studied him for a moment, then flipped open the Rolodex on her desk. "You won't find anything," she promised.

She was right. Dr. Chandra's apartment had already been rented. The building's owner spoke of relatives who had removed a few pieces of furniture. He'd purchased some other pieces from them. He knew nothing of any papers or photographs.

"It appears to be a dead end," Hugh Draper said. They had stopped in an Indian coffeehouse across the street to get their bearings and review the situation.

"Of course we may be all wrong about the plastic surgeon. Ali Baba might not have needed one here in New Delhi. He may have had transportation arranged out of the country. Or he may have gone to a different surgeon. Chandra's accident might have been just that—an accident."

"Perhaps we'll never know."

"I don't like loose ends," Rand told him. "There've been too many in this part of the world over the last couple of years."

That was when a tall, large man approached them, wearing a turban that identified him as a member of the Sikh religion. "Pardon me," he said in educated English, "but are you the chaps who inquired after Dr. Chandra?"

"We are," Rand admitted. "We were sorry to learn of his misfortune."

"I am Dr. Aafia Fareed, from Kolkata—or Calcutta, as the English called it. Dr. Chandra was a close friend. We went through medical school in England and served together in a bomb-removal squad with the Indian army before setting up our practices. I arrived at his former apartment just after you'd left. The manager thought he saw you come over this way."

Rand shook hands and introduced himself and Draper. "Do you know any details about his death?"

The turbaned doctor shook his head. "Only that he was run down by a truck last month while crossing the street to his office. The news was very upsetting to me, but I had surgery scheduled and could not get away until now." He motioned to an empty chair. "May I join you?"

"Please do," Rand said, feeling that this doctor might contribute something to their search. "Was the truck driver questioned by police?"

"I understand that he fled the scene, not unusual in these crowded streets."

"Are you a plastic surgeon like Dr. Chandra?" Draper asked.

Fareed shook his head. "Ear, nose, and throat. I perform corrective surgery, but nothing that is strictly cosmetic. We had been friends, for a long time, however."

Rand asked, "Were you in touch with him recently?"

"He phoned me from here the day before his death."

"And said what?"

"That he feared for his life. He had performed plastic surgery on a wanted man for a large sum of money, and already he was regretting it."

"Did you report that to the police?"

He shook his head sadly. "I did not take him seriously. The next day his office manager, Susan Withers, notified me of the accident. I could not be here for the memorial service, but I come now in hopes of learning something about his death."

"You believe he was murdered?"

"I do not know what to think."

Rand decided to tell him what they knew. "We have reason to believe the man Dr. Chandra operated on was the notorious terrorist leader known as Ali Baba. Apparently he escaped from Pakistan in the false bottom of a coffin which was delivered to a funeral home here."

"Ali Baba," Fareed repeated the name. "Some think he must be dead."

"But we think he's very much alive." Rand took the patient list from his pocket. "If we're right, the name he's using could be one of these seven. They're all of Chandra's male patients through the end of the year. Guijarey, Karni, Lakshmi, Masese, Mughal, Nautch, and Surai. Do the names mean anything to you?"

"Not a thing."

Rand stared at them again, and suddenly he was back at his desk at Concealed Communications, pondering an enemy cipher. The answer leapt out at him, so clearly that he wondered why he hadn't seen it at once. "This one!" he said suddenly, pointing a finger. "What address do we have for Masese?"

"Masese?" Draper scanned his list. "He lives in Jaipur. But how do you know it's him?"

"What word would be most important to a criminal using the name of Ali Baba? *Masese* is an anagram of *Sesame*."

Dr. Fareed, who knew the country, agreed to accompany them to Jaipur, a city about a hundred and fifty miles southwest of New Delhi. "It is called the pink city," he told them as they drove toward it along a wide paved highway with low mountains rising on either side. "The largest in the state of Rajasthan. By law, all buildings in the old city must be painted deep saffron pink. It is said the city was freshly painted in eighteen seventy-six for a visit by the Prince of Wales, and the tradition continues today." He spoke from the backseat, and Rand noticed he was trimming his nails with a pair of surgical scissors while he talked.

"I thought Sikhs wore small daggers inside their shirts," he remarked to the man.

"Many do, but I do not. These scissors serve most of my wants."

The old portion of the city was indeed pink, but that was only the beginning of the riot of color that awaited them. Women wore bright red and orange head coverings in the streets, and the men were no less colorful with their turbans. "Often you can tell a man's hometown and profession from his turban," Fareed said, "though I do not have that skill. You will notice this is a city of very wide streets, carefully laid out. It is also a city where much polo is played, not merely on horseback but on elephants and even bicycles."

Overlooking it all was the Amber Fort, a huge place on a hill north of Jaipur, with a commanding view of all around it. Begun in the eleventh century, it was later expanded to become a retreat for battle-weary maharajas. Originally, Fareed told them, it had to be reached by elephant up winding trails past seven fortified gates.

They passed an elephant being led by its keeper along the street. Its legs had been painted with a variety of intricate designs. "I wonder if he knows how pretty he looks," Draper said.

The address given by the patient M. Masese proved to be a convent of Catholic nursing sisters on Hospital Road. A gated fence surrounded the place and they could see an elderly gardener working among the flowers. It seemed like another dead end, but Dr. Fareed insisted that they investigate further. A short white-bearded priest who looked like a stuffed Father Christmas in his brown cassock and sandals came out to greet them. "Are you in need of nursing help?" he asked Fareed after the doctor had introduced himself.

"No, we are seeking a lost friend of mine, a man named Masese who gave this as his address."

"We know of no Masese here," the priest told them. "I am Father Briese of the Franciscan Order. I tend to the nursing sisters who reside here." His accent might have been French, but Rand could not be sure. "Let me call Sister Ruth."

They followed him into the convent with its dark woodwork and antique furnishings. It occurred to Rand that the place probably dated from late Victorian times, when the Queen herself had been proclaimed Empress of India. They waited a few moments until the priest returned, followed by a middle-aged woman in a white habit. "I am Sister Ruth," she said in a deep, almost masculine voice. "Welcome to the Convent of the Little Flower."

"We seek a man named Masese who is said to live here," Rand told her. "Do you know of such a person?"

She glanced over at Father Briese. "Do we? No, there are only the sisters here."

"We saw a gardener as we entered," Draper said. "Might he know something about this neighborhood?"

Sister Ruth peered out the window at the old man. "Cassim? He only came after his brother, our previous gardener, was taken ill at the beginning of the year. You might ask him if you wish. We have nothing to hide here."

Rand went out to speak with the old man, bent like a hunchback over his flowers. "Are you Cassim?"

"That I am," the man admitted, straightening up a bit. His English was good, probably dating back to the colonial influence on his country. "What do you want?"

"We're searching for a man named Masese. He may have been receiving mail at this address."

The name had sparked some recognition in his eyes. "I have seen him."

"What does he look like?"

The man did not answer at once, until finally Rand slipped him a few coins. Then he said, "Middle-aged, clean-shaven, about my height. Possibly an Arab. He paid me to pick up some mail for him and deliver it to an address outside the city. I did it just once. There has been no more since then."

"How long ago was this?"

"About a month, perhaps longer."

"The mail was addressed to him here, at the convent?"

"Yes. It was from a doctor's office in New Delhi."

Hugh Draper and Dr. Fareed had come out to join them now, and Rand told them what he'd learned. "Can you take us there?" Fareed asked at once.

The old gardener stared up at the sky, as if for some divine revelation. "It will be dark soon," he decided. "We could not reach the house before nightfall."

"It is important that we go now," Draper insisted, and this time it was he who gave the gardener some rupees.

The man laid down his tools. "This can be finished in the morning. It is already too dim for my poor eyesight. Let us go."

Rand told Father Briese that their gardener knew of the man they sought and was taking them to him. Then all four piled into Hugh Draper's car, with Cassim riding in back with Dr. Fareed. Rand was beginning to feel a bit like Dorothy in *The Wizard of Oz*, acquiring three traveling companions as she went off to see the Wizard.

"Drive west," Cassim instructed, "toward the desert."

"The desert is a long way."

"It is not that far to the house you seek. It is only on the outskirts of Jaipur."

They passed elaborate palaces and forts, spectacular even in the twilight. Draper was breathing hard. "You know, if this is the man we think it is, he'll be dangerous."

"There are four of us," Rand said to reassure him. He doubted if they would find the elusive Ali Baba this easily.

They passed the railway station and entered the residential part of the city, carefully laid out in square blocks. Presently they were traveling along a darkened highway. "This road leads to Bagru, but we will not be going that far," the gardener told them. "Do you see that sign up ahead?"

Rand could see nothing but after a moment Draper said, "Yes, I see it."

"Turn left there. We are almost to our destination."

They were on a lane much narrower than the highway, and Cassim had them pull off the road to park. All was in darkness, lit only by the moon overhead. As he left the car Rand could hear the distant haunting sound of a flute, which Dr. Fareed identified as a *satara*, actually a double flute. "It is the sound of the desert," he told them. "Melodious yet somehow strange."

Draper opened the glove compartment and took a small flashlight and pistol from it. "Better to be safe," he explained.

The old gardener hung back as they started for the darkened house with Fareed in the lead. It was a one-story stone building, no different from others along the lane. "No one seems to be home," Fareed said, using the knocker on the door. The music in the distance had ceased, and all was silence.

Draper reached around him and tried the door. "It's unlocked."

"You two go around to the rear," Fareed suggested, "in case he tries to escape."

Rand sent Draper to the back while he stayed at the front corner of the house, keeping his eye on Fareed and the gardener. Cassim still stood near the car, and had turned away from the house. Fareed carefully swung the door open, bending low as if to pick something up from the floor. The doctor stepped inside and suddenly yelled, "He's here!"

Rand hurried toward the front door as two gunshots sounded. He saw Cassim stagger and fall forward on his face. "Fareed!" he shouted.

"I'm in here, on the floor. Be careful!"

There was a smashing of glass at the back of the house and Draper came through the rear door. His flashlight picked out Fareed lying among some bottles and rags. Rand saw that Draper held the small automatic in his right hand. "I didn't fire," he said.

"Someone did." As he spoke, Rand remembered the old man out in front. He ran outside, followed by the others, and fell to his knees beside the body. They could see the blood from the wounds to his head and back.

"He's dead," Fareed said.

"Give me your gun," Rand demanded, holding out his hand to Draper. He put the pistol to his nose and sniffed. It didn't seem to have been fired.

"He's still in there," Draper said. "And we're sitting ducks out here in the moonlight!"

But Rand shook his head. "If he wanted to shoot us he'd have done it already. Come on, there may be another way out of there."

Using Draper's flashlight, he found a switch and turned on the room's only lamp. There were few furnishings, with some Indian-style miniature paintings on the walls. On a shelf lay a copy of the Koran. "A Muslim house, certainly," Rand said. He went quickly through the kitchen, bedroom, and bath, finding nothing. All the windows were locked, and Draper had only gained entrance by smashing the glass in the locked back door.

"Here's a trapdoor to the basement!" Draper called out. He lifted it slowly and Rand pointed the flashlight down, then started climbing down a rickety ladder. Draper and Dr. Fareed followed.

A pile of wooden boxes lined one wall of the small room. Rand lifted the lid on one, unable to decipher the stenciled Hindi printing. "Sticks of dynamite," he announced. "Enough to blow this house over the moon." He picked up a vest of heavy cloth. "It looks like he was fitting them into these vests for suicide bombings."

Draper had spotted something else. "This looks like a tunnel!"

"Ali Baba's escape route," Fareed said.

"Perhaps." Rand took the flashlight and Draper's gun, bending slightly so he could walk through the low tunnel. It had been carved from stone for most of its length, finally coming out over a hundred feet away. Rand brushed the spider webs from his path and stepped into another basement, obviously that of a neighboring house. He quickly searched both basement and upstairs, but the place was empty, devoid even of furniture. Like the first house, it seemed to have no telephone.

The others came along behind him. "Nothing here?" Draper asked.

"Not a thing. This was, as you say, his escape route. When he saw us split up to surround the house he knew he couldn't kill us all. Cassim was the unlucky one, probably because Ali Baba recognized him and knew he'd led us here."

"We must report the body and these explosives to the police," Draper said.

"We will do that, as soon as we find a telephone."

Off in the distance, he could hear the sound of the mournful flute once more drifting across the night air.

The following morning Rand awoke in his room at the Jaipur Palace, a medium-priced hotel some three miles from the city. Hugh Draper and Dr. Fareed occupied adjoining rooms. Rand thought about phoning his wife Leila at home in Reading, but then remembered it would be five and a half hours earlier there. Time zones were difficult enough to remember without the odd half-hour tacked on in some parts of the world.

The hotel was modern, though designed with the look of an Indian palace. He phoned Fareed and Draper, arranging to meet them at their doors for breakfast downstairs at nine. The tall Indian doctor was not yet ready when he knocked. He came out of the bathroom apologetically, in his underwear, wiping his newly washed hair. "Let me slip into my pants and shirt. I'll only be a minute."

Over a continental breakfast, with an Indian meal for Dr. Fareed, Rand raised the possibility that Ali Baba might not have been living at that house at all. "Someone who knew or suspected we would go there might have driven out ahead of us and laid a trap."

"That still makes it Ali Baba or one of his aides," Draper said.

"There is one thing we are forgetting," Dr. Fareed chimed in. "Plastic surgery can do amazing things these days. My old friend Dr. Chandra once gave a new face to a man who'd had a sex-change operation, helping convert him to a female."

"I doubt that Ali Baba has had a sex change," Rand remarked.

He had not given his name to the police when he called to report the killing and the stash of explosives. Thus he was surprised to see Father Briese enter the lobby accompanied by a police officer and point them out as they were finishing breakfast.

The uniformed lieutenant asked for identification and Draper pretended innocence, asking the priest what had happened. "Our gardener, Cassim, was shot to death on the road to Bagru," the chubby priest explained. "We cannot afford to lose two gardeners in such a short time. I told Lieutenant Kota that he had left with three visitors."

The officer smiled, enjoying his triumph. "It was an English voice that phoned in the report of the murder. With Father Briese's descriptions it was fairly easy to locate you."

Rand immediately accepted full responsibility, and when they went upstairs to his room he identified himself and gave the officer a number in London that he could call. He told the story of the search for Ali Baba.

"So," Lieutenant Kota said, "you are on the trail of the famous terrorist. You found him at that little house but he shot the gardener Cassim and escaped?"

"That's exactly what happened," Hugh Draper agreed, and Dr. Fareed confirmed it.

"But did you actually see Ali Baba?"

"No," Rand admitted. Perhaps the man was only a phantom, a profitable product for media headlines. And yet, the Pakistani undertaker was dead, Dr. Chandra was dead, and Cassim the gardener was dead.

"How did you trace him here?" the officer wanted to know.

"Dr. Chandra had been killed by a truck, the same as the Pakistani undertaker. We checked his male patients and discovered one of them was named Masese. It's an anagram for Sesame, if you remember your Arabian Nights."

"Would a terrorist killer likely engage in such word games, Mr. Rand?"

"I think he did. I think the explosives and the bomb-making equipment we found in that basement prove it was indeed Ali Baba."

"And you say he escaped through a basement tunnel to an adjoining house?"

"It was the only way out. The house had just two doors and the windows were locked. He couldn't have gotten by us, even in the dark."

"One of your party had a weapon?"

"I had a gun," Draper said, "but it wasn't fired."

Lieutenant Kota puzzled over their story. "Doesn't it seem strange that a terrorist in hiding would leave his front door unlocked?"

"Perhaps he was expecting someone," Rand suggested.

The police lieutenant rose to his feet. "I would like your pistol, Mr. Draper. I will return it to you after we've done some ballistic tests on the bullets that killed the gardener."

Draper handed it over. "Does this mean we have to stay around?"

"We'll know immediately if the caliber of the weapon is different. You could be free to leave by this afternoon."

After he left, they pondered what to do next. Hugh Draper walked to the window and looked out at the passing traffic. "We seem to be at a dead end regarding Ali Baba. If it really was him in that house, he could be across another border by now."

"Perhaps," Dr. Fareed said, "but never forget that India is a nation of illusions. Remember the famous Indian Rope Trick? And we once had a maharaja who rode into battle on a horse fitted with a fake elephant trunk. Enemy horses mistook it for an elephant and were intimidated by it, and even enemy elephants hesitated to attack it."

"Illusion," Rand murmured. "That's really what it's all about, isn't it?"

"To a degree."

"Any of the people we talked to might be Ali Baba. He might be that priest, Father Briese, or even Sister Ruth. Except—"

"Except what?"

"Except that Ali Baba was never in that house last night, was he?"

Both of them appeared puzzled. "He had to be!" Hugh Draper insisted. "Otherwise, who fired those shots?"

"A good question. Consider this: You were at the back door, Dr. Fareed had just entered the front door, and I was at the corner of the house. All the windows were locked. If Ali Baba or someone else in the house fired the shots that killed Cassim, his only means of escape was into the basement and through the tunnel to the adjoining house."

"We knew that last night."

"But I was the first one through that tunnel," Rand reminded him, "and I had to break through cobwebs on the far end. No one escaped that way last night. The shots that killed Cassim had to have been fired by one of you two."

"You smelled my gun," Draper reminded him. "It hadn't been fired."

"That's right. You might have had a second one, but I doubt it. You didn't break the glass until after the shots, when you reached in to unlock the door. Even if you were already inside, it would have been a difficult shot, firing around Fareed here, a large man, to hit Cassim out there in front of the house, lit only by moonlight."

"You're saying I shot him?" the doctor asked. "If I had a gun, what happened to it?"

"When I entered the house after you, I found you on the floor by a pile of rags. It would have been easy to slide the gun under them and retrieve it later when we left the house."

"Do you think that I am Ali Baba?"

Rand shook his head. "I know that you're not. You're a large man, and we established that he was small enough to have hidden in that coffin. I even considered the possibility that you might wear artificial legs, but I saw you this morning in your underwear."

"Then why would I kill that gardener?"

"I want you to tell me," Rand said. "I saw you stoop for something as you entered that house."

Dr. Fareed hesitated, and then said, "Chandra was my old friend. When I heard how he died I knew I must avenge his death. I brought the gun with me for that purpose. When I saw Cassim linger behind and then actually turn away as we entered the house, I remembered my bomb-removal training. I felt near the floor for a trip-wire used on booby traps, and cut it with my scissors. Then I turned and shot Cassim twice in the back."

"On that evidence alone?"

"Cassim said his eyesight was poor, yet he saw that road sign long before us. The house was prepared in advance for just such an eventuality. The terrorist Ali Baba had no brothers, but the legendary Ali Baba did. In the Arabian Nights his brother's name was Cassim, one more use of the old story, like his anagram of Sesame. You see, plastic surgeons can make a person look young, but they can also make him look older than his years if necessary. Ali Baba was the replacement gardener who came to the convent a few months back. Ali Baba was Cassim."

Rand sighed, knowing it was true, even though it might never be proven. He stared at Dr. Fareed and asked, "Now what am I going to do with you?"

Robert S. Levinson

Take My Word for It and You Don't Have to Answer

■ ■ ■

Robert S. Levinson is the bestselling author of the Neil Gulliver and Stevie Marriner series of mystery-thriller novels, the most recent of which is Hot Paint. *Other titles in the series include* The John Lennon Affair, The James Dean Affair, *and his debut novel,* The Elvis and Marilyn Affair, *which has been optioned for development as a film and a possible television series. Levison made his debut as a short-story writer in 2003 in the Warner Books/Mysterious Press anthology* Flesh & Blood: Guilty as Sin, *edited by Max Allan Collins and Jeff Gelb. He also debuted with short stories in both* Alfred Hitchcock's Mystery Magazine *and* Ellery Queen's Mystery Magazine. *He is also currently completing a second term as president of the Mystery Writers of America-Southern California chapter and recently was elected to a two-year term as director at-large on MWA's national board. He wins the prize for longest title this year with "Take My Word for It and You Don't Have to Answer," a tale that intertwines the heyday of Hollywood's Golden Age with the bitter reality of the folks who almost, but didn't quite make it to stardom.*

They found what remained of the body, really not much more than a gunnysack of bones, on the old, decaying Mabel Normand soundstage—a tall, narrow, triangular building, easy to miss, a block north of Sunset Boulevard where Effie Street collides with Fountain Avenue in the low-rent Silverlake area.

The soundstage was the least important landmark in the neighborhood, surrounded as it was by the outdoor location for Griffith's monumental *Intolerance*—now covered by a supermarket—the Monogram Studios, where Leo Gorcey, Huntz Hall, and the Bowery Boys turned out dozens of cheap movies—now home to a PBS TV station—and the ABC television lot up the street at Prospect and Talmadge, once a picturesque hillside owned by movie star Norma Talmadge, where Rin Tin Tin ran in movie after movie to rescue the three Warner brothers and their Vitaphone Pictures from bankruptcy.

Mabel, in her time the madcap queen of silent comedy, today would probably be entirely forgotten by anybody but the movie historians if it weren't for her love affair with the legendary Mack Sennett and her role as one-third of the love triangle that resulted in the still-unsolved murder of that suave playboy director William Desmond Taylor.

She bought the building after her split with Sennett.

Mabel intended to make movies on her own, but too much cheap booze and drugs got in the way and killed her career, as well as Mabel.

Who might be responsible for the bones buried in the gunnysack?

I already knew that, positively.

I knew that fifty years ago.

Only, I couldn't prove it at the time and I couldn't now, unless forensic sciences nonexistent in the 'fifties confirmed that the victim was who I thought it was.

If it happened to turn out otherwise, I'd be back at the intersection of Nowhere and Still Not Yet, burdened by a pacemaker losing ground by the acre to the passing years and a broken heart glued back together but never completely mended.

The story wasn't through playing out in videotape and words breathlessly spoken by a wide-eyed field reporter on the ten o'clock news, posing outside the ratty soundstage, whose walls were decorated in Technicolor tagging full of gang signs, sexual bragging, and a gallery of misspelled words in two languages, when I pulled over the phone and auto-dialed.

Harty answered halfway through the first ring.

Not bothering with a greeting, he said, "You think this is it?"

"Harty, how'd you know it was me calling?"

"You're watching the ten-o'clock. I'm watching the ten-o'clock. We always watch the ten-o'clock. I call you or you call me during the ten-o'clock. Hello, who is this? Is this you, Hale? So, okay, you feel better now?"

"It could be it," I said. "You ready for what happens if it's it, you sarcastic SOB?"

"You try to remember where you keep that damned pistol of yours and you come after me."

"Damned right, you still got that right."

"If I was going to forget anything, I'd like to forget you," Harty said.

"I wouldn't give you the opportunity. Take my word for it and you don't have to answer."

The catch phrase that put us over.

You remember?

How Harty would always challenge something I told him and I would shoot back, "Take my word for it and you don't have to answer"?

Like Abbott and Costello with "Who's on first?" Later, Berle calling for "Makeup!" or Buttons telling us, "Strange things are happening." Henny's "Take my wife . . . please!" The guy in the Fox newsreels reporting, "Monkeys is the craziest people."

Of course you remember.

Take my word for it and you don't have to answer.

Harty answered me anyway.

He said, "I don't need your help with anything. I'm quite capable of forgetting you on my own, thank you very much."

And a whole lot more, you bastard, I thought. *Take my word for it . . .*

We agreed to meet at nine the next morning, but I saw Harty hours before that, in my dream, a nightmare, really. It was the same one I've been having for fifty years, since the whole ugly business—what a *Daily* reporter called "The Hootchy-Kootchy Poochie

Caper"—happened. The name was stuck to this day, in a million books, movies, and TV shows; even a smash Broadway musical starring Ray Downe and Roy Durdy as a pair of stage greats modeled after Harty and me, even if the jury in our lawsuit didn't see the connection. When was the last time anyone in show business ever got a jury of his peers? (Take my word for it and you don't have to answer.)

As clear as if it were yesterday, there we are on the set of *Oh You Beautiful Girls*, our first day and still not believing we've made the giant leap from nightclubs to the big screen, and the queen of gossip, Louella O. Parsons, in her column in the *Examiner*, is already calling us "the first serious challenges for the mantle of Martin and Lewis."

In truth, it's more a hop, skip, and jump than a leap, because *Oh You Beautiful Girls* is a low-budget, almost-no-budget programmer, or why else would we be shooting on the run-down Mabel Normand stage and not one of the magnificent stages the size of airport hangars over at Metro or Fox?

The director is no Busby Berkeley, either. Harmon Von Howitzer was in the big time once, but when his phone rang nowadays it was usually a bill collector threatening to cut off his phone or gas and electric, the way the business had already cut off his career.

He got this gig only because his nephew, Bronco Von Howitzer, who'd trained on low-budget-no-budget seven-day wonders produced at Columbia by Sam Katzman and Joni Taps, and some pot-boilers for Brynie Foy, one of the Eddie Foy seven little Foys, over at Warners, was launching his Bomblast Productions with this sorry excuse for a musical comedy.

The songs, written by multiple Oscar losers Murphy and McCracken, would be performed by raucous Laura. Dane, in her first singing and dancing role, newcomer Brenda Lowe in the Ruby Keeler role, Tree Galleon, plucked from a Vegas chorus line by one of the investors who had an eye for guys, and Barkie, the movies' first and last talking-singing-dancing dog, a St. Bernard with sparkling eyes and an ingratiating smile.

Monogram Pictures had hoped Barkie would do for them what Rinny had done for Warner Bros. and Lassie for Metro in launching a series of Barkie musicals, like *Barkie of Broadway, Rock Around the Pound* and its sequel *Meet Me at the Pound,* and *An American Dog in Paris,* which won Barkie the last of his seven PATSYs, before his bark changed and he no longer could whine a tune.

Barkie was on the comeback trail with *Oh You Beautiful Girls*, while Harty and I were providing the comedy part of the "musical comedy" along with Jackie "The Judge" Johnson, a recovering A.A. who knew how to get to the bottom of a gin bottle five minutes before the cap was unscrewed.

Take my word for it and you don't have to answer.

So, it's our first day on the set and Harty and I are mostly in awe just to be here, because we're young—still in our twenties—with our future ahead of us, and everyone has to start somewhere, even with material like:

HALE

That Barkie knows how to carry a tune
as well as he carries a keg of brandy.

HARTY
(APPLAUDING)

A-paws, A-paws.

We're both oblivious to the fact that Judge Johnson is stumbling around Harmon Von Howitzer's ear, telling him how we're losing the laughs with our delivery and reactions and how he can make the scenes work much better if Von Howitzer wants to retake the scenes with him.

Laura Dane, meanwhile, has her own unhappiness about us. Laura is busy living up to her reputation for screwing everything that isn't screwed down on a soundstage, and so far, the way we hear it, seems to be losing only with Tree Galleon and us, Tree Galleon because of the aforementioned investor, and us because she sees Hale and Harty as a team and has remarked to the best boy and some others, "I like to save my threesomes for the wrap party."

We're glad for that, for lots of reasons, but mainly a reason that neither of us has foreseen.

On first sight, we've both fallen for Brenda Lowe.

It happens the moment she steps in front of the camera and we see her from our gawking position behind the boom.

Brenda is a raven-haired, dark-eyed bundle of beauty, charm, and elegance, radiating warmth and innocence as fresh and bright as a sunrise back home in Indiana.

HALE

She took my breath away. She's the girl
of my dreams. Believe me when I say I'm
going to marry that girl.

HARTY

Not if I marry her first.

HALE

I'm not kidding.

HARTY

Neither am I.

These words spring from our hearts. They're not in the script, although Judge Johnson, who has been tottering near us, at once lurches over to Harmon Von Howitzer and begins whispering in his ear.

Von Howitzer shoos him away and calls something at his A.D.

The A.D. shouts into his megaphone, "Quiet on the set!"

Judge Johnson, frowning at the director's order, has baggy-pantsed like a lost freeway motorist onto the set, a malt shop in Campustown, and appears to be stumbling for a grab at Brenda Lowe.

Barkie, sitting unleashed on a wood and canvas director's chair personalized with his famous paw-print autograph, begins a rumbling hum that turns into a growl, then ferocious barking as he jumps from the chair and charges at Judge Johnson.

Barkie leaps and is on target for the judge's back, in the air as Brenda pushes the judge aside, but instead lands on Brenda, knocking her backward and down onto the hardwood floor. Blinded by the speed and the suddenness, the bite he intended for Judge Johnson instead punctures Brenda's face.

Her scream is muffled inside his drooling mouth, teeth sunk deep and drawing blood onto Brenda's peaches-and-cream complexion, paws destroying her waitress outfit and ripping red streams into her shoulders and bosom.

The set is in instant, total turmoil, everyone yelling and screaming at once, aside from the judge, who is aiming for the nearest hiding place as fast as his straw legs will carry him, and the A.D., who's still demanding, "Quiet on the set!"

Within seconds, Harty and I are in the malt shop and pulling Barkie off Brenda, trying, anyway. Barkie is still confused. He doesn't want to let go. Brenda's eyes look up at me, pleading and near-lifeless, and she's making sounds like I've never heard before while I'm tugging and kicking at Barkie.

Von Howitzer has the megaphone now and he's shouting at me, "Don't hurt the dog, you moron! Don't hurt Barkie!" The A.D. is at his side, hands cupped at the corners of his mouth, echoing the demand, "Don't hurt the dog, you moron! Don't hurt Barkie!"

Harty has been missing for these moments, but from the corner of my eyes I see he's back, wielding a baseball bat he's found somewhere, getting ready to bring it down on the head of Barkie, when—

It's grabbed from Harty's grip by the dog's trainer, who pitches it away, pushes my partner aside, and sprints onto the set calling, "Barkie, ixnay! Ixnay, Barkie!" The A.D. shouts after him, "Barkie, ixnay! Ixnay, Barkie!"

Barkie opens his jaws and steps sideways from Brenda.

"Good girl," the trainer calls, softening his tone.

"Good—*girl?*" the A.D. says, confused.

"Sit, Barkie. Atta girl. Stay, Barkie. Atta good girl," the trainer coos at her, approaching Barkie with a doggie treat that looks like a slice of fresh liver not quite as raw as Brenda's mauled face.

"Girl?" the A.D. wonders inside his palms and looks at Von Howitzer for direction.

Von Howitzer tosses the megaphone at the A.D. and tells him, "Tell everybody to take five."

"Take five, everybody!"

"Make it ten," Von Howitzer decides.

"Take ten, everybody!"

As the crew disappears, Laura Dane wanders out from under someone, wondering in the cigarette-coarsened voice that could only be hers, "Where the hell's everybody goin' in such a hurry?"

She grabs a grip by the arm and starts leading him to wherever she came from—

Leaving Harty and me to watch over Brenda Lowe until the ambulance, a doctor, some help arrives, Harty as much in shock as I am, staring at the demolished beauty we'd both fallen for so hard so few minutes ago.

The donut place was around the corner from the old soundstage. Harty was already there when I arrived, sitting like a king at a window table for two, dunking a chunk of his plain donut in his coffee cup, and making faces at me for being late by ten minutes.

I pretended not to notice, him or his look, and got my own donut, a chocolate-covered, and a flavor-of-the-day coffee before I turned like I was scouting for a table and made like it was a big surprise finding him already there.

"You're late like always, so exactly who do you think you're fooling with that act, Hale, even if you were a good actor to begin with?"

"Whom," I said, settling onto the other seat. I took a nibble of donut, blew on the coffee before trying a sip. "Like you were ever a threat to Marlon Brando?"

Harty stared at me for a minute, then began studying the bottom of his cup like he'd run dry of punch lines and might find another one there.

Finally, he said, "Both of us, we were contenders. We coulda been champs. We coulda been somebodies." Not even looking for a laugh. The expression on his face as pained as it was painful to see. "Except for that damn dog."

"Actually, that damn Jackie "The Judge" Johnson. Take my word for it and you don't have to answer."

The catch phrase brought an upward tilt to the corners of his mouth, but only for a beat before he locked his lips in gloom again and said, "I was funny, all I ever wanted to be. I could have been big-time moving-pictures funny except for that damn dog. Just like Louella wrote about us—Martin and Lewis."

I nodded agreement and said, "Later, *Laugh-In*—it could have been us instead of Rowan and Martin. Was Hedda Hopper wrote that in the *Times*."

"Was Harrison Carroll in the *Herald*, back from seeing us open for Tony Martin in Vegas."

"Great pair of legs, that wife of his, Cyd Charisse. Tony Martin, not Harrison Carroll. A great, great pair of gams. You remember her with Kelly in *Singin' in the Rain*?"

At once, I regretted saying it.

Harty averted his eyes and said, "Remember her? By now you know how hard I try to forget her. I'm sorry I said it to you, about Harrison Carroll. I know better."

"Especially since it was Hedda Hopper," I said, trying to get off the subject.

I knew where it was heading, as usual, and it did after he finished staring out the window at some scavenger birds after crumbs on the parking-lot asphalt. Harty lived with his own ritual nightmare.

It was different from mine.

Harty's nightmare always began with that first vision of Brenda Lowe, but instantly, at once, Brenda was on the ground, screaming, and I'm battling Barkie, and Harty has lost the baseball bat to the trainer, this wimpy Rex Towel guy—"Rex the Wonder Wimp," we were already calling him—and the set's emptying and we're waiting for medics, and—

Harty can't take any more of watching Brenda suffer.

He finds the baseball bat and chases after Barkie.

Rex the Wonder Wimp senses what's on Harty's mind and tries to stop him.

Whack!

So much for Rex the Wonder Wimp.

Harty takes a slice at Barkie, but Barkie dances away from him, turns tail, and races off. Barkie's too fast for my berserk partner, but not so Jackie "The Judge" Johnson.

Harty finds the judge coming out of the john, trying to hide himself inside the emergency bottle of gin he had parked inside one of the overhead flush wells.

He swings and connects hard enough on the judge's arm for the bone crack to fill the soundstage. The judge is too pickled to feel the pain. He reacts with a silent, confused look before his knees fail him and he falls face forward.

Next, Harty goes screaming after Harmon Von Howitzer.

Von Howitzer's outside, stuffing a filter tip into his cigarette holder.

He recognizes the mayhem on Harty's face.

He orders him, "Too much. Take it down a notch."

Looks at his A.D. for confirmation.

"Take it down a notch," the A.D. tells Harty.

Harty swings, dropping the A.D.

"Too fast, slow down the tempo," Von Howitzer says.

He looks down at his A.D., who struggles unsuccessfully to get out the words and gets a dismissive look and gesture as his reward.

Harty steps in, like he's at home plate, takes deadly aim, and is about to let go at Von Howitzer when he's jumped by some crew members, and—

Wakes up screaming, "Watch your backside, you son of a bitch! You never know who's catching up with you!"

Sad truth is, Harty's nightmare is as real as mine.

Von Howitzer is through with Harty.

With us.

Before the night is over, after Brenda's been rushed to the hospital and the cops finish taking statements, and Bronco Von Howitzer has everyone agreeing not to press any charges, because he wants to save the publicity value to a time closer to the movie's release—

Our agent calls me, a bad-news bearer.

Hale and Harty are off the picture.

We've been branded *troublemakers*.

We're being replaced by Moe Yingg and Manny Yangg, a duo fresher than us and working dirty, which we never did, who'd come off the Playboy circuit and had been opening for Barbara Shore at the Rancho Vegas and the Fontainebleau in Miami.

Oh You Beautiful Girls is shutting down until Barkie is over his trauma and Jackie "The Judge" Johnson's broken bones heal.

I share all this with Harty the next morning, after I get him sprung from a holding cell at Ramparts, where the cops took him to cool off, my partner fighting to get free of them and warning the Day-Glo sky, "Watch your backside, you son of a bitch! You never know who's catching up with you!"

He listens like he doesn't care about anything, except to know how Brenda Lowe is doing at Cedars of Lebanon.

When I finish telling him, he shrugs. I can see that the humor he's always been so full of has left his eyes.

Harty's eyes and our act.

We keep working for as long as we can, although the venues get smaller and smaller and the bucks sometimes not big enough to cover airfare, carfare, motels with two-day-old dirty linen, and three squares.

Until nobody wants us, except for an occasional roast at the Friars, seats end of the dais and opening for kids a third our age, once even for Barkie.

One and the same.

Helped by that "Hootchy-Kootchy Poochie" business, the picture does boffo box-office, finishing in the top ten for the year.

It makes a star of the kid they brought in to replace Brenda Lowe. No voice and two left feet, and whatever else I don't care to speculate. I can't bring myself to mention her name, to this day.

It puts Barkie back on top, and not just with another PATSY.

His next movie, *For Whom the Bark Tolls* for Paramount, is even bigger than *Oh You Beautiful Girls*.

Comes the awards season, there's Barkie pulling them all, including a specially-struck mini-statuette on Academy night, the glorious golden statuette holding a St. Bernard in his arms.

Harty and I kibitzed about nothing in particular for another fifteen or twenty minutes, until I finally said, "We should walk over to the place and see what the cops have to say."

"I suppose," he said.

We took it slow, neither of us anxious to get there.

The loading dock by Bates Street was open and the only way inside, but we couldn't get past the yellow crime-scene tape or any of the close-mouthed cops guarding the place.

As if we were still living the good old days, we traded some more insults on the way back to our cars, and that was it—

Until about a month later.

Harty answered my call halfway through the first ring and, not bothering with a greeting, said, "You heard about the DNA?"

"You're the one with the hearing aid," I said.

"Top of the line," he said. "This little chippie thing so far down inside my ear I can hear my own itches. The bad news, hard as I try, I never miss a word you say anymore."

"Ignorance is bliss," I said. "I heard, yeah. I always knew, didn't I?"

"Says you. Come on over and I'll tell you what the TV news still doesn't know to tell."

"Listen on your chippie thing for the time. It's late. Better tomorrow, the donut place again."

The truth, after all these years of waiting . . .

I didn't know if I was ready for this.

I wasn't fooling Harty.

"Later than you think," he said. "Tonight. I'll make coffee by the time you get here."

Harty lived about fifteen minutes away, in one of the modest stucco bungalows lining a quiet residential street in Hollywood, below the A&M Studios at Sunset and Highland, what was originally Charlie Chaplin's studio and later Red Skelton's. He had the front door open and was on the porch urging me forward even before I'd covered half the fifty or so yards from my car past a neatly tended lawn and thriving flower gardens that were his passion.

The place smelled musty but otherwise hadn't changed much from the way I remembered it being my last time here, more years ago than I have fingers and toes.

It was like a museum that had put 'fifties living on display. Framed pictures of Brenda Lowe were everywhere—walls, table surfaces, the piano. Over the brick fireplace, a massive oil that captured her beauty and charm before the accident. A warm, sunny smile. Beaming eyes staring after a future bright with promise.

Harty had become something of a recluse after Brenda disappeared. She'd up and left him, cleared out one night never to be heard from again, leaving with nothing but his heart, he said, claiming the same on the missing person's report that made the "Hootchy-Kootchy Poochie Caper" thing bigger than ever.

Other things Harty said, hints he dropped, led me to believe something else, something worse, that he'd killed Brenda in some fit of rage or whatever happens when people find a way to hate each other with a passion equal to the way they love each other.

I knew they'd been arguing regularly, ferociously, in the weeks before Brenda turned up missing.

It was in 1952, and by then they'd been married almost two years.

He had started courting her while she was still in the hospital recovering from Barkie's attack.

She resisted him for months, feeling he was acting out of pity, but Harty eventually convinced her otherwise.

I was Harty's best man.

I still had a thing for Brenda, too.

Not like Harty, but the kind of lingering love that never goes away—

Strong enough to accuse him.

"I tell you what—" Harty said, not with the slightest trace of anger. "You ever can prove it, I want you to get a gun and come after me like you mean it. For keeps."

"I'll get a gun. You bet. Take my word for it and you don't have to answer."

Tonight, on the sofa in front of the fireplace, over a lousy cup of coffee that needed extra sweetener for flavor, he said, "My darling's career was destroyed by the damn dog along with her face, and Brenda never got over it, Hale, you know that part, and how she never worked again.

"That girl who replaced her in *Oh You Beautiful Girls*, she went on to a career bigtime. Brenda drowned deeper in her own misery over that. Deeper whenever someone else came along and made it singing and dancing. Got so I hated them, too. Didn't want to know from any of them. Debbie Reynolds. Ann Miller. Cyd Charisse. Mitzi Gaynor. Vera-Ellen. All of them could go to hell for all I cared, seeing what watching their pictures did to my darling." Tears began pouring down his tight, white, translucent face. "Finally, one night, she begs me harder than ever to put her out of her misery. 'Make me as happy in death as you have in life,' she pleads, and I, like a fool, never able to deny my precious Brenda anything else, after arguing and fighting over it for what seemed to become forever . . ."

He looked at me for sympathy and understanding before taking another swallow of coffee and replacing his cup on the coffee table.

"She already had a plan," Harty said. "Next thing, we go to the Mabel Normand soundstage, where her career began and ended. Some outfit's wrapping up a commercial shoot and we slip inside through the loading dock and hide out until everybody's gone.

"She's brought a huge gunnysack with her, the kind we use for cut grass, leaves, and refuse whenever we're outside gardening. We make love a little. We kiss a lot. We cry a lot. Then I put the bag over her. Tight. Suffocation tight. I lock out the air. I hold her close in my arms and keep on kissing her through the bag until I hear a sigh and a whisper that sounds to me like 'I love you, my dear one.' I hear a rattle. I feel her nude body go limp."

Harty needed a few minutes to regain control of his emotions.

Looking at me hungry for understanding and absolution, he said, "I seal her up in the bag good and tight. I find a place to conceal the bag, where I'm certain no one'll ever look and find her, there on the soundstage where she wanted to be, where she could have been someone . . ."

His voice faded inside his throat.

I said, "When she was a contender, like us."

His head moved left and right, over and over, like he was watching a tennis match in slow motion.

"No," Harty said. "We were contenders, but Brenda was always a star. Until the day she died. Still . . . You see how many years it took for the star to be discovered again?"

"I saw."

"Now, this DNA. Really something."

"Something."

We both sat quietly for a few moments.

"So, Hale," he said, forcing a smile. "You brought it like you always said you would?"

I pulled the .22 caliber pistol out of my windbreaker pocket.

Harty's smile broadened.

"You know what to do next, like you always swore you would if you found out the truth you suspected?"

I nodded.

His smile broader yet, like he was watching a miracle unfold.

"Do it, then, partner. Like you always swore. Like I'm ready for now. Aim good and do it. Do it because you love me and because you loved her, too." Harty arched his bushy white eyebrows. "Can you do it, Hale?"

I said, "Take my word for it and you don't have to answer."

G. Miki Hayden

The Maids

■ ■ ■

A member and board member of Mystery Writers of America, G. Miki Hayden has had a steady stream of short mystery fiction in print. Miki's novel, Pacific Empire, *lauded by the* New York Times, *was well received by readers, as was her psychiatric mystery,* By Reason of Insanity. *G. Miki Hayden, the author of* Writing the Mystery: A Start-to-Finish Guide for Both Novice and Professional, *a Writers Digest Book Club selection, is the immediate past president of the Short Mystery Fiction Society, which presents the yearly Derringer Awards. Miki teaches, coaches, and book doctors from her home in Manhattan. Her story "The Maids," from the MWA anthology* Blood on Their Hands *and a finalist for the short story Edgar Award, tells of the gap separating the hired help and the owners of a palatial mansion, and the crimes that can happen between them.*

When some of the cows dropped dead in their pasture, Little Marie merely laughed.

"Oh, that's terrible," I said, not understanding. "Those poor things—and now the children might not have milk for their breakfast."

Little Marie gave me quite a wicked look. "And why should the Benoit offspring have milk every day? Do my own children have such luxuries? No. They are whipped and made to fetch and carry for the master, with only what we ourselves grow for their food. If the Benoit children, like the cattle, drop dead, I will not care. And you should not either, Luisah. You have the pink stripes on your body from the mistress's whippings."

Little Marie and I spoke in the language we had taken with us from our home in West Africa. In the house, we were supposed to speak only French, so I glanced around nervously and hurried away, digesting the ideas she had given to me.

To wish the children of this house to die was wrong, was it not? I was a Catholic and must not think such things. Yet my back and my soul bore the marks of our mistress's malevolence. And I had many troubles in my life, the source of which were solely she and the master, who intended only, always, their own wealth and comfort.

Had I asked to be stolen away from my parents and brought to Haiti, or Sante Domingue, as this was called—the island of Hispaniola—when I was six? Had I asked to be put to work as a house slave from that age until now, so far eighteen years? Had I asked to be married to the slave Michel Benoit, a cruel man, and one of those who helped to oversee the field slaves? Or to have my two children torn from me and sold to a neighboring plantation? No. All this was at the wish of those who owned me. And Little Marie, a fierce adherent of the Vodou priest Ras Berbera, did not entirely shock me with her imaginings.

I brought the morning milk pail to the kitchen. And let that be the last of it for them to drink. I had many questions to ask Little Marie about what she had said. Yet so much work to do, as well. I must scrub the kitchen floor each day before breakfast and help the cook. Once the family was up, I must serve the food, and then begin to make a fire outside for a boiling vat. I must then strip the bedding and place the linen in the tub where I wash each sheet clean every other day. I then heat the iron on the stove and take the wrinkles from the cloth—so that when it goes back on their sweet-smelling beds, the feel and the appearance are just so, to Madame's satisfaction.

This is the start to my day that ends near midnight, when my husband, should he choose, takes the opportunity to abuse me. After which, I may have some six hours—the only ones in the day—to myself, and those spent in the dead sleep of exhaustion.

Angelina stepped up behind me and pulled my cap, setting my restless hair askew. I whirled and smiled. Might I slap her? Only if I desired to be hung from the tree behind the kitchen door, where I have seen others like me hung—black girls who misbehaved and were disrespectful.

"You are up so early, Miss Angelina," I said in French to the twelve-year-old. "Have you had sufficient rest?"

"I am riding to Cap François today, with Mama to buy many exquisite new frocks. A boat has come in from France with the latest fashions." She looked quite pleased at the prospect of making herself pretty.

For sure, she had the basic good looks to be a beauty, with flaming red hair—but sometimes the fiery temper to match. Her parents worried that the girl might not attract a husband because of her lack of amiability. I heard them discuss this. I listen to everything freely in the house, since I am a part of the furniture and nothing to notice.

"You shall be lovely," I declared. But somehow I thought of what Little Marie had said about the children dropping dead, and the idea failed to pain me. "In to breakfast with you, then."

After their meal, the mistress told me I would come to town today with her and her daughters—Angelina and Angelina's eight-year-old sister, Brigitte. If I behaved well, I might be given the job of personal maid to Mademoiselle Angelina, since her own black maid had died of a yellow fever the previous week. I curtsied in gratitude, although I was not sure I was exactly grateful. The new position meant I would dress the girl throughout the day and bathe her, in addition to the regular duties of my own. Such was the life here.

I rode on the outside of the carriage with the driver, Andre, a man who had come as a youth from his home in the Congo. We passed the place where the cows had died. A similar plague had broken out across many of the plantations, the master had told his wife at breakfast today. Madame did not pay particular attention, as she never cared to listen about business. The cows were being burned as we went by, so as not to infect the other livestock.

Death has a certain sense of comfort here, because those who die need not labor any longer. Since my two children were taken from me, I have learned to abort the *pauvres*—the poor little ones—before they are born. We maids have discussed this. We don't want our children to suffer our own fate. So perhaps *this* dying is good, too, for the animals. I do not know. Maybe the Fathers could tell us in church on Sunday, although I do not understand them or the language that they mostly speak.

On top of the coach, I broiled in the fierce sun of Haiti and was jounced mercilessly along the stony road. I thought further on the idea that the Benoit children might soon expire and was not perturbed. My own youngest had died soon after being sold to the master at a nearby plantation. Beaten to death. This was not unusual and no one thought of the matter again, save for me.

I went in with the ladies and helped Angelina and Brigitte try on new clothes. Angelina kicked me once in her displeasure at my clumsy buttoning of her dress. When they were done with me, I went out to wait, before going to the next shop. Finally, after all the dresses and some cloth were purchased and stowed in the coach, they entered the hotel for their lunch. Of course I had forgotten to bring either food or water for myself, but I stood on the square in the area where the slaves loitered in wait for their masters. We must stand somewhere, after all, must we not? Not being invisible.

In a few minutes, Andre, the driver, came across the open park from the carriage. "Come sit on the step of the coach," he urged. "You will find a little shade."

I accepted, and while I sat there, fanning myself with my hand, he brought a sweet yam grown in his own garden to share with me and, after, carried, in his own cup, water from the fountain for me to drink—not once but twice.

No man had ever shown me such kind regard. In fact, no other human had.

A little while later, I thought the mistress and her daughters might be coming back and I stood. Now I was on a level with Andre, where we could speak.

I broached the subject of my earlier talk with Little Marie. "Many of the plantations have dead cows and sheep," I said. "At some of them, the families, too, are dead. Do you think we black slaves can die from this awful disease, as well?"

"No," Andre answered me at once. "This is not an illness for the blacks to suffer. Just the whites and their animals. The disease is of greed and greed is not catching, the Vodou priests say. You must come and hear them."

Indeed, I was a Catholic and I feared the Vodou for more than one reason. "What do your priests tell you?" I asked, in curiosity.

"Not only the priests but the Maroon chief François Mackandal has talked to us. He was once owned by the Juin family, but set himself free. He says that we may rid ourselves of the plantation owners forever." A spark of excitement brought Andre's face to a life he had not shown before. "Mackandal said that in the homeland of the French, the peasants talk about revolt as well."

"Ah," I exclaimed. I had heard the Benoits speak of farmer uprisings in their native land, yet not with approval. But perhaps such a thing was now permissible. The Maroons, of course, I knew about—disobedient slaves who had run off to the hills. Had they a chief?

"The priest says the God of the French must be cruel, because they act cruelly in obedience to him, but our loa, the spirits we serve, are full of love only. Those of us who worship before the altars in the Vodou temple are loving to all who wish us well. The French do not, so we need not tolerate them any longer, but may seek out vengeance." Andre smiled, empty spaces showing where teeth were gone, either through beatings or simply because our teeth fell out from lack of nourishment.

I smiled, too.

"The houngans—our priests—and the mambos—our priestesses—say the bullets of the French will turn to water. They cannot touch us. Our God will protect us and theirs will fail."

I had a great deal to think about on the ride home, past fields of cane and sugar-cane presses, past cotton fields and land where the indigo grew. This island produced bountiful riches. The master praised it often for its cocoa and rum and molasses—none of which I knew by taste. What if those who worked the land were to own it? What if I had a fancy silk frock—ruffled on the bottom to keep off the mosquitoes? Perhaps Andre, who would work his own property, would buy me frocks and never hit me with his fists.

With our wheels rumbling deeper into the countryside, the stench of death grew. Fallen sheep lay scattered like logs in the neighboring pasture. Mistress must be frightened by the sight, revolted by the smell. In the distance, I observed flames and dense, black smoke. When we came nearer, I saw a plantation house on fire. The fine home was quickly consumed as we drove by, with slaves outside laughing, and no owner sending for water to fight the blaze. Where were the master and the mistress and their children? Dead of the plague?

I jolted awake the instant we reached the Benoit wrought-iron gate, and, soon, Andre fetched me down, daring to risk a moment's delay in opening the coach door to our mistress and the children.

I knew what all the slaves were told. Rules had been passed by our masters for us to live by and those rules said that no slaves might congregate during the day or night. We must not sing, except in the fields. And no drums were to be heard anywhere in Haiti. These things were expressly forbidden to us.

What I knew from listening to the master's conversation with his friends was that other rules had been passed in the colony as well—the Code Noir, which said we must be fed a certain amount of food every day and given two hours after lunch to rest. We must have Sunday off to say our prayers. But the owners laughed and continued on, as they chose. Yet the rule on the black slaves against our meeting together was strictly enforced. And that meant we were not to gather for Vodou ceremony.

I am a Catholic, as I have said, and always attended services with the family. As a Catholic, I know right from wrong and I have been told that the practice of Vodou is a grave wrong. But add to that, since it is not allowed, I am afraid to go because of the punishments. After I smooth the clothes with my hot iron, sometimes it is used to sear the skin of a slave who has misbehaved. Other times, a very bad slave will have honey poured on him and be staked to the ground, where he is eaten by insects. Other times . . . oh many evil things are done. Perhaps the Vodou priest is right. Perhaps their God, Jesus, is no good, since the acts of the whites are so very wicked.

Early the next morning, Little Marie invited me in quiet whispers in our tongue to come to the Vodou ceremony that same night.

I wondered what had inspired her to ask me that. "Has someone told you anything about me?" I inquired. I was jealous. Perhaps she and Andre were close and they had talked. Perhaps they were lovers. I must shake the dresses be would buy me from my mind.

The blankness in her eyes seemed to tell my answer. "We must know those we can count on," she said. "Not cook. She is old and unreliable." Little Marie darted her head around, watching to see if anyone spied. "Midnight," she murmured. "Toward the swamp. Past the stables."

This was out of the question. A Vodou ceremony was no place for a baptized Catholic. I practically shivered I was so afraid to think of it—although Andre would be there and many others. Could they crucify or hang us all? But they might. The idea was not entirely inconceivable.

Thus, when I found my weary self at something like midnight on the path to the swamp, I knew that I must turn back. I was a Catholic, which was enough, although many who were Catholic for Sunday were Vodou, too. But the Vodou slaves were those who had come here grown, who were already Vodou from their homeland. I had come here too young to know the ways of the loa—the spirits—or to worship them.

When I arrived at their meeting place, the bonfire was a small one and not a sound could be heard. The field slaves danced—and Little Marie and Andre—the only ones from those who worked in the house. The dancing was silent, since we were forbidden to sing or to drum.

Some on their knees or on the ground jerked in their bodies. I resolved not to do that because my dress must remain very clean. The difference between a house slave and a field slave is our clothing. Our garments are not rags like theirs. We must not offend the eyes of the family.

Andre, who saw me after a time, smiled. He came to meet me and pulled me into his circle. Was I now Vodou? The Catholic Fathers would say that this was wrong.

I did not feel wrong, however, only pleased, as the mistress is pleased when she goes to a ball at Cap François. I had never had such a time before.

After dancing and listening to the soft worship and the talk of the priest, I understood. The cattle had not been infected with a disease. They had been poisoned. The Maroon chief François Mackandal had given the slaves a deadly plant to scatter where the cattle grazed. At many of the big homes across the whole island, this poison was put even in the family's food. So, no wonder we blacks could not catch this illness which was for the whites only. And this, Andre had known. I was surprised.

Creeping back to the frond-thatched hut I shared with Michel, surnamed Benoit to mark him as their property, I wondered in regard to the rightness or wrongness of killing the whites. The Fathers might say that this went against the wishes of their Jesus, but the Vodou priest said the black people's God would strongly approve.

I always tried to act to please this powerful Jesus, who would be kind when I finally arrived in his heaven—but now I was not sure. If Jesus belonged to the white people only and the loa, like the Twins and Yemaya, to the slaves, perhaps I was more meant to serve the gods of the blacks. I did not know and could ask no one here. I might ask the Fathers if their God could love me as black as I was, but I already realized that the answer must be no. The French did not love me, so how could their God? Still, I had been a Catholic since I was six, eating the holy sacrament each week, and was thus claimed.

I could not have entered my hut more quietly. If Michel had been sleeping properly as he ought to have been, I would not have awakened him. But no, he had been lying in wait for me, which, tonight, only meant that he pushed me out of the bed onto the floor. I was used to sleeping on the floor when he preferred me to. I should not have gotten into his bed, though, because then he sat up, reached to me, and grabbed his hand into my hair, tearing at it. He shook me that way until my brain felt rattled and my neck nearly broken. Then he let go with another strong push. Although tears came to my eyes, this was not so bad as sometimes. I was not punched.

Without a word, Michel fell to sleep and I moved further away so that he could not reach me. I waited for my head to settle down before I, too, slept, my bruised body uncomforted by the packed dirt.

Over the next two weeks, I attended the Vodou several times more. Less frightened than I had been, I was, nonetheless, afraid. If we were caught . . . But at the Vodou, no one treated me badly. I was accepted as one of them. We danced, and no matter how tired I was from my work, I felt strengthened by what we did there.

I saw the future and pictured going on this way, until I perhaps died of the fever or of a beating from Michel. I had no idea that anything would change. How could it? What would change? More cows had died, and several of the horses, but new ones would be bought. We would go on as always. I would become a little more tired each year and my face and body more scarred and ugly. That was all.

"You must be the one to do it for us all," whispered Little Marie to me one morning. She pressed a small, closed wooden box into my hand and gestured for me to hide it in my apron. I placed it there, while she nodded approvingly. "Don't touch what's in there with your fingers," she warned. "It will kill you dead."

Naturally, my eyes went wide with great amazement. This was the poison fungus they talked about and I must hold it? I could not be calm.

Little Marie clenched her jaw grimly and went and looked into the other rooms to be sure no one was hiding there. Of course, we spoke the language of our own tribe, the Bagandas. But still. "You are the only one beside cook who handles the food directly and cook is not on our side. We cannot trust her."

We heard the rustling of a silk dress on the way down the hall, so we parted, and I was left only half comprehending what I must do. They trusted me—that was all I understood. I was trusted and cook was not. I was Vodou like them, even though a Catholic. But, of course, as a Catholic, I must not poison the family because Thou Shalt Not Kill. This was correct, was it not?

I felt fairly sure that I must not poison the Benoits, that Jesus, whom I was sworn to as a servant, and baptized in his name with the holy water, would not want me to. I must think of a way to say no to the Vodou slaves.

In the meantime, the wooden box seemed on fire against my body. Every step I took, it clacked and bounced. Would the poison come out of the box and attack me? It hit against the stove and made a noise. I jumped. I even broke a dish that day and cook tattled to the mistress, who slapped me hard across the face. "You stupid black girl. Why must I deal with these stupid blacks in this Godforsaken country?" Madame said.

Oh, if she would find the wooden box, I would be buried alive. I felt ill all day and went straight to bed that night, hiding the wooden box behind the cabin door, which Michel left open to get a little air. But I should not have stayed home that night for Michel abused me and then hit me many times for his extra pleasure. But he is neither Christian nor Vodou and only does the bidding of Pierre Benoit.

In the morning, Little Marie could only glare at me meaningfully. Again, the box was in my smock because I had no place else to hide anything that I might own. Luckily, the single possession to my name was an old wooden comb, and that I carried in my pocket always, though many teeth were missing from it and it did not comb my hair at all well.

That night I went to the Vodou ceremony. Where else was I to go that offered the company of friends, and solace? François Mackandal, the Maroon chief, was present and came to me personally during the dancing to whisper hot words into my ear. He called me a good girl, a smart girl, one who would help the blacks of this island claim our own—before the white men killed us off altogether, as they had the Indians who had lived here before. Where were those Indians? Dead slaves on the trash pile of the whites. I was a good girl, a smart girl. Only one answer remained for our kind.

Andre walked me quietly across the fields. "I'm afraid of the punishments," I whispered to him. "The whites will punish me with a great deal of pain."

"They will be dead," Andre assured me. "Too dead to punish. And we will all run off. We will be Maroons."

"I can't run off alone." I hesitated.

"We will *all* run off," Andre said, pulling me by the arm closer to him as we passed under the shadow of the stables. "You and I will run off together."

The horses inside snickered and we hurried on.

The next day, I got what little milk the milkers handed me and stopped before I reached the kitchen door. Carefully, I opened the wooden box with the hem of my apron. Inside was a gray powder. Would this make the milk look spoiled? I shook some in and the powder settled on the top, like dirt. I closed the box and placed it back in my apron. This was no good. The milk would not work. I could not get all of the poison in.

By the time I got the milk onto the pantry shelf, it looked the same as everyday cow's milk, white and foamy. But I had not placed enough poison in it, so the drink would probably only make the family sick. That was possibly better, since, as a Catholic, I was not actually supposed to kill. I would tell François Mackandal that the failure had not been my fault and Andre and I could still go to the Maroons.

Master came down early and I served him his coffee with plenty of the milk. "The coffee is too white, girl," he said. "It will not be hot."

"I'm sorry, sir. Will you drink that? I will run fetch you another cup." I went and stood in the pantry and stared into the milk, then I went back out to the dining room. "The coffee is boiling, sir. I will bring it in an instant."

The master's hand was on his chest and an odd look marched across his face. "Are you unwell, sir? Shall I go get Madame?"

He shook his head and I dared to stand in place and watch him, feigning concern. In a moment, he slumped to one side and collapsed on the floor. The poison must be very strong or the master must be very weak.

I did not feel at all bad, but I ran for Blanche, the mistress's personal maid. "Hurry upstairs and tell Mistress that the master is ill. She must come at once."

I passed the master on my way back into the kitchen. He did not twitch.

In the pantry once more, I stared at the milk, which looked quite ordinary still, though the froth was gone. I listened to cook in the kitchen banging her pans and waited for whatever was to happen next. I had not meant to kill him, possibly. That much powder had been very little. I would make my apology to Jesus later in a prayer and to the Twins and to the Dead, which I supposed now included Pierre Benoit.

Too nervous to stand still another minute, I went out the pantry door to the yard. I barely knew what I was doing. My only thought was to stay away from the master for a minute or two until the mistress was over her initial shock. But I might have been sorry for leaving the safety of the house because, unfortunately, Michel was out there.

"I have been banging on the door, you lazy black girl. Didn't you hear me? Go and tell the master I am here, as he called." Michel reached to give me a smack across my face, but I jumped out of the way in time.

"Oh, Michel, something terrible. The master is ill. He has the white plague."

Michel shook his head. "No, it isn't possible."

I wrung my hands. "Yes, it is true." I could barely keep a nervous smile off my face. But I thought with some sense of accomplishment that I had for once spoiled Michel's assurance of mind. He must worry about his own position on the plantation now, must he not? "Poor Michel," I added. "I hope this will mean nothing too bad for you."

I could not tell what was going on in that odd brain of his, since he had a way of keeping his thoughts to himself while acting superior, but I supposed he would be very glum.

"Don't talk so stupid, girl, or I'll give you a beating." He pretended he would advance on me, though I knew he would not. If the mistress saw him, she would chide him for wasting his time.

"Poor Michel," I repeated. "I feel sorry for you. But in any case, I will bring you a small cup of milk."

I ran into the pantry and poured my husband half a cup of the liquid, rushing out again, lest he go before he'd had his refreshment. If Jesus meant for him to die, Michel would be there and drink the milk and the poison would be sufficient to bring him low. And maybe he would only become very, very ill.

Michel wrapped his giant black knuckles around the delicate porcelain and I recalled that very fist cracking into my face and breaking the bone beneath my eye. I ran my fingers over the spot on my cheek, but quickly took my hand away and smiled encouragingly. He drank. I really hadn't served him much. I took the cup back and brought it into the kitchen. There, I set it into the trash, under a heap of eggshells and coffee grinds, so no one would drink from it accidentally. Cook was in the middle of preparing the meal.

I had not dressed Angelina yet this morning. She must be livid. I went back out to the yard.

"Oh, poor Michel," I cried out at once. He was on the ground, gasping. He had not died straightaway like the master. I supposed he was stronger. He might even live. "Are you not well?"

The day had been a brilliant one, but now some clouds covered up the sun. That would be a relief from the intense heat, making our trip to the Maroons in the hills that much easier.

Michel no longer seemed to be breathing and I reached over and pinched the flesh of his arm very hard. I wanted to see if he was dead or alive and that was one way to tell. Since he didn't move, I assumed the worst and dragged him into the outdoor larder, where the less perishable staples are kept. I saw no sense in leaving his dead body lying out for anyone to see.

"I'm sorry, Jesus," I said out loud. "But, Michel, you were not a very good man. Did you think nothing would ever come of your badness? That you would never be punished?"

I went into the house and the dining room, where a crowd was gathered around the mistress and around the master's body. "How terrible," I said, nearly wailing. "The plague has struck." Then the idea occurred to me, finally, that Jesus himself had used me as the instrument of his revenge. Was not their God a wrathful God? Oh yes. This was a very sensible and logical thought.

"Poor Mistress," I consoled her quietly, as I was suddenly tired and yearned to lie down. The killing of men, though it might not take physical strength, is an effort to exhaust one.

Mistress's eyes met my own and for once her face was fragile, as bone China is fragile.

I shooed the other slaves away from her presence and helped the mistress to a chair. "I will get you a coffee," I suggested. "The day will be a long one for you." Not actually, it wouldn't, however, and wasn't the right thing for her troubles to be over, too? Could a woman like her live without her husband? But in any case, I wasn't truly concerned with her best interests, simply eager to fulfill what had been asked of me by the Maroon chief and by God.

The milk was not running at all low and the liquid still appeared very ordinary. I gave Mistress the sugar to her coffee, as she preferred. I could have sworn for one moment when I handed her the cup that she almost said "Thank you." But she did not, and of course, I bobbed my head anyway.

She sent one of the men slaves for the surgeon, although the fact that the master was dead should have been quite obvious to her. "The plague, Mistress," I explained. "He has expired of the plague." I put on a sad face, since that was what one usually did.

I didn't like to watch her die, so I went back into the pantry and poured three goblets of the milk, one for each of the children—the two girls and the boy. I set them all on a tray and brought the tray out with me. As I passed the dining table, I saw a vomit coming out of the mistress's mouth. The poison in the milk had not lost its power, although it had already killed two men. Upstairs, I first brought the Benoit son, Henri, his milk. "Here, young sir. We are late with the breakfast. Have this to tide you over, until we serve."

I did the same for the two girls, but Angelina was in a rage. "I've not had my bath, you lazy, lazy girl." She hit me on the shoulder with the back of her hairbrush, then hit me again. I barely felt the blows because my mind did not think of them, spinning as it was with so much else.

"I am wrong, Mademoiselle, and I pray to Jesus Christ to forgive me."

With that, she was appeased and turned and drank down her milk.

So it was that I obeyed the summons given to me by God or the devil, I really don't know.

Downstairs, the house slaves milled about in some confusion with the mistress, too, dead on the carpet. Little Marie came over and hugged me. I didn't recall having been hugged ever before. "I will go and get the others," she said.

When she left the room, I went upstairs again to be sure the children were all dead. Like the cows in the field, they had each breathed their last. How quickly the Vodou poison worked.

Angelina lay sprawled across the floor in her nightdress, her plump white limbs quite akimbo, her soft, blazing-red hair shining in the sun. I took the silver comb from Angelina's dressing table top. In its place, I put my old wooden comb, a sign that I did not care to steal.

Andre was in the house when I went down and we nodded to one another as an acknowledgment that our work was complete. The field slaves would burn the Benoit house to cinders and the bodies of the family with it—along with the dead overseer, Michel. Andre and I headed toward the hills to claim and work our parcel of land.

And several decades later, I did not forbid my then-grown sons to go to Cap François along with the priest Boukman to overcome the still-ruling whites. A few years after that, Haiti became the country of the loa, with the Indians dead, the Spanish departed, the French overthrown, and only we blacks and some few mulattos left to harvest the island's rich and hard-won soil.

Shelley Costa

Black Heart and Cabin Girl

■ ■ ■

Shelley Costa's stories have appeared in The Georgia Review, The North American Review, Crimewave, *and* Cleveland Magazine. *A New Jersey native, she graduated from Douglass College, worked for two years in the trade division of Henry Holt and Company, then went on to earn a Ph.D. in English from Case Western Reserve University. These days she enjoys both Henry and P. D. James, and is a member of the Liberal Arts faculty at the Cleveland Institute of Art, where she teaches courses in creative writing. Her home is Chagrin Falls, Ohio, and she vacations in the Canadian Northwoods, the setting of the Edgar-nominated "Black Heart and Cabin Girl." The past comes back to confront the young woman at the center of "Black Heart," which was first published in* Blood on Their Hands, *and is an understated, powerful story about how decisions made years ago can haunt people ever after.*

Here is how the story ends: he buys an ax. It's a Sears Craftsman ax and it feels right in his hands, smooth and heavy, and he has always been satisfied with his Craftsman table saw and belt sander. Affordable and reliable tools, that's what he's always liked. Chopping yourself some wood? *the salesman asks, whose name pin says* JIMMY THIRTEEN YEARS OUTSTANDING SERVICE. Yes, chopping some wood, *he tells Jimmy, who smiles. As he signs the Visa charge slip, it strikes him that at some point a man starts to shape what he says to please. If he had started sometime before the final two days of his life, he wonders whether the story would end differently. Would he, for instance, be buying this ax? When he gets home, he stands the ax in the corner of the bedroom, then decides to move it to the basement because it seems cruel to alarm Diane, the woman he married four years ago after he drove Jo Verdyne forever from the lake. In a dark corner behind the furnace, he stands the ax against the cinder block foundation, next to the small wooden stool he had set there just yesterday to hold the straight razor that had once belonged to his father, who used to enjoy stropping it into a kind of fatal perfection. When he turns the blade softly against his hand, he marvels how, with the merest touch against his skin, a line of blood suddenly springs, and where that line begins is Black Heart, and where it ends is Cabin Girl.*

Jo sat alone on the port side of the water taxi, where she'd be able to see up the north arm of Lake Temagami on her first trip back in sixteen years. Seal Rock, Devil Bay, Point of No Return—even Stone Maiden Cliff. Places where the wind would kick up suddenly and churn the water into threatening white caps, places where the steep rock discouraged casual climbers before they discovered the warm, breezy lookouts at the top, scented with mats of brown fallen pine needles. She knew the taxi would turn west and head across the wide channel by Bear Island, the Indian Reserve, before the landmarks from her childhood would come into view, but she liked the idea that Temagami had gone on without her all these years. Half her life had been spent elsewhere, after all. Despite what she thought when she was a barefoot eleven and learned to clean fish and run the skiff almost as well as old Will Stanley, the caretaker at the lodge. Despite what she thought when she was twelve and the Hackett boy kissed her one night on the main dock only she wasn't sure she liked it very much even though she told him she did.

The water taxi Doral, with an outboard the size of a doghouse, sputtered through the No Wake zone at the landing, then flew her through the gap where the lake opened up, veering around shoals in a path rippled by a light wind from the southwest. The lake water, in some places hundreds of feet down to boulders left behind by the last Ice Age, was blue and green and gray, all the colors of clean and cold. She was five hours north of Toronto—and twelve hours north of Baltimore, where she taught baby chemistry for nine months a year at Johns Hopkins and had a townhouse she called home for want of a better term. It was May twenty-ninth, and according to Ellroy, the driver, who had the words SKATEBOARDING IS tattooed on one chunky bicep and NOT A CRIME on the other, the ice had gone out late just two weeks ago. He smirked at her, like the information was sexy somehow, and turned back to his windshield.

Three years ago her grandfather Carl Verdyne had died and left her the lodge Wendaban—a grand old two-story log building with eighteen rooms and a wraparound porch—which had been in the Verdyne family since 1904. Jimmy Stewart had fished there. Carole Lombard had lounged there. It had hosted titans and famous runaways and wonderful, wealthy derelicts who were looking for good food, drink, and a bed in a wilderness setting for a week. Those were the days of the great passenger boats that glided up and down the lake in a kind of ephemeral elegance. The days of fish crematoria, where all the uneaten bass and pickerel and lake trout were heaped and burned, days when an abundance of all things created only festive kinds of problems there in the Canadian Northwoods. Jo only heard about those days. By the time she was growing up, the movie stars were gone and the fish were an event, middle-class families from upstate New York were the guests, and the only wealthy derelicts who still came were completely uncelebrated.

For the first year after her grandfather's death, she denied the place, let the employees go, and paid the taxes. For the second year, she howled silently at the pain of the inheritance, fretted about the former employees, and wondered just how much longer the one-hundred-year-old logs of Wendaban could stand without any human attention. There were a couple of faceless offers to buy, during this time, and it was only the possibility of letting Wendaban go out of the family forever that made Jo realize she could never do it. She was no lodgekeeper, but maybe the beautiful Wendaban was no longer a lodge. In the third year after her grandfather left her the property where she had spent the first thirteen summers of her life—until the accident—or what she called the accident, the thing she could never name without capsizing into her own doubts—she gave up and hired a Toronto lawyer with expertise in setting up nonprofit organizations, a couple of Wendaban's former employees, and twenty minutes ago, Ellroy the water taxi driver, who, according to his tattered business card, also provided firewood and laundry service: WE GET YOU THERE, THEN KEEP YOU WARM AND CLEAN.

She moved into her grandfather's old room on the first floor of the lodge because it got the morning sun, and she took the handle "Cabin Girl." *When we're all grown up*, Christine had said when they were twelve, *we'll have our own VHF radios and you'll be Heiress and I'll be Cabin Girl and we'll call each other all the time*. Cabin Girl was all that was left of Christine, so Jo took it, though no one else knew why.

She put Kay Stanley, the old caretaker's daughter—Will Stanley himself had died in his bungalow on Bear Island just two winters ago—in charge of day-to-day operations, calling in the right people to check the septic system, overhaul the old Wendaban boats, install the solar panels, deliver the propane that still fueled the interior of the lodge because Carl Verdyne had liked the feel of it. Kay moved soundlessly the way heavy people do, her short arms swinging, her eyes disappearing into her muscular cheeks when she smiled.

It was Kay who hired Luke Croy, a handyman on the lake, to replace the rotten boards on the wraparound porch. He arrived one morning in a blue steel open boat that held clean pine lumber, backlit by the sun that was just edging over the pointed tops of the fir trees so she couldn't make out his face. When she could—Kay introduced them down at the dock—she could tell he was getting to be an old lake man even in his thirties, where all the colors of flashy city places settle over time and what's left are the browns that make a man indistinguishable from the wilderness. His long hair was pulled back neatly into a ponytail; his skin had a bright kind of windburn. He wore a loose cotton shirt and a leather carpenter's belt. She found his lack of conversation unsettling, so as he pried up the old boards with more care than she would have thought they deserved, Jo went back to sweeping the plank flooring of what was called the Grand Parlor at Wendaban. She kept an eye on him through the front windows as he measured and cut and sanded and hammered.

Over a week, Luke the silent handyman finished the porch repair and went to work on the roof over the kitchen, where water damage blackened the logs. At lunchtime, he disappeared up the lake in his blue steel boat for an hour or so—"Eating his lunch?" Kay shrugged when Jo asked if she knew what he was doing—and the rest of them planned the gala fundraiser for what Jo hoped would become the Wendaban Center for Environmental Studies. She and Kay and Benoit, the prickly cook from Québec that Kay had found, and Minette, a summer resident who was better connected on the lake than the hydro lines, were discussing whether it was more environmentally friendly to string Chinese lanterns or stake torchières, when the first call came over the VHF radio.

"Cabin Girl, Cabin Girl, Cabin Girl," the strange high voice leaped into the room from the small box Luke had installed on the mail table in the corner, "this is Black Heart. Over."

Jo didn't recognize the caller's handle, but as she loped over to the microphone, she could see Kay frowning. "Black Heart, this is Cabin Girl. Over."

"Cabin Girl"—it was a strained falsetto, not male, not female, filling every syllable with a kind of calculated insanity Jo had never known existed—"tell them what you did to Christine."

Tell them what you did to Christine.

She couldn't tell them: she didn't know. After sixteen years, she still didn't know. Jo left the others sitting there and walked stiffly up the creaking stairs to her room—her old room on the second floor of Wendaban, the one she had for thirteen summers, on the sunset side of the lodge, next to the back stairs, where the logs sloped and her friend Christine, the nurse's girl, would sneak in laughing in her long white batiste nightgown and crawl under the covers with her. At twelve they rubbed their feet together for warmth even in July because the Temagami nights were chilly. At thirteen they made tiny braids in each other's hair and applied lipstick to each other's lips and Jo told her how the Hackett boy had kissed her, which was okay, she guessed, if you like kissing a fish. *Someday I'll show you how it's done*, Christine sat back, erasing some of Jo's lipstick with her pinkie—*oh, not on me, silly*, she was quick to say, *on the mirror*. Christine's hair was white with moonlight as she flung herself back down on the mattress. *I know because I used to follow my brother around before he went to live mostly with our dad.* Then she folded her hands across her little breasts and smiled a smile that had nothing to do with Jo and her eyes only seemed to be looking up at the sloping logs but Jo knew she was looking right at whatever the knowledge was, which meant it was for real.

Tell them what you did to Christine.

Black Heart.

Someone named Black Heart knew how Jo ended up dressed only in a red shirt she had never in her life seen, floating unconscious in an old Wendaban skiff in the darkest part of the shallows, where the bay curved away from the lodge and the reeds were high, the night Christine died. Someone named Black Heart was saying it wasn't an accident.

For three days the only calls for Cabin Girl came from cottagers wondering whether Wendaban was open for dinner business. Otherwise, the VHF was a source of weather, messages relayed to youth camps from anxious parents wondering whether Johnny was managing without his teddy, and someone named Little Dorrit who sounded like she was a hundred giving a fruit and vegetable wish list to the long-suffering Irish Stu who went into town on a regular basis.

The fundraiser was a month away, and in addition to the indispensable Minette, and Walter, the Tums-chewing Toronto lawyer, the planning circle now included Cheryl, an event planner, and Guy, the University of Toronto professor working on putting together a consortium for the Wendaban Center. Providing them all with beds and food for as long as they needed reminded Jo of the old Wendaban, when a tough orange tabby patrolled for mice, and chess and bridge were played nightly by hurricane lamps in the Grand Parlor. Luke still stayed apart, stripping away the bad shingles over the kitchen—the day it rained hard he came inside and replaced a leaky seal around the toilet in #10—and when Jo climbed the ladder high enough to offer him a tumbler of lemonade, he shook his head, "Thanks, no," and turned back to his work. For some reason, Luke was one of her failures.

Jo heard the boat just as the motor sputtered to a stop and she set down the framed enlargement of the famous photo of Wendaban in 1904 that she and Kay were mounting over the stone fireplace. It was a black-and-white shot that found its way into any pictorial history of Lake Temagami: an Ojibway woman stood far back on the path leading up to the porch of the fine, solid lodge with its rough-hewn posts, set back in a stand of old growth pine in that decade before World War I. There was a grand stasis to the picture Jo always liked: everything was straight and plentiful, then, the jobs, the money, the pleasures, the people. She went to the double front doors and peered through the screen.

A man had tied up a runabout and was standing on the main dock, his hands in his pockets, slowly looking around. Jo held up a hand to Benoit, who was griping to her in two languages about these paltry inexcusable framboises, and asked Kay to take a look. The man was wearing a white polo shirt and nylon khakis, and in the sun that wasn't quite high enough yet, his skin was the olive gold that certain blonds have who get to spend a lot of time outdoors. When he moved over to the lamppost where the main dock abutted the rocky shore, she could tell it was the Hackett boy, some sixteen years after the experimental wet kisses in the same spot.

Tom Hackett.

Someone from those few summers before Christine died, when loon chicks slid on and off their mothers' backs and mayflies rose by the thousands over the lake like soft weightless gold shavings in the twilight and she wore her frilly halter top and one pair of shorts she didn't change for weeks because she was too busy chasing spotted toads into the woods until she either caught them or she didn't, her belly brown and showing in all the days of those early summers, when Carl Verdyne played the mandolin and guests leaned, listening, nearby. Tom Hackett. As she got to him he dropped his sunglasses and she thought it strange she should be so happy to see someone who only ever followed her around, someone she wouldn't let join her when she went out fishing because all he had to recommend him as far as she could tell was what her grandfather called the Hackett fortune even though he had great hands with a fishing pole because old Will Stanley had taught him, too, just like Jo, and even then he had a frank crinkly smile which to the twelve-year-old Jo was only disturbing. "I heard you were back," he said to her now, scratching the side of his nose as she held out her arms—amazed to find him standing on her dock—as if to say, *well here you are.*

"Cabin Girl, Cabin Girl, Cabin Girl"—Jo spun to face the radio—"this is Black Heart. Over." She didn't move. It was late afternoon and Luke had gone for the day and Minette was in town at a fish fry and Tom Hackett had ferried Benoit to the landing to pick up the Wendaban mail in one of the battered green group mailboxes. "Cabin Girl, Cabin Girl, Cabin Girl, this is Black Heart. Over." It was the same high sexless voice, a concentrated malevolence that sounded like no one she knew. No one she ever knew. Jo grabbed the mike just as Kay came out of the kitchen.

Her thumb was twitching as it held down the button. "Black Heart, this is Cabin Girl. Over." She let the button go.

"Cabin Girl"—the voice went higher, slower—"I know how you killed Christine."

Jo felt herself flayed open. She looked down to make sure, crossing her quaking arms over her torso just to hold everything in, not understanding why there was no blood or organs. Her first thought was to turn off the radio and give Black Heart no more access to her, but the radio was her sole connection with the rest of the lake, the only way she'd learn about fires or medical emergencies—the way the lake was hearing the harassment of her by someone calling himself Black Heart. Kay stood at her side as she held down the button on the mike. "Temcot, Temcot, Temcot," Jo raised the radio operator at the Headquarters for the Cottagers Association, "this is Cabin Girl. Over."

"Cabin Girl, this is Temcot. Over."

"Get me the police, Andy. I want to report a crime."

Millie T. called her, then, a middle-aged lady who told her to give the bastard hell.

Bar None called her wondering who Christine was.

Bevel Boy, who turned out to be Luke, saying he'd come back if she wanted.

My Blue Haven called offering legal advice.

Irish Stu, who wanted to know if she needed anything in town.

And Windjammer—Tom Hackett, who said he'd meet her on the dock of Wendaban for another shot at it—just to make her laugh.

But the Ontario Provincial Police who came in their blue and white patrol boat and took a few desultory notes told her what she already knew: there was no way to figure out who it was, not as long as Black Heart stayed on the VHF radio. He could be anyone anywhere—all he needed was an antenna—on one of the thousand islands of Lake Temagami, or within range on the mainland—or on a boat. She listened while the OPP advised her to get rid of the VHF radio and install a telephone with caller ID, not telling them it would be a betrayal of her grandfather, and she felt her eyelids droop in pain as it occurred to her that maybe her whole presence on the lake was now just a betrayal of another sort. When the cops asked about the Christine mentioned in the harassing calls, she told them the truth: Christine was her summertime best friend—the daughter of the nurse at Wendaban—who died in a fall one night the summer they were both thirteen, and she heard about the death the next morning. The lurid parts that only shimmered shapeless in her memory, all sixteen years that followed the event, she left out—left out because a speck of corrosion was beginning in the part of her brain where fear resides, and it was making her wonder whether the torment by Black Heart was, after all, correct.

Back inside the lodge Jo stood without moving in the Grand Parlor, her body just a broken mobile of dry bones, while Kay brought out dinner plates. The simple act of eating anything set before her seemed like the only joy left in the world. "Cabin Girl, Cabin Girl, Cabin Girl"—at the sound of the voice Jo let out a sob—"this is Black Heart. What happened to the red shirt you wore the night you killed her?"

She was undecided about the effects of suffering. Did it close over her like some kind of carapace and keep her safe from all sharpened speech and damaging looks? Or did it make her into a cluster of unprotected dendrons, a bouquet of stripped filaments completely incapable of blocking sensation? Benoit's incisors clicked when he spoke. Luke rubbed his left thumb and ring finger together before he ate. Kay had a smell of wet ashes when she passed. They were all becoming more formal with each other, which she realized is what happens when pain fills the spaces between people. Black Heart wanted her to suffer, wanted her to pay, that much she knew. *What happened to the red shirt you wore the night you killed her?* She didn't know. Didn't know what had happened to it. Didn't know why it was important. She remembered waking up in the skiff in the middle of the night—only the dock lights showed her she was back at Wendaban, only the dock lights located her somewhere in a world where she had always found comfort—thirteen and wet and bruised and naked in a large red shirt. *What happened to the red shirt you wore the night*—She had stumbled out of the boat someone had tied to the old crooked dock in the shallows near the back of the property—without Christine, who must have rowed them back, left Jo there, and gone up to bed. The shirt was mystifying, but she staggered noiselessly up the back stairs and fell into her own room. In the morning came the news, and in her grief over Christine—and her failure to confess to the events of the night before—Jo never wondered again about the shirt. But Black Heart had seen her in the red shirt. Or Black Heart had dressed her in the red shirt. She felt sick at the thought. *What happened to the red shirt*—The question was about a piece of clothing; there was no question at all about the killing. Had Black Heart seen it happen? Had she and Christine not been alone, after all?

Cheryl the event planner took charge of the RSVPs as they came in and kept insisting on floral arrangements, which Jo refused. Guy and Walter pushed for a short video presentation on Wendaban and Lake Temagami—"You've got to give people something for their money, Jo," they argued—and she agreed. A leaky shower pan in #16 led to water damage downstairs in #4, so for the week before the fundraiser, Luke appeared to be in at least three places at once, looking grim when he told her he couldn't get his hands on a new shower pan that would fit and he was damn well going to have to put in extra hours if she wanted all the repairs done in time. Jo paid her bills, handled the workers, and—when no one was around—ripped through old trunks and stashed boxes, looking for a red shirt.

Overnight the temperature dropped and Jo was up, cold, before daybreak. She went into the kitchen to start a pot of coffee. Outside the rain was soft and metallic on the pines and the bald rock. In it she heard the sound of everything she ever knew that flowed or healed, and without putting on a rain jacket, she took her coffee outside and walked the shore of Wendaban to the old crooked dock, where she sat. Rain added to the mug. Rain added to her face. Night was leaving, and a fine white Temagami mist was slung low, she could tell, over the water. A fish jumped. Jo cried for her grandfather, who had loved her—who sorrowed for her as much as for the dead Christine the morning he came into her room with the sloping logs and told her Christine had met with violence, which was just how he put it. Met with violence. Jo had no voice. He had gone on to say the girl was found dead on the rocks at the bottom of Stone Maiden Cliff. Her clothes were gone. They didn't know yet whether she had been—interfered with—he said, frowning, and she wasn't sure what he meant. But there were signs of a struggle at the top, and he was so grateful his Jo had been home asleep all night. Then, as he patted her shoulder in a gruff sort of way, she wondered, stricken, who did this to Christine?

Who did this?

And then she knew: she did.

And she started to scream.

She screamed because she had pushed her friend off Stone Maiden Cliff. She screamed because she could never tell anybody. She had been home asleep—just like her grandfather said—all night. All night. Every night. Home. Home asleep. The bruises were under the covers. The red shirt was on the floor. She could never look at any of it. She could never tell. *No one will know*, Christine had said, only she was wrong. Black Heart knew. All along.

Jo curled up tight on her side on the old crooked dock, fanning her fingers against the wood, like an underwater dying thing. A black dock spider eased a leg joint up between the boards. They weren't hand to leg, the two of them, but they were close enough. The rain was stopping. She heard a boat coming, making its slow small way to the main dock at Wendaban. Blue. Luke's boat. She curled up tighter, not letting herself feel relieved he was putting in more hours to get the job done. Without moving her head from the boards, she could see in the thin new daylight more world than she ever needed—a water skimmer rowing silently across the lake surface, a duck quacking softly along the near shore, the misty lower branches of the far pines. She heard him come over and stop just a few feet away. He set down his toolbox without making much noise.

"How long have you been here?"

Jo fanned her fingers. Her lips felt strange. Unfamiliar. "All my life." All he could do was grunt. She raised her face. "Why don't you like me?"

"Why does it matter?"

"Things matter."

"Do they?"

"Of course they do."

"Things like a red shirt?"

She jerked away from him. "What do you know about it?"

"I heard the call."

"I could use a friend."

"I give you good work for a fair price." He picked up the toolbox and started to walk away. "We don't have to like each other."

In the late afternoon the day before the fundraiser, Kay set out some cold cuts and store-bought potato salad—Benoit refused to handle them—for the helpers to grab a quick bite while they worked. At the crowded dock, boats were tied up to other boats, bumping softly against each other in the light wind. Minette was out front directing her teenaged son's friends on just where to hang the banner saying WELCOME TO WENDABAN in Ojibway that Kay had got some Bear Island children to paint. Tom Hackett was tying up the VHF radio with calls placed by the radio operator at Temcot HQ to the Ministry of Natural Resources, trying to get it straight whether torchières were considered open fires during a fire ban. Jo stood so long waiting for an answer that Luke took the bed linens out of her arms and went upstairs to make up the bed in #12. Minette's boy was trying to drive a torchière into the thin Temagami soil, poking it around for a better grip, then started bellowing out "John Henry." Jo stepped outside as his friends joined in, and for a moment everything was robust with youth and goodness. *Hammer be the death of me, Lord, Lord, hammer be the death of me.* The strong boys, the imperturbable clouds, Minette's laughter as the wind took the banner off one of its nails and it rippled sideways in a half-fall.

One of the old Wendaban skiffs was floating unmoored out in the wide bay, the result of too many lines being tied and untied, she guessed. She called Tom outside, who saw it right away, and they got into his runabout. "Let's go get the stray," he said, while she pushed them out from the other boats, and he backed up. She felt like they were running away—doing something daring going off together—the clouds, the boys, the fallen banner, even the voices getting more robust, *And he laid down his hammer and he died, Lord, Lord*—for those moments as he stood at the wheel and headed slowly toward the skiff, she believed in their own youth and goodness, and with no thought of the past she turned his face toward her and kissed Tom the golden Hackett boy who had, she was pleased to see, the good sense to shift into neutral while she did.

She liked it that he said nothing afterward and as they approached the skiff she took a boat pole to pull it alongside so she could grab the bowline. At first she thought it was a paint rag in the old rowboat, but she couldn't figure it out since no one had been using it. The hulls of the two boats were jostling as Tom kept the runabout in neutral. "We can just tow it—" he called to her, but she cried out and scrambled over the gunwales and into the skiff. There, laid out on the middle seat, was a very old red shirt.

Her head was coming off from a headache no amount of aspirin could reach. She slept badly, twitching in and out of sleep, and cried at the thought that the fundraiser for the Wendaban Center for Environmental Studies was going to find her pale and baggy-eyed and bedeviled. Yesterday she had wanted to load the skiff with rocks until it sank, bearing the red shirt to the bottom. But she folded the shirt instead and locked it inside the small steel safe in her grandfather's closet—just so it wouldn't disappear again. As she handled it, her fingers felt detached from her body.

By the time the guests started to arrive, she had changed into a yellow summer shift and managed to smile and pull off the handshakes, thankful that Tom Hackett and Guy eased into the void she couldn't help creating. Someone handed her a drink that was even paler than her face and she stood as straight as she could and listened to Tom Hackett tell an important dean from the University of Western Ontario that he was prospecting for diamonds in the province. And she listened to Guy tell a woman from the Toronto *Globe and Mail* that two of Wendaban's outbuildings would be converted into labs. And she listened to Benoit tell everyone that the tiramisu, if he must say so himself, was particularly excellent. Somewhere out back Kay and Luke—who had buttoned his top button and added a string tie for the occasion—were quietly hosing down a kitchen table they had dragged outside when the champagne punch bowl shattered.

Jo got through the video presentation without watching any of it. At ten-thirty Minette invited anyone who wanted to do wishing boats to come down to the dock. A few who were staying the night went upstairs, but Jo watched several others follow Minette, their way lighted by the Chinese lanterns Cheryl had driven all the way to North Bay to find that afternoon when they got the word from the ministry that the fire ban made torchières out of the question. Minette had unscrewed the dock lights and one by one the shadowy guests set out on the lake a flotilla of lighted candles fixed on cardboard squares, launched with silent wishes. In the windless night they were tiny flames adrift until the cardboard soaked through and they sank.

Jo watched them go from inside the double screen doors, while Guy, Tom Hackett, and the others were left looking at the architect's plans for renovating the outbuildings. "Cabin Girl, Cabin Girl, Cabin Girl—" *No, not now*, Jo pressed herself into the logs of the front wall, *not here*—the same awful voice—but she didn't have to answer and none of the guests would know she was Cabin Girl—

"Jo"—Tom Hackett moved toward her—"do you want me to get it this time?"

She shook her head as people turned to look at her.

"Cabin Girl," Black Heart—who knew she was listening, knew he didn't have to raise her again, knew formalities meant nothing when the accusation was murder—went on in that high, malevolent voice to a room that was completely silent, "tell them what you did with her clothes after you killed Christine." Jo started up the stairs as she heard Tom explain to the others that Jo had been the victim of a wicked joke. She nearly laughed at how reduced it all sounded, then found herself listening almost like a normal person to the woman reporter coming toward her who was wondering what Jo wanted her to do with the laundry in the bathroom of room #12. Jo said she'd take care of it.

She walked through #12 to the bathroom, and swung open the door. Submerged in the tub half full of water was a white sleeveless top and green shorts. She stared at them for just a second before she shrieked, seeing Christine peel them off at the top of the diving cliff. Luke was first into the room. "What the hell—?"

Jo stumbled out of the bathroom. "It's a mouse."

"It's not a mouse."

"Leave me alone."

"What happened?" He looked into the bathroom.

She saw it all. "You were in here today."

"So?"

"You made up the bed."

"So?"

"Who are you?" she hissed.

"Why does it matter?"

She yelled at him to get out—get out for good—and it was Kay who put her to bed in her old childhood room down at the sunset side of the lodge where the logs sloped and girls cuddled safe under the covers for years and years until they were very old women together. She knew it was Kay who kept the others out—she heard her arguing out in the hall with Tom Hackett and Minette—and little by little as the lodge grew quiet, she didn't know who had decided to stay overnight with the crazy screaming murdering lodgekeeper and who had gone, instead, to the mainland on a wild night ride with Ellroy the tattooed cabby. She felt an isolation she could never repair as long as she stayed at Wendaban, but whether she died in her sleep or lived to leave the lake forever was a matter of complete indifference as she pulled the covers over her head and she dreamed once again of Christine.

In the morning she rowed the old skiff the two miles to Stone Maiden Cliff, in a bay near the opening to the North Arm. Kay watched her go from the edge of the main dock. The sun was strong and the clouds were mountainous, cut sharply into the sky as the wind kicked up. At the base of the diving cliff she tied up to a stringy overhanging cedar and listened to the boat bang rhythmically against the small rocks as she started the steep climb. It was harder at thirty than it was at thirteen. Her feet slid back, her hands could hardly pull her up, she weighed more. She made it to the top of the twenty-foot cliff and rolled in the brown fallen pine needles, the way they always did, for flavor, Christine said.

It had been a quick, quiet row that night, sometime close to midnight when they were not supposed to be out. But it was July and they knew the lake well and they wanted to swim naked by starlight. They tied up out of the wind and scrambled to the top and lay there on their backs holding hands for the longest time. The moon was up, so the stars were fainter, but Christine pointed out Perseus. Then they stood up and stripped quickly, Christine peeling the white sleeveless top and green shorts, then kicking them behind her. At the edge they looked down at the cliff, the way it sloped in one place into a slanting shelf, the way a red pine sapling was growing bright and hopeless right out of the rock. They jumped together the first time, the way they always did, and crawled like naked dripping white monkeys back to the top. It was exhilarating, slamming into the water they could barely see in the black Temagami night. They clung to the sheer vertical face of the cliff as they treaded water, the little waves drawing them, pushing them, the rock so strangely warm still against their skin. They sputtered and groaned and laughed from the cold.

Then at the top Jo stood shivering and stamping her feet with a sudden chill, her arms tight across her chest. And in the next moment Christine changed their lives forever by stepping in close and putting her arms around Jo, who froze. Christine kissed her first just next to her mouth, then on her mouth, whispering, *No one will know.* And what happened next was a struggle that made her sick the minute it lasted—Christine saying her name over and over—Jo first trying to get out with a smile and ripping her brain apart to make sense of losing her friend forever while she had never held her closer—the soft kisses, a hand on her waist, the powerful foreignness of the flesh next to hers—and then she kicked—and then she pushed, oh yes, she pushed—and the scream was a gulp, but Jo was pulled over, too, aware all at once that she was stopped by the sapling and her head slammed into the rock, and the hands that slid down to her ankles dropped away and a terrible weight was gone for good.

Sixteen years later she lay crying quietly on her back at the top of Stone Maiden Cliff and thought about all the campers and canoe trippers and lovers who had been here diving since that night. She tried telling herself she had been thirteen and that tenderness is only something you can learn when you've been afoot in the world long enough to see how bleak all things are without it. Her name would cease to be a good name if she stayed in Temagami because Black Heart would see to it. Suffering, he was telling her, wasn't in recollection—it was in exile. Early that morning she had found her grandfather's old personnel files in a storeroom near the back of the lodge. The nurse, Aimée Delacroix, Wendaban employee for two years until her daughter died and she left Temagami, was divorced with one son—Jean-Luc Delacroix, four years older than Christine—"Bright young man, good with his hands," her grandfather had written in the margin. "Can we use him somehow?"

Here is how the story begins: night fishing with old Will Stanley some sixteen years ago. He begged the old man to take him out. Night fishing: flashlight when you need it, cigars for warmth and satisfaction, navigating by the moon, whizzing off the boat, even, now and then, a fish. They were anchored off the far side of Stone Maiden Cliff when the girls went over. The boy, who was in the bow of the boat, saw it happen. Will Stanley muttered shit *a couple of times and quickly started the motor. He and the boy nearly fell out of the boat to get to the one lying white and broken in the shallows.* This one's dead, *Will Stanley said to the boy who was trying to keep the discovery, the sight of all that death and nakedness, down in his stomach.* Leave her. *A loon called somewhere close by, and the boy jumped.* Leave her?

She'll be found in the morning and you're not even supposed to be here and I'm an old Indian standing here with two naked white girls and I only have just so much explanation in me, boy. *Will Stanley scrambled up the side of the cliff to the sapling on the shelf, where the other girl was knocked out, and managed to hand her down to the boy, who didn't know where to grab her. She was banged up and knocked out but he grabbed her around the ribs since it made some sense and yielded him a quick feel that was goddamn the least she owed him after what he had just seen—*

Will Stanley dressed her in his red shirt and set her carefully in the Wendaban skiff. Then he pulled the dead girl up farther on the rocks out of a kind of decency, the boy thought, and said, I'll row this one back and leave her out of sight. You give me half an hour and come after me, and I'll get you home as soon as I can. *The boy watched him row away toward Wendaban, bare-chested, an old man with just so much explanation in him, and he grew darker and more indistinct as he went. When he was out of sight, the boy sat near the dead girl until he couldn't take it any longer and climbed shivering to the top of the cliff to collect the clothing. It wasn't until later that he could see—with no more explanation in him than the old man—there was no easy way to return the clothing of the dead.*

It has taken two days since he set the ax next to the furnace to feel satisfied with the letter he wrote confessing to the events of four years ago, and the contents of the other envelope, a deed addressed to Cabin Girl. It is 2 A.M. *and sleeping upstairs is a woman named Diane he found and married just after he drove Jo Verdyne forever from the lake and then never answered any of her calls. Overhead is a single light, seventy-five watts, enough to work afterward with the razor.* A good light is everything, *Will Stanley used to say without much more in the way of explanation. But to Will Stanley, everything was everything.* A good net is everything, boy, *he'd say. And other times,* A good meal is everything. *But surely a good ax is something, Will Stanley? And a good razor?*

No one answers.

If he had a wishing boat, he would light the candle and launch it from the main dock of Wendaban, many hours away from this house in Nashville that has no meaning for him, and wish that he had never bought the Wendaban property through a holding company when Jo Verdyne put it up for sale and then never brought the wrecking ball in by barge. Much of the lodge had to be dismantled—dismembered, someone called it that day, and that seemed closer to the truth—and the very deep wrongness of it all didn't strike him until sometime after the rubble had been cleared away. He stood bewildered that he didn't feel more pleasure in getting what he had worked toward for months. And when the drilling yielded nothing, after all—not so much as a speck of kimberlite—he thought for the first time in his life that maybe he was a fool.

No, not a fool, exactly, because he had always been a clever man. No one, for instance, the night of the fundraiser at Wendaban, had seen him slipping his hand under the table where the VHF radio stood and detaching the Walkman he had Velcroed in place. By then Jo was shrieking in the upstairs bathroom and everyone was rushing over to the stairs. Black Heart's last message to Cabin Girl had been prerecorded and was just about as fine an alibi as a man could want.

He picks up the Sears Craftsman ax that someone named Jimmy sold him and starts up the basement steps. It is time to gather in those parts of him that will suffer when the letter is found. If he had a dog, he would have to gather it in for it would be the dog part of him that would remember forever what he had done. Now he will gather in the wife part of him that will only feel shame, but the blunt end of the ax is a good gatherer. And afterward the razor will draw a quick hard line below his chin and say there will be no more lies or false smiles from everything above this line. Do good for the people, when you grow to a man, you hear? *Will Stanley told him softly from the darkened stern of the boat as they fished quietly off the far side of Stone Maiden Cliff.* I will, I promise, *the boy said, but he stopped baiting his hook as the wind edged them closer to the front of the diving cliff and he looked up and saw something remarkable. Two naked girls kissing. He knew them. Their heads and arms and hips moved in the starlight that excluded him for all time.* You got the money, Tom, boy, but you also got a good heart. And a good heart is everything—

Marion Arnott

DOLLFACE

■ ■ ■

Marion Arnott is a Scots writer who teaches English at St. Andrew's Academy in Paisley. She has had some success in the world of the British independent press, particularly in Andy Cox's Crimewave *magazine, which led to a Crime Writers Association Dagger Award for her short story "Prussian Snowdrops" in 2001 and another appearance as a finalist for "Marbles" in 2002. Other highlights of her writing career include two appearances in Japan's* Hawakaya Mystery Magazine, *a place in Datlow and Windling's* Year's Best Fantasy & Horror *(volume XV), and in Maxim Jakubowski's* Best British Mysteries. *"Dollface" was also shortlisted by the CWA for 2003, and first appeared in her collection of short stories,* Sleepwalkers, *published by Elastic Press, a new publishing house specializing in short-story collections. She's back in this year's edition with another eerie tale where nothing is as it seems, and reality and hallucination blend in a spellbinding tale of a husband, his wife, and the child who is irretrievably caught between them.*

There's wide starless night and there's wide black water and the rowboat moves smoothly between. Charlie rows and keeps his eye on the small hooded figure hunched in the stern. His father is brooding and silent in the thick darkness. Somehow Charlie knows that he must find a safe shore soon. He rows and peers ahead, but wherever he looks, at sky or wide water, there's only impenetrable inkiness. He listens out for water being sucked on to land, but hears only the tiny splash of oars.

He rows steadily. Cool air soothes hint until the boat begins to rock; on a tideless, windless lake, the boat rocks violently from side to side. Charlie flattens the oars, but the boat leaps forward like a thing with a life of its own and skims across the surface of the water; then, with a stun of disbelief, he sees the hooded figure in the prow tip soundlessly over the side.

He drops the oars and leans out of the boat. There's no sound of a struggle, no cry for help. He gropes blindly in the murk for an arm, a leg, a head, but comes up with nothing but fistfuls of black satiny water. "Dad! Dad!" he yells, but his cries are stifled by the dark. For an agonized age, he gropes and scoops, and then a movement catches his eye: it's the hood, bubbled sodden on the surface of the water. Panting with relief, he hauls it into the boat, but it sags weightless over his arm. "Dad! Dad!" he sobs, and ferrets about in its folds until he's sure it's really empty. He buries his face in it, but it wriggles out of his numbed hands and plasters itself across his face. For a moment, he's blinded. Then it wriggles again and molds around his mouth and nose and it isn't empty: it's lined with a sludge that slithers into his mouth and nostrils. He claws at his face, desperate for air, but he's choking on rank liquid earth and there's no Dad, no safe shore, only a piercing sense of loss and the great terror that always comes with it. He's suffocating on a dark stinking sludge that floods thickly down his windpipe; he's stifling on foul blackness and there's a voice in his head, a quiet chant of "eternity" . . .

Everything began with the dream, and that began when Dad was dying. Dollface began then too, but the dream came first, ending each time on a chant of "eternity" in a cultured voice like Christopher Lee's. Always, as I opened my eyes, I realized groggily that it wasn't really Christopher Lee, that it was only Dad impersonating; and always, as I eased upright in the armchair, I thought I was a little boy again, giggling around one of Dad's building sites—I swear that, for a moment, I could hear the excavators gouging out earth by the ton, and saw myself running about challenging mummies, vampires, and ghouls to come out, come out, wherever they were, while Dad talked like Hammer House of Horror.

Always, about then, my vision cleared and I saw the bottle of Lucozade on the table, the white bed, the pallor of the dying man in it, and I knew I was in Dad's house, and that it was now, not then. In this room, the important past and impossible present met and mixed like whiskey and soda. I used to wake and see the hospital cleanliness of Dad's bedroom, but my nose was still full of the smell that followed the breaking in of the ground: dank earth and crushed mountain, old cold stone and stagnant water, all rancid with the stench of the living things the earth had swallowed and held until they rotted. Building sites smell like that, even on sparkling sunny days, and when I was little, the cold stench made me solemn with unease. Dad used to make me right again by grabbing me around the waist and talking like Christopher Lee—*"And now you know how the grave smells, Charlie. This is the smell of all eternity . . ."*—until I squealed with terrified delight. There was tickling then and a change of voice to Peter Cushing's prim precision—

"So gather ye rosebuds while ye may,
Old Time is still a-flying
And this same flower which blooms today
Tomorrow will be dying"

Big burly Dad used to fold to the ground like a lily in a heat wave and sigh wistfully when he got to "dying," a protracted polysyllabic dying and sighing, which made me scream with laughter.

But when Tomorrow came, and his long dying began in earnest, there was nothing funny about it. Dad lay tidy between the sheets, flat as an envelope ready for posting, and it was hard to believe that he wasn't really there, that everything that made Dad who he was had been sent on ahead somewhere: the rough and tumble games, the frowns, the half-shamed tendernesses, the rueful grin he faced the world with when things got bad, then worse and worse.

I talked to him a lot. The doctors had agreed that it was possible that he could hear me, or at least that it wasn't impossible. "Wasn't impossible" was good enough for me. I told him about my week, which didn't take long because the focus of my life was Saturdays and Sundays in that room with him. The rest of the time I ate and slept, and traveled fretting around the building sites—he'd never have forgiven me if I'd let the business slide—but stayed in the site office mostly, not liking the nightmare smell of the ground being dug up.

Dad never took to Dollface. We met her about six months before he sank into the morphine stupor. I came into his bedroom and found him sitting at his computer, cozy in his plaid dressing gown and blue cotton pajamas. He tried to hide the screen, but I saw he was in a Lonely Hearts chat room. An Adult Lonely Hearts chat room.

"Jesus, Dad! Betty Boobs? Hot4U? Foxon Heat?"

Dad looked at me, half shamed, half mischievous, an elderly wrinkled toddler about to be sent to bed. "I might be old and ill, son, but there's life in this old boy still." A comic downturn of the mouth, a sly wink. "And nobody in my life."

I looked over his shoulder, incredulous. "Dad, you're not Young Stud, are you?"

"Well, I was once, son." A rueful shrug; an explosion of laughter that I had to share, a laughter that became helpless as Dad explained to Foxon Heat how he'd acquired his nickname, and she replied in kind. Dad giggled till he coughed and spluttered. "It's just a bit of kiddology, Charlie. There's no way of knowing who's at the other end of these messages. We can be whoever we like."

And Dad wanted to be anybody but an elderly man who had begun dying.

It occurred to me over the next few weeks that Dad had never in his life had such fun relationships with women. He laughed and joked and talked dirty, they did the same, and all parties were satisfied. There were none of the usual disappointing revelations, recriminations, slammed doors, and leaving forevers. Just good, honest, dirty fun. He even inveigled me into competing for the attentions of Hot4U and Foxon Heat, but they beat me hands down when it came to sleazy snigger and soon returned to Young Stud. Then one Sunday afternoon, Dollface arrived. *"Hello, roomies,"* she said. *"Hi, Dollface,"* I typed. That was the start.

That first day, Dad shook his head at her chat: coarse sniggers were not her thing. She misunderstood or else she fell into an embarrassed silence. By silence, I mean of course that she didn't type a message for ages. How did I know she was embarrassed? I just did.

That first day she tried to change the subject—some chance—with a question about everybody's favorite films. She was answered with a royal flush of cinema's great erotic moments. *"Oh,"* she said. *"I haven't seen any of those."* Young Stud told her she ought to get out more, but Foxon Heat flashed the snigger smiley and told him there might be something interesting keeping her at home. Speculation about that kept them entertained for the rest of the afternoon.

Dollface didn't deign to reply, although she stayed in the room, and she was there every Sunday afternoon thereafter, not joining in and irritating Dad out of all proportion. He thought she was being superior, a big no-no in his book, and week after week, he teased her.

Come on, Doll, SHARE your dreams. We're all dying to know what rings your bells.

Dollface, we've showed you ours. Time for you to show us yours.

Hey, Dollface, you getting off on our fantasies? Are we helping?

Dollface, come on out and PLAY 'stead of sitting there taking notes.

She never responded. In the end, Dad gave up, and she and I lurked quietly together in dignified disapproval on the sidelines. After a while, occasionally and then more often, she threw in questions for me: films, books, hobbies—all that.

Now and again she made me smile. That Valentine's Day, she got on to the subject of romance and started spouting the Nation's Favorite Love Poetry. It was surreal, because simultaneously, some sad bastard calling himself BitOf Rough was looking for a lady to volunteer for a *9½ Weeks* scenario. *"I want to use a woman. I need to use a woman,"* he typed over and over, while the adult ladies waxed creative over leather masks and dog leashes. BitofRough swore he was willing to travel anywhere in the country and keep it confidential; Dollface quoted the love poetry of Keats, Shelley, and Burns, which she'd thrilled over at school.

Does anyone feel like that anymore? she asked. *So important to feel it, even once. Have you ever, Charlie?* I was spared the necessity of answering because Young Stud got in before me:

That's Fantasy, Dollface.
So's your stuff, Stud.
Don't see anyone else quoting Romance, Dollface.
Don't see anyone volunteering for a dog leash either.
More exciting than love, Doll.
In your world, not mine.
I don't live in Cloud Cuckoo Land.

She signed out then—I could *feel* her affront. And that annoyed me. She didn't have to come in the room; she didn't have to chat. The whole scene pissed me off anyway, both the roomies' relentless verbal masturbation and Dollface's resolute saccharine. You pays your money and you takes your choice, but I wouldn't have given you a bent franc for either. All kiddology, see? All of it. I've always known that.

The following week, she was back as usual, asking after my favorite books and films. That provoked Dad too. "Jeez, son, that snooty bitch's got her eye on you. She'll be wanting to know your astrological sign next—compatibility, all that. Waste of time, that one. Nice lady. The kind that gets on your nerves after a while, but."

She certainly got on his, which made me smile. Even at eighty, he liked to be the center of attraction, and her delicate getting-to-know-you questions were reserved entirely for me. I talked to her sometimes, just to wind Dad up a bit.

I didn't have that excuse by the time summer came. Dad slipped into his long deep sleep and I had a man in a white bed to talk to. I pm'd Dollface for the first time—she compelled politeness somehow—and told her my father was dying and that I wouldn't be around much now.

That's terrible, but. If you need a friend to talk to, I'm always here, Charlie. Three o'clock, Sundays.

Thanks, Dollface. CYA.

I had no intention, though. The chat room was Dad's idea of fun, not mine. And my next few weekends were taken up with pretending he was still there. I talked to him, and when I ran out of things to say, I read aloud the weekend papers (plus supplements) from cover to cover. I fussed over him: straightened his quilt, tucked him in, combed the silvery thickness of hair that flopped boyishly over his forehead. I chatted cheerfully—after all, he might be able to hear—and every now and then I'd say, "Still with us, Dad?"

There was no answer but the stupefied struggle for breath that forced his rib cage up and down. I couldn't stop listening to that. *Slowly up. Painfully up.* The breath took forever to reach the top. *Slowly. Slowly. Up. Up. Up.* I found myself filling my own lungs with air and holding it until I was dizzy, willing Dad to overtake me, dreading the silence that meant he'd broken down somewhere on the road. But Dad's breathing always reached the peak and was soon shuddering all the way back down.

And when listening exhausted me, and you would be amazed at how exhausting it was, I sat in the silence and watched over him. The silence in a sick room, the silence that attends your father's dying, is like a heavy weight, like boulders piled on your rib cage, crushing the life out of you; it's like a winter night, when you inhale needles of frost and they line your insides and you can't get warm; it's an empty place too, the shadow of tomorrow, that freezingly empty time that is no place to be alone; it is unbearable.

I'm always here, Charlie . . . OK, she was a stranger, but who better than a stranger to tell how you really feel? Who else *can* you tell? *Always here* . . . if she was, she would be the first woman who meant it, but then again, Dollface was definitely different, and the monitor was right there in the corner beside the window, staring blankly over at Dad and me, ready to spring to life at the touch of a button—maybe there was someone at the other end, someone who would dissolve the frozen silence of the dying room. I booted up, knowing she wouldn't be there, but . . .

Charlie! You're here.

Hi, Dollface.

How are you?

Fine.

I've been so worried about you . . .

I remember wondering if she was for real, and then deciding that it didn't matter. The Web is the home of charades and fantasy where you can make what you like of what you see. And that day I was glad to believe that someone was thinking of me. All that summer I was glad.

Dollface never told me much about herself, not that I asked at first. Too full of my own troubles, I came to talk, not listen: Dad, morphine deadness, loneliness, nightmares, loss—I spewed it all out, week after week.

Dollface, I keep having this nightmare.

Nightmare?

It's strange. I'm in the nightmare, but I'm looking on too.

I know that feeling.

It took an age to peck a full account on to the screen, but Dollface, as always, was endlessly patient.

That dream makes me shudder, Charlie. Really frightening.

Sunday wouldn't be Sunday without it.

Oh, don't joke. It's not funny.

I'm all right.

It's a fear of loss dream.

There's a surprise.

You must be very close to your father.

Yes. Morecambe and Wise. Laurel and Hardy. Lone Ranger and Tonto. All that.

Loss is a terrible thing.

Tell me about it.

But, Charlie, you never really lose people . . . not so long as you remember them. No one is really dead until they are forgotten.

He feels dead already.

I read once somewhere that death is no more than a stepping into the next room. You'll meet again. I believe that's true. It's a comfort.

What do you know about it, Dollface? You can't have been there if you can get comfort from that slop.

She exited the room, stage left, and I didn't care. Homilies of the Hallmark Greetings variety were a habit of hers and I usually smiled at them, but that day she got to me. I was angered by the slick sugary placebo she offered. Death is *enormous*, has *enormity* has *finality;* it's all the unhappy endings ever written rolled into a bullet aimed right at your head. I wanted to scream that agony at her, but at the same time, a terrible longing fluttered like a bird in my chest, a longing to believe something, anything, that would make living easier. It would have been good to surrender to that feeling, but deadly too, because hope failed is worse than no hope in the first place.

It was Dad saved me. I heard his great gust of laughter—just in my head, you understand, I'm not saying he was *really* laughing—and his voice sure and clear, saying the kind of thing I'd heard him say a hundred times: *"Another Thought For The Day, Charlie boy? She should be on Songs of Praise."* And then his chuckle rolled around the room. *"When you're dead, you're dead. Finito. Endgame. None of this Heaven and Hell, Pulse in the Eternal Mind malarkey. That was all invented to keep us behaving and fearing. Truth is, when you're gone, you're gone, and there's no coming back."*

You're gone. Or maybe you're only waiting in the next room. Two contradictory ideas. Dad, the toughest man I ever knew, faced the world with a scornful defiance I could only envy; Dollface believed in any kind of ludicrousness that made living bearable. I envied her too.

As the summer wore on, I began to wonder about her: who she was, what she was like. In a way, we had become close. She knew a lot about me, although I knew next to nothing about her. Not being used to confiding, I felt exposed somehow. After our quarrel over what happened when you died, I decided to keep off that subject, maybe get her talking about herself for a change. I felt guilty about snapping at her—after all she meant well—and the thought occurred that since the beginning, I had been hogging the show with all my troubles. That thought made me feel even more guilty. Why had she needed the comfort of "the next room"? I hadn't even asked. Maybe she had things she wanted to talk about, maybe she was as lonely and full of pain as me. Why else would she come into a chat room, for Christ's sake? I decided to give her the opportunity to open up a bit.

Hi, Dollface. How are you this week?

Fine, thanks. What about you and your father?

The same. Both of us. Let's talk about something else. You must get fed up with me and my miseries.

Not at all, Charlie.

You never say anything about you, Dollface. Tell me something.

Nothing to tell.

Come on! Must be something!

What do you want to know?

Anything—a/s/l?

Younger than you/female/somewhere and nowhere.

How do you know you're younger than me?

Women are always younger than the men they know.

I'm nearly fifty, Doll.

And I will never be fifty.

Very funny, Dollface. You a sweet little mystery, Dollface?

Definately, Charlie.

Behind me, Dad started muttering, which he did now and then, so I signed out with apologies. I was peeved at Dollface, anyway. OK, it's dangerous for women to reveal too much about themselves in chat rooms, but she and I had been talking for weeks. She *knew* me. I felt rejected. Why didn't she share her woes? Her life? Fair exchange, all that.

I sat with Dad, silently fuming. He had fallen silent again. I'd missed whatever it was he might have been trying to say. "You were right about her, Dad," I said. "Nice lady. Gets on your nerves, but," I sat grumbling for a while, then dozed off and plunged straight into the nightmare.

Charlie's heart is racing. Dad, hunched in the stern of the boat, turns his head slowly toward him. Charlie can't see the eyes in the dark, under that hood, but he feels them bright with fear, fixed on him. He knows the eyes are pleading. He knows. Dad's afraid! Charlie wants to touch his hand and tell him, "All right, Dad," although he knows it isn't. But words stick in his throat and he can't let go of the oars. He tries to wrench his hands off them, but they're stuck fast together. Charlie, frantic because he knows what happens next, struggles and splashes black evil-smelling water all over himself, while Dad tips over the side. He slips into the water, twisting slowly around as he falls. He's trying to get one last look at Charlie. He slides silently under black water and leaves his blind pleading gaze behind, burning cold as starlight on Charlie's face . . .

I woke up tasting filthy sludge again. I took a mouthful of Lucozade and swilled the dry sweet bubbles around my mouth. And maybe because I had got into the habit of Sunday afternoon revelation, I told Dad all about it.

"Hey, Dad," I said to the white bed after I'd described the choking sludge. "That was a real cracker, wasn't it, but? You'd have loved it."

The old childhood formula relaxed me. I heard Dad's gruff Hammer House of Horror chuckle once more, making everything all right, the way it did when I was little and we'd been watching our favorite Hammers on a Friday night. I loved them: *Dracula, Prince of Darkness; Frankenstein; Witchfinder General;* all the gory others. Scary fun with the lights out: Price, Lee, popcorn and Cushing, and me in my dressing gown snuggled up to Dad, covering my eyes when it got too much, but peering through my fingers because I didn't want to miss a minute. Then the bloodred credits and the eerie music at the end and Dad chuckling because I was all a-tremble. "Hey, Charlie," he'd laugh, "that was a real cracker, wasn't it, but?" And everything was all right again.

It was that day too because his chuckle flew straight as an arrow from the past into the present. "A real cracker, but," I thought, and found myself laughing in the old way. Who needed Dollface's soothing when I had Dad to laugh it off with?

I realized something else too: nobody but Dad ever said "wasn't it, but?" It was one of his Scottish-isms. He stuck "but" at the ends of sentences all the time. It doesn't mean anything except that the speaker hails from Glasgow. Dad's gravelly Scots accent had been refined over the years we'd lived in England, but he still said "wasn't it, but?" and "DEFF-in-ATE-ly" instead of "yes." Nobody in the whole city of Glasgow, he told me once, could spell "definitely" because in that part of the world they pronounced it with an "a." Dad did too, out of habit, or national pride.

And so did Sweet Little Mystery Dollface. *"Definately, Charlie."* And *"terrible, but."* She'd used the Glasgow "but" a few times, now that I came to think of it. What with hearing Dad's Friday Hammer chuckle, and guessing where Dollface came from, I suddenly felt better, as though I'd stolen a march on her.

Hi, Dollface. How's things in the far north?

No idea, Charlie.

But you're from those parts, aren't you?

Sorry?

Glasgow.

Once. Not now. How did you know?

Where now then?

No place in particular.

You're being mysterious again.

No. I move around a lot so I don't come from anywhere really. How did you know?

I couldn't resist a gloat about "definately."

Clever, Charlie. So you're from Glasgow too?

Originally.

Whereabouts in Glasgow?

Don't know. We moved away when I was small.

It's a beautiful city. I loved it there. I've never felt at home anywhere else. Do you remember it at all?

No.

That's a shame.

Except there was a park near where I lived.

Glasgow's full of parks—"the dear green place"—when I was small, I thought it was called that because of all the parks.

It was a green park, big, with a pond and a waterfall. I had a boat with blue sails. A swan attacked it once. I remember screaming.

Swans can be scary. They hiss. Have you ever heard them hissing? Beautiful though. I used to love feeding the swans, especially in winter.

I was always terrified of them.

Who rescued you from the swan? Did you get your boat back?

I don't remember.

But you remember the swan. People always remember the things that frighten them.

What frightened you when you were little, Dollface?

Being lost. Getting separated from my mum in the shops. Being left alone.

Like me and Dad.

Yes, but when you're little, it's your mum's loss you fear. She's the center of your world at that age.

I suppose.

I lost my mother when I was small.

Sorry to hear it.

I thought the world was ending when she died.

I know the feeling.

You never mention your mum, Charlie. Only your dad.

Never knew her. Not that I recall, anyway.

What happened to her?

No idea.

She made no response. That was a trick of hers. She'd leave the screen blank so long that it got to feel like a demand, and somehow, before I knew where I was, I was typing in more than I ever intended to say.

You still there, Dollface?

You know me—never far away.

Another long silence and an acre of screen waiting to be filled, Dollface waiting to be told, me resisting. I don't know why. My mother was old history and I had told Dollface about much more sensitive things.

Charlie, you still there?

Yes.

I thought you were going to say more about your mother.

No. I told you I don't remember her.

That is sad.

Only memories can be sad, Dollface. No memories can't be anything at all.

I suppose not. Terrible not to know your own mother, but.

Might have been even more terrible to know her. The kind of woman who runs away to Wales to find herself—

Find herself?

That's what she told Dad before she left. She had to find herself.

In Wales?

In Wales. Could have understood it if she'd fled to Paris or Shanghai. But Wales? With an insurance assessor? Reminds me of the man who ran away from the circus to become an accountant.

Lol—I see what you mean, Charlie, but it must have been awful for you to be left behind.

Could have been worse. She might have taken me with her. Imagine having to admit you came from Wales. She sent me a couple of postcards with views of the golden daffies. That's all I remember of her.

Still, your mother . . .

Dollface, Dad is restless. I have to go. CYA next week.

Bye, Charlie . . .

I signed off quickly. I could tell she was headed for one of her psychological analyses. It would, on past performance, go along the lines that the reason I'd never had good relationships with women was because of this early betrayal by my mother. Inability to trust and so on. And then she'd start in again on the necessity for me to make a life of my own once Dad had gone. Find a partner. Find Love. Start a family. She could never let that subject alone. Her sincere efforts to help drove me crazy sometimes; that day I didn't feel up to them.

I moved the chair over to Dad's bed. "Still don't know anything about her, Dad. I found out that she used to live in Glasgow, but then she changed the subject. Swans today. And then Mum and the man from the Pru. Dollface is still a Sweet Little Mystery."

Thinks she's making herself more interesting by being mysterious, Charlie.

That was something we used to laugh about a lot—the daft ideas that the females of the species have about what makes them interesting. There was a girl I brought home from uni, always dressed in black, always pale and soulful about some great unspecified tragedy that she would never get over. *"Tell her the answer's in Wales,"* Dad whispered as she was putting on her coat to go home. *"New South Wales should be far enough."* Then there was the one who claimed to be psychic and chanted *"Deep waters, black waters,"* over and over while Dad and I sat on cushions on the floor, staring into mirrors that reflected candle flames—I forget why, but my eyes were dazzled by little golden lights for hours after and Dad wound me up by going about the house chanting "black waters, deep waters" in Christopher Lee mode. There were a couple of intellectual ones too—*"Charlie,"* Dad said in wonderment, *"why do clever females always have flat chests?"* And in twinkly-eyed bewilderment at my marine biologist, *"The sex life of sea mice. Dead interesting that. What have I been missing all these years?"* And he laughed and laughed. *"Son, you're like your old man. Not much of a picker."*

FoxOn Heat and Hot4U were what Dad called knowledgeable about what hooked a man's interest. Both of them described themselves as blond, bouncy, and bounteous, green- or blue-eyed, leggy, mischievous, naughty when the moon was in the right quarter, naughtier when it wasn't . . . all that. *"Your Dollface,"* Dad said often, *"has no idea."* We speculated often about the reality of our roomies: wrinkled, toothless, decrepit, manless, and desperate, we decided, or else they wouldn't be touting themselves on the Net. Dollface was different though. We could never work her out. We laughed at all three, but especially her. Dad thought she was Mary Whitehouse's shade come to reform us, or Mary Poppins to sort us out, or the Virgin Mary to lead us to the good life—*"funny how all the Marys are virtuous,"* he said, *"except for Mary Magdalene, and she stopped being interesting once she was repentant."*

I laughed out loud remembering that, and then I had another of those whiskey and soda moments, because if I tried, if I really tried, I could hear Dad laughing, not in memory, but right along with me.

Hi, Dollface.

Hello, Charlie. How are things this week?

You've invaded my dreams, Dollface.

Me?

Swans. Big black hissing swans. The nightmare as usual, except that before Dad goes over the side, I hear hissing coming closer and closer out of the darkness, hundreds of hisses closing in on the boat. Then I see tall narrow black shapes writhing against the night sky. Snakes, I think, hundreds of them, standing on their tails in the water, hissing and writhing and churning up the lake. Then the air is filled with the beating of giant wings, and I see they're not snakes, they're swans unfolding their wings, rearing up on the surface of the lake and clapping their big wings so hard, the wind knocks me back onto my bench. Dad puts out his hands to ward them off and he falls right into that hissing mass. I search in the water for him, but the swans loop their necks around my arms and their feathers brush my face and their slimy webbed feet drum against my hands . . .

Stop! That's terrible. Charlie, I am sorry. I never meant for that to happen.

Sorry for what? It's my nightmare.

I should never have mentioned the swans and the hissing.

Don't be daft.

But you told me the swans made you scream. I should have dropped the subject there and then.

It was only a dream.

Yes, of a childhood fear. You see? I sparked it off by touching on an old fear.

No, it's not a memory. This is my fear of loss dream. Remember?

It's both. That rowboat and the black lake mean something. An old loss? An old fear? Your mother? That's how dreams work.

I don't think dreams mean anything very much, Dollface. Dreams are the place where we get to run safely insane.

They come from childhood.

I don't know . . . brb.

There was a stirring from the bed and a low moaning. I was across the room in two strides. Occasionally Dad surfaced for a while, sometimes because his morphine drip needed adjusting, sometimes for no reason. He never recognized me, but there was always the chance. I checked the drip, ready to ring for the nurse to come upstairs if he needed her, but everything was fine.

"OK, Dad?"

A murmur, a low rush of exhaled breath, "Challiechallie . . ."

Challie. My baby name. My eyes filled and I turned back to the computer.

Dollface, I think Dad's asking for me. Have to run.

He was moving his head feebly, his breath coming through his lips like the rustle of dead leaves. Challiechallie . . .

"I'm here, Dad."

He neither saw nor heard me. I sat by his bed, disappointed. He was still again, austere and dignified, his face lined and seamed like an Indian statue's. Well, he'd spared me Dollface's dream analysis at least. I didn't need it because I'd worked it all out for myself years before.

My mother shaped the lives of Dad and me. Everything we are, everything that happened or didn't happen, was down to her. The summer she left, I was so afraid that Dad too would go out the door and never come back that I wouldn't let him out of my sight. In the mornings, I clung to his legs when he was leaving for work, screaming till the street echoed; at night, I kept him awake with my noisy screaming nightmares. In the end, he gave in and took me with him when he went out to the building sites. I spent my time avoiding holes full of creepy crawlies and hating the smell of new turned earth; I built little houses with broken bricks and bits of planking to hide in if the excavators came near. Dad told me often that he could forgive my mother everything except that hellish summer and the state she left me in. *"But I got you through it, son, eh?"* And so he did.

He didn't come out of it so well. Never again in his life did he have a solid relationship with a woman. *"Trust's gone,"* he used to say and it made him difficult, which he was the first to admit. I lost count of the number of bouquets Interflora delivered on his behalf as an apology for loss of temper, unreasonable jealousy, a sudden slap. But it has to be said, some of them went out of their way to provoke him.

He explained to them all how difficult it was for him to trust—I've seen him cry as he explained—but they didn't listen and carried on in their own sweet way. They went on their girls' nights out and came home drunk and giggling and later than they said they would; they spent his money and lied about it; they practiced all kinds of cheap manipulations to keep him sweet; and the consequence was that they forced him into acting in a way that was different from who he really was. There would have been no trouble if they'd just gone along with the ground rules, but it was as if they enjoyed getting him going.

The last one in residence finished him with housemates for good. She took delivery of an "I'm sorry" bouquet, stuck it in the bin, and had the police supervise the removal of her belongings from the premises. *"As if,"* Dad said after, still pale from the police visit, *"I'd have tried to stop the silly tart leaving."*

There was never another one after her and I was glad. But one good thing came out of it all: I knew every trick in the female book by the time I was sixteen, and I never fell for a single one as I grew older. The only woman I ever *really* talked to was Dollface.

I needed her, irritating as her preaching could be. The summer Dad was dying, I went through a phase of thinking I was going mad. That time I heard Dad laughing with me—it wasn't the last time. As I remembered at his bedside, I *heard* him chuckle to frighten the ghouls and nightmares away, and I *felt* his rough stubble against my little boy cheek—*Daddy, will my face be scratchy like yours when I'm big?*—as he scooped me up in his arms and hugged me; a split second later, I was older and listening to him in the pub when his latest affair had gone wrong—*I'm a bad picker, son, always have been. Only good thing I ever got from a woman was you*—and I had a big lump in my throat because it never occurred to Dad that it wasn't his picking that was bad; it was just that there wasn't much to pick from.

I chatted to his bed, sometimes aloud, sometimes in my head, saying the things I wished I'd said at the time. The trouble was, he often answered, only in my head, but it felt real, as real as the cane chair I sat upon and the snowy sheets he lay between. I heard him.

Dollface, I think I'm going mad.

Why's that, Charlie?

And I told her all about the silence in the white room and how it pressed on me and squeezed the past out of my brain like toothpaste, and how I was never sure what and if and when I was hearing.

See, Dollface? I'm going mad.

No, you're not, Charlie. You're only taking on Death.

Come again?

Remembering everything. Replaying it all so that you can record it. All the good times. All the times you were close. This way he'll live on in your head. You should try and remember more, not less.

You're talking as if I'd forget him if I didn't try to remember.

No, you'll never forget him.

Dollface, my head's flooding so full with the past, it's nearly bursting. And I can't stand it because soon he'll disappear into a black void.

He won't disappear, Charlie. Nobody does completely, although some are harder to get in touch with than others. But they're always in your head somewhere if you let them be. Long after they're gone, they're there.

I don't understand what you're telling me.

You will. Let yourself remember.

How come you know so much about this remembering?

I've lost people. I know what helps. Memories are slippery things unless you pin them down with words. Give your memories words.

Dollface, I never heard so much garbage in all my life.

You'll see.

Sorry I said that.

No, you think you're right.

Yes. But I'm sorry if I offended.

You didn't. How could you?

Why are you so patient?

A troubled spirit with no one to talk to.

Are you, Dollface?

No, you are.

Who do you talk to, Dollface?

You.

Is there no one else?

No.

You don't take your own advice then?

About what?

Partner, family.

I was married once. I had a child.

Had?

The marriage ended. I lost my boy.

Then I really did feel guilty. All this time chatting and she'd never mentioned that.

What happened?

Death did. The how doesn't matter. Death is always the same: a temporary separation.

And you spend your time remembering him?

What else? I like to think of him being safe, being all right.

What was I supposed to say to that? "Dollface, he's dead. He doesn't need safe or all right anymore—he's beyond that." From far away, I heard Dad's voice, teasing in that faintly malicious way he had. *"See these intellectual spiritual types you go for, son? The whole pack of them rolled together wouldn't make one decent lay."*

Charlie? You there? I suppose you think I'm mad.

No, not at all.

Being polite doesn't suit you, Charlie.

OK, Dollface. You're just this side of mad, in the nicest possible way. To paraphrase, you're taking on Death in your own way. If it works—fine.

When you have a child, it's for life. For beyond life.

I must have been delivered without the instruction manual. I got dumped like the pup bought for Christmas.

She must have been a very strange woman.

Well, she wasn't like you, Dollface.

"Challie . . . Challie."

Dad's coming round. Better go.

OK, Charlie. See you next week.

Dad was restless again. His hands felt cold. The sun was streaming in the window in a big golden shaft right across his bed, but his hands were like ice. I turned the central heating on full, afraid suddenly that the cold meant a change coming, an ending.

"Dad?"

His head moved from side to side, a feeble "no, no" gesture that tore at my guts. His fingers plucked feebly at the bedclothes.

"Tray-sa. *NO!*"

Theresa. My mother's name. I felt a spurt of rage. I had no idea what filled my dad's mind in his coma, but if she was part of it, it was no good. I thought of him lying there helpless while memories crowded into his skull the way they did into mine, making him miserable, even on his deathbed, and I couldn't bear it. I sat on the edge of the bed and cradled his head gently—"Dad, Dad, remember the good things . . . only the good things . . . me and you and the football season and the summers in Scarborough . . . that homemade chocolate shop. Remember the violet creams? We ate them by the kilo . . ."

I don't know if he heard, but he relaxed suddenly, and when I held his hands, they were warm again and the fingers curled snugly into mine like a baby's. We sat like that for a long time, till I got cramped and moved back into my chair. I took my sweatshirt off, the room was so hot . . .

Charlie rows and rows. There's no light and no way to tell direction. Dad is silent in the stern, his head turned away, peering behind the boat as if there were some difference between the blackness behind and the blackness ahead. Charlie keeps on rowing. Then with a clenching fear, he hears the hissing again, long and steady and closing in . . . he rows frantically. Outrun them, he must outrun the snakey swans. He looks wildly around but he can't see where they are in the darkness. The hissing is a sibilant clamor, smotheringly close to his ear, fierce jets of steam spitting out of soft black feathers. Dad is looking at Charlie now, right at him. He lifts his arm and points ahead. Charlie turns and in the distance sees a thin pale blue line leap across the sky. Suddenly the water is below and the sky above, where they should be. The blue deepens and spreads higher up, trailing a rosy veil behind it and forcing the blackness out of the way. The sun is rising. Charlie glances around. The swans are there, hissing, jostling to get near the boat, gray outlines tinged with pink, then gray-white touched with rose. They are too close, too clamorous. He doesn't like the big snakey swans spitting at him. He closes his eyes and screams till the echoes hurt his ears . . . then he is scooped up into the air, high above the hissing. An arm holds him close, a hand rubs gently at his back. He buries his face in hair soft as feathers and huddles in close. She smells like flowers. When he looks down, the boat is a hundred miles below, tiny, empty, drifting, and a voice is lilting in his ear:

"Challie is my darlin', my darlin', my darlin'
Challie is my darlin', the Young Chevalier"

When I woke up, the room smelled sweet. It was a light clean scent, lily of the valley, gardenia, something like that.

No, Charlie, you didn't make it up. That's a Scottish song. About Bonnie Prince Charlie.

I've never heard it before.

You must have, or you wouldn't know the words. Maybe when you were small.

It's a right rumpty-tumpty tune anyway.

Yes, it is. They used to play it on TV along with the test card. A Highland mountain scene. Just before the children's programs. All the children used to sing it.

Maybe I heard it then. I'm surprised you admit to remembering it, you being so much younger than me.

Oops! But, then, I am ageless.

Lol. OK, Doll. You're ageless. I can't get that tune out of my head.

Why worry about it? It was a nicer dream than usual, apart from rumpty-tumpty music. You were rescued.

I didn't tell her about the perfume, how it cooled the room and stilled the air, and that somehow it upset me more than the rancid rot I usually woke to.

So what does the rescue mean, Madame Dream Diviner?

That there's light on the horizon. That things will work out all right in the end. Blue is the color of hope.

You made that up to make me feel better.

No. Blue comes with dawn and drives away the night. It's spring and summer and it's water that makes things grow. It's the chink of light through the curtains after a bad night.

OK, I feel better. If you make me feel any better, I'll combust spontaneously right here in front of you.

Very funny.

How'd you get over the loss of your boy, Dollface?

I didn't. I never lost him because he's in my mind all the time. I have valuable memories. I see him and hear him whenever I want.

You're madder than I am.

One day you'll understand.

When we're in adjoining padded cells?

Challie, you're such a darlin' sometimes . . .

That rumpty-tumpty tune rollicked around my head hour after hour. When I sat with Dad and the memories activated, it got in the way. He and I would be talking, or I was imagining we were talking, or remembering him talking in the past—I don't know, whatever it was that kept happening in that room—and that daft song would erupt in my mind, drowning out what he was saying. It shrieked away the pictures, too, of me and Dad and the places we went and the things we did. And the more I tried to hear him and see him, the louder it got and the faster it got, till my head spun with a jangling discord and ached from a sweet drifting scent.

One time, I was remembering *Witchfinder General.* I could hear Dad laughing at the plunging necklines and heaving bosoms belonging to all the daft trollops who went prowling around creepy places in their nighties in the dark, holding candlesticks aloft to light the way. We knew, just knew, they were going to run into the vampire or the ghost or the gang of drunken troopers. There was always one, with an awesome bosom but not so pretty as the heroine, who came to a bad end through night wanderings in her bare feet. Dad and I used to try and spot her before it happened—*Look for the one with the biggest boobs and the slight cast in her eye because she's the one who's not going to be rescued*—and if I spotted her first he gave me a Mars bar . . .

OH, CHALLIE IS MY DARLIN' . . .

"Women were women in those days, eh, son?" He said it every Friday night at some point. Once I remember chirping, *"Daddy, why does ladies have different chests from men's?"* and he said, *"To please the men, son."* I tried to remember his chuckling laugh, but I couldn't hear for the explosion of song in my mind—*Challie is my darlin', my darlin', my darlin'*—raucous and bold and thumpingly loud. I was furious. *"Daddy, why does ladies have . . ."*

MY DARLIN', MY DARLIN', CHALLIE IS MY DARLIN' . . .

"SHUT UP!"

It was Dad, in the voice that meant he was rowing with the current woman of the house. I actually jumped. And then there was blissful silence in my head. Dad looked peaceful, pale as his pillowcase, and I wondered dreamily which woman he was remembering. You'd think they'd leave him in peace on his deathbed . . .

Mummy is in the kitchen making soup. She shuts the door behind her, but Charlie can still hear the big soup pot clattering on the cooker. He is sitting under the table in the living room, playing with his boat. The sails are bright blue. "Like your eyes," she said in the shop, when he couldn't decide between the blue sails and the red. He hears the key in the lock. "Daddy! Daddy!"

"Where's my wee man?"

Peekaboo from under the tablecloth.

"Come out, come out, wherever you are!" Big laughing voice. Big laughing man. "I'm coming to get you!"

Cupboards opened, sideboard drawers, the hearth rug lifted. Peekaboo.

"Oh, where's my wee Charlie? Is he lost?"

Daddy cries into his big white hankie, Charlie crawls out.

"No, I'm here, Daddy. Here."

Up in the air. Toss. Catch. Toss. Catch. Toss—falling, falling—Catch!

"God, I nearly dropped you there, son!"

Huge sighs of relief. Big hugs. Giggle. Giggle. Daddy never drops him. Up in the air Charlie goes, around he swings, slaps the light shade twice, sends the shadows darting around the walls. Daddy slumps into his armchair, sits Charlie on his knee.

"And what did my wee man do today? I phoned and there was no one home."

"We went to the park."

"On an icy day like today?"

"Yes."

Charlie waits expectantly. Daddy jangles coins in his pocket: the memory game. He puts pennies in a row on the arm of his chair. And a whole sixpence. Charlie wriggles with excitement.

"Let's see if your memory is growing as big as the rest of you. The beginning?"

"Breakfast. I ate up all my cornflakes and toast. Mummy burnt two slices."

Pause. A penny from the chair to Charlie's hand.

"Mummy washed the dishes. I dried them. She says I'm a clever boy."

Another penny.

"And Mummy dusted and hoovered. I helped."

Another penny.

"Then we went to the shops for the messages."

No penny. Charlie frowns, remembering. "We got a loaf. And eggs. And strawberry jam."

A penny.

"And how did you come to be in the park, Charlie? That's a funny place to go on a snowy day."

"The butcher didn't have any ham bones for the soup. So we went to Gispie's."

"Gispies? Where's that?"

"Beside the park. The big butcher shop with the board with the picture of the cows on it."

"Oh, Gillespie's."

Daddy takes a penny back. "Tsk! Tsk! You didn't remember that one right, Charlie."

"And I saw a boat in the paper shop. And Mummy let me have it."

"To sail in the park?"

"No! Silly Daddy! The pond is frozed. It's for my bath."

"So what made you go into the park?"

"Mrs. Cameron. She was in Gillespie's as well. She said the pond was frozed and the birds were starving."

Two pennies surprise Charlie. Mrs. Cameron isn't a two-penny memory. Even he knows that. Daddy laughs. "You said Gillespie right this time, son."

Charlie whoops. Two pennies.

"Was it Mummy's idea to go to the park?"

Charlie shakes his head. "No, I wanted to feed the birds. They was hungry. We had a big loaf."

"And did she talk to anyone in the park?"

"Just me." The sixpence on the arm of the chair is bright and shiny. A new one. Charlie wants that sixpence and remembers hard. "She said afternoon to a man with a doggie."

"Did they talk long?"

"No. He said afternoon, then she said it, and he throwed a stick for the doggie and went away."

A long silence. Then Charlie smiles. "But she was talking a long time to the man in the paper shop. They was laughing and smiling, Daddy. Lots."

A sixpenny memory.

Charlie scrambles off Daddy's knee—"Remember, Charlie, don't tell Mum about all your pennies. She wouldn't like you having all that money"—and runs to his room. His piggy bank is nearly full. He has to cram his sixpence and his pennies in.

Something's hissing in the background. The soup boiling.

I had to get the doctor in that week. Dad's breathing was heavier. He checked him over, and said it was only to be expected: he was weakening, but wasn't in any pain. He kept looking at me. "You don't look so good yourself," he said. "Mustn't get ill." He mentioned the hospice again, not very hopefully because he knew my feelings on the subject. Later I looked at myself in the dressing-table mirror—black shadows hooped my eyes and my skin had a grayish tinge: too much time in the bedroom, too many hours in the site offices, too many bad dreams.

You have to take better care of yourself, Charlie. It won't help your father if you get ill too.

Dollface had lots of suggestions: fewer take-out meals (she was forever banging on about healthy food); early to bed and not so many nightcaps; walks in the fresh air; maybe a night out and some company, just now and again, to liven me up. In the beginning, her fussing had irritated me, but lately I had encouraged it, hinting at feeling seedy, being tired, all that. Childish. But it's a need, isn't it? To be cared for? To have someone bother about you? And no matter how vividly I relived Dad, he couldn't help me here.

How about nightmares, Charlie?

None this week. Just an odd dream.

I told her about the memory game.

Your fault, Doll, talking about valuable memories. I dreamed mine were worth a penny a go.

They're worth much more than that. This is a piece of your nightmare, Charlie. Your blue boat is in it. The one the swan attacked. You told me about it weeks ago.

I remember.

It must have been your mother who rescued you that day.

Dunno.

And maybe it's your mother who rescued you in the nightmare. The one who lifted you away from the swans.

Which mother? I had a fair few. Remember?

What did she look like? Your own mother? Like the woman in the dream?

I don't remember.

Try.

I didn't actually SEE her. I only talked about her.

Memories are breaking through, Charlie.

I didn't answer. She was always on about dreams and memories and my mother. Thought it was therapeutic for me. And it was mostly, except for my mother. I had no more interest in her than she had in me.

Charlie?

Here.

I was remembering something my mum taught me. When you close your eyes to sleep, if you think very hard about something, that's what you'll dream about. Maybe you could dream your mother.

Dollface!

Wouldn't you like to see her face? Just once?

I have enough nightmares.

She's something in your life that you avoid facing. For good or ill, you ought to. Maybe there are things you don't understand.

Dollface, will you drop it?

I was thinking about the memory game. Such an odd game for a little boy, don't you think?

There was no memory game. It's just a nightmare.

It sounded real to

I logged off then, didn't even say good-bye. "This is what happens when you tell people things about yourself," I said to Dad as I sat down by the bed. "Think they know better than you about your own life. Think they have a right to comment."

He lay white as an effigy on a tomb, and as silent. But I knew he would understand my anger—he had never liked interference in his own life. The last of his ladies had tried to cut down on his nights out, the number of pints consumed, the hours spent unaccounted for. "*Bloody women. They can never let you be. You're all that's wonderful until she moves in, then you can never be fine as you are again. It's called Lurv . . .*"

CHALLIE IS MY DARLIN', MY DARLIN' MY DARLIN'

Will you SHUT THE FUCK UP!

Charlie crawls behind the sofa. He wishes Mummy was good, then Daddy wouldn't shout, but she's bad. She makes men look. Charlie knows that's bad, and he got a penny for telling about the man whistling. He peeps out. She's going to get a smack because she's answering back. That's naughty. She's got her back to him and he can't see her face, but her shoulders are scrunched up. She's rubbing at red marks on her arms.

"But, Tommy, I was only going to the shops. It was just some daft boy passing on a bike . . ."

"SHUT UP! I KNOW YOU, TRAY-SA! CHRIST, I KNOW YOU!"

"Tommy . . ."

Slap!

Charlie closes his eyes. He doesn't want to see, but he can hear her crying. "Tommy! Tommy!" She's on the floor, rolling about, trying to get away. Daddy stamps hard. She mews like a cat.

I woke up sweating and shivering. The room was icy. I phoned the Gas Board to come out—*I've got an invalid here, a man's dying, and I don't care if it's Sunday get somebody out here to fix the heating*—and I went downstairs and waited. It was Gary the Gasman again. Gaz the Gas he called himself. His little joke. Third visit in six weeks.

"Afternoon, Mr. McCallum. Same old problem?"

I nodded. He went up to the room, tiptoed in out of respect for my father, fiddled about with the radiator.

"Seems all right now," he said. His tone was neutral, shading toward sympathetic. I couldn't stand it.

"It wasn't an hour ago. The room was freezing."

His turn to nod. "Want me to have a look at the boiler? Bleed the radiators? Maybe there's an air bubble."

We both knew there was no point, but I said yes, and he shambled off downstairs to the utility room. He banged about willingly enough. I made him coffee and put out the biscuits. He asked after my dad very kindly. I answered. He typed out a report on his laptop that said there was nothing to report, and left. "Call us any time, Mr. McCallum. We'll get to the bottom of this one day."

I took my time washing up the cups and sweeping crumbs from the table and decided not to go upstairs for a while yet. I might fall asleep and dream. I might stay awake and remember. That was the trouble, you see. I didn't know whether I was dreaming or remembering.

The nurse had the afternoon off, and so I had downstairs to myself. I couldn't help thinking about the dream. The stamping. The crunching bone. It never happened, so why did it feel so real? The house. The house it happened in—that couldn't be real. I'd have remembered that wallpaper around the fireplace. Christ, no one *could* forget that wallpaper! Purple with big sweetie pink, white-centered flowers. The stuff of nightmare. And that narrow coffee table with the out-angled legs and the black plastic gold-striped trim! And a glass top over a pink flower! Nightmare. Silly. Daft. I'd never been in a place like that. *So why did it feel familiar?*

I was beginning to see an answer, but I didn't have to think about it for long because the phone rang, shrill and shriller.

SHUT THE FUCK UP! SHUT UP! SHUT UP!

Dad's voice. Now what's he so angry about? Phones don't bother him, only bad Mummies. Rumpty-tumpty thought skidding about in my skull. Nothing to be mad about, Daddy. Only the phone ringing.

"Oh, quick, Challie. Daddy's on the phone." Charlie scampers up the stairs at the front of the house. One. Two. Three. Four. Mummy's hands are thick with bandages. She can't get the key in the lock. The phone is ringing, loud and angry. Challie can't reach the key. Too high, so she lifts him up and bangs his knee against the door. The key is stiff and he struggles to turn it. In his ear, her breathing's quick and fast. She smells like flowers. "Quick, Challie. Quick." It turns. She puts Charlie down and runs for the phone, but Charlie gets there first. "Hello, Daddy."

"Yes, I've been a good boy today."

"We was at the shops. To buy some pills. Mummy's hands is sore."

"We heard the phone. We was outside. Mummy couldn't turn the key. I did it."

"Yes, I'm a very strong boy."

CHALLIE IS MY DARLIN', MY DARLIN', MY DARLIN'

SHUT UP! SHUT THE FUCK UP!

Daddy closes the book and Charlie settles back on his pillow. Dreamily he watches shadows drowsing in the corner. Daddy doesn't tuck him up and say good night. He sits looking sad.

"Was Mummy complaining about her hands?"

"She said they was sore. She says you don't mean it."

"That's right. She makes me angry. She's not good like you."

Daddy's voice is deep and gruff and Charlie can't hear right. He looks at Daddy and his heart stops. Daddy's crying big fat tears. "Ah, son, you don't know how she hurts me. You don't know how bad a woman can make you feel inside. I don't want to hurt her. I'm good to that woman. You know I am. But she doesn't know what love is. She makes me do things . . ."

Dad sobs. Charlie can't stand it. He scrambles out from under his blankets and hurls himself at Daddy, crying and kissing better. "I love you, Daddy."

"I know, wee man. I don't know what I'd do without you. Will I give Mummy a surprise?" Charlie nods. "See, son, she thinks the living room is old-fashioned. How about we get her that stuff she thinks is groovy?"

Charlie nods. If Mummy is happy, maybe she'll be good.

Daddy dries his eyes. "So, when you went to the shops today, did you meet anyone on the way?"

The phone rang louder, as if it was shouting my name. There was no one on the other end of the line. Just the engaged tone. I slammed the receiver down. My head was jangling with voices and songs.

Daddy's smiling. Mummy loves her new curtains. Sweetie pink to go with the wallpaper.

"Floor length, for the big bay windows. Just like in the magazine, Challie. And that wallpaper—it's the very latest. Your dad's going to paint the doors white. The heavy varnish makes these old houses seem dark."

She bends down to kiss him, smelling like flowers. She has big white hoops in her ears, and she has eyelashes and little freckles on her cheeks "Like Twiggy, Challie. See?" she said when she was painting them on. She looks just like Twiggy in the magazine. Big, big eyes and hair like little bird feathers. But Twiggy's hands aren't all bandaged up.

"He's going to get started this weekend. The doors first. This time next week we'll be living in a new world."

Charlie helps. He has a little brush in his paint box and Daddy lets him paint around the door handles. Thick shiny paint and a strong smell that makes his head ache and his nose run. Open the windows, Daddy. Charlie hangs out the window, watches gray clouds tumbling snow onto the rooftops, sniffs the sharp clean smell of cold.

The phone screamed at me. Engaged again. I didn't hang up. Better the engaged signal than those pink curtains. I couldn't stand thinking about them: they made me angry; they made me feel sick. I listened to the phone instead. Whistles and clicks and a shrill whine. And somewhere in the whistles, a rumpty-tumpty tune. Not the engaged signal, definitely not the engaged signal. How could it be? It was the static you get when someone in the house is online. DAD!

I took the stairs two at a time and burst into the bedroom. His closed eyelids were curved closed like shells and the room was cool and still and piercingly sweet: lily-of-the-valley, gardenia . . . like that. I could have cried. The computer was on, a bright eye, unblinking, staring at me from the corner. My name was at the top of the private room along with Dollface's.

How did you get in here, Dollface?

Sorry, Charlie?

I logged off.

No, you were here all the time . . . showing online. I thought you had gone to see to your father. Or that you'd fallen asleep and had a nightmare. Thought I'd better wait for you to come back.

It's been nearly two hours.

Has it? I didn't notice. I was worried about you.

Thanks. Sorry. I thought I'd shut down.

What else could I say? I knew I'd shut down, I knew I had, but I couldn't be sure.

It doesn't matter, Challie.

Sorry.

It's all right. I don't mind. Is your father OK?

He's fine. No change.

Two hours. Nobody waits two hours.

I've forgotten what we were talking about, Challie.

So have I. Probably me as usual.

I know what it was—I was saying you could dream up your mother.

No, Dollface. No more today. Talk about you. Tell me about you. Tell me anything.

What?

Your marriage. Did it break up after you lost your son? Or before?

They happened at the same moment. What an odd question.

Together? What an odd answer.

I really don't like to talk about it, Challie. It's very painful.

I tell you painful things.

Yes, but some things are too painful. Your mother. My son. You understand, Challie.

What went wrong with your marriage?

That's old, old history.

Too painful?

Not now.

Tell me about it then.

It was nothing unusual.

Tell me.

It was a mistake from the start, Challie. He was much older than me. Thirty-five.

How old were you?

Just turned sixteen.

That's young.

Too young.

I played her trick and left the screen blank for long minutes.

Challie? Are you there?

Yes. I was waiting for the rest.

What rest?

Why it was a mistake from the start.

Long minutes. An acre of screen to be filled, Dollface resisting. And then

He pushed me into it. He was so SURE. And I wasn't sure of anything. Young girls never are. I was supposed to be going to university, but he didn't want that. Said it would waste too many years that we could have together. "Gather ye rosebuds while ye may," he said.

"Old Time is still a-flying"?

You know it? It's by Herrick.

It's a favorite of my father's. Only poem he knows.

It's a favorite with a lot of people. It makes sense. That's why I nag you. You mustn't leave it too late to live, the way I did.

You lived too soon by the sounds of it.

I didn't live at all. Not with him. He lived for both of us.

You left him, didn't you?

Long minutes. An acre of screen. What was I expecting? "Yes, Challie boy, I did. I went to Welsh Wales and then years later, you'll never believe it, I met up with my long-lost son in a chat room. Fate. Kismet. All that."

I don't know what I was expecting. Something. Some connection. I thought she wasn't going to answer at all but

No, I never got the chance.

?

He left me all alone.

From the corner of my eye, I saw Dad lift a hand: "ChallieChallie" in that dry gasping voice, then a sudden sharp, "No, Tray-sa! NO!"

Dollface, Dad's waking up again. I have to go.

No, wait. I want

Later. OK? I'll come back soon.

I shut down and checked I had done it right this time.

Dad was motionless in the bed, apart from a fluttering side to side movement under paper-thin eyelids. I could almost see the fierce gleam of gray eyes through those lids. His hand had flopped back onto the quilt.

"Don't think about her, Dad. Past is past and past fretting over."

Somehow I knew he was distressed. I rubbed his hands, warming them between mine. "Remember that time we were on the site in Manchester and I fell in the big crater? That was funny. I was floundering about in the water, screaming. 'Dad! Dad! I can't swim!' And I'm flailing my arms and legs and spouting water like a whale and you stood laughing at the edge of the pit. 'Dad, I'm drowning! Help!'

"And you shout, 'Well, stand up, you silly bugger!' And I did. And the water didn't even cover the top of my wellies."

I rubbed his hands some more, chortling. I hadn't thought about that day in years.

Stale water tasting like iron fillings in my mouth, running into my eyes and ears. And a tightness in my chest, a horrible clenching pain. Can't breathe. Can't. Gasping. Wheezing. And Dad jumps in the water beside me. "All right, son. It's all right" and he hands me up to one of the navvies and comes scrambling out after me. Hospital. Can't breathe. "Does your son suffer from asthma, Mr. McCallum?"

A panic attack. There'd been a few of those over the years. That was one of the more spectacular ones. Dad always blamed her for them. *See, son. There's nothing wrong with you. You're not going to die or stop breathing. This is emotional. Your mother leaving—you were too young. That's what caused it. You have to forget her, forget . . .*

A long scream of pain that swings into tune

CHALLIE IS MY DARLIN', MY DARLIN', MY DARLIN'

thumpingly loud, discordant, then softer, softer, lilting soft

"Challie is my darlin', my darlin', my darlin'
Challie is my darlin', my young Chevalier.
'Twas on a Sunday mornin', quite early in the year,
That Challie came to our town, the young Chevalier . . ."

"Is that song about me, Mummy?"

"You're the only Challie I know, aren't you?" A forefinger unfolds stiffly from under the bandages and touches the tip of his nose. Charlie laughs into her baby-blue eyes. They are in the café, but they have to hurry. Daddy comes home for lunch because he's working nearby in the park up the road. A new pond to be dug. A great big one. So he pops in and out of the house all day: for lunch, for a cuppa, to do a bit more painting and papering to help Mummy be happy. He doesn't like to come home to an empty house.

"Challie, you've not finished your ice cream. I have a wee message to go. Just across the road. If I leave you for a minute, will you sit here like a good boy?"

Charlie nods.

"What are you going for?"

"Oh, a comic if you're good."

Charlie sits at the window table, a good wee boy, licking his spoon. He watches her carefully for his daddy. He likes the way the winter sun shows the warm red in her hair. She goes into the big train station. She doesn't stay long. She comes running back over the road, her big earrings tossing, her black fun fur flapping behind her.

"Where's my comic, Mummy?"

"Oh, Challie. They didn't have any left." He knows she's telling fibs. Her face is red. She's biting her lip. "We'll get one tomorrow." Charlie is so angry, he doesn't speak to her all the way home.

I surfaced from that long walk home with my head pounding. I was still holding Dad's hands. I had that feeling you get when you know someone is staring at you. I knew who it was before I turned to look. Sure enough, the monitor was lit up, quietly waiting, quietly demanding.

"There's no way to tell who's at the other end of these messages, son."

"You're so right, Dad."

I pulled the plug on the pc, right out of the socket, and the screen turned ashy gray. I half believed it wouldn't, but it did, and I was relieved. I didn't understand what was going on, but I knew I had to stop it. I don't know why I thought cutting off the electricity would. I could silence her, but the past still rolled in like high tide. It rolled in before I even got back to my chair.

Mummy's humming, putting things in suitcases. His pajamas. And his blue and white sloppy joe. His sandals. He watches from the doorway.

"Hello, Challie."

She straightens up with his vests in her hand. She stops humming and her face is red.

"Challie. Can you keep a secret?"

Charlie nods. "It's a surprise for Daddy. A wee holiday." She folds the vests into the case. "Yes, a wee holiday. After all his hard work decorating." His socks go in next, his favorite stripey ones. "Now, you're not to say anything, It's a BIG secret."

She's humming again—"Challie is my darlin'"—and she's smiling but her eyes are sad.

The scene vanished like morning mist, although her humming hung on the air for a moment. Dad's hand tightened on mine. *"See when a woman gets hot pants for some-*

body, son? There's no stopping them. Nothing gets in their road—not even their own wee boy."

But she was packing my things.

"See, son, a kiddie just gets in the way. The new man doesn't like the reminder that she's used goods. You're better off with your daddy."

"She was going to take me with her."

And then I felt sick, churning sick. She started humming again and I turned that cold sweaty way you do before you throw up. I sat down and I spoke out loud, not to Dad, but to her. "I don't want to know. I really don't want to know." She hummed more loudly.

CHALLIE IS MY DARLIN', MY DARLIN', MY DARLIN'

The sky is black and the water is black. The air is thick with hissing and the soft ruffling of feathers. Charlie rows desperately to get away, to leave the swans behind. He's worried about Dad: his head is lolling on his chest; he is tiring. The hissing comes closer. Charlie feels rushes of foul sour air on the back of his neck. The boat begins to rock violently from side to side. On a tideless windless lake it rocks. Dad staggers to his feet and falls back onto the bench again. The boat tilts, and he's falling soundlessly over the side, twisting slowly around to get one last look at Charlie. The hood falls back. The face is small and white enough to glimmer through the dark, the eyes are big, the hair like birds' feathers. There are big white hoops at her ears and tears sliding down her cheeks.

"Oh, Challie! Oh, Challie!"

Such terror. Such longing.

And then she's slipping under the black water . . .

I wake up. The room is cold. The fire is out. I look around by the dim light from the hall. The big pink flowers are like faces laughing at me. I am looking for Daddy because he isn't in the bedroom and Mummy is fast asleep all by herself. But Daddy isn't here either. Then I hear footsteps on the gravel outside. I trot to the window, stand on tiptoe. The paint is still sticky. Daddy is putting something in the back of the van. It's Mummy's big suitcase. Funny. She's not to go on holiday. He shouted at her after tea when he emptied her handbag on the table. He waved little papers at her. *Two tickets! To Perth! Running away to your auntie? And taking my boy with you? You're going nowhere, doll. Nowhere at all.*

Daddy crunches back up the path to the house. I hide behind the sofa. I'm not allowed to wander about the house at night. I might fall downstairs. He comes into the living room, a tall wide shadow in the moonlight. He lifts Mummy's curtains, the new pink ones, from the sideboard, and takes them away upstairs. He leaves the door open. I shiver behind the sofa. It's cold. It's more than cold. The house feels funny. Too quiet. Too hushed. Not right. I shiver and shiver. Then Daddy comes downstairs slowly, heavily. He passes the door. The curtains are rolled up over his shoulder, a big bundle dangling down his front and back. I see bright hair flopping out of the end down his back. Mummy. She's stopped mewing now. That's good. She's not sore anymore. Daddy goes out to the van and I run upstairs and jump into bed.

My piggy bank is by my bed. It was too full for the new pennies and the half a crown I got, so they are lying beside it on the table. Daddy's going to buy me a new bank on Saturday.

I wake up early in the morning. It's still gray outside, dull and gray. "Daddy! Daddy!"

He comes right away. He's got his clothes on already.

"Challie! It's early. Go back to sleep."

"I waked up. Where are you going?"

"To the site. I've got some rubbish to dump. I'll sneak in early and shove it in a hole. We're laying the stone base for the pond today. That'll cover it up. Saves me going all the way to the dump." He puts a finger to his lips. He's smiling. I don't like that smile. "It's a secret." And he winks.

"I'm hungry."

He thumps away downstairs and brings me a biscuit and a mug of milk. "That'll tide you over till Mummy gets up. Now, you leave her in peace until I get back. No crawling in beside her. She was awful tired last night. And she has a headache." I'm puzzled, but already Mummy wrapped in curtains is becoming a dream. She's in her bed with a sore head and I'm not to wake her.

She ran away to Wales while he was out. He came back to find her gone away with the boyfriend he'd suspected all along.

I closed my eyes, too tired to take it in. I didn't want to stay there in that house, but I didn't know how to get back home. After a while, the room began to warm up, and then I smelled the rubbing alcohol the nurse used against bedsores. I opened my eyes. Dad was in bed and the Lucozade was on his table and the sun was shining in the window. It didn't feel like safe home, end of nightmare.

She was in the room with us, waiting. I knew what I would see when I looked over at the computer. The plug was out of the socket, but the monitor was glowing anyway. I went over and sat at the desk. I didn't want to, but I couldn't not go.

Challie! There you are. I've been so worried.

Hi, Dollface.

So what's been happening?

I think you know.

Long minutes. Acres of screen waiting to be filled. Both if us resisting.

Challie, how could you think I'd ever have left you?

Long minutes.

Challie, it wasn't your fault. You were only a wee boy.

Long minutes.

Challie, he was too clever for both of us.

Long minutes. I couldn't think of anything to say. Then I was angry.

Why'd you come back? After all this time? Why let me know all this now? Why spoil everything?

Challie, I was dying of being forgotten. You never kept me in your head. I couldn't get near you. He was too strong for me.

Until now. When he's dying.

Yes.

You should have let him die in peace.

Why? I have no peace. Never any peace. Not in life and not in death. I lost my little boy. I've missed you.

I didn't miss you.

Oh, but you did, Challie. All your life. You're a sour man because you missed me.

And knowing all this will make me sweet? You're mad. You're fucking mad.

Don't speak to me like that, Challie. You sound like your father.

I'd rather not speak to you at all.

That's cruel, Challie.

Sorry, Dollface. What shall we talk about? The night you died? Did he kick your head in or strangle you or what? Or maybe you'd rather tell about what it feels like being under a pond with the stone holding you down and the foul water lapping round you?

You already know what it's like, Challie. All your nightmares. That's what it's like.

Look, I don't see the point of this. You've only made things worse.

You need new memories. That's why I've come. And I have the right, Challie. After everything, I have the right to be in your memories. You're my son. And I didn't know you long enough.

Long minutes. My eyes were filled with tears. Her hair was red and it shone like fire. Her eyes were big and baby-blue.

There were good times, Challie. One of the best, the one I remember best, was that day we fed the swans. Oh, Challie, it was lovely. Try and remember. For me. Try.

What? Black hissing swans are a good memory? They haunt my dreams.

My fault, Challie. It wasn't meant to be like that. It's not easy to get through. Let me show you now.

Long minutes.

Challie, there was a time when memories were worth money to you.

I thought of pennies and sixpences and a whole half crown and closed my eyes.

Charlie skips along and kicks flurries of snow into the air. He holds his boat under one arm. He thinks about the one with the red sails, but Mummy likes the blue because they are like his eyes. He takes her hand and grins up at her. She peeps out from under the black fur hood of her coat, smiling down.

"Maybe you can slide on the ice, Challie, if it's thick enough."

"Slide on the ice?"

"Oh, yes. You can run on it—CAREFULLY—and then stick one foot out in front of the other and WHEEE-EEE you're sliding."

She lets go of his hand and shows him on the frozen path. He tries but slithers out of control and tumbles right into the big bank of snow piled shoulder high alongside the path. Snow scatters down on him from the bushes, but he keeps tight hold of his boat. She laughs and brushes the snow off his balaclava and anorak.

He can't see the pond because the snow is piled so high, but when they turn the corner, there it is. He gasps at the huge shining sheet spread out before him in the quiet cold. The sun is low in the sky and deep red rays shoot out from it, like the drawings of the sun in his comics. The day is ending early and the red beams stain the ice a deep pink. The snow around the edges is pink too, and the ice on the path. Everything is pink. "Mummy, can we slide? Can we?"

"Let me see how thick it is first." Her breath comes out in little white puffs. Charlie hisses like a steam engine and the white clouds hang around his head.

"Look, Challie. Look! Swans!"

There are lots of them waddling across the ice, their long white necks hooked and their heads hanging down. Mummy waddles like a swan, rolling from side to side with her head hanging down. Charlie does it too and makes her laugh.

"Aren't they clumsy on land, Challie? They're beautiful when they're swimming. But look at the poor things. Two left webbed feet. What's that they're doing?"

It takes a minute to work it out. The swans are sliding. Charlie and Mummy, hand in hand, stand amazed. A swan takes some lumbering steps, gathers pace, spreads its big wide wings and flaps till they make a snapping noise, then WHEEEE it's sliding right across the pond. When it gets to the other side it waddles back and joins a line of swans all taking their turn, one after the other. Waddle, waddle, snap of pink wings, WHEEEE!

It's funny. Charlie giggles and giggles. He wants to go on the ice with them but Mummy says he'll scare them away.

"Let's feed them," she says. She opens the loaf and tears off bread. Charlie throws it on the ice. A swan comes sliding across and gobbles it up, swallowing all the way down its long pink neck. It stands waiting, sharp black eyes watchful, fiery beak ready to snatch. Charlie throws more bread and the swans come skidding across the ice, crowding around, a seething mass of pink and white feathers, nipping at one another, hissing, crowding closer and closer around Charlie and Mummy.

"Mummy, they're like snakes!" screams Charlie, mesmerized by the undulating flexible necks. "Snakes!" he screams.

Mummy throws the rest of the bread far out onto the ice. The swans head off after it. She lifts Charlie high and hugs him. He drops his boat. One swan is startled and hisses at it. Charlie clings to Mummy, who's laughing still.

"It's all right, Challie. All right. The swan was frightened. See? They're all gone now."

And so they were, skidding and slithering after the bread. One slides so far it crashes into the snow banks around the edge and stands shaking its head, dazed. Charlie laughs, but he won't let Mummy put him down. She stoops to get his boat and then he rides balanced on her hip all the way to the park gates . . .

I opened my eyes. It was warm and cozy snuggled into her coat. And safe. And the swans—I had forgotten how it really was. What a sight they were . . .

Challie?

I'm here.

Wasn't that a good day?

I nodded, forgetting she couldn't see me. *Yes.*

There were lots of good days, Challie, and you've lost them. I want you to remember me. Let me live in your head.

Don't have much choice, do I? You'll never be out of my mind now.

Only the good times, Challie. The rest doesn't matter.

She let me go then. Dad drew me to him with muttering and mumbling, but he fell silent when I sat by the bed. What was there for him to say? What were the memories worth now? The odor of death and staleness clung to him. But behind me, on the warm breeze coming in the window, was the scent of sun-warmed grass and something sweet and light, lily of the valley, gardenia, something like that. She's always been there, always, somewhere and nowhere.

Rhys Bowen

Doppelganger

■ ■ ■

Rhys Bowen is the author of two mystery series, the Constable Evans mysteries set in contemporary North Wales and featuring policeman Evan Evans, and the Molly Murphy mysteries, with Irish immigrant sleuth Molly in New York in 1901. The first book in this series, Murphy's Law, *won the Agatha Award for best novel as well as the Herodotus and Reviewer's Choice for best historical mystery. The third book,* For the Love of Mike, *has won the Bruce Alexander Historical Mystery Award. Rhys's books and short stories have received numerous other award nominations, including a Bulgarian short-story prize. "Doppelganger" first appeared in the MWA anthology* Blood on Their Hands, *and was currently nominated for the Agatha Award. A fugitive from Britain herself, Rhys now lives in northern California. She is currently Norcal president of Mystery Writers of America. Just how far will a man go to ensure his future? The doppelganger of this story takes whatever means necessary—including murder—to secure a happy life for himself, even at a terrible cost to someone else.*

It was fate that brought Hofmeister and me together during the summer of '38. Fate, or in my case, luck. It was my final semester at the institute and funds were running low. My grandmother had died, her life savings already rendered worthless by inflation, and with her my only means of financial support.

Fortunately I only needed this semester to complete my diploma in engineering. I had just enough money to make it to July—with appropriate cost-cutting measures. No more eating in the mensa or restaurants, for one thing. No more drinking in the little weinstube around the corner and finally the realization that I would have to share a room in the student residence hall.

I had never shared a room before and the idea was repugnant to me. Having been raised an only child by my grandmother, I was unused to the company of other males. Their behavior at the institute always seemed to me a little too juvenile and boisterous after the isolation of my youth. I saw no need to participate in backslapping and horseplay. In any case, I had grown to prefer my own company and a good book.

Thus I entered that room in the Studentenheim on the twenty-ninth of April with much apprehension. What if he stank, or sang loudly in the bath, or smoked cigars or left wet towels and dirty garments strewn on the floor? What if he tried to sneak in women at all hours? So I was pleasantly surprised to find Hofmeister engaged in unpacking a modest suitcase and placing pairs of socks neatly in a top drawer.

"I've taken the bed by the window," he said, looking up as I came in. "Unless, of course, you'd prefer it?"

"No, take it by all means. I sleep better away from any form of light."

He came toward me, hand outstretched. "You must be Schwarzkopf. I'm Hofmeister."

We shook hands and clicked heels with the little bow that was customary even among fellow students. He didn't tell me his first name and I didn't suggest that he call me Jakob. I liked his air of aloofness and knew instantly that I should feel comfortable sharing a room with him.

It turned out that we had a lot in common. We were both final semester candidates for the diploma, specializing in the relatively new branch of aeronautical engineering. We were both somewhat quiet and withdrawn, orphans with no close family ties—he having been raised by an aunt who had died the previous year. And most remarkably, we looked alike too. The other residents started calling us the Twins. Since we were not very social and kept to ourselves, we gained the reputation of being snooty and standoffish. There were also hints that we were more than friends, for which there was no foundation, as neither Hofmeister nor I had inclinations in that direction.

We were both tall, slightly built, blond with angular features and the high cheekbones of the Slav. Perfect Aryan specimens, in fact. I often thanked my lucky stars that I had taken after my beautiful actress mother, rather than my dark and brooding playwright father. In fact, if she hadn't been stupid enough to marry him and thus give me a Jewish last name, then all would have been well. Especially since he had shot himself within a year of my birth. She, always fragile, had only outlived him by another two years and I had been raised as a good Lutheran, in the elegant town of Ludwigsburg by my maternal grandmother.

So I had passed through life pretty much unscathed and unaffected, avoiding the embarrassing street attacks, beard singeings, and rock throwings that befell more obviously identifiable Jews. I had come to believe I was immune when the director of studies summoned me to his office one day in May.

"You will take your final exams in July, Schwarzkopf. Is that correct?"

"Yes, Herr Direktor."

He sighed. "I am glad for you, for I have the unpleasant task of informing all my students of Jewish ancestry that they will not be welcomed back to the institute for the winter semester."

"Then I am indeed fortunate, Herr Direktor."

He looked at me for a long minute. "You are a gifted student, Schwarzkopf. You have maintained excellent grades throughout your time here. What will you do when you leave us?"

"I expect to be hired by one of the big aircraft companies. That is, after all, my sphere of expertise."

Another awkward pause.

"You haven't considered emigrating to, say, South America or the United States, where your qualifications would stand you in good stead?"

"I have no wish to emigrate, Herr Direktor. Any company in Germany would be foolish not to hire me when they see what I have to offer." I brushed a wayward lock of blond hair from my face. "Besides, in my case, I do not see that race will be a factor."

He sighed again. "I hope you are right. I wish you every success, Schwarzkopf."

When I recounted this conversation to Hofmeister, I was surprised with the vehemence with which he took the director's point of view. "I think you should seriously consider the Direktor's suggestion, Schwarzkopf—get out while there is still time, my dear fellow."

"But where would I go? I speak no Spanish and my English is also poor. Besides, I have no love for the American lifestyle. Too much noise and lack of moral fiber."

"It's a pity," Hofmeister said jokingly. "You'd have made an excellent Nazi."

"They invited me to join the Hitler Youth until they found out about my background, so fortunately I was spared countless singsongs and camping trips." I smiled. "What about you? I'm sure you'll make a wonderful Nazi yourself. Have they tried to recruit you?"

"Of course," he said. "Many times. But I'm not interested in politics. I just want to be left alone to conduct my research in peace. I'd like to be the first to develop a commercial jet engine."

"That would be a magnificent accomplishment," I said. "Jet propulsion also fascinates me. Wouldn't it be splendid if we were both hired by the same aircraft company and we could work on our research, side by side?"

"I've already applied to Dornier and Messerchmidt," Hofmeister said.

"So have I."

"Heard anything yet?"

I shook my head.

"Neither have I, but it's early days. They may want to wait for the results of our final exams." He got up and paced around the room. "I worry about your future, Schwarzkopf. You're a good fellow, but being a good fellow won't count when the Nazis finally crack down. That piece of paper with your racial background—that is all that counts, I'm afraid."

"Surely not." I gave a half-embarrassed laugh. "My mother was a popular performer in her time and my father was not just any Jew. His plays are performed throughout the world."

As Hofmeister said nothing, I continued. "Besides, I'm hoping to make myself indispensable to a major aircraft company. They wouldn't be stupid enough to hand over one of their most gifted research engineers. Not with a war in Europe brewing."

"The Nazis have their spies everywhere, so I'm told," Hofmeister said in a low voice. "Trust no one, Jakob."

I was touched by his concern for my future, but I still felt no real alarm. I would emerge with one of the highest diplomas in Germany. My research had been on aspects of aviation that the Luftwaffe would need to maintain air superiority in the coming war. And I looked like a true Aryan.

The semester drew to a close. We sat our final exams, and when the results were published, Hofmeister and I were both at the head of our class—although I outscored him by a few points.

"Now those aircraft companies will come beating down our doors," I said. "I wonder who will hear first, you or I?"

He gave me a crooked smile. "I've already heard from Messerschmidt," he said and looked away. "They've offered me a post at their research facility in Dresden."

"Dresden? That's a long way from anywhere." We were both from the Swabian area of South Germany and Dresden counted as a foreign country in our eyes.

"But a good position, nonetheless. Much of their topsecret research is being done there."

"Then I hope they will hurry up with an offer for me too. I think I'll write to them with my results to give them a nudge—and maybe I should ask Herr Direktor to give me a letter of recommendation."

Hofmeister moved away and stared out of the window at the hills that ringed our city of Stuttgart. "You may not want to put him in an embarrassing position, Schwarzkopf. To recommend you would be to compromise himself."

"But I had the highest grade in the class."

"And you are, unfortunately, Jewish."

"Half-Jewish," I said. "With parents who were both public figures. Surely these things count?"

"I'll tell you what counts in the eyes of the Nazis," he said. "Aryan. Non-Aryan. That's all. If Jesus were to come back today, he would not be welcome in Germany."

His message was finally beginning to register. "You are saying that no aircraft company will want to hire me, because I am Jewish?"

He nodded. "I fear that may be the case. I hope I'm wrong. They may want to, but dare not. You have a fine brain, Schwarzkopf, and on top of that, you are a good fellow. Without the name and the identity papers, one would never know that you were Jewish."

"Then you really believe that I should get out of Germany?"

"I really do, and as soon as possible, if you take my advice, or it may be too late."

I took his words to heart and made inquiries at various embassies. I found that it wasn't going to be easy. No country was welcoming Jews with open arms, especially penniless Jews like myself. And war was looming. The price of transatlantic tickets had doubled and tripled for those with a Jewish last name. Nevertheless, I sent off letters to aircraft companies in Britain and the United States and waited hopefully for their replies.

The semester ended. Those students who had homes to go to packed up their belongings and went home. Only Hofmeister and I had nowhere to go.

"I head for Dresden in two weeks," he said. "I want to get myself settled into my room and learn a little about the town before I have to report to work." He put a hand on my shoulder. "I wish you were coming too. I'm sorry things couldn't be different."

"I wish so too. Think of me as I spend my summer laboring in some farmer's fields, trying to earn enough money to pay for my ticket to America."

Uncharacteristically, Hofmeister slapped me on the back. "I tell you what—I've just come up with a splendid idea. We have to be out of here by tomorrow and I have no plans until I go to Dresden. Why don't we take a final trip together to the Alps. We can hike and stay in hostels. It shouldn't cost much."

I smiled. "Why not? One last look at the good South German countryside before we face strange cities and new lives."

So we stored our trunks and took the train south to Munich and then the little post bus into the mountains. Then we set off with rucksacks and no planned route. It was glorious weather—warm but not too hot for walking. We went from village to village, over mountain passes and down again, crossing green alpine meadows full of flowers and cows and goats, eating picnic lunches by tumbling mountain streams and sleeping the night in a peasant's hay barn when there was no hostel nearby. We both became fit and brown.

On the last day we attempted our most ambitious stage. The trail led right over the Laufbacher Eck and down to Oberstdorf. It was a strenuous climb, but well worth it. As we stood, panting, on the high ledge, it was like being on top of the world. Snow-covered peaks glistened around us. In the valley far below, a round blue lake reflected the sky. An eagle soared out below our feet.

Hofmeister spread out his arms. "This is the life, eh, Schwarzkopf. To hell with that nonsense down there."

The thought came to me in a blinding flash. I'm sure I had never considered it before, but maybe it had lain dormant for some time. I don't know. Anyway, I hardly had time to consider before I acted. I stepped up behind him and gave him a mighty push. He teetered for a moment, then waved his arms wildly, trying to regain his balance before plunging downward without a cry, his body bouncing from rock to rock like a rag doll until, at last, coming to rest at the foot of the cliff.

My heart was beating so fast that I found it hard to breathe. The world swam around me, so that I, too, was in danger of falling. I clung on to an outcropping of rock and stayed there with eyes closed until the vertigo passed. Then, with much difficulty, I climbed down to him. He was, of course, quite dead. Fighting back the nausea, I made myself go through his pockets and rucksack until I had replaced every piece of his identity with my own. Then I ran all the way down to the nearest hamlet to get help.

Everyone was very kind. They assisted me back to the nearest inn and gave me schnapps and warm blankets for shock. They wanted to know about poor Schwarzkopf's next of kin and were relieved to hear that there were none. I spent the night at the inn and then caught the train back to Stuttgart, where I retrieved Hofmeister's trunk from storage.

I was pleasantly surprised to find that he had just bought himself a new dark suit, also that he had a little money in his savings account. I used this, and the few days before I reported to Dresden, to visit his hometown of Ulm, where I acquainted myself with the facts of his childhood—the gymnasium from which he had matriculated, the apartment block where he had lived, the bakery on the corner. I found nobody who remembered him.

Thus reassured, I made my way to the city of Dresden and presented myself at the address where he had apparently already rented a room for himself. The landlady greeted me with deference and hoped that Herr Hofmeister would have an agreeable stay in her city. The room was spacious and well furnished and looked out over the old town. I decided immediately that I should enjoy living here. A letter had already come for me. The landlady pointed to it lying on my dresser.

It requested that Herr Hofmeister should report to the above address as soon as was convenient to meet with Herr Fischer and discuss his assignment. I put on the dark suit, which fitted me perfectly, and reported that very afternoon, anxious to be at work. The building was close to the city center, a faceless block of gray stone, among other similar buildings. There was no name plate on the outside, but I went up the steps and in through the front door. As I stood in the tiled central foyer, looking around at the various doors and staircases and wondering which to choose, a young woman came out and started in surprise at my standing there.

I gave her my name and asked to see Herr Fischer. She ran up the flight of stairs to my left then returned with a smile on her face. Herr Fischer welcomed me to Dresden. He would be delighted to see me, if I would just take a seat for a moment.

There were polished wood benches around the walls. I sat on one of these. After a couple of minutes the front door opened again and a man came in. He was shabbily dressed, mid-forties or maybe even older. He stood, looking around him, before taking a seat on a bench well away from me. He had removed his hat and clutched it in his hands, squeezing it out of shape as he played with it. Every time a door opened or footsteps were heard upstairs, he started nervously. At last he caught my eye.

"Who are you here to see?" he asked.

"Herr Fischer."

"You too." He dropped his eyes back to the battered hat in his hands. "I should never have waited. It was Hannah, you know. She was sick. And now it's too late, of course."

I wanted to ask him what he meant, and was phrasing the question in my head when footsteps came down the stairs. A young man this time, with close-cropped blond hair and wearing a black shirt and well-cut black trousers. "Herr Adler?"

The man sprang to his feet.

"This way. Room 224."

The older man shot me a despairing glance as he followed the black shirt up the stairs.

Now I was really confused. Why was this man so downcast at the thought of meeting with Herr Fischer? Perhaps, I decided, he was no good at his job and about to be fired. There was something disquieting about this place. It was gloomy and cold for a research facility, as faceless inside as it had been out. No pictures on the walls, except for the obligatory portrait of the Führer on one wall. No notice board, no buzz of conversation. Too quiet. I shifted uneasily on the hard bench. Would I enjoy working in these conditions? Or maybe this was just head office and the research facilities were somewhere else all together. Somewhere bright, out in the country. This thought cheered me. Then suddenly there was activity on the floor above. A door opening, running feet, a shout, and a single brief despairing cry. The young man in the black shirt came running down the stairs. As he passed me, he gave me a grin. It was not a friendly smile but a smile of triumph. I had seen it before when windows had been smashed and beards set on fire. A smile of cruelty.

Then a cold sweat crept over me as I realized where I was. This building had nothing to do with aircraft design. Of course the black shirt had looked strangely familiar. I was in Gestapo headquarters. Hofmeister had done his best to warn me. Their spies are everywhere, he had told me. I had scoffed at this idea, but he knew what he was talking about. He had been one of them. He had been planted at the institute and now he was to be their plant at the aircraft engineering facility.

My mouth had gone dry. I couldn't swallow. Even if Hofmeister had never met Herr Fischer before, it was only a matter of time before I ran into someone he knew, and then it would be all over. I couldn't imagine what they would do to someone who dared to impersonate a Gestapo spy. I looked around desperately, just as the man had done, and actually got to my feet. There was nobody down here. I could make a run for it. By the time they came looking for me, I could be across a border . . . That's when it hit me—I had nowhere to run.

The female receptionist appeared at the top of the stairs. "You can come up now, Herr Hofmeister," she said brightly. "Herr Fischer is ready to receive you."

Elizabeth Foxwell

NO MAN'S LAND

■ ■ ■

A longtime fan of historical mysteries, Elizabeth Foxwell has published seven short stories and won first prize in the 2003 Cape Fear [North Carolina] Crime Festival Short Story Contest. Her World War I story "No Man's Land," which was originally published in the MWA anthology Blood on Their Hands, *was an Agatha Award nominee for Best Short Story. An editor or coeditor of nine mystery anthologies, she edited the Malice Domestic serial novel* The Sunken Sailor *(Berkley, 2004), is a consulting editor and reviewer for* Mystery Scene *magazine, and serves as an at-large member of the Board of Directors of the Mystery Writers of America. Foxwell lives outside of Washington, D.C. Historical mysteries were a bit rare in this year's volume, with only a handful appearing. However, those that made the cut were uniformly excellent, like this twisting piece set against World War I.*

In the gray queue of ambulances I slumped against the painted red cross on my own, smoking the latest in a series of gaspers. In the distance, the guns boomed their incessant thunder, yellow bursts flashing ominously along the darkening horizon. This French countryside should have been quaintly bucolic with green grass and woolly sheep instead of ripped asunder, the long rows of trenches and barbed wire plowed remorselessly into the earth. Around the cigarette, my chapped fingers shook.

"Ta ra, Knox." It was my rangy Australian bunkmate, calling from the depot door. "Long run?"

I coughed, watching the cigarette smoke snake upward like a ghost in the mist. "Heaps of casualties plus two cases of spotted fever—and that blasted marker for Hospital Number Eight's turnoff has gone missing again."

"Dinky die. Almost slid into a ditch with my lot. Sodding mud. If I was a rum driver like—"

Involuntarily our eyes traveled to the sagging ambulance at the end of the queue—all ugly twisted metal and smashed windscreen. Aussie's habitual scowl softened.

"Don't tear yourself up, Knox. She's gone and good luck to her." She jerked a grubby thumb at a handsome staff car and the two tall, uniformed Tommies polishing its hood. "And now the Pommie brass are nosin' around with their fool questions. Bugger it. Little Turnip's a better sight off." She scraped her boots on the step. "We saved you some cocoa and stale biscuits. A sweet offer and no mistake. Come out of this damp."

"In a moment."

"Some happy new year, eh. Nineteen bloody sixteen." She glared toward the thumping distance. "Bloody guns." With a snort, she dove inside, the warped door as usual failing to completely close.

I should heed her advice, choke down lukewarm cocoa and hard biscuits, talk to the other girls, snatch at sleep on the narrow camp bed in the guise of a normal human being. It was difficult to be normal after the daily scrubbing out of my bus with its blood and vomit from soldiers mangled by shrapnel; hard to blot out the sobs of pain, the stench of gangrene and decay. The fortunate ones died before the hospital door, escaping the ordeal of amputation or the hemorrhaging of lungs from gas or the prospect of an alien and uncomprehending home front.

Others died instantly, shot through the head by a sniper . . .

I inhaled the blessed, steadying smoke deeply. Such was the work expected of middle- and upper-class women, bred for perfect marriages, idyllic motherhood, and the laundering of the battlefield.

Through the cracked door, the murmur of voices rose and fell.

"Was her ambulance in good order?" An older male voice, gruff and official.

"Certainly. Part of our duties, maintenance. Most likely she skidded in the snow. The ice can be fearful," said Finn, one of the other drivers.

"Could have been a tire," suggested another girl, Blake. "We puncture all the time. Did anyone look at the tires?"

"Of course, you twit," snapped Finn. "The left front is as flat as a board. But she smashed into the tree—she could have punctured before, during, after—it's anyone's guess."

"Perhaps," answered the gruff voice. "Or someone tampered with her brakes."

"Rubbish," returned our firm commandant. "Forgive me, General Ravenswood, but you wouldn't say such things if you were stationed here. This place is like Paddington Station. Who would have the opportunity?"

One of us, I thought. That's what was in the general's mind. One of us could mess about with Turnip's ambulance without challenge and spout something about assisting an exhausted friend. My resentment rose. In the grayest dawn and the blackest night, we drivers depended upon each other—was that trust to be destroyed by misdirected military inquiry?

"Another driver, Commandant," replied Finn, expressing my thoughts.

Aussie said a rude word.

"I have to agree with the sentiment of our Colonial cousin, if not her language," said the commandant. "My girls work hard, General, and don't merit idle accusations."

"No one is accusing anyone."

"Too right," said Aussie with scorn. "No sense to it. Can't see us fighting over Turnip's sparklers, or swish kit, or battalion of beaus—if they existed. The poor blighters are bleeding too much to paw us about."

"Not all of the men in France are wounded."

"We drive during the day," said Blake, "and are called out at night for the convoys. When we're not driving, we're usually asleep. Alone," she added with a gulp and probably a blush.

"The rules are quite clear about fraternization," noted the commandant, and I wondered if Blake was now the shade of a ripe tomato.

The general tried another tack. "May I ask where you all were when the incident occurred?"

"Oh, I see." Finn again, patrician and cool. "Gather the suspects into one room and someone will break down and confess?"

"I have to ask the question, Miss Finlay."

"If you must," said Finn. "Very well—we were on duty. At the time Turnip had gone west, I was driving a boy with pneumonia, two *poilus* with reeking cases of trenchfoot, and a Scottish sergeant with a terrific chest wound to Number Eleven. I'm sure they can vouch for me—if they were conscious, that is."

"I was transporting a doctor and a nurse," said Aussie. "From hospital to casualty clearing station and every aid station in between. Of course I could have gone walkabout between appointments, but the Doc would hardly wear it."

Blake was reported at No. 24—although longer than she should have been—and the other girls were either at the railway station or enroute to one of the other hospitals.

"And I was at the railway station as well. I hope those answers are sufficient, General?" said the commandant, satisfaction plain.

"For the moment, ma'am."

Another man—smooth, officious, somehow familiar—spoke up. "Was Miss Turnball troubled? Overwrought?"

"She wasn't unbalanced, if that's what you mean." Finn again, sounding more and more exasperated. "A little shallow, perhaps, a little silly, but not a lunatic."

"She did get all up in the air over that *Times* clipping," offered Blake.

"And came down again," Finn countered.

"Too right. You don't kill yourself over a society do," said Aussie. "So one of her mates got spliced to some posh fellow and is swanning about among the quality. A dead bore, if you ask me. Not worth a sausage."

"You never liked her," shot back Blake as if stung. "Said you'd wring her blood—blooming—neck."

"Because she nearly ran me and my lot off the road. Bloody stupid thing to do." I could practically see Aussie's shrug. "But it don't mean I was plotting to do her a bit of no good. Savin' that for the Huns and their ruddy guns."

"I think I feel sorry for the enemy," remarked the general.

"Ta, mate," said the gratified Aussie.

"Turnip could be thoughtless but she was as sane as any of us," asserted Finn. "Unless you believe, Captain, we all are on the verge of running off the rails?"

"It's a dangerous and difficult job—" started the captain.

"Perhaps we should be stowed away in a little ivory box in a high cupboard somewhere."

"Here, here," chimed in the irrepressible Aussie. "You tell 'im, Finn."

"We're not angels of mercy or delicate bits of porcelain. We have a job, Captain, the same as you. And we do it." Finn took a deep, aggravated breath. "Look, Turnip did not crash her bus due to a fit of the dismals. If she had cracked, she would have chosen something more dramatic."

"Such as—?"

"Wandering into the path of a convenient shell. Lord knows there are enough of them."

Finn was right. Athough dying behind the wheel would possess a certain glamour to the parents back home, it would be insufficient for Turnip. Turnball, I reminded myself.

Her real name. In our world, nearly every new arrival was rechristened with a shorter—and not necessarily flattering—form. We tended to forget the human being behind the amputated form . . .

I closed my eyes. She had only been nineteen and had lied about her age to the Red Cross to join up. "So handsome. So charming," she sighed about the officer she was secretly seeing under the nose of our hawklike commandant. Fresh from glittering balls and tennis parties and sophisticated nightclubs, she believed life could once again be gay. Only two years her senior, I knew otherwise.

"She was tired, poor cow," remarked Aussie. "Like all of us. And everyone knew she was a crook driver. She missed the turnoff and hit the tree. Dead easy. It's absurd that so many lives hang on a bit of ribbon."

"Ribbon?"

"Marks the turnoff. It's gone missing. Probably stuck in the mud like everything else."

"You said she nearly ran you off the road. How bad a driver was she?" asked the general.

"Don't you know? Christ." Aussie was contemptuous. "You should leave the chateau every so often."

The commandant rapped out a reproof—the man was a general, after all, and Aussie's behavior was unlikely to reap praise for either herself or the commandant.

"Let her continue," commanded General Ravenswood.

There was a distinctive snort—Aussie, uncowed. "Turnip cracked her bus up a fortnight ago and sent five of our boys to the graveyard before their time."

"Accident?"

So she had said. "It was an accident, Knox."

I held out a cup of Bovril, and she shook her head, lips compressing, almost turning green. "My tummy's giving me the gyp."

A common occurrence among us, given our strange hours and even stranger meals. I ignored it, occupied with the more vital issue. "I don't understand. There was a full moon. The road was clear. I checked that ambulance myself, just as you asked. What happened?"

"It's not my fault." Her tone was petulant. "The road is pocked with shell holes."

"If you wore your glasses—"

"I don't need them, silly. They're just for reading." She shrugged, leaning closer to her mirror. "Anyway, it's perfectly all right. I told the commandant a shell hit near me and knocked my bus off the road." She giggled, fluffing out her curls. "She swallowed it, the stupid sow."

I felt sick, as if I had the gypy tummy.

"They were bashed up pretty badly. They would have bought it in hospital, I'm sure."

My lips felt numb. "What about that man who did survive? He had two legs before the accident."

"Well, naturally I'm very sorry for him and all that, but I can't concentrate with all that beastly screaming and moaning. Honestly, how am I supposed to drive in the pitch black with all that racket?"

"Shock is hardly their fault, Turnip."

"They ought to have more self-control. They're trained soldiers, aren't they?"

"Training means little if you've just seen your mate blown to bits." A thought struck me. "How fast were you traveling?"

Her eyes skittered from mine and she did not reply, absorbed in her reflection.

"Turnip. How fast?"

"I don't recall."

I turned on my heel, marched by the chattering mess room, and headed for the wrecked Vulcan that had been dragged back to camp. On a hunch, I felt under the driver's seat and produced a bottle. A slightly cracked, very empty bottle.

"Just to ward off the damp," said she, flushed, at my elbow.

"You were drunk."

"For heaven's sake, it's only red wine. The Frogs practically are weaned on the stuff."

"They don't drink and smash up their wounded." I jerked back, slamming the door.

"Are you going to the commandant?"

"I won't, if you move to day duty."

"Can't be done," she said airily. "Franklin's been shipped home and Hills is in hospital with a septic thumb. We're shorthanded."

"Then you come out with me on your time off. We'll drive the routes together."

"I'd like to see myself," she sniffed. "I have better things to do in my precious few hours off."

"Then I'll accompany you when *I'm* off."

"Oh, really. I'm not taking on a minder, for heaven's sake. Too, too humiliating."

"Turnip. . . . don't you realize what you've done?"

"How you do rattle on, Knox." She cocked her dusky head. "I believe you're jealous."

"Don't be absurd."

"It isn't. I see it all. I have a chap and you don't."

"A *married* chap."

"You would say that. You want to spoil my romance because you don't have one. Well, I won't let you. He loves me and I love him." Her voice dropped to a purr. "And we don't just have tea and sandwiches, don't you know."

"Go on and sleep with the entire Royal Flying Corps if you care to," I retorted. "What I care about are soldiers with mothers, sisters, and sweethearts who won't be going home to them."

She pouted. "You used to be such fun; now it's Granny Sobersides day in, day out."

"This isn't a game, Turnip. I will tell the commandant."

"Go ahead. Tattle your head off. See what good it does you." She plunged a hand into her kit bag, withdrawing a brightly colored scarf. "Do you think this suits me? I thought so in Camiers but now I'm not so certain. It might do for Mother; she's been agitating for a souvenir to show her club."

"Don't change the subject."

"Then spare me the sermon, Padre Knox, do." She clasped my arm, wheedling. "You're ever so much nicer than that. You're like a sister."

I exhaled. "What do you want?"

"I need your help again . . ."

"Accident?" Aussie was saying. "Sure, you could call it that if an accident can be caused by her own vanity. She was shortsighted and wouldn't wear her glasses. Just a matter of time before she killed herself, I reckon. At least she took no poor sod with her this time."

"Sir—" The commandant cleared her throat, sounding less assured than when I had confronted her. "Nothing to be done, Miss Knox," she had said. "We are short staffed and new drivers won't be arriving from England anytime soon."

"You could borrow some drivers from Calais. Move her to a desk job—hospital—canteen—anything but behind the wheel."

"Calais is handling heavier casualties than we are. And her aunt is a prominent patroness of the Red Cross. Funds could be cut; questions would be asked—"

"God forbid," I snarled.

"You don't understand the situation. At home there is a vocal segment who question the wisdom and capability of female ambulance drivers. What do you suppose would happen if word got out about the wounded dying at the hands of Miss Turnball?"

I was very still. "Are you saying the Red Cross would shut us down?"

"Precisely."

"But you said yourself that we're overworked and there are no replacements. What are the wounded going to do—hail a cab?"

The commandant turned over her palms eloquently.

"We've done good work—Aussie was even decorated."

"No one said life was fair, Miss Knox."

Brilliant choice, I reflected. Expose Turnip, and we all were on the block. Keep mum, and the wounded were at risk. "No. I suppose not."

"Influence is the ranking officer here, I'm afraid."

"Yes, you're quite right, Commandant. Influence is the key."

"I'm as aware of Miss Turnball's connections as you are," said the general, all steel, echoing my thoughts. "But I should have been informed. Two accidents are significant. It would tend to confirm what Miss Finlay has denied—someone who was looking for a way to die."

"Look here, mate," interjected the unabashed Aussie, "If you really want to know about Turnip, you should talk to the driver outside. Turnip confided in her. Best in the unit. And before you ask the question, General, she was at Number Eight when Turnip bashed herself into potato and mash."

The voices murmured on. An officer emerged, straightening his service cap—a captain with a clipped mustache, clean chin, and shiny Sam Browne belt—the immaculate signs of a man well removed from the front line. I stiffened, dropping the smoldering stub of cigarette behind my back. Smoking on duty was not the done thing, especially by a woman. He paused, staring at me.

"Why, Miss Knox. This is an unexpected pleasure." The plummy male voice—no wonder it had sounded familiar. My mind raced as he strolled over.

"Captain Blight—Brightman." I bit back the near slip of "Blighty" and ground the forbidden cigarette under my boot heel.

"I remember that Eton Garden Party. Can it be—five years ago? There were roses on your hat." He smirked. "I pinched one of them for my buttonhole, do you know. And you wore a particularly fetching yellow silk frock."

With my hair now hacked off to discourage nesting fleas and the stained khaki uniform hanging from my ill-nourished frame, I was a faint shadow of that fashionable and complacent figure. Still, his eyes wandered over the curves of my bosom and my tightly belted waist as they had not dared to linger at the garden party, with my vigilant brother in attendance.

"And here you are doing your bit. Splendid. Much more useful than Somerville."

I swallowed sarcasm. More useful than he. At Oxford, I'd been favored for a First in English, whereas Anthony Brightman would barely escape with a Second in History. The dim Blighty, however, was entitled to a degree, while I, a voteless woman, was not. My brother, responsible for Brightman's new and more fitting name, had scoffed at the irony, declaring, "All the boys will be left behind by your brains, Kath."

Far behind.

His voice dropped. "I was sorry about your brother."

"Thank you," I said woodenly.

"Did you know we were at Cambridge together? Yes, I suppose you must; Geoffrey said you were close."

Close. An inadequate word that did not encompass impromptu and hilarious jaunts on his motorcycle; the patient, good-natured instruction behind the wheel of Daddy's balky motorcar; the ready ear and equally sympathetic shoulder to cry on during schoolgirl crises. And I would never know if I had returned that boundless generosity even in part, or if he knew how much I had loved him.

The smooth voice went on, oozing like treacle. "A good soldier, Geoff, very gallant. I could scarcely believe when we were posted to the same unit and I became his CO. He was fortunate to see more action than I. Served his country bravely."

I remained silent, my opinion about military intelligence best kept to myself.

"Perhaps we can have tea together soon. There is a very jolly hotel in Hardelot-Plage."

"Yes, I know." No doubt planning for after tea, the cheeky bugger. "It's not possible. We're rather busy here, Captain."

"Such formality. There's no need. The wife's in London, you know," he said confidently, as if I had never spoken. "A Lady-in-Waiting at the Palace. Safely away. Unless you're thinking of your dragon the commandant. Strict segregation between the sexes and all that tosh." He stepped closer to me, his fingers wandering down my sleeve. "You're a woman of the world. Surely you know the old rules don't apply here, Miss Knox?"

The hand intruded on more than just my sleeve, and I met his gaze squarely. "Indeed I do, Captain Brightman. I think you knew Miss Turnball?"

His eyes shifted. "We were—acquainted. Nice little creature. No one seems to know the cause of the accident. No witnesses. Pity."

So that was why he had accompanied the general—to put on a properly sorrowful countenance and ensure his name was not linked to the dead girl. "You must be so distressed," I cooed. "She spoke of you so often." My eyes bored into his, and his shifted again.

"Er, quite. I—I believe she missed home a great deal."

"She did." We all did. But home was a fairy tale now, a place of magical hot baths and faraway comforts and impenetrable ignorance, where war was noble and tidy. Not betrayal, not horror, not hopeless yearning for an only brother rotting in the ground with his comrades.

I swayed. Captain Brightman grasped my arm, and my hand brushed against his breast pocket.

"Are you all right?

"Yes, thank you." I straightened and stepped back. "I missed dinner. A momentary weakness."

"You should eat. Shall we go and—"

"I cannot, Captain. Waiting for the call out." To the trains and their inevitable cargo.

"Yes. Yes of course. Well." He took my hand and kissed it. His lips were damp. "It's been a pleasure, Miss Knox. Katharine." He lingered over my name. "I look forward to seeing you again."

Not likely, I reflected. How quickly was Turnip replaced. I pulled my arm free. "Goodbye, Captain."

With a puzzled glance at me, he walked off, no doubt accustomed to women fawning over an officer's uniform. For them, I had only to look as far as the letters from old school friends who were busily awarding white feathers of cowardice to young men in civilian dress. Those fortunate ones, safely out of it. As Geoff might have been. I scrubbed my fingers against my sleeve.

Aussie's "Pommie brass" emerged from the depot, pulling on his gloves. My patience in the cold twilight rewarded, I tugged my uniform tunic into more regulation shape. "Excuse me, sir?"

His grizzled face drawn, he snapped, "Who are you?"

"Katharine Knox. One of the ambulance drivers, sir."

"Oh. Right." Then he stopped and examined me more intently. "Half a mo—not Sir Peter Knox's daughter?"

I nodded.

"Well, I'm blowed." He grasped my hand warmly. "How do you do. He and I served together. Boer War."

"Yes, I know."

"Splendid on horseback. He had great panache then."

"Yes, sir. My brother Geoff and I thrilled to his stories." Too much—the skirmish in France had seemed an easy passport to the adventure of the Transvaal. So Geoff had declared and I, as usual, had to follow where he led.

"And Peter was a remarkably fine shot."

"He still is."

"Oh, does he still hunt?"

"On occasion. He's an engineer, sir."

"Building things instead of demolishing them. Fitting."

"He speaks of you with great affection."

"Does he?" The general brightened. "Good man. Knew his duty. You're like him—straightforward, blue eyes, fair hair. Dashed good-looking, if I may. Yes. Doing your bit now, I daresay, just as Peter did."

"Yes, sir. I came out with Geoff, but he died at Ypres. Sniper."

His craggy face sagged—he who must have seen an endless roll of death, in both wars. "Sad business. Damn waste."

I warmed to his laconic but honest sorrow. "Thank you. General, about the girl—"

He shook his head. "Strange. Received a message to come here—from your commandant, I assumed, but she tells me I was unexpected."

"I thought some of your questions sounded odd."

"Heard that, did you? Would have looked into the Turnball matter anyway. Niece of an old school chum who is now a Member of Parliament—wants answers." He rubbed his chin. "That rather brash Australian has very definite ideas about the case—and my own shortcomings, I must say."

"Aussie's a good sort, sir, and brave as a lion. She—"

But he waved off my defense. "I saw the Military Medal pinned to her tunic. Unlike some of my counterparts, I don't punish candor or transfer a good man for a frivolous cause. Your Miss Blake, however, may be an entirely different kettle of fish. If that girl doesn't have something to hide, I don't know who does. I can't remember when I've seen such a shade of crimson."

"It's not for a nefarious reason, sir. Blake's worried that the commandant will find out about her young man at Etaples."

He gave me a shrewd look. "I thought you girls had no time for anything but driving."

"Some do manage. Miss Turnball, for one."

"Excellent. I've been hoping to run into someone like you, Miss Knox. A lass I can trust who knows the people." He lowered his voice confidentially. "Absent the company of your very decided commandant and equally decided friends."

"They are that, sir."

"Well, two ambulance accidents so closely together do raise uncomfortable questions. Only natural to feel besieged and close ranks. You knew her well, I gather?"

"I did, sir." I hesitated delicately, like the properly bred young woman I was, and he prompted me.

"Distressin' for you, naturally. But if you know anything that can shed light on this incident, m'dear, you must tell me. Ease the family's grief."

"Yes, sir." I coughed, murmuring an apology for a throat taxed by cold, damp, and other unpleasantness while I weighed my words carefully. "Well, Turnip—Miss Turnball, sir—did talk to me. She was keeping company with Captain Brightman. I tried to warn her about regulations, but she was young and fancied herself in love."

"I see. And did he return her feelings?"

"She said so, General. But she did discover from the *Times* that he was married to an acquaintance of hers."

"Ah. So that was the way of it."

"Yes, sir. My brother was at school with Captain Brightman and served under him, so he couldn't pretend to me that he was unmarried."

"Risky. You could have told her."

"I did, sir. But it had no effect. She thought I was carping on her idol out of jealousy."

"Awkward business. His wife has deep pockets and pull at the Palace."

"So I gather, sir. And I have reason to believe Miss Turnball was in the family way." I had remembered the gypy tummy.

"Not a new tale. Poor child." He gave a gusty sigh. "Difficult to prove any of this, though."

"No, not especially. I expect if you search him and his belongings, you will find her letters. She was an indiscreet child, and Captain Brightman is, shall we say, sir, fond of trophies."

"Indeed. And if Miss Turnball was in the habit of writing letters to her uncle—" He fell silent and let the implication hang in the air between us.

"Yes, sir. Awkward indeed, for Captain Brightman."

The guns stopped, the abrupt silence equally deafening, and our heads turned as one.

"Ah. You will have to fill that ambulance soon, I regret to say."

"Yes, sir. I look forward to the day when I am out of work."

"As do I. Then perhaps your father and I can go bag some pheasants instead of more deadly game." He sighed. "My best to him."

"I'll tell him, sir, in my next letter." Softer than the harsher business of Geoff . . .

He saluted me, then marched to his aides milling by his car and barked a curt order. The commandant's whistle blew, the shrill summons to our convoy, and the girls rushed out of the depot to their ambulances. I cranked the engine, my coughing matching the engine's sputtering to life, the weather, tobacco, and the unaccustomed necessity of imitating the commandant on the telephone finally taking their toll on my throat.

I climbed creakily behind the wheel. In the swarm of people and vehicles, I saw Captain Brightman pushed into the staff car by the two very stern Tommies. The self-confident voice unleashed a string of protests as they rumbled away.

From my pocket I took out a fluttering of white ribbon, neatly snipped, and stared at it. The marker for the No. 8 turnoff. Because of the convenient "fainting spell," the other half now rested in Brightman's breast pocket, to be discovered by the ever-thorough military police.

Blighty was right. The rules were changed here—especially for Turnip, who saw no sin in betraying the men who had suffered so much and gave us their trust; and for Blighty, who had sent Geoff out on the perilous line while he, safely removed from the guns and the carnage, plotted his next sordid rendezvous. He deserved not to fall in battle, as more honorable men were doing, but hung by the neck until dead.

As the general had said, I knew my duty to my brother and my unit—and my Classics back at faraway Oxford. The Furies, pursuers of the murderer Orestes, were the daughters of Nox, or Night. Fitting my name, I had become a part of the black void all about me.

How simple it was to take a young girl's dreams of romance with an officer and twist them to one's own advantage. Listening to her confidences. Suggesting the route for a secret rendezvous at the jolly hotel in Hardelot-Plage. Making a few adjustments to her brakes.

Turnip was a casualty of war.

As were we all.

Repocketing the ribbon, I shoved the ambulance into gear and drove off into the dark.

Marcia Talley

SAFETY FIRST

■ ■ ■

Marcia Talley is the Anthony and Agatha Award–winning author of the Hannah Ives mysteries: Sing It to Her Bones, Unbreathed Memories, Occasion of Revenge, *and* In Death's Shadow. *She is also author/editor of a collaborative serial novel,* Naked Came the Phoenix, *where she joined twelve bestselling women to pen a tongue-in-cheek mystery about murder in an exclusive health spa. A second collaboration,* I'd Kill for That, *is set in an upscale gated community. Marcia's short stories have appeared in magazines and collections, including "Safety First" and "With Love, Marjorie Ann," both shortlisted for the Agatha Award. "Too Many Cooks," a wry retelling of Shakespeare's* Macbeth *from the viewpoint of the three witches, won both the Agatha and the Anthony Awards for Best Short Story of 2002. Marcia lives in Annapolis, Maryland, with her husband, Barry, a professor at the U.S. Naval Academy. Her story chosen this year, "Safety First," was first published in* Blood on Their Hands, *and was also a finalist for the Agatha Award. It shows what happens when the head of a small-town library takes his budget-tightening a bit too far.*

George stood on the steps of Lakeland Public Library—*his* library—and studied his reflection in the tall glass doors. Intelligent gray eyes set in a pleasantly round face, a full head of auburn hair, all his own, thank you very much. All in all, a cheerful sort of guy. Squinting at his reflection, he smoothed back an unruly lock with the palm of his hand, straightened his tie, and wondered, for the fourth morning in a row, why such a friendly-looking fellow deserved such punishment.

Years ago, sitting at a solitary cataloger's desk deep in the bowels of Lakeland Public, aspiring to be head of it one day, he wished he had known then what he knew now. Management would be simple, he told himself, if it weren't for all the people.

These doors, for example. He winced as the plain glass panels whooshed open automatically before him, followed by a blast of heat that ruffled his carefully styled hair. At their weekly staff meetings the circulation librarian, Jean McBride, had gone on and on about the old revolving doors. "That's the second time this week a mother with a stroller's been caught in that door, not to mention the indignity of forcing our handicapped patrons to use the basement entrance!" Counterarguments about the architectural significance of the doors—made of brass, glass, and ornately carved wood, part of the original building when Andrew Carnegie dedicated it at the turn of the century—

not to mention the added cost of heating the lobby, had fallen on deaf ears. When the readers' services librarian and the head of cataloging had stood in solidarity with their colleagues, George had capitulated. Now, fully 10 percent of his fuel oil budget was going to heat four parallel parking spaces on Cuyahoga Street and keep the blasted forsythia bushes warm throughout the winter. He had the bills to prove it.

"Morning, Dr. Hopkins."

"Morning, Jean." It annoyed him that no matter how early he arrived at work, that damned woman was there ahead of him. Already his stomach was in knots thinking about the staff meeting he'd scheduled for later that morning. He prayed they wouldn't gang up on him again.

Jean had been a particular challenge. When he'd first taken the directorship, Jean had been manning the circulation desk wearing tennis shoes, slacks, dumpy sweaters, and once, to his horror, a Mickey Mouse T-shirt. At his first staff meeting, he'd impressed on her, indeed on all "front office" staff, the importance of their appearance. "If we don't look professional," he had admonished, "how can we expect our customers (never patrons!) to treat us as such?"

Today he smiled at Jean, who wore, he was pleased to note, a frilly white blouse under a chic, navy blue suit. He pictured navy hose ending in black, patent-leather t-strap shoes, but could only imagine this without leaning very obviously over the counter.

George punched the up button and waited, pacing, while the elevator made a slow, creaking ascent from the basement. When the doors shuddered open, he climbed aboard and rode to the fifth floor, where his office was tucked into a corner with windows overlooking Lake Erie on two sides.

Lolly, his secretary, was already at her desk, head bent over her keyboard. When he pushed through the double doors, she popped up as if shot from a toaster. "Dr. Hopkins! Can I get you a cup of coffee?"

As he crossed the carpet to his office, Lolly orbited around her cubicle, keeping her body between her boss and whatever was displayed on her monitor screen. George's eyes narrowed. "Coffee will be fine, Miss Taylor." He took three steps toward his office, then suddenly turned, catching his secretary, already on her way to the coffee machine, off guard. "What's that on your monitor?"

Lolly smiled uncertainly. "Just a screen saver."

George squinted toward the monitor where manic dogs frolicked, gradually gobbling bits of the Word document Lolly had been working on. He scowled. "What's wrong with the one that came with the computer?" he demanded, thinking of the soothing, cloud-studded landscape that materialized on his screen whenever it had been idle for ten minutes.

Lolly's dark eyes bored into his, her lips forming a thin, hard line. She opened her mouth, then seemed to reconsider. "I'll change it back," she whispered.

George grunted. "What if a board member should come in and see that? Very unprofessional!" He unlocked the door to his office and slipped in, thinking this was not an auspicious start to the day.

For the next two hours, sipping the hot coffee Lolly periodically provided, hoping, vainly, to feel the revitalizing effects of caffeine surging through his system, George proofed the final draft of his annual report. On page twenty-seven, he added a paragraph that had just occurred to him about estate planning and the Friends of the Library Foundation. Then, exuding self-confidence after a short, but productively persuasive telephone conversation with an elderly, chronically ill donor, George gathered up the annual report, slid it into his secretary's in-box, and headed toward the conference room, smiling.

His confidence evaporated the minute he entered the room. Arranged in a horseshoe around the table was his staff, presided over like a malevolent Buddha by Claudia Fairfield, head of readers' services, narrow-eyed and unsmiling. Instantly, he regretted appointing Claudia head of the facilities management committee. Before he had time to pull up his chair, she thrust her triangular chin over the table and announced, "We have our report."

George swallowed, the coffee he'd recently consumed making an unwelcome comeback. On his left sat Jean McBride, hands folded on the table in front of her, quietly studying her painted thumbnails. On Jean's left was Belinda D'Arcy, the archivist, leafing through some papers and refusing to meet his eyes, still fuming, no doubt, over George's refusal to grant her request for leave without pay to take care of her mother. Next to Belinda sat Myles Nichols, the head cataloger who, with his floppy hair, flattish nose, and lipless mouth, reminded George of a lizard. Myles had an elderly mother, too. If George were to grant Belinda's request, soon Myles would be asking for leave, and the next thing he knew, the whole staff would be expecting George to bend over backward for them. There'd be no end to it. Time off to attend classes. Write a thesis. Get married. Go on vacations even.

George had done his homework on Belinda, at least. She'd threatened to quit, but George had been through her personnel folder and knew that the threat was an empty one. Just two years short of retirement, Belinda could hardly risk losing her pension.

As Claudia droned on about the annual picnic, vending machines in the staff area (including one that dispensed cappuccino), and electrical outlets in the ladies' rest rooms to accommodate their damn hair dryers, George zoned out. He found himself wondering about the package he was expecting from L.L. Bean and whether he'd have time to eat before his evening karate class.

"Overtime." The word sliced through his reverie like a knife. George had replaced his predecessor's rather lackadaisical approach to payroll with a computerized system, well aware that the institution of time cards would make him about as popular as mosquitoes at a nudist colony. But it had to be done. Now, it appeared, he was being punished for his pains. "Because of the Friends' meeting, I worked forty-nine hours last week," Jean was whining. "How does the library plan to pay me for it?"

Controlling his exasperation, George explained, for what seemed like the hundredth time, that overtime hours had to be approved in *advance*, and referred her to the new staff manual.

"Nobody told me I had to ask in advance," Jean complained.

"It's in the cover memo I sent out to all staff," George reminded her. He hastily finessed by referring Jean to the personnel office all the while knowing, with fear's cold fingers squeezing his gut, that before long he'd be summoned by the Brunehilde in charge of *that* office and forced to attend another session of "sensitivity training."

"And now," Claudia continued with relentless momentum, "we want to discuss some new concerns about library safety. As you know, Lakeland is an *elderly* library, and because of budgetary constraints, needed repairs have been shamefully neglected."

George knew all about budgetary restraints. He'd met with the Board of Governors just last week, and although he'd pleaded for more money, none had been forthcoming.

Indeed, the bond issue in November had failed; the library would simply have to make do with funding at last year's level. George doubted he merited the confidence the Board had placed in him. With automatic cost-of-living salary increases and the price of magazines and newspapers spiraling out of control, George was at his wit's end. Even if he fired that good-for-nothing gaggle of Madonna wannabees who shelved the books with all the speed of molasses in January, he'd save only enough to buy a one-year subscription to *Science Citation Index*. It was discouraging.

"Nevertheless," Claudia forged on, "we must address some safety issues."

"Which are?" George inquired.

Claudia raised an index finger. "One. The dumb waiter. It doesn't work half the time. Yesterday I looked up the shaft to see what was holding it up and nearly got decapitated when it suddenly decided to come down."

George suppressed a smile. If *that* happened, Claudia's mouth would go on flapping a full ten minutes after her head had parted company with her body. He nodded sagely, his fingers tented over his lips.

"Two. The compact shelving. The hand cranks are stiff and difficult for our older staff to manage." Claudia braved a sideways glance at Belinda. "Nowadays, they're *electric*," she added, as if George had just emerged, dazed and blinking, from a time machine sent from the seventeenth century. "With automatic shutoff controls. I shudder to think what would happen if someone was reaching for the Bryant Papers when somebody else decided to check out the World War II correspondence."

Myles, who had until this point been mindlessly tracing the lifeline on his palm with a ballpoint pen, raised both hands in front of his face and brought them sharply together. "Splat!"

Belinda glared at him from across the table. "Not funny, Myles." Myles shrugged and returned to his doodling.

"Three." Claudia soldiered on, like a suffragette on a mission. "We've got to get rid of the halon."

"Why?" George inquired. "It's the most effective fire retardant ever invented. And since it's a gas, it doesn't ruin the manuscripts as water would."

"True," Claudia admitted, "But it does deplete the ozone layer."

"Like freon," Jean added.

All around the table, George's staff nodded sagely. Good God almighty! He was captaining a Greenpeace vessel. "But surely . . ." he began, until Claudia raised a caterpillar-like eyebrow.

"No choice, I'm afraid. Halon gas hasn't been manufactured since 1994, and in 2003 it will be banned altogether."

With fat, ringless fingers, she started a three-page Internet printout on a circuit around the table. When it reached George, everybody waited silently while he scanned the document. Indeed, halon was being phased out in favor of an alphabet of substances like FM200 and ETEC Agent A, but it was the price tag that caught his eye. If he handed over his entire salary for a year, it would just about cover the cost of a retrofit.

"Besides, it sucks all the oxygen out of the air," Jean commented. "What if there was a fire and Belinda was working in the vault when the halon went off?"

Myles threw his head back, eyelids fluttering grotesquely over the whites of his eyes and gurgled like a clogged drain.

"Nonsense!" George scoffed. "There are safeguards." Although he didn't have the vaguest idea what they might be. "Let me study the issue and get back to you. Anything else?" His question met a wall of silence. "Good. Back to work, then."

George stood, shook the kinks out of his calves, and concentrated on shoving papers back into his folder. When he glanced up again, everyone had gone except Belinda. "Dr. Hopkins?"

"Yes, Belinda?"

"I was wondering if you'd reconsider your decision about my request for leave without pay."

George stared. "I thought we'd settled that."

"Well, I consulted the city employees' manual, like you suggested just now, and it clearly states that leave without pay may be granted under certain circumstances." A button dangled from her cardigan by a thin thread and she twisted it round and round. "I met a clerk at the court house yesterday who's on three months' leave just to study for her bar exam!"

George tucked his folder under his arm. "If you had read those regulations carefully, Miss D'Arcy, you'd have seen that such leave is granted at supervisor discretion. If I let you go for so long a time, it's as good as announcing to the Board of Governors that I don't really *need* an archivist."

A tear slid down Belinda D'Arcy's cheek and made a dark splotch on her lime green blouse. "My mother has Alzheimer's, Dr. Hopkins."

"So you said." George leaned against the doorframe. "Look, I don't wish to appear uncompromising and hardhearted, but I have a library to run, Miss D'Arcy. Surely there are, uh, arrangements you can make. Adult day care? Hospice? A nursing home? We certainly pay you enough."

Belinda turned and fled.

George stooped to pick up the button that had fallen from the archivist's sweater. "Wait! You've lost your button!" But the door to the corridor slammed, and Belinda was gone.

George spent the next week glued to the chair in front of his computer, plugging new figures into his Excel spreadsheet, moving them about from column to column like some elaborate chess game. If he put off the new photocopier acquisition until next year, he discovered, the dumb waiter could be fixed, but replacing the compact shelving and the halon system that protected the manuscript vault was simply out of the question, either now or in the foreseeable future.

Late one afternoon, with the cleaning staff busily emptying trash baskets nearby, George determined that the cranks on the compact shelving units did work a bit stiffly, but nothing that a little WD-40 couldn't fix. He worked the lubricant well into the crank mechanisms at the end of each row of shelves, then, beginning with the section where the atlases were kept, he knelt and began spraying WD-40 on the tracks that ran along the floor. He was so intent on his task that it took him a while to notice that the shelves were closing in on him. "Hey!" he shouted over the drone of the vacuum cleaner. "Someone's in here!" But the gap continued to narrow.

George scrambled to his feet and braced his arms, Sampson-like, against the shelves. "Hey!" he shouted again, feeling the flab on his upper arms quiver ineffectually beneath his sleeves. "Hey! Hey!"

It was an oversize *Atlas of the World. 1750, Volume IV* that saved him when he managed to wedge it into the narrowing gap between the shelves. Underarms ringed with sweat, he stepped over the blessed book and peeked out into the room. "Who's there?"

But he saw no one. Even the cleaning crew had vanished.

Later, relaxing at home with a cold glass of Chablis, his blood pressure and heart rate returned to normal, George almost succeeded in convincing himself that it was one of the cleaning crew who had moved the shelves but was simply too frightened to admit it. Yet a feeling of uneasiness hung about him like a cloud, and for the next couple of days, he rarely left his office.

Until Belinda D'Arcy called. "Please come down to the manuscript vault, Dr. Hopkins. I have something to show you."

George laid aside his *Publishers Weekly* and sighed. It had been a fine, sunny day. He had eaten lunch at a picnic table in the park. Later, his mother had telephoned to say that she was *not* coming for Christmas this year. Yes, a near perfect day. The last thing in the world George wanted to do was spoil it by talking to Belinda D'Arcy. "Can't it wait until tomorrow?"

"No."

"What is it, then?"

"I'll have to show you."

George checked his watch. "Okay. If it's that important, I'll try to stop by on my way home."

In the next few minutes while George packed up his briefcase, locked his office door, and caught the elevator to the archives on Sublevel A, he wondered what was bothering the archivist this time. A dead rat, probably. Or a bit of condensation on the pipes. He found Belinda waiting for him in the spacious vault, standing behind one of two long, narrow study tables, her plain face unflatteringly sallow under the bright fluorescent lights. "What did you decide about the halon?" she asked.

"We'll need new cylinders, pipework, and nozzles," George explained. "I'm putting them into the five-year plan."

"But it's dangerous *now*," Belinda complained, moving between George and the door.

"Look," George snapped. "I've studied the installation carefully. I've read the manual. Even if halon should suddenly fill this room, it would last only ten seconds." He pointed to a gridded opening near the floor. "After that, those big exhaust fans kick in and suck it all out. Nobody's in danger."

"Really." It was a statement, not a question. "I've left a report on the table," she said. "I suggest you read it."

Before he could reply, Belinda slipped out the door and slammed it shut behind her.

At first, George wasn't alarmed. It wasn't the first time Belinda had stormed out of a meeting; for someone in her sixties, she was surprisingly immature. The room was scrupulously neat so it didn't take him long to find the folder where she had left it for him, on the table farthest from the door. He skimmed over the report—something with an official-looking logo from a firm called Foggo, Inc.—but it didn't seem to contain anything he didn't already know. He put the report down and went to the door, but the damned woman had slammed it so hard that it was jammed. "Belinda?" Feeling foolish, he pounded against the door with his fist. "Belinda!"

Her voice was soft, and surprisingly close, just on the other side of the door. "I suggest you read the small print, Dr. Hopkins."

The woman had lost her marbles! George was caught up in some sort of macabre game, and if he wanted to get home tonight in time to feed the cat, the only thing he could do was play along. He grabbed the report and flipped through it again, noticing for the first time where someone—probably Belinda—had highlighted a footnote with yellow marker. *Caution. Do not place boxes, papers, or other objects on shelves or tables near the nozzles as they will be blown off by the extremely high velocities created by the gas shooting from the tanks. To minimize this potential hazard, install pegboard sheets at the ends of shelving units near the nozzles in order to allow penetration, but deflect the blast. Ceiling panels must be secured . . .*

George felt his face grow hot; blood pounded in his ears. He glanced quickly around the room. No pegboard sheets. Boxes all over the shelves. And how the hell was he supposed to know how the ceiling panels were secured.

"And by the way, *George*," he heard Belinda say. "I think I smell smoke!"

George's stomach lurched. "Belinda! Open the door!"

"Fire, fire, fire!" she singsonged.

George knew the klaxon would be loud, but he was totally unprepared for the ear-splitting sound of the halon being discharged. It exploded from vents all around him, knocking the boxes off their shelves, sending their contents—manuscripts and letters and antique photographs—swirling about the room in a furious hurricane. Floor tiles erupted from their framework grid, narrowly missing his head as they shot toward the ceiling. All around him, the air shimmered as halon mixed with the oxygen in it.

Ten seconds? It seemed to George like ten years.

A tile flew up, striking a shelf, which tilted. A bronze bust of Commodore Oliver Hazard Perry teetered on the edge, then toppled, falling on an aquatint of the barge *Seneca Chief*, dated 1825, shattering the glass. A glistening shard spun through the air, sliced through his collar, and severed his jugular.

By the time the exhaust fans kicked in, George was already dead.

Elaine Viets

Red Meat

■ ■ ■

Elaine Viets was nominated for three Agatha Awards in 2004, including two for her short stories "Red Meat" and "Sex and Bingo," both of which appear in this volume in a rare double feature. Shop Till You Drop, *the first novel in her new Dead-End Job series from Signet, was named one of the hot new series by* Publishers Weekly. *In each book, Elaine and her character, Helen Hawthorne, work a different minimum-wage job. "Shop" was set at a dress shop that sold bustiers to bimbos.* Murder Between the Covers *took place at a bookstore. For the third,* Dying to Call You, *Helen worked as a telemarketer—and so did Elaine. She was cursed coast to coast. Elaine is on the national board of the Mystery Writers of America. In "Red Meat," first published in the MWA anthology* Blood on Their Hands, *and the first of her stories in this year's volume, a man looking for a new lease on life gets more than he ever bargained—or asked—for when his every waking moment is taken over by the fitness trainer from hell, leaving him with only one way out.*

Ashley had a body to die for, and I should know. I'm on death row because of her.

You want to know the funny thing?

My wife bought me Ashley. For a birthday present.

I was turning sixty that July, and I could feel the cold wind at my neck. I wasn't bad-looking for my age. I still had all my hair. But that semipermanent twenty pounds of lard around my gut had turned into thirty. I had chicken skin on the insides of my elbows, like an old geezer. And women didn't give me appraising looks anymore.

Not that I need to look at other women. My Francie had kept her figure just fine. She was ten years younger than me, and worked out with a personal trainer. Recently, people had started asking if Francie was my daughter. I'd laughed it off, but it bothered me. I told Francie maybe she should dye her hair gray so she'd look her age. She said, "Maybe you should lose thirty pounds, Jake, so you'd look your age."

I'd thought about going to the gym. We had a good one, right here on Sunnysea Beach, Florida, owned by a former pro linebacker. I'd see Jamal Wellington out running on the sand. You know those fake-heroic chests guys strap on so they look like gladiators? Jamal had a real chest like that, and arms and legs to match.

Francie and I had a beachfront condo about a mile from. Jamal's Jym, but beach life makes you lazy. I never got around to walking down there. I'd think about joining the gym, but I'd always lie back down until the fitness fit passed. Instead, I'd pop another brew and watch another movie. I had a state-of-the-art entertainment system with five clickers (Francie put the clickers in a basket so I wouldn't leave them lying around).

Now that I was retired, I had time to catch up on my movies. I'd been comparing the classic Bond films starring Sean Connery to the later ones with Roger Moore. In my opinion, Connery was the one true Bond. Moore looked like a Sears shirt model.

When Francie came home from work that night, I said, "You can't trust movie critics. This so-called critic says *For Your Eyes Only* is a superior piece of escapism."

"I don't know what you need to escape," snapped Francie, slamming her briefcase down on the kitchen table.

I could tell Francie was peeved, so I put down my beer and took her to the Beachside Bar for dinner. I thought she'd be happy she didn't have to cook. Instead she glared at me when I mopped up my steak gravy with my butter bread. She got testy when I downed my third martini. By the time I ordered key lime pie with extra whipped cream, Francie was steaming. She didn't say anything, but the air around her got dense and crackly, like she was generating her own personal thunderstorm.

Francie's bad mood was gone by my sixtieth birthday, two days later. She smiled and slipped on her silky leopard-print robe I like so much.

"Happy Birthday, Tiger," she said, handing me a ribbon-wrapped box. "I got you a twenty-three-year-old blonde for your birthday."

"I like my fifty-year-old brunette," I said, patting her rump.

I opened the present. Inside was a gift card. It said I should meet my personal trainer, Ashley, at Jamal's Jym at 2 P.M. today for my first workout.

"Ashley? What kind of name is that?" I snorted. "She probably looks like a Russian Olympic gymnast. I bet she shaves more than I do." Then I shut up. I realized I was grumping like a sixty-year-old.

"Wait and see," said Francie, smiling.

I walked down to the gym that broiling July afternoon, feeling sorry for myself. I felt like I was walking barefoot across a hot stove. Sweat ran off me like rainforest waterfalls. I couldn't believe my own wife bought me a personal trainer to make me sweat more. I passed the WaterEdge condo building, its units hidden behind hurricane shutters. Those people had the sense to leave south Florida in July. I was stuck here with a bearded woman trainer.

At Jamal's Jym, I presented my gift card to a young guy named Barry. He wore only black gym shorts and running shoes. I wished he would put on more clothes. The guy's bare stomach was so flat you could bounce quarters on it. His muscles rippled when he typed in my name in the computer.

"Your wife got you Ashley," Barry said, with a knowing smile. "Welcome to the club." I didn't know if Barry was talking about the gym, or some other club. I didn't care, either. A blonde walked out of the Staff Only door, and I couldn't stop staring at her.

She looked like a cross between Wonder Woman and the captain of the girls' volleyball team. She was tanned to a golden brown and wearing a black Spandex sports bra and short-shorts that revealed eye-popping development, front and back.

She had muscles, but she wasn't gnarly and knotted, like those women in the bodybuilding magazines. Ashley was sculpted like a statue. Her breasts were high and round and real. Her eyes were blue-green, like the ocean on a summer day. Her long golden hair rippled in sunlit waves.

"I'm Ashley," she said.

"Jake," I said, which was all I could manage with my stomach sucked in.

Ashley had me work out with what she called light weights. After that, I had to do two hundred push-ups, then run on the sand for two miles.

I went home so exhausted, I fell into bed and slept until the next morning. I missed dinner, but I didn't mind. I dreamed of Ashley, looking like a blonde goddess in black Spandex.

I met with Ashley three times a week. Sometimes I slogged through the sand. Other times, I lifted weights. Always, she barked orders: "Slow down! Watch your form! Point those feet straight ahead. No penguinning!"

I was lying on a slant board while a beautiful blonde yelled at me.

I loved it.

I also loved that all the other guys stared when Ashley and I ran on the sand together. I was the envy of every man on the beach. Even the lifeguards looked at me with new respect.

"How'd you get so lucky to get Ashley?" asked Nick, the bartender at the Beachside Bar.

"My wife bought her for me," I said.

"Yeah, right, and my wife bought me Britney Spears," he said.

Nick didn't believe me. I could scarcely believe it, either.

Ashley had definite ideas about fitness. She wanted me to ditch my Diet Coke for bottled water. "Too many chemicals, dude," she said.

So I laid off the Diet Coke, and started drinking eight bottles of water a day, the way Ashley wanted. I wouldn't tell anyone, but I liked the taste better.

After six weeks, the chicken skin on my arms began to disappear. After eight weeks, my gut began to deflate. Women were giving me the eye again. My Francie started calling me "stud muffin." I hadn't looked this good in twenty years.

"I'm making progress, Ashley," I said. "But I can't seem to lose more weight."

"What are you eating, dude?" she said.

"Not much. That's what is so strange. I skip breakfast and lunch, then eat a big dinner."

She shook her head. "Bad idea. Your body can't run efficiently on no fuel. You're not eating enough."

"That's not what my wife says."

"You need to eat every three to five hours. But you need to eat right," Ashley said, firmly. Everything about her was firm.

She put me on a protein diet. I should have been happy living on mostly meat, but this wasn't what I called meat. Ashley wanted me to eat white meat of chicken and turkey, water-packed tuna, and broiled fish. I could have an egg-white omelet, but no butter or cheese. The only bread was whole wheat, and none of that after three in the afternoon. I could have a baked potato at lunch if I ate the skin, green vegetables like broccoli, and when I was feeling wild, graham crackers. That was it except for cranberry juice and two cups of coffee a day.

"Where's the steak?" I said. "Where's the hamburger?"

"Red meat's bad for you," said Ashley, looking commanding but adorable, like a dominatrix in a porno movie.

"Ashley," I said, "you are what you eat. I am two hundred pounds of red meat. I am a red-blooded male. I need my red meat."

"Mark my words, dude, red meat will kill you," Ashley said. She was right.

But I loved my porterhouses, filet mignons, even flank steaks. Red meat. Bloody meat, oozing deliciously on my plate.

I ate broiled chicken breast, though it tasted like warm Kleenex. I had whole wheat buns, though they were dry as old attic insulation. And egg-white omelets, though they tasted like nothing at all. I drank bottled water until I felt like one long stretch of plumbing. I sweated at Jamal's Jym, with Ashley barking orders, for two months on this dull diet.

I didn't lose an ounce.

"Hmm," said Ashley. "I know this diet can be slow to kick in, but you must be doing something wrong."

She gave me a little notebook and said, "Write down everything you eat each day."

The notebook was her first gift to me. "My diet diary," I joked.

It's amazing how your sins add up. I saw my life as one unending stretch of virtuous eating. I forgot about the jar of cashews I ate at four o'clock, the candy bar I sneaked at six, the occasional steak to break the monotony. I didn't think a little sour cream and butter on a dry baked potato was a big deal. I sure didn't think a couple of drinks were a problem.

But Ashley did. Lord, the lecture that woman gave me when she saw my diet diary.

"Listen, dude," she said. "I thought you were serious about this bodybuilding."

"I am," I said, mesmerized by her pectoral development. She'd built an amazing body.

"Then you've got to get serious about your food," she said, showing me those fat-free buns as she bent over to pick up a pencil. That improved my heart rate, let me tell you.

Ashley graded my diet diary like a kindergarten teacher. The turkey, fish, and egg-white omelets got smiley faces. The red meat got a frownie face. The martinis got "THIS IS TOO MUCH ALCOHOL!!!"

"Ashley, this is like being in prison," I said, because back then I didn't know anything about prison. "Even the doctors say a glass of wine is good for your heart."

"You can have one—only one—glass of wine with dinner," she said, sternly.

I showed Francie the Ashley-corrected diet diary. I thought she would make sarcastic remarks about the smiley faces, but Francie only patted my newly bulging biceps and said, "Ashley has done wonders, Tiger. Listen to her."

I smiled. Those thirty-two smile muscles were the only ones that didn't hurt.

That was something I didn't talk about. I hurt. All over. All the time. I looked better than I had in years, but those toned muscles let me know how they felt about getting back in shape. My shoulders hurt. My torso ached. My legs hurt.

When I say my legs hurt, I mean my calves, thighs, ankles, even my feet were sore. Each part hurt in a different way. My stretched calves were a dull ache. My sore feet were a sharp pain. My glutes shrieked when I sat down.

I was sixty years old, for god's sake. This was too much.

I told Ashley about the constant pain, but she only said, "No whining, dude."

Francie didn't take me seriously, either. "If that's all you have to complain about, you're doing pretty darn good," she said.

I admit all the compliments made me feel better. Take the night we were having an early dinner with four friends (I had to see Ashley at seven the next morning). They showered me with "you-look-terrifics," and "you've-been-working-outs." When I told everyone that Francie had bought me Ashley for my birthday, they could hardly believe it. The guys, Harry and George, winked and nudged each other.

Kaye said, "How do you feel about him working out with a twenty-three-year-old blonde, Francie?"

"Every woman should have an Ashley," she said. "For years, I've been telling him that he eats the wrong food, but would he listen to me? Oh, no, I was just a wife. I was just a nag.

"But when Ashley says he needs to eat more vegetables, it's bring on the broccoli, boys. When Ashley says he's eating too much red meat, he switches to fish and chicken. When Ashley says he drinks too much, he cuts back to one glass of wine a day.

"Could I get him to do that? Not me. I'm only a wife. But Ashley can. That's why every woman should have an Ashley. I wish I'd had her twenty years ago."

Everyone laughed, but I thought I heard a nasty edge. My delight in Ashley diminished just a bit.

I began noticing little things. Like how many times I saw Ashley running on the sand with paunchy guys between forty and sixty. Guys who looked ready to drop from exhaustion. I wanted to talk to them, but Ashley made sure they kept moving. She'd wave at me and never stop. The paunchy guys trotted along beside her.

So I asked her outright: "Those other guys you run with, did their wives buy you as a gift, too?"

Ashley said, "No talking, dude. It breaks your concentration."

Six months into the workout, the pain stopped. That's when I made my final, fatal mistake. I said, "Ashley, it doesn't hurt so much anymore."

I wanted to celebrate. But Ashley said, "Then we need to step up the workouts, dude. We can't have you enjoying yourself. No pain, no gain."

When she said those four stupid words, that was the first time I wanted to strangle her. Then Ashley brought out the blue bands.

They did not look like much: four feet of rubber tubing with triangular handles on the ends. Such simple things, but so many instruments of torture are simple. A simple electric drill in a kneecap can cause excruciating pain. A simple tire iron can break every bone in your body.

Ashley's exercise bands tripled my misery. She made me wrap them around a palm tree and pull them, while I held my hands and feet at impossible angles. We'd—no, I'd—work out in humiliating poses while fat red tourists, buttered with coconut oil, stood around and laughed.

"Come on, dude, work harder," Ashley would command. "Pull! Pull! Pull!"

I would pull until my arms quivered and my neck ached, but it was never enough for her. "Come on, you're not crippled," she would scream, entertaining the slug-butt tourists.

I smiled through my pain, but that night I went out and had a Diet Coca-Cola. Then I wrote it defiantly in my diet diary. It was my way of getting even. Diet Coke upset Ashley more than beer. She said beer at least had some natural ingredients. "Diet soda is nothing but chemicals, dude."

I felt ashamed when I drank my Diet Coke. I used to down martinis and single malt scotch. Now I was chugging Diet Cokes—and worse, feeling guilty. All because of Ashley.

I couldn't even get any satisfaction in my rebellion. Ashley only said, "You've come a long way, dude. Who'd have thought an old boozer like you would be sneaking sodas and feeling guilty about it?"

Then she laughed. The cords in her short, powerful neck stood out, ugly as tree roots. I was so mad, I wanted to kill her.

That night, I dreamed I strangled Ashley with one of her own exercise bands. I knew it was time to stop.

Next day at the gym I asked, "Did my wife buy you for one year?"

"A year? No, your wife got the deluxe package, dude. This is a life sentence." She smiled, but her mouth was harder than Arnold Schwarzenegger's abs.

"Life?" I said. I felt the prison doors closing on me. I would never know another pain-free day. I would never eat another steak without feeling guilty. I wouldn't even drink another sinless soda.

"Look, Ashley," I said. "This has been fun, but it's time to stop. It's been a year. Refund Francie her money and I'll go quietly. I'm sick of all this good health."

"Can't, dude," she said. "No refunds. Francie knew that when she paid up-front."

"Well, I'm sorry she'll lose her money," I said. "But I quit."

It felt good when I said that. I wanted my old life back, and if my old body came back with it, so be it. Maybe I didn't used to look good, but I felt good.

I saw myself ordering one of Nick's straight-up martinis with an oily slick of vermouth and a sliver of lemon peel. Then I'd have a long wet lunch of red wine and rare steak. Red meat for a red-blooded male.

"Quit?" said Ashley, and her lip curled. Even her blonde hair curled in contempt.

"What will you tell everyone? That you're not man enough to keep me? The whole beach knows we work out. Stop now, and I'll tell everyone you weren't tough enough to work out with a *girl*."

I remembered all those lifeguards and beach bums grinning as I made my proud progress on the sand, Ashley at my side. I remembered Nick the bartender's envy. I saw my friends at dinner, nudging each other. I'd never be able to explain how tired I felt. I'd be a laughingstock.

I'd been given a blonde for my birthday and I was too tired to enjoy her.

"I don't care!" I said.

Jamal came over then. I guess we'd been talking louder than I thought.

"Anything wrong?" he said, looming over me like a mountain.

I shook my head. I was too tired to do anything else. I hurt in places I didn't know I had.

I showed up as usual for my next session. I was tied to Ashley until death parted us. For the first time, I actually looked forward to keeling over on the sand. Eternal rest took on new meaning.

Now that I couldn't escape her, everything Ashley did irritated me. I hated that she called me "dude." I couldn't stand those silly smiley faces in my diet diary. Not that I saw many. I was not only drinking Diet Cokes, I was piling mayonnaise on my grilled chicken—at six fat grams a spoonful. Yet now I didn't gain weight.

"Can't you just lie like everyone else?" Ashley said, as she read my acts of dietary defiance. We were working out on the empty, sun-bleached beach.

"Who's everyone else?" I said, furious at all the frownie faces.

"The other guys whose wives bought me. I'm a paid nag, dude. It's my job to buff up the old boys, tell them to eat their vegetables and drink less. Wives pay me well so they don't have to say those things."

"You mean my wife . . . My wife knew that you . . ." I could hardly breathe, I was so angry. Ashley ignored my anger, just as she ignored my pain. She kept hitting me with her taunts. Each one was another slam to my tortured body.

"They all do. Every woman in Sunnysea would love to have me, but not the way you would. They know old guys are suckers for sweet young things." She laughed, a cruel, cutting laugh.

"That's what I am—one of your suckers?" I'd never felt more humiliated. Ashley didn't notice that, either. She handed me the hated exercise bands.

"Hey, don't bust a gasket, dude," she said, still laughing. "It's not your fault you can't get it up, old man. Energywise, I mean. Let's work on your upper body strength."

"It's fine," I said, wrapping the blue band around her neck and squeezing as hard as I could. I kept my elbows at a perfect ninety-degree angle. I kept my knees slightly bent to support my lower back. I kept my feet straight out, not splayed to either side, so Ashley couldn't say "no penguinning."

Ashley couldn't say anything. She was gagging, gasping, and clawing at her neck. She was strong, but I was stronger. I had another eighty pounds of solid muscle. She'd worked hard to build my arms. I pulled the band tighter. Her struggles grew more frantic. Her legs kicked futilely. I kept pulling, all the pain and rage I'd endured strangling my reason.

Ashley stopped struggling.

She was dead.

Slowly, I became aware of my surroundings again. I'd strangled a woman to death on Sunnysea Beach at two in the afternoon. I was fifty feet from a lifeguard cabana. But the guard, whose head was as thick as his neck, was staring at three squealing kids hitting one another with boogie boards. He didn't notice us.

The storm-shuttered windows of the WaterEdge condo were blind, too.

Even the tourists weren't out on the boardwalk in this heat.

If I'd lost my temper in the high season of December, some cop would be reading me my rights. But this was July. In Florida, on a summer weekday, the beaches could be as empty as a gym rat's head.

No one saw me. I was lucky. Better yet, I got out of half my class.

But how long would my luck last? I couldn't leave her there. Everyone at Jamal's Jym knew I worked out with Ashley at this time.

My condo was a mile away. No way could I carry her body there. How was I going to get Ashley off the beach?

Don't panic, I told myself. Think.

I unwound the blue band from around Ashley's throat and shoved it in my pocket. Her face looked awfully red. I put my sweat towel down on the sand, then put Ashley on top of it, lying on her stomach. I turned her head so her long hair covered most of her face. I put my water bottle near her head, to further block the view of her face. If you didn't look too close, she seemed to be napping on the beach.

No one noticed me doing this. More luck. I ran all the way home and got my car. A 1997 Lincoln has lots of room.

I found a meter, another lucky break, and parked a block from where Ashley was on the sand. I only had a quarter, which buys fifteen minutes in Sunnysea.

Now came the hard part, getting Ashley off the beach and into the car. I knelt down on the sand, and shook Ashley gently, pretending that I was waking her from a sound sleep. Then I talked to her, as if she could hear me. I wanted it to look like she was my daughter or my girlfriend, and she was a little sun-sick or tipsy.

I rolled her over on her back, then sat her up. She leaned against me. Her right arm flopped back down and nearly dented my quads. Her face looked swollen and awful, but her hair was hanging down, covering it. I got behind her, put my arms under her pits, and pulled her into a standing position.

I now knew what a real deadweight lift was. What did Ashley weigh? One hundred twenty pounds max? She felt like two hundred. I got her up and leaned her against me. She was oddly rubbery, but more cooperative than usual.

I draped her right arm over my shoulder and put my arm around her waist. She leaned against me like a drunk. That was good. I had a little spiel ready. "Out cold," I planned to say, with an indulgent smile. "Too many piña coladas."

I didn't see a soul when I carried Ashley to the car. It was my lucky day. I didn't even mind the ten-dollar parking ticket on my windshield. It was a small price to pay.

I opened the back door, and Ashley fell into the seat. She hit her head with a nasty THWAK! She didn't feel a thing, but I was hurting. She'd strained my already sore muscles. Soon those muscles would never hurt again.

But now I had to get rid of Ashley's body. I wasn't going to risk the ocean—it's too shallow here, unless you get about three miles out into the Gulf Stream. The canals were too risky for the same reason. But if I drove west, I'd be in the Everglades. The "river of grass," they call it. It was full of alligators. Perfect. I wondered if the gators would find Ashley as tough as I did. I smiled at the thought.

I was on Highway 27, which ran along the edge of the Everglades, in about an hour. I turned down a gravel road, bumping past a dusty-looking ranch and then a palm tree farm. The road petered out in the sawgrass, mud, and murky water that mark the start of the Everglades. They don't call it sawgrass for nothing. That stuff can literally slice your arm off.

I wrestled Ashley out of the car. I was sweating like a hog. I dragged her into the water, ignoring the mosquito stings and the sawgrass slashes on my arms and legs. The water was shallow and tea-colored. I didn't want to think about what was in there.

I looked for some big rocks to sink the body. But when I got back with my first rock, Ashley was gone. A few seconds later I heard a loud plop! It was an alligator, sliding into the water. My own stomach plopped a bit at the thought, but I knew Ashley was gone for good. I wouldn't have to worry about anyone finding the body.

I was home long before Francie got off work. She found me on the couch watching *You Only Live Twice*, sipping single malt, and eating salted cashews.

"Jake!" she said, surprised. "What would Ashley say?"

"Not a damn thing," I said cheerfully. "She's taking a long rest. So am I."

The scotch made my tongue slip. Francie didn't seem to know what my remark meant, but I'd have to be more careful. I'd have to make sure to go to Jamal's Jym at my regular time Thursday.

I didn't get a chance. Two police detectives, one fat and one skinny, were on my doorstep the next day. They told me Ashley's body was found in the Everglades by a fisherman. Jamal said I was her last appointment, and she never came back. No one had seen her alive since two o'clock yesterday.

I wondered why that alligator had not taken care of my problem, but I didn't say anything. I was cool. I told the cops that Ashley and I worked out as usual. The last I saw, Ashley was running south on the sand to Jamal's. I was headed north, toward my home. I may have sweated a little when I said this, but it was July, wasn't it? The detectives finally left. They seemed satisfied with my answers.

They were back the next day. The fat one asked me to describe my last afternoon with Ashley again. I said we'd worked out on the beach, then I ran home and she ran off the other way.

"You ran home?" the fat cop said.

"All the way," I said, smugly.

"Then why did your car get a parking ticket on the beach about the time that Ashley disappeared?" the skinny one said.

"Uh," I said, and shut up until my lawyer showed up. The cops got a warrant and impounded my car. I wasn't worried. I'd taken it to a carwash.

But the police found three of Ashley's long blonde hairs in the back seat and her sandy footprint on the inside door. I'd tipped the carwash guy ten bucks, too. Good help is hard to find in Florida.

There was no point in claiming we'd had a little afternoon delight back there because the police found traces of some nasty substances on the seat. The body sort of lets go, you know. No, I guess you wouldn't. You've never killed anyone.

The cops also found plenty of motive. Jamal testified that I'd had a "bitter quarrel"—his words—with Ashley at the gym and tried to get out of the contract.

My wife told the court about my strange behavior on the last day Ashley was seen. I couldn't believe my Francie would do that.

The jury, which was mostly men, couldn't understand how I could kill that gorgeous blonde. They didn't understand she was killing me.

So here I am on death row in Florida. Today is my last day on earth. The chaplain asked if I was sorry.

I am.

I am very sorry I didn't come up with a better body disposal plan. You can't depend on alligators. They don't really like humans, and only eat them if they're desperate or disturbed. It's crocodiles who find us tasty. I learned that in the prison library. I had a lot of time to read while my appeals were being denied.

The warden served up the final irony.

"You can have anything you want for your last meal, Jake," he said. "Even steak."

I couldn't stop laughing when he said that. I remembered what Ashley had said: "Mark my words, dude, red meat will kill you."

That's all we are. Red meat.

And Ashley's one hundred twenty pounds of red meat killed me.

Elaine Viets

SEX AND BINGO

■ ■ ■

Elaine Viet's second story, "Sex and Bingo," was published in the gambling anthology High Stakes, *and takes the reader and a hapless woman looking for work on an idyllic tropical cruise that is anything but.*

It was a summer of sex and bingo.

Where Helen came from, bingo had nothing to do with sex. In her hometown of St. Louis, bingo was a game for women gamblers. They were serious and gray-haired. Stick cigars in their mouths, and they'd look like the men who played high-stakes poker.

But on a cruise ship, everything was different. Even bingo.

Serious bingo was silent as a church, except for the intoning of the numbers and the hallelujah cry of "Bingo!" Here bingo players chattered like flocks of parrots.

Real bingo players would sneer at these frivolous women who played one card. Serious players could handle ten or fifteen cards.

Only one thing was serious about cruise-ship bingo: the money.

Twenty thousand dollars was the grand prize on this cruise. That was more money than Helen made in a year. And Helen couldn't win a dime. She worked on the *Caribbean Wave,* and cruise-ship employees were not eligible for bingo prizes.

But Helen was sure there was a scam. She knew an employee had walked away with a ten-thousand-dollar bingo prize on the last cruise. Now he was going to double his money and go for twenty grand.

She knew it, and she couldn't prove it. She was totally at sea, in all senses of the word.

Helen knew who to blame for that: her landlady at the Coronado Tropic Apartments. Good old Margery Flax.

Seven weeks ago, Helen had been exhausted by the discouraging job of looking for work in Fort Lauderdale. One night, as Helen trudged back to her apartment, hot, sweaty, dejected, and rejected, she was met by her landlady. Margery was wearing purple, as usual. Her purple shorts were spattered with red starbursts. Her red toenails were spattered with purple stars. The Florida sun had turned Margery's face as wrinkled and brown as an old lunch sack, but she had good legs, and liked to show them off.

"How'd you like to get paid to go on a Caribbean cruise?" Margery had said. Her landlady had on her best sweet old lady face. Helen was instantly suspicious. There was nothing sweet or old about Margery, even if she was seventy-six.

"I'd love it. I'd also like a million bucks, but there's no chance of that, either."

"But I can get you the cruise. My friend, Jane Gilbert, manages the fancy clothing boutique on the *Caribbean Wave* cruise ship. It's part of the Royal Wave cruise line, the best in the world. The service is superb. And the food . . . what are you living on these days? Peanut butter?"

"Scrambled eggs. Ninety-nine cents a dozen," Helen said. "I get six meals out of a carton."

"And a cholesterol count in the stratosphere," Margery said. She was puffing on a Marlboro. "Listen, take the cruise, and help out my friend. Jane broke her leg and won't be back in action for three months. Jobs on a cruise ship are hard to come by. Jane needs someone to take her job who won't take her job, if you know what I mean. I said you'd be perfect. You'll get room and board and make four hundred dollars a month. Cash." At the word "cash," Margery expelled a huge cloud of smoke. Helen waved it away.

Helen always worked for cash. It made her harder to trace.

"But, Margery—" Helen said.

"And commission," Margery cut her off. "You'll get a commission, too. There are some high rollers on those cruise ships. When they win in the casino, they buy big." More smoke.

"But, Margery, what will I do about my apartment here?"

"You won't have to pay any rent. My sister Cora's latest marriage just broke up. She wants to stay with me for a few months while she gets another face-lift. I can put her up at your place."

Margery was still blowing smoke, but suddenly it was all clear. Margery needed a place to put the much-divorced Cora, who she usually called "my obnoxious sister, Cora." In fact, Helen thought Cora's first name was Obnoxious. Helen wouldn't have been surprised if Margery had tripped Jane and broken her leg, just so Helen would go to sea and leave her apartment for Cora.

Helen took the job. She had no choice. She needed the money.

She'd only been on board the *Caribbean Wave* two days when she realized she wasn't being paid to take a cruise. She was being paid to stand ten hours on a hard tile floor. After a day in the shop, her feet hurt, no matter how sensible her shoes. Helen wore support hose, but she could feel the spider veins breaking out on her legs. When the sea was rough, the merchandise swayed and danced on the hangers and Helen's stomach shifted and lurched. The walls seemed to close in on her. It was worse in her room. Her inside cabin was the size of a coffin but not as plush.

But Helen loved the sea. She could stare at the ocean for hours. Some days it was the green of old Chinese jade. Other times, it was a brilliant turquoise with dark purple patches. On rainy days it looked like wrinkled gray silk, and when it stormed the water swelled and roiled like it was on to boil.

Today was a turquoise day. It was also her day off. Helen sat in a deck chair with a fat paperback, alternately staring at the ocean and reading about a woman who murdered her unfaithful husband. Helen hoped she got away with it.

She still remembered how murderous she'd felt the day she'd come home from work early and found her husband Rob with their neighbor, Sandy. Rob had always claimed he didn't like Sandy, but he could have fooled Helen with that liplock. In fact, he had fooled her. That's why Helen picked up the crowbar and . . . well, never mind. The crowbar made such a satisfying crunching sound. It was one reason why Helen had to leave St. Louis abruptly and change her name. She could no longer make six figures as an employee benefits director in a big corporation. She'd be too easy to find. Instead, Helen had to take a series of dead-end jobs that paid cash and kept her out of the computers. She rarely made more than $6.70 an hour. But if she had to do it all over again, she'd still do it all over again.

On a cruise ship, nobody cared that she was on the run. Everyone was running from something: old debts, old lovers, old lives. Nobody cared what she did, period. The seventies' hedonism wasn't dead. It had sailed away on the cruise ships. There were old drugs, new drugs, everything from pot to heroin and beyond. There was every combination of sex Helen could imagine, and some she couldn't.

Helen enjoyed the free atmosphere, but she didn't indulge. Drugs made her muzzy-headed. Love made her stupid. She was still recovering from a romance gone wrong. She'd made yet another bad choice in men, and she didn't trust her judgment. For this cruise, she was a noncombatant in the war of the sexes.

Helen just wanted to read her book and stare at the ocean. Now a huge shadow blocked her view.

"What's a pretty little thing like you doing reading that great big book?" said a good old boy voice. Actually, it sounded like, "Wad's uh purdy lil thang lack yew . . ."

Helen gave the guy her patented St. Louis glare, which could singe the hide off a rhino. It had no effect on him. He sat down next to her. He was cute, if you liked men who liked dumb women. He looked like Tom Sawyer, all grown up. His face was lean, tanned, and freckled. His hair was silky blond. One curl hung down over his eye. Nice muscular body. Friendly smile that stopped at his mean slitty eyes.

"Name's Jimmy," he said, extending a thick tanned hand highlighted with little golden hairs. "You're new. You work at the boutique. I'm the bar manager and bingo caller."

"I'm Helen," she said, leaving the hand dangling, untouched. "Even though I'm a woman, I can read and write."

"Aww, now don't take offense. It's just that somebody with those long legs shouldn't be wasting her time cuddling up to a book."

"I like smart things," Helen said, sticking her nose back in her book. Even Jimmy should get that hint.

He did. "You know pretty boxes kept on the shelf too long get so's nobody wants them anymore." His country-boy smile brimmed with malice.

"Beat it," Helen said. "Before I report you for sexual harassment."

"Plenty of ladies are happy to be harassed by me," Jimmy said.

"Can any of them read?" Helen said.

"Don't need to. What I teach them makes 'em forget all about books." Jimmy grinned, but it stopped before it reached his eyes. Then he walked off.

The creep was gone. But Helen's ocean view was still blocked. This obstruction was much better. It was Derreck, a muscle-bound cabin steward. Derreck looked like a god. Unfortunately for the women, he was a Greek god. Derreck was gay.

"I see you met the ship's legendary ladies' man," he said.

"That's him? He's disgusting."

"The small-town ladies from Michigan and Minnesota love him."

"I'd rather be marooned on a desert isle."

"I guess I better warn you about the Italian waiters, too. They're very macho and great womanizers. Don't tick them off. The waiters control access to the passenger food.

If you're ever hungry for a steak, the waiters can provide it—but you may have to provide something back."

"I lived on eggs for two months before I got this job," Helen said. "I can do without steak."

"I'm just trying to explain how a cruise ship works. Jimmy, as the bar manager, is an important person. His cabin has recessed speakers and other luxuries, all provided by thirsty staffers."

"Power I can understand. But I don't see how that slob scores with the women. Do you find him attractive?" Helen said.

"He's not my type," Derreck said, and shrugged.

"Is it true he has a new romance with a passenger every cruise, and most are married women?"

Derreck sighed. "Helen, Helen. You can take the girl out of the Midwest, but you can't take the Midwest out of the girl. Jimmy provides a public service. Our female passengers want a fling on their cruise. They also want it to be over when the cruise is over. They'll never see Jimmy again and he'll never see them. He gives them a nice guilt-free romance. You know, ships that pass in the night."

"One of those ships is going to hit an iceberg," she said.

"I doubt it. Jimmy excels at three shipboard activities: bartending, bingo calling, and banging passengers. He's never made a mistake in ten years."

"There's always a first time."

"What time is the midnight buffet?" asked a chunky gentleman in a red shirt splashed with parrots and palm leaves. He was about sixty, and looked like he was wearing a tropical disease.

"Twelve A.M.," Helen answered with a straight face.

The guy was buying the boutique's gaudiest cruisewear, so she was very respectful. Not only did she get a commission, she got the ugliest stock out of the shop. Mr. Shirt had won big at the blackjack tables and now he was showering his girlfriend with gifts.

"She's my little gold good-luck charm," he said, patting her round gold bottom. "I call her Lucky, and I plan to get Lucky all the time."

Lucky giggled.

The pint-sized blonde was definitely attracted to gold. Everything she chose shimmered and glittered, from the Gucci evening gown to the Armani jogging suit. Lucky was one of those women who looked like a knockout at first glance. She had a fabulous figure and blond hair to her waist. On second glance, she wasn't quite so stunning. Despite the clever makeup, her eyes were small and squinty, as if she used a jeweler's loupe to figure out the value of everything. Her lips were thin and her long blond hair was brassy and bristling with split ends. But she was built, no doubt about it.

Mr. Shirt kept patting her, as if to reassure himself she wouldn't disappear. Helen figured Lucky would stick with him as long as he had money.

"These platforms are cute. Do you have them in gold?" Lucky said. The shoe soles were the size of paving stones, but they looked sexy on her tiny feet. Helen noticed her toenails were painted gold.

"Let me check in the back." A quick glance told Helen there were no platforms in the small stockroom.

"I'll go look in the big storage room down the hall," Helen said.

"No problem. There are lots of clothes to try on here." Lucky held a black-and-gold beaded crop top to her jutting chest. Mr. Shirt beamed as if she'd done something clever.

Helen unlocked the storage room and nearly dropped the keys in surprise. She hadn't seen Jimmy since their encounter on deck at the beginning of the cruise. Now she saw more of him than she wanted. Jimmy was wrapped around a slender brunette passenger. She was moaning and writhing under him. He was lowering her to a table bolted to the floor.

The woman's white linen skirt was hiked up and her long dark hair had tumbled loose from its seashell clip. She had a wide gold wedding band on her left hand. Jimmy's large red hands were working their way across the woman's bare back, like two crabs on a beach. They had nearly reached the string on her green halter top. The woman's face was turned away from the door, but Jimmy saw Helen and gave that flat-eyed grin. The woman didn't notice her.

Helen found the gold shoes and tiptoed out. She returned to the boutique a little rattled, and talked too much to cover her confusion.

"So," she said to Lucky, "do you ever use that luck for yourself? Do you gamble?"

"Nah, she plays bingo," said Mr. Shirt, answering for her.

"That's gambling," Lucky pouted.

"Bingo is an old ladies' game," Mr. Shirt said.

"It is not! The last game of the cruise is at three this afternoon. It's a ten-thousand-dollar jackpot. So there. That's real money. You can see just how Lucky I am. Are you going to be there?" she asked Helen.

"You're wasting your time," Mr. Shirt said. "Blackjack is real gambling. Nobody with brains plays bingo."

If he hadn't said that, Helen might have skipped the bingo game. Now she felt it was a matter of sisterly solidarity.

"I can't play, but I'll watch," Helen said, thinking that described her life these days.

Helen missed lunch so she could take an hour for bingo. At two fifty-five, she put out the ON BREAK sign, and went to the Sea Star Lounge. It was packed with bingo players.

Helen sat in the back, sipped coffee, and talked with Trevor, the Bahamian bartender. Helen loved to listen to Trevor. He had the most beautiful accent.

Then Lucky flounced in, dressed in a tight gold-braided Escada pantsuit. She bought a bingo card and sat next to Helen. Jimmy got up onstage and told corny jokes like a third-rate comic: "You know why mice have such small balls? Because they don't dance."

The women lapped it up like cats with a saucer of cream. Finally he said, "You all ready to win?" At last he was calling the numbers. "I-18. B-4."

Lucky squealed. "That's two. See. I am lucky."

She had a long way to go. The grand prize was for a cover-all, all twenty-four numbers on the card.

Helen watched, comparing this game to bingo back home. Helen learned the game at the old city bingo halls in St. Louis. Her aunt Gertrude babysat on Sunday afternoon. Gert was supposed to take Helen someplace educational, like the zoo or the planetarium, but Gert and Helen were bored with them. Instead, Helen got an education in the bingo halls.

She learned to keep her mouth shut. If she said a word about their Sunday bingo games, she and Gert would really have to go to the zoo.

She learned to lie. Helen would come home babbling about the baby penguins or the star show until her parents tuned her out.

She learned that sometimes you had to take a risk. Gert lived mainly on her Social Security money. When she lost at bingo, she ate chicken necks until the next check. When her aunt won the five-hundred-dollar jackpot, she would have new slipcovers for the couch and filet mignon at Tony's, the best restaurant in St. Louis. She'd never get those on Social Security.

Helen learned that sin was more fun than virtue. Her mother made her eat sugar-free cereal, vegetables, and drink her milk. Her well-padded aunt let her have hot dogs, greasy fries, a chunk of chocolate cake the size of Gert's purse, and all the Coke she wanted.

Helen would sit and sip and watch. When she was seven, Gert got Helen her own bingo card. Helen attributed her number-crunching abilities to the reverent way the bingo callers said the numbers. B-6. G-54. N-43. You knew these numbers were important. They could change lives. They meant the difference between chicken necks and steak.

This cruise-ship game didn't seem like bingo to Helen. Bingo gamblers did not wear size-two Escada. Aunt Gert wore a JCPenney dress the size of a pup tent and smelled of Evening in Paris. She'd never touch the cute candy-colored bingo chips Lucky used to cover her numbers. Serious players like Aunt Gert used daubers, which were sort of like highlighter pens. Daubers were quicker than picking up little chips. Gert could handle fifteen cards per game.

Serious bingo players didn't say they were lucky. They brought their own luck. Gert had an orange-haired troll, a St. Christopher medal, and a plastic poodle lined up by her cards. She kept them in a purple velvet Crown Royal bag.

Serious players would never tolerate Jimmy, the jokey country-boy caller. Aunt Gert would have stomped out by now—or stomped Jimmy.

There were so many differences between cruise-ship bingo and real bingo, Helen couldn't keep track of them all. Her list was interrupted by Lucky's joyful shriek.

"O-66!" Jimmy called.

"Two more to go and I have bingo," Lucky said. "I hope someone else doesn't get it first."

"I doubt it," Helen said. "Jimmy's only called forty numbers."

Lucky looked at her curiously. "How do you know?" she said.

"I'm good with numbers, and I played bingo every Sunday with my aunt. A cover-all for a small crowd like this will take at least fifty-five to fifty-nine numbers."

"Bingo!" shouted a woman.

"Yeah, you really know bingo," said Lucky sarcastically.

But Helen did know bingo. It was technically possible, but highly improbable, to have a cover-all winner when only forty numbers were called. That bingo was either a scam or a mistake.

She'd seen a scam once. It had caused a huge scandal at St. Philomena's church. An investigation showed the crooked bingo caller was splitting the pot with her best friend. The pastor was so disgusted, he banned bingo for a full year.

Aunt Gert never went back. "Gambling is a matter of trust," she said. "When that's broken, it can't be fixed. Something is wrong there."

Something was wrong here, too.

A staffer who'd been holding up the back wall rushed to the winner's wildly waving hand. He began calling back the numbers. "And the last one is O-66," he said.

"That's it!" Jimmy said. "Congratulations, darling, you're the big winner. Step up here to get your jackpot prize of ten thousand dollars."

"Who won the money?" Lucky said.

Helen could see a woman pushing her way through the crowd to the stage. The winner had dark hair caught up in a seashell clip, a white linen skirt, a green halter top, and a gold wedding ring.

It was the woman who'd been in the storeroom with Jimmy.

"It's a scam," Helen said to Derreck that night. "Sure as I'm sitting here."

They were drinking in the crew bar above the rope deck, which was really the poop deck. Royal Wave ships did not use the word *poop*. Crew bar prices were cheap and the ship's staff sailed on an ocean of booze, except for the ones in dry dock at the onboard AA meetings.

Derreck was drinking with Helen to avoid a different temptation. The hunky cabin steward was in a committed relationship with Jon, a graphic artist in Miami, and didn't want to flirt with the crew.

"Are you sure?" Derreck said. "You don't like Jimmy. And it is possible to win after forty numbers." His jutting jaw was cleft, like George of the Jungle's. The man was ridiculously, heart-stoppingly handsome.

"What's the possibility that his current squeeze would win?" Helen said.

Derreck widened his already big blue eyes. "Really? The little redhead on the Panorama Deck won ten thousand bucks?"

"What redhead?" Helen said. "This was a brunette."

"Then you got it wrong," Derreck said. "He picked up a redhead this cruise. A schoolteacher from Akron. Divorced, cute, and a little naive, just the way Jimmy likes them."

"Oh, yeah? I caught him doing the wild thing with a married brunette, about an hour before the bingo game in the stockroom."

"Interesting," Derreck said, and took a thoughtful sip of his beer.

"I thought the crew couldn't fraternize with the passengers," Helen said. "I sure got a lecture on that subject."

"Well, they can and they can't," Derreck said. "Technically, the staff is forbidden. In reality, affairs by officers and uniformed staff like Jimmy are tolerated, but deckhands and belowstairs help would be instantly dismissed. It's sort of an upstairs-downstairs thing. You know, a Victorian lady could have a fling with her handsome footman, but heaven help her if she was caught with the bootblack.

"There is one unbreakable rule: No one on staff can take a passenger to his or her room. The cruise line put up cameras all over the crew sleeping areas to watch us. Cut the rape complaints way back."

"So where do the crew and passengers meet, besides my stockroom?" Helen said.

"Well, there are the lifeboats. We're always finding used condoms and wine bottles in the lifeboats. The top decks are another trysting place."

"I thought the security guards did rounds up there," Helen said.

"They do. Every thirty-five or forty minutes. They're easy to time. You just wait till the guard passes. Then you have at least half an hour."

"Are you speaking from personal experience?" Helen said.

"Not lately," Derreck said, and virtuously finished his beer.

"The crew has one more choice. In most ports there are fleabag hotels that rent rooms on an hourly basis. Want another wine?"

"No, thanks. How do you keep those flat abs when you drink beer?" Helen said.

"Beer has food value. It's made of all natural ingredients, malt, grain, and hops."

Derreck went for another beer. Helen stared out into the ocean's infinite emptiness. There was nothing, not even the lights of another ship. It did not make her feel lonely. She felt secure. No one could find her out here in this blackness.

Derreck returned with his beer and Helen returned to the subject of sex and bingo. "Why isn't the cruise director calling bingo? I thought that was his job."

"Because Jimmy's popular with the passengers and the cruise director is more interested in pleasing them than playing power games. Listen, even if Jimmy is guilty, how can you prove it?"

"I can't," Helen said. "Not this time. The cruise is nearly over. It was only seven days. We'll be back in Fort Lauderdale tomorrow. I'm going to watch him this next cruise."

"If he's crooked, that one is the big bait. It's twenty-one days, with at least twelve days at sea. Lots of sea days means more bingo games for the bored passengers and a big jackpot prize. Twenty thousand dollars."

Helen whistled. Aunt Gert would have thought she'd died and gone to heaven if she played bingo on a cruise ship with a prize that big. Gert had been dead for years, and Helen hoped she was playing bingo in some celestial hall with angel callers and golden daubers.

"Is there that much money in cruise-ship bingo?" she said.

"Gambling is big business on cruises," he said. "Along with bingo, there's Caribbean stud poker and the progressive slots. There's money in those, too, and cruise ships get a break the casinos don't. Casino jackpots have to keep going up each time the slots are played. Ships can roll the progressive slots back down after each voyage. Casinos can't get away with that."

Derreck's second beer was almost gone, but he still had questions. "Here's what I don't get: How do you cheat at bingo? It's basically a lottery. Is he fixing the numbers or what?"

"I'm not sure," Helen said. "I think he's getting his ladies to work with him somehow. I have a theory he has two girlfriends, one for show and one on the QT. That's the one he's cheating with. But this is a different game of bingo than I'm used to. These players are not all that sophisticated. It would be easy to get things past them. It's not right. Will you help me nail him?"

"Might as well," Derreck said. "Now that I'm faithful to Jon, I have lots of time for a cheater."

How was Jimmy doing it? That was the question.

How did that bingo scam work at St. Philomena's all those years ago? She couldn't ask her long-dead aunt. Helen couldn't call anyone in her family. Only her sister knew where she was, and Kathy couldn't tell a bingo dauber from a mud dauber. Aunt Gert's illicit bingo excursions took place before she was born, but Kathy would have never participated. She was a straight arrow.

The twenty-one-day Ultimate Caribbean Adventure embarked from Fort Lauderdale, and sailed the eastern and western Caribbean. Lucky and Mr. Shirt were replaced by other couples, some married, some not. There was the usual collection of single and divorced women, hoping for a shipboard romance, as well as older people enjoying the good meals and sea air.

The ship had barely reached Nassau, in the Bahamas, before Jimmy was flirting with a giggly little CPA who had a face like a china doll and thick, muscular dancer's legs. The CPA, whose name was Emma, must have been very good with money. She was staying in an eight-thousand-dollar Royal Wave suite with two oceanview windows, a king-size bed, and a Jacuzzi. Jimmy courted her with free drinks and bottles of wine at dinner. She giggled at his corny jokes.

Derreck pointed her out to Helen. "That's Emma, Jimmy's pick this cruise."

"That's his show girl," Helen said. "If he's running the same scam as last time, then he'll have someone else stashed in the background."

"That's going to be the tough part," Derreck said. "Keeping the second one secret. A cruise ship is worse than a small town. We all know each other's business. Speaking of which, Lordes, the Vista Deck maid, told me that guy that nobody wants to sit next to because of his awful BO doesn't shower. He hasn't touched a bath towel since the cruise started and his shower is dry as a bone."

"Sometimes," Helen said, "you can have too much information."

Working the boutique, Helen met most of the women onboard. She listened while they talked about their husbands, boyfriends, and exes. The Royal Wave operated on a cashless card system, and that seemed to encourage spending. Helen was fascinated. Before she'd picked up that crowbar, she spent as carelessly as they did. But now that she was on the run, she'd grown used to living on dead-end job money, six-seventy an hour or less. She'd learned to watch her pennies.

Nobody bought anything because they needed it. Men bought clothes for women to show off their own power. Neglected wives bought expensive outfits to punish their husbands. Women bought to celebrate a special occasion, get even with their man, or because they were on vacation and had to buy something. Emma the CPA spent lavishly, treating herself to delicate designs and light colors that flattered her china-doll face.

Occasionally, someone would lose too much in the casino, and then the trophy buys would have to be returned. Helen dreaded those times. The loud silences, unshed tears, the pulsating, palpable embarrassment nearly crowded her out of the room.

She listened carefully for the women to mention Jimmy, but they never did, not even Emma. He was a servant, part of the ship's fittings. She watched the storeroom like a cat watched a mousehole, but Jimmy never went near it.

He's too smart for that, Helen thought. He knows I know. He's found another hiding place. That would be easy. Cruise ships had more hiding places than the mountains of Afghanistan.

She followed him when he went ashore at San Juan, St. Thomas (which the crew staff called St. Toilet), and Georgetown on Grand Cayman Island. He did all the things the other crew members did. He ate in little local restaurants away from the crowds. He stopped at American fast-food places because traveling made you crave Big Macs and KFC, even if you rarely ate them at home. He drank in the bars and went for walks. Sometimes he took the giggly CPA with him, and sometimes he didn't.

"He's sticking with Emma. I've never caught him with another woman passenger," she complained to Derreck.

"Jimmy has become your great white whale," Derreck said. "You're following him like Captain Ahab." Derreck laughed when he said that, but Helen saw the concern in his eyes. Following Jimmy became an obsession.

"Helen, why are you doing this? You know the cruise line won't reward you if you discover Jimmy's fraud," he said. "They don't appreciate having their eyes opened to unpleasant things."

She knew that. But she couldn't stop.

"I'm tracking him for women like Lucky, who didn't know they were being cheated," she said righteously. Derreck gave her the fish eye but said nothing else.

Helen knew in her secret heart that she hated Jimmy and she hated cheaters. Jimmy was one of the destroyers, the men who preyed on unhappy women and shaky marriages. She thought again of her husband Rob, who'd made such a fool of her with their neighbor Sandy. That's why she wanted Jimmy, and that's why she was going to get him.

At first Helen was afraid that Jimmy might realize she was following him. But then she realized when the cruise ships docked in these Caribbean ports, they flooded the little towns with tourists. Crew members met one another coming and going. If she ran into Jimmy on a side street, well, she was trying to escape the crowds just like he was. She simply nodded coldly and kept walking.

Helen met Derreck in the crew bar the night before they docked in Cozumel, Mexico. She'd made no progress.

"I'm getting desperate," Helen said. "We only have two more ports."

"Something is going to happen," Derreck said. "Emma the CPA was giggling even more than usual."

Helen wanted to ask Derreck to go with her on the next shore trip, but he seemed distracted. He was suspiciously silent on the subject of Jon.

This time, Helen followed Emma off the ship instead of Jimmy. Some of the passengers went on the shore excursions. Others headed for the duty-free shops. Helen wondered how much Lalique, Royal Doulton, and Waterford people could look at.

Emma stayed by herself. The CPA wandered through T-shirt shops and souvenir stands, getting farther and farther from the cruise-ship crowd. Helen lost track of Emma in a shop that sold onyx bookends and coconut carvings. Half a block later, she spotted Emma again, but she was no longer alone. She was hanging on to Jimmy as if he were the last lifeboat on the *Titanic.*

The couple went to a dingy little hotel, blocks away from the bright new tourist hotels that lined the shore. It was painted turquoise, hence its name, La Turquesa. Helen was afraid they would see her. She was followed by swarms of grubby children selling souvenirs, begging for money, offering to show her the sights. Their older brothers tried to sell her drugs and themselves. But Jimmy and Emma were too wrapped up in each other to notice. Helen pushed her way through the begging crowds and went back to the ship. She didn't say anything about the tryst, but by the first dinner seating, the whole crew knew where Jimmy spent the afternoon. It was amazing how gossip spread on the ship.

"I've read this all wrong," Helen told Derreck in the crew bar that night. "He's not carrying on with anyone but the CPA. The cruise is almost over. Tomorrow there's a stop in Progreso."

Derreck grunted a response. He was in no mood to talk, but he did listen.

"You could say I've been gambling, too. Progreso is my last chance. The day after is our last sea day and the jackpot bingo."

Progreso was anything but, in Helen's opinion. It was a dirty little port city. Emma, like most passengers, took the shore excursion to the Mayan ruins at Chichén Itzá. Jimmy rode in the tender with the crew and began walking around Progreso. Helen followed, thinking how strange land felt. She was so used to the ship's movement she felt oddly flat-footed on land.

Jimmy stopped at a restaurant that had more flies and dogs than customers. Helen wasn't about to eat there. Instead, she went down the street to a pickup truck, where a man was lopping the tops off coconuts with a machete. She drank the sweet, warm coconut milk, then picked at the meat.

Finally, Jimmy came out of the restaurant talking to a tall, horse-faced blonde with elaborately curled hair. Helen recognized her from the cruise ship. She was Jackie, a beautician from Springfield, Missouri. She was married with two kids, she'd told Helen. She must have scraped together every penny to take this trip with her girlfriend, Lila. They shared an inside stateroom on the lowest deck, a shoebox-sized room. Jackie spent hours in Helen's boutique, looking at clothes she knew and Helen knew she could never afford. Eventually, she did buy a seashell hairclip. Jackie wore it today with what was obviously her best outfit, a peach dress with ruffles. She also wore a wedding ring.

Jimmy kissed Jackie. They walked up a steep rutted road, Jackie's high-heeled sandals slipping on the rocks and potholes, to a hotel that looked like a noir movie set: a single bare bulb, a whirring fan on a sagging registration desk. The lobby was painted a vile yellow. Helen hoped the beautician thought it was romantic.

Jimmy signed the register and paid the clerk up front. Bingo! Helen thought. She was right.

She couldn't wait to tell Derreck what she'd seen, but she waited anyway. He wasn't himself that night when they met in the crew bar.

He hadn't heard from Jon in six days. His lover wasn't answering his letters, phone calls, or e-mails. "Maybe he's out of town," Helen said. "Maybe his e-mail server is down."

Each excuse sounded lamer than the last and seemed to make Derreck drink more. Finally she gave up trying to make Derreck feel better before he was too trashed to help her at all. Besides, being sad only made him better looking. He wouldn't be lonely for long, Helen was sure of that.

"You won't believe what I saw today," she said. Helen told him about the fly-specked restaurant and the fleabag hotel.

"There seems to be an insect theme here," Derreck said.

"There was only one reason you'd go to that hotel," she told Derreck.

"To collect cockroaches?"

"I've got Jimmy," she said. "The beautician is his accomplice."

"But what have you got?" Derreck said.

That was what she didn't know.

Helen was determined to be at the jackpot bingo game early, to watch every move. Derreck was there, too, and rather grumpy. There was still no word from Jon.

Helen scanned the audience. Emma, Jimmy's show girl, was sitting up front, flirting outrageously with him. She'd bought her bingo card when she walked in the door, waiting in a long line. The only reason Emma had a seat up front was Jimmy had saved it for her.

Jackie the beautician was a little more savvy. She'd bought her card when they went on sale that morning and avoided the rush. She sat in the back. Helen wondered if Jimmy wanted her there. Helen liked the seating arrangement. She could see the beautician's bingo card.

"Remember, it's a cover-all," Helen told Derreck. "The winner has to have all twenty-four numbers on the card. There shouldn't be a jackpot until fifty-five to sixty numbers are called. If the cover-all number drops below forty-seven, it's a scam."

"So if he's cooking the numbers, why doesn't he just wait until fifty-five?" Derreck said.

"Because someone else could win, too, and they'd have to share the prize."

Jimmy had told his jokes, and the audience had oohed and ahhed over the grand prize of twenty thousand dollars. Finally, Jimmy started calling the numbers. The women were laughing and talking so loud, Helen could hardly hear the numbers.

"O-70. I-26. G-56."

She watched Jackie the beautician. She had covered all three of those numbers.

"I-30. B-1. O-69." Jackie had one of those numbers. Out of six called so far, she had four numbers.

Helen nudged Derreck. "Something's going on," she said. "Look how many she has already."

"How's she doing it?" Derreck said.

Helen didn't know. She stared at Jackie, but saw nothing out of the ordinary, except that she was covering her card at an alarming rate.

Helen looked at the stage and saw all the standard equipment: the bingo blower was puffing out the numbers. The display board lighted up when Jimmy placed a ball in the masterboard slot for that number.

"N-34," he called. The number went up on the display board, and Jackie covered yet another space.

"How many numbers have been called?" Derreck said. "Have you been keeping track?"

"Yes. Thirty-eight. It's going to happen soon. Jackie only needs two more."

"Three," corrected Derreck. "The center space on her card is empty."

"That's the free space," Helen said. "You're hopeless."

But she was, too. She stared at the stage. Jimmy was laughing, flirting, and flapping around like a wounded crow. But something was off. Something was missing. She couldn't remember what it was. It nagged at her. She thought back to her bingo games with Aunt Gert. What was missing?

"O-63. N-36."

"Bingo!" Jackie screamed.

"Balls!" Derreck said.

"That's it," Helen cried, and sprinted for the stage. Suddenly everything had fallen into place, and she knew what was wrong. She knocked Mrs. Edmond McGregor, sixty-one, off her motorized scooter, but Helen kept going, running as fast as she could.

Jimmy saw her charging through the audience and tried to pick up the balls he'd called, but Helen threw her body over the master board. Jimmy grabbed her and tried to pull her away. But Helen hung on to the master board and kicked him hard in the crotch. He fell to the floor.

"Arrrgh. My balls," screamed Jimmy. Helen wasn't sure if he was yelling about the bingo balls or something more personal and tender.

"My hip," howled Mrs. McGregor, the woman Helen had knocked off the motorized scooter.

"My money," screamed Jackie the beautician. "Where's my three thousand dollars?"

Three? The jackpot was twenty thousand dollars. The last piece of the puzzle was complete.

"You cheated on your husband. And you cheated on bingo," Helen said, enraged. The stage microphone picked up her voice, and it rang forth from the speakers, the voice of an angry goddess. People were screaming in panic now, and running from the room, knocking over chairs and tables, spilling drinks and bingo cards.

Jackie fell to the floor, weeping. "I just wanted a little fun," she said.

"Bingo is serious," Helen said, and her voice thundered through the room. Six security guards and the chief purser stormed through the doors. Bingo was serious indeed.

"So what happened after the purser and security showed up?" Derreck said.

They were in Helen's cabin. Her door was open to let the crew know everything was on the up-and-up, but the staff avoided her like a rabid lionfish. Only Derreck came to see her while she packed. She would be escorted off the ship first thing tomorrow.

"I couldn't see anything," he complained. "The room was closed and locked and the rest of us were thrown out. Except for Mrs. McGregor, who went to the ship's hospital."

Helen winced and stuffed a pile of T-shirts into her suitcase. "I'm so sorry I flipped over her cart. How is that poor woman?"

"Alive and well and calling for her lawyer."

"Ouch," Helen said. Three pairs of shorts followed.

"What made you try a flying tackle on Jimmy?"

"I had to," she said. "If he got those bingo balls, I couldn't prove how he was cheating. I'd been staring at that stage. I knew something was missing. When you yelled 'Balls!' I realized what it was. Nobody was onstage verifying the numbers Jimmy called.

"That's the fastest way to have fraud. It's so easy on a cruise ship. The players don't know the game. In a shoreside bingo hall the other players would scream foul if someone wasn't called up from the audience to verify the bingo numbers as they're called. Even then, you can get collusion. It happened in a church bingo game when I was a kid. That's why many serious bingo halls have video surveillance with monitors the players can see. They wouldn't tolerate this lax security."

"But I still don't know how Jimmy did it," Derreck said.

Helen threw her tennis shoes on top of the shorts. She wondered if the dirty soles would leave marks on her clean clothes, but she didn't care enough to rearrange her suitcase.

"First, he found an accomplice. He knew how to pick them. The women liked to cheat and some of them, like Jackie, didn't have much money. Three thousand dollars was a lot to them.

"Jimmy would find his mark, romance her, and then say, 'How would you like to win three thousand dollars?' "

"Three? The jackpot was twenty thousand," Derreck interrupted.

A pair of sandals followed the tennis shoes. "Jimmy couldn't help cheating any way he could. He couldn't even split the winnings with the poor woman, Jackie. He told her—and probably all the others—that he also had to split the take with a greedy housekeeper. Jackie believed him. The cruise line says there was no crooked housekeeper. Jimmy was taking that share, too."

"At the risk of repeating myself, let me ask again: how did he do it?" Derreck said.

"Cruise-ship bingo cards are sold ahead of time on the day of the game. He asked his accomplice, Jackie, to buy a card when they first went on sale that morning. Then Jimmy had her call him and read all her card numbers to him. He wasn't in his cabin, but Jackie left the message on his answering machine. He didn't even bother erasing the tape. The cruise line has him cold."

"He got lazy," Derreck said. "Jimmy's been working here for ten years. I wonder how long he's been scamming the cruise line?"

"He didn't say. In fact, he wasn't talking at all. But Jackie sure babbled. She was scared to death. I don't know which she was more afraid of—divorce or prosecution."

Helen found a pair of socks on the floor and crammed them into the suitcase.

"When Jackie called with her card numbers, Jimmy was in the lounge to verify the setup of the game. The stage staff, the grunt labor, did the actual physical installation of the bingo blower and display board. Jimmy stood around and supervised. He simply excused himself for a moment, went to a phone, and retrieved the message with the bingo numbers Jackie had left for him."

"I still don't get it. How did he get the blower to put out the right numbers?" Derreck asked.

"He didn't," Helen said. "The ball would be B-5, but he'd call Jackie's number, B-12. Then he'd drop it in the B-12 slot on the master board and it would flash on the display board, because the system doesn't know the real number of the ball that's dropped in the slot. It just knows if a ball is there. Only the most sophisticated machines actually verify the ball is put in the correct slot, and cruise ships rarely have those.

"A bingo hall would have someone from the audience come up onstage and verify that the number was being accurately repeated, but most cruise ships don't. Jimmy conveniently forgot that step. And I couldn't remember it. My aunt Gert would have never let him get away with it."

Helen found more socks in the drawer and stuffed them inside her tennis shoes.

"Jimmy would call out forty numbers or so before making his girlfriend the winner. Once the girlfriend called 'Bingo!' a second cruise staff person would go to her seat and call her numbers back.

"This person was not in on the scam. Jimmy, the caller onstage, confirmed the numbers and announced, 'That's a winner!' The winner was handed a bundle of cash—most of which she later handed back to Jimmy. But she was happy with her earnings. She knew it was more money than she would have made in an honest bingo game."

Helen made a final search of the tiny cabin. Her clothes for tomorrow were laid out on the single chair. She was ready to go.

"Jimmy was fired," she said. "He's confined to quarters until the cruise is over and banned from any Royal Wave ship for life. Do you think he will go to jail?"

"Not a chance," Derreck said. "The Royal Wave line does not want any bad publicity. I suspect Jimmy will retire in comfort with his ill-gotten gains."

"At least he won't be ruining any more shipboard bingo games," Helen said.

Derreck told her good night. Helen wished him good luck with Jon, but they both knew that romance was over. Helen suspected Derreck was relieved. Celibacy did not suit him.

Helen got a rather chilly thank you from the cruise line, and a not-so-gentle hint that she was no longer welcome as a boutique employee, even if it was a subcontracted position. But Jane Gilbert was tired of sitting around the house. Her broken leg had healed and she was happy to return early to her job on the cruise ship. She gave Helen a nice thousand-dollar bonus in commissions. So Helen was happy.

Helen's landlady, Margery Flax, was happy to have an excuse to put her obnoxious sister Cora on the plane home a week early.

Helen's little apartment seemed big as a mansion after so many weeks in that cramped cabin. She enjoyed sleeping in her own bed. She dreamed of Aunt Gert and a piece of chocolate cake as big as a purse.

Jackie the beautician was allowed to catch the next plane back to Missouri. She was barred from Royal Wave cruises forever, but the cruise line did not prosecute her, nor did they tell her husband. She was happy, too.

No one got the twenty-thousand-dollar jackpot money. But someone did win the jackpot.

Mrs. Edmund McGregor, whose motorized scooter tipped over in the bingo debacle, settled out of court with the Royal Wave line for an undisclosed amount. It was rumored to be two hundred thousand dollars.

Despite her unfortunate experience, she did take another cruise—on the *QE II.*

David Edgerly Gates

ACES & EIGHTS

■ ■ ■

David Edgerly Gates lives in Santa Fe. His short fiction has appeared in Alfred Hitchcock's Mystery Magazine *and* Ellery Queen's Mystery Magazine, A Matter of Crime, Story, *and* Best American Mystery Stories, *and been nominated for the Shamus and Edgar Awards. "Aces & Eights," first published in the December issue of* AHMM, *was a finalist for the short story Edgar Award and is the fifth of the bounty hunter stories, a series of period Western mysteries. David says about his lead character, "Placido Geist is an accidental character. He was introduced about a third of the way into 'The Undiscovered Country' as a previously unthought-of story element, but as soon as he stepped onto the page he was fully fleshed, and demanded his time in front of the camera. He was just waiting in the wings for the right part." The times may be a'changin' for old Placido, but the nature of his job sure hasn't, and in this story he's back to his old tricks, dealing with desperate men who sometimes get a bit closer than he would like.*

The card game in the Alhambra was headed for trouble, anybody could see that, and when the cardplayers kicked back their chairs and turned over the table, Placido Geist hooked his elbows on the bar to watch the entertainment. In the bad old days, somebody would certainly have pulled a knife or a gun, and the argument would have ended with one or another of the men in the game dead on the floor, but this was the tail end of 1917, after all, and even in the Texas Panhandle civilization of a kind had arrived. The bouncers stepped in, and a town constable showed up in short order. One of the cardplayers gave the constable some lip, and the constable slapped the man with the barrels of his shotgun. It laid the damn fool's scalp open, and the sight of his injury sobered the others up.

The constable, a man named Billy Dollar, walked over to the bar and stood Placido Geist to a whiskey.

Billy himself drank rarely. He had Kiowa blood in him, and claimed that liquor gave him windy bowels, but some people said he didn't trust a drunken Indian, himself included. Placido Geist had been acquainted with Billy the better part of twenty years, off and on, and he'd never seen him drunk or foolish. He thanked Billy for the drink, and took a cautious taste. It was coarse stuff, grain alcohol cut with bitters and Jamaican ginger, flavored with tobacco, watered milk passing for cream. Like so much else these days, you couldn't trust to appearances.

"The last I heard, you were chasing renegades, south of the Rio Grande," Billy Dollar remarked.

"I found them," Placido Geist said.

"There was a fair reward posted, as I recall."

Placido Geist nodded. "I'm headed into Amarillo to collect from the railroad," he told him.

Billy nodded. "You were to stay over, me and the missus got an extra room, indoor lavatory right down the hall," he said, smiling. "Few improvements, civic and otherwise, the last time I recollect you were in these parts."

Placido Geist glanced around the saloon and turned his gaze back to Billy Dollar.

"All right, it ain't much," Billy admitted.

Buffalo Flats had been one of the tough cowtowns on the trails north, but went into decline as the railheads were pushed south and west, and made the big cattle drives unnecessary. Then the oil boom came, and the Flats filled up with wildcatters and roughnecks, along with the usual custom that followed them for the easy money to be had, whores, dips, cardsharps, barbers and bankers, clergymen and carpetbaggers.

Billy Dollar cleared his throat. "You be in the market for a commission?" he asked.

Placido Geist was a bounty hunter by trade. He was well past sixty, and Billy wasn't far behind. The question sounded a trifle wistful.

"The reason I ask," Billy went on, "is that I know of a man in difficulties, with need of private law."

"Why private?"

Billy sucked on his teeth, awkwardly. "He's an Indian," he said, at last.

"Kiowa or Osage?"

"Kiowa, my mother's second cousin," Billy said. "He's a rich Indian, mind you. He can afford to pay the freight. Plain fact is, though, he can't leave it to local authorities."

"What's it about, Billy?" Placido Geist asked him.

"His daughter's been kidnapped. For ransom. Jennie's nine years old."

Jacob Nighthorse had made his money in the oil business. He had leases in the Cimarron Strip of Oklahoma that brought him substantial royalties. Nighthorse made no pretense of being a plain man. His house was Greek Revival, three stories high, with yew hedges planted as a windbreak outside and oak wainscoting in the halls. Placido Geist met him in the study. The slate for the billiards table had been brought overland from St. Louis, and the books ordered from Philadelphia and Boston. The felt on the billiards table was scuffed from use, and the bound books had every evidence of being read. Nighthorse was a widower, with time on his hands.

Placido Geist looked at the shelved titles. Bought by the yard, but much handled since. Dickens, Trollope, Sir Walter Scott. He took down a copy of Scott's *Quentin Durward* and leafed through it. A somewhat silly book, as he remembered, but an exciting one, filled with daredevil adventures and hairbreadth escapes. A pallid hero, but vivid villains. He returned the novel to the shelf. Jake Nighthorse offered him a drink. It was imported whiskey from Oban, Scotland, and Placido Geist didn't turn it down.

Billy Dollar stood quietly to one side, watching them. The oil man hadn't offered Billy a whiskey.

"How long has she been missing?" Placido Geist asked.

"Just over a week," Nighthorse said.

"And how much are they asking?"

"A hundred thousand dollars."

"Can you raise that kind of money?"

"I already have."

"You intend to pay it?"

"I want my daughter back," Nighthorse said.

Placido Geist took a sip of his single malt. "And where do I deliver the ransom?" he asked.

"You're to meet a man in Palo Duro, those are my only instructions," Nighthorse said. "From there, the arrangements are up to you." Nighthorse seemed like a man who was keeping his feelings in check, but the fury radiated off him like an odor, or the chime of a bell. His posture in the dim light of the library was almost blurred with anger. "I mean to *leave* the arrangements to you," Nighthorse said, significantly.

"You're giving me a fair degree of latitude," Placido Geist remarked, choosing not to read his meaning.

"I trust you to get the job done," Nighthorse said.

Placido Geist deliberated, but there was no delicate way to put it. "What if your daughter is already dead?" he asked.

"Find the men who took her," Nighthorse told him. "I don't expect them to be brought back alive."

Placido Geist had understood this from the first.

Nighthorse handed the bounty hunter a small lacquered box, figured with elaborate joinery. Placido Geist opened the lid. There was a linen handkerchief folded inside. He undid it cautiously. It took him a moment to realize what he was looking at. He hadn't seen anything like it since he'd scouted against the Apache. The artifact was pale and perfect, and curled at the edges, as delicate as the wax impression of a Nautilus shell or the petals of a rose pressed between the pages of a book.

It was a child's ear, severed from the scalp.

"I mean to come along, provided you'll have me," Billy said. "I can still sit a saddle, if you can."

Placido Geist nodded. "I figured as much," he said. "Not that I wouldn't appreciate the company, but how does your wife feel? And you're taking time away from your job. The town pays your salary, not Nighthorse."

"A hundred a month and found," Billy Dollar said. "I think I can do better, as does my wife."

"Your share of the reward, provided we're able to find the girl." Nighthorse had made it clear that his hundred thousand dollars was blood money. Failing the recovery of his child, the ransom was a bounty on her kidnappers.

"I mean to earn it," Billy said.

"You intended this from the first," Placido Geist said.

Billy nodded. "You were approachable," he said.

"And you used me as leverage."

"Nighthorse was reluctant to put the business in my charge. You have a reputation I can't match."

"My reputation, as you call it, is questionable."

"I've got the stomach for killing, if it comes to that."

"It may," Placido Geist said. "Is this family feeling, you and the Nighthorse girl?"

"She calls me Uncle Billy," Billy said. "It's a courtesy title. My own girl died of the smallpox when she was nine. Jennie Nighthorse is that age, now. Could be I'm trying to make it up to her."

His daughter, did he mean? "Do your explaining at home, Billy, not to me," Placido Geist told him. "I can't give you an alibi."

"I don't need one," Billy Dollar said.

He'd tried his hand at other things over the years, but he had a gift for tracking men. It was his calling, you might say, and it had made him something close to famous in the border country, although nothing on the order of the Pinkerton's agent Charlie Siringo, who'd pursued Butch Cassidy, or some of the frontier lawmen of an earlier time, like Hickok or Earp. Nobody had yet written a dime novel about Placido Geist, and even someone who knew his name wouldn't have recognized him if they passed him on the street. Short and rumpled, and in fact rather stout, he cut an unremarkable figure on his bandy legs, and looked the part of a broken-down old cowboy. It wasn't common knowledge that he'd killed forty men in his career, more than the notorious Texas gunhawk and braggart Wes Hardin. He was of mixed blood, his father a German immigrant, his mother *mestizo*, which accounted for his queer name. *Placido* means "tranquil" in Spanish, and he had a quiet air about him. His father's surname meant "ghost" in German, and some on the Mexican side had taken to calling him *el Espectro*, since it was said you never saw him until it was too late, but he'd grown up in a stern school, where the margin for error was the difference between staying alive or winding up dead.

Placido Geist and Billy Dollar boarded a train in Amarillo, which took them south through the Tierra Blanca to the whistle stop at Nazareth. Jacob Nighthorse had arranged for a car and driver to meet them there, a 1904 Oldsmobile that could run on either alcohol or gasoline, serviced and driven by a cheerful Negro named Jupiter Cox. He loaded their gear into the car and the three of them proceeded over the unimproved road to Palo Duro, wearing dusters and goggles to protect them from the alkali of the Llano Estacado, which blew into the open vehicle, sticking to their exposed skin and sifting down inside the scarves around their necks. They coughed and chugged their way into the town, looking as if they'd been dredged in flour, the grit caught in their throats. The wind scoured the pueblo with particles so fine they would have passed through cheesecloth. Billy Dollar dismounted from the automobile and went off to find them a hotel room, hopefully one that provided running water. Placido Geist got down more slowly, feeling his age, and brushed at his coat.

The livery stable also served as what the owner was pleased to announce on his sign as a GARAGE, which meant some of the stalls stored other cars, and he now offered repairs. He was an eager young man, and his farrier did double duty at the forge, turning out the odd replacement part as well as shaping horseshoes. They were much taken with the Oldsmobile and the ground it had been able to cover. Placido Geist asked if he could hire a decent pair of horses, but when he saw what was on offer, he determined to shop around for outright purchase of mounts. He wasn't keen to spend money he hadn't yet earned, but Nighthorse was being generous with expenses.

Their driver, Cox, unpacked the luggage on the porch of the hotel and said he'd sooner spend the night in the stables with the automobile, in which he took a proprietary interest, before starting north again. Placido Geist saw no harm in this, and respected the man's dedication, although it was tempered by necessity. Cox was responsible for the car. Placido Geist went up the steps and into the hotel.

Billy Dollar had gotten them adjoining rooms on the second floor, with a shared private bath in between. The hotel had steam heat from a boiler in the basement, and there was a tub with spigots. Billy had already run a bath, and he was soaking in it. Placido Geist unpacked his gear, laying it on the bed. Billy talked to him through the open door as he soaped up in the tub. "You figure they'll contact us here?" Billy asked.

"They know we're coming," Placido Geist said. He set out his toiletries on the bedspread and unwrapped a break-top Smith & Wesson .44 with a nine-inch barrel, along with a box of cartridges. He also had a smaller gun, a single-action Colt Sheriff's Model with a three-inch barrel that he carried at the small of his back, next to his kidneys. In his experience, it didn't matter whether you hid a gun in your hat. If it was always there, you knew where to find it. The big guns, his own .45–70 Sharps Borchardt with the heavy barrel and Billy's .32 Winchester, were over in the corner of the room with their saddles and other tack. Placido Geist had brought along an ornate Mexican saddle, chased with silver and absurdly heavy. The bellman had struggled with it, carrying it upstairs, and complained that gold coins or lead fishing weights might well have been stitched into the saddle skirts. Placido Geist tipped him a paper dollar.

"If they think we have the money with us, they may well try and take it away from us," Billy Dollar remarked.

"They well might," Placido Geist said. He opened a small case on the bed and thoughtfully assembled a stubby shotgun. It was a twelve-gauge Parker hammerless side-by-side with double triggers, the barrels taken off at eighteen inches. Inside twenty feet, the spread of shot was palm-sized. Beyond that, it was ineffective. He loaded double-O buckshot in the left-hand barrel, which fired first, and a lead slug in the right. The slug was split across the face, so it would fragment when it hit bone. He closed the breech.

Billy Dollar sat up in the tub, rinsing off his upper body, and began lathering his face to shave. For a man who was part Indian, his beard was heavy enough to shave every other day. "Tell me," he said, talking around the brush, "what do you make of Nighthorse?"

Placido Geist was stripping off his clothes. "He wants his daughter back," he said. "Absent that, he wants the bandits that took her dead. Or preferably both. Any man who cuts off a child's ear to show he's in earnest is vermin."

"You ever take scalps?" Billy Dollar asked him.

Placido Geist sat down on the edge of the bed and tugged off his boots, grunting with the effort. "Are you going to run me a fresh bath, or did you expect me to use that greasy water a second time?" he asked.

The hotel featured a dining room that was the nearest thing to a decent restaurant Palo Duro had to offer, and the townsfolk crowded in on Thursday nights for the house special, chicken and dumplings, mashed potatoes and gravy, and a helping of soggy greens on the side that came out of a tin. Individual tables were hard to come by, so there was family seating, like a boardinghouse. After the two old hired guns took a place, they were joined by a whiskey drummer from El Paso and a smartly dressed octaroon who looked to be either a pimp or a gambler. It was the octaroon who caught their attention when he looked down at the food and made a sly remark about a sow's ear and a silk purse, and then winked at them gravely before picking up his silverware.

They met him after dinner in the saloon bar. He introduced himself as Aristide L'Ouverture.

L'Ouverture obviously expected Placido Geist to spring for the drinks. He asked for cognac. Placido Geist bought the Creole a brandy. "What else are we buying?" he asked him. "Not a sow's ear."

"Not a full-grown pig, but a young farrow."

"Damaged goods," Placido Geist commented.

L'Ouverture smiled. "We take each other seriously, no?" he inquired. "Or would you like to see her other ear?"

"You've made your point," Placido Geist told him.

"Where, however, is the promised silk purse?" the Creole asked him, with his Cajun lilt. "Not in your automobile, I rest assured. So, where?"

"The money will be paid on delivery," Placido Geist said to him, mildly. "I'm to make the arrangements at my discretion."

"Excuse me," L'Ouverture corrected him. "Arrangements will be made at *my* discretion."

"There are only two of us," Placido Geist said, indicating Billy Dollar. "We were sent to conclude a deal, nothing more or less. A time and a place. The price is already agreed."

"Then we negotiate a time and a place," L'Ouverture told him. "South of here is Sulphur Draw, no more than a day's ride across the Llano Estacado. You know this country well enough to find it?"

Placido Geist nodded. "Below the Caprock," he said.

"You will be met there."

"How do we make ourselves known?"

"You had no need of it here," L'Ouverture said.

"How do we know the girl's still alive?"

L'Ouverture grinned. "How do I know you have the money?"

"If the girl's already dead, you won't see a dime," Placido Geist said.

"Men of goodwill act in good faith," L'Ouverture said.

"I have no reason to trust you," Placido Geist told him. "You've mistreated a child, disfigured her, even murdered her by now. You mean to kill us both and steal the ransom."

"Let's be frank," L'Ouverture said. "You're hard men to kill, or you wouldn't be here. I wouldn't be here, if it weren't for the money. And if the girl is dead, there's no trade, so I have nothing to gain. This is a simple business transaction. There's no personal animus involved. Why can't we be dignified about it?"

"Then why not make the trade here?"

L'Ouverture shrugged. "We're suspicious of each other, and with good reason," he said.

"I won't cheat you, if the girl's alive, and if not, you'll get what you deserve."

The octaroon smiled. "If you try and cheat us, the girl will get worse than she deserves," he said. "I have associates, even more prudent than I am. You have heard the name, perhaps, of Balafré?" He pronounced it, teasingly, in the French manner, BAHL-a-FRAY.

Placido Geist gave no sign of it. "We'll do what you ask," he said. "Sulphur Draw, the day after tomorrow."

"Two days' time, then," L'Ouverture said, not unpleasantly. He put his empty glass down on the bar and sauntered out.

"No better than a Comanchero," Billy Dollar muttered.

"No worse, either," Placido Geist said.

"Worse would be hard to stomach," Billy said. "There's something shifty about that Creole, not just being a high yeller in a dude outfit."

"It's my belief he means to murder us in our beds," Placido Geist commented.

Billy nodded. "I mean to sleep light," he said.

They took turns sleeping, as it turned out. Billy had the first watch. They'd plumped up pillows under the bedclothes, and Placido Geist slept in the bathtub fully dressed, with his knees up, hunched in a blanket. Billy Dollar sat on the commode with the sawed-off shotgun in his lap. It was past midnight when they changed places, Placido Geist restless and stiff, and Billy complaining of sore hams. Billy folded his big body into the tub and shifted around awkwardly, but made no more remark about it. He settled down after a spell, holding his pistol to his chest, and was soon breathing loudly through his mouth, his face slack as an infant's. The only light came from a gas lamp outside the hotel, shining in the bedroom windows, but it was almost completely dark in the lavatory. Placido Geist let himself relax and listen to the background sounds, the building shifting its weight, the groan of plumbing, a drunk stumbling by in the street below, the sigh of Billy's breath. If you stayed too alert, you'd jump at every noise. He was waiting for a noise that might seem out of place, but none came. He peered at his biscuit watch and then put it away.

He considered his sins, which were many.

The old manhunter came out of a light doze, listening hard, and reached out to lay a hand on Billy's chest.

Billy started awake and then lay absolutely still.

There was the faint scrape of metal on metal again, perhaps a brass key turning in a tumbler lock. Billy sat up carefully and got his legs underneath him. Placido Geist rose to his feet but didn't move away from the toilet.

Billy eased himself up to his full height. He cocked his weapon thoughtfully, pressing the trigger and closing his other hand over the the cylinder as he brought back the hammer, so there was only a single stifled click as the cylinder turned and locked. Billy let the pressure off the trigger.

Placido Geist slid his right foot across the floor, and followed with his left. The floorboards didn't squeak. He leaned against the doorjamb and peered out of the lavatory toward his bedroom door. He saw the knob begin to turn, slowly and deliberately. Placido Geist glanced at Billy. Billy put one leg out of the tub, let it take his full weight, and quietly followed with the other. Placido Geist held his breath.

Billy moved silently, heel-and-toe, into the opposite doorway, that gave on the adjoining bedroom. He looked back and nodded.

Placido Geist didn't wait for the men in the hallway to signal each other. He planted his feet, rested the butt of the scattergun against his hip, and let off a round. The buckshot in the left barrel blew out a six-inch hole around the doorknob and shattered the hand that was holding it, taking it off at the wrist. The man shrieked.

Billy's gun boomed three times in the other room.

Placido Geist fired the second barrel of the shotgun. The split slug caught the man in the corridor just below the breastbone, knocking him into the far wall. Placido Geist broke open the shotgun and reloaded before he stepped through the splintered door into the hallway. His man sagged to the floor dead, with staring eyes. Fifteen feet away, the Creole lay helpless, two rounds through his chest. Billy came out of his door, glancing right and left, and then looked at the men they'd just shot.

"Only two of them?" he asked.

"There were only two of us," Placido Geist said.

The breath rasped in the octaroon's lungs, and even as they stood by, he choked on his blood and died.

Placido Geist sucked on his teeth, frustrated.

"This may be awkward to explain to Aristide's associates in Sulphur Draw," Billy remarked.

"Not if they knew him for the greedy scoundrel he was," the old bounty hunter observed.

It was unfortunate that the Creole was dead, instead of merely disabled, but in matters like these it was unlikely you'd be given much selection.

There were five of them in the gang. Three of them had taken the girl, and two had stayed behind, to deliver the ransom demand to Jacob Nighthorse, and to see what steps he took. They didn't expect immediate pursuit, not if Nighthorse wanted his daughter back alive. L'Ouverture had devised the kidnapping as well as the method of letting Nighthorse know they meant business. He'd peeled the girl's ear off himself, fastidious as a surgeon, and taken savage pleasure in its neatness. He considered himself both stylish and clever, but proved to be too clever for his own good. Death had come to him as a rude surprise, as it comes to most men. The man called Balafré would not have been surprised by L'Ouverture's death.

Balafré was brutal, but cautious, and thought the Creole a preening fool, overconfident and condescending. The scar that gave Balafré his name split his upper lip and nostril and scored his cheekbone, up alongside the corner of his left eye. He was probably lucky the Mexican with the knife hadn't blinded him, but the Mex was lucky he died quickly. Balafré would have preferred to take more time with it, but he was in more of a hurry to stay alive. Once a thing was done, it was done. You played what cards you were dealt, and only learned the game when you played for more than you could afford to lose.

They'd brought the girl down the western slope of the Caprock escarpment, skirting the tableland and keeping to the trees, where there was both water and cover, and deadfall to make campfires. The girl hadn't whimpered, although the skin of her inner thighs was chafed from days on horseback. The man with the scar respected her for it, putting it up to her Indian blood. He himself was part Mescalero, and didn't trouble her with conversation. He knew she was already as good as dead, and unlike the octaroon, he had no need to make her suffer unnecessary humiliations. When he killed her, he meant to do it cleanly, without fuss or warning. The girl had no way of knowing this. She was perhaps too young to anticipate such a thing as her own sudden end. Balafré had grown old in the ways of death, having seen so much of it. He was unsentimental about his own chances, or anybody else's.

The other two men were not of his choosing. One was an albino boy, quick with a gun or a knife, and good with horses or pack animals, but without social skills. He kept to himself, once camp was pitched, and spoke little. The second man called himself Beaudry but probably answered to half a dozen others. He made more of an effort to keep the girl comfortable, but she shrank from his clumsy courtesies. She mistrusted his solicitude, and chose the man with the scar as more reliable, or at least indifferent. Her confidence was of course misplaced, but Balafré understood it. He didn't trust Beaudry himself, and chose not to leave him alone with the girl for any longer than necessary. Beaudry had unhealthy appetites, like the Creole, and was only waiting for an opportunity to indulge them. If the albino boy were odd enough, with his stringy, pale hair and washed-out eyes, and his unnerving manner, cringing like a dog who'd been badly treated, but all too ready to snap if you made to pet him, he was still dependable. He wouldn't try and rape the Nighthorse girl. Then again, he probably wouldn't try to protect her, either, so Balafré determined the sensible course was simply to cut Beaudry's throat when the time came. And that time would come soon enough.

They were holed up in an old adobe under the Caprock, some distance from the settlement at Sulphur Draw. This was the part of the Creole's plan that disturbed Balafré. It was isolated, but isolation wasn't safety. Balafré didn't think the men Nighthorse would send would be careless or inexperienced, and he already suspected what had happened. The octaroon had counted on being able to ambush Nighthorse's men in Palo Duro, and he'd hinted at some obscure advantage, but nothing was that easy. Balafré was more patient than most, and knew the value of stillness, but he also knew that other men were not to be relied on. The only sure thing you could count on was the unexpected.

In this case, that might prove disagreeable. He was probably better off to cut his losses, but he was divided in his mind. There was a lot of money to be had if he waited. It was unsettling. Usually his decisions were severe and arbitrary, like the weather. He found it confusing, having to balance this equation, and had to study on it.

They found Jupiter Cox dead in the stable, his skull split.

"This is a wicked bunch," Billy Dollar said, somewhat taken aback. "That man was harmless."

"One of us should have warned him last night, after we spoke with L'Ouverture," Placido Geist said. "I entirely forgot about Mr. Cox, and now I'm responsible for his murder."

"We have to wire Jacob Nighthorse, to send somebody for the automobile," Billy said.

"L'Ouverture as good as told us he'd had somebody search the car," Placido Geist muttered, still aggravated with himself.

"They killed him when he got in the way," Billy said.

"They murdered the Negro for sport, like as not," Placido Geist told him. He hitched the heavy saddle onto his hip and hoisted the big Sharps. "Whether or not we find the girl alive, these are surely men who'd benefit from a hanging."

"You think she's still alive?"

"I can't think otherwise," Placido Geist told him.

"Let's get to it, then," Billy Dollar said.

It wasn't yet sunup. They'd answered what questions were asked by a Palo Duro deputy marshal after the shooting had woken up half the guests in the hotel, but the marshal had taken them at their word it was self-defense. Billy carried a badge, after all, and Placido Geist had a reputation that went before him. The marshal had told them to go back to bed, and present themselves before the town magistrate in the morning. They took advantage of this parole to gather their possibles from the hotel and repair to the garage. The dead chauffeur was an inconvenience as well as an affront, a possible obstacle to their leaving, and Placido Geist felt time was short. Much as he regretted the insult to the deputy marshal's courtesy, he had no choice. Any later difficulties could be papered over with Nighthorse's money, but in the meantime, there was more pressing business.

Billy woke the sleeping stableboy, no doubt lucky not to have been awake earlier to witness the murder, and Placido Geist picked out the two best-looking horses he could find from the sorry string in the corral. They were in no position to dicker. Placido Geist simply left two hundred dollars with the boy, an outrageous price, and hoped the owner would see at least part of it. They were already in flight from a manslaughter inquest, and being charged with horse theft would only make things worse.

They rode south. The country was so featureless that a yucca on the horizon was a landmark. The Llano Estacado, the Staked Plain, took its name from the early days of Spanish exploration. The first white men to traverse this barren landscape had marked their route with stakes, a method handed down from the Roman centurions who crossed North Africa, to find their way back. The soldiers of the Catholic majesty of Spain had left their bones in this dreary expanse. Only the colorful name survived, but little else. The color itself was bleached out of the ground. To the human eye, it was an unforgiving waste, hard as an anvil, the sand itself hammered and calcified, like the bones of the conquistadors.

"Hard to imagine they took Jennie Nighthorse across this," Billy Dollar said. "A sheltered nine-year-old, convent-bred. I doubt she'd stand the journey."

Placido Geist's horse stumbled, and then found her footing again. He straightened in the saddle and glanced at Billy. "We can only hope she's a young woman of stamina," he said.

"I'm running low on stamina, myself," Billy said.

"Try not to run low on spit," Placido Geist remarked.

They had water enough for the horses, if they were short on it themselves, but it wasn't worrisome.

More troubling was the Creole's mention of Balafré, or Cicatriz, as the Mexicans called him. Placido Geist had heard of him before. His given name was Vermilion, and he was a ruthless outlaw, by reputation, but to the old bounty hunter's knowledge he'd never raided north of the Pecos or been party to so carefully executed a crime. It was out of character. The man was reported to be cruel but uncalculating, a methodical killer, but not the sort to think through such a scheme as the Nighthorse kidnapping. He was unlikely to chop logic, or bargain for the girl's life, and would as soon murder both his hostage and his partners, and make a run for Mexico alone, to live another day, leaving the money behind him. Such a man was difficult to outwit, since he *lived* by his wits, and had neither character nor vanity to play on.

They made good time, and reached Sulphur Draw near sundown, after pushing the horses hard. At first blush, the settlement looked to be a sad and stunted ghost town on the edge of nowhere, but as they rode closer, they saw the telegraph line coming up from the south, and some new buildings scattered about the outskirts, the lumber still raw.

"Signs of life," Billy Dollar remarked.

"Few and far between," Placido Geist said.

They pulled up and sat their tired horses in the thickening twilight, gazing across the dusty ground at the town.

"I don't imagine the hotel has indoor plumbing," Billy said to the bounty hunter. "My bones could use another hot soak."

"We'll be lucky if there *is* a hotel," Placido Geist said to him. "Or even a livery."

They rode on in, and dismounted in the last light of day. The town seemed as weary and dispirited as they were. There was a stable, though, and they were able to board their horses.

They walked up the street, stopping at the jail, but there was nobody there. They crossed over to the nearest saloon, an unprepossessing establishment that didn't have much custom. The bartender directed them to the faro game at the back, where they found the local sheriff sullenly losing. He was in a poor temper, and showed a marked disinclination to involve himself in their business.

They retired to the bar. Placido Geist ordered a whiskey, and was mildly surprised when Billy did the same. Billy knocked back his drink with alacrity and asked for another.

"He lacks enthusiasm, for a lawman," Billy Dollar said.

"Nothing in it for him," Placido Geist said.

"We could sweeten the pot, or don't you want to share?"

"It's not the money, or the credit we might get," Placido Geist said. "If we let it be known what we were carrying, we could generate a little too much enthusiasm. The bandits might get scared off. Let alone the fact that we'd be worth more dead than alive to anybody who wanted to try their luck. Better safe than sorry."

"They tried it in Palo Duro, and we fought them off."

Placido Geist had been thinking about Palo Duro, and it bothered him that the Creole seemed to think he could get the money without an assault heavier in manpower, but he didn't voice his doubts out loud. "Let's wait and see if our man makes an offer we can shake hands on."

Billy Dollar picked up his shot glass and regarded Placido Geist with what might have been misgiving, but made no comment before he drank. They bought the bottle and removed to a nearby table.

The two of them sat there the better part of an hour, watching the flies circle and making idle conversation. Billy, unaccustomed to drink, was feeling his liquor, growing downright lugubrious.

"You recall a man named Bright?" he asked. "He was the law in Sweetwater for a while."

"Tall, boisterous sort? I believe he got himself killed in Abilene a few years back."

Billy nodded. "Working the door in a whorehouse."

"I'm sorry to hear he'd sunk so far," Placido Geist said, pouring himself another drink. "No more corrupt than most, as I remember. Affable enough, in a coarse way."

Billy looked around the bar, measuring his future. "Not much to look forward to," he remarked. "Carrying water for the Pinkertons, breaking strikes, or working as a bouncer, listening to whores complain about the custom."

"Don't go mournful on me, Billy," Placido Geist said.

"I prefer to think of it as contemplative," Billy said.

Placido Geist smiled, gently. "We could tell one another lies all night," he said. "Let's wonder about dinner and a place to bed down. The men we're here to trade with will likely find us without our help."

Billy shifted his weight, uneasily. "I think they already have," he murmured, as if to nobody in particular. He pointedly didn't look toward the door.

Placido Geist raised his glass unhurriedly and took a careful sip, letting his eyes rest briefly on the man who'd just come in. He was of middle age, wearing charro pants with silver conchos, and a woolen jacket, his sombrero pushed back. When he turned to face them his scar was vivid. The puckered seam caught the light like snakeskin. He lifted his hand amicably in their direction, affecting to have just seen them. Placido Geist put his glass down and left both hands on the table. The man with the scar came over. Billy pushed his chair back to give him room, but the man with a scar was too wary to sit without an invitation.

"Would I recognize your name, you were to give it?" the man with the scar asked Placido Geist.

Placido Geist told him who he was.

The man with the scar nodded to himself. "That sounds about right," he said. "Jacob Nighthorse would want the best money could buy." He tipped his head toward Billy Dollar. "And the tame Indian?"

"You look part Apache to me," Billy said to him. "Mimbreño or Mescalero?"

"A man with no head for whiskey shouldn't drink," the man with the scar said. "I never met a half-breed Kiowa yet who had any head for whiskey, or the stomach for a fight."

Placido Geist made no remark.

Billy sat back, crossing his legs, and brought his hand up from under the table without haste. He laid the barrel of the .45 Bisley Colt alongside his thigh, and when he cocked the hammer, it made no more noise than a cricket's wing. Nobody six feet away would have heard it, or even noticed the gun, but the man with the scar was closer than that. He allowed himself a small smile, respectful but disappointed, as if his expectations had been answered.

"Accidents happen," he said to Placido Geist.

"A little accident happened to your friend the Creole, back in Palo Duro," Placido Geist said.

"I figured as much," the man with the scar said. "Do we deal?" He looked slowly and insolently at Billy Dollar.

Billy remained still and watchful.

Placido Geist bobbed his head.

The man with the scar pulled out a chair and sat down.

Placido Geist was leafing through a mental catalogue. "You'd be Dick Vermilion, called Balafré, or Cicatriz, by the Mexicans," he said. "Known to be a murderer and desperado. I'd have taken you for an older man."

Cicatriz grinned, hugely. "A man is as a man does," he said. "And as for age, I'd have thought you might have dried up and blown away by now. They call a man *el Espectro*, you expect him to be skin and bones. You two look fat and sassy to me. No offense," he added, glancing at Billy.

"None taken," Billy said.

"She's alive," the outlaw said to Placido Geist.

"That's a start," Placido Geist said.

"You'll want a look at her first," Cicatriz said.

"That would be prudent."

"The two of you come down here to kill me?"

"Only if the girl's already dead," Placido Geist said.

"The octaroon must have underestimated you."

"I think he overestimated himself."

Cicatriz smiled. "How do you want to work it?" he asked.

"Which outcome would you prefer?"

"All of us still standing afterward."

"You've got the advantage of the ground," Placido Geist said. "The element of surprise. You've had time to go over the terrain and set up an ambush."

"So you have a suggestion to even the odds."

"I don't trust you not to kill us, and the girl, too."

Cicatriz shrugged. "It goes without saying," he remarked. "Just as I don't trust you to let me ride off with another man's money."

"I'm instructed to bring Nighthorse's daughter back to him alive," Placido Geist said. "Failing that, to kill every one of you. It's your choice."

"You're not leaving me room to swing a rope."

"I don't mean to."

"I've still got the girl, though."

"Which is all that's keeping you alive."

Cicatriz sat back and studied him for a moment. "I believe I might have met my match, old man," he said.

"If you believed that, you would have dry-gulched me at the earliest opportunity. We wouldn't be having this talk."

"L'Ouverture enjoyed spinning out a talk," Cicatriz said.

"Conversation was his weakness," Placido Geist said.

"He was all talk and no sand," Billy Dollar commented.

Cicatriz looked him over with closer attention. "You'd be Nighthorse's cousin, the constable," he said. "Getting his girl back means a preferment for you."

Billy didn't bother to answer that.

"What if just the two of us meet, out in the open?" Placido Geist asked Cicatriz.

"How does that further?"

"That's what it comes down to, in the end."

"You're probably right enough," Cicatriz said.

"You care to pick the place?"

"About three miles west of here there's a dry wash, and a broken-down adobe. You can make it out from a distance. The two of you come at daybreak, but stand clear of the cabin until we take each other's measure." He grinned. "Outside of rifle range. I'll meet you halfway, close enough to keep you covered from the adobe. If the Kiowa has me in his sights, neither side has the advantage of the other."

"I don't know how many men you've got."

"I'm not spoiling for a fight," Cicatriz said.

Placido Geist nodded. "Done, then," he said.

"You're known to be a dead shot. I'd suspicion of you, you were to send this Indian in your place."

"You kill me, you won't get the money," Placido Geist said.

"You kill me, you won't get the girl," Cicatriz said.

Placido Geist nodded again. "Fair is fair," he said.

The man with the scar stood up from the table. "I'll be waiting for you, then, tomorrow morning, out in the scrub," he said. He glanced at Billy and smiled, without humor. "There'll be less talk, and more sand."

They were in position well before daylight. It was bitterly cold, with a sharp wind off the escarpment, and the two old men blew on their hands and shuffled their feet, huddling up against the horses for warmth.

They'd dismounted a ways back and led the animals forward in the dark. Billy had the better night vision, and signaled a halt when they came to the slight rise. He crept up it to scout the terrain ahead while Placido Geist held the reins.

Billy slithered back down and got heavily to his feet. His breath frosted in the starlight. "It's about a mile distant," he said. "Looks pretty much deserted, but that's what you might expect."

"They wouldn't be showing any light," Placido Geist said. "Vermilion knows better than to build a fire if he figures us to be here early, which he does."

They both understood it was probably a trap, but they hadn't been able to work out any better way. Agreeing to the rendezvous was their only chance of recovering Jennie Nighthorse alive, even if it got them killed.

"He'll likely have two or three others," Billy said. "They won't all be inside the adobe."

"No," Placido Geist said. "I'd box the compass, if it were me. Put a man off to either side, six or eight hundred yards from the rise, here. It's a consistent feature in the landscape and you'd think it gave us a natural advantage."

"Come dawn, we'd have the sun at our backs," Billy said.

"Makes for a good target, in silhouette."

"You ride down to meet Vermilion, and I show myself, giving you cover, but still out of range of the adobe. One of the men in the brush picks me off, and then Vermilion kills you. I'd do it the same way."

"Simple enough."

"Simple enough if we're dead," Billy said. "I don't admire being taken alive by a breed Apache."

"Then again, if he has his men already in position, they're lying on the cold ground right now," Placido Geist said.

"I'd be getting uncomfortable, it were me," Billy said.

"Might get drowsy, or distracted," Placido Geist said to him. "Go to picking stones out from under my bedroll, restless, wanting the time to go faster."

Billy Dollar grinned. His teeth shone very white in the darkness. "A man as careless as that might get himself killed," he said.

"See that you don't," Placido Geist told him.

They hobbled the horses, and the two of them moved off in opposite directions, first circling back, behind their position, and then flanking forward, to cast a wider net.

The albino boy was the better shot, and given a task, wouldn't shrink it, or turn tail and run. Beaudry had too many weaknesses to be dependable. Cicatriz had already determined he should be disposed of as soon as it was convenient. He'd sent the ash-blond boy into the brush, with instructions about who was coming, what to wait for, and when to shoot. Beaudry stayed where Cicatriz could keep an eye on him. Beaudry had at least a single virtue, in that he was predictable.

It was the girl who was behaving oddly.

At first, the man with the scar had put it up to her captivity, a resignation to her situation, an eagerness to please her captors and escape punishment. Many white children taken by the Comanche or other tribes had been known to lose their white ways and adapt to Indian life, refusing to be ransomed back by their birth parents and choosing to stay behind with the savages. Cicatriz had of course said nothing to raise any false hopes in the girl, but she seemed to sense the possibility of deliverance, perhaps to shrink from it. Cicatriz felt the girl's dependence on him was understandable, even natural, given her circumstances, and although he treated her curtly, he found himself unaccountably protective, keeping her from further physical harm, or sexual injury at the hands of Beaudry. But there was more to it, somehow. Here, she was a necessary part of the plot, valued in a way she wouldn't be if she was returned home. Or so it seemed, from her apparent devotion to him, as if *he* were her rescuer, not those two old men he meant to torment, and kill, when the time came. His own ambivalence bothered him. He didn't like being of two minds. He reminded himself that Jennie Nighthorse was a commodity, not a person, to be handled like livestock: she was only the means to an end. Still, he was having second thoughts. The girl posed a riddle, or harbored a secret, or perhaps represented the answer to a question he'd never asked himself before.

It was all very troubling, almost painful. Cicatriz felt as if his head were being squeezed tight in a vise. He knew his anger was unhelpful. It needed an object.

The boy had remained absolutely still, once he'd taken up his position in the scrub, and waited uncomplaining in the chill darkness for sunrise. He didn't shift his weight, or scratch at insect bites, or relieve himself. Hunkered down inside his heavy coat, his hat beside him on the ground to make his outline less pronounced, he might have been a rock or a stump.

It wasn't sound or movement that had given him away, and Placido Geist almost missed him. Crouched low and moving counterclockwise, careful of noise, the old bounty hunter had noticed a pale blur, only a few yards away, and took it for a patch of bare ground. He crept closer, not sure of what it was. It was the crown of the albino's head, his hair almost white.

The wind blew hard off the caprock. The hiss of scraping sand covered the bounty hunter's approach. Only at the last did the boy sense somebody coming up behind him, silent as a ghost.

He looked to save himself, but it was too late. Placido Geist did what had to be done, dispatching the boy quickly and without fuss, using a knife. The albino bled out quickly, jerking only a little as Placido Geist held his face in the dirt. He wiped his knife off and sat back, breathing heavily and listening for any sign he'd been heard. There was just the faintest blush of light to the east, the stars beginning to fade, and he was able to better make out the near ground. He debated whether to try and get closer to the adobe. He figured the man with the scar could have as many as four men with him, but he didn't think it likely. He'd already lowered the odds, and if Billy had chanced to pick off another one, Cicatriz might be down to only one gunman to protect his back, or none, and the one left behind might be a poor marksman. Placido Geist decided to get back to the horses.

Billy wasn't there, and Placido Geist wondered what his own chances were if the deputy had been taken by surprise himself, out there in the scrub. Billy rose slowly from his hiding place in the brush, cradling his six-gun.

"Wasn't sure it was you," Billy said.

"I wasn't sure of you, either, for a minute," Placido Geist said. He was relieved to see him.

"You run across any bandits out there?"

Placido Geist told him what he'd found, and what he'd done.

"One down, then," Billy said.

Placido Geist explained his line of thought afterward.

Billy nodded. "I wouldn't choose to think we're safe as houses, but it takes the edge off," he said. "You still intend to step out there and bandy words with that half-breed, or can I just shoot the son of a bitch when he gets in range?"

Placido Geist went over to his horse and took the Sharps out of his saddle scabbard. He brought it back to Billy. "I'd put more faith in a .45-70 than a .32 Winchester carbine at that distance," he said, handing Billy the buffalo gun.

Cicatriz slept like a cat, in snatches, and he was instantly alert when he woke. He heard the girl whimper again, and the murmur of Beaudry's voice, cajoling. The man with the scar uncoiled noiselessly and got to his feet. He was across the adobe in less time than it takes to cock a pistol, and when Beaudry looked up at him, no pistol in his hand, taken by surprise and his face thick with goatish stupidity, Cicatriz drove the knife into his throat with such force that it pinned Beaudry's head to the wall.

Cicatriz gathered the girl up in her thin woolen blanket, leaving Beaudry to flop helplessly, clawing at the handle of the knife with both hands. The man with the scar carried the girl away. She seemed fragile as a bird. Beaudry kicked at the earthen floor, suffocating in his own blood. Cicatriz set the girl down in the open doorway and hunkered next to her, brushing the hair back from her eyes. Her eyes were hot, but not from weeping. Beaudry scuffed his heels on the ground, weakly, and then stopped altogether. She paid him no mind. Cicatriz began speaking to her softly in Spanish, the language for horses and children. She didn't understand the words. He spoke on, not watching Jennie Nighthorse, but looking out through the doorway into the rising sun. It wasn't high enough to warm her, yet, but the liquid syllables, even in Cicatriz's harsh accent, seemed to bathe her in light. She took his hand.

Cicatriz glanced down and felt a hollow and abiding sadness deep in his chest. He fell silent.

The girl had spoken little on their journey, but now she did. She told him a story. It was about a king, who had lost his wife and had only a young daughter for company. The king was ill-served by one of his trusted advisers, but the princess saw through the man's self-interest. She tried to warn her father. The king was preoccupied with affairs of state, and paid her no heed. Unhappily for the princess, the wicked vizier had long ears, and word of her tale-bearing soon reached him. He hatched a scheme with a band of Gypsies, and they carried her off to sell into slavery, but the Gypsy chieftain took pity on the girl, and in time fell under her spell. In the end, knowing she was of royal blood, he made her a queen of his own people.

It was, we imagine, only a childish fancy.

Cicatriz had listened with close attention. His stormy, disfigured face relaxed. He saw that the wound on the side of her head was completely scabbed over and showed no sign of infection. If her hair were artfully arranged, there would be no visible sign of her injury, later in life, if she were to have such a life. Cicatriz pictured her, dressed in white. He could read between the lines of the fairy tale, even as he was charmed by her earnest telling of it. There was a dark history hinted at, but perhaps a happy ending, and he desperately wanted it to come true for her, if not for him.

Jennie Nighthorse had of course read many of the books in her father's library, and had been in fact encouraged to read them, so what she told the man with the scar was taken from those fables and romances. But she had her own experience to draw on, for all this, not that she could quite bring herself to put it into words.

Through the binoculars, Placido Geist could see the man with the scar crouched in the doorway, and the Nighthorse girl. She was still alive, at least. He couldn't make out her condition, or what Cicatriz was up to. He was crouched next to her like a bird of prey, but something in his posture seemed more like that of a supplicant, pleading an awkward case.

Placido Geist put the field glasses away and mounted his horse. Billy had moved down off the rise into the brush, to give himself a better field of fire, closer to the target. Placido Geist sat his horse in the flat morning sunlight, the tableland receding to an infinite weary distance even as the horizon appeared to draw closer. The sun was a few diameters above the edge of the earth, like a disk punched in a piece of paper. Everything was crisp and oblong, early shadows taking on definition, their outlines foreshortening.

Cicatriz stood up and stepped through the doorway, into the light. He shaded his eyes with his hands, and then tugged his sombrero over his head from behind, squaring it. He started forward. Placido Geist nudged the horse with his spurs and urged her down the slope, the mare still skittish and uneasy from a restless night. She swerved her head from side to side, looking to crop a cholla blossom or some greasy desert grass. Placido Geist pulled the bit back, not sawing at her mouth, but straightening her neck. The mare moved sideways a little, recalcitrant. He pulled up and got down, leading her on by the reins. He and Cicatriz walked slowly closer to each other, both afoot now.

He could use the horse for cover, putting her between him and the adobe. Placido Geist thought it was curious that Cicatriz hadn't brought a horse with him. It spoke to the man's carelessness, or his lack of fear. Placido Geist didn't think the man with the scar was careless. He must figure he had an ace up his sleeve, but Placido Geist didn't know what it might be. It didn't matter, if they got caught in the open. They stopped, some twenty paces apart, taking one another's measure. The two men regarded each other. It was the classic distance for a gunfight. They both wanted to get closer, if only to make a rifle shot harder, for either party, but Placido Geist was thinking particularly about someone watching from the adobe. He had every confidence Billy Dollar could notch the wings off a fly at a quarter mile with the Sharps, and the man with the scar obviously thought likewise.

"I see you left your saddle gun behind," Cicatriz said.

"This comes down to the two of us," Placido Geist told him. "I killed the boy in the scrub an hour ago."

"Age counts against youth," Cicatriz remarked, idly.

"What's your play going to be?" Placido Geist asked him.

"You can't have her back," the man with the scar said.

"We agreed on the price, a hundred thousand dollars."

"You can keep the money," Cicatriz said.

"She belongs with her family," Placido Geist said.

"She's safer with me," Cicatriz said.

"Safer than with her father?"

"She's not safe with her father," Cicatriz said.

Placido Geist didn't understand. "What are you saying?" he asked.

"She's being interfered with," Cicatriz said.

"Interfered with?" Placido Geist stared, baffled by the man. "Are you trying to tell me that Jacob Nighthorse is taking liberties with his own daughter?"

"Not her father. He's blind to it. He can't keep her from harm," Cicatriz told him.

"Who will, then?"

"*I* mean to."

"You're on the run, a wanted man," Placido Geist said.

"That's no disqualification."

"The girl can't stay with you. She needs medical attention and family affection, an education, some kind of future."

"I'll take her south of the border to Zacatecas, and leave her with the Sisters of Guadalupe. There the nuns can raise her properly. She'll be better off."

"An orphan, in a Mexican convent."

"I was a foundling," the gunfighter said.

"Look where it's gotten you," Placido Geist said.

"I won't give her up," Cicatriz insisted, stubbornly.

"I find it hard to credit that you're a man of sentimental nature," Placido Geist said.

"Think whatever you want," Cicatriz said, "but why would I be caught in a lie, when by rights I should be indifferent as to whether the girl lives or dies?"

Placido Geist had the nine-inch Smith stuck in the front of his belt, but he suddenly didn't want to fight the outlaw. He realized that Cicatriz, like any other man, had once been a child, himself unprotected from adult predators. But it made little difference why. What counted was that there had been an abrupt shift in the balance between them, and Placido Geist felt less than confident where his loyalties lay.

"What would you do in my place?" Cicatriz asked him.

"Much the same, if I believed it to be true," Placido Geist admitted.

Cicatriz allowed himself a slight smile. "We believe what we choose," he said. "Did you bring Nighthorse's money, or were you going to ambush us, one by one?"

"I brought it," Placido Geist said.

"How much did you get to keep, when you hunted us down?"

"All of it, if the girl were dead."

"That's a fair price to put on a man's head."

"Just your ears," Placido Geist told him.

Cicatriz nodded. "Take the money back to Nighthorse," he said. "Tell him my ears were too expensive. Tell him his life is cheap." He turned away.

"Vermilion," Placido Geist said. He drew the .44 Smith.

Cicatriz kept his back turned. "I'll kill you to keep her," he said quietly, "or you'll kill me to get her. It's not needful, either way."

Placido Geist blew his breath out and lowered the gun.

Cicatriz pivoted slowly, his arms out at his sides. His own pistol was in a cross-draw holster under his vest. "Did the Creole tell you more than you wanted to hear, in Palo Duro?"

"Damn your eyes," Placido Geist said, exasperated.

Cicatriz shrugged. "Why isn't she already dead?" he asked.

"Walk away from this."

Cicatriz grinned. "I would have shot you in the back, old man," he said, keeping his hands spread. "I might, if I get the chance."

"Do you want such a chance?" Placido Geist asked him.

"Only if I can give the girl one," Cicatriz said.

"You're asking something I can't offer."

"I offer myself," Cicatriz said, simply. He folded his arms, his hand moving that much closer to his gun, but still not quite reaching for it, deliberately provocative.

The .45-70 Government was a slow bullet, that tumbled at a distance, but it hit before the sound carried. The heavy slug caught Cicatriz just to the left of his collarbone and nicked the aorta, shattering his left shoulder. It knocked him clean off his feet in a spray of bloody gristle, and he skidded across the hardpan, smearing bright arterial blood on the sand.

Placido Geist took a startled step backward, bumping unexpectedly into the horse. The boom of the Sharps racketed over the alkali and died away. The old bounty hunter dropped to the ground, but there was no fire from the adobe. He crawled over to the man with the scar. "How many others?" Placido Geist asked him. "Who else is in the shack with the girl?"

Cicatriz was panting. He was short of breath, and his eyes had gone wide and staring, the pupils enlarged.

"How many others?" Placido Geist demanded hoarsely.

Cicatriz tried to focus. "That damn Kiowa," he muttered. "He's better than I thought." He coughed up wet tissue from his lungs.

"I'll see that she's safe," Placido Geist said. "I promise you that."

"Who'd trust a bushwhacker?" Cicatriz asked him, grimacing. He coughed again, and died with a sudden shudder.

Placido Geist got to his feet. He saw the girl standing in the doorway of the broken-down adobe, watchful. Nobody else appeared, and she seemed to be alone. Placido Geist gathered the reins of his horse and walked her ahead, letting her shy away from the dead man on the ground. He wasn't looking forward to this.

The girl took a step toward him, coming out of the doorway, and then hesitated, looking past him.

Placido Geist glanced back over his shoulder. Billy had caught up his horse and mounted, and was riding down to the adobe to meet them. Placido Geist turned back toward the mud hut, still leading his horse. He wanted to get there first. How many others? he thought. The girl was concerned about something, but it wasn't somebody behind her. He thought about the dead outlaw Cicatriz, and the bargain he'd made with himself that led to his death. There was a piece missing.

Placido Geist was seized with a chilly certainty, as if a shuttered window had opened in his heart, and now a cold wind blew in. He quickened his pace. The girl watched him approach. Her gaze was listless and resigned.

Placido Geist stopped a few steps short of the adobe. "Your father sent me to bring you home," he said to her, gently. "Is there anybody else inside?"

She shook her head. "He killed him," he said.

He knew she meant the man with the scar.

She looked past him again, biting her lip. She seemed less sure of herself. The look on her face was one of dread.

"Get back under cover," Placido Geist told her.

Billy rode up and got down off his horse. He was carrying his .32 lever-action, the big Sharps in the saddle scabbard. He was pleased with himself. "Got the last of them," he said.

The old bounty hunter had stationed himself in the doorway. "All but one," he said.

"He still inside?" Billy asked, puzzled.

"I wouldn't turn my back on him," Placido Geist said.

Billy squinted at him, less than jovial now, as he read Placido Geist's meaning, but he kept the carbine pointed down at his feet and made no move to raise it.

"You in on it from the first, Billy?" Placido Geist asked him. "Or was it simply an opportunity, something that presented itself?" He sounded honestly interested in the answer. The .44 Smith was in his waistband, but he had his hands clasped behind his back. "I'm only wondering whether you were meant to kill me in my sleep."

"I never intended to hurt anybody," Billy said.

"You knew where the money was, stitched in my saddle. What gave you second thoughts?"

"Jacob Nighthorse swings a lot of weight," Billy said. "It could have swung my way, I did this right."

"Not if he knew you were scratching his daughter."

Billy's eyes were pinched and wary. His breath came short. "Don't go down that road," he said tightly.

Placido Geist saw he was dangerously close to the edge. "I didn't go down that road, Billy," he said.

"I didn't think they'd mutilate her," Billy said.

"What difference does it make? You don't want her to be brought back alive, not and tell her father about you. You came along to make sure she died."

"There was no need for her to suffer."

"You threw in with scoundrels and scum. You wanted the money, and you wanted the girl dead, and you wanted Nighthorse in your debt. You've lost on all three counts. You took the devil's coin, and killed a better man, out there on the hardpan. There's no backing down from it now."

"I meant no injury," Billy said obstinately.

"You're a black liar, Billy Dollar," Placido Geist said. "You're a coward, and a thief, who broke faith with a child, and you're holding a dead man's hand. Aces and eights."

Billy swung the Winchester up, thumbing back the hammer as the barrel came level. Placido Geist brought the .45 Colt Sheriff's Model out from behind his back and shot Billy twice in the chest with it, slip-hammering the single-action. Billy sat down heavily on the ground, the wind knocked out of him. He seemed disappointed, both in himself and the way things had turned out. He looked up at Placido Geist with a puzzled expression. "I didn't mean for things to get this far," he complained. "I never thought I'd have to use you for an alibi."

"You told me you didn't need one," Placido Geist said.

"I needed more than that," Billy said. His eyes glazed over, and his sagging body slackened, toppling sideways. He was quite abruptly dead.

Placido Geist had seen a great deal of death, but he felt an unaccountable loss. He turned away and went inside the adobe to find the girl.

She'd made no effort to hide herself, but stood just behind the door, trembling slightly, her eyes cast down.

"He's past hurting you," Placido Geist told her.

"Uncle Billy was a bad man," Jennie said, looking up at him with a child's grave conviction.

"He did some bad things," Placido Geist agreed.

"But my father trusted him," she protested.

"Men you can trust are in short supply, unhappily," Placido Geist said.

"My father's better off, now," she said, her voice firmer.

Placido Geist thought back to the last time he'd seen Jacob Nighthorse, outside his grand, empty house on the edge of the prairie. Placido Geist had looked back, but Nighthorse had made no gesture of farewell. He stood rigid and solitary by the wind-blown hedge, frozen against the unforgiving skyline like a dead tree with withered branches. Whatever he might have known, Nighthorse knew he'd failed to keep a promise.

"The man with the scarred face, he wasn't a bad man."

"No worse than most," Placido Geist told her.

"He tried to be kind to me," she said.

"A man is as a man does," he remarked, and when he said it, he heard an echo. Cicatriz had told him exactly that.

There is no such thing as love, Placido Geist supposed. There are only proofs of love. He went out to his horse and got a spade to dig the graves.

Jeremiah Healy

PROPORTIONATE RESPONSE

■ ■ ■

Jeremiah Healy is the award-winning author of the John Francis Cuddy private investigator series and (under the pseudonym "Terry Devane") the Mairead O'Clare legal-thriller series, both set primarily in Boston. Healy has written seventeen novels and over sixty short stories. The Mairead O'Clare legal thrillers are Uncommon Justice, Juror Number Eleven, *and* A Stain Upon the Robe, *which has been optioned for Hollywood by Flatiron Films. Healy's later Cuddy novels include* Rescue, Invasion of Privacy, The Only Good Lawyer, *and* Spiral. *A stand-alone private eye thriller,* Turnabout, *appeared in December 2001, and the second collection of his Cuddy short stories,* Cuddy Plus One, *was published in 2003. The first collection of Healy's non-Cuddy stories,* Off-Season and Other Stories, *also appeared in 2003, making it a great year for aficionados of Healy's shorter work. "Proportionate Response," an original story that was first published in* Off-Season, *takes a simple premise—two cabins on the opposite sides of a lake, and spins it into a story of loss, redemption, and new beginnings.*

ONE

Raymond Hammett leaned into the next stroke a little, the paddle blade making that satisfying hiss through the water, the afternoon air over the lake so still he could hear the sound. As his paddle passed the side of the canoe at his seat in the stern, Hammett drew it free of the water, the resistance from the lake like a lover's gentle tug. Despite the black flies, heaven come to earth as a sunny Saturday in early June.

Softly, he said, "You'd have enjoyed this, Hildy." And she would have said, "Colonel, you speak the truth." Even after Hammett retired from the Army at age forty-two, his wife called him "Colonel," though they got to enjoy precious little of their hard-earned time together. She died in an air crash on her way back from the funeral of an aunt. At Hildy's own wake, a well-meaning neighbor had tried to tell Hammett how ironic that was. The widower had just stared back at the jerk.

It was that or choke the man to death.

Other people had tried calling Hammett afterward, at intervals of two weeks, then a month, then longer or not at all. Couldn't really blame them, he knew. Probably took a lot for a person to pick up the phone, facing what would be an evening sitting across a dinner table from . . . his face.

The landmine had done a job on it, all right. Strictly speaking, it wasn't a landmine, but a Claymore that some Viet Cong had strapped to a tree trunk and triggered by a tripwire. Took out three troopers and his R.T.O., the heavy radio the last was humping absorbing most of the shrapnel but not the piece that caught then-Captain Hammett on and through the left cheekbone. The medics had done what they could, the evac' hospital even more. But you need something to build from, and the shrapnel hadn't left much. Back in the days Hammett still looked at his face in the mirror, it seemed to him that the long-term effect was something like melted wax where the feature should be, causing the left eye to sag downward.

Goddam good thing I don't need glasses. Hate to see the optometrist bending the frames to try and line up the lenses.

After Hildy's funeral, Hammett had grieved for over two years. What seemed like a reasonable period, but wasn't long enough. Not by a mile. He'd used the "surviving-spouse" settlement the lawyer had gotten him from the plane crash to move back east, picking Maine for the smallmouth bass fishing, and the serenity, and the . . .

"Privacy," prompted Hildy. "Admit it, Colonel. You wanted to be off by yourself. Where nobody had to see you every day."

And I've got that. For sure.

A puff of wind passed over, making the upright fly rod whistle and sing like the rigging on a sailboat. Hammett had used a thin, metal broom-holder and some Velcro strip to fashion a frictiony little clip that secured the rod vertical at its cork handle just north of the reel. Screwed the clip right into the thwart of the canoe, which he knew would offend a purist because the boat was a beautiful, cedar lapstrake, naturally stained a deep, nicotine-yellow both inside the hull and out. But aside from the clip, Hammett babied the caned-seat canoe, taking care not to crash it into rocks or scrape it along the gravelly bottom of the lake's shallows. He even put the ballast rocks (that had to ride in place of a passenger up-front) in a black, plastic battery box with side handles, so he could lift the extra weight from the hull without scratching the finish.

Then the puff of wind steadied and quartered to the northwest, blessedly keeping the black flies at bay. Might make casting a little difficult, though, unless I get in the lee of the far shore.

Looking that way, Hammett spotted a couple of boys, fooling around with diving masks and fins at the water's edge. The lake was clear enough, the snorkeling ought to be pretty good (if a bit cold), though these boys didn't have "snorkels," too. Hammett had liked snorkeling before the Claymore day, but thereafter, the left side of his face couldn't take the pressure of the mask's rubber. And so he'd given up that endeavor.

Among others.

Drawing closer to where he'd pass the boys, Hammett could see them a little more clearly now. One was maybe eight or so, with sandy blonde hair that couldn't seem to make up its mind what color it would be when he grew up. The other boy was a year or so older, his hair more brown, maybe what the younger one's had to look forward to. Both were skinny, the meager flesh stretched over loose-boned frames, but there was something in the way the younger one canted his head that made him seem the leader of the pair to Hammett. You're in the service long enough, you learn to watch for that sort of thing.

"No, Colonel," Hildy would have said. "It's just that you think you know who they are."

And she'd have been right, too. That little point they were swimming off should be about due-downhill through the woods from a ramshackle farmhouse, the name "PEELE" on the side of its rural mailbox. The house kind of slumped at the head of the L-shaped lake road which took a right-angle turn at its foot to service Hammett's and three other cottages. Or "camps," as Hammett had come to realize Mainers called any lakefront properties. Driving by the Peele place, he'd occasionally seen a woman—getting out of an old station wagon or tending the flowerbeds—but no man. Of course, Hammett had never tried to call on the people there, either.

Thanks to the "privacy," don't meet many new folks anymore. And just as well.

The canoe was drawing even with the boys now, maybe fifty yards away. Close enough to be sure it was the two from the farmhouse, even to see the brown-haired one had a purple mask, the sandy-haired one a yellow. That sandy, younger one reminded Hammett of an Australian lieutenant he'd known in-country.

Back when I was a captain. Wonderful guy around the Saigon bars—"Here, have another pint, mate?"—and I'd started to like him. Until I noticed there was something off about the guy. The way he canted his head, too. What was off turned out to be wronger than wrong: the Aussie had caught a six-year-old Vietnamese boy pilfering from their stores. Took a machete to the child, stuck the small, severed head on a post at the entrance to their compound before a superior officer made him take it down.

That was all, too. Just made him take it down and bury it, before any members of the press got wind of the photo-op and arrived with their cameras.

"I don't get it, mate," the Aussie had tried to complain to the American captain. "Proportionate response, right?"

Hammett hadn't thought so.

Shaking off that memory, he eased up on his paddle as the canoe passed the point. Both boys looked toward him, shading their eyes like Indian scouts from the sun behind him. Hammett waved, and the older, darker-haired boy waved back. The other didn't, that younger boy even dropping his shading hand back to join the other, both balled now into fists on his hips.

Raymond Hammett started paddling again. "This distance, Hildy, that brown-haired boy probably doesn't have the eyesight to see my face against the sun."

"Stop waving, you dweeb," said Curt Peele to his older brother.

Dropping that hand to his side, Jeff Peele turned to the boy who was always giving him orders, even though there was nearly two whole years between them. Giving orders like his dad used to before the divorce, which Curt was almost too young to remember. Once in a while their mom would even say Curt reminded her of their father.

When she told them that, though, it somehow didn't sound like a compliment.

Jeff pawed the ground a little with his big toe. "But it's the man who bought the Ward camp."

"So?"

"So, he's like a neighbor, and besides, he waved first."

"Yeah, and you want somebody to see you, waving to a geek?"

Jeff had no answer to the question. Frankly, he wouldn't want anybody to see him doing that, but he also felt kind of sorry for the man, with his face and all. Who wouldn't?

Now that Jeff had obeyed him, Curt was ignoring his older brother again. As usual. "Look at him."

Jeff turned back to the lake. "Look at what?"

"The geek, what the hell we been talking about?"

Jeff strained his eyes, but couldn't see anything special.

"What about him?"

"All he does with that canoe is cruise around the lake fishing. Or not fishing. Just grossing everybody out with that geek face of his."

"So?"

"So," said Curt, taking in the little point of land with total scorn, "we want to go swimming and diving and stuff; but we're stuck here."

"Here's not so bad."

"Here's boring."

"So, we can walk someplace else."

"Yeah, right. And get eaten alive by the bugs?"

Jeff took that moment to look down at his leg, swatting a black fly that had landed there. Then he realized there already were three more bites on that same leg, the drops of blood dribbling down from where the—

"Stop messing with those and answer me."

Jeff was afraid he'd missed the question entirely. "What?"

Curt sighed like he was saddled with the dumbest brother in the state. "I said, wouldn't it be cool to go anywhere we wanted to?"

Jeff didn't like the turn this was taking. "Canoes cost too much. Mom said."

"All right. With *his* canoe, we could go all over the lake."

Jeff pawed at the ground some more, his big toe starting to hurt now. "Mom wouldn't like that, and you—"

Curt leaned in toward him, cutting him off. "Yeah, right. And who's gonna tell her?"

Jeff looked down again, realizing his big toe was bleeding, and not from a fly bite.

Lifting the single smallmouth bass he'd kept from the afternoon's fishing, Raymond Hammett left the canoe on the ramp, both paddles inside the hull. Two hand-carved, cedar paddles had come with the boat, seemed no reason not to leave them there as well.

"'That's the great thing about Maine, Hildy. You don't have to lock everything up. It's America like she used to be, back in the fifties."

Hammett carried his fish toward the dry sink bolted into a stout maple. He began cleaning the bass quickly and deftly with a Swedish filleting knife—lot homier heft to it than the jagged-edge commando one he'd used in the war. His work today produced a pair of fillets, maybe six ounces each. Skimpy for two, but just right for one with a simple salad and some white wine.

Healthy too, you didn't count the accumulated mercury. But Fish and Game said in one of their circulars that so long as you limited yourself to one smallmouth per week, your own level wouldn't get too high.

Hammett walked up the path through waterfront pines for a hundred feet to the cedar camp. Same wood as the canoe, and same color, too. Old Man Ward had done himself proud building both.

Hammett paused for a moment before washing the fillets at the kitchen faucet. How long before they'll be calling me "Old Man Hammett"?

"If they don't already," Hildy would have said.

Her husband barbecued most things—briquettes rather than gas—but bass was better in a fry pan. Before breading the fillets, Hammett made a salad of Boston lettuce, baby carrots, some smoked cheese diced into cubes, and a tomato. Not a great tomato, but then it was early in the season to have any at all.

Reaching for a canister of breadcrumbs to coat the fillets, Hammett noticed he was running low. After checking the pantry and the fridge, he decided on a drive to the country store in the morning. Coffee, hamburger. Salad dressing, too. And maybe a rib-eye steak, to have with that Zinfandel he'd bought down in Augusta.

Hammett started the smallmouth fillets cooking in the fry pan, thinking about the first time he'd ever tasted red Zinfandel. "Rafanelli" was the name, unfiltered wine from old vines. After his convalescent leave, Hammett and Hildy had been stationed at the Presidio outside San Francisco, and they'd begun driving north to the wine country, stopping once in the town of Healdsburg, where a waiter had recommended this local red with their dinner. After that, Hammett studied up on wine a bit, even subscribing to some of the reviewing magazines. It got to be a joke that if one of the other service couples asked them over to dinner, Hildy would say, "On one condition." And when they'd ask "What?," she'd say, "That the Colonel gets to bring the wine."

Now he laughed a little at that, almost burning one side of the fillets.

A few minutes later and settled in at the dining table, Hammett raised his glass—a nice Beringer sauvignon blanc, $5.99 at that same wine store—and said, "To the lake, to the house, to us."

What he thought Hildy would have liked as a toast, every night.

After Hammett finished dinner and cleaned up the kitchen, there was still a little sauvignon blanc left. He corked the bottle, put it back in the fridge.

Finish the wine on the screened porch after my shower. Maybe hear that owl again, the one with the long, funny call. "Hoo-hoo-hah-*hoo*, hoo-hoo-hah-*hoo*-ah." The last part almost identical to the sound Al Pacino made in that movie, *Scent of a Woman*.

"You mean 'Owl Pacino'?" Hildy would have said, and Hammett laughed for both of them.

This time of year, he showered and shaved at night. Sleep clean, the sheets last a little longer between laundries. Also, you shave in the morning, the insect repellant stings like the blazes. At night you're going to be on the porch, anyway, so you don't need it against the mosquitoes.

Stepping out of the shower, Hammett closed the curtain behind him so the vinyl wouldn't stand wet and begin to mildew. He opened the medicine cabinet and took down the shaving cream from next to the sleeping pills.

Those pills. Hammett had gotten a prescription for them just after Hildy died. Doctor had been real good about it, said they'd last a while. In case he needed one in the future, "if, for example, you should suffer a 'flashback.' "

No doctor had to tell him what "flashback" could be like, though. There wasn't a soldier who'd served in-country that didn't flash back to the worst times now and again. But there were good times, too, and you couldn't close the door on everything without leaving in the cold some of the memories you'd want to have come visit.

Hammett lathered his face, the daubing with his fingers not so different from applying charcoal before a night mission, cut down on the reflected glare off pale, bare skin. The beard to the left of his nose was surprisingly patchy after that Claymore day. In the mirror, of course, the sides were reversed, and he sometimes found himself marveling.

For shaving, you still see the skin, but somehow you've learned not to appreciate the face.

"Just as well, Hildy," said Raymond Hammett, drawing the double-edged razor carefully over the left side. "Just as well."

TWO

"You boys still sitting out there?"

"Yes, Mom," said Jeff, looking at his brother Curt, who himself was looking at the road and petting their dog. Fiver—a mixed breed the size of a German Shepherd, bought from the animal shelter for five dollars—was lying in the dust of the driveway. The boys swatted at the flies, but Fiver just blinked them away without bothering to move because moving rarely seemed to help.

Evelyn Dana "E. D." Peele stepped outside the front door. She watched her two sons, same father but different characters. No, different species, almost. Jeff, the older, was more like Fiver than he was like his brother. Or like his dad, Matt.

For which maybe I ought to be grateful, huh?

But E. D. still felt something was wrong. It was a glorious Sunday morning, even with the black flies, yet her sons were just sitting there. "You both okay?"

"We're okay, Mom," said Curt, eyes fixed on the road, hand stroking the head of the one other creature E. D. was sure he loved.

She looked from one boy to the other. Some kind of "son-spiracy," like over the scuba masks. They'd worked on her for almost a month last summer, saying they knew the country store would put them on sale after Labor Day. And the boys proved right, the masks marked down to fifteen dollars each. Curt insisted on the yellow—the "better"—color, Jeff yielding to him and taking the "dorkier," purple one. The fins were only ten for the pair, but E. D. had drawn the line at snorkels. No, she'd read in the *Kennebec Journal* about a little girl who'd drowned using one on a coastal lake. Seen the news photo of the mother, too.

E. D. shuddered. No photo like that of her was going to be in the paper, not if she could help it.

Though, truth be told, the masks and fins were worth the money I paid and more. Keep the boys occupied when they'd most miss having a father around them. Not that I much miss having a husband around. Matt's kind of husband, anyway.

Most of the time.

E. D. hugged herself as Fiver rolled over. Another father-substitute. Show the boys some of the responsibility they should have—

The dog heard it before Curt did, and Curt before Jeff, she could tell by their heads moving. Car coming up the road from the lake.

Raymond Hammett approached the house he thought the two snorkelers without snorkels called home. Through the windshield of the Jeep Wrangler—"The Colonel likes to stick with a vehicle he knows," Hildy would say—Hammett examined things a little more carefully. "Ramshackle" might give the wrong impression, he decided. The

Peele place looked okay in a cosmetic, landscaping way. Flower-beds tended, lawn mowed and raked before it got lost in the surrounding brush and tall grass. But the paint was peeling, and the roofline sagging, and a few shingles were missing in spots where Hammett suspected a man would've replaced each as it got pulled off by wind or storm.

A man. "Colonel, mind your own business, now," said his wife's voice inside his head.

Hammett slowed as he approached the house, as much not to kick up dust from the dirt road as to look more closely at the people in the front yard. Two boys in shorts and sneakers were sitting by a fair-sized male mongrel. Them for sure, too. Look at the way that younger one—the "Aussie"—cants his head. Body language, best identification system there is, at any distance.

Their mother stood framed by the doorway, whisking one hand at a fly. Sturdy woman, but a very feminine gesture. Wearing blue jeans and a print shirt—blouse, Hammett corrected himself—and watching him. Plain-featured, not a face you'd look at twice.

Then Hammett thought of his own. Not a face you'd look at even once, except to stare maybe, in shock or disgust.

The Jeep had slowed so much, the dog started to roust up, woofing at it. The Aussie boy took hold of the mongrel's collar, and Hammett noticed a chain around a big tree. Probably for tethering the dog when the people were all away or inside for the night.

Then the woman waved. Must recognize the car, know who it belongs to, but she isn't turning away. Instead, she's waving. The brown-haired boy, too. Even the younger one.

Raymond Hammett waved back, thinking as he passed the house that the Aussie was smirking a little.

"Poor man," said E. D. To the Jeep's rooster-tail of dust.

Curt muttered from the corner of his mouth. "Geek's more like it."

"Curt, I'll not have you talking that way about anyone, especially somebody as admirable as that Mr. Hammett."

"What's 'admirable' about being a geek?"

"He is not a geek." E. D. let her voice settle down a register. "No one is a 'geek,' period. And his wound comes from the war. Mr. Hammett fought for his country, not like your . . ." Their mother's voice trailed off, but not in time.

"Like our what?" said her younger son, as though he really didn't know.

"Never mind." This attitude of Curt's, the reason I'll have to leave the office early on Tuesday, attend that parent-teacher conference.

But, first things first, "You boys want to take a drive somewhere today?"

Before Jeff could speak, Curt said, "No, thanks, Mom. We're going diving."

E. D. looked at the poor dog, now rolling in the dust against the flies. "Take Fiver with you, let him get some water relief from the bugs."

"Can't," said Curt, tugging Jeff up.

E. D. Peele thought her older son looked a little reluctant, but she also knew he'd never resist his younger brother's decision. "Be careful," was the last thing she said to them as they headed with their mask and fins across the road and down through the woods.

THREE

"Hildy, you'd have loved this place, too."

Raymond Hammett made his way along the aisles of the country store, a bit of everything on the shelves and walls around him. Foodstuffs, hardware, sporting goods—including some snorkeling masks. Even a bulletin board that had index cards tacked to it for "WANTED TO SWAP," "LOST-AND-FOUND," and "CAR-POOLING."

Hammett carried one of those wire-handled baskets on his forearm. Getting the steak and hamburger last, he went up to the counter, where a nice but stringy-haired teen-aged girl was just finishing up with another customer. The cashier's name was "Tessa," Hammett knew, and she had a stringy-body too. Not at all like the woman back at the Peele . . .

Hammett was shaking his head (before Hildy could prompt him) when Tessa turned his way and flinched. Poor girl, she always did that, and there wasn't a thing he could say that would make a difference, because he'd tried everything he knew. And Hammett knew also that he couldn't blame her.

Tessa mustered a smile. "Will you be needing anything else today, sir?"

Hammett thought briefly of all the things he "needed," but instead said, "No. Thank you."

The girl said "Super," yet never once lifted her stringy-haired head until she had to count out his change.

"This is so wicked awesome."

It was Curt who had spoken, but Jeff had to agree. The wind through their hair as they paddled furiously, Curt in the stern clunking the side of the canoe only once in a while now, and Jeff, with slightly longer arms, clearing it every time. There was a great sensation of going fast without noise, like coasting down a long, paved hill on a bike. Even the interior of the canoe was kind of cool, his shoes and mask and fins resting on all this polished wood in funny shapes, the way *National Geographic* showed a whale's ribs on television.

Jeff noticed the bow of the canoe started to point toward shore, near where they usually went swimming. "We going in already?"

"Just so's I can pee."

"Do you think we should go some slower?"

"No," said Curt.

"But what if there're rocks or—"

They banged into something that made the whole canoe vibrate. Jeff tried in the next few seconds to remember if he heard a crunch sound, like they'd broken the outside. "So now what?"

Curt said, "So now we go around the thing."

They used the paddle blades to push off whatever the problem was, producing, a screechy, scraping noise. Curt made the canoe move in a curve, and they got to the sandy shore without any more problems.

And without going so fast.

Jeff got up from his caned seat first, the canoe tipping some, the way it had when they first got it in the water. They couldn't quite beach the bow without him having to wade a little, which was why his shoes were off and Curt's were still on. After Jeff went over the side, he reached for the front of the canoe to pull it up on shore, and the older brother didn't like what he saw.

"Uh-oh."

"What's the matter now?" said Curt.

"The front of this. It's all, like, mushed in."

"So? It's not leaking or anything, right?"

"No. But the man's going to be able to see we screwed it up on him."

"How's he gonna see that?"

Jeff looked at his younger brother. "When he comes down to his dock and looks at it."

"This isn't his dock, dork-brain."

"I mean, after we take the canoe back there."

Curt just shook his head.

"Hey," said Jeff, "we are taking it back, right?"

"You are such a dweeb."

"What?"

"While I take a pee, you're gonna get some brush, cover the canoe up like the Indians did. That way, we can come down here and use it any time we want."

Jeff didn't say anything.

"It's ours now," said Curt, striding up into the woods like he owned the lake and everything around it.

Jeff stood there for a minute, then took his stuff out of the canoe and set his mask by a tree while he put on his shoes.

Trying to swat the black flies headed for his legs. And trying to think, too.

Raymond Hammett watched the sun setting over the far ridgeline. All afternoon, he'd puttered around inside the camp, where the bugs weren't a problem. Once the sun was low, the black flies stopped flying, and you could go out for a nice, Sunday evening of casting in the lingering daylight.

Carrying his fly rod and plastic tackle box, Hammett was almost to the water's edge before he registered that the canoe was gone. He stopped cold, forcing down his anger and looking around for what the ground could tell him.

Footprints. Sneaker treads, from the pattern of them. Smallish for a man, though. And, you looked a bit closer, two pairs were involved, one a little . . . bigger than the other.

Had to be.

"No," Hildy would have said. "Just 'could be.' No real proof it was the same two boys."

Swallowing the anger rising in his throat, Raymond Hammett marched back up the path to his camp.

FOUR

Turning from the kitchen range, E. D. Peele said, "You boys were gone a long time."

"We got a lot done, though." Curt winked at his older brother.

"A lot of diving you mean?"

"Yeah, Mom," said Jeff, dropping his fins outside before stepping through the door.

"But where's your mask?" she said.

Jeff was transfixed for a moment, then looked down at his empty hand.

Curt said, "Uh, we must've left it down by the lake. The bugs were some fierce."

"Well, you can get it tomorrow."

"Tomorrow?" said Jeff, a forlorn tone in his voice.

"Yes. After school."

"Why not now, Mom?"

"Because dinner's almost ready." E. D. gestured toward the oven. "Tuna casserole, and I want us to eat while it's hot."

"But, Mom—"

"No "uts' about it. We're eating, period." She turned back to the range. "Besides, your mask'll be safe. Who'd steal it?"

E. D. Peele couldn't understand why that simple observation would make her younger son burst out laughing so hard he had to run from the kitchen.

"State Police, Trooper Outlaw."

Raymond Hammett stared for a moment at the telephone, wondering how much abuse the woman must take for having a name like that in police work.

"Hello?"

"I'm sorry. My name's Raymond Hammett, and I'd like to report a theft."

"Of what item, sir?"

"My canoe."

"Your location?"

He told her.

"And phone number?"

Same.

"Now, this canoe, can you describe it?"

He did.

"And the approximate value of the item, please."

"I don't know, but given how old it is and the great care the former owner took to keep it in condition, the 'item' probably could be fenced as an antique."

"Well, we don't know yet whether that's likely."

"How do you mean?" said Hammett.

"Lots of times, it's just kids."

"Kids," thinking again of the footprints and the house at the head of the camp road.

"Yeah. Especially the younger ones. They'll boost a canoe like their teen-aged brothers would a car, go joyriding for a while. Then they leave it someplace on the lakeshore."

"You really think that's what happened here?"

"Well, sir, I don't know for sure. But I guess I'd suggest you try looking for the canoe before I do a real formal report on the incident."

"Thank you."

"Uh, and sir?"

"Yes?"

"I were you, I'd wait till the morning light to go looking."

"Thank you," said Raymond Hammett as neutrally as possible before hanging up.

"You think maybe we should sneak down there tonight?"

Jeff floated the question from his one position of honor, in the top bunk of their bedroom. Floated it softly, so their mother in the next room wouldn't hear. And phrased it in a way that might lead Curt to respond positively to the implied suggestion.

The same way Jeff used to ask questions of their father.

"No," came the answer from the lower bunk, sharply.

"But what if—"

"Yeah, right. The geek's going to come out in the dark, trying to find his canoe?"

"Maybe."

"No 'maybe' about it, dweeb. He's not. Probably doesn't even know it's gone yet."

Jeff heard Fiver clanking the chain outside their open window, woofing a little, like some small creature was in the brush nearby. "Curt, the guy goes fishing like every afternoon."

"Hey, we see him once in a while. That doesn't mean he goes out at night, too."

The chain noise stopped. "I don't know."

"And besides, even if he does start looking for the thing, how's he gonna find it, the way we moved all those branches and stuff?"

"I don't know," repeated Jeff, lamely, feeling again like he was talking with his father.

"Yeah, right. You *don't* know, dork-brain." Curt rolled over in the lower bunk. "So quit bothering me and just go to sleep."

Jeff tried hard to do that. He really did.

FIVE

Raymond Hammett thought to himself, This is a lot like walking through the bush in-country.

Before leaving his camp on Monday morning, he'd bloused the tops of his pants into his hiking boots against both black flies and deer ticks. Then he'd selected a long-sleeved, tight-buttoned shirt and the long-billed baseball cap he used for fishing on sunny days. Dousing every exposed area of skin with insect repellant (which somebody had once told him didn't really "repel" insects; it just masked your human scent so they thought you were a tree), Hammett began walking the perimeter of the lakefront. Past an occasional summer house already opened for the season. Past many more that were still shuttered, the owners figuring there was little sense in driving a couple hundred miles only to be hot lunch for the bugs.

But it was pushing through the still-undeveloped parcels along the water that reminded Hammett of being back in Vietnam. He'd always been an officer there, some poor enlisted man having to walk point. Everybody needed to know what to look for, though. The tripwires would be attached to mines and other booby-traps. What you did was cock and recock your head, not moving the rear foot till the front one was planted safely. You shifted your line of sight often enough that way, you might pick up a reflection of moisture on the strand of wire. Or maybe even the wire itself.

Or maybe neither, like the morning the Claymore got my face.

But no need to worry about that kind of thing here. Raymond Hammett had to smile. No, aside from the flies and ticks, Maine was safe.

"Except for canoes, Colonel," Hildy would have said, and her husband stopped smiling.

Bouncing along the potholed road in the school bus, Jeff Peele made sure the books in his knapsack hadn't tipped over and squashed his peanut-butter-and-jelly sandwich, like they once did. Then, quietly, he said, "I don't think we should tell people about the man's canoe."

Next to him on the bench seat, Curt glanced toward his older brother but sideways, like what Jeff had to say really wasn't worth a full-face look. "You mean *our* canoe?"

For the rest of the ride, Jeff didn't say anything else to Curt.

It turned out to be easy to spot. Once you'd been searching for a while, learning the feel of these particular woods.

The leaves were turned the wrong way.

Raymond Hammett circled the little glade of oaks behind a notch of sandy beach between the rocks. "Right about where I saw those boys from the Peele farmhouse swimming," he reminded Hildy.

Hammett went into the glade, stopping by one of the branches that angled unnaturally away from the sun. When he grasped the branch, it wanted to come away in his hand, revealing a swatch of stained cedar beneath. Thirty seconds later, he'd uncovered the whole canoe and finished his quick inspection of her.

Both paddles were under the thwarts, but her bottom was deeply scratched and her bow worse gouged, like they'd run the little lapstrake beauty into a rock at ramming speed. Mistreated her, and badly.

Then Hammett began to look for sneaker treads. The ground was too leafy, though, and besides, even if he matched a track by the canoe to the ones by his boat ramp, that wouldn't necessarily prove those two Peele boys were the thieves.

"No," Hildy would say. "Just means the thieves were both places, Colonel. Which you already knew."

Hammett shook his head, and that shifting of view let him catch the reflection of sunlight off something made of glass, closer to the lake. Walking over, he knew what it was before he could formally make the thing out.

Stooping, Hammett examined it. No snorkel, and purple, but was it the same mask he saw the older boy with Saturday afternoon? He closed his eyes, tried to picture it. The memory wasn't clear enough.

"Not enough to go confront them, Hildy."

Then Raymond Hammett had an idea.

SIX

"It's not here."

"You sure?" said Jeff.

Curt Peele looked at his brother with all the righteous contempt an eight-year-old can manage. "Are you retarded, too?"

Jeff didn't see how answering that would help, so he just nudged one of the dead oak branches with his shoe. "Paddles, too."

"What?"

"The paddles. They're gone, too."

"Of course they are, dork-brain. How do you think that geek got back to his camp?"

Jeff never understood why his younger brother always had to answer him with a put-down. Even when they were div—

"Aw, no. No! Mom's gonna—"

"Now what?" said Curt.

Jeff still couldn't speak for a moment.

"You look like you're gonna cry, dweeb."

"My . . . mask. It's not here, either."

Curt looked southward, though the old Ward camp was a good mile from where he stood. "That geek stole our canoe back."

"And my mask."

"Come on," said Curt, repeating himself as he stomped through the woods up toward their house.

Behind the counter of the country store, Tessa flinched. Damn, I wish I wouldn't do that to him, poor man.

He said to her, "Do you have any chain?"

Tessa tried looking him in the eye. The right eye. The left side of his face wasn't so bad, that way. "You mean like a length of chain?"

"Right."

"Sure. We got them on big rolls back there in hardware. You're welcome to take a look, but maybe if you told me what you have in mind . . . ?"

"I need to secure my canoe."

"Secure it? Well, then, we got this braided cable, comes all wrapped in like clear plastic tubing."

"Cable. So, it's lighter?"

"And some cheaper, too," said Tessa. "What we can do for you is form like a little loop at both ends. This vise-thing you pound with a hammer makes those loops pretty much impossible to pull out. Then you can run one loop and the cable through something on the canoe and around a tree trunk. After that, just hasp the two loops together with a combination lock. You following me, sir?"

"I think so. What would it take for somebody to cut through the cable, though?"

"Cut it? Oh, gee, bolt-cutters, I'd guess. Or maybe a hacksaw, only they'd have to cut each one of those braid wires in the cable, and that'd sure take a while."

"I don't think I have to worry about that."

"Oh, so you just need something to kind of keep honest people honest?"

Tessa thought the poor man looked at her like he couldn't understand what she meant.

Her back to the kitchen door, E. D. Peele swung her head around just enough to see who it was coming into the house. "Well, where were you guys, diving again?"

Curt said, "He wishes."

Jeff swallowed hard. "I think some—"

"He lost his mask, Mom."

E. D. turned all the way from the sink this time, grabbing for a towel. "Oh, no." She looked at her older son. He just stared at the floor, so depressed.

E. D. thought about the situation. Admit it: if Curt lost his mask, you really wouldn't feel so bad. But you'd have to replace it, because otherwise he'd just take Jeff's. And diving's one of the few things they do together that your older son seems to enjoy.

"Don't worry, we'll take care of it," said his mother, trying real hard to figure out just where she could squeeze fifteen dollars from this month's cash budget.

As Tessa doled out his change for the cable and lock, Raymond Hammett put the purple diving mask on the counter. "By the way, do you sell these here?"

The cashier picked the thing up by the head strap, making the face part twist a little. "Don't know much about them, but it sure does look like one of ours, yessir."

"I found it while I was taking a walk along the lake."

"With the flies and all? You're a brave man."

Hammett saw Tessa flinch again, probably thinking she'd reminded him of his wound. And she had, but somehow he got over it almost before he realized it.

Hammett took out the three-by-five index card he'd block-printed back at his camp. "I wonder if I could post this on your board over there?"

Tessa read the note. It said, "FOUND: DIVING MASK NEAR LAKE. IF YOU CAN DESCRIBE IT AT THE COUNTRY STORE, YOU CAN CLAIM IT."

She looked up, into his right eye. "Sure. You want me to hold on to the mask, then?"

"If you would."

"No problem."

"Just one other favor?" said Hammett.

"Yessir?"

"I don't want any credit for finding the thing, but if somebody does claim it, could you call me?"

A kind smile. "Sure. That do it?"

A smile back. "I think it will."

Curt told Jeff he wanted to wait till it was good and dark, so they did.

"You ready?" said the younger brother from the lower bunk.

Jeff nodded in his.

Curt sighed. "I said, you ready?"

"Guess so."

"You got Mom's flashlight?"

Jeff said, "You think we're gonna need it?"

"It's night out, dork-brain. How're we—"

"There's a full moon."

Curt stopped. His older brother never interrupted him, but—looking out the window—Jeff was right. For once in his life.

"Okay, so no flashlight," said Curt. "Just slow us down, anyway, and one more thing for you to lose."

"I just thought of something else."

"Now what?"

"Fiver's gonna bark outside when he sees us, and Mom'll wake up."

"No, she won't."

"Sure she will."

"Mom's not gonna wake up because Fiver's not gonna bark. He's our dog, retard. He knows us."

Jeff couldn't think of a comeback to that.

"All right," said Curt, swinging his legs out over the edge of the bunk. "Let's go and get that buck knife Pa left here."

"Knife?" Jeff pictured it, his father unfolding the blade till the whole thing was almost a foot long. "What do we need that for?"

"You think even that geek's so stupid he's not gonna have our canoe tied up this time?"

Our canoe.

"Well, do you?" said Curt.

Jeff didn't answer, but no, he didn't think Mr. Hammett in the old Ward camp was stupid at all.

Sitting on his screened porch in the silence and the dark, Raymond Hammett was swirling the remainder of Monday night's wine around the inside of his glass when he heard the sound of rustling branches down near the boat ramp.

That's what they always told him in Officer Basic before he went overseas, one of the few things that proved to be true there. If I see you before I hear you, then I'm probably dead, because you've managed to sneak up on me. But, if I hear you before I see you, then probably you haven't seen me yet.

And that means you're the one's not going home walking.

Hammett set the glass down and waited until the rustling sound near the water gave way to an abrupt, scraping noise. Then he eased up from his chair and out his porch door.

"It's, like, some kind of . . . plastic rope."

"What is?" said Jeff, crouching down by the boat ramp.

The other voice grew snotty. "I can't see it good enough without the flashlight you said we didn't need."

And I don't need this, thought Jeff. Uh-unh.

Curt said, "Let's see if I can cut the plastic with Pa's knife."

The older brother heard the younger one snap open the blade. Loud enough to carry across the lake, much less a hundred feet or so to the camp. Jeff forced himself to look up the hill, but still didn't see any lights on inside, even with the gritty, sawing sound now coming from beside the canoe. Might be Mr. Hammett's away for the evening, like out to dinner or something.

I wished we'd checked to see if his Jeep was—

"Damned thing!" said Curt.

"What?"

"The geek's got some kind of wire under the plastic. Knife won't cut it."

So, forget about the canoe. "You see my mask?"

"He wouldn't keep it down here, dweeb. That face of his, how's that geek gonna use a mask for diving?"

At the next noise, Jeff nearly jumped out of his skin.

Hammett lowered his hands from his mouth. Their father must have been gone from the scene before teaching the boys how silhouettes stand out in moonlight. Or how voices carry through quiet woods.

No need now for the country store to telephone me, either. Pretty clear who the canoe thieves are.

Raymond Hammett put both hands to his mouth and made the call again. Grinning a little, liking the way his "Owl Pacino" echoed in the night.

Curt said, "It's just a bird, retard."

"I don't think so."

"What do you mean?"

Jeff tried to swallow, couldn't. "You ever hear an owl on the ground?"

The noise came again, closer this time.

"Look," said the older brother, "it's not right to cut the man's chain."

"It's not a chain, dork-brain. I told you, it's—"

A third time. The same noise, but much closer.

Jeff straightened up. "I'm getting out of here."

Curt almost shouted at him to wait, until they both heard the sound again and a flapping noise, like the biggest winged predator in the world was coming for them through the bushes.

And then they both began to run pell-mell along the lakefront.

Raymond Hammett had to clamp a hand over his mouth. It would have been good to laugh, but he wasn't sure the boys were out of earshot yet.

And Hammett had heard enough to tell that the older one was leaning to good, the younger to bad. "Both need a lesson, though, Hildy. And the mask business might not be enough to teach them about . . . proportionate response."

Hammett waited a little longer, then climbed back through the undergrowth toward his driveway. He'd make better time on the road, and there was no need to follow them, since he knew exactly where they were headed.

Her heart in her mouth, E. D. Peele wasn't sure why she was suddenly awake until Fiver's barking registered. Probably just a possum or a porcupine, because he'd already learned the hard way about skunks.

Then she heard the sound of something coming through the woods. Running, and running hard.

Turning to her night table, E. D. opened the drawer the boys were never to touch. Took out the handgun and checked the load, the way Matt always told her to do.

One of the many things he'd always told her to do.

Fiver was near frenzy now. Over the sound of the barking, E. D. yelled toward her sons' room. Got no answer.

And vaulted out of bed faster as a result.

Jeff was afraid his lungs would explode. He tried to remember feeling that way before, just running up the hill from the lake. In the past few years, he'd done that run a hundred times—a thousand, maybe. But he couldn't ever recall being so out of breath, or the tree branches reaching out to whack at him, or the roots reaching up to trip him.

The dog's good, thought Raymond Hammett, lying in the tall grass. But she's even better.

The spunk of her, framed by the doorway. Enough presence of mind to think of the gun and the outdoor floods, though she did forget how the interior lamps would backlight her, wearing nothing but a tee-shirt that barely reached her thighs.

Unh. "Sorry, Hildy," Hammett whispered to himself, the dog going from noisy to nuts, straining at that chain.

Then the two boys breached the woods and came onto the road. Chests heaving, feet stumbling, they had to be scratched up pretty bad, too. Their mother sounded at least as relieved as mad, though Hammett doubted her sons could appreciate any ratio in the mix.

"What in the world are you doing out here?"

Aussie, the younger boy, spoke first. "Tried . . . to find . . . Jeff's . . . mask."

"I thought you already did that after school today."

Younger again. "It . . . wasn't . . ."

"And why were you running so hard? You could've broken a leg, even your necks."

Now the older. "Sorry . . . Mom."

"Well, come over here, let me look at the both of you. And don't ever do anything like this again."

"Mom," said the Aussie, "we—"

"—won't," finished the other brother, and Hammett watched their mother seem surprised, as though he'd done something special or new for her.

"It's okay," said the Peele woman, first toward the dog, still straining against the chain. "It's okay," she repeated, this time to the older boy, before shooing both her sons back into the house.

The dog stopped barking, but stayed alert, woofing a little once in a while as his nose tested the wind.

"He senses me, Hildy. Not sure what I am, just something out beyond his reach that he has to treat as . . . threatening."

Then the floodlights went out, and Raymond Hammett got another idea.

SEVEN

Entering the country store Tuesday morning, E. D. Peele yawned. She hadn't been able to drop back to sleep after all the excitement the night before, and getting the boys up and off to school had turned into a real chore. But given the parent-teacher conference on Curt coming up that afternoon, E. D. wasn't sure she'd have time to stop on her way home. And, since even her younger son was apparently willing to risk his skin looking for his older brother's diving mask, E. D. wanted to be sure she had a new one to give Jeff over dinner that night.

If Tessa had any in stock.

Sitting on his deck—well, kind of reclining, really, in a redwood lounge chair—Raymond Hammett began his checklist. Important things, checklists.

"Wouldn't attempt a mission without one, Hildy."

After looking down at the counter by the cash register, Tessa looked up from the red diving mask in the blister pack. "Didn't you buy one of these last year?"

"Two of them," said E. D. Peele. "But Jeff lost his."

"When?"

"Just over the weekend."

The cashier got a coy expression on her face. Nice girl, Tessa, but she could be aggravating, now and then. "E. D., you see the card on the bulletin board?"

"Which card?"

"Take a look. It's all printed out in capitals."

E. D. walked over to the board, then came back a lot faster. "The lake's where he lost it."

"The person found the mask said he wanted somebody to describe it."

Apparently this was going to be one of Tessa's aggravating times. "Like the new one here, only purple."

A coy smile now as the cashier's hand reached under the counter. "We have a winner."

E. D. looked down at the purple mask, feeling a little knot of money worry unravel deep inside. "Tessa, that's super. Who posted the card?"

Even coyer. "Why?"

"So I can thank him."

"How do you know it was a 'him'?"

E. D. tried to keep her teeth from clenching. "Because a minute ago you said, 'he wanted somebody to describe' the thing."

"Well, *he* also said he didn't want any credit for finding it."

"Tessa, please? I'm going to be late for work."

"Okay, okay. It was the man who bought the old Ward camp."

"Mr. Hammett?"

"If that's his name. He just wanted me to phone and let him know if somebody claimed the mask."

"Thanks, Tessa. But don't bother about calling. I'll do it from the office."

"Easier than visiting him, I guess."

"Easier?"

"Account of . . . you know, his . . . deformity?"

E. D. Peele realized that wasn't how she thought of Mr. Hammett's face.

The telephone rang several times intermittently during the morning, but Raymond Hammett ignored it. As with most tasks, there was a right way to compose a checklist, and that was by the application of total concentration. Picture the mission from beginning to end. Even walk through it in your head, so you know what might be needed.

Dark clothes? Check.

Hamburger? Check.

Pills? Check.

Pliers? Check.

Commando knife?

He thought about that last one a little more. Then Raymond Hammett forced his mind to walk through the end of this particular mission, the possible contingencies nobody could eliminate, and he made a tick mark next to "Commando knife," too.

E. D. Peele hung up the telephone in her office. She'd tried three times, once an hour or so, but gotten no answer. Probably out fishing.

Then she considered thanking the man in person. From what I've seen of him, he's certainly impressive despite the . . . Tessa called it a "deformity," but really it's just a wound, and wounds heal. Not perfectly. Thanks to Matt, I can attest to that. But heal they do, and you can move on from there.

I can attest to that as well.

E. D. drifted back to visiting Mr. Hammett—God, he's not so much older than me, I'd call him by his first name, if I knew it. But directory assistance had only a first initial, "R". For "Robert", maybe. Or "Richard"?

Anyway, I can just stop by casually, after work. Tonight, for instance—no. No, I've got to be at Curt's parent-teacher thing. And besides, that might be his supper hour, anyway. So after dinner, then. Tomorrow, say, and with the boys, so that Jeff can thank him personally.

Sure, that's even better. So why didn't I think of visiting before I tried phoning? It's almost a blessing the man didn't answer.

Because, if he did, I wouldn't have an excuse to go see him, now would I?

E. D. Peele found herself smiling in a way she hadn't for quite some time.

"Okay," said Curt on the ride home in the school bus, now not glancing to the side but turning full-face toward Jeff on the bench seat. "What are we gonna do about this geek?"

"He's not a geek."

"All right, all right. But what're we gonna do?"

Jeff said, "I'm thinking on it," but what was really going through his mind was how much last night had seemed to shift things around between his brother and him. Hard to see why, but ever since I kind of cut him off in front of Mom in the yard there, Curt's been the one asking me stuff instead of making me ask him. Or telling me what we're gonna do.

Only problem with that was, Jeff couldn't think of anything *to* do. Especially since whatever might occur to him would probably mean going back to the man's camp sometimes, and that scared Jeff more than Curt—or his father—ever had.

"I've got a surprise for you."

It was Jeff's turn to clear the dishes, so he didn't realize she meant him until he turned around, saw his mother with one hand behind her back,

She was smiling, too, like you didn't hardly see anymore. Then out whipped the hand, and Jeff saw what was in it.

"Well, aren't you happy?"

The older brother looked to Curt, who was shrugging in a way their mother couldn't see.

Jeff said, "Where did . . . ?"

"Mr. Hammett found it."

"Mr. . . . Hammett?"

"You know, that nice man who bought the old Ward camp. He found your mask by the lake and left it at the country store."

"He . . . found it?"

"Yes." E. D. couldn't understand why Jeff wasn't jumping for joy. "That must be why you boys didn't see it. By the time you went searching, he'd already picked the thing up and brought it in to Tessa."

"But why?" said Jeff.

"Why?" This really was strange. "I suppose because he saw the other masks on display there."

"Yeah," said Curt's voice, "that must be the reason, all right."

E. D. Peele turned to look at her younger son. His voice, maybe, but his father's tone, the one the teacher had talked with her about that afternoon. A tone E. D. didn't like, especially when, as now, she didn't understand what Curt meant by it. But Jeff thought he did. And liked it even less.

Raymond Hammett dressed in the dark clothes before putting the pliers in his pocket and the commando knife in its sheath on his belt. Then he examined himself in the bathroom mirror, the watch cap already pulled down over his forehead. Burnt charcoal from a used barbecue briquette had been applied in slashes under his eyes and across the bridge of his nose.

So the pale skin would blend in more with its surroundings, not gleam in the moonlight.

Hammett could feel himself becoming energized. Like the old days. For the first time in years, he had a mission, something to accomplish. Even the edge of risk to it, small though the personal danger might be.

After a deep breath, Hammett reached into the medicine cabinet, took down the vial of sleeping pills, and shook three out into his hand. Dropping them in the pants pocket opposite the pliers, he moved to the kitchen for the freezer bag of defrosted hamburger.

Then Raymond Hammett made his way out into the night.

"He knows," said Curt from the lower bunk.

"I know."

"He gave that mask to Tessa at the country store so she'd tell him who claimed it—"

"—which would also tell him who stole his canoe."

"Our canoe."

"His canoe, Curt. Period."

"What do you mean, 'period'?"

"I mean everything's even," said Jeff. "We took his canoe, he took my mask, and now everybody's got what's theirs again."

"You think the geek feels that way, too?"

"I told you, Mr. Hammett's not a geek."

"All right, all right." Then Curt did something he never, ever did.

He hesitated.

In fact, it was a good count of five before the younger brother spoke again. "Well, do you think he thinks we're even or not?"

If you'd asked Jeff two days ago, he'd have admitted that hearing such an edge of fear in Curt's voice amounted to a good thing. Now, though, the older brother was already more afraid himself than he'd ever admit to anybody.

Than he'd ever been before, for that matter.

The dog barked at his approach. Nothing you could do about it, of course. A good dog'll let the folks in the house know something's wrong outside.

From his prone position in the tall grass, Raymond Hammett watched the floods come on, despite knowing they'd ruin his night vision for a while. That was okay, though.

He had more than a while.

Hammett watched the Peele woman come to the door again, too. Same spunky attitude, though this time without the gun. Maybe because tonight things were happening a little earlier, even if it was full dark already. In civilized places, people tend to measure danger by the clock.

The woman hushed the dog, who hunkered down into that woofing attitude again. Then she turned off the floods, and Hammett waited.

Waited until everything was nice and peaceful.

That's when he took out the freezer bag of raw hamburger, shaped a glob of it like a baseball, and used his left pinky finger to embed one of the sleeping pills deep inside the core of it. Then, holding the ball of meat ("The 'meat ball,' Hildy") in his right hand, Hammett lobbed it like a grenade toward the dozing dog.

The ball landed almost at the mutt's nose. He started but didn't bark, seeming more interested in the hamburger than how it had been delivered. The dog sniffed once, licked twice, then chomped hard, hoisting the chunk of meat up into his mouth and swallowing with benefit of tongue more than teeth.

Raymond Hammett grinned, checked his watch, and settled in to wait a while longer.

"Mom?"

"What is it, Curt?" E. D. Peele called back.

"Everything okay outside?"

"Yes. Fiver probably just heard a porcupine or something."

"You sure?"

"Curt?"

"Yeah?"

"Go back to sleep."

Half an hour, and Raymond Hammett was surprised the dog's snoring didn't wake up everybody in the old farmhouse. Glad I tried just the one pill first.

To be absolutely sure, though, he doctored another glob and heaved it toward the dog, actually hitting a forepaw this time. No reaction from him.

Quietly nevertheless, Hammett moved to the dog's side, waiting a full two minutes more before going to work.

EIGHT

"Maybe it was a bear," said Curt the next morning.

"It wasn't a bear." E. D. looked at her younger son, thinking, That's the sort of worst-case thing I'd expect Jeff to raise instead. "We all would have heard Fiver trying to . . . We all would have heard something."

Her older son was examining the chain at its end. "Looks like he just broke through it, like." There was a link bent open on the ground. "Twisted this enough, and it let go."

Looking at what Jeff had in his hand, E. D. had to agree with him. "Good bet. Well, they say little kids and dogs always roam along the path of least resistance."

"What does that mean?" said Curt.

"It means downhill or with the wind." To Jeff, "I'm going to call work and school. You two start by going down through the woods toward the lake, and when I'm off the phone, I'll take the road toward the camps. Keep calling Fiver's name."

Her younger son said, "But what if we don't find him?"

There was a whining tone to Curt's voice that E. D. couldn't remember him using before. "Then meet me at the old Ward camp."

"No."

"Yes, Curt. The man might have seen Fiver, but even if he hasn't, at least we can thank him for finding Jeff's mask."

"No!"

"Yes! Jeff, make sure you and your brother get there."

"I will," he said.

Very evenly for him, thought E. D.

"State Police, Trooper Outlaw."

The phrase "closing the circle" went through Raymond Hammett's mind as he identified himself into the receiver. "I believe I spoke to you Sunday about my missing canoe?"

"Yessir," she said. "I believe you did."

"Well, thanks for the advice. I found it."

"Terrific. Appreciate your calling to let us know."

"Oh, one other thing?"

"Yessir?"

"I'm afraid I also found a sick, stray dog on my property. I've tried the family I think owns it, but first the line was busy, then I got no answer."

"Do you want to give me their name, sir?"

"Maybe I'd better. In case they call in, to report the dog missing or something."

There was a slight tension on the other end of the line, like Outlaw had heard something in Hammett's voice she wished could be checked by seeing his face.

Be glad you can't, Trooper, he thought.

Then the officer said, "The family's name, sir?"

"What're we gonna do?"

Jeff glanced sideways at his younger brother as they walked into the woods. "Look for Fiver, what do you think?"

"But you know he took him."

"Then Mom'll find him before we will."

"But what if he killed—"

"Fiver?" yelled Jeff at the top of his lungs. "Fiver?"

"Oh, thank you so much."

Raymond Hammett nodded. Seeing the Peele woman from the road—or even from the tall grass around her yard—didn't do her justice. Not so much a plain face as a strong one, more character in it than make-up on it. And not shy about rough-housing a little with the dog, getting her cheek slurped in the bargain.

"Noticed him moping around late last night," said Hammett, "like he'd eaten something didn't agree with him. I was pretty sure he was yours, so I waited till a decent hour to call. But first your line was busy, then I got no answer. After that, I contacted the State Police about him."

"I'll call them myself, let them know everything's okay." She looked up at Hammett from a kneeling position next to the dog. Looking right at me, too, with nothing off about her reaction. "I also want to thank you, Mr. . . . Hammett, right?"

"That's right. Raymond Hammett."

"What do you go by?"

The retired colonel found he was unprepared for her question but wanted to answer it right. "Your choice," he said, and tried a smile.

She smiled back. "I like 'Raymond.' "

"So do I."

That's when they both heard running feet slapping the gravel of his driveway.

Jeff's legs gave him a better stride, so he got to them sooner, though if he'd stopped to consider it, he'd have had to think long and hard to remember another time when he'd beaten his younger brother in a race. Understanding what he saw might take even longer.

There's Mom, getting to her feet from petting Fiver, who's rearing up on his hind legs and waggling his paws like he's begging for food. And there's Mr. Hammett, too, standing close enough to her he could touch a shoulder. Somehow, his face doesn't look so bad up close, like I imagined it worse from the canoe and the Jeep than it really was. And Mom has that smile again, like from when she gave me the mask last night after dinner, only more—

That's when Curt caught up and went by, running hard to Fiver, who started jumping all over him, almost knocking the younger boy down.

E. D. Peele said, "Jeff and Curt, I want you to thank Mr. Hammett for finding Fiver."

"Thank you," said Jeff, thinking, Wow.

"Thanks," said Curt, not thinking anything beyond how glad he was to have Fiver back.

Their mother's face returned to her older son. "And thank Mr. Hammett for finding your diving mask, too."

"Thanks, Mr. Hammett."

"That's all right. I lost my canoe a couple days back, forgetting to secure it at my boat ramp." The man stopped, but not a hesitation. "I know how easy it is to lose something, not to mention how happy you can be, getting it back."

And somehow Jeff knew that was all the man would say about the subject, now or later.

His mother waved a hand. "You boys take Fiver back to the house. I'll be along in a minute, then I'll drop you at school on my way to work."

As they walked up the driveway, the dog running figure eights around and between them, Curt said to his brother, "I can't believe Fiver just ended up there."

"Me neither."

"So, how do we get even?"

"We don't," said Jeff.

"But—"

"Look, Curt. That man was ahead of us all the way, from the minute we stole his canoe on. I'm not ever—repeat, *ever*—doing anything like your stupid stunt again."

"But—"

"No buts. Period."

"Nice-looking boys," said Hammett.

"But a lot to handle alone."

E. D. Peele suddenly looked at him, then flinched and looked down. "I have to get to work, Raymond."

"Before that, what do you go by?"

"Well, my full name's 'Evelyn Dana Peele,' but everybody calls me 'E. D.' for short."

" 'E. D.' or 'Evie'?"

A smile without a blush. "Your choice, Raymond."

Hammett nodded. "Thanks, Evie."

She nodded, too, her next words tumbling out in kind of a hurry. "Look, how about if my sons and I say a proper thanks by having you to dinner tomorrow night?"

"Dinner?"

"Oh, nothing fancy. Maybe chicken, if you like that. And potatoes and a green vegetable?"

Raymond Hammett felt Hildy prompting him but somehow not talking to him. "On one condition, Evie,"

"What's that?"

"I get to bring the wine."

The two of them smiled and nodded until each felt a little, well, giddy.

Joyce Carol Oates

The Hunter

■ ■ ■

Joyce Carol Oates is one of the United States' most prolific and versatile contemporary writers. With a career that spans more than thirty years, she is the author of more than one hundred books, including novels, short-story collections, poetry volumes, plays, literary criticism, and essays. Her writing has earned her much praise and many awards, including the National Book Award for her novel them *(1969), the Rosenthal Award from the American Academy Institute of Arts and Letters, a Guggenheim Fellowship, the O. Henry Prize for Continued Achievement in the Short Story, the Elmer Holmes Bobst Lifetime Achievement Award in Fiction, the Rea Award for the Short Story, and in 1978, membership in the American Academy Institute. She also has been nominated twice for the Nobel Prize in Literature. Recent books include the novel* Rape: A Love Story, *and the nonfiction book* The Faith of a Writer: Life, Art, Craft. *She is also a regular contributor to* Ellery Queen's Mystery Magazine, *the source of her story, "The Hunter," and she is certainly in fine form with this complex tale of love and betrayal among civilians and ex-cons of an American prison, and how the relationships that spring up behind bars can have devastating consequences on the outside.*

At the phone booth outside the Kwik Shoppe on Route 31, Spedwell, New Jersey, there she stood bathed in light. My eyes knew to follow such light. Hair shimmering-pale falling to her hips. Face turning to me like a crescent moon. Quick shy smile. She would say *It was meant for us to meet, that was why I smiled.* For she had dialed the number of one who failed to answer and if he had answered she would not have turned restless and anxious and her eyes lifting to mine across the oil-stained pavement to where I stood beside my pickup about to climb inside. Ignition key in my hand.

In that instant in such a way our lives were joined forever.

Hannah her name was: an old name. Out of the past. A name you would see chiseled in gravestones, in the oldest churchyards.

I had known in that instant seeing Hannah across a distance of perhaps thirty feet that there was this about her, young as she was and her body lean as a boy's and the sparrow-bones of her shoulders revealed inside her loose tank top I wanted to caress, and to kiss, so fragile a sudden blow might shatter them. I had known that Hannah's soul was not a child's soul but predated her years on earth as my soul is an ancient soul out of place in these times of godlessness and a mongrel mixing of the races.

Liam Gavin I was named, for I was of the hawk, a hunter of the sky. Liam Gavin my grandmother-born-in-Galway named me, for my young mother abandoned me at my birth to be raised by my grandmother.

Hannah and Liam Gavin were our names then, together. As if always our names had been together like carvings in stone.

She came to live with me. My place I was renting in Spedwell. Upstairs over the pet-supply store with the dusty display window, that was so often closed over the summer. Five minutes' walk from Luigi's Pizzeria where I worked. And Hannah wished to work, but was too young. But Hannah came by the pizzeria to assist me often. There was no harm in this, my employer did not object. On deliveries Hannah rode with me in the van to keep me company after dark. Walking with me to customers' front doors, ringing the bell. If it was Hannah, with her long shining hair and smile like a candle flaring in the dark, that handed them the pizza in its big flat cardboard box, the tip would be as much as one dollar more than if Liam Gavin had brought them the pizza instead.

Did Liam Gavin resent this fact?

Certainly I did not. For all facts exist to be considered, and utilized.

In small towns like Spedwell you see through lighted windows in the evenings. In summer especially, when windows are open. Often a front door will be ajar, or fully open. Even if you wish not to see at such times, to resist temptation, your eyes lead you to see. For in a small town like Spedwell they don't trouble to pull down their blinds. There is quiet here mostly, and trust.

Hannah said, I love it that people see us together. I love it that they see Liam and Hannah.

It wasn't clear until we had been together for some weeks that Hannah did not always speak the truth. Small untruths I would catch her in. That she would deny, shaking her head like a deceitful child. Long hair rippling and the scar tissue on her face shiny as teeth. There were men she smiled at in the pizzeria when she believed I couldn't see her face. On the street, a car or a truck passing and Hannah would narrow her eyes, staring. Telephone calls she made in secret, that I had reason to know of. When I spoke to her of such things she denied them, always she denied what I knew to be true which was an insult to me. The man she'd tried to call, that day by the Kwik Shoppe, was a trucker whose route was Newark to Atlanta, and I had learned that Hannah had ridden with him in his truck before coming to live with me. And there was the mailman who parked his van at the curb and climbed the stone steps to the building where we lived, that was built on a small hill at the end of Main Street. Six days a week this mailman, a black man of no clear age, their skins are so smooth-dark and their behavior so friendly-seeming. This Negro with a thin black moustache like it was drawn in crayon on his upper lip.

Six days a week he would come to place mail in the row of mailboxes outside our building, that were made of cheap metal and rusted and their locks long broken. It was rare that I would see him, for I was at work, but I understood that Hannah would see him, seated on the front stoop in the sun her thin legs bare and pale and her feet bare, and there she would paint her toenails. My portable radio beside her. Hannah's deceitful face uplifted, her slow smile. The ugly scar on her face did not deter her from offering herself to even a black man whose odor would cling to her for hours.

Saying, Hi there. No mail for me today again I guess?

Never any mail for Hannah. Who had no last name.

Lonliness I would write *eats at the heart. All my life I have been lonly. But I have faith, this will change somday soon.*

Our teacher's name was Mrs. Knudsen. We were instructed to call her Mrs. Knudsen and when she said, at the third class meeting, Please call me Evvie, Evvie is my name, some of us were unable to make the switch. Because you don't want your teacher to be somebody like yourself. There is a need to believe that your teacher is somebody different from you.

Mrs. Knudsen she was to me then. Saying, This is very good work, Liam Gavin. The way you express yourself is clear and direct and your vocabulary is well chosen and what you say is always interesting. Except you have misspelled a few words, I will show you.

She showed me in her own handwriting that was so beautiful:

loneliness someday

There were about twenty of us in the class. The number changed each time. Men were released from the facility, or somebody new signed up for the course. Improving Your English Skills it was called. Tuesday and Friday mornings at ten A.M. This was Red Bank Correctional where my sentence was eleven months to two years but would be reduced to seven months for good behavior. For always in such places Liam Gavin is a cooperative prisoner, a Caucasian.

Word was out in Red Bank, the English teacher Mrs. Knudsen was a good-looking sexy woman, which was true in a way of speaking, but Mrs. Knudsen was not the type of good-looking sexy woman the average inmate at Red Bank would desire. For Mrs. Knudsen was not young. Later I would learn she was thirty-seven. She did not look anywhere near that old, but you could see she was not young. Her hair was graying-brown and looked like she had washed it and combed it through but nothing more so it was frizzy and limp. Her face was solid and creased around the mouth from years of smiling. In the fluorescent lights you could see lines beside her eyes. Some days she wore a dark lipstick that did make her look sexy, her mouth like something you would wish to kiss, or to bite, but other days her face was pale and a little shiny as if she'd rubbed it hard with a rag. Most days she wore slacks and a turtleneck sweater or a shirt and jacket. It is likely that Mrs. Knudsen was instructed to wear loose clothing to come into the facility, which is intelligent advice. It is the advice I would give to any woman.

The thing you noticed most about Mrs. Knudsen was her laugh. A quick loud laugh like she was being tickled. You liked to hear that laugh. In a prison facility, nobody laughs much. But when we had our classroom "discussions" Mrs. Knudsen attempted a sense of humor to put her students at ease, treating us like you'd treat older high school guys, and it was true that most of Mrs. Knudsen's students were younger than her, in age at least. In Red Bank as in other state facilities there are few men beyond a certain age, most of us were younger. By young I mean under thirty. Many young Negro prisoners who know one another from the street and do their business in prison, or try. There are some men not from cities, though, but from small towns, or rural parts of the state, and these were mostly white men. I was one of these.

Improving Your English Skills was a course that ran all the time at Red Bank when they could get teachers to teach it. The teachers were volunteers. I took the course only when Mrs. Knudsen taught it. And only for ten weeks because my parole came through.

For good behavior as I have said. In such places the guards who are mostly white like me, and trust me. Mrs. Knudsen liked me, and trusted me, and I have reason to believe she wrote a good report on me for the parole board. This was clear for when we met again, five weeks after I was released, by accident we met at the Medlar Mall, Mrs. Knudsen smiled at me right away and put out her hand to me as nobody ever did in Red Bank or anywhere, and said, Liam, is it? Hello!

Like it was such a surprise, and it made her happy. Like I was somebody she knew and had a fondness for.

The fiery light in Mrs. Knudsen's eyes. I was not sure that I had seen it before, in Red Bank. Beneath her loose clothes it had been hidden. I saw now that her eyes were warm and dark and hopeful.

Let me buy you a cup of coffee, Liam Gavin. You're looking very well.

You're looking very well is not something anyone would say to me, of people that I know or work with. Yet when Mrs. Knudsen uttered these words, I felt very happy.

Starbucks! Not a place I would ever go. Yet Mrs. Knudsen insisted, and inside seated at a small table I inhaled the smells, I looked around and saw that it was okay, nobody was staring at me or wondering who I was. *You are not one of us, you don't belong here*—these sneering words I would have expected, yet did not register. For so many people look like me now. White guys in their twenties, even high school kids. Mrs. Knudsen had her way of putting me at ease, asked me questions in a kind of slow searching voice like teachers do, how was I, what was I doing now, did I have a job, did I have a family, where did I live. Saying with her smile that made creases sharp as knife-marks beside her mouth, You were one of my best students, Liam. You were always so attentive. You sat so straight. You wrote such interesting compositions. You made me feel less . . . despair.

I was surprised to hear this. I didn't know where to look. The coffee mug in my hand was heavy, and shaky.

Mrs. Knudsen laughed, saying in a lowered voice sometimes yes she did feel despair. There was embarrassment between us for you don't expect your teacher to say such a thing but there was excitement too at such a confession. Mrs. Knudsen's hand too shook a little holding her mug of coffee. There was a look like a girl's—daring, flirty, pushy—in her face I had not seen at Red Bank where Mrs. Knudsen had asked us to call her Evvie but mostly we had not, out of politeness and clumsiness we had not called her anything to her face. Where she wore loose clothes and no makeup most days never looking like she looked now at the Medlar Mall, never in sexy trousers that showed the curve of her hips and a sweater tucked into the waist of the trousers, and her mouth shiny with lipstick.

In a scolding voice saying, Evvie, please call me! I call you Liam, don't I?

Evvie, I said. Ev-vie.

But the word was strange on my lips, like a foreign word I could pronounce but did not comprehend.

Mrs. Knudsen was telling me of her family. Her husband who was a very busy man she said, an accountant. Her son who was fourteen and no longer needed her. Not even to console him when he's feeling blue. He just goes to the computer, and the door to his room is shut. Everything is e-mail, e-mail; that damned e-mail. Of course I understand he's no longer a little boy, I understand that. I wouldn't want him to remain a child. I love him too much. My husband . . .

In this strange intimate way Mrs. Knudsen talked to me in Starbucks. Like we were old friends meeting after many years. She was leaning forward with her elbows on the table. She had three cups of coffee, and I had two without finishing the last. She asked if I was hungry and I said yes so she ordered chocolate chip cookies which I ate trying not to drop crumbs onto the table. This first time we met in the Medlar Mall that would seem to be, if you'd seen us, by chance. Mrs. Knudsen would consider it so. She had no idea I had moved to Medlar. When I was released from Red Bank I looked through telephone directories for three counties until I found the right Knudsen family. Medlar was not too distant, the parole board allowed me to live in Medlar so long as I had a job there, as I did. And so I moved, and so I came often to the Medlar Mall at different times of day. I did not drive past Mrs. Knudsen's house. I knew the address, and I knew where the street was, but I did not drive on that street. Nor did I telephone that number even to hear Mrs. Knudsen's voice. I would not do such a thing. I was on parole, and I knew better. Mrs. Knudsen knew better too, it was not allowed to see people from Red Bank outside the facility if they are on parole. I thought *She is forgetting this. She is pretending to forget.* The knowledge made me happy, for it was our secret between us.

After the Starbucks, Mrs. Knudsen asked if I needed a ride anywhere and I said yes, that would be good. So Mrs. Knudsen drove me a few miles north on the highway to the place I was staying in, that had been a motel but was converted now to one-room efficiency apartments. Mrs. Knudsen said it must be lonely here, this is a melancholy place, and I shrugged and said, It's okay.

Close-by was the Amoco where I worked. To get to the mall I took the local bus. Soon I would have a car. I waited for Mrs. Knudsen to say she'd like to see my apartment, see how I'd decorated it, but she did not.

But Mrs. Knudsen took my phone number. And two days later Mrs. Knudsen called me. For she believed I must be lonely, she said. I had told her that my family was scattered, which was true. She understood how hard it must be, on parole like I was. In Red Bank you did not inquire why another inmate was inside, nor did Mrs. Knudsen inquire why I had been sent there. In one of the papers I wrote for Mrs. Knudsen I spoke of my conviction for aggravated assault, a fight I had gotten into with a man I didn't know, and had not meant to hurt so bad as I did, in a bar in Trenton. This was two months after Hannah betrayed me but still I was in that mood, quick to flare up and wishing to hurt even a stranger who pissed me off by the way he looked at me. But of this charge, and whether my sentence was fair, Mrs. Knudsen never spoke, nor would she.

The next week, on Wednesday when I was working half-day, Mrs. Knudsen took me to lunch at a restaurant in Pinnacle, and afterward to a bookstore called the Bookworm. In a big old wood-frame house, and down in the cellar was the Paperback Treasure Trove, that smelled like a graveyard but Mrs. Knudsen seemed to like it, shelves of moldy old paperbacks for prices low as 50¢—25¢—10¢. Mrs. Knudsen picked out a dozen paperbacks for me saying, Oh Liam, you'll like *this!*—you'll love this! excited as a young girl. It made me smile to see her. Some of these were young-adult books, *The Solar System, In the Age of the Great Dinosaurs, The Red Pony.* Biographies of John F. Kennedy, Babe Ruth, the first astronauts. In Mrs. Knudsen's warm brown eyes I saw the hope of something like pain, it came so strong. Her eagerness to believe something of me I could not comprehend, still less name.

The moldy old books, I wanted to toss down in disgust. I was not fifteen years old. I was not a mental deficient. Instead I thanked Mrs. Knudsen for her kindness. For the books, and for the lunch. Mrs. Knudsen touched my wrist saying in a scolding voice, Now Liam, call me Evvie, please!

Between us there was that flare of light, so fierce you would not believe it could ever go out. But I have grown wary of such, and distrustful.

Liam Gavin I was named, yet there was a being deep inside Liam Gavin who could not be named. This being had never been baptized in any church. No woman had sung lullabies to him cradling him in her arms.

This being seemed to reside in my eyes, I thought. Sometimes in the region of my heart. Sometimes in my belly. And sometimes between my hard-muscled legs.

Between my legs, a fist-like thing that grew rigid and angry with sudden blood.

This thing had no name. It came of a time before there were names, nor even words. Before God spoke with a human tongue.

This woman of all women, I did not wish to harm. In her arms I wept and she was forgiving of my weakness. As women are forgiving of weakness if it is a bridge to their strength.

A light played about her head that was small and sleek, hair cut short. She had had chemotherapy she said, her hair had been thick and had fallen out and when it grew back it was light and fuzzy, soft as a child's and of no color, like thistledown. So she cut it short herself with a scissors, that she need not think of it any longer. As she ceased, she said, thinking of all vain things.

She was a potter and a weaver. So many created things were displayed in her house, you stared at them in wonder. Inside this house of bright colors like flowers, and a smell of modeling clay and paint. And baking bread she made herself, and fed to me: coarse whole grain with nuts, raisins, sunflower seeds. Meals she prepared for me in stoneware crockery, wild rice, polenta. Liking to watch me eat, she said. For she had so little appetite herself, yet yearned to feed others.

Her skin was pale as parchment. Her very face seemed shrunken. Her eyes were ringed in shadow yet became alert and glittering when she worked. Speaking to me, if she was not tired, she lifted these eyes and I felt something turn in my heart, they were beautiful in a way no other man could see. For Liam Gavin has been blessed in this, to discern beauty where another man, careless and crude, would not see beauty.

I was not certain of her age. She might have been older than Mrs. Knudsen. Yet she might have been much younger. She was of a smallness different from Hannah. In my arms she required protection. I thought *Here at last is one who needs me more than life itself.*

Outside her windows were feeders for birds. I helped her hang the newest of these, from a corner of the roof. She thanked me and her eyes filled with tears like precious jewels. Inside her kitchen we would watch cardinals, chickadees, juncos, house finches, jays at the feeder beating their wings in the air, lighting on the perches. These birds she would identify for me. The male cardinals' red feathers bright as blood, astonishing to see. If she was tired we would lie on her sofa beneath one of her handmade quilts in the late afternoon as the sun slanted in the sky and dusk came on and we would watch the birds unseen and hear their small cries. Sometimes we slept, the birds' cries mingled with our dreams. And sometimes we shared the same dream, of the two of us lying together beneath a handmade quilt watching birds at a feeder, their small wings flailing the air.

It was a happy time for me. My happiest time I think. But it was a strange time. For Olive was the only woman I had known who could peer into my soul as through a window. The others, it was a mirror they had seen. Their own faces they had seen, and adored.

My love who was so frail, as if her bones were hollowed out. Yet when I was trapped in one of my nightmares, she would wake me. She would grip my face that burned with fever between her small cool hands and she spoke to me as you would speak gently to a child, to wake him but not to frighten him.

Liam! Liam Gavin. I am here, I will always be here. You are safe with me.

When Olive was first missing, they came to ask me questions. For it was known, I was Olive's friend. I had been living in her house for five months. So many questions they asked of me, yet I answered these questions. I did not attempt to flee. You would suppose, I was puzzled as anyone was, and alarmed, that Olive had gone away. They asked how had we met, and I told them of how passing through this small town Upper Black Eddy on the Delaware River I saw an arts fair beside a church, and stopped, and marveled at the rich colors of certain of the vases and pots, and there were weavings of a kind I had never seen before, and such paintings—! I could not look away but stared and stared.

I did not tell them the complete truth: that the pots, vases, weavings, by Olive or by others, scarcely interested me. What held my attention was a single small painting of a boy of about twelve, with my face.

An angular Irish face it was, strong-boned, frowning, pale blue eyes and lank hair the hue of burnt copper, a shade lighter than my own had been at that time in my life.

Olive did not paint much any longer, she said, but formerly she had done portraits, and this was a "dream portrait" as she called it, of one who had appeared to her in a vision, but was not known to her.

I did not tell them how I saw the small name written in the corner of the canvas: *Olive*. Of how I knew that *Olive* would be my fate, before I looked up to see the woman observing me from only a few feet away.

Softly this woman uttered one word only, as I turned to her.

You!

I did not tell the police officers such truths, for these were private and sacred to me. For I knew I would be misunderstood.

Numerous times I was asked what I knew of Olive Lundt—for that was her full name—and where I believed Olive might have gone and I could repeat to them only that I did not know. That there were many things in Olive's life of which she did not tell me. For Olive was an artist and not an ordinary woman, and because of this she led a life of inwardness and secrecy. In Upper Black Eddy it was known that Olive often went away, by herself. She stayed with friends at the Shore. She stayed with friends in the Poconos. In cold months she drove to Key West where she lived with artist friends. She had been married, years ago. She was not close to her family who lived in Rutherford, New Jersey. She had many friends but certain of these friends did not know of one another, for Olive wished it that way. That no one know very much about her. During times of sickness, she did not want her friends to see her. It might have been a time of sickness now, I told them. It might have been her cancer returning. When Olive would wish to be alone.

They did not want to believe me, for of all the persons they interviewed in Upper

Black Eddy Liam Gavin was the one they suspected. Or wished to suspect. Because I was a parolee, and had what is called a criminal record, and had shared a house with Olive. Yet these police officers were men like myself. Like the prison guards at Red Bank, they knew a certain kinship with me. I answered their questions honestly. I had made no attempt to leave Upper Black Eddy. I spoke without guilt. I did not speak with the air of one who has been hurt or betrayed. More, I spoke in stumbling bewilderment. Wonderment. That Olive would depart one night without saying goodbye, and without explanation.

Would you take a polygraph test? I was asked.

I would! I would gladly.

At the start Olive was so trusting, she gave me her checks to cash. She gave me money to shop for food. Many times Olive said, I could curl up in your heart, Liam Gavin.

Later I came to believe the woman was testing me. She was testing her faith in me. As if half wishing I might steal her money and disappear. For then she would have smiled saying *It was to be. I am meant to live alone.*

In the third month I was living in Olive's house, her son came to her. She had told me that she had a son but he had not seemed real to me. The boy was eight years old. At the time of Olive's cancer he'd been five and six and she couldn't care for him so he went to live with his father and his father's new wife in Tom's River in south Jersey. He was a quiet child, small-boned like his mother. But sullen and guarded in my presence. I vowed I would win this boy's trust. I would win his love. I spoke softly in his presence. I took him canoeing at the boat rental in New Hope. I repaired his broken bicycle. Yet he would not smile at me, rarely would he speak to me. Soon in the household the boy became a seed or a small bone in my throat I could not swallow, yet could not cough up. I did not hate him. I took care to hide my impatience with him. For there was a hope in my heart at this time that I would love him, and I would be a father to him. For it was time for me to marry. Seeing me with her son Olive said, I love you, Liam, that you love my son! The tragedy of his life is, his own father does not love him.

Olive did not seem to see that her son did not love me, there was this strange blindness in one who used her eyes so shrewdly in her work. I would come to perceive that this is the willful blindness of the artist, who sees only what she wishes to see. For Olive in her innermost heart lived not for others but for *her work* as she spoke of it.

There came the hour when the boy shrank from me even when I smiled at him, and I thought *He will have to die*. It was a calm thought, as a hawk, high in the air, sights its prey far below on earth, and prepares to strike, swiftly and yet without haste. Then in my arms in our bed one night Olive began to weep, that the boy lay sleepless—she knew!—in his room, and she felt such guilt of him for she could not love him as a mother should love her child. Oh Liam, Olive said, I gave him up, when I believed that I would die. I wanted to spare him. I pushed him from me. I made him live with his father and his stepmother, he has never forgiven me. He will never trust another woman in his life.

I had to acknowledge that this was so. I felt a rage of pity for him. This boy so like myself whose mother could not love him, who had turned her face from him. And I knew that I could not lift a finger against him.

After this, it happened that I began to test Olive by certain measures. I wished to know if she loved Liam Gavin, or if she loved *her work*. For she spoke of *her work* fiercely yet tenderly as if she both hated it and loved it, *her work* deep in her body as an eye in its socket, or a bone encased in flesh. *Her work* she valued beyond her son. Through clumsiness I overturned a tall earth-colored vase Olive had spoken slightingly of yet in that instant I saw her eyes flash fury at me, and I knew that she had pride in the vase, as she had pride in all her created things, though she spoke and behaved in humility. It was the first time any woman or girl had looked at Liam Gavin in such a way. My hand leapt out, the back of my hand striking Olive's parchment face. Astonished, she fell backward, she was sobbing, shivering. Yet there was an exaltation in her, that at last a man had dared to strike her as she deserved. Yet I ran from the house through a marshy field to the edge of the river where in broken pieces like crazed eyes the moon was reflected and where some minutes later the woman came to me, to touch my arm gently. For I understood that she would come to me, she would not expel me from her house and her bed. I understood the woman's pride was such, she had convinced herself she was without pride.

She would send the boy back to his father, she said. As a way of placating me. For she thought it was the boy who had come between us. She would do this for me, telling herself it was for Liam Gavin and not for herself, that the boy was a burden to her, a hook in the heart, a reminder of weakness she had no wish to recall.

We were tender as new lovers that night. For I had not wished to hurt this woman, truly. She was so shrunken and frail: the bone of her skull nearly visible through her wispy child's hair. Forgive me, I asked of her, and she forgave me of course, it was a sign of the woman's strength to forgive a man's weakness. Yet in that instant when the vase had shattered at my feet I understood that Olive had no need of me. She was a potter, a weaver. She had *her work*. She was not yearning and hungry for love as Mrs. Knudsen had been. She had not the innocence of Hannah who was a child in deception as in love. In her heart Olive betrayed me every minute of every day for in her heart there was no room for any man.

Yet I did not act upon this knowledge at once. The way of the hawk is to ascend, to contemplate his prey from a great height. The way of the hunter is swiftness yet not haste. And there was a sweetness to our lovemaking, that required me to be so gentle, like lovemaking to a child, that excited me, and when I was angry, the excitement that passed between us too was sweet. When the fire coursed through my body, Olive dared to approach me, and hold me. Olive dared to approach me, and hold me. Olive was strong enough for such, and took pride in it. Saying, You see, Liam, I am your lightning rod! I can save you from yourself. My love, you're safe here with me.

That polygraph I passed, like the others.

Peter Robinson

THE CHERUB AFFAIR

■ ■ ■

Peter Robinson's first novel, Gallows View, *introduced Detective Chief Inspector Alan Banks. It was shortlisted for a best first novel award in Canada and for the John Creasey Award in the U.K. It has been followed by more than ten more, including* A Dedicated Man, A Necessary End, *and* The Hanging Valley, Past Reason Hated, Wednesday's Child, *and* In a Dry Season, *most of them nominated for many awards, including the Edgar. The latest Inspector Banks novel is* Cold Is the Grave. *He has also published many short stories in anthologies and in* Ellery Queen's Mystery Magazine, *including "Innocence," which won the CWC Best Short Story Award, and "The Two Ladies of Rose Cottage," which won a Macavity Award. He has taught at a number of Toronto colleges and served as Writer-in-Residence at the University of Windsor, Ontario, 1992–93. Peter lives in Toronto with his wife, Sheila Halladay, and enjoys music, walking, reading, travel, good food, and good wine. The story that appears in this year's anthology comes from the pages of* EQMM. *"The Cherub Affair" finds a new character from Robinson, a professor-turned-private-detective tackling his first real case, and all the troubles that entails.*

ONE

Dazzling sunlight spun off the glass door of Angelo's when I pulled it open and walked in at eleven that morning, as usual.

"Morning, Mr. Lang," said Angelo. "What'll it be?"

"I'll have a cup of your finest java and one of those iffy-looking crullers, please."

"Iffy-looking! All our donuts are fresh this morning."

"Sure, Angelo. I'll take one anyway. How's business?"

"Can't complain."

"Watch the game last night?"

"Uh-huh."

"Don't tell me, they lost again, right?"

"Uh-huh."

Angelo is a diehard Blue Jays fan. He gets depressed when they lose. He's been depressed a lot this summer.

Angelo looked over my shoulder, out to the street. "Hey, wonders never cease," he said. "Looks like you've got a customer."

"Client, Angelo, client. You get customers. I get clients."

"Whatever. Anyways, this one you'll want to see." He whistled lasciviously and sculpted an impossibly voluptuous shape in the air with his hands.

Curious, I took a plastic lid for my coffee and, juggling the cruller in my other hand, tried to make a dignified exit. Could this be it, after all this time? The legendary beautiful blonde of private-eye fiction come to life at last. In *my* office?

I took the stairs two at a time and saw her standing there in the hallway, about to knock on my door. She turned, and I could see an expression of distaste on her face. I couldn't blame her. She was Holt Renfrew from head to toe, and the place doesn't get cleaned often. Under the dim glow of a bare sixty-watt bulb, the old linoleum was cracked and veined with years of ground-in dirt.

Angelo's mimed shape hadn't been far wrong, if a tad over-generous. She was certainly beautiful, but there was something else. I knew her. Damned if I could remember from where, but I knew her.

She smiled and held out her hand. "Mr. Lang. It's nice to see you again."

I gestured her into the office, where she brushed crumbs off the chair with her white-gloved hand before sitting down, crossing her legs, and turning her nose up at the view. It's not great, I know, but it's cheap. We're in a strip mall on the Scarborough side of Kingston Road, opposite one of those clapboard hotels where the government houses refugee claimants. I parked my coffee and cruller on the cluttered desk and sat down. Now I knew where I recognized her from, but the name still wouldn't come.

She peeled her gloves off and gave me another smile. "Susan," she said, as if sensing my embarrassment. "Susan Caldwell."

"Of course," I said. "Nice to see you again, Susan."

Susan Caldwell. She had been one of my students ten years ago, in another life, when I was a teaching assistant at the University of Toronto. Now I remembered. Susan had been notable mostly for her long blond hair and a rather ill-advised essay on Darwin's influence on Wordsworth's thought. The blond hair was still there, along with the dark blue eyes, button nose, long, shapely legs, and a nice curve at the hips. Impure thoughts passed through my mind, but she was only about five years younger than me, and she wasn't my student anymore.

"What can I do for you?" I asked.

"I need help."

"Why choose me?" Nobody else ever does, I might have added, but didn't.

"I remembered that article about you in the paper awhile back."

Ah, yes, the famous article. When I couldn't find an academic position after getting my Ph.D. in English, I followed my adolescent fantasy, fueled by years of Hammett and Chandler, and enrolled in a private investigator's course. I got the qualification, served my apprenticeship with a large firm, and now I was out on my own. LANG INVESTIGATIONS. It had a ring to it. Anyway, the newspaper had done a feature on me, labeled me "The Ph.D. P.I.," and it sort of stuck. Embarrassing, but it brought in a curious client or two, and now here was the lovely Susan Caldwell sitting opposite me.

"People who need me are usually in trouble," I said.

"It's not me. It's my brother."

"What's the problem?"

"He's been arrested."

"What for?"

"Murder." She leaned forward and rested her hands on the desk, so bound up in her plea for her brother that she didn't even notice the dust. "But he didn't do it, Mr. Lang. I *know* my brother. He wouldn't harm a fly."

Now that she mentioned it, I did remember hearing something about the case. I don't usually pay a lot of attention to true-crime stories, especially when they involve celebrities, but sometimes you can't avoid picking up a few details, especially if it's close to home. "Tony Caldwell, right?" I said. "The famous fashion photographer. He's accused of murdering his wife."

"Yes. But he didn't do it."

"Ms. Caldwell, Susan," I said, "I don't usually investigate murders. The police don't like it, for a start, and I try to stay on good terms with them."

"The police." She spat out the word as if it were a cockroach. "Don't talk to me about the police! They've just decided Tony's guilty and that's that. They're not even looking for the real killer."

"They must have a good reason," I said.

"Well, maybe they *think* they have a good reason, but they don't know Tony like I do."

"What could I do that the police can't?"

She looked me in the eye. "You could believe me, for a start," she said. "Then maybe you could talk to him. At least you could keep an open mind."

She had a point there. There's nothing the police like more than an open-and-shut case; it's neat, like balancing the books, and it makes the statistics look good. And most cases *are* open-and-shut. Why should Tony Caldwell's be so different? Because his sister said so? If I killed someone, I'd hope that *my* sister would refuse to believe it, too, and defend me just the way Susan was defending Tony. Still, I was tempted to give it a try.

"Where is he?" I asked.

"He's staying with me. He just came out on bail. Our parents live in Sarnia, and Tony's not supposed to leave Toronto."

"Give me the details," I said.

Susan sat back in her chair and spoke softly. "It was about one o'clock in the morning. Tony and Val—that's Valerie Pascale, his wife—had been out, and they just got home."

"Where do they live?"

"The Beaches. Or Beach. I never know which."

"Either's fine with me. Go on."

"The neighbors said they heard them arguing loudly. Then, after it had been quiet for a while, Tony called the police and said his wife was dead."

"Is that exactly what he said?"

"On the phone, yes, but when they came, before they warned him or whatever they do, they say he said, 'I didn't mean it. I'm sorry, Val.' "

That didn't sound good. "Did they argue often?"

"They loved each other very much, but it was a pretty volatile relationship. Valerie grew up in Vancouver, but she was half French," Susan added, as if that explained it all.

"Did Tony explain what he meant by the comment?"

"He said that he was apologizing for the argument, that he was sorry the last words they'd had together were angry, and that he'd never have a chance to make up."

"Did he say anything else?"

"He admitted they'd had a quarrel, and said he stormed off upstairs. I know this might sound odd, Mr. Lang, but he had a shower. If you knew Tony, you'd know he's a compulsive showerer, and he always does it when he gets upset. Ever since he was a kid. When he went downstairs about twenty minutes later, he found Valerie dead in the living room, stabbed. He says he doesn't remember much after that."

"You say she was stabbed. What about the knife? Did the police find it? Were Tony's fingerprints on it?"

"It was just a kitchen knife, I think. He said he'd been using it earlier to cut the string on a parcel."

"So his prints *were* on it?"

"Only because he'd been using it to cut the string."

Again, it wasn't looking good. "Did he confess?"

"No. Of course not."

"Was there any other reason the police charged him so quickly, then?" I asked, almost dreading the answer.

"Well," said Susan, shifting uneasily in her chair. "I suppose so . . . I mean, you know, when they got there . . . it *might* have looked bad."

"Yes?"

"Well, when the police arrived, Tony was kneeling beside her body holding the knife, and he was covered in blood. Valerie's blood."

TWO

The police refused to talk to me and warned me off the case, as expected, so I decided to have a word with the accused next. Susan Caldwell lived in a two-bedroom apartment in the Yonge and Eglinton area, or "Young and Eligible," as it was known locally because of the hordes of singles who filled the apartment buildings and frequented the restaurants, bars, and clubs every night. Susan was waiting when I arrived, and without further ado she showed me into her brother's room.

Tony Caldwell lay sprawled on his bed reading a photographic magazine. He looked more Queen Street West than East in a white T-shirt with Japanese characters scrawled in red across the front, black jeans, hollow cheeks, and gelled, spiky blond hair. Handsome if you liked that sort of look, effeminate if you didn't. I didn't care either way.

I introduced myself, and he gestured me to a hard-backed chair by the window. We were on the twelfth floor, and below I could see lunchtime swarms of office workers hitting the trendy Yonge Street bistros and trattorias.

"I really didn't do it, you know," Tony said. "It happened exactly the way I told the police."

"Tell me about that evening. Who was there? What were you doing?"

Tony propped himself up on a cushion. "Val and me, Jacqui Prior, my business partner Ray Dasgupta, and Scott Schneider and his wife Ginny. We were supposed to be celebrating. Jacqui had just been chosen as the new Cherub girl. It's a whole range of soaps, bath oils, shampoos, and stuff due to be launched next year. Major multinational campaign. Anyway, Jacqui was the face, the look, and our studio got the contract for the still photography, so we all had a lot to celebrate. Scott is Jacqui's agent, so he and Ginny were over the moon, too. You've no idea what a boost that will give Jacqui's career—not that she's done badly so far, but it's a whole new ballgame for her. For all of us, in fact. It's like we've all suddenly moved into the big time."

"When did things start to go wrong?"

"Just before the cappuccino. We'd had quite a bit to drink, and Val had been moody all evening. Finally, she hit us with the news. When everyone got around to toasting Jacqui for the fiftieth time, Val said something about her face not being so photogenic if she didn't keep her hands off me. You can imagine how that heated things up."

"Was it true? About the affair?"

"I'm not proud of it, but I won't deny it."

"How did Valerie find out?"

"I don't know. I thought we were discreet."

"Could someone have told her?"

"I suppose so, but I can't imagine who. I didn't think anyone else knew."

"What happened next?"

"Well, there was a very embarrassing scene in the restaurant, and Jacqui had to take Val to the washroom to quiet her down."

"Didn't that surprise you, Jacqui and Val going off together after what had just happened?"

"I never looked at it that way. They'd been best friends for an awful long time. But Val was a lot calmer when she came back, and Jacqui left almost immediately with Scott and Ginny. Val and I stayed a bit longer with Ray, drank some more, but it was obvious the party was over. We started arguing again in the cab on the way home. When we got there, the fight went on. I tried to calm things down, but Val was really wild. She's always been extremely jealous. Anyway, I was looking for a distraction, and I remembered there was a package of books I wanted to open. Modern first editions. I hadn't had time in the morning. I got a kitchen knife to cut the string, then Val started on at me again for being more interested in the books than in what she had to say, which, to be honest, was nothing really but a string of insults aimed at me. That was when I threw the knife down and went for a shower—they always seem to calm me down—and when I came back she was dead. That's all there is to it."

"You didn't hear anything?"

"Nothing at all. The shower's pretty loud."

"Could someone have got in the house while you were showering?"

"I don't see how. The front door was locked and bolted, with the chain on."

"And the back?"

"The door was open because it was a warm evening, and we get a nice breeze from the lake, up the ravine, but the screen door was locked. I know because the police kept going on about it when they were trying to get me to confess. They kept telling me how it couldn't have been anyone else, that there were no signs of a break-in."

"How long had you been seeing Jacqui?"

"Only a couple of months."

"Was it serious?"

"I don't know." Tony sighed, running long, bony fingers through his hair. "She's a hard one to fathom. I thought I was serious, but maybe I was just infatuated. Jacqui's a fascinating woman, complicated, very difficult to get to know."

"You say she and Val were old friends?"

"Yes. Had been since high school. They both went into modeling, out in Vancouver first, then they came to Toronto about five years ago. That was what hurt Val most—that it was her closest friend. It wasn't so much that I'd been with another woman, though that would have been bad enough, but that I'd been with Jacqui. We'd always flirted a bit in public, you know, just in fun. But one time we were alone and things just got out of hand."

"Can you think of anyone else who might have had a reason to hurt Valerie?"

"So you *do* believe me?"

I remembered Susan's plea. "I'm keeping an open mind."

Tony thought for a moment. "No," he said. "Since Val gave up modeling, she's been doing a bit of teaching at the agency. Deportment, public speaking, that sort of thing. She gets along well with everyone."

"Did she have any lovers?"

"Not that I knew of, and I'm pretty sure I would have known."

"Okay," I said, getting up to leave. "Thanks a lot, Tony. If anything comes up, I'll be in touch right away."

Tony seemed surprised and alarmed that I was leaving so soon. He sat up abruptly and crossed his long legs. "You are going to help me, aren't you? You do believe me?"

"What I believe doesn't really matter," I said. "It's what I can get the police to believe that counts. But don't worry, I'll do my best. One more thing: Do you think I could have the house keys? It would help if you'd write down the address, too. I'd like to have a look around."

"Sure. You can take Valerie's set," he said. "I picked them up last time I was over there, after the police let me out. I couldn't stand to stay in the house, not after what happened, but I didn't like the idea of them just lying around like that."

I took the ring of keys. A Mickey Mouse key chain. Cute. "Do you know what all these are for?" I asked.

Tony started counting them off. "Front door, back door, studio, agency. That one I don't know."

There was one key left, but it didn't look like a door key to me. Too small. I thought I had a pretty good idea what it was.

"Did Valerie keep a safety-deposit box?" I asked Tony.

He seemed surprised by the question. "Not that I know of. Why?"

I held up the key. "That's why," I said.

THREE

I wanted to find out where the safety-deposit box was located and what its contents were, but I didn't know whether I'd be able to get into it even if I found it. Technically, Tony would inherit everything of Valerie's, unless her will specified otherwise, but criminals aren't permitted to gain financially from their crimes. On the other hand, Tony hadn't been convicted of anything yet. Something to talk to a lawyer about. In the meantime, I had asked Tony to check with Valerie's bank, and there was plenty of digging around for me to do.

The Caldwell house looked like a cozy English vicarage right out of *Masterpiece Theatre*. I parked my 1998 Neon across the street among the BMWs and Audis, and, feeling vaguely ashamed of its unwashed state and the dent in the front right wheel arch, I walked up to the door.

Outside the house stood a huge old oak tree, and I wondered if it would provide an intruder enough cover from the nosy neighbors. Even so, anyone who wanted to get in would have to get past the heavy door, which Tony told me had been locked, bolted, and chained. There was no porch, just the dark, paneled door set in the sandy stonework. The key let me into a small hallway, and a second door led into the living room. The police had taken the carpet, leaving the polished wood floor bare.

Three of Tony's photographs hung on the wall. They were very good, as far as I could tell. I'd expected modernistic effects and cut-up contact sheets, but two of the three were landscapes. One looked like a Beach sunset, showing the Leuty lifeguard station in effective, high-contrast black-and-white, and the other was a view of a rocky coastline, probably in Nova Scotia, where the cliff edges cut the land from the sea like a deformed spine. Again, Tony had used high contrast.

The third was a portrait signed by Valerie, along with what I took to be her lip prints, dated two years ago. She was posing against a wall, just head and shoulders, but there was such sensuality about her Bardot-like pout and the way her raven's-wing hair spilled over her bare, white shoulders. There was something about the angle of her head that seemed to challenge and invite at the same time, and the look in her dark eyes was intelligent, humorous, and questioning. For the first time in the case, I had a real sense of the victim, and I felt the tragedy and waste of her death.

Upstairs, I rummaged through her bedside drawers and checked out the walk-in closet, but found nothing I didn't expect to. I assumed the police had already been through the place before me and taken anything they thought might be related to the crime. On the other hand, if they believed they had caught the criminal and had enough evidence against him, then they wouldn't go to the expense of an all-out, lengthy crime-scene investigation. Not exactly *CSI*; they'd leave their lasers and Luminol at home. Valerie's clothes were high-quality designer brands, her underwear black and silky. I felt like a voyeur, so I went back downstairs.

Next I moved into the kitchen, where the parcel of books still lay on the table, brown paper and string loose around it. The books, first editions of early Mavis Gallant and Alice Munro, were from an antiquarian dealer in Halifax, I noticed, and the string was a quaint, old-fashioned touch. The only thing missing was the knife itself, which the police had taken as evidence.

The door opened onto a back stoop, and my intrusion scared off a flock of red-throated house finches from the bird feeder. Judging by the untidy lawn surrounded by its flagstone path, neither Tony nor Valerie had been very interested in gardening. At the far end, the lawn petered off into bracken and roots where the ravine threatened to encroach, and finally the land dropped away. I walked to the end of the garden and noticed that the ravine was neither too steep nor too overgrown to be inaccessible. There was even a path, narrow and overgrown, but a path nonetheless. You certainly wouldn't have had to be a mountain lion to gain easy access from the back.

The ground had been hard and dry at the time of the murder, I remembered, and we'd had a couple of heavy storms in the last week, so there was no point in getting down on my hands and knees with a magnifying glass, even if I had one. I stood at the end of the lawn for a while enjoying the smell of the trees and wild flowers, listening to the cardinal's repetitive whistling and the *chip-chip* sounds of warblers, then I went back inside.

Fine. Now I knew that it was possible for someone to get up and down the ravine easily enough. But how about getting into the house? I sat at the kitchen table toying with the string. I could think of no way of getting through a locked screen door without leaving a trace, unless it were either open in the first place, or somebody had opened it for me. Valerie might have opened it to someone she knew, someone she felt she had no reason to fear. If she were distracted by her anger at Tony, her surprise at seeing a friend appear at the back door would surely have overruled any caution or suspicion she might otherwise have felt. On the other hand, if the door was locked when the police arrived, that was a problem.

As I sat twirling the string around my fingers and idly glancing at the two first editions in their nest of brown paper, I became aware of a niggling discrepancy. It was unconscious at first, nothing I could put my finger on, but as it turned out, it was *on* my finger. I unraveled the string and tried to fasten it around the books. It didn't fit. Much too short. I looked around on the floor but saw no more, and I could think of no reason why either Tony or the police would secrete a length of string.

I went over to the screen door and examined the catch, which looked like an upside-down earlobe, and surely enough, when I looked closely, I noticed scuff marks around the narrow neck. Making sure I had the house keys in my pocket, as an experiment I opened the door, hooked a length of string over the catch, then shut the door, standing outside, holding the string. When I tugged gently, the catch engaged and the screen door locked. I let go of one end and pulled the string toward me. It came free.

I still had nothing concrete, no real evidence, but I did have the solution to a very important problem. If Valerie *had* let someone in through the back, whoever it was could easily have killed her, left the same way, and locked the screen door from outside. Now I knew that it *could* be done.

FOUR

Jacqui Prior, my next port of call, lived in an apartment off The Esplanade, close to the St. Lawrence Market, the Hummingbird Centre, and all the wine bars and restaurants that had sprung up around there. I found her in torn jeans and a dirty T-shirt, lustrous dark hair tied back in a ponytail, busily packing her belongings into boxes she had clearly picked up from the local LCBO store. While she seemed surprised to see me, she was also curious. She said she was just about to take a break anyway and offered me a cup of Earl Grey, which I gladly accepted.

There was a superficial resemblance to the photograph of Valerie Pascale I had seen at Tony Caldwell's house, but Jacqui seemed somehow unformed, incomplete. She had the kind of face that was beautiful but lacked personality. I imagined that was probably what made her a good model. She must be the kind of person who would shine and sparkle in front of the camera, given a role to play. Her olive skin was smooth as silk, perfect for beauty soap, shampoo, and bath oil commercials, and I could imagine her looking wholesome in a way that Valerie Pascale didn't.

"Where are you moving to?" I asked.

"I've found the perfect little house in Leaside."

"Leaside? Won't that be a bit quiet for you after all this?"

She smiled, showing perfect dimples. "I like things quiet. I need my beauty sleep."

There wasn't much I could say to that, so I sipped some Earl Grey.

Jacqui frowned. It could have been real, or it could have been a model's frown. I didn't know. "It's awful about Valerie and Tony," she said. "I feel terribly responsible in a way, but I don't see how I can help you."

"It's not your fault," I said. "People do what they do. I'm just not convinced that Tony Caldwell did what he's been accused of."

"Oh? What makes you think that?"

"Just a few inconsistencies, that's all. You and Valerie were old friends. How did you meet?"

"We were at high school together, then we both went to UBC. We shared an apartment in Kitsilano."

"So you knew her pretty well?"

"As well as one could know Valerie."

"What do you mean by that?"

"She wasn't exactly an open book, you know."

"She had secrets?"

"We all have secrets. Valerie could make the most innocent thing into a secret. It was her nature to be mysterious, enigmatic. And she liked to be in control, liked to have the upper hand. She needed to feel that, ultimately, if the walls came tumbling down, she'd be safe, she'd have an escape route."

"Didn't work this time," I said.

Jacqui wiped away a tear. "No."

"Who told her about your affair with her husband?"

Jacqui looked shocked, and I was beginning to feel more and more that I was being treated to her repertoire of faces. She was good. "Do we have to talk about that?"

"I'm trying to help Tony."

"Yes. Yes, of course. I'm sorry. I don't know how she found out. I'm sure nobody knew about us."

"What happened when the two of you went to the washroom?"

"Nothing. We just talked it out, that's all. Sort of made up."

"Sort of?"

"I told her I'd end it with Tony. She was still upset, but she accepted my word."

"Would finishing with Tony have been difficult for you?"

"A little, perhaps. But it's not as if we were in love or anything."

"So it was just an affair? A fling?"

"Yes. Oh, don't sound so disapproving. We're both adults. And it's not as if I was the first."

"Tony had other affairs?"

"Of course."

"Did Valerie know?"

"She never said anything to me."

"Are you sure you don't plan to go on seeing Tony now that Valerie is conveniently out of the way?"

"I don't like what you're implying. I've lost a very good friend. There's nothing 'convenient' about that."

"A good friend whose husband you stole."

"I didn't steal him. Don't be so melodramatic. These things happen all the time."

"Where did you go after you left the restaurant that night, Jacqui?"

"I came here. Scott and Ginny dropped me off. They'll tell you."

"Did you visit Tony and Valerie's house often?"

"Sometimes."

"When was the last time?"

"About a month ago. They had a barbeque. We were all there. Me, Ray, Ginny, Scott."

"So you knew the ravine well enough?"

"We all went for a walk there, yes, but look—"

"And you had plenty of time to get back out to the Beach the night Valerie was killed, if you wanted to."

"I don't drive."

"There are taxis."

"They'd have records."

"Maybe. But Valerie would have let you in the back door, no problem, wouldn't she?"

"What are you talking about? Why should I go to the back door?"

"So you wouldn't be seen from the street. Because you went with the intent of killing Valerie. You just didn't know that Tony would get the blame. When you found out he was in the shower and Valerie was alone, you seized the opportunity and killed her."

Jacqui stood up, hands on hips. "This is ridiculous. On the one hand you're saying I went there with the intention of killing Valerie, which is absurd, and on the other hand you accuse me of seizing the moment. Which is it? It can't be both. Look, I don't want to talk to you anymore. You're not a real policeman. You can't make me."

She was right. I had no special powers. Standing, I reached in my pocket for the key. "Recognize this?" I asked.

She looked at it, pouting. "No."

"It's a safety-deposit key," I told her. "Were you ever aware of Valerie having a safety-deposit box?"

"No. But I told you she could be very secretive."

"Any idea what she might have kept in it if she had one?"

"I don't know. Money? Now, if you don't mind, I've got more packing to do."

Jacqui's response to the whole safety-deposit-box issue was just a bit too rushed and casual for my liking. I followed her to the door trying to decide whether I believed her or not. I wasn't sure. The problem was that Jacqui Prior wasn't a WYSIWYG sort of woman. Tony Caldwell had called her complicated, but in a way she struck me as shallow, empty without the role to assume, the correct expression to wear or gesture to make. As I rode the elevator down to my car, I found myself wondering if I was being manipulated. Just how much did Jacqui and Tony's affair have to do with what happened to Valerie? In my mind's eye, I saw myself as Charles Laughton riding his stairlift in *Witness for the Prosecution*. Had they planned it between the two of them, I wondered, and was my getting Tony off part of their plan? Was I being used in their game?

If Tony Caldwell or Jacqui Prior hadn't murdered Valerie, then who else might have done it? Discounting the passing-tramp theory, my money was still on one of the dinner guests: Jacqui, Ray Dasgupta, Scott and Ginny Schneider. Valerie would have let any one of those four in the back door. But which one? And why? And what part did the safety-deposit box play? Maybe I would find out something from the others who'd been at dinner that night.

FIVE

I found both Scott and Ginny Schneider in the office of their modeling agency just off Spadina, in the garment district. On the surface, Scott seemed very much the outgoing, charming type, while Ginny was more reserved. They were both in their late thirties, and I'd guess from her cheekbones that Ginny had probably been a model herself in the not-too-distant past. Her husband looked more like a trendy stockbroker in casual business attire.

"I thought the police had settled the matter of Valerie's death," Scott said.

"They've arrested Tony Caldwell, if that's what you mean," I said. "But that doesn't settle anything."

"How so?"

"I'm just not convinced. I understand Valerie worked for you?"

"She helped out sometimes, yes. She'd been a model herself, and quite a good one, too, so she was able to work with some of the girls and with the clients, help us with our selections. It's an important part of the business, and it can be very tricky, matching the model to the product."

"Was anything bothering her around the time of her death?"

"Her husband's affair with Jacqui Prior, I should imagine."

"Did she talk to you about that?"

"No. We only found out at the dinner, along with everyone else."

"You, too?" I asked Ginny.

"Yes."

"And were you surprised?"

"Naturally," said Scott, looking over at his wife. "We both were."

"Do you have any idea how Valerie knew?"

"I'm afraid not. We certainly didn't tell her."

"Well, you couldn't tell her if you didn't know yourselves, could you? You must have worked closely with Jacqui, though. Did she ever let anything slip?"

"Nothing. Look, Mr. Lang, I'm very sorry about Tony and everything. I've known him for a number of years and count him as a good friend as well as a business colleague, but don't you think the police know what they're about? He and Valerie did have a terrific row—we all witnessed that—and not long afterwards, she was dead. It makes sense. Any one of us could snap under pressure like that."

"Indeed we could," I said. "Any one of us. Where did you go after you left the restaurant?"

"We dropped Jacqui off at her apartment, then we went home," Ginny answered.

"Did anything unusual happen on the way?"

"No. Scott had had too much to drink, so I drove."

"Where's home?"

Scott answered this time. "Scarborough, down near the bluffs."

"So you weren't too far away from Tony and Valerie's place?"

Scott's bonhomie vanished in an instant, and he stuck his chin out. Ginny looked on coolly. "What are you getting at?" Scott said. "You come around here asking damnfool questions, and then you start accusing *me* of murdering Valerie?"

"I haven't accused you of anything," I said.

"You know what I mean. You certainly implied it."

"I merely implied that someone other than Tony could have done it." I looked at Ginny. "Did either of you go out after you got home?"

Ginny looked down at her hands folded on her lap before answering, "No."

"Of course we didn't," Scott snapped. But something was wrong. Ginny didn't want to look me in the eye, and Scott was blustering. Was she protecting him?

I took the safety-deposit-box key from my pocket. "Have either of you seen this before?"

They both looked genuinely puzzled. "No," said Scott.

"Never," said Ginny.

"Okay. Thanks for your time." I pocketed the key and headed back to my car.

Tony Caldwell's photographic studio was located in that urban wasteland of movie studios and sound stages between Eastern Avenue and the Gardiner, where Toronto pretends to be New York, London, and even a distant galaxy. At least parking in one of the vast empty lots was easier than around Spadina, which had cost me a small fortune. The studio had an empty feel to it, but Ray Dasgupta was in the office working at the computer. He stopped and looked up when I knocked and entered. I told him who I was and what I was doing.

"You probably think it's odd, me working here while all this is going on," he said.

"I suppose it takes your mind off other things," I said. "And no doubt there's work to be done."

"Mostly bookkeeping."

"What's going to happen to the studio now?"

"I don't know. Tony was the real creative energy behind us. I'm not much more than a glorified administrator. Oh, I know a shutter speed from an f-stop, but that's about as far as it goes. Tony has a flair for striking up relationships with his models . . ." He paused. "That wasn't meant to come out the way it did," he said. "I mean behind the camera."

"I know what you mean," I said. "But seeing as you mention it, how much do you know about these other relationships?"

Ray sucked on his lower lip, frowning.

"It's not that tough a question, Ray," I said. "Jacqui wasn't the first, was she?"

"How do you know?"

"Never mind. But if anyone ought to know, it's you, his partner. How many? How long?"

Ray squirmed in his chair. "Always," he said. "As long as I've known him, Tony's been chasing women. He couldn't seem to help himself."

"And Valerie didn't know?"

"I don't know whether she suspected or not, but she never acted as if she did. Not in public."

"And you think she would have done something if she'd known?"

"Yes. Valerie is a proud woman, and jealous, too, not someone to take an affair lightly. She might not have divorced Tony. After all, she'd given up her own career, and she liked the lifestyle, but . . ."

"Maybe she'd have killed him?"

"But he's not the one who's dead, is he?"

Still, it was another possible scenario. Maybe Jacqui was the last straw. Perhaps there'd been a struggle, Valerie with the knife, trying to kill Tony, and things had turned around. That didn't help me much, though, as he hadn't even tried to claim self-defense. "What do you think of Jacqui?" I asked.

Ray's lip curled. "Jumped-up little slut. It's not as if she can't have any man she wants. Why Tony? Why steal her best friend's husband?"

"And Valerie?"

Ray looked away, clearly disturbed by the question.

"Ray? Something you want to tell me?"

"Look, I . . . I would never have . . . I mean . . ."

"Were you in love with her, Ray?"

His silence told me all I needed to know.

"Was it you who told Valerie about Tony and Jacqui?"

Ray jerked his head in an abrupt nod, then turned damp brown eyes on me. "How could he? How could he treat her like that? Oh, she never looked at me twice. It's not that I thought . . . or even hoped . . . but I couldn't bear to see it anymore, them carrying on the way they did, and Valerie not knowing."

"So you told her."

"Yes."

"When?"

"Just before dinner."

"Did you kill her, Ray?"

"Why would I kill her? I loved her."

"Maybe you went round to the house later and found her alone, Tony in the shower. You thought you were in with a chance now, but she turned you down, laughed at you, and you lost it. Is that how it happened, Ray?"

For a moment, I thought he was going to confess, then he said, "No. I didn't do it. But I'd have a closer look at Jacqui Prior if I were you."

"Why's that?"

"Because of something Valerie said when I told her about the affair."

"What did she say?"

"She said, 'I'll ruin her. The little bitch. You see if I don't. And don't think I can't do it, either.' "

SIX

"You'd better not have come around with more of those ridiculous accusations," Jacqui Prior said, flopping on the sofa and crossing her long legs.

I took out the safety-deposit-box key and held it in front of her. "I've been talking to Tony," I said, "and we've been through some of Valerie's papers. According to her Visa bills, there's an annual fee of forty dollars at a BC credit union. The people there were not forthcoming, but they did admit that Valerie rented a safety-deposit box. I asked myself why she kept a box in Vancouver when she lived in Toronto."

"And?"

"It's my guess she got it while she was still living there, and she doesn't need frequent access."

"So it's probably empty."

"But why keep paying? She can't have forgotten about it. The annual bill would remind her."

"So what's your explanation, great detective?"

"That there's something in it she wants to keep."

"And how does that relate to me?"

"The two of you grew up in Vancouver."

"So?"

"What's in the box, Jacqui?"

"I've no idea."

"You're lying."

"How dare you!"

"What's in it? Was it worth killing her over?"

"I didn't kill her."

"So you say. But the way it looks to me is that you had the best motive. You were having an affair with her husband. She threatened you. And she was keeping something in a safety-deposit box in Vancouver that may be related to you."

"That's just conjecture."

"But it's pretty reasonable conjecture, you must admit."

"I'm admitting nothing."

"Well," I said, standing to leave, "the police will probably be less polite than me, and there'll no doubt be media interest. Your choice, Jacqui. If you're innocent, you'd be far better off telling me the truth. I don't have to tell anyone."

I could see her thinking over her options: Whether to tell me anything. How much to tell. How many lies she might get away with. In the end, she came to a decision. "I need a drink first," she said, and went over to the cocktail cabinet and poured herself a Pernod. It turned cloudy when she added a few drops of water. As an afterthought, she asked me if I wanted anything. I said no.

"Strictly between you and me?"

"Of course."

"When Valerie dropped her little bombshell and all hell broke loose, I took her to the washroom."

"I've always wondered what went on in there."

"She told me she'd ruin me."

"How?"

"When Val and I were students," Jacqui said, "we were . . . well, to put it mildly, we were a bit wild. We got into coke and stuff in a fairly big way and it can skewer your judgment. There was a man. We thought it would be fun to make a video. He didn't know. No copies. Only the original. Need I say more?"

"The three of you?"

"Yes."

"And Valerie kept this?"

"I told you she liked control."

"Why would she want to have control over you?"

"Not me, you fool. Him. He was a politician. Still is, and climbing the ranks."

"So Valerie used it to blackmail him?"

"She never used it for anything, as far as I know."

"But that gave him a motive for killing her. Who is he?"

"He didn't even know about it. I'm sure of that."

"But Valerie threatened to use it against you?"

"Yes. This Cherub contract is a really big deal, and I need to be squeaky-clean. It's a family line, so if it got around that their cherub wasn't quite as cherubic as they thought, I think you can see where that might lead."

"The unemployment line?"

"Exactly."

"You do realize, don't you, that you've just given me another motive for your killing Valerie? If she made the video public, you'd have been ruined."

"No. You don't understand. There was no video."

Now it was my turn to look puzzled. "What do you mean?"

"You don't think I wanted that thing lying around, do you? I can make myself look enough like Valerie to fool people, especially strangers behind the counter in a bank, and her signature is easy enough to forge. One day, while she was at the dentist's, I borrowed her key and her ID."

"So you're saying—"

"Valerie didn't know, because she never checked from one year to the next, but the video was gone. I destroyed it. That safety-deposit box was empty."

"Then who . . . ?"

Jacqui put her hand to her mouth. "Oh, no," she said, turning pale. "Oh, God, no!"

"You again," said Scott when I called at their Scarborough home early that evening. I had spent the rest of the afternoon doing the sort of digging I usually do when I'm not investigating murders. Ginny walked through from the kitchen and nodded a curt greeting.

"What can I help you with this time?" Scott asked.

"When you were driving Jacqui home from the restaurant the night Valerie was murdered, you asked her about what went on in the washroom, didn't you?"

"So what? I was curious."

"And she told you that Valerie had threatened her with something that could ruin the whole Cherub deal."

"She did? I don't remember."

"Oh, come off it, Scott! You mean to tell me you were so curious you can't even remember what she told you?"

"What does it matter?"

I leaned forward. "It matters because it gave you a motive to kill Valerie."

"That's absurd."

"No, it's not. I've been doing a bit of research this afternoon, and I've discovered that your precious agency is in serious financial trouble. You're in debt up to your eyeballs—second mortgages, the lot—and you can't afford to lose the Cherub contract. When you thought that was in jeopardy, you knew you had to get rid of Valerie. Maybe you planned on killing them both, but when you saw Tony wasn't there, you changed your plan."

"It's an interesting theory," said Scott, "but that's all it is."

I knew he was right. What I'd discovered, and what Jacqui had told me, might point the police in Scott's direction, but they'd need much more if Tony were to be set free.

"You know what the sad thing is?" I said. "You did it all for nothing."

"What do you mean?"

"Jacqui was upset. All she said was that Valerie had threatened to ruin her. What she didn't mention was that she no longer had the means to do it. You killed Valerie Pascale for nothing, Scott."

Ginny turned pale. "What did you say?" she asked.

"Don't, Ginny!" Scott warned her.

But it was too late. Ginny glanced at her husband, turned back to me, and said, "Do you think for a moment I would let her destroy everything we'd worked for?" She looked over tenderly at Scott, who was gnawing on a fingernail. All his deepest fears had now come true. If he wasn't an accomplice and had, indeed, passed out, he must at least have suspected and worried that the truth would come out. "She deserved to die," Ginny went on. "She was going to ruin all of us just because of a stupid adolescent affair. And now you tell us it was all for nothing." Her laugh sounded like a harsh bark.

"You still have no evidence," Scott said. "Ginny will deny everything. Do you realize what you're doing? You could ruin all of us, Jacqui, Tony, Ray included."

I stood up to leave. "Jacqui will survive. And so will Ray. The one thing neither of you seem to have given a moment's thought to," I said as I headed for the door, "is that Tony Caldwell is awaiting trial on a murder charge. A murder he didn't commit. Think about that when you lament your business losses."

After I'd shut the door behind me, I slid my hand in my inside pocket and turned off the tiny digital recorder that had been on the whole time I'd been with Scott and Ginny. Maybe it wouldn't stand up in court, but it would be enough to get Tony free and reopen the case. And, who knows, perhaps Susan Caldwell would be grateful enough to have dinner with me. We could talk about Darwin's influence on Wordsworth.

John Vermeulen

THE CORPSE THAT LOST ITS HEAD

■ ■ ■

Three of our foreign authors have appeared in previous editions of The World's Finest Crime and Mystery Stories, *and this year we begin with Belgian author John Vermeulen, who published his first novel (juvenile science fiction) at the age of sixteen, and became a full-time professional writer in 1979. Since that time, he has written more than thirty books: science fiction, juvenile books, several thrillers, historical and erotic novels. He has won several prizes, and his work has been translated into German, Japanese, and French. Two of his historical novels reached the bestseller lists in Germany and Switzerland. He has also written many short stories for magazines such as the Dutch editions of* Playboy *and* Penthouse, Chez, *etc. A sailing addict, he worked for a long time as a water-sports journalist for several magazines and was editor-in-chief of the Belgian sailing magazine* Yachting *for a decade. This year's story, with the matter-of-fact title "The Corpse That Lost Its Head," first appeared in the Dutch edition of* Playboy *in 2003, and concerns a man who wishes to come up with a foolproof way of murdering his wife. Naturally, things don't go as planned—especially on a sailboat . . .*

Killing my wife turned out to be more difficult than I had expected. Getting away with it without being caught didn't seem to be a big problem, but it was the deed itself that made me shiver. I hate violence and I can't stand the blood. Time and time again I had rehearsed it mentally, but when I was staring at the back of her head, with the wooden hammer in my hand, an icy hand struck me. Maybe I had dreamed too much about my new life without Greta and with Kathleen, and perhaps I hadn't thought well enough about the sound of her cracking skull and the sight of her breaking eyes. Or maybe it was just my conscience. After all, Greta couldn't help it that I had started hating her, she was the kind of person she was. A wet dog can't help it that it smells, right? And I knew she loved me, in her own possessive way. But if I wanted to get a divorce from her, her lawyer would leave me completely broke, she had assured me when at one point I had brought the question on in a rhetorical way. Bye-bye the beautiful house, bye-bye my sailing yacht *Cash Flow* in the south of France, bye-bye the fat salary in her old man's firm . . . I hadn't mentioned the word "divorce" anymore. Not even rhetorically.

But Kathleen was young and sparkling fresh, she was bright and fun to be with. And she was also damn attractive. From the first time I saw her smile with her glittering white teeth, my life had taken a 180-degree turn. Soon we became lovers, and from then on Greta started to be a serious obstacle.

Oh, yes, I do believe in romantic love without the need of expensive cars and half a dozen gold cards, but not for long. Women like Kathleen don't like losers, no matter how good they are in bed. So, I had to do something about Greta, something drastic.

If I killed Greta on board the yacht, all I had to do was throw her in deep water with an anchor around her neck. And then report her missing. Crew members do disappear sometimes, especially if they stumble into the water during the night without wearing a lifeline. And well, who puts on a lifeline on a quiet night on the Mediterranean anyway? I had it all figured out in less than ten minutes. However, to find a clean way to kill Geta, I needed several days. In the end, the painful conclusion was that just a little bit of violence would be inevitable. The idea was to knock her out with a blow on the head, before I put her over the side of the boat. I should do this with a wooden hammer, because by using an ordinary hammer, I risked knocking a hole in her skull. And like I mentioned before, the color of blood makes me sick.

It wasn't unusual for us to leave our mooring in Port Camargue in the evening for a sail to Montpellier or one of those other nice places. After a hot day with little wind, it can be very pleasant at sea when the last daylight is disappearing. So, Greta didn't ask any questions when I started the engine and cast off. She kept silent until she saw that I steered the boat into the sea instead of following the coast to the northeast. Then she asked me: "Do you intend to sail to Africa or something like that?"

I had my answer ready: "We go on motoring for a few miles, that way we don't have to tack later on to Montpellier."

Greta didn't understand much about sailing. To her, a boat was just a floating thing you could use for sunbathing. So, she accepted my answer and disappeared below. There she sat by the navigation table, with one of her stupid crossword puzzles.

Three miles off the coast, the echo sounder gave a reading of seventy-two feet, more than deep enough. The sea was silvery enlightened by the full moon, and in the wide environment there was no other ship in sight. The coast was a convivial ribbon of twinkling lights.

I put on the autopilot and took the wooden hammer out of the trunk beneath the starboard cockpit seat, where I also kept the spare anchor with a chain on it.

By the muffled light above the navigation table, I could see the back of Greta's head. She sat there puzzling, slightly bent forward; unaware of what was about to happen. Just one firm blow and everything should be over. The world wouldn't miss her, and neither would I.

At that moment, Greta looked up. "You need help?" she asked. She had to raise her voice because of the noise of the diesel engine.

I kept the hammer behind my back. "No need to, I can handle it," I said. It was a bit strange; normally she never volunteered to help me with the boat.

She shrugged and got on with her puzzle.

I was standing behind her now, staring at her crown, my heartbeat camouflaged by the thumping sound of the engine. What to do if she wasn't knocked out by the first blow? Looking her in the eyes, the moment she would understand what was happening, should be something unbearable. Greta sometimes had a frightfully coercive glance; maybe in a former life she had been a witch or something like that.

The moment I raised the hammer, my ears began to sough and I felt a faint coming up. I wanted to be a thousand miles away, with my head between Kathleen's satin posterior. That latest thought helped a bit, I remembered why I stood there staggering at the point of no return.

Greta's pen stopped writing, and one frightful moment I thought I heard her unpleasant sharp voice in my head: *Come on now, you moron, or don't you have the guts . . .*

Savagely and almost blindly I hit her on the head. It was almost as if I was defending myself in panic against a monster that was trying to eat me. It felt like I hit a piece of wood. Without a sound, Greta collapsed with her face onto the navigation table.

I stood there motionless, staring down at her, with a sudden and intense feeling of remorse. That damn conscience again!

Her limp body weighed heavily, I had to heave her on my shoulders in order to get her into the cockpit. Greta wasn't dead; I felt her breathing just before I let her glide down painfully on the teak bottom of the cockpit. In the pale moonlight her wide-open mouth looked like a black hole in her ghostly white face and she was drooling. I averted my eyes from it and took the spare anchor out of the trunk. The chain made a hard, rattling sound on the edge of the cockpit seat, it startled me. The gray sea was still deserted.

Fumbling, I enwrapped the chain around Greta's neck and put the whole shebang over the side. First the anchor went in. Its weight gave a hard pull on Greta's body. Headfirst it followed the anchor and disappeared under the surface. The rest of the chain rattled again, tearing splinters of polyester out of the guardrail of the cockpit. Right at the moment the last bit of the chain fell into the water, *Cash Flow* experienced a bump that almost caused me to lose my balance. At the same time the engine came to a sudden halt.

Nervously I pressed the starter button. The diesel fired right away, but it was killed again when I put it in gear. It sounded as if the propeller was fouled.

The anchor chain! I had expected it to sink right to the bottom of the sea. To be honest, I hadn't thought at all about the possibility that it could block the propeller. My mind had been too busy with other things.

"Damn!" I cursed. I sat down on the cockpit seat and tried to think.

With a bit of luck and handiness, a diver could free the propeller, but I wasn't a diver. Dammit it, I couldn't even swim properly! And moreover, it was dark.

Right then, despair gave me an idea. I could disconnect the prop shaft. That wasn't so difficult, all I had to do was remove just one pin and loosen the bearing, and then the thing would fall out of its hole. And I had the sails to navigate back to the marina.

Two minutes later I was lying on my stomach in the narrow engine room, fumbling with the pin of the prop shaft by the light of a small flashlight. Within my reach I had a cotton rag to close the hole of the shaft against incoming water.

The pin came out easily, but the shaft didn't move. It looked like the chain completely blocked the stupid thing.

Cursing didn't help. I was sweating in the cramped space with its nauseating smell of diesel oil, so I crawled back into the cabin where I sat on the starboard bench, defeated.

The second idea—also born in despair—came by a beeping sound of the echo sounder. It was the shallow depth alarm that sometimes went off when a shoal of fish was swimming underneath the boat.

I jumped on my feet and spread the sea chart on the table, on top of the ladies' magazine with Greta's crossword puzzle. The anchor was dangling about forty-five feet deep beneath the yacht. If I sailed into shallow water, the thing would dig itself into the sea bottom. Even at a modest speed, the twelve tons of weight of the boat should cause quite an impact, possibly enough to pull the propeller shaft out of its bearing.

According to the chart, I had to sail a mile or so in the direction of the coast. There were no other shallows in the environment.

I set sail and steered *Cash Flow* shoreward. There was just a faint breeze and the extra weight I was towing under the boat had the effect of a handbrake, so my speed was less than three knots, but fortunately I had the time.

After a while, the echo sounder indicated that the depth beneath the keel was lessening. Now and then I let my eyes wander over the sea. At some moment I saw the lights of three fishing boats close to the shore. They were steaming to the southwest. Besides this, everything kept quiet.

I passed the forty-five-feet depth line and braced myself. Anytime now, the anchor could get stuck between the rocks at the sea bottom. And then it happened indeed. In spite of the low speed, the impact was severe. However, *Cash Flow* did not lose her burden. She lay motionless now, regardless of the still pulling sails, kept on her place by the anchor.

For the second time I crawled into the engine room. I could have saved the effort; the propeller shaft was still solidly in place.

"You dirty bitch!" I shouted. I was getting the idea that even dead, Greta was still badgering me.

I lowered the sails, not knowing what to do next. Now I really was in deep shit, with a boat that couldn't go anywhere and the anchor chain firmly enwrapped around the dead body of my wife. And Kathleen didn't seem the kind of woman who would visit a murderer in jail. I hated myself for being so stupid.

But despair kept inspiring me. What if I sank the yacht? There was a small rubber dinghy to get to the shore. I could tell the authorities my wireless was out of order. If I gave them a false position, they probably would never find the wreck. Suppose they should make the effort to send out a search party. Which I doubted. Forty-five feet or so of water was not that deep, but thanks to its fin keel, the yacht would lay down on her side and there was a good chance that the blue hull (a choice of Greta's!) wouldn't be spotted from the air. There even was a possibility of recovering the loss of the boat from my insurance.

The next moment I was busy unscrewing the fasteners of the several water inlets and outlets at the bottom of the yacht. After that, I opened the valves. The seawater started gulping in from half a dozen holes. A true nightmare for every sailor, but I had other worries.

I took the folded rubber dinghy out of its stowage and inflated it with its air cylinder. After that, I took the paddles and put the dinghy over the side. At that moment, I remembered my documents. Hurriedly I went back into the cabin where the water stood a couple of inches above the floor now. Apparently it had reached the batteries, since the lights were slowly fading. I grabbed my car documents and passport out of the navigation table and, with squishing shoes, climbed back on deck.

A shapeless, dark figure was floating in the water next to the dinghy.

My heart started pounding like crazy. Reluctantly I climbed into the small boat. Only then I discovered how the corpse had come free from the anchor chain. Greta's head was gone, it probably sank. The force of the chain around her neck when the anchor had stuck had jerked the head off of her body. I reached that conclusion as soon as I had stopped vomiting. At the same time it struck me that there was no longer a need to sink the yacht.

I clambered back on board to close the valves. In the meantime, however, the water in the cabin had risen too high. I couldn't reach the valves without plunging my head into the water, an impossible exercise for a nonswimmer, especially in the dark. I just couldn't do it.

Dripping wet and shivering despite the sultry night, I let myself down into the dinghy again. As if they were pulled by a magnet, my eyes slid to the jagged remains of Greta's neck. Silvery fish were swimming around it, their movements causing a greenish fluorescence on the surface of the water.

My brains were whirling. The corpse had to go, and definitively. But how?

The solution of my problem floated right before my nose, bubbling and gargling. I had to put the corpse into the sinking yacht. And pray the wreck would not be found indeed.

I switched my brains to nonactive and dragged the decapitated corpse into the dinghy. Groaning, I heaved the heavy, almost unmanageable thing on my back in order to climb with it over the guardrail of the yacht. This guardrail was already a good deal lower than before, but that barely helped.

And then, Greta grabbed me by the throat. All of a sudden her arms closed around my neck with enormous strength. *Rigor mortis!* I realized after the first terrible shock. I jerked and struggled in order to free myself from those cold arms that were trying to strangle me with much more strength than the living Greta had ever possessed. I staggered, after which my left knee collapsed. Together with my horrible burden, I came down painfully on the cockpit floor. Some way or another, I tumbled head forward into the cabin where I splashed into the still rising water. The submerged corpse loosed its grip, and all of a sudden I was free. Furiously I pushed the now stiff body away from me and gasped for air.

There wasn't much time left, the water had already reached my breast.

With my last bit of courage, I pushed the corpse into the forecastle and shut the door. This way, it would not float out of the yacht when it was sinking to the sea bottom. Breathing heavily, I wrestled myself back on deck and into the dinghy. I took the paddles and rowed about twenty yards away from the yacht. There I paused, out of breath and dizzy, to watch *Cash Flow* going down.

Right before the water reached the deck, the rear end of the yacht started sinking much faster. For a moment it looked like one of those torpedo-struck ships in an old war movie, with its bow in the air. Then it disappeared soundlessly into the deep.

After a while, amid the stream of air bubbles, some stuff surfaced. A cushion, two half-empty bottles, an empty canister, a wooden hammer . . . With some vague idea to bury the rubbish somewhere, I collected the stuff in the dinghy.

I sat there motionless for quite a while, even after the very last air bubbles had disappeared, staring at the gray water. Together with Greta and the yacht, an important part of my life had vanished.

I reached the shore without being seen and there were no night wanderers on the beach. Maybe I should have felt relieved, but the truth was that I felt as if I had received a blow with a wooden hammer myself.

At first, the local police reacted annoyingly, as if they wanted to accuse me of being an irresponsible sailor. Their attitude changed when I started to snivel. As a rule, the French are relatively sensitive about emotional situations. And sniveling was something that came quite spontaneous at that moment.

The police let me go home, to Kathleen.

"I think that accident was the best thing that could have happened to me," I said to Kathleen. "But you know what they say: if you remove your dog's fleas, the poor bastard will miss them."

"Your fleas will soon be forgotten," promised Kathleen.

She had the kind of body that could make the primitive beast in me slobber, and she expertly made use of that quality. After a couple of days, I was so full of her that even a whiff of her perfume was enough to give me an erection.

The day my father-in-law heard about Kathleen, he went berserk. "My poor daughter's corpse is not cold yet, and you already are shacking up with that bimbo!" he shouted at me.

"You don't understand," I tried to defend myself. "I need Kathleen to cope with my grief!"

He sure didn't understand it. "Get rid of that hooker or you'll get the sack!" he snarled.

Well, I didn't want to lose my job, more so because there was a problem with the life insurance of Greta. In order to pay me, the company needed to see her corpse. Since there was no corpse, it would take quite some time before I would see any money. So, I rented a small flat in my neighborhood for Kathleen, and from then on I waited every day to visit her until it was dark. That way, appearances were kept up.

And then the nightmares started.

"You talk in your sleep," Kathleen told me one morning, after I had spent the night in her apartment. "A bit weird it was, you mumbled something about a chain."

"About a chain?" I asked, alarmed.

"A chain, yes. And also something about a propeller jam. What's a propeller jam?"

"Oh, that," I said, glad to see a way out. "Propeller jam is when the propeller of a boat stalls because something is wrapped around the shaft. I did tell you the misery with *Cash Flow* started when after the collision, the anchor chain got caught by the propeller, didn't I?"

"You were dreaming about that?"

Usually I forget my dreams, so I couldn't remember. "Greta never told me that I was talking in my sleep."

"Very smart of her," said Kathleen. She smiled knowingly.

Two days later, she didn't smile any longer. In the midst of the night she woke me up. "What the hell is happening?" she asked, irritated. "That entire hullabaloo! Do you want me to get in trouble with my neighbors?"

This time I *did* remember bits and pieces of a nightmare, something about a decapitated black corpse trying to strangle me.

I stood up from the bed and walked to the bathroom for a glass of water, needing some time for myself. The mirror above the sink confronted me with a pale, hollow-eyed face with gleaming sweat on the forehead.

When I went back to the bedroom, Kathleen eyed me suspiciously. "You were terribly scared. What's wrong?"

"It was a monster, a kind of . . . eh, zombie." I fumbled at my throat.

"A zombie named Greta?"

I sat down on the bed. "My wife has drowned and I lost my yacht, wouldn't that be a bit of a traumatic experience? Wouldn't it?"

Kathleen ignored the sarcasm. "Maybe you are missing your fleas more than you thought you would," she said. She pulled the blanket up under her chin and looked unfriendly.

The next night I was screaming, *"Her head is gone!!"* when Kathleen woke me up. I could still hear the echo of my own voice in the room. I was sweating all over and I started trembling. Seeing Kathleen's glare didn't help.

"John . . . did you kill her?"

Telling her the whole story, putting that weight off my shoulders, the temptation was enormous. But I wasn't that sure about Kathleen, her reaction was unpredictable.

"Perhaps I'm feeling guilty," I said. "Maybe I could have done more to avoid the accident."

Kathleen's dark eyes were still poking into mine. Just when I could no longer stand it, she looked the other way. "Maybe it's better we don't see each other for a while," she said. "And maybe you better go see a shrink."

I felt relieved, because I was afraid the nightmares would get worse. And in my own house I had no neighbors who could hear me.

Sleeping pills didn't help, the bad dreams broke right through the sedation. And then, one early morning, when I was still dazed and sick as a result of another miserable, god-forsaken night, I was summoned to the police station.

"They found your boat," the inspector, named Rutz, said. "The net of a fisherman was hooked by the rigging of the yacht." Rutz looked up at me, investigating. "It seems the boat lies quite a distance from the coordinates you gave the authorities in France."

I had no quick answer to this. Images from my nightmares were spinning through my mind and I felt giddy. The inspector waited patiently until I said, "An error is not impossible. You see, under the circumstances . . ."

Inspector Rutz shrugged. "You can tell me whatever you want about that, sir. Yachts!" He shook his head. "With my salary . . ."

Up came the question I barely dared to ask: "Did they . . . eh . . . did they lift my boat?"

Rutz nodded and my heart jumped up in my throat. "They said the wreck was lying in a dangerous position." He tinkered with the papers on his desk. "According to my French colleagues, you intentionally sank your boat," he said casually. His eyes locked to mine.

I looked away and stared to the floor. "They're right," I answered. *The corpse?!* a voice was screaming in my mind. *What about the corpse?!* "I . . . I couldn't go back home, not without my beloved wife. And then . . . I must have blown a fuse, I didn't want to live any longer. You see, I can't swim and . . ."

"So you sank your boat?"

"I suppose there must be a psychological explanation for my behavior at that moment. You see, the yacht was my dearest possession, after my wife that is."

"Hm . . . But then you changed your mind?"

"I panicked, I couldn't find the courage to . . ." The bastard doesn't believe one word of it! I thought.

"You told the French police your boat sank after a collision with an unidentified floating object . . ." He smiled. "That's an UFO." The smile disappeared. "Why did you tell a lie?"

"Because of the insurance."

The inspector nodded. "Of course, I hadn't thought of that." He straightened his papers and made a gesture at the door.

I eyed him unbelievingly. "That's it?"

"For the moment, yes. Until I get the final results of the French investigation. I suppose you're not planning to leave the country?"

It was raining outside and I welcomed the cold drops on my heated forehead. Not a word about the corpse, it was hard to believe. Maybe the fish, little sharks that prey on cadavers, ate it. They lived everywhere in the sea, also in the Mediterranean. But after all that bad luck, it seemed illogical to have such luck. Maybe it had drifted away, with the chance that it would wash ashore someday. Or maybe they found it already and they kept silent about it in order to lure me into a trap. Bitch! I once more thought bitterly.

The same day I got a call from the insurance company. They told me I could wave my claim good-bye. I even would have to pay myself for the cost of the salvage of the wreck. They did not sound very friendly.

I was in desperate need of a bit of warmth, so I drove to Kathleen's apartment. She wasn't there and all her personal stuff was gone. I didn't leave the place until I was done cursing and kicking the furniture.

Back at home, I swallowed the remaining sleeping pills and laid down on the couch, waiting for unconsciousness to hit me. My eyes were barely closed when black, dripping, decapitated corpses came crawling to me out of all the corners of the room. It was a good thing I had no neighbors.

Eight days later, out of France came the laconic message that the wreck of *Cash Flow* was released by the authorities. It was mine again, on the condition that I would pay the attached invoice concerning expenses for the salvage.

Where the hell was the corpse?!

I didn't feel like driving to Port Camargue, I was afraid of ambushes. As a matter of fact, I felt like doing nothing at all. I didn't even go to the office anymore; my job could go to hell. My father-in-law kept his peace. He probably was glad he didn't have to face me.

I tried to get drunk a couple of times, but after two or three drinks my stomach would throw it all up again.

One day I couldn't stand it anymore. I took a plane and flew to the south of France. Driving had become too dangerous, with all those decapitated corpses that came popping out of all kinds of hiding places. Even during the daytime now.

Cash Flow stood ashore on a quiet corner of the marina. The chain and propeller were gone. Besides a bend in the mast about six feet from the top, the yacht almost looked normal.

It was broad daylight, the sun was shining, and people in colorful clothes were walking all over the place. This gave me the courage to take a ladder and climb aboard.

The boat had dried out, but the interior was badly damaged by the salty water. I stood there in the middle of the cabin and looked around, sweat pricking in my neck.

The door to the forecastle was open, but I didn't dare go inside. Dizzily I stared at the magazine with the crossword puzzle and the wooden hammer at the navigation table. After I blinked, the table was empty.

Dirty witch! I wanted to snarl, but all of a sudden I was afraid to make any sound. Then the panic set its sharp tooth into my nerve system. One way or another, I managed to climb down the ladder without breaking my neck and I ran out of the marina without looking back. I would never see the yacht again.

The Air France air hostess looked like Kathleen. I almost started crying when she asked with concern if everything was okay with me.

The following night, the dreaming started to get really nasty. It started with an innocent ball game, but when the ball fell into my hands, it turned out to be the snatched-off head of Greta. After that, I tried to stay awake, but the combination of pills and exhaustion makes me doze off again. And then the next nightmare grabbed me by the balls. Compared to this, Dante's *Inferno* looked like Disney World.

The following morning I realized that I was heading for either madness or suicide. You couldn't run from something that lives in your head. After pacing up and down for an hour or so, I went to the police station.

"I killed her," I said to the inspector. At first he didn't seem to know what I was talking about. "My wife," I explained. "In the south of France, on my yacht."

"You look terrible," he noticed. "Are you feeling okay?"

"I can't stand it anymore, I want to get rid of it."

Inspector Rutz leaned backward on his chair and folded his arms. "Please tell me."

"I snatched her head off her body, with a chain."

He looked surprised. "Did you? I suppose you had to pull quite strongly?"

"I used the boat to do that."

"Oh! Like that, yes."

"But first she got a stroke of a wooden hammer."

The inspector shook his head. "Tsk, tsk," he muttered.

"But even without her head, the bitch tried to strangle me!"

"Well, some women are hard to kill." Inspector Rutz reached toward the button of his intercom.

"Her head didn't surface anymore." The memory made me shiver. "And the corpse keeps on chasing me."

"Once I saw a decapitated chicken running like hell," Rutz said. He pushed the button.

I began to realize he was acting strangely. "I'm telling you the truth!" I adjured him.

Inspector Rutz rose from his chair to open the door for an officer. "Sir, you can't stay drunk all the time," he said to me. "You need help." He looked very understanding and he gave me a comforting pat on the shoulder. "The officer will bring you to the right place."

Aghast, I looked at the inspector. "You think I'm crazy!"

"I just think you're a little bit overstrained," he corrected affably. "But given some time, you will be okay." With gentle coercion he pushed me in the direction of the door where the officer took over. "The officer knows the way, sir," he said. "All the best."

The psychiatric institute was nice and cozy and the personnel were extremely friendly. After they had shown me a few things, I decided to stay for a while. You know, during the ride in the police car I had done some thinking about the reaction of Inspector Rutz.

The shrink who treated me was a pro. In less than a month he cleaned my head of the idea that I had killed my wife. Of course it helped that I did my very best to work with him.

Well, I didn't really sing and dance when I finally walked home, but it sure was a long time ago since I had felt so good. I suppose the Prozac also helped.

It took my lawyer two years to make the company pay me the life insurance money of my lost wife. It sure was a lot of money, but I didn't buy a new yacht.

The corpse was never found, but one day I saw an article in the newspaper about some tourists at the Mediterranean who got sick by eating shark. Perhaps it had nothing to do with it, but to be honest, I always had found Greta a poisonous bitch.

Gradually the nightmares stayed away. Anyway, Tina, that new gorgeous girlfriend of mine, never complained about me talking in my sleep. Now and then, I would still have an ordinary dream about the drama. But nowadays I'm not always sure that Greta is playing a role in it. You know, it's not easy to recognize a corpse that has lost its head. Ha ha, I can already laugh about it now . . .

Chris Rippen

The Best

■ ■ ■

Chris Rippen was born in Haarlem in The Netherlands in 1940. He studied Dutch language and literature at the University of Amsterdam, and currently teaches literature and writing in Amsterdam. He has had several crime novels published, including the novel Playback, *which won the prestigious Dutch mystery award The Golden Noose, as well as a collection of short stories. A former president of the Society of Dutch/Flemish Crime Writers, he is also the chairman of the Dutch/Flemish branch of the IACW. His novels and short stories have also appeared in Germany, Spain, Bulgaria, Japan, and the United States, including the following story, "The Best," which appeared in the anthology* Nachtboot *(Nightboat), his own short-story collection, and which is a classic police procedural about murder at a football (in the U.S. it would be called soccer) game.*

It couldn't get any worse, temporary sergeant Munck thought, looking at his first corpse.

It had been such a quiet, by police standards almost peaceful, Sunday afternoon. The supporters of the visiting team had arrived by special train of which not even one coach had been demolished. Under a bleak but promising February sun they had marched toward the stadium, mingling with the flow of people who had come by car, most of them supporters of the home team, on the way. They didn't actually behave like church-goers but there was a kind of festive mood that was quite rare for a match considered, and therefore handled by the authorities as high risk.

They had sung their songs, made their little provocations, but nothing of the sort that would cause police intervention. Whatever it was that had caused this almost serene atmosphere, the general opinion was that it was in line with the new police strategy to keep all standby auxiliaries hidden from view. So all horses, assault vans, water cannons, and the riot squad were present as usual, but only visible to the inhabitants of the home for the elderly on the edge of the Eastside park.

During the yells, singing, and waves there had only been one riot, in section K, of course, and strangely enough almost at the end of the match, something involving fire-works and lots of smoke, but that was all. Even the very mediocre match by twenty-two overpaid but uninspired football players ending in a goalless draw couldn't disrupt the amiable mood and the supporters left as they had come. Except for the man in the dark blue ski jacket on one of the lower benches in section H, beside the players' tunnel.

While two of the stadium's medical officers examined the body, careful not to touch it, temporary sergeant Munck peered at the moist, dark stain on the lower back of the jacket and the cut it surrounded. The man's face or at least that part of it he could see, reminded him of someone, but he couldn't place him until he caught a name. Terwiel. Yes, Robin Terwiel.

Alerted by the images on one of his monitoring screens, Munck had left the command post outside the stadium, sensing from the panicked gesturing by one of the officials that something was seriously wrong in the stands, a heart attack or something like that. But this was so bad he couldn't do anything more than wait for his colleagues from the detective force and keep the curious members of the board at a distance. Because he was only an ordinary reserve officer, not authorized to handle this horrible event that had turned this almost peaceful Sunday into its opposite.

Munck spoke to the man who had found the body, not an official but some steward or other by the look of the badge on his lapel, a lean man in his late forties with a somewhat bitter mouth. After the match a spectator had called him from his post at the entrance, saying someone was down and looking sick but when he'd arrived on the scene he saw at once that this was something different.

"I can't believe it," he kept saying in a thin, monotonous voice, which could have referred to anything including an unobserved body in a crowded stand. Munck didn't ask.

When the man had to leave, he stuck out his hand and Munck took it, a little touched. He looked at the empty stands, bare skeletons around the green far below, on which toilet paper streamers swirled in the wind blowing in through the open gates, and he shivered.

And then his portable phone rang and he ran back to the command post as the alarmed voice of his colleague continued to report that war had broken out downtown, the riot squad were on their way as were the water cannons, so it was business as usual for a high risk match on a Sunday afternoon.

That night on the television news in a football fragment of a few years earlier, Munck watched the dead man in section H, as he had been in life. He wondered why he hadn't recognized the former football international Robin Terwiel at once. It couldn't be just the beard.

"Have you never looked at the wall above my bed?" Philip asked. It sounded like a reproach, but the eyes of his twelve-year-old son showed only fascination, pride even. His father had been there.

"People look different when they're dead," Munck said.

The newsreader had called the tragic death a new low in the history of football hooliganism and it had dominated over the news of the vandalism after the match.

"Wasn't it horribly frightening?" his wife asked when they went to bed.

He thought about it for a while. "No," he said. "But afterward everything felt quite different." She didn't ask any further. He knew she didn't approve of him being a member of the reserve police force. You're a tax inspector, she used to say, not a cop. You shouldn't take people's money twice.

Next morning the front pages of most newspapers combined the stories and pictures of the body in section H and the rioting supporters under one big headline. No one could explain why Terwiel had been killed. He was no longer active as a player. Former teammates, contributing to his necrology, described him as a solid, often hard, but never unfair defender and a loyal colleague. Two years back he had finished his career at FC Roma, where he had been under contract for six years. He was currently attending a trainers' course in Holland and regularly visited the matches of his old club, Utrecht. The police were still looking for witnesses and had no comment at all except for the cause of death. He had been stabbed. Only one newspaper queried the outburst of violence on such a peaceful and friendly match and why the hooligans had waited so long.

At the police debriefing on Monday evening there was a sharp comment from the commissioners about the lack of alertness. The murder of Robin Terwiel was considered a crime on its own and left out of the actions discussed in the debriefing. The homicide division took Munck's statement and they watched tapes with him, partly his own that they had already confiscated, but all they saw was a blur of faces. They would need to ask the lab for a blowup. They all agreed it was astonishing that, so far, no real witness had come forward. The few people who had phoned had only recognized Terwiel earlier on. As far as they knew he had been on his own.

Later that week Philip asked his father to come to his room. Three walls had now been covered with team posters, illustrating Robin Terwiel's career. His first period with FC Utrecht, then the glory years with Rotterdam, his decade in the national football team, and even two portraits taken during his exile in Rome. Munck looked at the face with the firm chin and the stern look, growing firmer and sterner with each photograph. "That's him all right," he said to his son. "Great. Where did you get all these posters?"

"I just asked. I already had a few of these, you know. Every club has its own promotion office. No problem getting stuff there. And this one I traded with Don." Philip's friend Don was the real expert on football and Philip was his loyal disciple.

"Was Robin Terwiel your favorite?"

"No, but he was good. Difficult to pass."

"I know," Munck said. He could hear Don saying it. "I do watch matches on TV now and then." He looked at his son. "Aren't you and Don a little sad?"

"Sad? Why? He didn't actually play anymore, so . . . you know."

Munck nodded. For a moment, he looked at the faces on the wall that had formed the sporting entourage of the man who had died in section H. A lot of them were vaguely familiar to him but he could only remember a few names. History was hard on heroes, he thought. Out of sight, out of mind. Behind him Philip was saying something and he turned. "What?"

His son giggled shyly. "Don's brother says one of his girlfriends knifed him. He was a womanizer."

Munck stared at his son. "Don's brother," he said. "Well, well. He's a man of the world. How old is he?"

"Fourteen," Philip said.

Because of a completely unexpected cold spell the football competition was suspended for several weeks. A combination of heavy snowfall and a temperature of minus ten degrees, which was exceptional for March, made most football pitches unplayable. During the vacuum the small stream of speculations around the murder of Robin Terwiel trickled on for a short while—it ranged from personal problems and mob contacts to a case of mistaken identity, none of which was confirmed or denied by the remarkably silent police—then the whole thing was overshadowed by an unprecedented but typically Dutch doping scandal among the professional speed skaters. It was winter time, after all.

Only once Munck was called to assist on traffic duty as a reserve cop, during some international congress. It was a cold, boring job and his wife complained about his coughing and sneezing in the days after.

Every time Munck dropped in at his son's room he looked at the football pictures for a moment. After some time Terwiel's face stood out, he knew where to look. Then came the others, he recognized them now and noticed how some of them stayed with a team for a long time while others disappeared and didn't return. Philip often joined him, mentioning names and commenting, saying something like "super" and Munck felt his son was waiting for him to make comments of his own. So he asked for the names of other players, where and when they had played after leaving the club on the photo. Meanwhile he looked aside at his son. All of Philip's friends were decorating their bedroom walls with photos and flags and he wondered how much the game itself meant to him. Every time it was his turn to drive his son's team to an away game, Munck watched his son from the sidelines. Around him were other parents, family members, shouting encouragement or cursing. Philip played in a shy and absentminded way, with unfinished rushes and movements, almost halfhearted. When he got the ball it was almost always by accident. Sometimes he glanced at his father. His coach, a rough but good-natured tradesman, always spared him any comments.

They seldom talked about Terwiel, it seemed they were both avoiding the subject. Munck was interrogated by the homicide department twice. He watched the blow-ups of the tapes and tried to focus on the people next to and behind Terwiel, which was made difficult by the constant switching between cameras. He didn't recognize anybody except for the official he had met, standing higher up in the stands.

"If I wanted to kill somebody, a crowded stadium wouldn't be my first choice of location," he said to the interrogating officer as they were having coffee afterward.

The other man smiled. "Yes, but you're not a murderer. Look at the trouble he's giving us. This was very cleverly done. I think he did it during the fireworks, shortly before the final whistle."

On the first football Sunday after the icy spell a man was found sitting against his car in the members-only parking lot of the FC Rotterdam stadium. It was several hours after the match and already dark. Two members of the board recognized old Pim Mulder, the club's medical adviser, who had left the post match drink five minutes before they had, and his gray Volvo 70 S. Because of the alcohol on his breath—and the fact that there was no other physician at hand—they had concluded he was drunk and carried him inside. When they'd unbuttoned his overcoat they saw he was covered in blood. He died that same night without having regained consciousness.

There was no other connection to the Terwiel case than the cause of death. But it was so conspicuous that every newspaper started digging around in the records of both dead men. At first the results were not spectacular. They had known each other but had not been friends. Mulder had been the national youth team's doctor for some years and Terwiel had occasionally consulted him during his period in Italy. Not a reason for getting stabbed with the same knife, as one sports commentator mentioned, there had to be more to it. Why were the police so quiet about the contents of the trunk of Mulder's Volvo? When it was revealed that Mulder had also been medical adviser to one of the Frisian speed-skating teams, the connection with the doping scandal and Terwiel's Italian mob connections was easily made and soon mud was flying everywhere in the entire sports world.

From pictures in the paper Munck recognized Pim Mulder on Philip's posters. He was on a few of them, standing next to the coach and the assistant coach of the national youth team, Jong Oranje, of 1984. A plump, friendly-looking man with a heavy mustache. Not exactly the witch doctor the press were creating at the moment. With Uncle Pim you could have fun.

Munck looked at the team. They were all very young, even the stern-looking Robin Terwiel. The breeding place for the national selection. Thanks to Philip all names and faces were familiar to him now, except for a blond boy in the first row, two places to the left of Dr. Mulder. "Who is this by the way?" he asked Philip. "Here he is in Jong Oranje, and he's also on one of the FC Rotterdam posters of one year later. But he's not on anything after that."

For the first time there was no reply from his son.

And then, finally the police made their first arrest. It was a football association employee whose activities had brought him in regular contact with both Mulder and Terwiel. The press conference following the arrest could not alter the feeling that the police were more in need of an arrest in order to ease pressure from the press and public opinion than that they had a real suspect. Out of curiosity Munck phoned the detective from homicide. "Well, you've got your dark alley killing," he said. But his contact was not very communicative. Munck understood that the case was no longer any of his business.

One evening Philip and his friend Don were waiting for him when he got home.

"Dad, remember that football player on the photo?"

"Which one?" Munck asked. It had been a long day.

"You asked me who he was, the blond one in the national youth team. Remember?"

"Yes," Munck said. "Did you find out?"

Smiling proudly, Philip pointed to his friend. Munck bowed. "Mr. Expert," he said. "I'm listening."

"His name is Jan Postema." Don had a piece of paper in his hand that he was turning over and over without looking at it. "Born in 1965, center forward and left wing. Played with Cambuur and FC Twente. Four caps in the national youth team. Rotterdam got him under contract in 1984. Six goals in '84/85. In 1988 he was rejected for the team."

"Why?" Munck asked. "Do you know what happened?"

"I only know he was heavily injured and never fully recovered."

"That's bad," Munck said. "Where did you get this information?"

"The Internet, and a book on football of my brother's."

Munck nodded. "I've heard about your brother."

That night Munck and his son looked at the players of the national youth team with renewed interest. "Strange, don't you think?" Munck said. "Success for one and bad luck for the other. But you can't tell from the picture, can you?"

Some days later, during lunch at the office, when some of his colleagues were talking about the football competition, Munck asked if anyone had heard of Jan Postema. Vaguely, someone said, it was a long time ago. He was a forward, a bit of a show-off, but . . . Vitesse, wasn't it? Or . . . Then Herman Voskamp raised his voice and all faces turned toward him. Herman was like Don, Munck thought, but without an elder brother.

"A miracle," Herman said. "Since when are you interested in football?"

"Since he finds dead players," a voice said.

Munck grimaced. "Since my son papers his wall with posters of football teams," he explained. "I wonder if Postema's still playing."

"It would be a miracle if he is." Voskamp put his elbows on the table. "It may have been twelve or thirteen years ago but I still remember the sound."

"What sound?"

"Of his knee. Kneecap broken, ligaments torn off like Velcro, everything."

They shivered. "You could hear it?"

Voskamp shook his head. "In a way. From the way his leg was twisted when he went down one could immediately see that it was as bad as it gets. I could feel it in my own knee and my stomach turned." The memory distorted his face.

"What was the match?" Munck asked.

"FC Rotterdam versus Vitesse 198 . . . let's see, I think it was seven. Yes, that's it." He turned to Munck. "And do you know who did it? Who came in from behind with a flying scissors kick that crushed anything in the way? Your Robin Terwiel, that's who. What a coincidence, huh? So, to answer your question: to my knowledge Jan Postema doesn't play anymore and has never played since the incident. But I don't know where he went or what has happened to him since then."

Munck looked at his watch and rose. "Thanks, Herman, where would the world be without experts?"

At five o'clock that afternoon, as he was leaving the office, he met Herman at the elevator.

"How about a pint in the pub on the corner?" Munck asked.

"Just a quick one," Herman said. "It's my chess night."

As they settled at the bar with two beers Herman said, "Well, out with it. You're not the type to hang around in bars with people from the office, so it must be you want to talk about Postema."

Munck grinned. "You're right. But it's not just him, he's just one of my hunches. My son has at least two posters with Terwiel and Postema on the same team. Rotterdam and Jong Oranje, so they played together for quite some time. But in the match you told me about they were on opposing teams. When did that happen?"

"We're talking . . . 1987, the '86/87 season, I remember it was in the spring. If I recall correctly Postema had been with Rotterdam since 1983."

Munck smiled. "It was 1984, according to my fourteen-year-old informant."

"He's right," Herman said. "It was '84. That first year his place on the team was secure, although he scored fewer goals than expected. In the second year he spent more time on the bench, there was a lot of rivalry and some trouble. After or maybe even during the season he was loaned to Vitesse."

"Loaned?" Munck asked. "How does that work?"

"It often happens with players who have not come up to expectations yet. Their club doesn't get rid of them because they were too expensive or there is still hope for improvement or whatever. Other clubs with fewer possibilities to invest like to borrow them. It is also a way for the players themselves to keep their hand in."

Munck nodded. "What happened with Postema?"

"Jan Postema was a bit of a problem case as I recall. Highly talented, I think, but not yet fully matured. Hard on himself, hard on others in the game. He was not very popular and perhaps already a little spoiled. He was about nineteen when Rotterdam bought him, a bit young to transfer to the highest level of competition. But I don't think the club wanted to sell him yet. Maybe they hoped he would mature in a team at a lower level. But after the injury it all came to nothing, of course."

"I have a feeling I can ask you anything about football," Munck said. "So please tell me about that tackle by Terwiel. Was he sent off for it?"

Herman closed his eyes for a moment. "No, he wasn't. Things would be different today. He only got a yellow card for it."

"Did he do it on purpose?"

"Crush his opponent's knee? Of course not. Terwiel played rough but rather fair. But I do believe he handled Postema roughly intentionally. A matter of tactics. And Postema was the kind of player that attracted rough tackles. Artistic, a virtuoso, selfish. And a bit of an actor. He played the dying swan when he was tackled. He was often accused for stealing penalties or fobbing off a sanction on his opponents." Herman emptied his glass.

"Another beer?" Munck asked.

"I remember now," Herman said. "When Terwiel tackled him a lot of people in the stadium believed he was faking it again. They were yelling '*Schwalbe.*' But I knew better."

"Schwalbe?"

"Swallow, the common term for someone faking a fall. It wouldn't have been the first time he'd pulled a stunt like that. There was also a hostile atmosphere in the stadium. After Postema scored for Vitesse, the Rotterdam supporters turned against him. I think they felt he'd sort of betrayed them. The crowds chorused some nasty chants at him and the stadium commentator also stirred up the public against him. Not very nice." Herman looked at his glass and beckoned the barkeeper. "OK, just one more. But this one's on me."

Then he looked at Munck. "Now tell me something. Do you really think all this has anything to do with Terwiel's death?"

"I never said that."

"That's true," Herman said.

"As a matter of fact this is the first time I've heard of this. I was just following a hunch. Maybe I was trying to impress my son." Munck told Herman about Philip and in return Herman told him about his two daughters. They were already married but still . . . and then they talked about fatherhood until their glasses were empty again and they left.

"Do you actually like football?" Herman asked when they got outside.

"Not really," Munck said. "Not anymore, anyway."

"I do," Herman said. "But only the game itself, nowadays." He laughed. "It's the same with religion. You no longer need the organization to be a believer."

Late that night the phone rang. It was Herman, apologizing for the lateness of the hour.

"When I got home I looked in some of the yearbooks to check up on what we talked about earlier, and I was right. So, if you want to follow another hunch, here's one for you. Guess who was the attending physician on Postema's injury?"

Munck was silent for a moment.

"Are you still there?" Herman asked.

"Yes."

"Because Postema was still under contract with Rotterdam it made sense that Pim Mulder who was team doctor at the time was in charge of the treatment. Small world. By the way, I lost the chess game this evening. Thank you very much."

"Thank you," Munck answered.

It took Munck the rest of the week to catch up with Jan Postema. The trail led him to a shabby bungalow in Reeuwijk where a tired-looking blond woman with nice eyes that watched him suspiciously came to the door.

"What do you want with him?" she asked and when he'd explained she naturally asked why he was still interested if he wasn't a reporter. Normal questions to which he could only have replied satisfactorily by telling the whole truth, but he only wanted her to know part of it. The whole time her fingers were playing with the hair of the little girl who was holding on to her mother's skirt with one hand and keeping the other in her mouth.

He was feeling uneasy and was already on his way back to the gate when the woman relented by giving him the address of Postema's mother.

"It's up to her now," she said. "I can't be responsible anymore."

Because the mother lived all the way up in Friesland, Munck asked for Postema's address by phone and to his surprise he got what he wanted. "Would you please give him my love, sir?" the friendly voice said. "Tell him I'll come again on Tuesday."

In a clinic in the wooded outskirts of Arnhem a man in white walked Munck along a corridor and stopped at a window. "There he is," he said, "left of the palm tree."

Munck watched the man in the wheelchair looking out of the window of his room into some kind of winter garden. The curly blond hair, already thinning on top, was the only thing he recognized. The man was wearing a cloth neck brace. Underneath the brace his shoulders were round and big and his upper arms were muscular. One of his legs was in plaster and the sling he had his right arm in was decorated with multicolored pins. He turned his head stiffly and looked at them. His eyes were dark and expressionless. "He can't see us," the male nurse said. "This is a one-way window."

Munck nodded. He had seen the perimeter fence around the grounds and knew the outside windows were made of armored glass. This wasn't just any clinic.

"When did this happen?" he asked.

The nurse opened the file he had looked up when Munck arrived. "You are a police officer?" he had asked when Munck had put in his request, and Munck had decided to leave out the "reserve" just this once. "We're checking everything, just in case."

"February 14," the nurse answered. "The day he was turned down for the training course for coaches, on grounds of his physical condition. On his way home he crashed his car into a tree."

"What about his physical condition?"

"As far as I know one of his knees won't bend. And the last few years something's also gone wrong with his hips. Of course, this is nothing to do with the injuries he sustained during the crash."

Munck looked at the man in the wheelchair. "Do you think he did it on purpose?"

The nurse was silent for a moment. Then he said, "He's done something like this before. I'm afraid his physical condition wasn't the only reason he was turned down for the training course. He's been under psychiatric care for over four years now."

Munck watched the inert figure in the wheelchair. "Does he get any visitors?"

"A few. His mother comes by every fortnight. Sometimes his ex-wife and the children. And every Saturday a man takes him out in the garden. I don't know who he is. Jan calls him coach."

"Any journalists?"

"None. Do you want to go in now?"

"No," Munck answered. "I know enough now."

On his way home he felt both relieved and sad, but refused to analyze his feelings.

On the second Sunday after the icy spell something grotesque happened. Approximately five minutes before the final whistle, with the scores at two–two, about twenty thousand football aficionados attending the match Rotterdam v. Excelsior heard the excited voice of the stadium commentator change into something midway between an orgasm and a death struggle. The public voiced its preference for the first option in loud en masse encouragement, but when a member of the board finally went to take a look, the latter option turned out to be closest to the truth. The commentator was transported to the hospital in critical condition with a knife wound, approximately fifteen centimeters in length, in his abdomen.

Munck heard the news on the car radio while driving home after a family anniversary party. When he got home Herman Voskamp had left a message on his voice mail, but he switched on the TV sports program first. The sports commentator left out all the spicy details but his perturbation showed clearly on his face. Stadium commentator Jack Belterman, the grand old man of his profession, praised for his enthusiasm and love of the game, was the third victim in a row and the football community was baffled as to the reason behind the murders. The police were also still interrogating stadium personnel because the studio had been easy to get into. As he walked to the phone Munck saw Philip watching him. Herman answered the call after the first ring.

"This can't be called a coincidence anymore," was the first thing he said.

"I assume Jack Belterman was the commentator you mentioned?" Munck asked.

"Yes, A first-rate asshole in my opinion, but everybody seems to like him now. He was a twelfth player when he was commentating, if you know what I mean. In the past they had a lot of trouble with him but Rotterdam never sacked him. He was very popular with the crowds."

"It can't have been Postema himself," Munck said. He had told Herman about his visit to the clinic.

"No, but you're on the right track. You have to inform the police now, Munck. I mean the regular police. This isn't something you can do on your own."

"I know."

"Three people dead!" Herman said. "OK. Two and a half. Some madman is taking revenge for him and no one knows where it's going to end."

"Is anyone else involved as well then?" Munck asked. "Who is next?"

"To a lunatic it could be anyone. If you don't go to the police, I will."

This time the blond woman refused to even come to the door. From his car Munck could see the little girl sitting at a table. He waited for some minutes and then drove off. Once again he was relieved, he hadn't known how to put his questions to her. He had just wanted to sit with her and listen to her story of life with Jan Postema. He realized he was not capable of investigating a murder case, he was just a tax officer playing at being a cop. He could not ask her who on earth loved Jan Postema so much they would kill for him. Herman was right, tomorrow he would notify the homicide department.

When he got home his wife looked surprised. "You're very early, what happened?" He cracked a joke about being sacked and went into the garden. After a while Philip called him from the kitchen doorway. "Dad!" His friend Don appeared beside him. Munck waved.

"Come inside, Dad, please," Philip begged.

The boys coaxed him along into the dining room and pointed to a medium-size poster, spread out on the table. A football team, very young players, no older than twelve or thirteen, wearing green T-shirts that clashed with the grass and the red capital letters above their heads. FC Cambuur, he read. An old, bad color photograph.

Philip looked up and Munck nodded his approval: "Very nice, boys. Is this from the famous Don collection? Let me guess, Robin Terwiel again?"

"Wrong!" Philip nudged his friend. "Look for yourself, Dad!"

But the real expert was getting impatient. "Championship district North, season 1977/78: FC Cambuur, Junior team C," Don explained.

Munck put his hand over Don's mouth. "My turn, professor. Please."

He bent over the poster and looked. His finger went from face to face, then stopped. "This one. Jan Postema. Am I right?"

As the boys talked on, Munck looked at the blond boy who was sitting on his haunches in the front row, squinting against the light, then at his teammates. You couldn't tell by looking at a picture, he thought.

"Why is he holding the ball?" he asked.

Philip looked at his friend. Don answered, "Because he scored the most goals."

"He was the best," Philip added.

And then Munck's eyes caught the man in the training suit on the right. Legs apart, arms folded, his face firm and proud. A lean face. Munck stared.

"Who is this?" he asked.

"The coach." Don's expression showed what he thought of people you had to explain everything to.

"I have been waiting for you," the man said.

Munck looked at the lean face with the bitter mouth. "For me?"

"Ever since that afternoon in the Utrecht stadium. You looked at me in a peculiar way and I knew you knew. We shook hands when I left. A signal."

Munck was silent. The sun on his back was still warm. In the garden behind the wrought-iron fence, most of the patients had already gone inside.

"When I saw you sitting here, I knew you had come for me, which suits me just fine because I've finished."

The first time the wheelchair had passed the bench where he was sitting, the man known as coach hadn't looked at him, but Munck knew he'd seen him. With his eyes he'd followed the figure behind the wheelchair walking on the lawn for as long as he could and then he'd waited. The second time, half an hour later, the man had nodded a greeting to him. In his dark sunglasses Jan Postema looked like a blind man. From their movements he could see they were talking now and then. Later, Munck had seen the man coming through the gate, an inconspicuous man with an unobtrusive face. A man who might have remained unnoticed in a crowd and invisible in a dark alley.

"They destroyed him. One crushed his knee, and another put him down. The third acted medically unwarranted. Between them they destroyed both his career and his life. Now I have destroyed them." He sat upright, his hands on his knees, a man ready to go.

"He was the best. I already knew when he was twelve. The best I ever had. Jan had a unique pass move, the like of which you could find among the truly great: Cruyff, Keizer. On a good day he could win a match on his own, like Johan Cruyff." His voice weakened. "In that match, that final match he was having a good day. He was untouchable, no one could stop him. Then Terwiel came in and stopped him."

He looked at Munck. "That Sunday in February, I didn't have a plan at all. I just had a knife with me. I've had it for years, I hunt. Two weeks earlier I heard Jan had tried to kill himself again. Something snapped inside me. I had been hoping and waiting too long. You've got to believe me, it was pure coincidence that I bumped into Terwiel in the stands. I'm an assistant there on weekends. I saw him and knew I wouldn't be able to stop myself."

He was a hunter, Munck thought. He knew when and how to kill. Unobtrusive, unnoticed. I don't even know his name yet.

Munck got up.

"He really was the best," the man said.

Helga Anderle

THE RIVAL

■ ■ ■

Austrian author Helga Anderle is our newest foreign author to make an appearance in The World's Finest *series, but she's no stranger to U.S. publishing, having had a story in the landmark collection* Women on the Case, *edited by Sara Paretsky. This year she returns with "The Rival," first published in the anthology* Ingeborgs Fälle, *a story that begins with two women on a train, and swiftly becomes much, much more.*

Karin almost couldn't believe her luck when, dragging her trolley behind her along the aisle, she found a compartment in which there was only one passenger. It was a woman in her best years: well groomed, dark blue pantsuit, grayish hair cut in an elegant bob. On her knees she was balancing a briefcase. In her left hand she held a thick stack of paper, in her right a pen. The reading glasses on the tip of her nose gave the impression she was intensively studying important notes. When Karin entered, the woman merely shot a brief glance at her, answered her greeting, and returned to her reading. Probably an academic, or a lawyer, or a university lecturer, or something in that line, Karin assumed and went to get settled into the opposite window seat. After having disposed of her coat, which was completely soaked through on the shoulders, and heaving the trolley onto the luggage rack, she began rubbing her wet hair with a handkerchief. "Wow, I'm glad to be in the dry. It's raining cats and dogs outside," she remarked.

The heavy rain kept hammering on the windows and lightning illuminated the black sky like fireworks. "Do you mind if I close the curtains?" asked Karin. "I know it's childish, but I am scared of thunderstorms!" Without awaiting the woman's consent, she rose and closed the blinds.

Apparently the woman was not keen on entering into a conversation; she scribbled busily at her notes, wanting to be left in peace. But Karin couldn't be considerate, she needed somebody who would listen to her and her sixth sense told her that this woman would be perfect for it. Karin moved restlessly in her seat, trying to find a good opening. The first words would be decisive. The bait would have to be chosen with care to capture her listener from the beginning.

The woman rustled her notes, took the glasses off, yawned behind her hand, and used index finger and thumb to rub the bridge of her nose. Now, this was her chance! Karin cleared her throat, and before her courage faded again, she hastily asked, "Do you think women should wear sexy lingerie to keep their husband from going astray?"

Dumbfounded, the woman shook her head, as if she couldn't believe what she had just heard. Karin blushed in embarrassment and continued without stopping. "Excuse me for bothering you with such an intimate and delicate problem, but right now I wouldn't know . . . please listen to my story . . . perhaps afterward you'll understand . . ."

Resigned, the woman heaved her shoulders as if accepting the inevitable, lifted the briefcase from her knees, put her notes aside, and made a gesture, which Karin interpreted as an invitation to get started.

"There is this woman, Nina by name, who one day rummages through the storage room. She rarely sets foot inside—it's crammed with old stuff and tools—taboo for her, it's Willy's domain, Willy is her husband. She is looking for her step trainer, because she suffers from low blood pressure and the doctor ordered her more sports instead of pills. Since she couldn't find it anywhere, she assumed that Willy must have locked the trainer up somewhere because its squeaking got on his nerves when he watched the sports program on TV. As Karin scours the upper shelf to reach the shabby carton behind her discarded ice skates, the whole lot crashes down on the floor, almost smashing her toes. The white box, which suddenly lands at her feet, must have been hidden in it. It's not much bigger than a chocolate box, has no label on it, and is only tied with a thin thread. She cannot resist opening it. Wrapped in barely crushed paper she finds an exquisite set of lingerie."

Karin paused to await her listener's reaction. The woman looked stunned but remained silent, and so Karin continued. "Bra, garter belt, and slip emit an exquisite scent, as Nina examines them upside down, looking for a label. There is none. The set looks as if it were exclusively made for a sultan's favorite concubine: precious soft red silk, cream-colored laces, and expensive embroidery studded with pearls. A refined accessory of seduction, a blunt attack on the senses, as if made for a mysterious odalisque out of a thousand-and-one-nights, who is aware of the beauty of her body and knows how to use this asset to her advantage."

Karin registered delightedly that her vis-à-vis's lips curled into a smile. She had been prepared for disgust, for indifference, and even for being scorned off. But none of these occur. On the contrary her listener seemed to enjoy herself. A woman with imagination—just perfect.

"As if she had burnt her fingers, Nina hastily wraps up her discovery and restores order, so that Willy won't notice. She decides better not to remark on it to her husband for the time being. She observes him suspiciously when he returns from work, but she cannot detect any change in him, Willy behaves as usual. His veiled brown eyes reveal no secrets whatsoever. Agitated as she is, Nina finds no sleep, the question of whom the frivolous *dessous* could belong to turns around endlessly in her head.

"One thing is quite clear though: they are not destined for her. Not for a woman who despises her body, feels ashamed when naked, and has worn solid white cotton underwear since childhood. Nina can't wait for her husband to leave in the morning. The temptation to put on the *dessous* is overwhelming, even if she knows in advance that she will look pitiful wearing them. And it's true. In the mirror she sees herself as the underdeveloped fourteen-year-old girl, who used to borrow her mother's clothes and put on bizarre makeup to sneak into a movie not allowed for minors."

No smile from her listener this time, but an earnest look. "The discovery must have been quite a shock to her, I assume."

"More than that," Karin confirmed eagerly. "It's the big bang that throws her world upside down. She had always trusted Willy, believed her marriage to be a happy one, there were never any serious quarrels. Concerning the marital duties, Willy wasn't exacting. At the beginning she had feared that if she rejected him he would brutally rape her. But this never happened, he didn't force himself upon her against her will. Once, it must have been in their first year of marriage, he had invited her to celebrate her birthday in a posh restaurant. Candlelight, champagne, lovely music. Nina had been slightly drunk and in a romantic mood. At home, Willy had shyly handed her a beautifully wrapped box containing lovely lingerie and asked her to put it on. But instead of being happy about it, Nina sobered up on the spot. 'You don't expect me to pose for you in this thing? If you want to get horny you'd better go and see a strip show!' she had cried and angrily threw the box into a corner. Willy had looked like a beaten dog, but he hadn't said a word and thereafter there was never another incident of this kind.

"Nina blamed her mother for being so prudish and inhibited. Already in school Nina had been like that. When her classmates told stories about their petting experiences, she could never contribute anything, and they had mocked her as the Iron Maiden. It had been a privilege that they let her come along when they went to hunt up some exhibitionist in the Prater—a popular class sport. It had been an easy task to track down these perverts. They always used to hide in the bushes near the playgrounds, waiting for a victim to come along and scare her by exposing themselves. Strangely enough none of the girls was ever afraid. Instead of being shocked and running away, they had giggled hysterically. One or two of the girls who were courageous enough had even made some insolent remarks and thus spoilt the fun for those disgusting old lechers. Nina would have never dared to do this by herself, but in the group she had felt strong and had enjoyed the common excitement.

"Who knows what her mother would have done had she known? Even when Nina had met Willy she kept it a secret as long as possible. As expected, her mother had been against him from the beginning and had tried everything to break up the relationship. She didn't like men in general—her great love had abandoned her when she became pregnant—and this shattering experience had not only traumatized her but also embittered her for life. Nina had already been twenty-nine years old and was still a virgin when she met Willy on a Russian language course. If it was love she couldn't say, but she enjoyed his company and better even their similarities: Like herself Willy was a loner, introverted, shy, not a big talker. No Adonis, no charmer, but serious, reliable, and successful in his job. When he proposed to her, Nina didn't listen to her mother, but said 'Yes.' "

Karin was relieved when her listener nodded approvingly as if agreeing with Nina's decision and took it for granted that she should continue with her story.

"Nina functioned like a robot. Her head was a mess. Constantly, all her thinking turned around the question of who this superwoman for whom the *dessous* were designated could be and where Willy could have met her. She tried to envisage the women at his office—barely dressed—one after the other, but none seemed to fit. Eventually the idea popped up that she had to find out where Willy had bought the lingerie, perhaps one of the saleswomen would remember him and whether he had been in female company. Methodically, she scoured the exclusive lingerie shops on Kärtnerstrasse and Graben, equipped with a Polaroid shot of the *dessous*—she wouldn't have dared to take the original along. At the end of the week she had blisters on her feet from running around, but her playing detective had not led her anywhere. In the beginning, the idea that Willy could have a mistress had seemed utterly absurd to her, but there was no other explanation. Although she felt mean to be sneaking into his private sphere, she rummaged his suit pockets, his desk, and even the stuffy cellar, without finding any proof of his infidelity."

Suddenly the door of the compartment was opened and the conductor came in asking for their tickets. "Gee, what a complicated itinerary! At 9:10 P.M. you could have taken a direct train," he remarked as he returned Karin's ticket.

"I travel lightly, I don't mind having to change trains," she replied.

The door closed with a bang.

"Did Nina succeed in getting a clue where the *dessous* came from?" asked the gray-haired woman when they were alone again.

Karin shook her head. "Not really, it remained a mystery. There were only assumptions; one saleslady believed that they could have been custom-made abroad . . ."

"Well, in my opinion this Nina seems quite naive. I can't believe there were no previous signs that there was something wrong . . ." remarked Karin's vis-à-vis.

"You are quite right," Karin exclaimed. "In fact, there were quite a lot of indications that Willy was hiding something from her. Lately he had been more withdrawn, more taciturn than ever, even when she asked him he revealed nothing about his work or his trips abroad. And for quite some time he hadn't tried to make love to her. In bed, he turned his back to her like a stranger. Inhibited as she was, Nina didn't care much about sex, but she liked it when Willy cuddled her in his arms. It was pleasant to feel the warmth of his body on her skin and she loved to stroke his bare, hairless chest. Amazingly his skin was as smooth, soft, and silky as her own and when he embraced her and she could feel his heartbeat under his ribs, she felt sheltered and safe like a baby at its mother's breast."

"Couldn't she have talked with her husband about her suspicions?"

"Of course, but she lacked the courage. And besides, apart from the white box with the lingerie there was no proof that he was betraying her."

"But how could she go on living with this uncertainty . . . it would drive me nuts!"

"Well, Nina was going nuts indeed. The whole situation was like a nightmare. If she ever could find peace again, she had to tail her husband, no matter if she disliked it. So the very next day she hid in the doorway on the opposite side of the street and waited till Willy came out of his office—then, her heart beating like a hammer, she followed him at a discreet distance. Willy lingered on his way home, stopped for coffee, listened to a street musician, bought the evening paper—but there was no indication that he was indulging in any extramarital excursions. However, one evening he stopped at a hairdresser without Nina noticing any change in his hairdo afterward. And she couldn't figure out what was behind it."

"He could have met somebody, couldn't he?" suggested Karin's listener.

"Wait, wait, you'll hear in a moment," Karin replied. "On Friday, when Nina was already getting tired of tailing her husband, she was rewarded for her patience. When Willy left work he was with a woman. As you can well imagine poor Nina was totally shaken, but as soon as she regained control of herself she tried to visualize the attractive, elegant blonde on Willy's side in the red lingerie. Judging by her shapely figure the *dessous* could fit her. Superficially, the woman looked cool and inaccessible, but Nina had seen enough Hitchcock movies to know that underneath the surface these icy blondes were explosive volcanoes. Somehow, the woman looked familiar to Nina, but she couldn't figure out where they could have met. It hurt to register that the couple seemed to be comfortable with each other. Nina followed them till they entered an impressive turn-of-the-century building near the Ringstrasse."

Karin's vis-à-vis straightened and exhaled loudly. "So her suspicions were right . . ."

Karin nodded and went on. "Nina crossed the street and studied the nameplates at the entrance. There was a lawyer and a tax consultant and in addition there were a number of private apartments. Quite possible that her rival lived there and was already slowly and provocatively peeling off the red *dessous.* Or that she and Willy were drinking prosecco and discussing their common future while she, the betrayed wife, got wet in the rain. Soaked to her bones, ice cold, and deeply depressed, Nina went home and waited till Willy returned. With some effort she kissed him on the cheek as usual, but secretly she sniffed for traces of the perfume of this other woman. It didn't calm her a bit that she could only smell Willy's usual aftershave."

"She must have reached boiling point. Surely she made a scene?"

Karin laughed bitterly. "Anybody else would have, but Nina didn't. She is too much of a coward and scared of the consequences. What if Willy planned to dump her and asked for a divorce? However she does ask him why he is so late, and Willy answers dryly that he had been to see the firm's lawyer. Unsatisfied, Nina keeps on questioning him, until he admits that he had been in the company of the bosses' new secretary. Of course! Suddenly Nina remembered that she had met the attractive blonde at some party. She had been hired as a replacement for old Frau Novak, who had looked like a female KGB officer. 'Not only attractive, but also very competent,' Willy assures her. 'A stroke of luck, that we have her,' he adds. Nina has heard enough, fighting back tears, she storms into the kitchen, wondering whether this Stroke of Luck not only accompanied Willy to the lawyer but quite probably also on his frequent trips abroad."

"Well, that's a good guess, it happens all the time," her listener mumbled. Karin felt like hugging her. Besides being a good listener, she was empathic and seemed to take a deep interest in Nina's fate.

"I haven't asked you yet where you are going?" Karin asked, secretly hoping that her listener would stay with her until they reached H.

"Oh, there is still some time to go before I get off," the woman answered vaguely, after having looked at her watch.

"I hope you don't mind my talking so much? I have to change trains in H and since I haven't slept much lately I must try to stay a awake. If I stopped talking I'm sure I'd fall asleep right away."

"Oh, don't worry, that's okay . . . I needed a break anyway . . . and I must admit you are a very good narrator."

Karin blushed as usual when somebody praised her. It happened rarely. "Good, then I'll go on . . . where was I? . . . Oh, yes, Nina's rival is no longer a phantom, she is real, and there is no way she can escape those images of Willy and his lover, which haunt her obsessively. Desperately she decides to visit her mother—there isn't anyone else to whom she could tell her story and ask for advice. Willy takes her to the station. 'Don't you worry about me, stay as long as you want, I'll be alright by myself,' he says when he kisses her good-bye and Nina can't help to think that he is glad to have her out of the way.

"Her mum isn't surprised at all. 'Haven't I told you thousands of times that men are no good? What made you think that your Willy should be an exception? . . . But how silly of you to run away and leave him prey to your rival instead of fighting for him!'

" 'But what should I have done?' cries Nina desperately.

"Mummy shrugs. 'What do I know? The usual . . . scratch her eyes out, kick her teeth in, inform her boss about the true nature of his blameless assistant . . . '

"Nina is disappointed. She had expected compassion and understanding, but instead her mother only served her three hefty meals a day—'Look at you . . . nothing but skin and bones, have to feed you up a bit'—accompanied by some melodramatic advice not helping her at all. But at a distance Nina begins to see things in a different light. Why should Willy be satisfied with her, an unattractive child-woman with a figure like an ironing board, when he could have a real eye-catcher instead? A voluptuous woman who enjoyed wearing sexy underwear and indulging in wild sex? It was obvious that Willy, like the vast majority of men, got a kick out of women in sexy lingerie. And what was wrong with that? A harmless pleasure, nothing perverted. So why didn't she do him the favor, if she could win him back this way and save her marriage?"

Karin stopped, her mouth felt dry from talking and she was glad to find some mint drops in her coat. She put one in her mouth and also offered some to her companion, but the woman refused.

"Isn't it strange that no refreshments have been brought down the train? I'd love to have something to drink, I'm very thirsty," Karin said.

Her listener straightened and pushed the bottle of mineral water on her tray in Karin's direction. "Help yourself, there isn't much left, I'm afraid."

Karin thanked her and gulped down what was left directly from the bottle. Then she looked at her watch. "There'll still be enough time to tell you the end of the story. In H, I'll have to change trains.

"The more she thinks about it, the more Nina feels the urge to go home. She doesn't call Willy, she wants to surprise him. Shortly after nine o'clock she is home and already in the hall she notices that his coat isn't hanging in the cloakroom. There is complete silence everywhere, only her steps clatter loudly on the wooden floor, so she takes off her shoes and walks around in her stockings. Kitchen, living room, bedroom, everything is neat and untouched. Without making a sound she sneaks around, feeling like an intruder. Her joy at the thought of seeing her husband is gone, and suspicion returns. When she approaches the bathroom she notices a weak streak of light under the door and hears the splashing of water. Curiously she squats down and peeks through the keyhole. There are candles around the bathtub, making it difficult to see anything in this dusky light. Slowly it dawns on her that Willy isn't bathing alone in this festive setting. Nina feels as if somebody has punched her hard in the stomach. How could he dare to bring his lover into her apartment! *I'll spoil this fun for you, you wait and see! The naive wife isn't as dumb as you think! You'll soon see a new side to me!* she fumes, outraged. But instead of rushing in and throwing herself like a fury on the adulterers, she prefers to wait a little. While staring through the keyhole and straining to pick up any noises—a pearly laughter, a sensual sighing, a soft groan—she is suddenly overwhelmed by a feeling of omniscience. Like God, invisible, but seeing and hearing everything."

Karin's vis-à-vis had closed her eyes a while ago. Hands folded in her lap, she seemed to be dozing. Just as Karin stretched out her hand toward her, the woman suddenly opened her eyes and took a gasping breath.

"I'm not boring you, am I?" Karin asked watching her intensively.

"Oh, no . . . on the contrary, your story is really exciting, please go on!"

"From her keyhole perspective Nina's view is restricted, she can only see pieces of a puzzle, fragments. At first, water splashing over the edge of the tub and a white arm emerging out of the foam peaks. Next the soft shape of a round hip appears, then blond curls falling down to the waist, dripping water. When her rival steps out of the tub, and turns toward her, Nina catches a look at her bosom and almost chokes in a fit of admiration and envy. She had always longed to have such breasts: perfectly formed, pointed, as if sculpted by an artist, with beautifully rounded pink nipples. For a brief moment, Nina wonders where Willy is, but she is too consumed by the storm of her emotions to worry. The stranger seems to feel quite at home as she cuddles into a towel and reaches out to switch on the light. With the towel knotted around her waist, the woman turns toward the mirror. When Nina tries the door, she finds that luckily it isn't locked. She pushes the handle and opens it noiselessly . . . She feels hot and cold shivers running down her spine as she watches the woman caressing her breasts, before slipping into the red bra and hooking it expertly at the back. She then puts on the slip and at last fastens the garter belt around her wide hips. Nina fights the impulse to dash in, throwing herself at her rival, scratching and biting. Instead, she pushes carefully against the door to widen the crack . . .

"Heavily perfumed clouds of vapor envelop her, but nevertheless she takes in the scene quite clearly, although it doesn't make any sense to her. A blond, curly wig, carelessly thrown beside the washbasin. A razor blade, slowly gliding over soapy cheeks, leaving narrow pink lanes in the white foam. The mirror almost blinded by steam, reflecting a pair of eyes—hugely opened in terror—staring at her. Willy's eyes! A high whimpering sound rises from his throat as Nina bends to pick up the razor blade that he had let drop. But he doesn't defend or protect himself as she thrashes out manically at him to destroy those perfect breasts. Again and again she hacks at them, sobbing and shouting, until the red silk is hanging in threads."

The thick silence that follows is suddenly interrupted by the announcement to the passengers that the train will reach H in five minutes. Paralyzed by sheer horror, Karin's listener is struggling to find any words. Only when Karin rises to get her luggage, the woman quickly says: "Please wait! I adored your story. Why don't you write it down and mail it to me. Here is my card!"

Karin says good-bye, expresses her thanks for listening to her, puts the card into the pocket of her coat, and leaves the compartment. Her next train leaves in ten minutes, she has to hurry. While rushing to the platform, she thought that it was quite senseless to keep on running like a rabbit trying to wipe out her trails.

She was certain that the woman in the train had seen through her story and guessed the truth, yet at the same time felt sure that she had nothing to fear from her. What worried her more was that tomorrow the cleaning lady was expected and she would inevitably find the mess in the bathroom.

Wasn't it a stroke of luck that she had conveniently met this woman, an editor, on the train? A lot of people had written books while in jail and become famous writers. Why shouldn't she give it a try?

Frauke Schuster

African Christmas

■ ■ ■

Our next story is by Frauke Schuster, whose tale "Two Sisters" graced the pages of The World's Finest Crime and Mystery Stories, Volume 4. *Born in 1958 in southern Germany, she spent the greater part of her childhood in Egypt, then returned to her native land where she studied chemistry, was awarded the OBAG Cultural Prize for her doctoral thesis in 1984, and worked for a scientific magazine. She started her writer's career with various short stories, and in 2002 her first crime novel,* Atemlos *(Breathless), was published by KBV, Germany. Her second novel,* Toskanisches Schattenspiel *(Tuscan Shadow Play), was published in May 2003, along with this small gem of a story, "African Christmas," first published in the German anthology* Schlaf in himmlischer Ruh *(Sleep in Heavenly Peace), wherein a disgruntled employee wishing harm upon her coworker falls instead under the spell of an "ancient" curse.*

Silent Night" from the bakery on the left, "The Little Drummer Boy" from the hat shop on the right. In between, the narrow lane, in gray December light, slippery under an icy rain mixed with a first few flakes of snow. As icy as Sybill's feet, in those bootees that unfortunately were more elegant than warm. Feet that had to be laboriously dragged forward these merry pre-Christmas days.

Christmas shopping. Year after year she had enjoyed plunging herself into the chaos of the pedestrian precinct, fighting her way through cardboard reindeer sleighs, Christmas trees powdered with synthetic snow, and chubby-faced plastic angels, trying out her talents in that modern jungle war for perfume, champagne flutes, and other last-minute gifts, but this time . . .

Christmas. Season of love, of joy, of endless money spending. And after Christmas she would be out of money, out of a job. Financial problems in the company, Eileen—"Ms. Boss"—had stated, her regard appropriately somber. Economy measures, ordered from above. Consulting companies wrote red numbers these days. But Sybill still had felt safe after the solemn lecture, had supposed it would be Ted who had to leave. Ted, just half a year in the company and already getting on everyone's nerves. Not everyone's, she corrected herself bitterly. He never got on Eileen's nerves. Only into her bed. What she herself, in her dumb naiveté, had only realized when she received the letter telling her the company regretted, but in their house they didn't see a future for her any longer.

The disgusting wind tried to rise into a storm, as if even the elements had conspired to destroy her every pleasure. The icy rain froze on her red-blond mane, her feet felt like snow-sculptures, her fingers like tiny, icy spears. Grimly she imagined one of those spears penetrating Ted's skin, passing his thin ribs, piercing his deceitful heart. At first he'd continuously waylaid her, but having once understood where the wind blew from or, to be more exact, where it blew to, he changed the bed and his feelings like decent people would do with their socks.

Damned frost! A junk shop attracted her attention, not because of that jumble of antiques and trash in the window, but because she glimpsed a fireplace inside, with a real open fire, embers glowing in an orange light. Only the sight of it made her feel warmer, if not in her heart, but at least in those deeply frozen feet.

The next moment she stood in the dim light of the shop, amid dusty chandeliers, their fake silver coating glittering, yellowing lampshades and dark oil paintings displaying fog-covered mountains and sinking ships in storm-ridden seas. Somehow the whole shop seemed enveloped in a kind of anti-Christmas gloom. There was no "Silent Night" or "Jingle Bells" music here, only the strangely slow ticking of a clock, which Sybill suddenly thought really provoking. You couldn't simply ignore Christmas, a few days before the Holy Night!

She positioned herself in front of the fireplace, warming her bottom in the hope that the shop owner, who presumably stayed in the back room, would grant her and himself a nice rest till asking the inevitable question of how he could help. Maybe she would even find some interesting stuff in such a shop, for her friends, fitted to her not overly loaded purse?

Feet and fingers comfortably thawed she left the fire, curiously looking around in the much too quiet room. That box there? Silverware, a true antiquity, the price sticker too small for the dishearteningly high sum that was written there. Had the thing once belonged to the King of France, or what? That brass chandelier on the next shelf would be cheaper, but too baroque; neither Louise nor Anna would like that.

Sybill had just decided to leave and to search the next department store for cheaper, more conventional gifts when suddenly she found herself face-to-face with the statue.

Carved ebony—which genius had whispered that suggestion, as far as she knew she'd never seen ebony before?—decorated with ivory inlays. Black Africa, she supposed, and given the looks of the wood, rather antique. The price label—oh, two hundred and seventy-five euros! Louise would love that thing; following her last year's Asia-mania, she just fancied all that African stuff these days, but for that price—No, thanks!

Regarding the figurine more closely, she thought the eyes—yellowish ivory with pupils made from some black, shiny mineral—showed an uninviting, slightly malevolent expression. Sybill suddenly shivered, but it might just be a draft of cold air coming from the window.

"Congo, seventeenth century," a low voice murmured at her back. Sybill spun around. Unnoticed by her, the shop owner had emerged from the back room, a withered old man, white hair combed upward, which gave him the strange looks of a drowsy owl.

"Seventeenth . . . ! That's what makes it so expensive," Sybill said, and the merchant sighed.

"Considering its age it's much too cheap. But—it's said to be cursed, to carry some lethal African curse. And the expression of the eyes—you might have noticed . . ." His gaze obviously avoided hers. "The former owner died under mysterious circumstances, the heir wants to get rid of the thing as fast as possible. Bur no one's interesting in buying it, though everyone keeps telling me they're not superstitious . . ."

Sybill stared at the statue—and the figurine stared back at her, with unblinking eyes. A curse. Lethal. Superstitious? Of course she wasn't, what with living in the twenty-first century! Well, admittedly she wore that Chinese charm bracelet, hid that lucky stone in her handbag, but nevertheless . . .

One hour later, back in her apartment, she set the statue down on her kitchen table, where it looked completely out of place between all those bread crumbs and used coffee mugs. Immediately Sybill hunted for the gift wrapping paper. "Two hundred and seventy-five euros," she murmured. "You'd better be worth your money, otherwise . . . !" A beam of sunlight parted the clouds, flooding the kitchen table, and all of a sudden the stony eye of the statue glinted menacingly, as if the weird thing had understood her very words . . .

Charm bracelet and lucky stone or not, she didn't like keeping the statue in her apartment for too long, took the oblong parcel to the post office as soon as she had scribbled the direction on the front. Happy Christmas, dear Ted, I hope to see you dead soon . . .

Maybe he would wonder why she of all women would send him a Christmas gift. On the other hand—as she had come to know him, he'd probably attribute it without any suspicion to a natural tribute to his everlasting manly charms that she was still interested in him.

And she hummed "Jingle Bells" on her way back home, where she wrapped up the gifts for Anna and Louise in the best mood possible.

Next morning, while enjoying her coffee, she imagined Ted undoing the parcel, setting up the statue in his room. Luckily she had already taken her leftover vacation days, didn't have to go to work anymore, didn't have to meet him in person. But maybe he already was . . . ? She turned the radio on, listened to all that pre-Christmas merriment. Would he be one of those rare, disciplined people who actually waited till Christmas Eve before unwrapping the gift, or would he do it that very day . . . ?

Amid "Hark! The Herald Angels Sing" and "Joy to the World" she wondered how the statue would work, imagining the various scenarios she would like to see him in . . . Falling down the stairs, maybe, breaking his too seductive neck . . . Muggers in the dark, masked guys carrying pistols, a shot, his white shirt turning red—exitus! Or maybe somewhat more subtle? Some incurable, lethal disease befalling him from out of nowhere? And when she, Sybill, would meet him once more, in a couple of weeks, he'd look pale, hollow-eyed, and haggard, wearing the mark of one doomed to premature death on his forehead?

Peace on earth and mercy mild . . . It had been way too long since she had enjoyed her breakfast that much.

Next morning she studied the local paper with increased attention, and the following day as well. Heart failure while driving? No, the deceased one was beyond fifty, Ted barely thirty. Mugging in the pedestrian precinct? Oh, no, just the simple robbing of a woman's shopping bag! Somehow, Sybill felt disappointed, till she remembered that fatal illness. These old curses might prefer to work slowly; in former times the only thing people had in abundance was time. No comparison to the hectic pace of modern days.

She took her latte macchiato to the sitting room, comfortably settled down in front of the TV. Answering job ads could wait.

At eleven o'clock the doorbell rang, the postman pressed a parcel into her arms. "Addressee has moved to unknown place!" And he hastened down the stairs, always in a hurry, and today, two days before Christmas, more so than ever.

She knew the parcel at first sight, undid it mechanically. And there the statue lay, in the wrapping paper, its black pupils piercingly staring in Sybill's face.

"Forget it!" she said aloud. "You, a menace? Only to my finances, it seems, because I spent two hundred and seventy-five euros on you, all in vain! You can't even find the right guy!"

Partly in anger, partly feeling relieved, she put the statue upright onto the table, so that the thing faced the wall. What kind of nutter had she been, believing all that nonsense?! And where, all devils, was Ted? Where had he moved to, just before Christmas? All of a sudden! She'd never heard the slightest hint about his seeking a new abode . . . And, suddenly, she knew: Ms. Boss had got her divorce, plus the huge, empty villa . . .

Ms. Boss . . . Every year, Sybill had dutifully sent her a gift for Christmas, a sunny weather gift, for sunny working conditions, so to say.

Again she took up the statue, looking into these strangely live eyes. "So, you'll be promoted. Special gift for the boss. It was your choice, don't forget!"

The old wrapping paper was torn; it had been the last remnant as she noticed with a surge of anger. Another shopping trip? Never! Finally she unearthed a bit of ribbon in the green shade people's thoughts connected with venomous African snakes, tied it around the long neck of the statue. The effect proved to be more ridiculous than decorative, and Sybill gave a mirthless laugh.

"We'll go there and simply put you down at the doorstep. And if I'm lucky . . ." She didn't talk on, new, bloody horror scenarios rising in her head: a fire in the house, at the dead of night, and none of the inhabitants could be saved . . . A gas explosion, an earthquake, there were so many possibilities . . .

"Away in a Manger" the voice in the radio sang in exaggeratedly sweet tones when Sybill's Fiat went along the snow-covered road, following the bank of the Danube as Ms. Boss was living in a suburb, in the most expensive and luxurious one, to be sure.

The statue was lying at the passenger's seat, wearing the horrible ribbon, and when Sybill furtively glanced over the eyes suddenly flashed up in a beam of sunlight. All of a sudden she felt dizzy, as if something would try to strangle her . . . Her foot hit the accelerator; the sooner she got rid of that thing, the better! The car gathered speed, racing down the road and then . . . !

"She must have been driving like a lunatic!" the gray-haired officer said when he regarded the wreck of the car. "With these conditions, snow everywhere! I guess she got onto a sheet of ice and . . ." His gaze drifted away from the tree, over to the mortuary van.

"Look here!" His younger colleague had discovered a wooden statue, about thirty centimeters in height, which had probably been flung out of the car at the impact of the accident. "Might have been a gift for somebody . . ."

The older man stomped over, took the statue, shook his head disapprovingly. "Not another one of these!"

"Meaning what?"

"At the moment you meet these things all over antique shops and flea markets. Sellers tell you they're seventeenth century, somewhere from Black Africa. In truth they're cheap mass production, artificially trimmed to look old." The officer laughed grimly. "And mostly they come with some gruesome, hair-raising story of fatal powers or curses, to make them more interesting for eventual buyers."

"Gosh!" his younger colleague said. "You can't really think anyone would be thick enough to fall for such shit?!"

Sharyn McCrumb

THE GALLOWS NECKLACE

■ ■ ■

Sharyn McCrumb, an award-winning Southern writer, is best known for her Appalachian "Ballad" novels, set in the North Carolina/Tennessee mountains. The latest of these, Ghost Riders, *is an account of the Civil War in the Appalachians and its echoes in the region today. Her novels include* New York Times *bestsellers* She Walks These Hills *and* The Rosewood Casket, *which deal with the issue of the vanishing wilderness, and* The Ballad of Frankie Silver, *the story of the first woman hanged for murder in the state of North Carolina. Her other works include the* New York Times *Notable Books* If I Ever Return Pretty Peggy-O, The Hangman's Beautiful Daughter, *and* The Songcatcher. *Her honors include the 2003 Wilma Dykeman Award for Literature given by the East Tennessee Historical Society, AWA Outstanding Contribution to Appalachian Literature, Chaffin Award for Achievement in Southern Literature, Plattner Award for Short Story, Virginia Book of the Year nomination for the Best Appalachian Novel, SEBA Best Novel nomination, St. Andrews College's Flora MacDonald Award, and the Sherwood Anderson Short Story Award. Her books have been translated into more than ten languages, and she was the first writer-in-residence at King College in Tennessee. In 2001 she served as fiction writer-in-residence at the WICE Conference in Paris. A graduate of UNC Chapel Hill with a MA from Virginia Tech, she has lectured on her work at Oxford University, the Smithsonian Institution, the University of Bonn, Germany, and at universities and libraries across the country, where her books are studied. She lives and writes in the Virginia Blue Ridge. Last year she put her own inimitable stamp on Sherlock Holmes with "The Vale of the White Horse," and she makes another appearance this year with "The Gallows Necklace," first published in* The Dark: New Ghost Stories, *edited by Ellen Datlow.*

When Neville Gordon realized that the elderly man by the window was his old schoolmate Edward Seeley, he felt as if he had seen a ghost. Surely, he thought, given the date and the purpose of his journey, this encounter could not be coincidence. Gordon stood in the doorway of the first-class railway compartment still staring at the car's only other occupant, an old man gazing out the window of the train, watching the green lawns and hedgerows flash past. After the lawns of outer London would come clumps of woodland and stretches of golden fields and then a more exalted group of gray buildings as the train pulled into the station at Oxford.

The train rocked a bit as it rounded a curve, and as Gordon put out a hand to steady himself, his newspaper slid to the floor, but he made no move to retrieve it. He was still staring at the man beside the window. He had the leathery look of an old soldier, now retired from some tropical empire outpost, but still fit and military in his bearing. His clothes were not new, but they were well cut and of good material. Despite the patina of age that had seamed his face, he still had the look of that earnest schoolboy Gordon had known in his youth. *So,* he thought, *Seeley went abroad after the tragedy. He prospered, and now after all these years he has come back to England in his retirement. How extraordinary to meet him today.*

"It's Seeley, isn't it?" he said aloud, settling himself in the opposite seat. "Mungo?"

Upon hearing that old school nickname of so many decades past, the gray head turned, and the man's look of wariness changed to a hesitant smile. "Why, it's Neville. Neville Gordon!" he said. "Good heavens, it's been a long time, hasn't it? But I'd have known you anywhere, anywhere at all. You haven't changed—well, of course you have . . . not a lad of twelve anymore, but all the same . . . know you anywhere."

They shook hands. In a few moments of staccato conversation Gordon filled in the gaps of a lifetime. After their school days at Winchester, Seeley prepared for his military career by attending Sandhurst, while Gordon had gone on to Oxford to read law. Now he had been a solicitor in the family firm for more years than he cared to count. He had married an earl's daughter, dead these ten years now, and there had been one son, a fine, bright lad, destined to follow his father into the firm, but it was not to be. The boy had died on the Somme. In his lawyerly way Gordon had endeavored to convey the bare bones of his life story with a flat recitation of facts, but his voice shook a little when he spoke of the death of his son. He was still practicing law, he said. Work was all he had really. No reason to stop now. Gave him an interest in life. Gordon kept too busy to dwell upon the aches and pains of his advancing age, but now, seeing the change the years had wrought in Mungo Seeley, he felt the full weight of the decades pressing down upon him.

"And what about you, Seeley?" he said. "You were a soldier from the look of you. You must have been in the war as well?"

"No. I was posted in India. I was too old for any real fighting, I'm afraid, so they left me out there to see to things while better men carried on the fight in Europe."

Gordon nodded. "And have you a family as well?"

Seeley looked away. "No . . . No. I never married. Not after—No. I never did."

Not after the tragedy, he had been about to say. His face twisted with the effort of suppressed emotion, and Gordon knew that courtesy required that he change the subject to something less painful for Seeley to discuss, but he could think of nothing else. They had been schoolmates, but after so many years, they had nothing in common. Any reminiscences would invariably led up the same path and therefore back to Sarah. Today of all days he must think of Sarah. Surely this meeting of old acquaintances on the 11:25 to Oxford—surely this could not be coincidence?

"Have you kept in touch with Sarah?" asked Gordon, looking away from that stricken countenance. "Perhaps a card at Christmas?"

"No," Seeley whispered. "I went right away. Wanted to forget all of it. Couldn't." He glanced down at the newspaper, still on the floor of the compartment. "The date! Gordon, it was *today*."

"Yes, of course it was. Surely you remembered. Are you not on your way to Oxford to see her?"

Seeley looked pale. "No. I had no idea she was there. Last place in the world . . . No. I wanted to do a bit of research in the Bodleian. Project of mine . . . Got the idea while I was out in India, don't you know . . . A history of Hindu superstition. Saw some amazing things out there. Saw a dagger once with a curse on it that . . ."

"I am going to see Sarah," said Gordon, stemming the tide of explanations. "I am her solicitor, you see."

Seeley mouthed the words to himself. He leaned forward with a look of timid eagerness, and said, "So you see her still?"

Gordon nodded. "From time to time."

"How extraordinary!" said Seeley. "What became of her? What is she like now? Still beautiful, of course?"

Gordon permitted himself a tight, lawyerly smile. "Well, she is a handsome woman still, though at sixty-three I should hardly call her beautiful. Her hair is silver now, instead of gold, and her face is lined, but when she is exceptionally pleased or angry, those incredible blue eyes of hers can still pierce you heart. She married, you know . . ."

Seeley's eyes widened and he gasped. "I—I never thought she would. Not after—"

"Oh, yes. Ages ago. She is a grandmother now."

"I cannot imagine it," said Seeley, shaking his head.

"No, I suppose not," said Gordon. "It's odd, isn't it, how people we have not seen for a long time remain unchanged in our imaginings. We know the years pass. We see time's effect on our own countenances in the mirror, but still we picture absent friends as if they were immune to time. Why, seeing you was a bit of a shock, Seeley, for you have been twenty in my mind's eye lo these many years."

Seeley scarcely seemed to be listening. "So she is old now," he murmured.

"Up in years, but not frail. Why don't you come along and see for yourself, Seeley? I'm sure she'd be delighted to have you turn up. I am here on a matter of business, but our meeting will not take a great deal of time, and she always has me stay to supper afterward. Do say you'll come along. It's always pleasant to meet old friends. I know she would agree."

"I might bring back unpleasant memories . . ."

"You can hardly think she needs reminding of them. And there have been more horrors since then. The war, you know . . . She lost her son and I lost mine. We will talk of happier days."

"I will come," said Seeley. "If you are certain that my visit will not be a burden to her in any way. Er—perhaps I ought to dine elsewhere?"

Gordon laughed. "Sarah will hardly grudge you your cutlet, Seeley. She is rather well off, even in these uncertain times. There was an inheritance from her mother's family, and then she married well—an older man of private means. He was wealthy enough to do whatever he fancied in life, and he chose to pursue his muse, which was poetry, at the university. He was, as I said, a good bit older than she, and he died three years ago, but Sarah has been fortunate enough to keep her health, and there is sufficient money to keep her in comfort, so I should not call her life a tragic one at all—mindful of course of what the Greeks said."

"Eh—the Greeks?"

"The ancient ones, Seeley. They said: *Call no man happy until he is dead.* We learned that in old Brunson's class at Winchester, you know."

"Oh, that. Course we did. Couldn't think what you meant at first." Seeley gave him a tentative smile. "Imagine Sarah still being at Oxford. Been there all her life then."

"Well . . . she went away for a bit, you know, after the inquest. I believe it was during her stay with relatives in Cornwall that she met Sir Alfred. She is Lady Beldon now. I'm afraid people made rather a joke of the name at first. One of the picture papers printed her photograph with the caption *The Beldon Sans Merci* . . . They were still angry, of course."

"Angry?"

"That she had not been hanged."

Riparian, the home of the widowed Lady Beldon, lay well beyond the outskirts of Oxford, amid wide lawns and well-tended gardens that sloped down to a grove of trees on the banks of the Thames itself. From the low wall that separated the property from the lane, one could see an expanse of lush green grass, and on a rise beyond that stood the long, low Queen Anne house of mellowed rose brick, its rows of French windows opening out onto a flagstone terrace. The windows caught the light of the early afternoon sun, and the old bricks shone in the heat of the September afternoon, giving the scene a warm and drowsy air. Just beyond the property, the road ended in a dusty circle at the edge of a wood.

"End of the lane," said the taxi driver, nodding toward the house. "Lovely place, innit? Looks right out over the river at the back, lucky souls. Enjoy the day while you may, gentlemen. Clouds coming in afore dark."

"Yes, indeed," said Gordon, counting the coins out into the driver's outstretched hand. "I don't doubt you're right." He was relieved to know that the local people had forgotten the Darcy tragedy, as the case was called then. It was natural enough, he supposed. The taxi man had not even been born when those events occurred. But Sarah herself had not forgotten. The windows of her sitting room on the back of the house were heavily curtained, and even in high summer they were never open to the view of the river. He turned to Seeley. "Let's go along in," he said. "And, Mungo, do try to be cheerful."

Seeley wondered later just what he had been expecting when he met Sarah Darcy after all these years. Despite what he had said about being unable to imagine her old, he had imagined being ushered into the presence of a stooped and gaunt old woman, wreathed in black mourning clothes, and somber with the weight of that old tragedy bearing down upon her spirit. But he had been wrong.

As soon as Gordon and Seeley set foot upon the checkered marble floor of the entrance hall, they were met by a smiling woman whose hair seemed more blond than gray, and whose elfin manner was as sunny as the primrose tea gown she wore with such careless elegance. The years had indeed been kind to Sarah Darcy. She was no longer a girl of nineteen, it was true, but she carried the decades lightly with no trace of sorrow for herself . . . or for anyone else. Before Seeley could dwell on that last thought, she had enveloped him in a brisk hostessy hug, brushing his cheek with her lips, and exclaiming,

"But it's dear old Mungo! I cannot believe it. Neville, you are an absolute wizard! Where on earth did you find him?"

Gordon smiled. "I can take no credit for that conjuring trick, I'm afraid. He turned up in my compartment on the train, and I insisted that he come along with me. I knew you'd be pleased."

Her smile flickered only for an instant. "Why, of course!" she said. "I'm too delighted to see you both, and you must promise that you will stay to dinner and tell me every single thing that you have been doing since I last saw you."

Mungo's tanned face turned a deeper shade of red. "That shouldn't take long to tell," he said gruffly. "Been a soldier for most of the time. Knocked about the world a bit. Never married, y'know. Just me now."

Sarah nodded. *"Just me,"* she said with a trace of sadness in her voice. "It all comes down to that in the end, perhaps." She turned back to Gordon. "You mustn't mind me," she said, tapping him playfully on the arm. "Just a sad moment. But we have things to attend to, and it will be better to have it over with, so that I can enjoy your visit."

Gordon nodded. "We shan't be long."

"Well, perhaps a bit longer than usual," said Sarah. "I have some papers for you to look over, concerning the Beldon properties in London."

Gordon nodded. "Of course. We must go over those as well as . . . the other. Perhaps Mr. Seeley will excuse us for a bit."

"Yes, that would be best," said Sarah, tugging at a bellpull. "Cunningham will show you into the library, Mungo. I know how much you've always loved poring over musty old books. And we shall be out to take tea with you before you know it."

A tall, sepulchral manservant arrived as if on cue, and to conduct Seeley away to the library. As they left the marble entrance hall, he heard the drawing-room doors close behind Gordon and Sarah. It occurred to him then that the lawyer had not carried a briefcase with him. "He hasn't got any papers with him," Seeley said aloud. "How can they be conducting legal business?"

Cunningham permitted himself a discreet cough. "It is not my place to comment upon the mistress's affairs," he said. "But perhaps sir knows about the ritual imposed upon her ladyship many years ago at the . . . er . . . um . . . the trial."

Seeley stared. "The trial . . . Of course, I remember . . . but that was forty years ago. Surely they abandoned all that ages ago?"

"Oh, no, sir," Cunningham intoned. He had stopped in front of a carved oak door, almost black with age. "The judge's instructions were quite specific on that point. Miss Sarah must always wear the hangman's noose about her neck, and upon the anniversary of the tragedy her compliance with the order must be witnessed by an officer of the court. If she should ever have neglected to carry out this directive, she was to be hanged." He paused and flung open a carved oak door. "The library, sir."

Seeley sat in the leather armchair beside the unlit fireplace, sunk in the gloom of the dimly lit room, with its musty smell of unread books. Apparently the library had been her husband's refuge, and no one had taken an interest in it since his death. Above the mantel hung a full-length portrait of the young Sarah, resplendent in a low-cut blue gown that matched her eyes. It had been painted before the tragedy, then, for she was never to wear low-cut gowns thereafter. The painted image of her loomed over him, flaxen-haired and impishly smiling, with the gold necklace of Burmese turquoise shining against her pale throat.

They had found the necklace clutched in Jack Rhys-Taylor's clenched fist.

Seeley glanced up at the portrait for a moment, repressing a shudder, and then at random he pulled a volume of Tacitus's histories off the shelf and began thumbing through it, scarcely taking in the sense of the words on the page. He had not looked at a line of Roman history since his school days, but still, it was something to keep him occupied while Gordon and Sarah performed the bizarre ritual that had saved Sarah from the gallows. It had been so many years now that he had nearly forgotten the details of the judge's edict: the hangman's noose perpetually worn. The peculiar penance in lieu of execution or a prison sentence had been much remarked upon at the time. Some people had approved of the mercy implicit in the sparing of the prisoner's life, but there were newspaper editorials questioning the mental fitness of the judge, who had indeed retired before the year's end, but despite the comments his curious ruling was left to stand. The consensus was that the deaths caused by the accused were the result of folly, not deliberate malice, and that Sarah would never be a danger to society. As a well-born young woman the authorities seemed to think that she would suffer as much from the prolonged symbolic punishment as a lesser mortal might feel at the gallows itself. In his later years Seeley might have questioned the arrogance of such a verdict, but at the time his own regard for the defendant had made him grateful that her life was spared.

He wondered what it had been like all these years—to wear the hangman's noose about her throat. Because of her rank—the granddaughter of a duke—rather than out of consideration for the fact that she was a woman, Sarah was permitted to wear a silken rope instead of the coarse hemp actually used in hangings, and she was permitted to conceal the silken rope beneath her clothing. The court had not deemed it necessary for the rope to be visible to all and sundry, but Sarah had been made to give her word that she would wear it always. Because she was a member of the aristocracy, the authorities assumed that she would be honor-bound by that promise, and presumably she was.

Seeley recalled that Sarah had taken to wearing blouses of high-collared lace, or brightly covered scarves about her throat to conceal the ever-present gallows necklet. Unless people knew who she was and what had been her penance, they might never suspect that she wore the rope at all. Seeley supposed that the punishment was gentle enough, and the judge's trust had been repaid, for indeed Sarah had led a blameless life ever since. Seeley had been away from England for many years, but the newspapers and society gossip followed the British armies to the most far-flung outposts of the empire, and had there been a breath of scandal connected to Sarah's name, he would have heard.

"Hello! I'm sorry. Did I startle you?" The young woman in the doorway seemed at first an apparition to Seeley.

When she appeared in front of his chair, he gave a cry of alarm, and the copy of Tacitus tumbled from his lap and lay facedown and forgotten upon the hearth rug.

I am dreaming, he thought. *I had nodded off in this chair, waiting for Sarah and Gordon, and now I find myself transported back before the war.* Or perhaps he had dreamed everything that had transpired since those days of his youth. How wonderful it would be to wake up and find himself still young and Sarah untouched by tragedy after all, to find that the Great War that had been such a nightmare for the world had in fact been only a private nightmare of his own . . . In the time it took to form those wistful thoughts, Seeley's mind righted itself to full alertness, and he realized the war and the present were unchanged, and that the fair-haired young woman in the doorway was not a ghost, nor was she Sarah. The resemblance was familial, not phantasmal.

"I am sorry," she said. "I've startled you. I had not realized that anyone was in here."

Seeley struggled to his feet and stammered a hasty introduction. "I am an old friend of your—of—of Lady Beldon . . ."

The vision of the young Sarah smiled at him. "I am Lady Beldon's granddaughter. My name is Marguerite, and so of course everyone calls me Daisy." She nodded toward the portrait. "I look rather like her, don't I? I can see that it must have given you a shock to wake up and find me standing over you. It must have been some time since you had last seen her."

"Ages," said Seeley. "How ever did you know?'

"Well, your reaction, for one thing. You still think of my grandmother looking as I do now, and that has been quite a while ago. Besides, I have been living here for several years now, ever since my mother died of influenza at the end of the war. I should have recognized you if you had visited us since then. I do hope you'll join me for tea?"

Seeley nodded. "I should be delighted," he stammered.

"Oh, good. *Grandmère*'s lawyer has come down for his annual visit. They shut themselves up for ages, talking business, I suppose. They emerge in time to change for dinner, but hardly ever in time for tea. So I am glad that they provided me with company for a change. I can't think what is taking them so long!—Well, I can. *Grandmère* said that she had some questions about the London properties to put to Mr. Gordon, but still, it is tiresome of them."

She does not know, thought Seeley. He was shocked that this should be the case, but a moment's thought told him why this should be so. Of course the secret of her grandmother's tragedy would have been kept from a small child, and the girl's parents had died before they thought her old enough to be told the story. She must be now about the same age that Sarah was when the whole thing happened. It did not seem long ago at all.

There had been a party in Oxford that September evening . . . Seeley could no longer remember the details of that. Later events had swept the memories of the early part of the evening right out of his mind. Seeley had taken the train up from Sandhurst, on the pretext of visiting old school chums, but really to see Sarah. They had all been moths hovering around the flame that was Sarah Darcy. She was a golden girl, as elusive and insubstantial as a will-o'-the-wisp, and they were all in love with her, or at least infatuated beyond all reason.

In those days Mungo Seeley was a tall, awkward boy from a Glasgow military family, bound from the cradle for a soldier's life, and he knew that Sarah Darcy would never consent to be an army wife in some outpost of the empire, but from the moment he met her, Seeley had refused to consider the impossibility of a match between them. Willingly he had joined the throng of her admirers.

How had he met her?

Through Jack Rhys-Taylor, he supposed. Or perhaps it was Albert Candler or Tom Spenser. He had been at school with all of them, and when they went up to Oxford he often visited them, allowing himself to be hauled along to dances and party suppers with that careless, laughing crowd of young people, and the beautiful Sarah Darcy was foremost among them. She was not a student, of course, but her father was the dean of one of the colleges, and she had drifted into the world of the revelers as naturally as a bee finds a rose garden.

That fateful night, after the early evening dance had become too tame for them, they had all converged on the riverbank for a late evening of punting on the Thames. The party consisted only of Sarah and her swains. Surely her prospective suitors had danced with other girls that evening, but if so, the ladies were overshadowed by Sarah's golden radiance, and they were left behind in the headlong dash to the river's edge. Amid laughter and shouts of encouragement, the boys and Sarah had piled into three of the small punts belonging to the nearest college—not that they asked anyone's permission to take them. They cast off in the moonlight, a flotilla of boisterous, drunken youths, determined to impress their fair lady with song or seamanship, according to their lights.

Sarah had been in the boat with Jack, Tom, and two fellows from Trinity—Robbie Graham and Arthur Laurie. Arthur poled the first punt upriver, while Sarah leaned back against the bow, trailing her hand in the water, and smiling lazily at her fleet of admirers. From time to time she would call out to the other boats, or join them in the chorus of a song as they drifted along the dark ribbon of water. Neville Gordon, who was steering the second craft, kept shouting to his two passengers to pipe down and stop rocking the boat before they all ended up in the river. Seeley, the visitor from Sandhurst, rode in the third punt with a shy and spotty divinity student from Merton. They took turns poling the craft, and Seeley was regretting that he had not had more to drink, because he felt suddenly cold on the dark river, and the raucous singing of the others only served to remind him that he was an outsider. The boat had drifted along well astern of the other two punts, perhaps because neither he nor the Merton chap had been industrious in their poling. They knew that they stood little chance of being noticed by Sarah, and now the whole idea of the expedition had begun to seem silly.

Seeley was just thinking to himself that he would ask to be put ashore so that he could walk back to his lodgings when he heard a great splash and then shouting.

"Anything wrong?" someone called out.

"Only Jack being a hero!" someone called out in the darkness. "Sarah has dropped her necklace in the water, and he's gone over the side to fetch it!"

"What, in the river?" said the divinity student. "It's pitch-black down there. He'll not find it."

"No, I shouldn't think he would," Seeley agreed. "The weeds seem quite thick here as well. It's like poling through a hedgerow. Perhaps it's clear where the others are."

They heard Sarah's voice drifting over the water. "But I mustn't lose it!" she cried. "Mummy will kill me. It was my grandmother's necklace. Oh, please do find it! I shall . . . I shall give a kiss for it . . ."

More laughter. Then another splash, and more voices calling out, "Arthur, you fool! It's quite deep here!"

Seeley peered ahead at the dark shapes adrift on the river, but he could not make out any faces. One of the boats rocked as its occupants peered over the sides, and there were more splashes and shouts of "Steady now!"

A minute or more passed, and Seeley took up the pole and began to maneuver the punt toward the other boats, where all had suddenly gone quiet.

"It's been two minutes, hasn't it?" he heard someone say.

"I say, Jack?" another of the shadowy figures called out.

"Can you see him?"

"Did he swim to shore?"

"Has anyone seen Arthur?"

"Jack!"

Seeley turned and scanned the tree-lined bank of the river, but he could see no human form in the shadows cast by the moonlight. He leaned over the side, trying to see ripples in the black water, but he could make out nothing. "Hasn't he come up yet?" he called.

"No," came the reply from the second boat. "And here's why!" A hand was thrust at him and he felt the cold slime of wet foliage against his hand. "They are tangled in the weeds!"

"We should go in and see if we can free them!" someone called out.

These exchanges were punctuated by the sound of Sarah alternately screaming and breaking into floods of weeping.

"But shouldn't someone go for help?" asked Seeley.

"I expect so," said the calm voice. "Won't be time to save them, of course, but . . . I expect so. Why don't you take your boat ashore, then? I'm going after Jack!"

The conversation ended there.

"Right, I'll go for help then," said Seeley, half to himself, because nobody seemed to be paying him any mind.

The fellow from Merton stood up in the boat. "Can you manage it on your own then?" he said. "I just thought that I might be more useful here. I can swim." He took off his jacket, folded it and laid it on the seat, and eased himself over the side, careful not to upset the punt. "Be as quick as you can, though, will you?" With that, he was gone.

The cries and the splashes faded as Seeley poled downstream a few hundred yards toward the lights of a distant house. He was thinking that the divers would be hauled to safety long before he could return, and perhaps he'd better ask for a flask of tea to take along in case they had taken a chill. He was calm and without any foreboding of tragedy when he lodged the punt in the reeds on the riverbank and waded ashore.

He had been wrong, though. When he returned some twenty minutes later with some men from the nearby cottages, they found that no rescues had been effected, and the shouts to the divers had ceased in the face of their certain death. The only sound was Sarah Darcy's soft, persistent weeping, and no one was bothering to comfort her.

The rescuers worked with boat hooks by lantern light, but the sky was already turning gray with the first light of dawn when the first of the bodies broke the surface of the dark river. Three of the revelers had drowned—Arthur, Jack, and the divinity student from Merton, who had gone in to try and save the first two. Robbie Graham had also dived in to attempt a rescue, but the others had managed to pull him back aboard before he, too, became trapped in the weeds.

Seeley wondered later if he should have insisted on taking Sarah away with him, but he doubted that she would have gone, and although he was ashamed to admit it, the thought had not even occurred to him at the time. Perhaps he had wanted to get away from her screams as much as he had wanted to help, but he pushed that thought out of his mind.

He had stayed for the inquest, come back for the funerals, and back again for Sarah's trial, though his testimony had hardly mattered. Both he and Gordon had testified that it was all a dreadful accident, that Sarah had meant no harm when she dropped the necklace, but the jury had listened stone-faced to their protestations. What was a young lady doing out on the river late at night, unchaperoned with a gang of varsity students, they wanted to know. No better than she should be, their stern faces said. Perhaps she did want to be rid of at least one of the young gentlemen. Who's to say she didn't? There was no mercy to be had from them. Sarah's position was made all the worse by the fact that Jack Rhys-Taylor had been the heir to a baronetcy. His people were said to be distraught by his untimely death, and at the time of the trial there were whispers that their influence had been brought to bear on the case to ensure that the foolish young woman did not get off scot-free. And indeed she had not.

Now a lifetime had passed, and Seeley found himself looking again at the necklace that had caused the tragedy. It sparkled around the neck of another lovely girl, almost the image of the young Sarah herself, and the sight of that necklace made him shiver. The young woman sat there at his elbow, pouring tea and smiling, and he made replies to her conversation, with what words he scarcely knew, and all the while his mind roared with the memories of those cold, pale bodies stretched out on the riverbank, wreathed in the tendrils of water weeds.

It seemed strange to him somehow that Sarah had gone on to have a life, and that those three young men had not. He had never got over the uneasiness of having survived the incident. Everyone had said that Seeley did the correct thing by going for help, but he could not overcome the fact that he had risked nothing while his friends were drowning. He might not have been able to save them, might even have died himself, but he had never quite escaped the guilt of not having tried. In the long army career that followed for Seeley, no act of valor had ever quite compensated for his inglorious prudence that night on the river.

And what did Sarah feel after all these years? He wondered if she ever thought of those who were drowned. She recalled the tragedy, of course. How could she not? But did she ever think of those three young men as bright and happy individuals, or were they now simply the authors of her discomfiture?

Daisy Beldon stood up. "Have you finished your tea, Mr. Seeley? I have. And it's such a lovely warm evening for September. The mist is coming up, but there's still a bit of daylight left, and it seems a pity to stay cooped up inside all day. Would you like to go out and see the garden? The roses are gone, but we have autumn flowers in the borders, and of course the herb garden."

It was precisely the sort of reasonable suggestion that a well-bred hostess might make to a visitor to the house, and Seeley, who was quite tired of sitting anyhow, got up without a moment's thought, and followed her down the passageway and through the curtained French windows that led to the garden . . . that led to the river.

He saw that the twilight had deepened the sky to the color of pewter, and skeins of darker clouds now hung in the air. There couldn't be more than half an hour's light left, for although the afternoon weather had been perfect, it was late September and the days were short. On the river, a mist was rising.

"It's so peaceful in the garden," said Daisy, wending her way around a stand of rose trees. "I love to look out over the flowers and to watch the river drift by. *Grandmère* never comes out here, though. I pick the flowers and take them in to her so that she can arrange them in vases. She does lovely flower arrangements. It's the sort of thing that girls in her day had to learn."

Seeley smiled. "I remember those days," he said. "I remember your grandmother carrying a nosegay that she had made herself. We were at a dance. She was wearing that very necklace, as I recall."

Daisy reached up and touched the necklace at her throat. "You remember seeing her wear this necklace? How odd. I've never seen her put it on. Once when we were searching for a pair of earrings for me to wear to a dinner party, I saw the necklace tucked away in her jewelry box, and I asked her why she never wore it. The stone matches her eyes, don't you think?"

Seeley nodded. "I always thought so," he said. "And now they match yours as well."

Daisy Beldon prattled on with the assurance of a pretty young girl who thinks that all the world looks kindly on her and takes an interest in the minutiae of her existence. "It's curious," she said. "When I asked *Grandmère* about the necklace, she said she didn't care for it. Then she said I'd better have it, because when she was nearly my age she had got it as a gift from her own grandmother."

"A family heirloom. Yes, I do recall that," said Seeley politely.

"I'm fond of it. In fact, I wear it all the time," she said with an uneasy titter of laughter. "I only wish I could stop dreaming about it."

Seeley turned to stare at her. "I beg your pardon. Did you say that you dream about this necklace?"

"Yes. I shouldn't have mentioned it, really. I know it's very silly of me, but it is beginning to worry me a bit. I only got the necklace last spring, and since then I've had the dream a time or two, but just lately it has happened nearly every night."

Seeley stared out at the river now swirling in evening mist. After a moment he said, "Would you think it terribly impertinent of me, Miss Beldon, if I asked you to describe your dream for me?"

"I shouldn't mind telling you about it, Mr. Seeley, only you must promise not to tell my grandmother. I mustn't worry her." She waited for his nod of assent before she continued. "I see the necklace tangled in a clump of weeds . . . not a garden, exactly . . . They are strange willowy plants that seem to float as if the wind were blowing them, but I feel no wind. I reach out my hand to grasp the necklace, and suddenly I cannot breathe. I try to run, but I cannot. I wake up choking and gasping for air."

Seeley felt the sudden chill of the evening. The darkness had deepened now, draining the color from the garden, and when he turned to look at the river, he found it completely swathed in mist. The sky was growing darker now, giving him the sensation that a silver cover had been placed over the house and grounds, blotting out the world outside. He found himself longing for the comforting sight of the paneled library, with a fire in the grate and a decanter of whiskey on the tray before the armchair.

"A most unusual dream," he said. "Perhaps you ought to put the necklace away for a while."

"I know. I've tried." Her voice dropped to a whisper. "A few days ago I began to take it off before I went to bed, but in the morning when I awoke, I found I was wearing it again! I suppose that I am so attached to the necklace that I cannot bear to be without it."

"Perhaps if you asked that it be locked away in the safe, that would settle the matter," said Seeley. "Rum thing, you're dreaming like that. Puts me in mind of India . . . tales I heard . . . We should go in now. It's getting dark."

She turned to look at him. "It is chilly, isn't it? The dark comes so quickly in autumn, I always think. Why don't you go back inside, Mr. Seeley? I just want to pick a few flowers for my room in case a rain tonight spoils them, but I won't be long. I'll join you shortly."

With some misgivings, Seeley turned and went back into the house. Although he was concerned about the young lady, he was not sorry to leave the garden, beautiful though it might be. He found that he no longer wanted to be within sight of the river, especially not in the presence of that infernal necklace that was the origin of that long-ago tragedy. He had almost reached the library when he heard Gordon calling out to him.

"There you are, Seeley! We couldn't think where you'd got to. Will you join us for a drink before dinner?"

Gordon and Sarah bore down upon him, smiling with relief that the yearly ordeal was over, but despite their gaiety the feeling of oppression did not leave him. "I was just walking in the garden with Miss Daisy," he told them. "A most charming girl. She is outside still, gathering flowers. Perhaps we might call her." He gestured toward the drawn curtains covering the French windows.

Sarah shivered. "Daisy is always mooning about in that garden," she said. "Let us go in to dinner. I'll send Cunningham to fetch her."

"No," said Seeley. "She's just outside. Let me go." Even as he said it, he felt a stab of misgiving, and he suddenly realized that he did not want to go back out into that dark garden, but he knew that he must. Perhaps this feeling of dread was only an old man's fancy, or the oppression of a coming storm, but what was he to make of the dream? His years in India had taught him not to dismiss such things lightly.

Before Gordon and Sarah could argue further, Seeley fumbled with the curtained French windows and jerked at the catch, and plunged out into the deepening twilight. He stood there on the flagstone terrace, blinking, as his eyes became accustomed to the dim light.

"Miss Beldon?" he called out. He had not spoken loudly because he thought she would be close by, but his voice echoed in the darkness and no one answered.

Seeley did not see her at first. He had expected to find her still cutting flowers in the borders of the terrace, but when he perceived that she was not there, he scanned the expanse of lawn, and saw a dark figure walking toward the river. He called out again, but when there was no response, he began to run toward her.

He was only yards away from Daisy Beldon and the river, when he saw that she was not alone. Standing at the water's edge beside Daisy Beldon was a taller figure, his head bent as if the two of them were in conversation. Seeley hurried on. There was something familiar about the silhouette before him.

As he drew near, he heard the lazy drawl of a man's voice saying, "We're just going punting down the river for a bit . . . won't you come?"

Seeley stepped out of the mist and clasped the girl by the arm. "Hello, Jack," he said softly.

Jack Rhys-Taylor looked just as he had on that other night on the river so long ago. He was still dark-eyed and handsome, regally slender, and wearing a look of well-bred coolness that was the antithesis of fear. He was still twenty. At the sound of his name, he turned to look at Seeley, puzzled, perhaps, by the sight of this old man who seemed acquainted with him.

"It's me, Jack," said Seeley in answer to the unspoken question. "It's Mungo."

"Hello, Mungo," said Jack, in the same jaunty tone he had always used. "We're just going out on the river. I say, doesn't Sarah look lovely in her necklace?"

Seeley turned to look at Daisy. She stood at Jack's side, dazed and silent, like a sleepwalker. In the faint light, her resemblance to her grandmother was remarkable. Beyond her, Seeley could see the shadowy form of a punt, just beyond the reeds at the water's edge. More dark shapes sat in the boat—waiting.

Words hovered on Seeley's lips, but he had the absurd thought that it would be discourteous to remind Jack of the fact that he was dead. "It has been a long time," he said at last.

"Not a bit," said Jack softly. "We only just left the party a little while ago. Lovely evening for punting. I know Sarah is keen to go along. And we mean to take her with us."

Seeley wondered if his fear at seeing the apparition had caused him to imagine the undercurrent of menace in Jack's voice. The lights from the house caught in the gold of the necklace, making it shine in the darkness. Without thinking, Seeley snatched at the pendant, tearing the chain from Daisy Beldon's throat. "This damned necklace! It has done enough," he said, and he threw it far out into the river.

Daisy seemed to come to then, with a cry of alarm. "*Grandmère*'s necklace!" she cried. "Oh, I can't lose it!" With the toe of one slipper, she began to kick at the heel of the other, struggling to get them off. "I must go after it!"

Seeley looked back at the old woman, standing in the glow of light on the terrace. He wondered if she could see them—and if it would matter to her. She made no move toward them, as she had made none on that other night on the river.

Seeley pushed his way past Daisy Beldon, who now stood alone on the bank of the river. He waded into the dark current that swirled about the reeds. "No, my dear, I'll go in and get it," said Seeley quietly. "You go back to the house now. I shan't be long."

Brendan DuBois

ONE SHOT DIFFERENCE

■ ■ ■

Brendan DuBois is the award-winning author of eight novels and nearly eighty published short stories. Besides the United States, his work has appeared in several foreign countries. He is the author of two acclaimed suspense thrillers, Resurrection Day *and* Betrayed, *both of which received starred reviews from* Publishers Weekly. *He is also the author of* Six Days, *another thriller, and the novels in the Lewis Cole mystery series:* Dead Sand, Black Tide, Shattered Shell, Killer Waves, *and* Buried Dreams. *His short stories have appeared in* Playboy, Ellery Queen's Mystery Magazine, Alfred Hitchcock's Mystery Magazine, Mary Higgins Clark Mystery Magazine, *and numerous original anthologies. He has twice won the Shamus Award from the Private Eye Writers of America for Best Short Story of the Year, and has been nominated three times by the Mystery Writers of America for an Edgar Allan Poe Award for his short fiction. "One Shot Difference," our selection for this year's anthology, once again details the failings of a relationship—something that DuBois, despite the military edge often found in his work, is very good at bringing to life.*

The training session that day took place in an area of the decommissioned Air Force base that had once stored nuclear weapons for the B-52s and FB-111s stationed there. The Air Force bombers were long gone and it was mostly civilian aircraft that were now using the mile-long runway. Other parts of the base had been cut up and subdivided for high-tech firms, a passport-processing office for U.S. customs, and a regional bus system. Since no one had come up with a commercial use for the two dozen concrete bunkers half-buried in the soil, they had been abandoned when the base had closed years earlier. Each bunker was long and curved, covered with soil and grass, with a ventilation shaft poking out from the center. They looked quiet and peaceful, not at all like a place that had once stored weapons capable of incinerating a city and killing millions in a matter of seconds.

Craig Francis leaned against the hood of a Porter police department cruiser, watching the SWAT team members from a half-dozen local towns get suited up and ready for the day's session. His arms were folded and he was enjoying the early-morning sun. He was also enjoying seeing the cops goof around, eating donuts and drinking coffee and tossing footballs back and forth. Most of them were much younger than he was, quite muscular and strong, and they had the cocky attitude that came with being healthy, young, and on top of their game. He, on the other hand, was on the wrong side of forty years old, had never walked more than a mile at a time in his life, and had long ago ceased being cocky. Except for a young woman who worked as a dispatcher, talking to a couple of the cops, he was the only civilian among the early-morning crowd. His real job was owner and manager of the Francis Farms convenience store in Porter, a popular place for the Porter cops. No cop ever paid for a cup of coffee or snack at his store, and in return, they kept an eye on the place and responded quickly whenever he needed them, for something as small as a teenage shoplifter or somebody who passed a bad check, or something as bad as a holdup.

It was a good arrangement, a comfortable arrangement, and sometimes it came with a few perks, like today. The cops from Porter and other towns that belonged to the regional SWAT response team were conducting a training session, and they needed a couple of volunteers to serve as criminals, to make the training more realistic. Craig had done it a few times before and found it fun; though he usually ended the day with bumps, bruises, and once, a bloody nose, it had always been worth it.

But today . . . well, today was going to be different. He looked around at the cops as they put on their protective vests, their Kevlar helmets, their kneepads and gloves, and saw one Porter cop tossing a football to another. Even among the other cops, he stood out. Dirk Conrad. Twenty-seven years old, black hair shorn quite short. Even with the protective gear and body armor, it was easy to tell from the swell of his upper arms and chest that he spent a lot of his time working out.

Dirk spotted Craig looking at him, grinned, and gave him a big wave. Craig waved back with a smile. Craig knew a lot about Dirk: where he had grown up, where he had gone to school, and how he was doing with the department. Dirk was a crack shot, tough on the streets, was on a fast track for promotion, and made it clear that he intended to get out of the department one of these days and try for the FBI or CIA. He had big plans to go with those big muscles, and Craig knew that, and more.

He shifted his weight on the cruiser and lifted his head up to the sun. For Craig also knew that young Dirk Conrad was having an affair with Craig's wife Stacy, and for that, Craig planned on ending Dirk's life today, in the midst of all his fellow cops.

The thought and the bright sunshine on his face made him smile.

And the hell of it was, he had never intended to run that damn convenience store. It had belonged to his father, and he had worked plenty of afternoons and weekends—giving up school activities like track or band or the school newspaper, and especially dances and proms—to help out the family and make some pocket change. Sacrifices, Dad had said. To get ahead you need to make sacrifices. But once he had gone to college and nailed his Business Administration degree, he was ready to shake off Porter and raise some hell and make some money, and forget about sacrifices for a while.

But Dad had gotten a rare blood disease that seemed to eat him from the inside out, and since he was their only boy—his three older sisters had already found husbands and had children by then—Dad had pleaded with him not to sell the store. Francis Farms had opened in Porter in 1902, with Craig's great-grandfather, and Dad didn't want the store and the name to die with him.

Fine. A promise to a dying man and he had given it, knowing he had other plans, other ideas, and yet . . .

The trap had been set.

He had taken over the store and within a week knew that the reverse was true: The store had taken over him. Each day was a rolling morass of problems to be solved, problems to be addressed, problems to be ignored. Employees who didn't show up or who showed up late. Delivery trucks blocking the parking lot for the customers. Health inspectors. Youngsters with fake IDs trying to buy beer. Liquor inspectors. Employees who stole, customers who stole, people wandering by the front of the store who stole. Water bill, tax bill, oil bill, electricity bill . . . Mother of God, the amount of money spent each month on electricity (for the freezers and coolers and lights and everything else) was as much as he spent on renting an apartment while going to college! Sweeping up and cleaning up after some three-year-old girl who, racing through, knocked over a display of grape-jelly jars. People coming in looking to put up posters in the window, people looking to sell raffle tickets, people looking for donations to this charity or that charity and don't you know, it's the duty of business owners to support the neighborhood?

Trapped. Within a week, it felt as if the chains of responsibility had been gently but firmly clasped around his ankles.

Oh, he could have given up after a month or so, but there was that streak of stubbornness in him, combined with the promise he had made to Dad, dear old Dad, to keep the damn place running.

Sacrifices.

And so he had remained, in a life of work and not enough sleep and never any real days off, until the day Stacy came by next-door, to open a hair salon.

And then it had all changed.

One of the police officers—who had a thick moustache and was wearing a bright orange vest with TRAINING stenciled in black, fore and aft—stepped out into the middle of the crowd and said, "Listen up, people, listen up. It's time to get started."

The cop went on about how the SWAT team would split up into different groups and work through different scenarios during the day. Two of the old bunkers would be used during the training session. Some years ago, the cop explained, Navy SEAL members had come to this very place and had constructed in the bunkers rooms made of wooden doors and plywood walls. Craig thought about that, and as the cop went on and on in great detail about the training that was going to take place, he wandered over to the closest bunker. The metal door—rusting at the hinges—had been propped open, and he stepped inside, the interior cool and damp. The floor and the walls and curved ceiling were concrete, and there was faded paint on the concrete, marking some sort of grid. Before him, just a few yards in from the entrance, was a wooden warren of rooms and corridors. He slowly walked through them in the dim light, wondering how it felt to race through here, even in a training session, knowing that something bad was waiting for you.

He paused and touched the walls and a nearby door. He shivered, remembering what the training officer had said. Navy SEALs—elite warriors—had been in this same room, had built these rooms to help themselves train, and now, well, where were they? Afghanistan? Iraq? Yemen? So far from home. He wondered if they ever thought about the training they had done at this old air base in New Hampshire, and he wondered what they would think about what he had planned for the training session today.

He had a feeling most of them would understand.

Craig turned and went back outside.

Stacy Moore had come in one summer day to introduce herself, and Craig couldn't remember much of what he said to her, for he was struck by how beautiful she was. She had on tight jeans, a white knit sleeveless shirt that was unbuttoned far enough to show a fair amount of cleavage, and her blond hair was tied back in a simple ponytail. She said she had taken over the lease next-door, was opening up a hair salon—"Stacy's Hair Design"—and could he do her a favor?

Absolutely, had been his reply. She had needed power—"Damn Public Service is late in coming by"—and would he mind if she ran a power cord from his store to her place?

Thinking about that request had taken about a second or two.

Not a problem, he had said. He had even helped her bring in some supplies, admiring the way she filled out her clothes, admiring her laugh, and when he was through moving things and hooking up things, she had blushed slightly and said, Well, I wish I could pay you back for your help.

He had laughed. My pleasure, he had said. Really.

She had folded her arms, exposing even more of her cleavage, and said, Well, how about a free haircut?

And in a matter of moments he had been seated in one of the chairs, warm water cascading over his head, her strong fingers working at his scalp, working in the shampoo, and he looked up at her figure and her smile, and he knew without a doubt that he was falling in love.

Outside, he joined the dozen or so cops, nodding at all the Porter cops he knew, and even Dirk managed another smile in his direction. The training officer lined everyone up—except, of course, for Craig and the young woman dispatcher named Sarah—and started referring to a clipboard held in his hand.

"All right, let's get a move on, we've only got a few hours to work with," he said. "You know the drill, you know the scenarios. Now it's time for a safety check. Everybody check your weapons, check your belongings. No live rounds. No edged weapons. This is just training. Leave the real stuff behind."

Before the line of cops were two long folding tables, and on the tables were plastic ammo boxes, opened up, showing round after round of simulated ammunition. Craig wandered over and examined one of the bullets, recalling when he had first seen these little bundles of power. They had the same brass jacket as any other semiautomatic 9mm. round, but the amount of powder inside the cartridge was smaller than for a regular bullet, and the slug at the top was a type of paintball. It stung and left a brief red splotch of paint, and that was that. Every cop here today would load their weapons with these fake rounds, and while they stung some, it sure beat the hell out of the real thing. And it helped with the training, especially with two "bad guys"—him and Sarah—deep within the rooms, waiting in ambush for the squads of SWAT members to come barreling through.

He put the fake round down and then, almost absent-mindedly, he put his hand in his pants pocket where he felt something small and hard and metallic.

Another 9mm. round, just like the ones on the tables.

Except this one was the real thing.

He smiled, went back, and joined the cops.

Craig had been thrilled and thankful when Stacy had agreed to go out with him, and soon they were a couple. It had been so easy at first, with her working right next-door to him, and he had made a habit of popping in and out during the day, bringing over drinks and sandwiches at lunch, and sometimes they had managed to have lunch out on the sidewalk, watching the people of Porter go by. He would check with her as she closed up, making sure she could get to the bank all right with her deposits—the block they were on could be rough at certain times of the night during certain times of the year—and he would juggle the schedules of his workers so he could have at least one night a week with her.

She was from Dover, the next city over, and was a high-school grad who just wanted to have her own business using the only skills she really had, as a hairdresser. After a while, when she had learned about his business-school experience, she had shyly asked him to examine her books. He had made a dreadful joke about having already examined other personal parts of her, and her books would be relatively easy, but he stopped laughing when he looked at her piles of receipts and bills.

Stacy's Hair Design was in debt, was sinking faster than the *Titanic*, and unless something drastic happened, and soon, she would be facing personal and business bankruptcy.

After telling her this, and after seeing the tears erupt, he had offered something drastic: marriage.

And happiest of days, she had said yes.

With the briefing over, the training officer came over and handed him a revolver. "Still know how to use this, Craig?"

"Without a doubt," he said.

"Sorry we only have one spare," he said. "Looks like you and Sarah will have to share."

"Not a problem."

Before going into the bunker, he put on his own protective gear: gloves, old fatigue jacket, a thin vest that covered his back and front, and a foam-lined plastic helmet with a clear plastic front. It was hard to talk with the helmet on, and when he and Sarah got into the bunker, he lifted up the helmet and said, "You want to have the gun first?"

Sarah was small and thin, with brown hair and big brown eyes. Earlier he had learned she had been a dispatcher with the department for only six months. She lifted her own helmet and grinned.

"Really?"

"Sure," he said. "I've done this before. You go ahead and have fun."

She took the large revolver in her small hands and said, "Oh, you know it. Lots of these guys love to give me crap on the job. It's gonna be fun to get some payback."

He smiled back. "I know the feeling."

So a month after their marriage, she had come to him and said that as much as she hated to do it, it was time to close the hair shop. And he had said, Not a problem, you can work at the store. As assistant manager. Not a problem. Which was true. Stacy's Hair Design had gone out of business, his new wife had moved six feet over to her new job, and then, well, it began to crumble.

Simple things at first. Working with the spouse, the whole day long, just a few feet away from each other, meant no quiet time, no alone time. Little quirks of hers that earlier had been fun and amusing started to grate on him. Her humming. The way she picked at her fingernails. And the way she always seemed to dress with her cleavage exposed. And there was more to follow. She didn't like the way he arranged the shelves, he didn't like the way she'd chat away with a customer while a line formed. She thought he was too bossy, he thought she took too much time on breaks.

Their life revolved around the store, the store, all glory to the store, and lots of times, at the end of the day, they would both fall into bed, speak only a few words to each other, and then fall asleep. The only difference in the days of the week was that on Sunday, the newspapers for sale in the store were fatter.

That's when he started to become frightened that everything was beginning to fall away with his life and marriage. Sacrifices, he thought, when do the damn sacrifices stop?

But then hope came, from a most unlikely source: the federal government.

SCENARIO ONE:

The SWAT team was breaking into a house with two known drug dealers, one of whom was believed to be armed. Craig's role was to be the first drug dealer spotted, and he was sitting in a plastic chair, hands in his lap. The training officer said he was to cooperate and not put up any fuss, which was fine. There would be plenty of time for fuss later. Young and eager Sarah was somewhere deeper into the rooms, and he had wished her good luck and good aim.

Sounds. Booted feet tromping on the floor, low whispers, and then, like some nightmare vision from an Orwell book, the armed and well-equipped police came through the door. Even though he was expecting it and had done this several times before, his heart raced at the sight of these bulky armed men coming right at him. They had on goggles and helmets and protective vests and black fatigues and gloves and military boots, and some were holding out 9mm. pistols while others were carrying 9mm. submachine guns, and the moment Craig was spotted the screaming started, words tumbling over one another, echoing in the confines of the bunker.

"Police!"

"Search warrant!"

"Down on the ground!"

"Down on the ground, now!"

"Show us your hands!"

"Now!"

"Now!"

"Now!"

Craig's heart was really thumping and he held out his hands and dropped to his knees on the concrete floor, and then stretched out. Hands expertly searched him, looking for any weapons—and a horrid thought suddenly came to him: Suppose the real round of 9mm. ammunition was found?—and when somebody yelled, "Hands to your back!" he moved his hands to his back and crossed his wrists. There was a squeeze at the wrists and another voice said, "Secure!" and he turned his head, seeing the booted feet fly by. Another part of the training. No handcuffs, no plastic restraints. He was now a prisoner, and he played along and waited.

Some other noises, of voices, as the police moved into the other rooms.

"Clear!"

"Okay."

"Checking . . ."

"Hold on . . ."

"Gun!"

"Gun!"

And the gunfire erupted into the short and ferocious *pop-pop-pop* of practice rounds being expended, and more yells, more shouts, and then a whistle was blown by the training officer. Scenario completed.

Craig rolled over and sat up, removed his helmet. The SWAT members came back in as he stood up, some laughing, a couple of them looking embarrassed, with splotches of red paint smeared across their black fatigues. One guy said, "Hah, look at that, you got nailed by a girl," and the other cop responded, with some bravado, "Man, the number of times I've nailed girls, I just decided it was time to let one of 'em have some payback."

Then Sarah came in, smiling, her helmet off and her hair matted down. Her protective vest was smeared with a half-dozen paintball rounds, and she was shaking one of her hands, as if she had just burnt it on a stovetop. The other hand held the large revolver. "Man, that stung! Man, did that hurt! But I got some of you back, I surely did." And she laughed.

"All right," the training officer said. "Time for a debriefing. Sarah and Craig, if you can excuse us, please."

"Sure," he said, walking out of the bunker and blinking in the sunshine, helmet under his arm. Sarah was with him, still smiling. "That was some fun, but you know what?" she said.

"What?"

"I knew they were coming, I knew what they were going to do, but I was still scared. I was breathing hard and when they came into the room, I almost peed myself. Funny, huh?"

"No, same thing happens to me, all the time," he said.

She wiped at her face. "How come they did that?"

"Did what?"

"Asked us to leave."

Craig said, "So they can have a debriefing without a couple of civilians hanging around, that's why. In some ways, we're just guests here. That's all. Nothing to get offended about."

"Oh, I'm not offended," she said. "Just curious."

"Good."

She then smoothed her hair and said, "I fired off all six rounds. Time to load up."

"Go right ahead," he said. "It'll be awhile."

So he sat on the grass while she went over to the table with the simulated ammunition. She undid the cylinder of the revolver, emptied out the spent brass cartridges, and then reloaded with the paintball rounds. Young Sarah worked quickly, efficiently, and Craig smiled at her hurry, since the cops were all still in the bunker taking part in the debriefing session.

He turned his head up to the sun and waited.

The news had come first from a story in the Porter *Herald*. In some mysterious way, grants from the Department of Housing and Urban Development were trickling into the city of Porter. Some of that money was going to be used in the neighborhood where the store was located, as part of "Renovation" and "Revitalization" and "Revamping" and other words that began with the letter R.

Interesting enough, he had thought, leafing through the newspaper as he waited for a young boy to count out seventy-five pennies so he could buy a candy bar, but the news got even more interesting when a couple of real-estate developers wandered by. And that had been the deal: They were going to grab a chunk of that development money, and if Craig and his suffering wife were interested—were they ever!—then the store and the building would be purchased at a very reasonable price, and would then be turned into low-price apartments for welfare recipients or higher-priced apartments for senior citizens, depending on which interest group was making the most noise that year.

And his eyes had watered with tears, real tears of sheer joy, at seeing the proposals the real-estate agents had provided, for it meant a lot of money, enough for some time off and a fresh start for him and the woman he had married.

Maybe the time for sacrifice was over. And for the first time in months, things had been looking up.

At least for a while.

SCENARIO TWO:

A raid on another drug den. The cops coming in weren't told how many people were in there or how they were armed. Sarah seemed eager to be the shooter again, and Craig said that was fine. His role was to be half-hidden in the corner of one of the rooms, and the training officer had told him to freelance, to do whatever he wanted.

Such an invitation.

So this time, Craig stood flat against a wall with his hand down at his side. It was a bit of a gamble, but he had taken one of his black gloves off and had rolled it up to make a cylinder. That was at his side, and he waited, breathing hard, the plastic on his helmet fogging up. Somewhere in there, Sarah was waiting with eager anticipation, and in a way, so was he.

Voices again, the sounds of the boots on the concrete.

He waited, heart now thumping merrily along.

They were closer now, in the other room. Voices, low and indistinct.

He could see the play of flashlight beams on the far wall.

Very close.

A cop came into the room, holding a 9mm. pistol in front of him, two other cops behind him, and Craig stepped out, quickly raising his arm, holding out the rolled-up glove and—

"Gun!"

Damn, he could actually see the muzzle flashes erupt from the barrel as the cop coming into the room fired at him, and the paintball rounds struck his chest with a soft thud. He dropped and rolled onto the floor, letting the glove fall out of his hand, and he heard the cop who had just shot him mutter, "Oh hell, did I screw up," when he realized Craig wasn't armed.

On the cold concrete floor, Craig smiled.

More movement, more voices, and then another shout, deeper inside the bunker, of "Gun!" and more gunfire. Craig kept on smiling as the whistle blew and he sat up. The cop who had shot him had lifted up his helmet, and the smile faded as Craig realized who it was: Dirk Conrad.

Dirk shook his head. "Man, you got me, you really did."

"It happens," he said, feeling good at seeing the shocked expression on that usually confident face. Dirk had on the usual SWAT gear, but he noticed something else, as well: a yellow smiley-face button, right in the center of the vest. Like some sort of mocking talisman or good-luck charm.

The training officer came over, his face set. "Time for a debrief. Excuse us, will you?"

"Sure," Craig said, and he was outside again, joined shortly by the police dispatcher. Sarah frowned and said, "They were better this time. I don't think I got anybody but they really nailed me good. What about you?"

"Held up a glove and got shot."

She laughed. "That's something."

Craig found a spot and sat down on the cracked asphalt, leaned back against the concrete wall of the bunker. Sarah joined him and he caught a whiff of her perfume. Something young, something sporty. He suddenly found that he was envious of her youth, her wide-open future.

"Sure, that's something," he said. "But it can also mean a lot of trouble for Dirk and for the department, down the road."

"How's that?"

He rubbed his chest where it still stung from the shot by the paintball, even under the protective pad. This time tomorrow he'd have a nice purple and green bruise there to remind him of this day, as if he would need any additional reminding.

"Thing is, let's say in a year or two Dirk's involved in a shooting of a suspect. Could be clear, could be a righteous shooting. Still, the guy's defense attorney might want to find out the background of the nice cop who shot his client. So he'd subpoena the department's training records for Dirk, to see if he found anything questionable. Bingo, there's a record that during this particular training session, he fired at a person holding nothing more threatening than a glove. See the trouble?"

"God, I guess so," she said, the revolver large and still in her lap. "Tell me, how do you know so much about cops?"

"Experience," he said. "Simply experience."

Sure, things had been looking up for him and Stacy and the store, until something happened. That was the way of the world now. You made plans and thought things through and thought everything would work out, and then Something Happened. This time, the something was a bit of Congressional backstabbing and backslapping that meant funds allocated for Porter went to Portland, Maine, or Portland, Oregon, or some other place. Which meant the eager real-estate agents who had been sniffing around the store went away and never came back. Which meant that a week after he had turned down an offer for the store from one of the agents—confident that a counteroffer would come back later that was larger and better—Stacy just looked over at him from behind the store counter, lining up lottery tickets, and said with quiet bitterness, "Some life, huh? Some life."

And what could he have said? That there would always be sacrifices?

So he had gone along, done the best he could to run the store and work and live with Stacy, and then, well, something clicked. It had just seemed to him that the only times she was happy, smiling, and engaged were when there were cops around the store. Pretty funny, eh? Cops who were supposed to serve and protect were now making his wife happy. And one night . . . well, he had gone back to the store by accident. Or had it been accidentally-on-purpose? He still wasn't sure. All he remembered was that he had left some receipts at the store and when he got back there, had gone through the door, the little bell jangling, there had been Stacy, and there had been Officer Dirk Conrad. Stacy had been leaning over the counter, buttons on her tight black sweater undone just so, and Dirk had been grinning the grin of somebody who had seen this sight before and had enjoyed it very much.

And the look from the both of them, as he unexpectedly came up the main aisle, told him everything he needed to know.

The third scenario was delayed until after lunch. For a while the SWAT team members trained by themselves in the two bunkers, learning how to better enter and sweep the rooms. Craig and Sarah were left alone for a while, and while Sarah got on her cell phone and talked for long and dreary moments to her boyfriend Toby, Craig went over to a sunny side of the bunker and stretched out his legs. Before him was grassland and then a tall chain-link fence topped off by razor wire, and on the other side of the fence, the ground was cleared out for about fifty feet to the treeline. Up on the slight rise leading to the access road was a locked gate, so that the cops wouldn't be disturbed. All of this land where once nuclear weapons had been stored, and where armed Air Force security police were authorized to use deadly force, was now a nature preserve. The officers out here at night, armed and ready, had probably thought this place would last forever.

But things change, he thought. Boy, do they ever change.

Late one afternoon a couple of weeks ago, he had been in their living room in their apartment, waiting, a black videocassette cartridge in his hand. It seemed heavy enough to be made of lead. A few weeks earlier, he had gone into the back office of the store and rewired and reconnected an old security-camera system that kept watch on the store and the back office. He supposed he should have told Stacy. Right. He guessed he should have, but he hadn't, so there you go.

So what now?

A voice whispered inside of him to toss it aside, get rid of it, never to view what might be stored forever on the magnetic impulses on the thin tape. Little impulses of energy that had the power to destroy his marriage. All right there.

He juggled the tape with some difficulty, cursed under his breath, and then went over and slid it into the VCR on top of the television set. On top of the VCR was a framed photo of him and Stacy on their wedding day, and blinking hard, he turned the photo around and picked up the remote.

Grainy images inside the store, not much going on. He used the fast-forward button, toggled it hard, until . . .

Until there he was. Dirk Conrad. Alone in the store with Stacy. There was no sound, so he couldn't tell what was being said between them, but what the hell. He knew they weren't discussing the latest zoning-board proposal. The screen was split in two. The left-hand side showed the countertop where Dirk and Stacy were conversing. The right-hand side was his office, and it was blank, since the lights weren't on.

And then it happened. Stacy and Dirk slid out of view on the left-hand side, and then the right-hand side of the tape lit up, and there was the interior of his office. Dirk brought Stacy around to his desk—his own damn desk!—holding her hand, and that little betrayal right there—holding another man's hand, even though Craig knew what was going to happen next—bore right through him like a drill bit from an oil rig, churning its way into his chest.

Stacy started unbuttoning her blouse. Craig got up and switched everything off, and then went into the bathroom to vomit.

Lunchtime. The overhead sun was high up and it was hot, and as in the other training sessions, sandwiches and drinks and snacks were produced from little portable coolers. The cops stripped off their helmets and gloves and vests and weapons, and dumped them on one of the long tables where the ammunition was stored. Young Sarah brought her revolver over and did the same thing, and he waited, waited long minutes, like the time waiting for a retiree to find a dollar bill in his wallet for a lottery ticket, and when he thought the time was right, he went over to the table. Some cops were now in the tall grass, dozing, while others tossed a football back and forth. Craig got up and stretched and reached into his pants pocket for the real 9mm. round. He went to the table and did his work quickly and efficiently, and then went back to the bunker and waited.

"All right, people," the training officer said, "time for the third scenario."

And when Sarah came back, holding the revolver in her hand, Craig held out his hand.

"Do you mind?" he asked. "I'd like to have a chance at shooting someone."

She smiled and handed the revolver over. "Sure, why not. I've already done it twice. Why should I have all the fun?"

He smiled in return. "Exactly."

Ever since he'd viewed the tape, it had been odd, but Stacy had been kinder and gentler to him, as if she was feeling sorry for him or something. A hell of a feeling. The tape had remained hidden and unviewed, and he was still trying to decide what in hell to do when one day, Dirk Conrad had shown up at his store.

Talk about your challenges. Underneath the counter of his store he had a sawed-off baseball bat, and wouldn't Dirk have been surprised if that had been swung at his noggin when he came over to chat after getting another in a long series of free cups of coffee. Instead he gritted his teeth and held his ground, and made small talk with Dirk as he got his free newspaper and free cup of coffee, and he imagined in some way that Dirk probably thought the free wife from the store owner went with everything else.

So. All those thoughts were tumbling through him and again he was wondering what to do when Dirk said, "Hey, next week we're going up to the base again, doing another SWAT training session. You interested?"

Hell no, was his thought, but he decided to be polite. "I guess so."

Dirk nodded, put the folded-up newspaper under his arm. "That'd be great. We could have some real fun."

"Sure," Craig said, and damn it, that could have been the end of it, except for one thing.

As Dirk left the store, he looked back and winked.

Pretty simple.

A wink, as if he knew he was pulling something over on Craig, knew it and enjoyed it, and Craig was surprised at how the anger just roared through him, making his ears echo with the noise, and by the time the door closed behind Dirk, Craig knew that he would go to that SWAT training session and end Dirk's life.

SCENARIO THREE:

An armed gunman was hidden in a house with an accomplice who was unarmed. They had earlier robbed a bank, and the armed gunman was threatening to kill anybody who came in.

Sarah gave him a pat on the shoulder and said, "Good luck," and Craig said, "Thanks," as he took a long series of deep breaths, the revolver fat and heavy in his hands. Sarah was deeper in the rooms, waiting, and he wondered what she would think about this particular scenario, which came up in his mind like so:

Real scenario three: Porter resident and store owner takes revenge against cop having an affair with his wife.

He was in the second room, hidden behind a table and chair. His breathing sounded harsh in his protective helmet. He waited.

And wondered briefly what Stacy would think when this day was over. She had covered the day shift for him so he could do this training session, and amazingly so, she had kissed him on the cheek when he had left and had murmured, "Have fun."

Have fun. Did she really mean it? Was she now regretting what had gone on between her and Dirk? Could it be over? Seeing her standing behind the counter, just as he was leaving, he had been stunned by his feelings of warmth and love and affection for her, even though she had betrayed him.

But who had betrayed whom first, with all the long hours, the sacrifices, the demands placed upon her?

Voices, outside. He raised the revolver, found his hand was shaking so hard he had to hold the gun with both hands.

He could not afford to miss. Could not afford to shake.

The approaching voices grew louder.

Two days earlier, he had sat in the apartment looking again at the black videocassette tape. He hadn't viewed it since that first day, and had hidden it in a rear closet behind some shoes. He knew what he was planning, and when it was all said and done, when things were wrapped up, he wasn't going to have this tape in his home. So among the other plans, he made plans to get rid of it, and soon.

Quick, quick, quick, he thought, Jesus, it's going to be quick. No more time to think, no more time to reconsider, it was way too late for that.

"Police!"

"Search warrant!"

"Hands up!"

The forms came into view and he raised his gun and waited, waited until he saw the SWAT team member with the little yellow button on his chest, and he pulled the trigger and pulled the trigger and the shots started ringing out and the fire continued and *BAM!* something struck his chest with the force of a telephone pole being swung by a giant.

Cold. Wet. He opened his eyes, could hear voices in the distance, yelling and screaming. Hands were working over him, tugging at his clothes, getting them off. His chest ached and ached and he couldn't catch his breath. It was as if he had run the race of his life and everything was now still. He opened his eyes and saw the glare of flashlights being trained down upon him.

He thought he was still in the bunker.

Cold. Wet. And now the wetness was warm.

And he thought he could hear sirens, off in the distance, and hoped somebody would remember to open up the gate in time.

And he closed his eyes.

It took some waiting, but eventually they did arrive in his hospital room, a couple of days before he was due to be discharged. The bullet wound in his chest was healing nicely and the pain was now just a manageable ache. Two solid-looking men in business suits, looking both professional and slightly embarrassed, came in and sat down. They mentioned their names and he forgot both names instantly, but in his mind he called one of them Lawyer and the other Cop. Both had thin black briefcases, which they balanced on their knees.

The cop started it off. "Mr. Francis, once again, I want to offer my personal apologies, as a member of the Porter Police Department, for what happened to you last week."

He nodded. The lawyer jumped in as well. "And for the city of Porter, too, Mr. Francis—you also have our apologies."

"Thank you," he said, keeping his voice low and hoarse, though truth be told, he was doing better than he had expected when he had planned the whole thing out, when the utter insanity of what he came up with struck him and he thought about all the sacrifices he had made for that damn store, and now, he had made his final sacrifice. A big one, but one that would count. He knew Dirk was a crack shot, knew he would aim for the center of his body, and chances were, his heart or any other vital organ wouldn't be struck. A chance, a crazy chance, but what the hell. The other options seemed worse. He did not want to lose Stacy . . . Stacy, who had come in blubbering and teary the day he had been admitted, and had Confessed All.

The cop said, "Before we go on, Mr. Francis, I need to talk a bit about the status of Officer Conrad."

He said nothing. The cop looked embarrassed and said, "A day after the shooting, a videotape arrived at our Internal Affairs office, mailed anonymously. Um, I'm afraid the tape was from a surveillance system at your store. You do have such a system, do you not?"

"I do," he said, keeping still.

The cop said, "Well. It seems that, um, the tape showed . . . well, it showed a woman I believe to be your wife and Officer Conrad in a rather intimate encounter. In your store. Mr. Francis, we believe somebody at the store, perhaps a disgruntled employee or somebody like that, mailed the tape to the department."

He tried to put a bit of shock into his voice. "Why are you telling me this?"

The lawyer stepped in. "We believe that when Officer Conrad's future is determined, the local news media might find out about this tape. We're sorry, but we felt you should know about this beforehand. I mean, well, were you aware that Officer Conrad and your wife were . . . involved?"

He turned his head on the pillow and said, "I really don't want to talk about it."

Stacy, in this room, begging forgiveness, begging understanding, willing and able to do anything he wanted to make it right.

The cop came back. "We understand completely. And Mr. Francis, you should know that by the end of this week—even though his union might make a fuss—Officer Conrad will be off the force. His shooting of you, combined with the relationship he had with your wife . . . it makes his continued future with our department and in any law-enforcement department in this country impossible. He may even face criminal charges when all is said and done."

He knew they couldn't see his face, so he allowed himself just a brief smile. "I see."

It was the lawyer's turn. "Mr. Francis, if I could have your attention for just a moment. As counsel for the city, we have an interest in reaching an equitable settlement so that this doesn't have to go to court, waste your time and the city's time, cost you attorney's fees and so forth. I'm prepared today to make such a settlement offer to you."

The lawyer opened his briefcase and passed over a sheaf of papers, and clipped to the top of the papers was a cashier's check. Craig kept his emotions in check as he looked at the numbers. He looked at the lawyer and the cop.

"I sign this and drop any claims against the city, and this check is mine?" he asked.

"That's correct."

He handed the papers and the check back to the lawyer. "Change the five on the check to a seven and you got yourself a deal."

The cop looked at the lawyer, the lawyer looked at the cop, and there was the briefest of nods back and forth. The lawyer put the papers back in his briefcase and stood up. "Then we have a deal, Mr. Francis. We'll be back within the hour."

He smiled at both men as they left his hospital room, and checked the time. Stacy would be coming by shortly, and then, well, he'd pass the news along. The store would go up for sale, and combined with the city settlement, there was plenty there to start new, start fresh, and get out of Porter. He had taken a bullet for his life and his marriage, and that was the fact. And with the size of that check . . . he was in a forgiving mood toward Stacy.

The time for sacrifices was over, and it just took one shot.

Not a bad deal.

Liza Cody

Woke Up This Morning

■ ■ ■

Liza Cody grew up in London. She studied painting at the City and Guilds of London Art School and the Royal Academy Schools. She has worked as a painter, furniture-maker, photographer, and graphic designer. Her first book, Dupe, *won the John Creasey Award for the best first crime novel of 1980 and was nominated for an MWA Edgar Award in the USA.* Under Contract *was shortlisted for the Gold Dagger Award, and in 1992 she won the Crime Writers' Association Silver Dagger Award for* Bucket Nut. *In 2003 she published a collection of her short fiction, which is where "Woke Up This Morning" first appeared. The idea of the unreliable narrator is brilliantly worked in this short story, with Cody's sure hand and style leaving almost everything in doubt for the befuddled, hungover young woman who is just struggling to remember what she did last night—and did her activities include a murder?*

Woke up this morning—nothing on my mind. Under the window a man and a boy talk: high voice, low voice. Across the wall children quarrel with their mother: tune, harmony, descant wailing. Downstairs a woman walks in wood-soled shoes on a stone floor—clip-clop, do-wap. The fan hums. This is the way the world sings before you open your eyes—shoo-wap-she-wah—when the only conversation is in a fading dream of one man saying, "It's all right, 'nother day." And a second man says, "She lost it. She lost the bit that matters."

As I climb to the surface I'm already forgetting what mattered but I do know that I was the one who lost it. Being blamed, in dreams and real life, is normal.

Nothing on my mind, strange melodies of morning in my ears: I could be anywhere or nowhere. But the climb out of dreamland into somewhere is hard. My legs ache. There is a bruising weight on my neck. My mouth is a dust bowl. Eyelids, mortared together with foul secretions, feel like bricks. Nausea rises with consciousness. This is a bad wake-up, and it gets worse. I open my eyes and I don't know where I am. There is this vast boat of a bed. It's on a platform, in a bedroom the size of a small house. And that's not the worst of it: I am stark naked and I'm not alone.

The old man beside me sleeps on. An appalling crumpled reptile with an old man's smell. No morning music from him. Dear God, what did I do last night?

I slide out of bed with the speed of an escaping snake. A door leads through a sickly mirrored dressing room to a bathroom: two basins, two showers, two bidets, one imperial-sized sunken tub. This is luxury, but I've never seen it before. Nothing is familiar. I stumble toward the window. A gauzy white curtain billows and reveals, for a moment, a sunny walled garden with a romanesque swimming pool in the center.

This is the world I woke up in and it is not my world. Behind the thick loo door my private choir is silenced. I sit, head bowed, morale in tatters, and try to connect last night to this morning. My guts churn, my head thunders, and my skin oozes. I hope I've caught flu, that I'm really ill. I don't want to think that this is a hangover, that I did this to myself. Sick, and lying in bed with a naked old man, his swollen knuckles bunched under his loose chin, his chicken legs and yellow clawed toes. Who would do a thing like that of her own free will?

I wash until my skin is fresh and brown again but I don't feel clean. I dry my hair on a soft white towel that has the name Lisette embroidered across one corner. I gaze out past the drift of curtain to the unbroken turquoise water of the pool. I slither into last night's clothes—the black satin trousers, the scrap of tunic top. I stand beside the huge bed refusing to look at the decrepit remains of manhood. But at the last moment, surprised by a pang of rage, I steal his gold watch and a fat handful of notes from his tan wallet. Whoever he is, he owes me something.

What is it that makes you creep away with your high heels in your hands? Shame? Last night my shoes were on my feet and my feet were defiantly, proudly, on the platform. I was bopping around behind my keyboard and we played "High Heel Sneakers" with a Latin lilt. Our little joke in honor of the Chaux-du-Gard Bullfighters' Club. Everything, no matter how inappropriate, had to have a touch of tango, mambo, samba. With a sprinkling of "La Vida Loca" for the kids. Only a sprinkling, mind; the kids don't pay for the band. The club worthies do that, and there ain't one of 'em under the age of fifty.

Shoes in hand, hand on heart, heart in mouth, I pad down stone stairs to a vaulted cave of a living room. Great arched doors open on to a graveled courtyard and the August sun hits me in the face like a burning hammer. This must be a converted olive mill. I've seen a lot of them, though none as big and grand as this.

How do you tiptoe, barefoot, across gravel? On the other side of the courtyard an iron gate stands ajar. Beyond the gate is freedom from this great, grand domain. Somewhere in the cavernous shadowy house, women talk, water gurgles, footsteps echo. Maybe one of the women answers to the name Lisette and I really, truly, don't want to meet her. I have dried my toxic skin on her clean embroidered towels and God alone knows what I've done between her silky white sheets.

In the end, I ran for it. I was too thirsty, too disgusted, to wait any longer. Why should I tiptoe? I'm not a silly teenager living in my father's house. I'm a grown woman, working out the summer in the south of France and I'm old enough to make my own decisions.

But, oh God, oh God, creeping around with my shoes in my hand is so much a part of me. Coming home from clubs, underage, under the influence. Hiding the fact that I'm out of my skull. Washing garments to hide the stains. The last few years I spent in my father's house were one big cover-up. Is it any wonder I feel like a guilty schoolgirl?

I can hear my father's voice even now: "You smell like a dog—like a bitch in heat. Get out of my sight. One of these days I'll find you dead in the gutter and I won't care because I'll know you put yourself there."

If he could see me now, stumbling across a field of young olive trees, taking a short-cut to the main road, avoiding the critical gaze of nosy neighbors, he'd say, "Put on your shoes and kick yourself to death." And he'd mean it. I'm sweating in last night's sexy stage clothes and I feel sick as a dog. On top of that I have, tucked between tight black strides and hip bone, a wad of stolen euros and a heavy gold watch. A consolation prize? What sort of consolation was that? Why did I want to make a bad time worse?

And now I have to face Evert who thinks that because I've shared his bed a few times I am his girlfriend. I can't afford to lose him the way I lost Dieter. Evert plays sax and cannot be replaced. Whereas when Dieter stormed off in a jealous snit at least we had a drum machine. And we decided we were better off without him because he was a crap drummer, we could split the fees three ways instead of four, and there was much more room in the van without his battered old drum kit.

What I didn't take into account was that Evert would see Dieter's departure as a victory. He acted as if he'd won me in battle when in fact all that happened was that on a couple of occasions I just happened to fancy him more than I fancied Dieter. I was not Dieter's girlfriend. I am not Evert's girlfriend, but he thinks he's my boyfriend. He refers to us as "we." "Get over yourself," I say. "Don't be so suburban." But then he acts all Dutch and polite and won't take a blind bit of notice. Will he notice now?

So I walk across a red field of young olive trees in the burning sun and I don't know where I am. When I reach the road, which road will it be and which way should I turn? Evert and Chaux-du-Gard. There's a wall in my mind. Yesterday on one side; today on the other. I cannot see through it.

We played with a wall behind us last night. The stage was set up against it. The canopy was festooned with fairy lights—supplied by the Bullfighters' Club. I was out front as usual, with Evert behind me on my left and Noah on my right. Evert and Noah would be sneering at each other while doing a pretty competent job.

To put it as simply as possible: sometimes I don't want to sleep alone. But I would never sleep with Noah because he is shorter than me. Long ago when I was a kid, bunking off school, watching some love-flick in the cinema, I said to my friend Su-Rita, "When I grow up, I'll never, ever go out with someone runty."

"You're a snob, Jasmine," she said, sucking sweets, not taking her eyes off the screen.

"It looks ridiculous," I said. "Tall girl—midget man."

"Even if he was famous?" she said. "Or a millionaire? Or in a rock band?"

"I didn't say I wouldn't stay in with him. But he'd have to be mega-mega."

Noah is not mega-mega. He's a good jobbing guitarist with a nice bluesy voice and a sweet feel for harmonies. I like him; I probably like him better than Evert. But Noah's a short-arse and Evert is a six-footer. End of story.

I get to the road remembering that Su-Rita married a computer programmer from Hendon when she was eighteen. I couldn't believe it: romance swapped for a terrace house in Hendon. I went to the West End and hooked up with two buskers. We were going to be the next youth explosion as soon as someone important noticed us. Dreams; fuck 'em.

I limped into Chaux-du-Gard and didn't put on my sandals until I was at the bottom of the winding cobbled lane that avoids the town center. I didn't want to walk through the square, among the plain trees, café tables, and old men. I'd had more than enough of old men. Young men too. It would've been nice to avoid Noah and Evert but Noah was sitting, smoking, at the bottom of the iron stairs to the flat above the *charcuterie*, our digs for the night.

"What time do you call this?" he said. "We were supposed to be on the road an hour ago." He looked at the red earth caked like dried blood between my toes. He stared up into my poached salmon eyes. "Where've you been? You look like shit."

"What's it to you? You're not my father."

"Father?" he said, surprised. "It's not your morals I'm questioning—it's your judgment. And your bloody timekeeping."

I should've apologized. Instead I sat on the step beside him and took one of his cigarettes. He sighed and lit it for me.

"Noah," I said, "what was I drinking last night?"

"Everything they put in front of you, you dumb bitch. And don't say we should've stopped you. We tried."

"Everything?"

"Wine, anise, cassis, Pernod . . ."

"Oh, shit."

"And you called Evert a tight-arsed, anal retentive Nazi when . . ."

"Well, he is."

"That's what I like to see," Noah said cheerfully, "remorse."

I said, "Y'know, I'm sick of playing this jive Latin crap to old men with a bloody drum machine. You can't play samba and stuff without proper drums."

"Well, who deep-sixed the drummer?"

"He walked."

"Jasmine, you are a living example of why bands crack. When this gig's over, I'm only ever going to play with men."

"You don't mean that." I leaned my head against his shoulder. It was a good strong shoulder. Pity he's such a shorty.

"Met an old guy once in Tennessee," Noah said, "really run-down, broken old bastard, scratched a living cleaning kitchens after the bars closed. But when he wasn't blind drunk he played guitar like a dream. He'd been in this one town for fifty years . . ."

"Why're you telling me this?"

"Shut up and listen. He used to be one of those traveling musicians—they'd breeze into town and the party was wherever they sat down and played. Like Charley Patton."

"Like us."

"Hell, no!" Noah's voice went sneery. "Just 'cos we're gigging 'round the south of France does *not* make us Charley Patton. We just pretend, 'cos there's sun and money and we don't want to admit we're faking it."

That shut me up because he was on the button enough to be really depressing.

"Anyway," Noah went on, "this old guy. I asked him why he got stuck in this one-horse town and never moved on. He said, 'I married a woman here, only her husband objected. And one day he came in with a gun and shot my toes off.' 'Even more reason to move on,' I said. But he just shook his head. He said, 'When I die, I wanna die in the same county where they buried my toes. That way, when the Lord come, he won't have to search far to find them.' So I asked what happened to the woman, and he said, 'Between a guitar an' a gun there's no contest.' So there he was, rotting. Never moved on, never recorded, never made his name, all because men don't ever act rationally around women."

"Don't blame the women. It's not our fault you're all barmy."

"It's your fault when *you* don't act rationally. You're the one got rat-arsed last night and made a fool of yourself lap-dancing the oldies. But I suppose you *could* say it isn't your fault Evert wants to kill you."

Even more depressed, I said, "Where is he?"

"And that's another thing." Noah was pitiless. "Why are you humping Evert? You don't even like him." Pitiless and nastily accurate. "Are you pretending to be Janis Joplin or Billie Holiday? Getting trashed and humping the band? 'Cos you're no more one of them than I am Charley Patton."

"Fuck off, Noah." I stood up. I was sick of being told. Shoulder or no shoulder I was sick of Noah too.

"Sort it," Noah said. "And hurry."

I dragged myself up the iron steps to my fetid little room. Aspirin, wash, pack, I thought, in that order. It took fifteen minutes. The bottom of my case was rank with grubby clothes rolled up, neglected, and the jeans and shirt I put on weren't exactly laundry fresh either. I thought about the huge bed with its silky white sheets and the towels embroidered with the name Lisette.

Noah poked his head around the door. "Evert's back with the van. Better get your story ready."

"What story?" I said, struggling with the zip on my bag and not, oh definitely not, looking at him. "I haven't got a story. There's nothing to tell. I can't remember what happened and I woke up in a field of olive trees." Unlike the first cigarette, the first lie of the day saps your energy and makes you want to hide.

"Olive trees." Noah leered. "Yeah, *right.* You'll have to do better than that, Jasmine."

"It's true. I've just washed all the red earth off. Look at my towel if you don't believe me."

"It ain't me you got to convince."

"Evert can go screw himself too. It's none of your business. I turn up on time. I play. I sing in tune. That's what I owe you."

I hauled my bag off the bed and dragged it to the door. Noah watched coldly. He didn't offer to help.

Baum, ba-da bada-baum, the bag slid down the iron steps like a drumroll. Evert stood at the bottom, eyes unreadable behind black shades. The hot sun glistened off his white-blond hair.

"As for singing in tune," Noah muttered from behind me, "that was the worst 'Mi Caballo Blanco' I've ever heard last night."

"In the second set," Evert said, "you embarrassed us."

I could not remember the second set. I know we ended the first set with "La Vida Loca." Everything up to there was the usual blur of familiar, much repeated licks and links, but after that was a blank.

I stood on the fire escape, between Evert and Noah—the rock and the hard place—struggling to remember. The wall began there; between "La Vida Loca" and the remains of the night was a soundproof, opaque barrier. And here were Noah and Evert, who rarely agreed about anything, telling me I went tits up in the second set.

Evert said, "Get in the van, Jasmine. In the back. I do not want to talk to you and I do not want to see you." To Noah he said, "We have to go now to the clubhouse for our money. I went, before filling up, but the treasurer was not there. They did not know where he had left the check."

"Shit," Noah said, "it's not going to be one of those, is it? I don't want any hassle about money."

We drove in stony silence through the narrow streets of Chaux-du-Gard to the scene of last night's disaster. Evert pulled into the courtyard and got out. I kept my head down. I didn't want to see or be seen. This was not something I could creep away from, shoes in hand.

After a while Noah said, "What's he doing in there? How long does it take to pick up a check?"

I said, "You know, I think I've got flu. I've never felt like this before."

"You won't get any sympathy from me," Noah said. "If you throw up anywhere near my guitar cases Evert won't need to throttle you. I'll save him the bother."

"You're all heart."

"Shut up, Jasmine. You aren't the victim here."

Then Evert was wrenching the driver's door open. He jumped in as if a junkyard dog were snapping at his heels.

"Did they cough up?" Noah asked. But Evert was too busy revving the engine and reversing out of the courtyard onto the street to reply. The back of his neck was red and sweating.

Drivers hit their horns as he emerged without warning.

"What the fuck?" said Noah. But Evert threw the stick into first, crunching through the gearbox, and pulled away with a sickening jolt. I slid back into one of the amplifiers.

"Ow!" I yelled. "Take it easy, you *plank*."

"Plank, am I?" Evert hissed. "What, then, are you?"

"Just slow down," Noah said. "You'll kill someone."

"Kill someone? Me? Oh, no—that, I think, is Jasmine's job." He steadied, and settled more sedately into the flow of traffic while I glared at his neck and sweaty blond hair. "You want to know what has happened, why there is no check, Noah? I tell you: it is because the club treasurer, the former mayor of Chaux-du-Gard, has just been found dead in his bed. And you want to know what else, Noah? This is the same former mayor that our dirty little friend here went home with. What do you think of that, Noah?"

"No shit!" Noah twisted around in his seat and stared at me.

"Don't look at *me*," I said. "I haven't done anything."

"No?"

"No?" echoed Evert. "Then tell me this: what happened after you kicked my shin and told me to leave you the hell alone, and I left you the hell alone to get into the Mercedes with the club treasurer who is now dead?"

"Did I do that?" I asked Noah.

"Was it a Mercedes?" said Noah.

"I don't *know*."

"Of course it was a Mercedes," shouted Evert. "A big, cream, deluxe coupé with the roof down. Which is by far too much car for an old man. What does a little old man want with so much power? It is obscene."

I woke up in a field, I woke up in a field, I said to myself. There was no disgusting chicken-legged old man in a bed. You woke up in a field with red earth between your toes. Nothing else. Nobody saw you. There was no *moulin*, no bedroom suite as big as a house, no swimming pool, no little old lizard with his claws bunched up under his chin. Was he really dead? Was he really the treasurer?

"Jasmine?" Noah said. "This is serious. What the hell happened? You can tell us. We won't turn you in."

"Don't count on it," Evert growled at the windshield.

"I woke up in a field," I said. "I keep telling you—I don't remember anything after 'La Vida Loca.' Really. Nothing."

"This is not possible," Evert said. "She is lying as always."

Did I wake up in the same bed as a dead treasurer? Why didn't I know he was dead? Surely I can tell the difference between old and cold.

"We should go to the gendarmes." This was from Evert. While he is coming he shouts, "Oh, you, you, you." I felt sick.

"Ah, Evert, man, take it easy," Noah said. "What would we gain from that? Think, man: we're playing again tonight."

Outside the van, the stone houses of Chaux-du-Gard give way to fields, and a long way behind them the dusty green and silver knuckles of the Alpilles punch, impotent, at the unforgiving blue yonder. I want to be talented, beautiful, and free but instead I'm trapped in a searing hot metal box with two men who despise me. Sweat slides down the insides of my arms into the palms of my hands. A handful of sweat: it's something Charley Patton might have sung about. Me, I just sweat.

Evert said, "Maybe she killed a man. She goes home with him and in the morning he is dead. What can we make of this?"

"She must be one helluva fuck." Noah sighs. "But, man, what did he die of? Was he killed or did he, like, just pass away?"

"This they did not say."

"Seeing he was such a wrinkly," Noah said, "maybe she was too much for him."

"Is that what happened?" Evert drilled me with angry eyes through the driver's mirror.

"What a way to go," Noah mused almost to himself. But not quite.

Evert's red neck turned purple. "I think certainly she should talk to the gendarmes." He took his foot off the gas, looking for somewhere to pull over.

"Don't be a jerk," Noah said.

I'll never know if Evert was going to drive on or turn back because that was when the engine cut out and the van rolled to a stop in the middle of the road.

"Clogged fuel line," said Noah.

"Electrics," said Evert. Neither of them knew.

I thought, if they just jiggle the battery leads and the van starts then everything will be all right. I woke up this morning in an old man's bed and, I thought, if I were talented, beautiful, or free enough, none of this would have happened. Then I realized I was afraid of Evert. So I left the van, climbed down through the ditch, and walked into the stony dry field on the other side. From there I observed Noah and Evert as they failed to start the engine and make everything all right.

There was nothing I could do but watch the traffic concertina behind them and the bad-tempered way the other drivers waited for the chance to overtake. Most of them hooted. Even from my field I could see Evert's face, red with frustration. Red for danger. I rubbed my hands dry on my thighs and that was when I first picked up the sound of a police siren from the direction of Chaux-du-Gard.

The traffic in both directions pulled over allowing the car to whiz up the wrong side of the road. It stopped in a cloud of dust, askew in front of the van. Two chunky cops, belted and bristling, stepped out and started forward, waving their arms and shouting. Noah took one look and then slowly shrugged his shoulders. His French is worse than mine. We always left the talking to Evert.

Done for, I thought. I sat down on the powdery earth because there was nowhere to hide. I won't say a word, I thought. There's no way to explain any of this in French. Evert won't believe me in French, English, or Esperanto. I can stick to my story, but with him translating, him telling French cops what I'm like, I'll be *pommes frites en merde.*

Four men stood on the road deciding my future. All I ever wanted to do was have a good time—to say what I want, do what I want, go where I please. Why should I sit in a field and be afraid? Because I won't be what Evert wants. Evert says, "You've had enough. You drink too much," when I've only had two glasses of wine. Before I slept with him he didn't say anything at all. Now he says, "You're cheap, you look at men all the time." He's like my father—he wants me to be afraid of living. "Do you want the neighbors to think I am the father of a whore?" my father asked once. I was ten and a boy held my hand walking back from school. I didn't want the neighbors to think anything at all so I said, "I didn't *do* anything," and he locked me in my room and shouted scriptures through the door for two hours. What did the neighbors make of that, I wondered.

The fattest cop stood with his hands on his hips listening to Evert. The other one was directing traffic around the van. Noah beckoned and I *was* afraid of life.

As I negotiated the ditch under the contemptuous gaze of the fattest cop I heard him say, *"Elle est arabe, la gonzesse?"* So I stuck my hands on my hips and said, "He is a moron, the fat fuck?"

"Get in the van," Evert roared.

Noah muttered, "You never know when to keep your stupid mouth shut, do you?"

"Aren't they going to take me away?" I offered my wrists for the cold kiss of handcuffs.

"Get in the fucking van and shut the fuck up."

"Speak slowly," I said, "I'm only an ignorant Arab."

"You a shithead or what?" Noah said.

That's about right, I thought. I got in the van and sat with my arms around my knees like a trussed goose in an oven. Cooked, I decided, grease dribbling down my sides, ready to be carved up. Girls just want to have fu-hun, I thought, queasy. You have a little too much to drink and go to bed with one little guy, and look what happens. According to my father I should be a teetotal virgin or a teetotal wife with six kids, guardian of all virtue, keeper of the faith, blameless, sexless. Because if you make a little music, dance a little dance, live a little life, you're lost and gone forever. According to him I should be at home right now, teaching my poor daughters how to look after a husband, how to hide their hair, how not to have fun. Another generation of sad little girls behaving like my poor dead mother, who behaved like her mother, even though she ended up living and dying a stone's throw from the Edgware Road.

Me? I snuck into cinemas to escape. I dreamed the romantic comedies. I hung out in the record shop and bought CDs I wasn't allowed to play at home. Bought the CDs, and bought into the whole rebel-rebel song and dance—the greatest escape of all, which led slowly but surely to a dead man's bed, and a fat French cop with a gun snuggling up to his meaty haunch and a neat line in racist patter.

Noah's right: I'm not Billie Holiday or Janis Joplin, except in that they didn't get away with it either.

Noah said, "Don't say a single word." He scrambled into the front seat and slammed the door behind him. "Especially when Evert gets in. For your own good. Just this once, Jasmine, button up."

Five minutes later, to my surprise, a tow truck turned up. Evert and the fat cop helped attach the chains. Evert got behind the wheel, and with our front end hoisted up, we moved off. I couldn't believe it. My head swam and vomit rose in my throat. From the back window I watched the two cops recede like dark clouds blown away on a strong wind.

Ten minutes was all I could stand. I said, "Stop. Please. I'm going to throw up."

"Evert! She's not kidding."

"Shit," Evert said. He hit the horn and rolled down the window to signal to the tow-truck driver. I tumbled out of the back door while we were still moving. I thought I was going to heave up my liver and spleen as well as everything else. This was championship spewing, and it was done right next to a wrought-iron garden gate. I hung on to the bars for support.

An old man appeared from behind a rosebush. Another old man, I thought. I never wanted to see another old man again. My legs were cold, wet pasta.

Noah said, "God, Jasmine, did you *have* to?" And the old man said, "Are you British?"

"American," said Noah. "*She's* British."

"She needs water," the old man said. "Better bring her in."

"That's okay, sir, we'll manage," Noah said. But the old man opened the gate and drew me to him with one big gnarled hand. Evert shouted something from the van, and Noah hovered uncertainly. I didn't care. I let the old man lead me up a crazy stone path to the shadows of his porch. Was that what happened last night?

"Michelle," he called, and a middle-aged woman in a blue smock came to the door. She helped me inside and upstairs to a small bathroom, tutting and humphing at the state of my T-shirt and jeans. She filled the basin with cold water and gave me a washcloth. Then she left me alone with the cool glazed tiles.

I washed my face and the ends of my hair. I rinsed my mouth. The only way I could deal with my T-shirt was to strip it off and run the tap over it. Now I would look like an entrant in a wet-shirt contest. That would help my reputation no end.

On the windowsill was a pot of scarlet geraniums and a terracotta figure of a woman soaping her armpit. I took the hint. My legs were shaking so badly I had to sit on the rim of the bath. I couldn't bear to look at my reflection in the mirror over the basin—*la gonzesse*, naked from the waist up, staring back at me like my own distorted passport photo. Who would ever believe a face like that—a foreigner, even to myself?

The woman called Michelle came in without knocking. She gave me a glass of water. "Drink," she ordered. I drank. "Undress," she said, pointing to my wrecked jeans. Then she gave me a shirt. It was huge, faded by years of sun and softened by years of care. It hung down to my knees.

"Drink more," she said, "and go down to speak to my father. You feel better, yes?" Her accent was a mixture of French and American.

On the way down I noticed what I'd been blind to on the way up. The house was bustling with little stone and bronze people. Pictures jostled for position like a crowd on a dance floor. Faces peered from canvases. Trees swayed in the mistral. Every domestic scene—cups, coffeepots, stripy cushions, corners of tables, blowing curtains—appeared on the walls like windows into another house. It wasn't peaceful but it was fun.

The old man was out on the porch with Noah. They sat in canvas chairs and Noah nursed an ancient guitar on his lap. He turned to me, his eyes bright with discovery, and said, "Henry knew Woody Guthrie in New York. Unbelievable."

The old man said, "Are you feeling better? Sit down."

"Henry says Woody might have played this guitar." Noah stroked the yellowing wood with a reverent thumb.

Henry sighed and said, "Your young friend looks as if she might like to sit. Would you fetch another chair from the shed?"

While Noah went to the shed I sat on his chair. I pulled the shirt down and said, "Thanks for taking me in."

Henry got up. "Don't move. I'll be right back."

I sat there, all empty and wobbly, looking at the old man's garden that was tangled but well watered except for a patch by the fence where the hose wouldn't reach. Two old men in one day were too many old men. Henry seemed okay, but who knows, maybe the dead guy had seemed okay too. I couldn't remember. Why would I go in a Mercedes with a creepy old man? I don't like old men.

Noah came back with the extra chair and said, "Y'know, Henry's a piece of living history. In the 1940s he hung out with Woody Guthrie. Woody stayed in his loft. How about that?" Noah did like old men. Or maybe he just liked their stories.

Henry came back with a drawing board and said, "Shut up, everyone. I need twenty minutes," and that suited me just fine. There was a breeze that smelled of wet grass and I could sit still and wait for the world to stop tumbling.

After a while Noah got up and went to look over Henry's shoulder until Henry said, "Shove off, young man. I can't work with you breathing down my neck."

Michelle came out with a basket of crusty bread and a bowl of fat green olives. "Papa," she said, "you want to eat?"

"Yep," he said, "thank you." But he didn't. It was Noah who attacked the food.

I yawned and stretched and immediately Henry said, "Hold it like that—arms behind your head, legs—yes, just like that." Then he was off again, with his color sticks and drawing board, in a world of his own. A world that hardly included me, even though it was my arms and legs he was concentrating on. Michelle sighed and went back into the house. Noah strummed quietly on the yellow guitar. And I thought about how restful it was to be looked at by someone who kept his distance. I imagined Henry and my father sitting side by side on my father's blue velour sofa. A preposterous image: Henry in cramped gray London. But my father would never come to France—he nearly had panic attacks if he had to leave the Edgware Road. Maybe that is why I'm here.

It was serene: Noah, not talking, doing what he did best; old Henry, not talking and doing whatever it was he did. And me, not talking, doing nothing at all.

Then time ran out and Evert barged through the gate, leaving it to clang shut in his wake. He was halfway across the garden when he started shouting: "I was going to give you to the gendarmes, but no. They are racist pigs, even though it is me you call a Nazi. So I save your ass."

Henry said, "Excuse me?"

"Take it easy, man," Noah said. "this is Henry—he knew Woody . . ."

"And again," Evert shouted, "you are without any clothes, coming on to a strange man. When the gendarmes call you a slut and an Arab, I save your ass . . ."

"Up *yours,* " I yelled. "Why do you always think the worst?" I tugged the vast shirt down to my knees. "What in hell have I done to you?"

"Get a grip, Jasmine," Noah said, "and shut up."

Henry got slowly to his feet. In spite of his age he was an imposing man. "You are in *my* yard," he rumbled. "Mind your goddamn manners. *All* of you."

"I'm sorry, sir," Noah said, "we have an ongoing situation here."

"Too right it is a situation," Evert said. "This is my girlfriend . . ."

"*Not!*"

". . . and she is a whore who has killed a man . . ."

"Wait a goddamn minute," Henry said, "and explain, *quietly*. If you can't do it quietly, get out of my yard."

"I didn't kill anyone," I said, "and I'm *not* his girlfriend. I woke up under the olive trees."

"She says she can't remember anything," Noah said. "She says she has the flu . . ."

"I will explain," Evert said. "If she is not my girlfriend, why did she sleep with me? If she is not a whore, why did she go with the mayor in his Mercedes? And where did she get *this*?" He reached into his pocket and held up the fat wad of euros. "*And*," he went on triumphantly, "if she did not kill him, where did she get this?" He flourished the gold watch in front of us like a conjurer. "It says on the back something . . ." He pretended to read the back of the watch. "Oh, yes, it was awarded by the grateful citizens of Chaux-du-Gard on the occasion of his retirement."

"You searched my bag," I cried. "You fucking *freak*."

"Of course," Evert sneered, "because you are a liar." Oh, you, you, you.

Henry held up his hand. He said, "It seems to me, young man, that if you are lucky enough to find a pretty girl to sleep with you, even once, you should not call her bad names."

"They are true."

"Then you are stupid to sleep with someone you despise."

Evert blinked at Henry as if he were waking up and seeing him for the first time.

Noah said, "They're both crazy. They neither of 'em should have anything to do with each other."

"Life is too damn short," Henry said with authority. And it sounded like he was granting me a divorce. Instead of being just another old man he became in that moment a man of experience and judgment who should be listened to.

"You're right," I said. "Evert, I apologize for sleeping with you and for the way it messed with your mind. I promise it will never happen again."

Evert turned purple. "You cannot do that."

"Let it go, man," Noah said. "It wasn't doing either of you any good."

"You say this because you want her for yourself."

"Aaaagh—fuck it." Noah spread his hands in frustration.

"Are you really a band?" Henry asked. "I mean, do you get it together and play tunes, harmony and rhythm? How?"

The three of us turned to stare at him, and for a minute all we could hear was the breeze rattling the stiff rhododendron leaves.

Then Evert said, "But this explains nothing. Jasmine, you must tell us." He still had the watch and the money in his hand and he shook them in my face.

"I don't know," I mumbled, miserable. New beginnings, good intentions, I thought, crash when they meet old lies and evasions. "They were there when I woke up."

"In a field," sneered Noah.

"Ah yes, the famous olive trees," said Evert.

Henry reached out and plucked the watch from Evert's hand. Carefully he perched a pair of reading glasses on his nose and examined the back. "He died, you say? Hell, the old buzzard was younger than I am."

That surprised me. Henry was tall and broad. His hands, though knuckly, looked strong. His feet, in their leather sandals, were spades that dug into the ground.

"Did you know him?" Evert asked.

"Better than I wanted to." Henry gestured with his thumb at the house behind him. "Anyone who wanted planning permission had to deal with him. He owned a construction company. So, you hire his workmen, you use his materials, and you pay whatever he decides to charge, and bingo, he gives you planning permission. That's local government."

"Sweet deal," Noah said.

Henry nodded. "There's an ordinary, everyday level of corruption that's just accepted around here. If you want to get along you play along."

"He was also the treasurer of the Bull Fighters' Club," Evert said. "Jasmine went with him in his Mercedes after our gig last night and this morning he is dead and we do not get paid."

"Seems like you gotta whole fistful of money in your hand right now," Henry said.

"This is not our money," Evert said primly. "This is money Jasmine will not explain."

"Lemme count it," Noah said, snatching it away from Evert.

"Can you explain it?" Henry said to me. And because he was simply asking, not accusing, I looked into his faded blue eyes and said, "No, I can't. They say I was drinking with all the old men at the club. They say I played really badly in the second set. They say I got in the mayor's car. But I can't remember any of it. I would've had a drink with the clients after the first set. But that's because Evert and Noah want me to."

"Keeps 'em sweet," Noah said.

"But she is supposed only to be polite," Evert said. "She is not supposed to sit on their laps and go with them in their cars."

"Is that what you did?"

"That's what they say. But I swear I don't remember."

"You mean it's all a blur?"

"No, it's a blank."

Henry stared at me and I stared back. If he believed me, maybe I would become truthful.

He said, "Drink some more water. You're looking ill again."

I sipped from the glass beside me. The water seemed to slide across my tongue and fall into an empty space. I couldn't understand why I felt so hollow. My life is always messy, I know it is, but I can cope with a mess. I can't cope with a void. A whole night of my life is missing. I woke up in a dead man's bed. Something happened and I don't know whose fault it was.

Henry said, "Maybe you should eat something now. Maybe we all should."

As if she had been listening from behind the door, Michelle appeared on the porch. She said, "Why are you concerning yourself, Papa? You will tire yourself and then you won't work. When you don't work you feel bad and you lose your temper."

"Do you want me to kick them out?" he asked, smiling.

"Yes," she said. "They come here shouting and I have to clean the bathroom. We don't know them." She picked up Henry's drawing board and gazed at the drawing. She looked at me critically. Then she sighed and said, "There is soup."

"Thank you, my dear," he said.

We followed him into the kitchen at the back of the house. A polished wood table was already set for five with green pottery bowls, baskets of bread, and a steaming tureen of soup. Michelle, I thought, was a woman who anticipated defeat.

She said, "You're a stubborn old man, Papa. What you need is peace and quiet. You don't need these young people with their jealousies and their scandals."

"Now then, Michelle." He patted her hand soothingly. "We'll be back to normal soon enough, and you know a little scandal is like a little spice."

"You're as foolish as you're stubborn," she said and started ladling out the soup. Behind her, through the window above the stone sink, I noticed my jeans and T-shirt flapping on a line. I thought, I want to let Henry adopt me. I'd pose for him sometimes, and then I'd go out and racket around town and come back with interesting stories to tell him. Maybe he'd let me call him "Papa" like Michelle does. Papa and father seem such different concepts. Father knows exactly what his daughter should be like. He curses her when she doesn't match his blueprint. Papa looks but doesn't touch. He listens but he doesn't judge.

Henry said, "Okay, we should eat and enjoy, and talk of something else. But I'm curious: I want to know why you two boys choose to disbelieve your friend here."

"Is it a matter of choice?" Noah asked.

"Of course it is. Unless you know for certain what she does or does not remember, you can't tell me she's lying when she says she remembers nothing."

"We think perhaps she has committed a serious crime," Evert said.

"Pah!" Michelle said unexpectedly. "She is not a serious person. She isn't serious about anything."

It felt like stinging criticism. More stinging by far than Evert calling me a liar and a whore or Noah calling me a shithead.

Henry said, "Perhaps a crime was committed *against* her. Have you thought of that?"

"Whaddya mean?" Noah said.

"I'm talking about abduction and rape."

"She got in the car of her own will," Evert said, "and she called me a Nazi when I tried to stop her. She knows nothing of the history of Dutch resistance in the war."

"Well," Henry said, "I guess none of you was alive in World War II. But I was, and it taught me that the difference between a victim and a villain isn't near as clear-cut as they teach it in history class. Which brings me back to my question: why are you two so convinced your young friend has committed a crime?"

"Because they aren't my friends," I said. "I thought we were friends—we play together, and we travel together. . . ."

"And we sleep together," Evert said viciously.

"Only three times—and look what's happened there—it should have been fun . . ."

"Pah!" Michelle interrupted.

"Well, it should've brought us closer together . . ."

"Do you really think that sex makes people kinder?" Michelle asked. "Then you are sillier than I thought."

"Life has taught Michelle to be a cynic," Henry said. He leaned across the table and pinched her middle-aged chin as if she were a ten-year-old.

"And you, Papa, have the *naiveté* of an artist." She batted his hand away, but she didn't seem displeased.

"Why are you taking Jasmine's side?" Evert asked. "When you do not know her."

"I don't know any of you. But maybe I have more information than you do. I've lived in these parts for half a century and I hear the rumors. A lot of people resented the old mayor. He had a stranglehold on this area, like I say, but he would've died in office if he hadn't been forced to retire a coupla years back."

Michelle said, "I thought you didn't believe that story."

"Maybe I didn't then, but maybe I do now. Or maybe I'm just reassessing it."

"What story?" Noah asked.

"Two German girls complained to the gendarmes—or their parents did. Sisters—they'd been to one of the local shindigs, like the bull festival you guys just played at, you know, dancing with the local boys. On their way home they said the mayor offered them a ride so they got in his car. They admitted they were tipsy but they thought it was safe because he was the mayor and an old man. But the next morning they went to the cops and said the old bastard had spiked their drinks and raped one of them."

Michelle said, "But of course they were tourists, and they don't behave themselves like the local girls." She gave me a cool glance before going on. "So half the town thought this was a story they made up to explain to their parents why they didn't come home."

"The other half believed everything the girls said. More than that, they said that he had been preying on young girls for years, since his wife died, and that he went to Marseilles regularly to buy Rohypnol."

"Some say Viagra also," Michelle put in.

While Henry was speaking I had a sudden vision of my hands, balled into fists, pummeling a man's naked chest. They were like dream fists, with no strength in them, and it was as if I were observing them from a slit in black cloth. I squeezed my eyes shut trying to bring the vision into focus but it slid away.

Henry said, "Of course the cops did nothing. But the mayor resigned suddenly, giving ill health as a reason."

"So he's pulled this kinda shit before?" Noah said, looking at me.

"How would I know?" Henry shook his head. "This is just another story for you to believe or disbelieve, as you choose."

As I could choose to believe in my vision of fists. I could choose to believe that I had a memory of helplessly fighting someone off. Or it might have been a dream. Was it a dream or a memory? I knew which I wanted it to be.

"But here's a thought," Henry said. "How come, when you went to the clubhouse for your money, no one asked to speak to Jasmine? You'd think someone would say, 'Jasmine was the last person to see the old bastard alive,' and they'd want to hear her version of events."

"It's true, everyone saw how she behaved," Evert said. "And many of them saw her get in his car. But no one this morning said a word about it."

"Like they don't want to know," Noah said. "And when we broke down and the cops came, I was shitting myself they'd come for Jasmine. But all they wanted was to get us out of town as fast as possible. No wonder the tow-truck turned up so quick."

Henry slurped his soup and said nothing. He looked tired. I closed my eyes and tried to recapture my vision of fists. Dream or memory? And if it was a memory—well, I've been pushing away unwanted guys all my life—so which memory was it? Was I a victim or a villain? I didn't want to be either one.

Later, days later, I was sitting in Henry's studio, and I said, "I never thanked you properly for sticking up for me."

"Hold still," he said, without looking up from his maquette. Then he said, "I didn't stick up for you."

"But you believed me when the two guys who were supposed to be my friends didn't."

"I never said I believed you," Henry said. "I didn't disbelieve you, which is different. But all that money, the watch. Come *on.* I wasn't born yesterday."

I know I'm a liar but I didn't want to lie to Henry, so I kept still and said nothing.

"You were sick and in trouble," Henry said eventually, "and it had very little to do with the ex-mayor of Chaux-du-Gard. It was more to do with how the world treats reckless young women. And, y'know, young men are so goddamn sure of themselves."

Tonight, maybe, I'll play for Michelle and Henry again. I can do a passable "God Bless the Child." They won't think I'm Billie Holiday, but it might make Michelle change her mind about me not being serious. I don't think I'll do "La Vida Loca" ever again.

"What're you smiling at?" Henry's fingers are gloved with drying clay.

I say, "Can I call you Papa, Henry?"

"I'm not your goddamn father," Henry says, and laughs.

The tap in his studio sink drips, ta-doo, ta-dum.

Clark Howard

THE LEPER COLONY

■ ■ ■

Clark Howard has been a full-time professional writer for more than thirty years. His work ranges from twenty-one contemporary novels and true-crime books, to more than two-hundred short stories and articles in the mystery, western, and true-crime genres. He has won the Edgar Allan Poe Award and four Ellery Queen Readers Awards for short-story writing, and has a dozen nominations in the short-story and true-crime categories from the Mystery Writers of America, Western Writers of America, and Private Eye Writers of America. He has also written a boxing column for The Ring *magazine, and has had his work adapted for both film and television. "The Leper Colony" features a very unusual department of a big-city police force, handling the crimes that no one else in the department will touch, and all of it is done with Howard's usual economy, grace, and style.*

At the end of a long, wide marble hallway in the county courthouse, half a dozen men in suits and neckties sat on wooden benches or stood leaning against the wall, forming a loose group around large oak double doors, on one of which was a polished brass plate that read: GRAND JURY.

The men seemed tense, edgy, nervous. One of them, who was pacing back and forth a few steps, pulled his coat back to reach for a handkerchief. His coat caught for a second on a holstered revolver on his belt. Just in front of the revolver was a police captain's badge. Straightening his coat, he used the handkerchief to blot perspiration on his forehead.

"Why don't you relax, Pulaski?" one of the seated men said.

Pulaski stopped pacing. "Relax, Connor? How the hell can I relax? Four or five of the best cops in my district are probably being crucified behind those doors, and you want me to relax?"

Connor tried to placate him. "It may not be as bad as we think. Turino's one of us. He's a captain, just like the rest of us. He might come through for us."

"Yeah, right," replied Pulaski. "And I might win the state lottery, too—but I doubt it." He began pacing again. "Turino's a straight-arrow and you know it. Every one of us out here is going to lose some good cops before this investigation is over. Sure, some of them take a little on the side once in a while—from bookies, after-hours joints, card rooms, even a few pimps running girls—but nothing big, nothing serious, no drugs, no strong-arm stuff, no organization money. The rest of the time they're out keeping our districts clean. Does a little taking mean we gotta lose good cops?"

Connor shrugged. "I don't like it any more than you do, Pulaski. But taking is taking. Remember, Turino didn't blow the whistle on anybody; he just got called to testify, like we all did. We've got a new mayor; he's promised to clean up the police department."

"We could've cleaned our own house," one of the other captains in the group said.

"Yeah, but we didn't," another pointed out.

"Face it," Pulaski said. "Turino's gonna torpedo us."

At that moment, one of the big oak doors opened and Captain Vincent Turino, in full uniform, walked out. He was a man of perhaps fifty, obviously trim and in good shape, his black Italian hair thinning and graying. The expression on his face was fixed, determined.

Pulaski stopped pacing again. All of the men in the hallway fell silent and stared apprehensively. After a moment, Connor stood up and, with Pulaski, confronted Turino.

"Tell us you didn't do it, Vince," he said. His tone was almost a plea, but there was hopelessness in it.

Turino was a rock, unyielding. "I did it," he told them flatly. "I did what was right. I told the truth."

With that, he walked past them and down the hall alone. More alone than he'd ever been in his life.

The next morning, Turino, in civilian clothes, sat ramrod straight in a chair facing the desk of Police Commissioner Harvey Munro. The commissioner's expression, normally amiable, was distinctly dour this morning, as if someone had put curdled cream in his coffee.

"You're a damn fool, Vincent," he said without preliminary.

"I told the truth," Turino said. His tone indicated that as far as he was concerned, nothing else was of consequence.

"Sure, sure, the truth," said Munro. "The truth is that you shot the careers out from under nineteen cops with a combined total of a hundred and sixty-seven years of service."

"Nineteen cops who were taking payoffs," Turino reminded him.

"Sure, sure," said Munro. "Gambling payoffs," he pointed out. "After-hours drinking clubs. A few poker rooms. A few poor girls trying to earn a living on the streets. Victimless crimes, Vincent."

"Not," Turino said stubbornly, "when they involve bribing police officers."

The police commissioner shook his head and slumped back in his chair. "You're not only a fool, Vincent, you're a sanctimonious fool. You and I worked the street together, remember? How many free lunches did we eat at Calzone's restaurant? How many free drinks did we have off-shift at Doyle's bar? How many—"

"That's different," Turino reasoned. "That was social. That didn't involve money. The nineteen cops you're talking about were running a *business*. They had regular paydays, Harvey!"

Munro sighed wearily. "Talking to you is a waste of time. Just remember, you made your own bed, Vincent. I'm relieving you of your command and transferring you out of your district. From now on, you work down in the basement at headquarters. You'll be in charge of the Probation Squad."

A knowing smile surfaced on Turino's face. "The Leper Colony, huh?"

"That's what they call it," Munro confirmed. "And frankly, I can't think of a more appropriate place for you—since you've made a leper of yourself in the department now."

At noon that day, at a little side-street Italian cafe, Turino sat across a table from a mature, full-bodied woman with silver-streaked hair, dressed in a stylish St. John knit suit. Her name was Abigail Lang and she had a master's degree in business finance. Six years earlier, she was head cashier at a local bank branch that had been held up. Turino was in charge of investigating the crime. Today, Abigail was a vice-president of the same bank chain, and she and Turino, both divorced, had shared an apartment since four months after they met.

At the moment, Abigail was frowning across a bowl of penne with pesto. "The Leper Colony?" she said. "What on earth is that?"

"It's a special squad for cops who have unofficially been put on probation for one thing or another, or who are simply trouble-makers in general. It's really a place for people the department would like to get rid of but don't have a legitimate reason to."

"What are they on probation for?"

Turino shrugged. "Could be anything. Repeated incidents of minor insubordination. Disrespectful language to a superior. Inability to get along with peers. Just about any kind of conduct that falls below the level where the department can bring charges for dismissal."

"I get the picture," said Abigail, nodding. "They make them into kind of outcasts so they'll get disgusted with the whole drill and resign."

"Exactly. But there's more to the picture. See, department regulations won't permit a cop on duty to simply be idle; he has to be given work of some kind. So they give the people assigned to the Probation Squad every scut case that other squads don't want to handle."

"The dangerous stuff?" Abigail asked uncomfortably.

"No, no, nothing like that," Turino assured her. "The scut cases are the aggravating, irritating, irksome ones that drive cops crazy. Neighborhood disputes. Ongoing domestic arguments. Juvenile shoplifting. Crank complaints. That sort of thing."

"Neat," Abigail said. She took his hands across the table. "I've been meaning to talk to you about something, Vin, and now seems like the perfect time for it. Our chief of security at the bank has only a year left before retirement. He's been trying for months to find someone to go to work for him now and take over the job when he leaves. You'd be a natural for it. It's a high-level job, responsible for the main offices and thirty branches. You'd make an easy fifteen thousand a year more than you do now."

The expression on Turino's face told her that it was a futile suggestion. Since he had been a young man fresh out of the Marine Corps and back from Vietnam, he had never been anything but a cop. From conversations both casual and intimate, Abigail subconsciously knew that he would never be anything else. She squeezed his hand.

"Not interested?"

He smiled a half-smile and squeezed her hand back. "Thanks anyway, sweetheart. But I couldn't. I'm a career police officer."

Abigail nodded wryly. "Sure. A career police officer who's now a leper among his own."

"I'm still a cop," Turino said firmly.

The following morning, Turino, briefcase in hand, paused in front of a headquarters basement door with a cracked opaque window in it, and a plastic sign next to it that read: PROBATION SQUAD. Scotch-taped beneath that sign was a second one, cardboard, on which was carelessly lettered with a black marker: LEPER COLONY. Turino opened the door and walked into a seedy little squad room with peeling paint, scarred wooden desks, missing floor tiles, and inadequate lighting. Lounging around the room in various stages of uniform and civilian dress were five men and one woman.

All conversation ceased when Turino entered. Closing the door behind him, he paused. His eyes swept the room, studying each of them perfunctorily, as their collective eyes examined him in the same way. If anything, they were more curious about him than he about them. No one as highly ranked as a captain had ever been assigned to the Probation Squad before.

After a moment, Turino, without speaking, walked through the room to a frosted-glass cubicle at the rear. Inside, he hung his coat on the back of a chair, opened his briefcase on the desk, and removed six manilla file folders, each about an inch thick. They were the personnel records of the six officers currently assigned to the squad. Sighing quietly, resignedly, Turino opened the top file and summoned the officer whose name was on it.

"Detective Ryan Riley, come in here, please!"

A tall, square-jawed, lean man with a blond crew-cut, in street clothes, came in and sat down in a chair that Turino pointed to.

"According to your file, they call you 'Rambo' Riley, that right?" Turino asked.

"That's right, Captain," Riley confirmed.

"You've been with the department for eleven years and you've had eighteen excessive-force complaints. You must have a pretty short fuse."

Riley shrugged. "I believe in hitting before I get hit."

After another minute or two of conversation, Turino dismissed Ryan Riley and called in another officer. "Officer Lewis Calder!"

Calder was handsome almost to the point of being pretty, with a perfectly proportioned, muscular physique.

"Your file indicates that you study ballet dancing in your off hours. That right?"

"Correct, sir," the uniformed officer confirmed.

"And you belong to an unapproved radical organization called the G.L.F. What's that?"

"Gay Liberation Front, sir."

"Why is it disapproved by the department?"

"When we stage protest marches, we carry perfume to spray on demonstrators who confront us."

"So?"

"So, Captain, the department says the spray bottles are weapons."

Turino dismissed Lewis Calder and called, "Officer Cornell Robinson!"

Robinson was black, stoic, unsmiling, and unblinking. He had hardhead written all over his face.

"Robinson, you've had two white partners shot up while on duty with you, and you came away unscathed. Why is that?"

"Luck of the Irish, Captain."

"Very funny. Both of your former commanders say you can't get along with your fellow officers—white *or* black. That true?"

"Must be. White police captains wouldn't lie. *Sir.*"

Oh boy, Turino thought.

"Officer Angela Danner!"

Through the door came a face that was plain but still pretty, offset by a body that clearly was more suited to a Victoria's Secret catalog than a police uniform.

"Officer Danner, your transfer sheet just says 'Ongoing contrary behavior' to your former commanding officer. That's kind of vague. Can you give me some more details?"

"There's only one detail," Angela Danner told him. "I like to pick my own bed partners."

Turino looked sceptical. The captain who had transferred her was a devout Catholic family man. "You expect me to believe you were transferred to the Probation Squad because you refused to go to bed with your captain?"

"No, I don't expect you to believe it at all," she told him flatly. "But if you'd care to try your own luck, I'll be happy to prove it to you—*Captain.*"

As she walked out, Turino could see why the previous commander, family man or not, had tried.

"Detective Al Marshowitz, please!"

In came a Serpico type. Scruffy beard. Cocky beret. Bracelets and earrings. A Hebrew-language newspaper sticking out of his pocket.

"Your sheet says you're a 'nonconformist.' Aside from your appearance, how do you not conform?"

Marshowitz shrugged. "I smoke a little pot. Snort a little coke at a party once in a while. Pick up a hooker if I feel like it. Oh, and I've got some good friends in the joint."

"Sounds like you should be on the other side," Turino observed.

"Maybe I should be." Marshowitz paused for effect, then smiled slyly. "But I'm not."

Turino let him go.

"Officer Arthur Holden, please!"

Holden was short, almost pudgy. He looked affable but confident at the same time.

"Says here your nickname is 'Doc.' Why is that?" Turino asked.

"I'm a Ph.D.," Holden told him. "Sociology."

"You could be making maybe fifty thousand a year more practicing or teaching," Turino said. "How come you're a cop?"

"I'm still learning," Holden said. "For me, being a cop is like being in life's schoolroom."

"I guess you were a lot smarter than your captain, right?"

"Right," said Holden. "I'm a lot smarter than *any* captain."

When he had finished interviewing them all, Turino put his face in both hands and shook his head. He remembered the commissioner's words: *You made your own bed, Vincent.*

Putting the personnel files back into his briefcase, he closed it and walked back through the shabby little squad room to the door he had entered. Before leaving, he turned around and said evenly, "You're all dismissed for the rest of the shift. Be here at seven-thirty in the morning for roll call. And be here ready to go to work."

There were chuckles behind him as he closed the door.

The next morning, Turino was waiting there for them as each one straggled in. He stood in the middle of the room, coat off, sleeves rolled up.

"All right, listen up," he said in his best authoritative voice. "I don't know how long any of you are going to be in this squad, or how long I'm going to be running it. But as long as we're here, we've got police work to do and we're going to do it. You all know without me telling you that the work they throw down here is the cases nobody else wants to work. They're the dead-end cases, the crank cases, the ones where the cops working them can get caught in the middle of something sticky."

Fists on hips, Turino walked up and down among them. Deliberately, he stared down each one of them.

"You're all in this squad because someone higher up didn't like you but didn't have anything on you that would be grounds for discharge in a departmental hearing. That won't be the case down here. I don't like or dislike any of you; I don't even know you. But I do know *this*: The refusal to accept a case assignment *is* grounds for departmental dismissal, and I'll use those grounds if you make me. If any of you want to resign, do it; if you want to get fired, refuse an assignment; but if for some reason of your own, you want to still be cops—*good* cops—then let's go to work." He went into his cubicle. "Come inside for your assignments as I call your names. . . ."

Rambo Riley, with his chiseled face, crew cut, and ham-sized fists, and Al Marshowitz, with his Serpico beard and gypsy attire, were the first two summoned.

"I want you two to hit the streets and find a guy named Luis Ortiz," Turino said, tossing a police report across the desk. "He's wanted for overtly threatening the life of a deputy public defender named Charles Hill. He came into the public defender's offices yesterday with a knife, looking for Hill. Got away before deputies could apprehend him. The only known connection between the two is that about two years ago, Hill was assigned by the court to defend someone named Gildardo Ortiz on a burglary charge, and Gildardo was convicted and sent to Coldwater Prison. There may be a connection between the two men, may not; as you both probably know, the name Ortiz is not uncommon in the barrio.

"So—I want two things done: one, find out *why* Luis Ortiz wants to knife Charles Hill; and two, find a way to resolve whatever's between them, if you can. If not, bust Ortiz for stalking with a weapon. That's all."

Cornell Robinson, with his angry black face, and smug Doc Holden, with his Ph.D., came in next. Turino tossed another report over.

"There's a gang dispute building up on the West Side. Two gangs: the Aztecs, who are Hispanic, and the Rattlers, who are black. Their turfs are divided by one block on Maypole Street. A white line has been spray-painted down the middle of the street.

"Yesterday, a black magazine writer who grew up on the block returned for the day to see his old neighborhood. The Aztecs grabbed him on their side of the street, took his wallet, and pushed him across the line into Rattler territory. Word is, the Rattlers are working up to an act of retaliation for what they perceive to be an insult. The Street Gangs Unit doesn't want to handle it because they're afraid it'll blow up in their faces.

"So we get the call. Hit the street, Officers. Try to get that magazine writer's wallet back. And try to keep the peace on Maypole Street."

Next to come in were the gay advocate, Lewis Calder, and the body to die for, Angela Danner.

"An old guy over in Little Italy may or may not have disappeared," Turino said, giving them the report. "His name is Vito Carbone, age seventy-seven. Apparently he's been missing for several days, nobody's sure exactly how long. Now, three times before he's been gone for a couple of days while engaged in marathon card games with some cronies of his. Missing Persons considers it a crank complaint and has elected not to work it. But the case has to be cleared by somebody, so—"

"So they give it to us," Lewis Calder finished the statement for him. "How sweet of them."

"Have fun," Turino said wryly.

"We'll try, Captain," said Angela Danner. She winked at Turino as they left.

Before the squad dispersed, several of them returned individually to Turino's office to adopt attitudes.

Rambo Riley said, "Look, I'll work with this freak Marshowitz, Captain, but understand that as far as I'm concerned he's not much better than this stalking spic punk we're after. If this little creep tries to interfere with me, I'll bust him up as quick as I would the punk. Maybe quicker."

Cornell Robinson made it known that, "If you think sending me out with a honky Ph.D. is some kind of clever move, Captain, you're wrong. Think this guy is going to get inside my head and find out why I can't get along with none of my partners? Fat chance."

And Lewis Calder declared, "It isn't really necessary to partner me with the only woman in the squad, Captain. I mean, come on. I can be trusted with a male partner, really. Especially the ones in this squad. I mean, I do have *some* taste."

As they all left, Turino announced, "I'll be making field checks during the day, so I'll probably catch up with all of you on the street."

Filing out the door, members of the Leper Colony left a chorus of moans and groans in their wake.

After the squad left, the two captains who had confronted Turino in the Grand Jury hallway walked in. Turino stepped out of his cubicle to meet them. There was a moment of silence, then Connor, who commanded Uniform Patrol, said to Pulaski, "He looks right at home in this hole."

"He should," said Pulaski, of the Fugitive Squad. "He's a leper just like the rest of them down here."

Turino did not respond to the slurs. "If you've got business in here, state it. If not, take a walk."

"Talks tough, don't he?" Connor said.

"Oh yeah," Pulaski agreed. "Talking is what he's good at."

"State your business," Turino said flatly, his words now a warning.

"Our business," Pulaski said with a cold smile, "is to advise you that Jacob Kalb is at large as of about three o'clock this morning. He overpowered a night-shift guard at the hospital for the criminally insane and escaped. Your name is on the 'Advise If Released' list. You helped send him up and I believe he threatened to kill you if he ever got out. So consider yourself advised."

"Of course, we'll do everything we can to protect you," Connor added sarcastically. "After all, us cops got to stick together, right, Turino?"

As soon as they left, Turino called Abigail Lang at the bank. "I may have a little problem," he said. He told her about Jacob Kalb's escape. "The guy's a psycho rapist I caught and helped send up before you and I met. He's never killed anyone, but I don't want him starting with me—or you. I'd like you to stay away from the apartment when I'm not there."

"But how could he possibly find out where you live?" Abigail asked. "The phone and utilities are in my name, and the police department doesn't give out home addresses, does it?"

Turino grunted softly. "In my case, they might make an exception. I got the distinct impression from Connor and Pulaski that if they apprehended Jacob Kalb, they might happily give him my address and turn him loose. Anyway, promise me you'll stay away from the apartment until we can be home together."

"Of course, Vin, if that's what you want. I'll stay in my office until I hear from you."

On the street making field checks later that morning, Turino located Calder and Danner working the Vito Carbone disappearance case.

"Any progress?" he asked.

"Not really, but the plot, as they say, seems to be thickening," Calder replied. "Apparently there's *another* old guy involved in the picture."

"Yeah," said Angela Danner. "Guy named Luigi DiRenzo. He and Vito Carbone have always been kind of friendly enemies, until recently, when Luigi's granddaughter wanted to become engaged to Vito's grandson."

"That's when the two became *real* enemies," said Calder. "Luigi, as head of the DiRenzo family, refused to bless the engagement. Supposedly that meant that the two young people wouldn't be allowed to see each other."

"We know this sounds far-fetched, Captain," Angela put in, "maybe even archaic. But these are a couple of very traditional Italian families—"

"I understand, Danner," the captain assured. "My name is Turino, remember? Go on."

"Okay, well," Calder picked it up, "we've learned that Vito came up with a proposition. They both have the reputation of being very fierce card players, see? Been gambling together for forty years, each claiming to be better than the other. So Vito offers to teach Luigi a new game of solitaire, on condition that if Luigi can't beat the game in two weeks, he'll bless the engagement. And if Luigi *does* beat the game, Vito will publicly acknowledge that Luigi is the best card player in Little Italy."

Angela shrugged. "It was a challenge that Luigi couldn't refuse. So Vito taught him this game called 'Prisoner.' Luigi started playing it. The story we got was that he played it all day, every day, for two weeks, but wasn't able to beat it once. A few days ago, Luigi stood up and threw the cards against the wall, uttered some Sicilian curse, and stormed out of the house. That night, Vito Carbone disappeared."

"Some members of the two families are afraid Luigi might have done away with Vito," Calder added. "But Luigi won't discuss the matter one way or the other. The only comment he's made is that Vito's 'fate is in the cards.' That's all he'll say."

"Maybe it's got something to do with fortunetelling," Turino speculated. "My grandfather's ninety-three and he sees a Sardinian fortuneteller once a week. Insists that it's his secret of longevity." Turino thought a moment. "Tell you what, you two split up. One of you go home, get into street clothes, and stake out old Luigi; maybe he'll lead us to something. The other one check out all the gypsies in the area who use cards to tell fortunes; see if there's any possible connection there."

After leaving the two officers, Turino radioed Central Dispatch. "Any progress on a fugitive named Jacob Kalb?"

"Spell that, please."

"K-A-L-B."

"One moment, please." Then: "Nothing in the computer, Captain."

The escapee was still at large.

Next, Turino drove to the neighborhood where detectives Rambo Riley and Serpico Marshowitz were trying to locate Luis Ortiz, who was stalking deputy public defender Charles Hill. They had been checking the various barrio poolrooms and other dives that Ortiz was likely to frequent.

"No luck locating him," Riley reported. "But we did come up with a possible motive. The man Hill defended, Gildardo Ortiz, is Luis's brother. And Gildardo's wife, Esperanza, divorced him after he was sent up this last time. The mother of the Ortiz brothers told us that Esperanza later started dating Charles Hill. Then she moved out of the neighborhood."

"Wonderful," Turino said irascibly. "Luis probably thinks Hill got Gildardo sent up on purpose."

"Wouldn't you?" Marshowitz asked.

"Shut up, weirdo, I'm giving this report," Riley said coldly. Marshowitz's eyes narrowed dangerously. *They're like oil and water,* Turino thought. *Better keep them apart from now on.*

"Try to find out where Esperanza lives or works and go see her," Turino instructed. "See if she knows where we can hook Luis, and find out if she even knows what's going on. It's possible that she could be in more danger than Hill is."

Turino left the two acrimonious detectives and drove away. Once again he radioed Central Dispatch. "Anything on Jacob Kalb yet?"

Again there was nothing.

Turino drove to the block on Maypole Street where a spray-painted white line divided the turfs of the Aztecs and Rattlers street gangs. There, in a candy store on the Rattlers side, he found black officer Cornell Robinson and Ph.D. Doc Holden talking to two men, one white, one black.

"Captain, this gentleman is Phil Davis, the store owner," Holden said, "and this gentleman," he indicated a casually but smartly dressed black man, "is Jason Harper, a staff writer for *Today's Truth* magazine."

Turino was shaking hands when into the store burst four members of the Rattlers, all dressed in black berets and slacks, and white crew-neck shirts.

"Those Aztec bastards!" one of them shouted to Officer Robinson. "They didn't even give this guy a chance to explain who he was! Just took his wallet and threw him across the line!"

"You don't get out of my face, boy, I'm gonna throw you somewhere!" the black officer shouted back, louder. Doc Holden immediately got between them.

"Calm down, Eddie," the white store owner urged. "Let me explain this to the officers." He turned to Turino. "This is Eddie Feen, Captain, the leader of the Rattlers. I let his boys hang out at my store and he sees that don't nobody give me no trouble. Jason here is an old friend of mine; we both grew up right on this very block. 'Course, now Jason's a famous writer and lives in a fancy apartment in a classy highrise, but once in a while he comes down to see me. He hasn't been down since the Rattlers and the Aztecs divided up the block, so he didn't know he wasn't supposed to be walking on the Hispanic side of the street. And *they* didn't know that *he* didn't know—"

"All right," Turino said, holding up a hand, "I think I understand the dynamics of the situation." He turned to Eddie Feen. "I intend to avoid a gang war here, you understand me?"

"I only understand one thing, Captain," the black youth replied defiantly. "The Aztecs took a black man's wallet and threw him over the line into our yard. That's a slap in the face of the Rattlers. And the Rattlers don't take slaps in the face."

"We understand that your group integrity is at stake," Doc Holden interjected. "All we want you to do is stay cool until we can talk to the Aztec leader."

"Has anybody gone over there and explained to the Aztecs who Mr. Harper is?" Turino asked.

"Not yet, Captain," said Cornell Robinson. "Only a few minor Aztec members are over there right now. But someone's gone for the leader and the war chief." The tall black officer stepped over and locked eyes with Eddie Feen. "You'll cool it for just a little while, won't you, boy?" he asked, with just a touch of menace.

"Yeah, okay," the Rattlers' leader agreed. He returned Robinson's confrontational stare. "But I ain't no boy, *man*. And don't you forget it."

Robinson smiled a cold smile. "I won't."

Deciding to stifle any potential altercation, Turino came over to Robinson. "Do me a favor, will you, Robinson? Get on your car radio and ask Central Dispatch if there's any news on a fugitive named Jacob Kalb."

"Sure, Captain."

Robinson broke off his stare-down with Eddie Feen and went out to the patrol car. On the radio, he identified himself and said, "Anything on a fugitive name of Cobb?"

"Spell that, please."

"I'm not sure. C-O-B-B, I guess."

After a moment, the dispatcher came back on and said, "The name clears the fugitive list. Subject must have been apprehended."

Robinson reported back to Turino. "Looks like that fugitive's been caught, Captain."

"Thanks, Robinson." Turino felt a slow flow of relief wash through him. Excusing himself from the group, he went to a pay phone at the back of the candy store and called Abigail Lang at the bank. "Looks like Kalb has been picked up, honey. It's safe for you to go home now. I'll be along as soon as I can." He returned to the arguing group trying to avoid a gang war.

Back at Central Dispatch, Robinson's call-in came up on the computer screen on the desk of Captain Pulaski, commander of the Fugitive Squad. He immediately called his friend, Captain Connor.

"Turino just had someone check on Kalb, but they got the name wrong and it was keyed in as C-O-B-B. It came back negative. Turino's probably been told that the guy's been caught."

"Isn't that a crying shame," said Connor.

"Yeah, isn't it," Pulaski replied.

Downtown in the Civic Center, an unsmiling man wearing a stolen raincoat over his prison hospital jumpsuit entered the records office of the Registrar of Voters.

"I'd like to get an address for a Mr. Vincent Turino," he told the clerk.

"What's the purpose of your inquiry, sir?" the clerk asked.

"He's a cousin I haven't seen in many years. I'm visiting for a few days and thought I'd contact him, but his telephone number is unlisted. Voter registrations are public records, aren't they?"

"Yes, sir, if the inquiry is legitimate. Fill out this form, please."

Fifteen minutes later, Jacob Kalb left the office with Vincent Turino's address.

In another part of the city, officers Lewis Calder and Angela Danner had split up as Turino had instructed. Danner, having changed into jeans and a windbreaker, was loitering outside a corner grocery, waiting to see if old Luigi DiRenzo was going to leave his building. Calder, still in uniform, was cruising the neighborhood, stopping whenever he saw a "Fortunetelling" sign to ask the occupant if they could interpret Luigi's cryptic comment that the missing Vito Carbone's fate was now "in the cards."

Eventually, Angela's wait paid off as she saw Luigi emerge onto the street and walk to a nearby deli. Through the window of the deli, she saw the old Italian buy a bag of food to go. Angela followed him as he left the store and walked back toward his own building. Instead of entering by the front door, however, he turned down an alley and went in by the basement door.

Across the alley, Angela took her radio from under her windbreaker and contacted Lew Calder. "Something funny's going on here," she said, telling him where she was and what she had observed. "I'm going in there," she added.

"Wait for me to get there, Danner," Calder cautioned. "You know the procedure: Always wait for backup. I'll be there in about seven minutes."

Angela went in alone anyway.

Slipping quietly through the basement door, she found a small room behind the building's furnace, and there the missing man, Vito Carbone, sat tied to a chair, his mouth covered with adhesive tape. Luigi DiRenzo sat at a small table in front of him, spreading out his bag of food to eat.

"Okay, Mr. Smart Guy," Luigi said, "I'm gonna sit here and play this stupid game of Prisoner while I eat. If I beat it, I untie you and give you something to eat." He smiled tightly. "But you an' me, we both know I won't beat the game, don't we, Mr. Smart Guy?"

Angela watched from the shadows as Luigi began to deal out the tableau for a game of Prisoner: a straight line of cards from which the player can take three from the right end or two from the right end and one from the left end, as long as the value of the three cards totals ten, twenty, or thirty, with face cards worth ten.

Quickly and deftly, his gnarled hands belying their appearance, Luigi went through the deck—and failed to beat the game. "I lose again," he said. "Surprise, surprise."

As he shuffled for another game, chewing away on a slice of hard salami, Angela, behind him, eased her service revolver from under her jacket and moved farther into the room. "Police officer, Mr. DiRenzo!" she said firmly. "Put the cards down and keep your hands on the table! You're under arrest for kidnapping!"

Luigi DiRenzo sat very still and did as he was ordered. Angela moved around the table and peeled the adhesive from Vito Carbone's mouth.

"Shoot him!" Vito ranted weakly. "He's a madman! He's had me tied up like this for two weeks without food or water!"

"Liar!" Luigi retorted. "Two days only!" He looked at Angela and said aloofly, "I am punishing him for being a man without honor. We had a wager and he tried to make a fool of me, teaching me a card game that cannot be beaten—"

"*You* are the liar!" Vito rebutted. "It *can* be beaten!"

"Not," Luigi claimed stolidly. "You lie through your Sicilian teeth!"

"No, he doesn't," a new voice interjected. They all turned to look. Officer Lew Calder had arrived. He was holstering his weapon. "I just learned all about the game from a gypsy over on Keeler Street. The game is hard to beat, but not impossible. The gypsy said that she herself has beaten it seven times over the past twenty years."

Luigi stared incredulously at the cards. As Angela handcuffed him, Calder untied Vito and helped him upstairs. Angela followed with Luigi. As they started to leave the building, various members of the DiRenzo family came out of their apartments. Before the officers got to their cruiser at the curb, members of the Carbone family were hurrying from their own building directly across the street. The two families congregated and merged, all seeming to talk at once. Vito's grandson, Frank Carbone, came over to Calder.

"Officer, may I speak to you in private for a moment?"

Calder stepped aside with him. For several minutes, they engaged in quiet, somber conversation. Then Calder rejoined Angela and they put Luigi in the grille-protected rear seat of the cruiser. Behind them, the two families began to separate, the Carbones taking a shaky Vito into their building. Before the officers got in the cruiser, Angela asked, "What was that all about with the grandson? He try to get you not to take the old man in?"

"No," Calder replied easily, "he asked me if I had any ideas about how he could get out of the wedding engagement. He doesn't want to marry Luigi's granddaughter. The match is being forced on him by his family."

Angela rolled her eyes. "You're a cop, not a marriage counselor. Why ask you?"

"I know the guy slightly," Calder admitted. "I've seen him at some gay bars."

"Oh, I see," Angela said. She glanced around at the departing families and the stoic old man in the back of the cruiser. "Sure would have saved both families a lot of trouble if he'd just told everyone, wouldn't it?"

"Yeah. Saved a lot of trouble—and maybe *caused* a lot, too," Calder replied quietly. "It's hard to know when to stay in the closet and when to come out."

The two officers got into the cruiser to take old Luigi DiRenzo to jail.

Detectives Riley and Marshowitz, unable to determine Esperanza Ortiz's address from anyone in the Hispanic neighborhood, decided to go directly to the victim of the threats made by her former brother-in-law, Luis Ortiz. But when they arrived at the County Building, they learned that deputy public defender Charles Hill had gone home early that day because of some kind of family emergency. Riley and Marshowitz talked to Hill's supervisor, an assistant public defender, and obtained Hill's home address.

Charles Hill lived in an upscale apartment building on the near North Side. The eyebrows of both detectives went up when they saw two names beside the doorbell: C. HILL and E. ORTIZ.

"No wonder Luis is out for blood," said Riley.

Marshowitz rang the bell. At first there was no answer, but after two more rings, both persistent, the door opened just the length of a safety chain.

"Charles Hill?" asked Riley.

"Yes—uh, what is it?" The man at the door was pale and nervous.

Riley identified himself and Marshowitz. "May we come in for a minute, Mr. Hill?"

"No, I'm sorry. I, uh—I'm sick today—"

Over Hill's shoulder; both Riley and Marshowitz saw in the reflection of a wall mirror that behind Hill stood an Hispanic man holding an open switchblade to the throat of a terrified Hispanic woman. Riley quickly drew his gun.

"Wait, man," Marshowitz said urgently, grabbing Riley's arm. Riley jerked his arm away.

"Back off, weirdo," he snapped. "I know what I'm doing—"

Shoving Marshowitz away, Riley shouldered through the door, tearing the safety chain from the wall, pushing Charles Hill roughly aside. Marshowitz bolted after him; again grabbing Riley's gun arm.

"Luis, let us speak to you, please!" he shouted in near-perfect Spanish.

"Are you crazy!" Riley yelled. "He's threatening that woman with a deadly weapon!"

"Don't shoot him, Riley!" Marshowitz got between his partner and Ortiz. "Luis, don't move, please!" he ordered. "Don't cut Esperanza! If you hurt her, this cop's gonna kill you!"

Riley stared in outrage at his oddly attired fellow officer. "You say 'cop' like it's a dirty word, Marshowitz. Why don't you tell him you've got a badge, too; tell him you're carrying a gun same as me!"

"He's right, Luis, I'm carrying a gun. But look at me, man, I'm not *holding* it. I don't want to shoot you, I want to help you."

"Well, I want to help *her*," Riley growled. "He's got a knife at her throat, you moron!"

"Helping him *will* help her!" Marshowitz insisted. He turned to Ortiz. "Listen to me, Luis. You're making a bad mistake here. Your brother Gildardo wouldn't like this."

"You wrong, man!" Luis Ortiz snarled, speaking for the first time. "My brother is *proud*. He would want me to avenge him. This *cabrone*, this bastard, let him go to prison so he could steal his wife!"

"That's a lie!" Charles Hill snapped, stepping forward. "I didn't even *meet* Espe until six months after Gildardo was sent up!"

"That is the truth, Luis," said Esperanza in a trembling voice, the switchblade point just a fraction from her throat. "Gil and I had already decided to divorce before he was arrested the last time. That's why I didn't even go to his trial; it was all over between us. I only met Charles when the lawyer handling our divorce had me take him the consent papers to send to Gil up at the prison."

"You think I would believe you two?" Luis said with a sneer.

"Why don't you ask your brother, then?" Al Marshowitz suggested casually, removing his beret and sitting down on a convenient chair. "Call him right now and ask him."

"Call him? Are you crazy, man? He's in Coldwater Prison. They ain't got phones in the cells, man!"

"If I get him on the phone, will you talk to him?"

Luis stared dumbly at him but did not answer. Marshowitz took a chance and picked up the phone. "Operator, this is a police emergency. I want you to connect me with the warden's office at Coldwater State Prison near Lenox City."

At the candy store on Maypole Street, Turino and his two officers, Cornell Robinson and Doc Holden, watched as the leader of the Aztecs, a tall, pockmarked youth named Terry Pilar, walked boldly down the opposite side of the street and stood glaring over at them in an obvious challenge.

"You going over to talk to him, Captain?" Holden asked quietly.

"No, you are," Turino replied. "You're smarter than me, remember?" Next to Turino, Robinson grunted a laugh.

"Right," said Holden. He walked out to the center of the street and stood at the white line. Terry Pilar sauntered over to face him. "I'd like to find out how this misunderstanding can be settled," he said to the Aztec leader. "Is there any way you would agree to give back the wallet you took from the black man?"

Terry smiled. "Is that all you and the Rattlers want? Hey, no pro'lem." He gestured to one of his gang and the wallet came sailing through the air and landed at Holden's feet. Holden picked it up and returned to the candy store.

"Easy as can be, Captain," he said smugly.

"Yeah, too easy," Turino said suspiciously.

Eddie Feen, leader of the Rattlers, put down a Coke he was drinking and stepped over to them. "Check for the money," he advised knowingly. Turino looked in the wallet. The currency section was empty. He turned to Jason Harper, the writer to whom the wallet belonged.

"How much did you have in it?"

"Probably a couple hundred," the writer replied, shrugging.

Turino turned back to Holden. "Right now we've got a misunderstanding. But if we don't get the money back, we've got a felony. Tell them that."

Holden returned to the white line in the middle of the street. Before anyone could object, Eddie Feen strode out to join the officer.

"We need to talk about the money that was in the wallet," Holden said to Terry Pilar.

"Nothing to talk about, man," the Aztec leader said, shrugging. "The money has been confiscated." He smiled widely. "Tha's a word I learned from the *chota*," he added. From the police.

Eddie Feen jabbed the air with a threatening finger. "You can't just take a brother's money, man! It ain't right!"

"If we got a good enough reason, it's right," Terry Pilar replied flatly.

Feen started to argue, but Holden, suddenly interested, stopped him with a touch. "What would be a good enough reason, Terry?" he asked.

"Well, like if we was making up a fund, man, for a girl over on our side who's gonna have a kid, you know?" He turned accusing eyes on Eddie Feen. "A kid that one of *your* guys made, man."

Feen drew back as if struck. "My guys don't have nothin' to do with foxes on your side of the line, man."

"One of 'em does," Terry countered. He signaled to a follower, and a young Hispanic girl, obviously pregnant, was escorted out of a nearby building. When she got to the line, Terry said, "Tell him who got you pregnant, Teresa."

"Leave her alone!" came a sudden shout from the Rattlers side of the street. A tall youth with dreadlocks strode forward, anger flashing in his eyes. Feen stared incredulously at him.

"Leroy? You did this?" He grabbed the youth by the shirt. "You broke the rules and went with a girl from the other side?"

"Yeah, I did!" Leroy said defiantly, knocking Feen's hand away. He straddled the white line and put a protective arm around Teresa. "She's my girl an' we're gonna get married—even if I have to fight everybody on *both* sides to do it!"

Feen shook his head. "I don't believe this."

"We got to talk, man," said Terry Pilar.

The two of them walked down the white line a short distance to speak in private. Turino and the others came out of the candy store. Holden walked back to explain the situation to them. Presently, Eddie and Terry returned.

"We made a decision here," Eddie announced loudly. "Leroy and Teresa can go together and nobody from either side is gonna bother them."

"Yeah," added Terry, "they gon' have their baby, and when the kid is old enough, the kid can decide which gang it wants to belong to."

"Right," Eddie Feen affirmed. "Now this problem is over, hear?"

"Not quite," said Turino, walking up. "There's still the matter of the two hundred dollars."

Robinson said, "Captain, let me have a moment with Mr. Harper?" Turino nodded consent and Robinson led the black magazine writer off to the side. After a brief conversation, they returned.

"Captain Turino," the writer said, "I'm afraid I owe you an apology. I was mistaken earlier. There wasn't any money in my wallet after all."

At the apartment of deputy public defender Charles Hill, Luis Ortiz, with the knife still at Esperanza's throat, was now holding the telephone in his other hand.

"Sure, Gil," he spoke quietly into the receiver. "It's just that you're my *carnal*, my brother, and I'm the only family you got now. I didn't want you to think I'd let anybody dishonor you—"

The others in the room waited tensely until, presently, the telephone conversation came to an end.

"Sure, okay, Gil. Yeah, I will, *carnal*. Okay, I promise, man."

Luis handed the receiver to Detective Marshowitz. "Hello, Warden? Yessir, I want to thank you for helping us out down here. I know this was a pretty unorthodox request—" Then, after a pause, "Yessir, well, maybe it did some good at your end, too. Thank you again, sir."

As Marshowitz hung up the phone, Luis laid the switchblade on a table and slumped back against the wall. Esperanza hurried into the arms of Charles Hill. Marshowitz turned to Rambo Riley and looked pointedly at his drawn gun. "What do I have to do to convince you that you don't need that cannon?"

"Cuff him," Riley replied, picking up the evidence knife.

Marshowitz stepped over and handcuffed Ortiz's wrists behind his back.

"I guess I'll be joining my bro in the joint now," Luis said glumly. Charles Hill came over to him.

"You got any priors, kid?" he asked.

Luis shook his head.

"No, man, not yet. An' I jus' promised Gildardo I'd stay clean."

Glancing at Esperanza, the lawyer thought about it for a moment, then said, "Let me defend you in court. I may be able to get you off with probation. Deal?"

"Yeah, man, deal," Luis said gladly. He turned to Esperanza with tears forming. "I'm sorry, Espe. Please forgive me."

Brushing her own tears away, Esperanza nodded.

As Marshowitz and Riley took Luis out to their unmarked car, Marshowitz said, "I'll ask the captain to give you a new partner tomorrow. You won't have to work with me anymore."

"Who said I didn't want to work with you anymore?" Riley asked gruffly.

"We're two different types of cop," Marshowitz reasoned. "We'd spend half our time together arguing."

"So?" Riley challenged. "What's wrong with a good healthy argument? Besides, maybe I'd learn something." His tone softened a touch. "I just learned something in there." He faced off with his outlandish partner. "Look, I'll give it a try if you will."

Marshowitz studied the tough cop for a moment. Finally he nodded. "All right. Okay. Maybe I'll learn something, too."

Vincent Turino, in his patrol car, had left the divided block on Maypole Street and was driving back to headquarters. Odd, he thought, how individual cops could screw up by themselves, but with the right partner could mesh into one half of a damned good team. The black officer, Robinson, would never have been able to get through to the Aztecs, and Doc Holden, for all his education, probably wouldn't have thought of asking the magazine writer to forget about the money in his stolen wallet.

He hoped the other teams he had put on the street today had bonded as well. Wouldn't the big kahunas downtown be surprised if the Leper Colony turned out to produce first-rate police officers—

His thoughts were interrupted by an all-points bulletin being broadcast over the radio. "Attention, all units. All units, attention. This is an updated ID on wanted fugitive Jacob Kalb. Subject is now believed to be wearing a tan raincoat over his institutional clothing. Kalb, a convicted serial rapist, escaped last night from Union Hospital for the Criminally Insane outside the city. Subject is Caucasian, age thirty-seven, six feet tall, one hundred sixty pounds—"

Turino's eyes widened. Snatching up the radio's mike, he called Central Dispatch. "This is Captain Turino," he said urgently. "Confirm an earlier report that fugitive Jacob Kalb is in custody."

"One moment, Captain." Turino waited, breaking sweat on his brow as he listened to background voices in the dispatch center. Then his operator returned to the line. "Captain," she said, "subject Kalb has not been apprehended."

"I want you to patch through an emergency telephone call for me," he said, and gave her Abigail Lang's number at the bank. A secretary answered.

"I'm sorry, Captain, but Ms. Lang has left for the day."

Getting back to Dispatch, Turino said, "Try this number, operator," and gave her the number at the apartment he and Abigail shared.

While Turino was trying her office number, Abigail, wearing a robe, was in the kitchen putting a casserole dish of chicken breasts in the oven to bake. As she turned on the controls of the oven, she thought she heard a noise at the front door.

"Vin, that you, honey?" she called.

There was no answer. Frowning, she went to the door and looked out the peephole. As far as she could see, the hallway was deserted. Shrugging to herself, she went into the bathroom. She smiled, thinking how when Vincent was home, they showered together, but when she was alone, she liked to languish in a warm, fragrant tub of water. Reaching down to the faucet handle, she started running a tub.

In the bedroom, the telephone rang, but Abigail could not hear it.

Out in the hall, Jacob Kalb pressed one ear to the apartment door and heard nothing, not the sound of the running water, not the ringing telephone. From under the stolen raincoat he was wearing, he took a small crowbar he had picked up earlier at a construction site. In mere seconds, he had pried open the apartment door.

Once inside, he heard the sound of water running in the tub, and the ringing of the telephone. As he stood there listening, the telephone stopped ringing. Smiling, Kalb made his way to the kitchen. From a wooden holder on the counter, he pulled out a thin-bladed carving knife.

Then he moved through the apartment toward the sound of the running water. On the way, he took the bedroom phone off the hook.

Four blocks away, with his emergency flashers and siren on, Turino turned into a line of stalled traffic. He called Dispatch again and asked that the apartment number be retried. This time, when the operator came back on, she said, "Captain, that number is now busy."

Looking up ahead, Turino tried to see what was holding up traffic. He could see the flashing yellow lights of a tow truck. *An accident. . . .*

He could neither proceed forward nor go backwards. Cursing silently, he turned off the motor and snatched the car keys from the ignition. Then he got out and slammed the door shut, and desperately began running along the line of stalled cars.

In the apartment, Kalb peered around the edge of the bathroom door and watched as Abigail removed and hung up her robe. As she turned to step into the tub, she saw Kalb move into the open doorway. Jumping back, terrified, she screamed and instinctively reached for her robe again. Kalb grabbed her arm and shoved her roughly back against a floor-to-ceiling mirrored wall, cracking the glass.

"Don't be afraid," Kalb said calmly. "I'm not here to hurt you." His eyes grew excited at the sight of her body. "We'll just have ourselves a little fun before the person I really want gets home—"

Kalb stepped toward Abigail, then there was a thunderous explosion as a close-range shot was fired behind him. A .40-caliber slug from a Glock automatic tore through his transverse thoracic muscle and blew apart the wide end of his vena cava. The escapee pitched sideways into the partly filled tub and lay facedown, half submerged, blood bubbling from the entrance wound in his back, turning the water pink, then red.

In the doorway stood Captain Pulaski of the Fugitive Squad; directly behind him Captain Connor of Uniform Patrol.

"Nice shot," said Connor. Stepping around Pulaski, he draped Abigail's robe around her trembling shoulders.

Three minutes later, Turino burst in, gun drawn, panting from his run.

Later, with crime-scene investigators, photographers, medical-examiner's assistants, two deputy district attorneys, and an Internal Affairs officer all milling around the apartment and hallway, Turino left a finally calm Abigail in their small, cozy den with the landlady attending her, and went into the kitchen where Pulaski and Connor had helped themselves to cans of Coke from the refrigerator and were sitting at the table.

"How'd you know Kalb would be here?" he asked.

"Just a guess," said Connor. "Pulaski knew you got an erroneous fugitive report and would think your place was safe."

"We figured we'd keep an eye out for him until you got here," Pulaski added.

"I don't suppose either of you want my thanks," Turino said.

"We didn't do it for you, Turino," said Connor. "We did it for a nice lady we know who now happens to live with a leper."

They got up to leave.

"Incidentally," Pulaski said on their way out, "you've got a broken mirror in your bathroom. That means seven years of bad luck. We hope you get every day of it."

The next day at roll call, Turino passed out a printed form to each member of the Probation Squad.

"These are resignation forms," he said. "The commissioner wants all officers and detectives who are on probation to be aware that the department will process without delay or further inquiry any resignation request received from this squad. He stated in a memo accompanying these forms that he realizes that personnel assigned here may resent it and therefore feel that the police force is not the right career path for them. He assures you that he understands that and will personally see that your departure is considered a voluntary termination of service with no unfavorable notations on your records." The captain glanced around. "Anybody interested?"

Officer Arthur "Doc" Holden shook his head. "I've got to go back out on Maypole Street and make sure everything stays peaceful between the Aztecs and the Rattlers."

"*You've* got to go back out there!" Officer Cornell Robinson snorted. He tore his form in half. "A loaf of white bread like you would probably get run off if you didn't have some colorful backup like me."

Detective Ryan "Rambo" Riley rolled his form into a ball and tossed it to Detective Al Marshowitz, who today was dressed in torn jeans and a Disney World sweatshirt. Marshowitz rolled it into a larger ball with his own form and tossed it all the way across the office to a waste can, into which it dropped without hitting the rim. Riley grinned and held up two fingers. A basket. Two points.

Officer Lewis Calder folded his form neatly into thirds and used it to mark his place in a gay-advocacy magazine he had been reading. Officer Angela Danner opened her purse, removed a lipstick, and scrawled a large "NO" on the form. Then she opened a compact and touched up her lips a bit.

Vincent Turino suppressed a smile and reached for a freshly delivered stack of case files.

"All right then, you lepers," he said, "let's see what kind of garbage they sent down for us to work today."

Honorable Mentions

■ ■ ■

Alexander, Gary, "Comic," *Alfred Hitchcock's Mystery Magazine*, February.
Alexander, Skye, "Life, Death, Love, and Baseball," *Undertow: Crimes Stories by New England Writers*, Level Best Books.
Barnard, Robert, "Rogue's Gallery," *Ellery Queen's Mystery Magazine*, March.
DuBois, Brendan, "Always Another," *AHMM*, Jul./Aug.
Ellis, Kate, "Les Inconnus," *Crime in the City*, Do-Not Press.
Ellis, Kate, "Wonders of Technology," *EQMM*, January.
Fallis, Gregory, "Dem Bones, Dem Bones," *AHMM*, October.
Fry, Susan, "Peat," *AHMM*, December.
Gates, David Edgerly, "Smoke Follows a Liar," *AHMM*, April.
Giencke, Jill, "A Kindness Returned," *Austin Layman's Crimestalker Casebook*, Spring.
Gold, Glen David, "The Tears of Squonk and What Happened Thereafter," *McSweeney's Mammoth Treasury of Thrilling Tales*, Vintage.
Halstead, William, "Tootoo," *EQMM*, February.
Hayden, G. Miki, "War Crimes," *A Hot and Sultry Night for Crime*, Berkley Prime Crime.
Helgerson, Joe, "The Case of the Breathless Martian," *AHMM*, May.
Hinger, Charlotte, "Any Old Mother," *Blood on Their Hands*.
Hockensmith, Steve, "Dear Mr. Holmes," *EQMM*, February.
Howe, Melodie Johnson, "The Talking Dead," *EQMM*, June.
Kinman, Gay Toltl, "Death in Russia," *Detective Mystery Stories*, #37.
Lakey, Babs, "Jesse James' Radio Caper," *Futures*, Summer.
Levinson, Robert S., "Good Career Moves," *Flesh & Blood: Guilty as Sin*, Mysterious Press.
Lippman, Laura, "The Babysitter's Code," *Plots with Guns*, Web site.
Marston, Edward, "The Hunchback and the Stammerer," *EQMM*, February.
Matteson, Stephanie, "The 13th Card," *EQMM*, Sept./Oct.
Powell, Megan, "Favors," *Shred of Evidence*, November.
Randisi, Robert, "Henry and the Idiots," *High Stakes: 8 Sure-Bet Stories of Gambling and Crime*, Signet.
Riordan, Rick, "A Good Day's Work," *EQMM*, Sept./Oct.
Rowan, Iain, "The Chain," *EQMM*, December.
Rzeltelny, Harriet, "Amazing Grace," *AHMM*, February.
Schreiber, Norman, "Call Me Wiggins," *My Sherlock Holmes*, Web site.
Stirling, Elaine, "Death by Donuts," *AHMM*, June.
Vachss, Andrew, "A Piece of the City," *EQMM*, February.
Wilson, John Morgan, "Anything for Olivia," *EQMM*, March.
Wright, Eric, "The Lady of Shalott," *A Killing Climate*, Crippen & Landru.

About the Editors

■ ■ ■

Ed Gorman has been called "one of suspense fiction's best storytellers" by *Ellery Queen*, and "one of the most original voices in today's crime fiction" by the *San Diego Union.*

Gorman has been published in magazines as various as *Redbook*, *Ellery Queen*, *The Magazine of Fantasy & Science Fiction*, and *Poetry Today.*

He has won numerous prizes, including the Shamus, the Spur, and the International Fiction Writer's Award. He's been nominated for the Edgar, the Anthony, the Golden Dagger, and the Bram Stoker Awards. Former *Los Angeles Times* critic Charles Champlin noted that "Ed Gorman is a powerful storyteller."

Gorman's work has been featured by the Literary Guild, the Mystery Guild, the Doubleday Book Club, and the Science Fiction Book Club.

He lives with his wife, author Carol Gorman, in Cedar Rapids, Iowa.

Martin H. Greenberg is the CEO of TEKNO BOOKS, the book-packaging division of Hollywood Media, a publicly traded multimedia entertainment company. With more than nine hundred published anthologies and collections, he is the most prolific anthologist in publishing history. His books have been translated into thirty-three languages and adopted by twenty-five different book clubs. With Ed Gorman, he edits the 5-Star Mystery line of novels and collections for Thorndike Press.

In the mystery and suspense field, he has worked with at least fifteen bestselling authors, including Dean Koontz, Mickey Spillane, Tony Hillerman, Robert Ludlum, and Tom Clancy.

He received the Milford Award for lifetime achievement in science fiction editing in 1989, and in April 1995 he received the Ellery Queen Award for lifetime achievement for editing in the mystery field at the Fiftieth Banquet of the Mystery Writers of America. In 2004 he received the Lifetime Achievement award from the Horror Writers Association, becoming the only person to win major editorial awards in all three genres. He lives in Green Bay, Wisconsin.